Governey

a novel

Constance Eve

House of Hawthorne Publishing
Grosse Pointe, Michigan

ISBN 13: 978-0-9786641-0-7
ISBN 10: 0-9786641-0-8

Cover design by Todd Clements
Page design by Lee Lewis Walsh, Words Plus Design,
www.wordsplusdesign.com

Acknowledgements

If no man is an island, then it is particularly so in reference to the art of writing. A special thank-you to my valued mentors, Yuri Dia Konov and Gwenn Samuel. I am also grateful to family and friends who assisted me with any editing, research, proofreading and, in particular, for their support and encouragement, namely: Todd, Kjersten, Joanna, Nina, Theresa, Vito, Marco, Sarah, Francesca, Marie, Lillian, Caryl, Sam, Brian and staff, The Ohio Theatre, Dr. Hale and Dr. Heneke.

Lastly (as the best is often saved for last), I thank God for my husband Bill whom I can always count on to be the loving and devoted partner which he has steadily proven to be for the past 39 years.

Author's Note

What you are about to read is the product of a troubled mind…a mind conditioned from early childhood to conceive sexuality as something forbidden and dangerous. A mind incarcerated by shame, fear, angst and guilt. The crime? Being born into a Catholic, Italian-American family in the early 1950s. The book? A subconscious attempt to resolve lingering nightmares accompanied by a willful determination to prevail, cherishing the blessings of faith, courage, and an unwavering passion for freedom along the way.

"The horse is made ready for the day of war,
but power to overcome is from the Lord."

— Proverbs 21:31

"Those who would give up essential Liberty
to purchase a little temporary Safety
deserve neither Liberty nor Safety."

— Benjamin Franklin

part 1

Samuel

chapter 1

An Inconvenient Predicament

Inside the meticulous kitchen, Samuel Governey shoved a rolled newspaper under his armpit and yanked a few polishing supplies from a utility room shelf. Anticipating the demeaning task ahead, he gritted his golden molars. *One of the wealthiest gentlemen in this toe-kissing town and I'm bamboozled into sprucing up my own wretched pair of shoes!* Giving the dull porcelain sink a passing glare, Samuel stomped over the coarse stone tiles toward a knife-ridden butcher block. *If I'll be wearing my wing tips to the club this evening, they had better bloody well be perfect!*

Though Gothic in style, the elaborate kitchen of the Governey mansion was equipped with every modern convenience including a Frigidaire with its own ice-making compartment. Mahogany cabinets stocked with crystal and china hovered above an expansive marble counter. At the far end of the room near an arched entrance, a wilted arrangement of calla lilies adorned a cherrywood table. Seven chairs, forming a broken circle, were positioned precisely around the table's edge. The eighth, pried from its place, suffered the intrusion of Samuel's dark suit jacket and straw hat, each article of clothing irreverently shrouded with the unforgiving odor of formaldehyde.

Samuel dropped the polishing supplies on the counter, pushed the sleeves of his starched white shirt to his elbows and unrolled the newspaper upon the butcher block. After pausing at the headline on the Lindberg murder, he shrugged his shoulders as though dismissing a fleeting concern. In spite of the hot August afternoon, he could feel the coolness of the limestone tile beneath his stocking feet as he placed the Oxfords on the paper and started to unlace them. The sun's rays, weakened by an overcast sky, filtered through the cathedral windows, exposing the sloppy workmanship of the shoes even more than he had previously noticed. The deep blue edges of the wing tips were smeared by the polish of the black toe caps. Samuel's face reddened as he rubbed a chamois skin into the thin black shadow which marked the fine leather. *Damn that Zachary,* he silently cursed. *Just had to get a hold of that poisoned liquor! Now I get some incompetent Negro at the barber shop to polish my shoes. Damn darky should be back in Africa painting the natives instead!* As if on cue, the blunt, irregular sound of a crudely crafted wind chime breezed its way through the screened window. It reminded Samuel of his former excursions into Sudan. In exchange for a few western trinkets bestowed upon avaricious head tribesmen, he had purchased the privilege to partake in their most exotic rituals. Slender, painted bodies with partially shaven heads participated in stick fights among members of their own tribe, wielding six-foot staffs with carved phallus tips. By rubbing ash into small cuts on their foreheads, natives inflicted rows of scars resembling pellets to establish tribal identity. To increase their worth in marriage, women attached to their lower lips wooden plates the size of hotcakes. But Samuel considered these amusements trivial compared to the thrill of witnessing the sacred rites of a young girl's passage into adulthood. An intoxicating satisfaction would dominate his senses as he observed the victim, her legs forced apart, screaming under the grasp of numerous women while undergoing the horror of having her genitalia sliced open by a sharpened stone or, if the natives preferred, a broken bottle, razor blade or the scissors which Samuel had so generously provided. With the aid of Acacia thorns and catgut, the two sides of her vulva would then be stitched up, leaving only a tiny opening enforced by a sliver of wood for the passage of urine and menstrual blood. The mutilated genitals would be saturated with citrus juice sealed in cow dung and her legs bound together until she was healed. The unsterile nature of these procedures had not concerned Samuel, nor had the fact that occasionally a young girl, whose vital artery had been severed, would bleed to death. His only disappointment was being denied the opportunity to participate in the procedure itself, but he eventually would find another way, after his return home, of making amends.

As the crooked sound of the wind chimes faded into the humid air, Samuel frowned. The fact that he was standing here polishing his own shoes continued to gall him. He had specifically stated in the ad his need for a servant with general nursing experience, preferably male. Yet, when questioning potential employees about simple medical procedures, more than half had failed to answer properly. The others had been too God-fearing, badly groomed or lacked domestic experience. He especially remembered the woman with a nest of red hair who reeked of moonshine whiskey. After leaving her alone for merely a moment, he had caught her filling an oversized handbag with anything she could grab hold of. *Should've hauled her off to the slammer instead of booting her ugly ass out the door,* he muttered while buffing his shoes to a superior shine. *If only I could get my hands on another morphine addict. Attentive to my needs and easy to control.* Zachary, an orphan since childhood, had been the perfect choice for a domestic servant. Besides room and board, the only other comfort Samuel needed to provide his former employee was the required amount of morphine each day. No more, no less. It worked for 13 years.

After inspecting every inch and pore of the shoes' fine leather, Samuel gathered the polishing supplies and breathed a sigh of resolve. At the very least, he could always depend on Pete the barber to give him the best shave and haircut in town—even knock 10 or 15 years off of his appearance by restoring his hair color to a dashing blonde. Gathering the supplies in one arm to render a free hand, he brushed a wavy strand from his high forehead. It was wet. He hadn't realized he was sweating. Stooping to avoid the door frame, he stepped into the utility closet and reached inside his pocket. In spite of the smell of formaldehyde still lingering upon his skin, Samuel could detect the flowery scent of perfume on the embroidered cloth, a token of his erotic rendezvous at Madame Charlotte's earlier that morning. Disguised as a luxurious cottage situated upon 20 acres of farmland just a few miles north of the Governey estate, this prestigious brothel was the only place Samuel frequented to satisfy his carnal needs. Since Madame Charlotte ran a clean house, the chance of contracting a social disease was virtually nil. In all the years he had patronized the gentlemen's roadhouse, the routine of cleaning and inspecting a customer's private parts for urethral discharge had never been neglected. And no gentleman appreciated this hygienic practice more than Samuel Governey. His medical schooling did, of course, arm him with the necessary knowledge regarding certain social diseases. But, it was not merely this education that made him so appreciative of the Madame's explicit precautions. Rather, a pivotal encounter Samuel had experienced at the volatile age of 16 provided him with all the instruction he would need for the rest of his life. Her name was Violet Stimple.

chapter 2

An Ill-Fated Discovery

Initially, the young Samuel had tried to avoid the flagrant advances of Violet, a suffragette campaigning at the University of Pennsylvania during the autumn of his freshman year. It wasn't because the young student didn't find the spirited graduate attractive, but Samuel had an unsettling feeling about the ladies—especially those who didn't seem to know their place. Yes, he had planned to take a wife some day, but when that day came, it would be on his terms. He certainly wasn't going to settle for some curvy-hipped hussy who, besides blatantly flaunting her intentions toward the inexperienced lad, pranced around Rittenhouse Square in pantalettes waving a large sign and shouting some nonsense about equal rights. In spite of her wrongheadedness, however, at least she and her good-for-nothing lady friends had sense enough to choose their words carefully, Samuel later reflected. *She was a suffragette, alright. Equal enough to give me the bloody clap. Made me suffer plenty!*

First it was the burning. Then the discharge of pus. It all started a week or so after finally succumbing to Violet's bold advances. Although Samuel suspected that this ailment had been the result of his indiscreet tryst, he delayed seeking immediate medical treatment. Perhaps under more fitting circumstances he would have been willing to confide in his father about the matter, but that possibility was out of the question. Instead, Samuel attempted to treat himself with an over-the-counter medicinal salve. But, when the infection had finally reached the point where the urgency of urination along with bleeding prohibited him from attending classes, he finally visited the attending physician on campus who administered the necessary dosage of silver nitrate over the next several months.

Maybe if the situation were different, Samuel would have been willing to forget about the pain and the time-consuming trips to the college physician. After all, Dr. Maurice had told him it could have been much worse, spreading into his bloodstream causing arthritis. Or, ultimately, death. But in spite of his restored health, the gonorrhea had not released its ugly grasp without leaving an indelible mark. Since he had not sought immediate treatment, the disease had more than likely left him sterile.

Upon learning of his inability to father a child, Samuel became obsessed even to the point of neglecting his studies. It wasn't that he had his heart set on having children—he didn't especially care for those little brats anyhow. What did disturb him so deeply, though, was the gnawing feeling that he was now half a man. And all because of some 22-year-old wench who ran around town demanding equal rights. But what about *his* bloody rights? Didn't they matter? He, Samuel Randolph Governey, the sole heir-apparent to the Governey legacy, had been stripped of the right to father a child. Not just any child, but the only successor who could perpetuate countless generations of his father's noble lineage. And all of this jeopardized by a woman who surely had more experience with intimate matters than himself. Despite the fact that it was he who delayed the necessary medical treatment, the fault still lay in the luscious lap of that good-for-nothing slut. After all, not only had the enticing brunette infected him, but it was she who had pursued him in the first place with those "come hither" eyes, dark as poison. And the whore wouldn't let up either. Not until finally having her way with him. Then she discarded him like a piece of garbage. Hadn't wanted anything to do with him since. Probably knew she was infected too. Knew and didn't care a pin. He could have stomached being stripped of anything else—even his new made-to-order "Silver Ghost" Rolls to which he, the privileged son of a British earl, was entitled. Or a good part of his future inheritance, for that matter. But the loss of his manhood was intolerable. It ate away at his mind and soul not only on campus where he would occasionally encounter Violet Stimple's cold shoulders, but throughout the remainder of the day and during the night. Especially at night. In his dreams. No matter how hard Samuel tried, he couldn't wipe that smart-ass smirk off her Jezebel face. *This is your first time, isn't it?* her sugary voice would taunt him as she'd shake down dark, thick hair. *Don't be so shy now*, she would tease, brushing firm bare breasts against the boy's naked chest while her long, commanding fingers attempted to unbutton his peg-top pants. But it would stop there. He hadn't allowed her hands on him then and he wasn't going to allow it now. It was he who would do the handling. He was the one in control. Or at least that had been the case during their erotic escapade within the private walls of "suffrage headquarters." But she had the upper hand now. Stole his family jewels. And she was going to pay.

chapter 3

Revenge

It had been several months since his initial encounter with the incorrigible libertine that young Samuel last walked across the narrow cobblestone path leading to suffrage headquarters. As the winding walkway guided the vindictive college student toward the front of the building, it occurred to him that by continuing straight on, he would find himself at the edge of the Schuylkill River. Samuel grimaced, wondering why this thought had occurred at such an inopportune time. Immediately quickening his pace, he focused on an orange brick building bordered by two gas lamps and draped by a faded awning. The headquarters, located within a foundering publishing house, displayed a soft beam of light through its front paned window, accentuating a row of shops which had closed their weary doors for the evening. The odor of horse manure mingled with the sweat on Samuel's brows as he placed his left hand into his khaki cloth pants to once again finger his pearl-handled jackknife. Peering through the scratched window of the publishing house door, he felt his temperature rise as he observed Violet under the revealing light of a brass parlor lamp. Perched behind a crude desk, with her black hair pulled up in a bun, Miss Stimple seemed as focused as a shifty raven while addressing a stack of manila envelopes. Directly behind her, the open door of the large printing room revealed only darkness. She appeared to be alone. Good. He had known that the proprietor allowed the suffragettes to use the premises after hours, but wasn't sure if Violet had still kept to Friday evenings. Or if she would be entertaining another male visitor. But as far as he could tell, she was all by herself.

Before making himself known, Samuel reviewed his strategy. He would start by giving Violet a friendly greeting as she opened the door. When they were both locked inside, he'd expose the knife and address her in his most sinister voice. Grab her by the throat. Threaten to slash her genitals. Shock her so much, she'd tremble like a weak-kneed sailor. Beg for mercy. Cry like a baby. By the time he was done with her, *she'd* be the one having nightmares—hopefully for the rest of her bloody life. As Samuel raised his hand to the door, the rattling of an electric fan inside the office reduced his angry knock to a light tap.

It took Violet Stimple a few seconds to realize that the tapping on the door was not another loose pamphlet flapping under the whirling fan. After locating the source of the noise, she put down her fountain pen and glanced toward the scratched glass, immediately recognizing Samuel. Damn! It was that awful schoolboy. What the hell did he want after all these months? Violet leaned her unbridled bosom against the desk and picked up a smoking cigar from a nearby ashtray. She had a mind not to even answer the door, she thought, and drew heavily on the panatela. Rich bastards like him were nothing but trouble. Give 'em a large cock along with a fancy English accent and they think they're the key to some fucking buried treasure. A guy like that wouldn't know how to treat a lady if she approached him stark naked and wrapped her legs around his prissy face. *Hell,* she complained under her breath while exhaling the cigar's sweet cherry scent, the stuck-up asshole wouldn't even let her touch him. She may as well have been a cadaver!

Hoping he would go away, Violet placed the cigar back on the ashtray and proceeded with her work. No longer able to tolerate the persistent knocking, however, she reached for the cigar once more and rose from her seat. She'd get rid of the son-of-a-bitch soon enough, she resolved, while stamping low-vamp heels across the hardwood floor. Upon releasing the bolt and opening the door, Violet looked up at her unwelcome guest but remained quiet, waiting for him to say something.

Samuel maintained the appearance of a reserved disposition while his mind seethed. That pompous tart had the audacity to be smoking right in front of his face. And a bloody cigar at that! He removed his hat and ran manicured fingers through his hair, regretfully eyeing the alluring cleavage above the neckline of Violet's white cotton blouse. At least she had the decency to wear her hair in a refined manner. Hell, she wasn't even wearing a corset. "Hello Violet." He paused for a moment, waiting for her to close the door, but she just stood there, saying nothing. "I wanted to see you," Samuel went on. "It has been a while, has it not?"

The priggish son-of-a-bitch was always so goddamn regal, Violet thought. She couldn't even bring herself to call him "Sam." "Yes, it has," she answered curtly, raising her brash voice above the noise of the fan while contemptuously blowing smoke into her guest's face. "Can I help you with anything?"

"Well, perhaps," he answered, "you may start by closing the door, if you do not mind."

Violet pursed her rose-painted lips while following Samuel's request. There was no reason to ignite his peculiar disposition, but she would keep the door unlatched.

The loud, steady rhythm of the fan played on Samuel's mind as he looked into Violet's dark brown eyes. He hesitated to expose the knife. She should be in a more vulnerable position. Perhaps it would be better to slowly seduce her and then proceed with his plan. Get her warmed up a bit.

"I was wondering how you were getting along, Violet."

"I didn't think there was anything to speak about," she curtly answered, tapping her sharpened fingernail against the cigar band while standing near the closed door.

Samuel forced a patronizing smile. "You look tired, Violet. I am sorry to have interrupted your work, but perhaps it is for the best. Come," he gestured toward a large Roman chair at the side of her desk. "Have a seat if you wish."

Violet took one last deep draw from the cherry-scented cigar and snuffed it out on the ashtray while still glaring at her unwelcome guest. Sitting on the edge of the chair, she continued to exhale a heavy stream of smoke while simultaneously placing delicate forearms, shadowed by soft wisps of hair, upon the armrests and crossing shapely legs. Samuel stepped toward the coat rack near the corner of the room, hung his cassimere cap above her handbag and turned off the fan. The room became startlingly quiet.

Violet's stomach suddenly turned. She wished she had her gun.

"Now," Samuel said, approaching her once again, "A lovely lady such as yourself should not be addressing this many envelopes. Your pretty little fingers are much too delicate to be pressing against a fountain pen for that long. You will blister them terribly."

Violet pulled her hand away and started to rise from the chair. "Samuel... I'm on my period so why don't we just call it a night and not waste each other's time, alright?"

Samuel stood silent for a moment as he watched her start toward the door. In an instant, he grabbed her arm, pushing her against the front of the desk.

"Get your *fucking* hand off me!"

"Do you know why I really came to see you, Violet?" he hissed, squeezing her arm even tighter. "It is because you have given me something truly special and now I am going to show you my most grateful and sincere appreciation." He reached into his pocket with his free hand and pulled out the knife. Exposing the blade, he held it to her lips. "I just want you to know, my dear, how totally overwhelmed I was to learn you had given me gonorrhea. Not every gentleman who beds a lady so lovely is fortunate enough to end up with such a precious memento."

The color started draining from Violet's face. "Sss...aamuel. Please. I...I really don't know what you're talking about. I would never do that to you...or anyone. Now, let go or...!"

"Quiet!" he demanded while clenching her arm even more and pushing his knee into her crotch.

Violet's perspiring breasts heaved under the weight of her attacker. "Samuel...please! Please don't hurt me! Let me go!" she begged, grappling for something at the side of the desk.

"Because of you, Violet, I am no longer able to have children," he sneered. "My father's heritage traces back generations and you, *my sweet*, have irrevocably severed the tree. I think it only fair that I return the favor." Samuel eased his knee away from Violet's heated crotch while lowering the blade of his knife from her quivering lips to her jugular. With vengeful anticipation, he envisioned the knife's edge ever-so-slowly gliding across the pointed nipples of her soft breasts. Teasingly, the blade would trifle with her clinging skirt, encircle the tiny hollow of her navel, and then abruptly halt its tip directly between the tufts of her legs. He would hold it there for a minute or two...maybe several as she would squirm and plead for mercy. But before he could contemplate any further, a gut-wrenching pain immobilized him. Instantly he dropped the knife, cupping himself with both hands.

Samuel watched Violet kick the knife under the desk as he lay on the bare floor in a fetal position. Towering over his curled-up body like a triumphant warrior, she defiantly gripped a long, thick pole attached to a suffragette banner. Her dark hair hung wildly about her flushed face. "You crazy son of a bitch! Get the fuck out! Get out of here right now…! You deserve what you got…! A fucking asshole like you should still be sucking on your mama's tits!"

As though a surge of electricity had jolted through him, Samuel, fighting off the pain, sprang to his feet and lurched forward, grabbing Violet's waist with both hands. Feeling a light blow to the head, he realized he had been struck with the suffragette banner. Swiftly, he grasped the thick neck of the electric fan with his right hand while still holding onto Violet with the other as she clawed sharp nails through his shirt. Ripping the fan's plug from its socket, he gave one hard blow to Violet's head, knocking her onto the crude floor. Enraged by her struggle to recover, he dropped to his knees, pinning the beaten woman down. Then, clutching the fan's thin cord, he wrapped it around Violet's neck, entangling it in long, black strands of hair. Seconds turned into minutes as Samuel persevered in tightening the cord, stretching its length to maximum breadth. Feeling like a member of a spellbound audience witnessing a skillful actor engaged in a diabolic plot, Samuel experienced a depraved satisfaction upon hearing the brash voice turn into choking gurgles. His long, thin lips broke into a demonic scowl as Violet's porcelain skin quickly transformed into a dark purplish hue, her outstretched hands grappling about in thin air. Then, at last, after what seemed to be an excruciating performance, his surrendering victim struggled no more.

Completely exhausted, Samuel sat slumped beside the dead body. Continuing to catch his breath, he stared at Violet. She looked like a tattered rag doll. Her full lips and proud nose were pressed into the hardwood, but mercifully buffered by a mop of raven hair. The dirt-stained skirt was now up to her waist, exposing a pair of ruffled drawers. Noticing her dark, torn stockings, Samuel reached out to touch the milky white skin underneath. She still felt warm. Slowly, he moved his hand upward, sliding it beneath her crumpled bloomers, stroking smooth, rounded buttocks. Spurred on by the heat of passion, he decided to undress her. Ravish her right there. It would be the perfect union. He couldn't have children and now neither could she. As he turned the body over, the smell of cherry tobacco spilled from Violet's lips while a cascade of hair fell away from a bruised, welted neck. Holding her limp body in full frontal view, Samuel noticed the thin cord still wrapped around Violet's neck and suddenly came to his senses. He, Samuel Randolph

Governey, a 17-year-old college freshman and blueblood by royalty, had just become a common murderer!

Immediately releasing Violet's body, Samuel gazed through the window, focusing on the enveloping darkness. There wasn't a soul around, he concluded, still breathing heavily. He'd better get the bloody hell out of there. Chances are, he would get away with this dastardly deed. He *must* get away with it! Another thought occurred to him as he sprang from the floor. Uncovering fingerprints was the latest technique now. He had left fingerprints on the fan. And on the floor. Could they be traced back to him if there was a thorough investigation? What if there wasn't an investigation? What if there was no body? He could wrap Violet in the scarlet blanket she had hidden in the cloak room, put her in the back seat of his Rolls and drive her to his home on Chestnut Street. Hopefully, with his father's long-standing habit of drinking and staying out late, there would be no problem secreting her body into the colonial mansion. He could stuff her in a steamer trunk and lock it in the fruit cellar. Then, when the time was ripe, he would rent a boat in the middle of the night and drop the trunk into the river. Sneaking her remains out the back door of the publishing house would be his first move, though. The Silver Ghost was parked right there. Before leaving, he would tidy up a bit to give the appearance of Violet having unexpectedly left town. Although it had been a messy struggle, it was still a relatively clean kill. No great loss of blood—just a few scratches, he thought, noticing the dried slivers of blood piercing through his wrinkled, yellow shirt. Hell, the whore hadn't even soiled her drawers.

Samuel quickly went about his business, first wrapping the body in the scarlet wool blanket. Satisfied that his inspection of the electric fan showed no sign of foul play, he then placed it back on the cabinet and pushed the plug into its socket. As an extra precaution, he took a piece of stationery from the desk and thoroughly wiped down any area of the fan that he had touched, repeating this procedure over the rest of the room. After pocketing the retrieved jackknife, he opened the top drawer of the desk and placed the fountain pen next to a set of keys, using the piece of stationery as a glove. Eyeing the burned-out cigar in the ashtray while experiencing a twinge of déjà vu, he decided to leave it alone. Dismissing the unexpected discomfort, he sighed. In spite of the terrible struggle, the desk was still in fair order.

After donning his cap and removing Violet's handbag from the coat rack, Samuel extinguished the parlor lamp. Waiting for his eyes to adjust to the darkness, he lifted the blanketed body and hoisted it over the handbag upon his stiffened shoulder. Finally, in a last effort to rid the room of any evidence, he stooped down to pick up the suffrage banner, the word "LIBERTY" ripped apart. Clenching the sign underneath his free arm, he quickly headed for the back room. Treading his way across the creaky floor, his footsteps, becoming slow and heavy, suddenly ceased. The printing press and work tables which idly sat upon the ink-stained floor appeared strangely sinister as he stood at the room's center where, within the throes of one particular crisp autumn evening, he had bedded the vibrant suffragette upon the scarlet blanket and, for a lingering moment, Samuel could detect the faint outline of Violet's shapely body beckoning him to stay. Feeling as if a pair of weights bore down upon his kidskin shoes, he carried the body toward the back of the room. There, he paused for a moment, attempting to catch his breath. Then, with his heart beating wildly, he slipped out the door.

In time, the investigation blew over. The authorities, finding no evidence of foul play and wishing to avoid panic on campus, attributed the suffragette's disappearance to a case of free-spirited whimsy. This behavior, they attested, was not unusual for women of her character who were willing to leave town not only unexpectedly, but unchaperoned as well. Upon finalizing his sinister plan and many years thereafter, a satisfied smile would every so often chisel its way into Samuel's face at the thought of Violet Stimple decomposing beneath the dark, murky waters of the Schuylkill River, her long, black hair, like battered seaweed, escaping through the holes he had drilled between the heavy clamps of the basswood trunk.

chapter 4

Parental Ties

Being a descendant of British nobility, Samuel's father, Randolph Eugene Governey, had been endowed at birth with the aristocratic title, "Earl of Cheshire." Having also inherited homosexual tendencies, however, the earl remained an unwed highbrow until the seasoned age of 47. But Randolph Governey's decision to marry was not the result of the social mores often facing aristocratic playboys of his time. Rather, the earl's flagrant spending habits during his bachelorhood, leaving him virtually penniless, had prompted him to seek a rich American wife.

Bringing along his best attire as well as a few precious heirlooms, he set sail across the Atlantic aboard the *RMS Etruria*. Knowing that the prestigious ocean liner would be occupied by several wealthy American heiresses and hopeful that at least one title-seeking maiden would be eager to latch on to a tall, dashing English earl, he shrewdly staked out his future wife. As fortune would have it, on the second evening of the three-week voyage, his plan proved well worth the wager. For under a cool star-filled late summer sky on its promenade deck as the great ship headed westward, the homely 31-year-old daughter of an American oil tycoon, Louisa Beth Langley, was overcome by the earl's warm-heartedness as he offered her his monogrammed jacket.

———◦———

Louisa Beth Langley, residing in a Philadelphian mansion with her long-widowed father, Frank Lawrence Langley, grew up as a child often shunned

15

by her playmates. Even though Louisa's nursemaids would dress her in frilled lace or smartly-styled day dresses, the lonely heiress would take on the appearance of a bug-eyed scarecrow. With a nose too long for her drawn, freckled face and unruly chestnut-colored hair cropped above droopy shoulders, the boyish young lady yearned to win the admirable glances bestowed upon her younger twin sisters, Cassandra and Beatrice.

By the time Louisa reached adolescence, the discriminating scales between the unattractive heiress and her younger siblings remained grossly unbalanced, weighing heavily upon the dejected debutante's social life. Plagued with an unsightly complexion and breasts which made her gaunt body appear overstuffed, Louisa promptly would have joined an abbey if not for the required vow of poverty. To make a bad situation worse, at the age of 25 when Louisa herself should have been well-settled in marriage, the gangly spinster reluctantly served as maid of honor for her sisters' elaborate double wedding. At the reception, she purposefully caught one of the brides' bouquets, immediately closed her eyes and wished for a reputable husband of her own. Later, upon bringing the fragrant orange and white blossoms into her home, she untied one of its knotted ribbons with spindly fingers, hoping, according to the old superstition, that her bridegroom would soon appear. But to Louisa's disappointment, the only man who kept reappearing along the embellished corridors of the opulent mansion was her silver-haired father, offering his broken-hearted daughter what little consolation he could.

Although Louisa was initially jealous of her sisters' good fortune, she was glad that they had married two brothers from New York. Since the attractive twins would be living a good distance from Philadelphia, she would no longer be subject to the intolerable attentions they encouraged. But even these expectations fell along the wayside. Not only were the Martin brothers handsome and affluent, but the refined young men had been appointed "Patriarchs" by Mrs. William Backhouse Astor, the queen of New York's highly-esteemed Knickerbocker society. As a result, their privileged wives would often send lengthy letters to Louisa on personally-embossed stationery describing their fashionable lives near Central Park. All the more envious of her siblings' good fortunes, Louisa would dream of attending the lavish affairs and parties of the "crème de la crème," particularly the renowned party of the century, the great Vanderbilt ball. But her protruding lips would gradually curl into a heavy pout as she realized that she probably never would experience waltzing with a husband of her own in an immense ballroom filled with extravagantly-costumed guests. Or, for that matter, walk arm-in-arm with her new groom down Fifth Avenue after attending early Sunday morning church services.

But on the evening of September 12, 1888, on a luxury cruise designed to cheer her spirits, Louisa, on the threshold of despair, trusted that she had miraculously found the answer to her prayers. Gazing into the frothy, fleeting black water of the Atlantic as her corseted chest cushioned the *RMS Etruria's* varnished oak rail, Louisa Beth Langley felt her heart leaping upon hearing the voice of Randolph Eugene Governey. The reserved heiress was stunned by her own reaction; she had, after all, heard the warm familiar "How do you do?" directed toward pretty maidens a number of times. *However,* she soon realized, apart from the owner of the princely voice, the only other person occupying the large, open space of the promenade deck was herself.

"Excuse me for being so forward," the tall, mustached stranger apologized, presenting a black wool dinner jacket, "but my conscience could not allow another moment to pass without offering my assistance." Aware that the single heiress was at a loss for words, he sympathetically added, "The chill…it will be the death of you. You are shivering and in need of a warmer wrap." As a hesitant smile crossed the heiress's blushing face, Randolph Governey placed the jacket around her taffeta-covered shoulders. "Allow me to introduce myself," he exclaimed with a graceful bow while reaching for Louisa's hand. "Randolph Governey, Earl of Cheshire."

Louisa pressed the lapels of the jacket against the high lace neck of her pink satin gown as the earl's deep blue eyes fell upon the back of her hand in preparation for the customary kiss. She could not help but notice upon his forefinger the elaborate gold & onyx ring encrusted with a coat of arms as he pressed his soft, warm lips against her skin. Aware of the impropriety of speaking to a stranger without being formally introduced, she nevertheless replied elegantly as the earl returned her hand. "Louisa. Louisa Langley. It is indeed a pleasure to make your acquaintance."

chapter 5

A Royal Marriage

In an elaborate wedding ceremony at St. Peter's Episcopal Church on an overcast day in June of 1889, Louisa Beth Langley, the last of Frank Lawrence Langley's three daughters, married Earl Randolph Eugene Governey. After walking with her new husband down the red-carpeted aisle of the crowded church adorned with orchids and filled with the music of a chamber orchestra, the virginal bride, bedecked in a wedding gown with a train of five yards, declared this day to be her happiest. Following a procession of gilt-laden carriages led by matching gray horses, the wedding party and guests attended a lavish breakfast served by a number of white-wigged footmen adorned in purple plush breeches. During the evening's reception, sitting amidst numerous wedding gifts mostly of crystal and sterling, Louisa flauntingly eyed her sisters with their common American husbands as Frank Langley presented his daughter with a diamond tiara in celebration of her newly-acquired title, "Countess of Cheshire."

Although it was customary for an aristocratic couple to complete their honeymoon in the south of France before taking residence at the groom's ancestral estate, the newlyweds opted instead to spend their entire vacation in America. Randolph, desiring to avoid the issue of physical intimacy as a result of his sexual disposition, declared that after the honeymoon, it was incumbent upon him to personally visit his London manor with its neglected grounds where he would oversee the commencement of requisite restorations. Then, after transferring all details to a trustworthy overseer, he would return to America and reside with Louisa in New York for however long it took to complete the project. This would not only enable his dear wife to avoid the unpleasantness of dwelling in a barely renovated home located in an unfamiliar country, but seeing how she had taken a fancy to the thought of living in New York for a while, it was a comfortable situation for both to accept. The extended honeymoon, which at Louisa's insistence lasted two months, took place in Newport, Rhode Island. Fortunately for Randolph, since the upscale town was the favorite summer romping ground for America's foremost citizens, a heavy schedule of activities helped relieve the homosexual groom from his nuptial duties. Louisa, on the other hand, having been sheltered and raised as a puritanical Christian lady, was not quite sure what to expect in the marriage bed, but had the gnawing feeling that it involved more than a complimentary good night hug and peck on the cheek.

Prepared to change into as many as ten flamboyant outfits throughout the day, the newlyweds, after having spent the previous night dining, dancing and theatre-going, would enjoy breakfast on the terrace of their private chateau. Next on the agenda was the usual equestrian ride about the elm-shaded town, after which the couple would occupy the later part of the morning shopping on Bellevue Avenue and viewing a game of tennis. Noontime activities included swimming on the rocky shores of Bailey's Beach and eating lunch, either served on a steam yacht or on tented grounds complete with all the china, silver and personal service to which royal couples were accustomed. Mid-afternoon found the honeymooners at the polo field followed by a late afternoon promenade of carriages. Flaunting a six-carat diamond upon her gloved hand and with a white lace parasol closed tightly beside her, Louisa, sitting alongside Randolph in their personal coach, would excitedly nudge her husband upon recognizing several faces she had seen in the society section of the *Philadelphia Times*. However, regardless of Louisa's newly-attained status, she knew better than to give the likes of the Astors as much as a nod before being properly introduced. Having been raised among the "nouveaux riches," she understood the discriminating etiquette of those having a history of generational wealth, knowing that it sometimes took years for debutantes in the same social circle to become one of their "elect."

Tea on the couple's terrace at five o'clock had initially left Louisa hungry for more than crumpets and lobster salad. Yearning to trade a token of herself for a few passionate kisses, the new bride would first wait for the attending servant to clear the dishes and leave the room. Then, declaring how uncomfortable summer finery was, she would remove her feathered hat while asking Randolph in the sweetest voice to help unbutton her bustled gown. Finally, upon turning to face her husband, Louisa would pucker her lips into one budding beak. However, Randolph's response to her affectionate overtures was to declare that they best utilize the time by catching 40 winks before dressing for eight o'clock dinner. Despite such disappointment, she would defer to her husband's wishes and, after several days, resigned herself to the fact that in spite of his passivity in the bedroom, she had gotten a good bargain after all.

Although she found the honeymoon to be rather disappointing, Louisa's spirits were eventually lifted by a visit from her sisters at the chateau after which, to her utmost delight, she was introduced to Mrs. William Astor and other prominent members of the Knickerbocker society. Finally the countess and her husband were not only mingling with America's aristocracy, but were being invited to luncheons and dinners at their most pretentious Newport homes. It was like a dream come true for Louisa and from that point on, the honeymoon elapsed more swiftly than a high-nosed snub toward an undeserving lowborn.

After the honeymoon, the newlyweds promptly moved into their opulent new home on New York's Park Avenue. Although a few of the Knickerbockers skeptically assumed that the tall, dashing earl had married a homely Philadelphian strictly for her money, the royal marriage was received readily by the majority of New York's elite. Upon their arrival at the train station, a welcome committee complete with a five-piece band and gift-bearing horses awaited them. Then, the very next evening before the earl's departure for England, a going-away party was given, leaving no time at all for the exhausted couple to share more than a good night's sleep in the master bedroom.

Sorry to see her husband leave for Europe just a couple of days after their arrival, the Countess of Cheshire was nevertheless content with residing, for the time being, in the city of her dreams. Preoccupied with decorating the impressive three-story townhouse as well as socializing with New York's upper crust, Louisa patiently awaited the day when she and the earl would proudly stroll their newborn child, preferably a male heir, down Park Avenue. At first, the virginal wife, still pitifully ignorant of conjugal intimacies, had been hopeful of already being with child. She did, after all, share a bed with her husband every night since their marriage. Wasn't that how a woman befell such a delicate condition? By sleeping with a man? Why, ever since the honeymoon, even their bare feet had touched underneath the satin sheets plenty of times.

Having gotten over the initial disappointment of not conceiving a child, Louisa occupied more of her spare time in the late autumn months replying to the increasing number of letters received from her husband overseas. Unlike the first messages of a long remaining summer which were few and far between, the countess noticed an enthusiasm about the earl's writing to which she was not previously accustomed. The renovations of his estate were not only coming along, but had exceeded his expectations. A renowned Parisian decorator was doing a splendid job enhancing the great hall and supervising the re-carpeting of the grand staircase while the master masons were refurbishing the mansion's stone facing. The gardeners, having labored all summer underneath the intermittent British sun, had finally completed their duties for the year.

Although Louisa wished she could be with her husband for the holidays, she was nonetheless excited with the arrival of the Christmas season, especially after being invited to Mrs. Astor's home during the week of the Nativity holiday. The Astor residence, located on 34th and Fifth Avenue, was an extravagant four-story brownstone with one of the few private ballrooms in New York. Looking forward to wearing her diamond tiara and red velvet gown designed for the occasion, she anticipated mingling with other guests while sharing delicious tidbits of her prospective London residence. And since her husband, the earl, would not be there to accompany her, Louisa's father readily agreed to travel all the way from Philadelphia to take his son-in-law's honored place. Unfortunately, however, she received a short message from her father stating that as a result of his feeling out of sorts, he would be unable to tolerate the trip after all. Presuming that it would not be proper to attend this affair unescorted, the countess developed a most terrible case of melancholy. The realization that she would not be attending Mrs. Astor's party, the one event she had looked forward to all season, brought her to the brink of utter despair. Even the servants who had decorated the halls of her home with holly sprigs and spice-scented candles could not lift the gloomy mood from their mistress. Louisa resorted to sitting alone in the darkened drawing room after dinner, sipping hot butter rum in an effort to soothe her spirits. On one particularly frigid, blustery evening in late December, she was especially perturbed upon being interrupted by the parlor maid.

"Excuse me, madame," the servant meekly inquired, "but there are carolers at the door! I thought they might cheer you up a bit, ma'am."

Louisa lowered the mug from her lips and forced herself to swallow the warm brew. It was annoying enough that the footman had so rudely interrupted her about the placement of the Yule log. "Marjorie, I instructed you specifically that under no circumstances was I to be disturbed!"

"Madame, I beg your pardon, but I just thought that...."

"What business do they have coming around so early anyway? It's not even Christmas Eve. Next thing you know, we'll be decorating the halls in November! We may as well go ahead and light the Yule log!" Noticing the maid's subservient silence, she added, "Give them each a nickel and a piece of ginger cake and send them on their way."

"Yes, madame, as you wish."

The parlor maid wiped the sweat off her brow as she headed toward the foyer to let the carolers inside before going to fetch their meager tokens. What a tyrant this one was! She, Marjorie Blair, a reputable employee, whose ancestors had loyally served a number of royal families, came all the way from England for this? Why!...working for the Tsar of Russia would have been much easier and the traveling less. And the woman was ugly. Ugly as a cross-eyed toad! If it weren't for all that money of hers, she'd be out on the streets begging too. It was no wonder the master was staying in London!

Upon opening the front door to the chorus of "The First Nowel," the maid was suddenly startled by a strong flurry of snow slapping her face. As if nothing out of the ordinary had happened, the five young merry wishers dressed in winter rags and wet, scant shoes, continued their song. But the maid, instead of inviting them in to warm themselves, stood mute, blinking the wintry wetness from her eyes. Then, in total astonishment, she focused on the prominent figure before her. The tall, unexpected visitor wearing a familiar cassimere coat and top hat carried a stack of brightly-wrapped packages piled up to his chin. Behind him, on the sleeted street, stood a snow-covered coach accompanied by an attentive footman and a set of matched grays.

"Why!...why, my God! If the devil ain't playin' tricks on my bloody eyes ...It's Master Governey!"

"Good evening, Marjorie," the earl replied, raising his baritone voice above the refrain of "Joy to the World." Scrutinizing the merry group, he then added, "Another welcoming committee? How on earth could you possibly have known of my arrival? It was supposed to be a secret!"

Marjorie let out a bright, warm smile while nervously adjusting her white cap. "Sir, I was on my way to fetch them each a nickel and a piece of cake. The madame's instructions. She will be so happy to see you, sir!"

"Well, in that case, let me save you the trip," the earl offered. "If you will be so kind as to take a couple of these gifts from my hands."

Randolph signaled the footman to retrieve the rest of the gifts and then accompanied the singing group inside while reaching into his coat pocket. The carolers stopped mid-phrase as the lordly gentleman handed each of them a crisp dollar bill. Randolph was equally spellbound as his penetrating dark blue eyes gazed upon a remarkably beautiful pubescent lad. At last, he instructed the rosy-cheeked boy to remove his cap. The youngster's full, shivering lips instantly spread into a wide appreciative smile as the generous master of the house ruffled his matted blonde hair and dropped a five-dollar bill into the sock-like hat. Suddenly, upon hearing a familiar voice, Randolph reluctantly tore himself away from the speechless poppet.

"Randolph!"

"Louisa, my dear!" the earl exclaimed, still viewing the young lad from the corner of his eye. He then stepped forward to greet his wife with a generous hug. "How marvelous to be back in your arms. How I missed you so!"

The countess broke into tears as she clung to her tall, handsome husband. "Oh, my dear Randolph," she cried, clutching the padded shoulders of his overcoat. "It has been absolutely awful here without you. I did not want to let on in my letters, but now that you're home.... Oh Randolph, this is the nicest surprise I have ever been favored with!" Quickly, she helped him remove his wet, heavy overcoat, ordering Marjorie to hang it upon the garment rack to dry while the other bustling servants carried Randolph's bags into the house. Then, arm-in-arm, the countess accompanied her earl into the pine-scented hallway leading to the foot of the stairs while the excited voices of the carolers faded into the frigid night. Briefly pausing to admire the eight-foot Douglas Fir decorated with shiny bulbs, sugarplums, and a multitude of tiny, unlit tapers, the couple then ascended the winding stairway to freshen up in the regally-bedecked bed chamber.

Louisa visited the boudoir to reapply freckle ointment, examine her tightly-pinned hair, and retouch her dark pink lipstick while Randolph, anticipating a lavish dinner in comfort after seven days of rugged travel, removed his suit jacket, vest, and damp shoes. Ever appreciative of the circumstances that had afforded his newly-found wealth, he carefully placed a brand new platinum pocket watch upon the washstand before stepping into a pair of slippers. Opening the drawer of the matching golden oak dresser, he then donned a silk brocade smoking jacket which, along with several other items of clothing, had awaited his return over the past few months.

While re-waxing his handlebar mustache in front of the dresser's scroll-framed mirror, Randolph could already smell the chicken Dijon warming in the oven. In an instant, however, the delicious aroma of the earl's late evening meal was impudently replaced by the smell of heavy perfume as Louisa appeared before him looking, in his opinion, considerably worse than when she had greeted him at the front door. Preferring instead the boyish looks of her natural features, the earl nevertheless complimented his wife before escorting her down the stairs.

A single place setting of Herend china and Louis XV sterling silver, along with a glass of cognac awaited Randolph as the couple entered the mirrored dining room. Within a few minutes, Randolph's full meal, reflected in splendid presentation, was set before him. With his countess beside him, the earl ate and drank heartily while listening to her account of the upcoming Christmas extravaganza at the Astor's. But at that particular moment, attending a stuffy party with her New York friends was the most remote matter on Randolph's mind. Patiently listening to his wife's babbling, the earl contemplated the imminent grandeur of the Governey estate back in England while reassessing his plan to produce an heir to the family's noble lineage.

Having already requested the first floor maid to prepare the parlor and bring in two glasses of wassail spiked with red wine, Randolph retrieved one of the smaller gifts under the candled tree in the entrance hall and accompanied his wife into the cozy curtained room. He then directed Louisa onto a tufted loveseat, allowing the crackling fire to provide them with ample lighting. Besides radiating a welcoming warmth throughout the room, the yellow-blue flames mercifully accentuated the scent of the mantle's large pine wreath, softening the harsh smell of Louisa's flowery perfume.

"Louisa," he began, bearing the beribboned package while comfortably seating himself aside his wife on the velvet seat, "I know that things have been rushed along since our wedding. Believe me, darling, when in London, I thought of you every day and regretted that we had not chosen an unhurried place for our honeymoon." He reached for his wife's oversized hand while holding the gift with his other. "My darling, when in England I searched everywhere for something that would express my profound and unending love for you," he emphatically stated, referring to a family heirloom he had paid a local English jeweler to reset.

"But Randolph, my dearest," Louisa protested, hiding her eager delight. "You should not have! It's not even Christmas yet and besides, I haven't gotten you a thing. If only I had known...."

"Hush, my dear," Randolph answered while squeezing Louisa's hand. "My most precious gift is already sitting before me. Come now," he nodded, releasing his grip. "Unwrap the gift. I am anxious to see how you like it."

Without further protest, she unwrapped the package and slipped the velvet case from its box. Her drawn jaw dropped even lower as she opened the case and stared at a sparkling ruby pendant, considerably larger than her thumbnail, surrounded by a garland of diamonds. A string of perfectly-formed miniature pearls, resembling polished smoke, displayed a luster her ruddy complexion had never known. "Oh Randolph! It's perfect...it's absolute perfection! I can't wait to wear it to the Christmas dance. It will match my dress beautifully!"

"Turn the pendant over," the earl insisted.

Acquiescing, Louisa read out loud the inscription engraved upon the 18-carat gold plate. "*Louisa & Randolph, Christmas, 1889.*"

"I want us never to forget our first Christmas together," the earl explained.

"And it is indeed a special Christmas. Oh, Randolph darling!" Louisa cried while stroking her fingers along his cheekbone. "The best gift you could ever give me is your own sweet presence!"

Randolph eyed the tiny gold spheres on his wife's thumb-shaped earlobes. "There are also earrings to match," he explained, taking the velvet case from Louisa and removing the necklace from the box. "The jeweler will be sending them from England. They will be arriving shortly." After unlatching the diamond clasp, he draped the heirloom around the lace-collared neck of his beaming wife. The ruby's shimmering clarity against her dark silk dress emphasized even more the dullness of Louisa's bristly hair. "There!" he exclaimed. "The necklace will never grace a more fitting subject!"

Straining her neck to better view the exquisite pendant upon the yoke of her dress, she sighed, "Oh, Randolph! It's absolutely beautiful! I shall never want to take it off!"

"Then don't," he interjected. "Wear it as long as you wish. It is yours to do with as you please. Now, my dear, let us toast our blessed marriage." He then handed a glass of the cinnamon-sprinkled wine to Louisa, hoping that in early fall of the ensuing New Year, she would be the mother of their new-born son.

As the crackling flames within the hearth of the ivory fireplace continued to devour the crumbling logs, the couple engaged in small talk, filling each other in on misplaced details of the last five months. Louisa, intoxicated from the events of the entire evening as well as the wine-filled drink, felt especially passionate and restlessly waited for her husband's cue to retire for the evening. As the mantle clock chimed ten, beckoning Elsworth, the head butler, to place more logs among the dying embers, Randolph unexpectedly stopped him. To the countess' immense satisfaction, he told the servant to precede them upstairs to the bed chamber and tend to the fireplace there. With eager trepidation, Louisa followed her husband up the winding stairway and into the bedroom, viewing with a new perspective the satin sheets the chamber maid had recently turned down for the evening. After impatiently waiting for the butler to check the vents and restock the fireplace with dry birch logs, Louisa coyly dismissed him. Listening for Elsworth's footsteps to fade down the long staircase, she turned toward her husband and asked him to unfasten the back of her dress. But this time, after guiding the last cone-shaped button through its yielding crevice, he did not turn away.

chapter 6

Dreams and Schemes

Despite the rekindled fire warming her flushed cheeks, Louisa shuddered as the earl's agile fingertips tickled her collarbone. His forceful hands had so fluently helped her out of her gown and petticoat that she hardly had to wiggle, she noted, aware of the emerald-colored gown, its perfumed bodice stiffly standing atop the puddled skirt. And now, here he was...her dear, dashing earl, unbuttoning the front of her corset cover, her bare arms and silk-covered legs in full, frontal view. And here *she* was, allowing him to unsheathe her, so unlike the chaste lady she *ought* to be. And how far would he go? How far would she permit him to undress her? Louisa blushed as the answer became as apparent as the ruby and pearl necklace which would, no doubt, linger amid the cleavage of her bosom. *Yes...*she would let him take off *everything.* Even her corset and muslin drawers if he so desired.

Louisa let out an undignified gasp as Randolph began to unlatch each garter of the corset, the black silk fabric of her stockings falling to her ankles. Instinctively freeing each foot from the loosened stockings, Louisa, trembling, looked up toward her husband. With a determined gaze storming dark blue eyes, he pressed his ringed forefinger upon her gaping mouth. Before Louisa could attempt to comprehend such a gesture, she was feeling the weight of gold and onyx as he firmly traced her silent lips. Suddenly aware that Randolph was hindering her feminine appearance by smearing the rose-colored lipstick, she was tempted to pull away, but her concern was quickly forgotten as the intensity of the earl's eyes reflected a never seen before look...a look much more than mere desire. Although she could not define it, Louisa believed in her womanly soul that it was the look of deep wanting...the look of magnified lust. Breathing with relief upon being reassured of her husband's unconditional love, she allowed herself to relax once again, continuing to savour the passion which burned inside.

As Randolph began to untie her corset, Louisa felt her bosom swell like a replenished poinsettia. With quick, even breaths she awaited her husband's response. This was the first time he would be viewing her completely unclothed. As the strings of the corset grew longer with each liberating pull, she felt an intense desire to tear it off herself...to grab Randolph's hands and brand them to her firm, full breasts. Her anticipation was further ignited as the stiff cotton fabric finally bursting forth, spilled her ample bosom, as if unleashing two resplendent turtledoves. Abashedly aware of her pert, crimson nipples, Louisa stood bewildered as Randolph stepped away and proceeded to undress himself behind her back. Although the thought of seeing her husband in such an exposed state inflamed her curiosity, she did not turn around, fearing the experience too overwhelming for her maidenly eyes. She had, of course, beheld paintings and sculptures of the male form in cathedrals and art museums, finding them fascinating. But, after all, they were mere imitations. And even so, an intruding fig leaf, or worse yet, some cruel and deliberate castration had often prevented her from experiencing the wondrous pieces of art in all their masculine glory.

Louisa's virginal musings were suddenly enhanced as the earl's aristocratic hands, reaching from behind, cupped her taut waist. Instantly, she let out another gasp, feeling the muslin drawers, along with stern fingers glide down her hips and along the full length of her legs. Finally stepping out of the last piece of underclothing, Louisa could hardly bear it. Except for the radiant necklace gracing her bosom, her blissfully aching body was now exposed in all its innocent splendor.

Puzzled by her husband's request to lie face down upon the bed, Louisa obediently complied, though self-conscious about her boyish buttocks which, up until a few moments ago, had been cleverly camouflaged by the padding of her undergarment. No longer bridled by the shackles of modesty, she entertained the idea of disregarding the earl's instructions altogether so that her finest feminine feature...abundant breasts crowned by ripe, berry-like nipples...would be available for him to see...fondle...even squeeze...the sensations racing downward through her midriff and toward her abdomen until she would somehow, some way, find herself bursting into sudden shards of ecstasy. But before she could act on such an impulse, Randolph's strength was holding her down, his hands pressing into the small of her back as he slowly kneaded his way toward her narrow hips and unshapely buttocks.

Louisa, by now frenzied with desire and longing to be ravished in places she had never before dared to imagine, rose to her knees as the earl attempted to enter her. Kneading her own breasts with one hand while trying to satisfy the throbbing desire between her moist thighs with the other, she suddenly shrieked upon feeling her virginal flesh tear away. Her pleas for Randolph to stop lasted only a fleeting moment before she understood that beyond this threshold of pain was the promise of incomprehensible pleasure; her formerly sacred, undefiled pool bursting into a turbulent ocean with quickened force. Relaxing her stiffened body and resuming the aid of her own man-sized hands, Louisa begged the earl to continue as she deliriously witnessed the satin sheets quaking beneath. As the hearth's blazing fire enticed the frost upon the velvet-draped windows to melt into tiny, sweat-like droplets, Louisa remained oblivious to her surroundings. In spite of the fierce winter storm which continued to rattle the heavy panes of the streaked, clouded glass, she could hear no more than the feverish roar which raged within her fiery soul.

Deliriously surrendering her savage sensations, Louisa let out several long screams while the earl, achieving his own victorious climax, clenched her tightened buttocks with both hands. Though his grip began to loosen, Louisa, oblivious to the easing weight of her husband, continued to bask in self-induced ecstasy. Finally exhausted by enduring abandon, she collapsed upon the blood-christened sheets. Breathing heavily, Louisa clutched the embroidered pillow and contemplated her husband, peacefully lying on his side with eyes closed, looking no less magnificent than Michelangelo's "David" or Titian's "Adonis." Gingerly, she shifted her gaze toward her husband's glistening thighs, hoping to catch a glimpse of that special manhood which, only minutes prior had accompanied her into the throes of insurmountable pleasure. Though mostly hidden by a reclining posture, the placid appendage looked more like a wax ornament withdrawn from a warm oven. Louisa sighed while reflecting upon her naiveté. Perhaps at last she would now bear their child. Being careful not to disturb him, she cautiously reached for Randolph's warm, unresponsive hand and pressed it to her bejeweled bosom. Then, stretching her arm across his smooth, muscled chest, she relished his rich, seductive scent which, like a potent opiate, lulled her into a sound and peaceful sleep.

chapter 7

Solitary Labor

During one fretful November evening in the year of our Lord 1890, as the fierce autumn winds heralded the impending arrival of another brutal winter, Louisa Langley Governey, confined to the same canopied bed upon which she had experienced abounding ecstasy, comprehended once again the bizarre courtship between pleasure and pain. Going into labor two weeks before the announced due date, the countess was immediately accompanied to her room by Gerta, the recently-hired Swedish midwife. The earl, doing his best to insure that his wife would bear a healthy child, immediately called for her obstetrician, Dr. Otto Gruben, who arrived within the hour. Disregarding Louisa's desperate cries, Randolph instructed the doctor to do all he could for the baby which, he had learned shortly before the obstetrician's arrival, was in transverse breech position. Deciding there was nothing more for him to do, the earl conveniently isolated himself within the library. Located on the first floor near the back of the house, the mahogany-paneled room filled with robust furniture and displaying a showcase of leather-bound books, was the most effective way of shielding the earl from his wife's irritating moans. And, since dinner had been so tersely disrupted, he demanded that Marjorie bring in a tray of freshly-cooked mutton. He also made it a point to remind Elsworth to fetch his nightwear, since he intended to sleep upon the plush Verona davenport that was painstakingly carried in from the parlor.

After taking one last bite of his potatoes lyonnaise, Earl Randolph Governey placed the monogrammed sterling silver fork upon his dish, removed the linen napkin from his lap and reached for a snifter of half-century old cognac. Swirling the potent drink and inhaling its sweet bouquet, he surveyed the sumptuous room, grateful that only the hearth's crackling fire hindered its welcome silence. Placing the glass to his lips, he congratulated himself. Never in his wildest dreams had he expected to procure such an exceptional dowry. He had done damned well after all. Replacing the crystal glass upon the silver tray, Randolph wondered how his wife was coming along. Would she bear him the son he was hoping for? He winced upon considering the alternative. It had been a welcome relief during the past nine months to refrain from marital relations after bribing Dr. Gruben to concoct a convincing account of the dangers involved; the thought of having to repeat the whole pathetic sexual charade numerous times was more than he could stomach at the moment. That is, if his wife even survived the birth.

Randolph took one last swig of cognac, hoping Louisa's labor would not last past the morning, yet long enough to allow for a hardy night's sleep. Although the library was comfortable, being cooped up in one room for an exaggerated amount of time was not his forte. Even Armand, his current Viennese lover, could not persuade the earl to linger in his embraces for more than a few hours. Placing the empty sniffer aside, Randolph envisioned Armand, the blonde, curly-haired architectural student half his age. Having known the young man for a mere three months, he was growing rather weary of him; somewhat like a piece of parchment handled once too many times. Perhaps it was time to move on.

Randolph opened his desk drawer and removed a small enameled container. Unsnapping its lid, he noted the bright red inscription, *"English Legend,"* sprawled across the faded ivory image of a British castle. After placing the cap upon the embossed leather-framed blotter, he pinched a clump of firmly-packed snuff between his thumb and ringed forefinger. Being careful not to disturb his moustache, Randolph raised the wad to his nostril and snorted the rum tobacco. Having repeated this process to the other side of the nose, he wiped his flared, reddened nostrils with a silk handkerchief and recapped the container. Focusing once again upon the illustration gracing the lid, he reflected upon his own magnificent dwelling in Cheshire. Although the medieval structure had been on the stocks since late June, and its overseer was certainly competent, the progress of the castle's renovation had been temporarily hindered due to shipping delays and inclement weather. Replacing the snuff box inside the desk drawer, Randolph surmised that the early spring of 1892 would not only provide waters calm enough to cross the Atlantic comfortably, but also allow an aristocratic family of three to take residence in the refurbished castle without any foreseeable regrets.

Reclining against the back of the tufted leather chair, Randolph reached for his pocket watch. Half past ten. It was time Elsworth cleared the dinner tray and brought in his nightwear. Firmly snapping the case of the watch, he eyed a silver crown smoothly etched upon brushed platinum. Hopefully, the earl aspired, before the night was out, another set of male hands with tiny royal fingers would claim this prospective heirloom and eventually pass it onto another generation. Realizing that he would be undressing in a minute or two, he placed the watch upon the desk and summoned the head butler who, while helping Randolph into his nightwear, anxiously stated that Louisa was still going through a most wretched time. After dismissing the servant, Randolph, feeling he had experienced a most trying day himself, settled upon the oversized sofa underneath its downy layers of bedding. Reassuring himself that his son could not be delivered by a more competent set of hands than Dr. Gruben's, he closed his tired eyes.

Although the solemn atmosphere of the library had initially cooperated with Randolph's wishes for tranquility, he gradually awoke from his peaceful slumber upon hearing a faint, howling noise. It most probably was a stray cat, he groaned, reaching for the usual feather pillow to place about his ears. But upon feeling the soft walls of the davenport closing in on him, Randolph realized he was not in his own bed. Suddenly aware of the surroundings of the library, he started to recall the circumstances which had led to his refuge there. It was Louisa. She had unexpectedly gone into labor, but not without complications. The baby, lying crosswise against the womb, was not settled in its usual birthing position. He pictured Dr. Otto Gruben stroking his goatee while expounding upon the difficulties involved. Since this was Louisa's first child, chances were that the labor itself would be atypically prolonged. When the baby was ready for birth, manual repositioning would be necessary in order to allow its buttocks to emerge. And, finally, most likely with the help of forceps, the infant's head would be guided from the womb. Although the doctor seemed confident that Louisa could successfully deliver the child in this manner, an operation might be necessary allowing removal of the baby through the abdomen. Whatever the case, the obstetrician had promised, he would do everything possible to deliver not only a flourishing, robust baby, but to preserve Louisa's excellent health as well.

Anxiously ruffling the down-filled layers of bedding, Randolph propped himself against the stiff, tufted back of the davenport. Squinting his eyes, he looked about the library. Although the remaining embers within the fireplace were lively enough to provide adequate warmth, their diminished intensity contributed an eerie glow to the room. As far as he could guess, it was probably close to dawn. But, being that the lined, velvet curtains were shut tight, it was hard to tell for certain. While Randolph pondered whether to walk across the room to retrieve his pocket watch, his thoughts were once again interrupted by the same howling which had, just moments before, disturbed his sleep. This time, however, being fully awake, he identified the sound more clearly. It was a scream. A long, high-pitched shriek. A woman's voice. Louisa! Could it be? No. It was absurd. Her voice would be too far away to penetrate the mahogany shelves lined with volumes of books. But yet...was it possible? Continuing to remain still for what seemed to be several minutes, Randolph, now hearing only the snapping embers of the dwindling fire, lay back down on the davenport, pulled the fluffy covers over his body, and once again shut his tired eyes. But this time before he could fall asleep, a loud, urgent knock on the door caused him to jerk violently, compelling him to quickly clutch the bulky sides of the davenport to avoid tumbling onto the rug-covered floor. The strained, urgent voice of Elsworth accompanied it.

"Master Governey! Master Governey, sir!"

Without a second thought, Randolph flung the covers aside and grabbed his silk robe at the foot of the davenport. Shoving his arms into the garment, he felt for his slippers and swiftly slid them on. Before he could reach the opposite end of the room, Elsworth burst open the door.

"Master Governey!...Good sir, Master Governey!" the servant declared, gasping between breaths. "The doctor asked me to fetch you right away, sir. It's the missus. She's...she's had her baby sir!"

At that instant, Randolph shoved Elsworth aside and headed down the hall toward the back stairway. Racing up the stairs while glancing over his shoulder at the tailing butler, the tongue-tied earl was barely able to spill the inevitable question from his stammering lips. "What...what...is...is it a boy?"

Following his master's heels on the second flight of stairs, Elsworth responded after a slight pause. "I don't know, sir. Gruben didn't say. All he said was to get down there and wake you, sir. He was stern. Too stern for any questions."

"Good God, Elsworth! Is the baby alright, then?" Randolph demanded while heading down the third-floor corridor toward the master bedroom.

"Sir...I don't know, sir. I really can't say. I...."

Before his servant could utter another word, Randolph dashed into the bed chamber. Like a whirlwind suddenly snuffed from the sky, his heart still beating wildly, the earl stood sheepishly, sights upon Gerta contentedly snuggling a white blanketed bundle to her stalwart bosom.

"Congratulations, Randolph," a familiar male voice proclaimed. Looking toward the source of the forthright voice amid the intrusive smell of alcohol, the earl noticed Dr. Gruben washing his hands in a large porcelain basin. Pompously eyeing his disconcerted client, the doctor continued. "Good sir...I am proud to announce that you are now the father of a healthy nine-pound baby boy."

Finding himself totally speechless, Earl Randolph Governey, taking a cleansing breath, scrutinized the sleeping child as the midwife stepped forward to present the newest aristocratic member of the Governey household. A bit alarmed at first by the baby's misshapen head and reddened face, but reassured by Dr. Gruben that the abnormalities would soon disappear, he proudly assessed his newborn son. With only its tiny face visible, he could already discern the defined cheekbones and other outstanding features of his family heritage. And, although the infant's fragile eyes were closed, its long, light lashes and peachy wisps of hair revealed the promise of superb English ancestry.

"Louisa is faring well," Dr. Gruben casually interjected while drying his hands on a white linen towel. "Much better than she actually looks. I administered a tonic to help her relax."

Feigning concern for his unconscious wife, Randolph gave the child a gentle stroke on the cheek and suggested that Gerta rock him in the nursery. With a solemn expression on his face, he approached the canopied bed, stepping upon the trampled white sheets which had been strewn across the patterned carpet. Standing at the side of the bed, he stared in disbelief at the unrecognizable figure before him. Resembling a drained corpse, Louisa lay motionless except for the slow, steady breathing which barely troubled the cotton blankets tucked about her swelled abdomen. Surrounded by the dawn's pale light, her sallow face gave her unkempt hair a dark, savage appearance. Clinging to her limp neck like soiled fragments of frayed rope, the sweaty, mop-like mane did not belong to an eminent countess, but a wretched commoner who had futilely engaged in some unforeseen, violent struggle.

"She has been through quite an ordeal, Randolph," Dr. Gruben explained. "But, your wife is extremely fortunate." The obstetrician extended his calloused hand toward Louisa, feeling her forehead. "After several hours, I was able to maneuver the child in a position favorable for vaginal delivery," he candidly volunteered, overlooking the role Gerta's indispensable hands had played in sparing Louisa from the German physician's insatiable scalpel. Dr. Gruben then placed both hands in the pockets of his blood-stained smock and, looking up at the face of his most prestigious client, continued. "She is still bleeding heavily, but no more than usual under these circumstances. I have cancelled my appointments for the remainder of the day in order to personally monitor her progress. I assure you that in a day or two, with plenty of rest, your wife will be well on her way to recovery. So," he firmly stated while extending his hand toward Randolph, "if there are no other concerns then, will you please have one of your servants show me to my quarters?"

Satisfied that his newborn son was in good health, Randolph pulled the doctor from Louisa's side and proceeded to address him in a subdued tone. "What are her prospects for the future, Otto? I mean...will she be able to bear any more children?"

Lowering the intonation of his own voice, the physician shrugged his shoulders while releasing Randolph's hand. "At this particular juncture, my good Randolph, I believe my prognosis is positive for a full recovery."

The earl, ever searching for a convenient excuse to avoid further intimate relations with his wife, weighed the next question more cautiously, all the while avoiding the doctor's comprehending eyes. "Is there not even the slightest possibility, then, that another pregnancy could endanger Louisa's life?"

Immediately understanding his client's intentions, Gruben stroked his trim goatee. "Well, my dear Randolph," he replied, again shrugging rounded shoulders. "Anything is in the realm of possibility."

Randolph then leaned toward his confidant, firmly grasped his upper arm, and whispered in his ear. "Once again, Otto, would a substantial amount of compensation influence that prognosis, then?"

The calculating physician, remembering the exorbitant fee earned from the earl's prior proposition regarding Louisa's pregnancy, gradually unmasked an understanding grin. "Well, Randolph, perhaps your wife is not as well as I originally diagnosed. Of course, you understand," he discreetly added, "It is still a bit too early to tell."

chapter 8

Waiting

Strengthened by the intense desire to mother her newborn child, Louisa soon recovered and, within days, was cradling little Samuel to her breast while rocking him in the nursery. Contentedly eyeing the exquisite christening gown which had been placed across a frilly day bed, Louisa reflected upon her son's name. Chosen for her husband's paternal grandfather, the countess was especially pleased since it reminded her of Sir Samuel Cunard, founder of the transatlantic steamships preceding the luxury liner *Etruria* on which she had met her husband, subsequently leading to her blissful marriage. As little Samuel continued to suckle, Louisa recalled the conversation she had with Dr. Gruben informing her that any impact upon the uterus for the time being could cause extreme hemorrhaging and possible death. Despite the diagnosis, Louisa was nevertheless elated that she had at last borne a healthy baby boy. And, since the pangs of labor still lingered within her memory, the required abstinence was, at the present time, a most welcome situation.

As the affluent City of New York dressed its frigid streets for the festive Christmas season, a christening celebration was held in honor of Samuel Randolph Governey, Park Avenue's newest member of nobility. Earl Randolph Governey was particularly overwhelmed as nearly 500 guests filled the great ballroom of the Waldorf-Astoria to pay homage to his beautiful newborn son. Besides proudly fathering a child who would continue his family's noble lineage, he appreciated the array of handsome young men who attended the lavish affair, particularly those who were unattached or under-age. Influenced by an overbearing amount of holiday cheer, the earl's lascivious overtures were not only obvious to the objects of his desire, but well noted by several of high society's strait-laced matrons as well, including the socially influential Mrs. William Backhouse Astor. Consequently, from that memorable day forward, like an unbeknown torrent swirling about the base of a sand castle, Earl Randolph Governey's sterling reputation as a devot-ed and loving husband had begun to erode.

As Christmas day approached, sending last-minute shoppers scurrying and frantic servants bustling about, Louisa once again fell into the habit of isolating herself in the darkened drawing room of her cheerfully decorated home after nursing little Samuel to sleep. Every day for the past two weeks, she had waited for a footman to arrive from 34th and Fifth Avenue bearing an invitation to the Astor's Christmas gathering. Hoping to settle her wor-ried mind, she finally called on her sisters who hesitatingly confirmed that the Astors were indeed having a party and, supposedly, all invitations had been sent. Moreover, when Louisa suggested looking further into the matter to rule out the possibility of some overlooked postal error, her siblings vehe-mently discouraged her. They stated that perhaps Mrs. Astor, having acquired new acquaintances throughout the year, had been obligated to limit the number of guests her private ballroom would accommodate. Yet, as they attempted to offer an acceptable explanation, Louisa could detect evasiveness in their eyes and a troubling intonation in their voices. Broken-hearted by such a disappointing outcome, she returned home and confided in her hus-band, who, kissing her tenderly on the cheek, reassured her of their good fortune, stating that the New Year was sure to bring further prosperity and happiness.

But the New Year proved no better as the countess, volunteering her usual services for charity, increasingly sensed an aloofness from her cohorts with curious glances as cold and tainted as New York's snow-covered streets. Upon the arrival of spring, her suspicions were increased when, unlike the year before, she had not received even one invitation to a country picnic or garden party. Furthermore, upon hosting a tea party in her own home, only a few of the less prestigious ladies had attended. And, confiding in her sisters once again was unsatisfying since neither of them would offer any reasonable explanation for such an obvious snub by those within the respectable circle of upper-crust society. If it were not for her undivided preoccupation with little Samuel and the loving reassurances of her devoted husband, Louisa Longley Governey, like an ostrich in quicksand, would surely have sunk into the depths of despair.

As the year 1891 spawned a renewal of life in all its blossoming beauty, Louisa's melancholy was sorely magnified upon receiving a final prognosis from her obstetrician regarding her last postnatal examination. Once again, according to Dr. Gruben, her uterus had failed to heal properly despite the passage of nearly half a year. Therefore, the good doctor reiterated, remembering the substantial bribe he received from Randolph, it was vital Louisa refrain from sexual relations. Unless, of course, it was her wish to risk another pregnancy which would most likely not only result in severe hemorrhaging and possible death, but carry irrevocable consequences for the unborn child. "Of course," he had offered, "you are most welcome to seek another opinion if you like. Perhaps you will eventually find a physician who will tell you what you want to hear. Although, in my fervent opinion, any doctor who would contradict such advice is not fit to treat a common pauper." Having been brought to her senses by the highly-esteemed physician, Louisa, though fretfully dismayed, was nevertheless relieved that she would no longer be subject to further embarrassing gynecological examinations or suffer the pangs of childbirth ever again.

As spring wilted into the past, ushering in the new summer, Randolph Governey, having recently jilted another lover and anxious to clear the stagnant atmosphere created by his wife's sullen mood, proposed that they celebrate their second wedding anniversary by spending a week or two in Newport. Not only would it be a delightful remembrance of the honeymoon, he suggested, but the heavy schedule of activities provided by the prestigious resort was sure to take her mind away from all troubles. Leaving little Samuel behind with his nanny and wet nurse, Louisa coaxed herself into enjoying the impromptu vacation. And, for the first few days, dressed in extravagant outfits and reveling in the company of America's elite, she had succeeded in lifting her spirits. However, in only one split fraction of a second, while unexpectedly encountering Mrs. William Backhouse Astor, she felt as if her face had been flung against the rocky shores of Bailey's Beach. For in that one instant, the queen bee of New York's prestigious society had given her a "cut direct"—the ultimate insult—the most degrading snub of all snubs. Louisa had amusingly witnessed the demeaning technique before, and never imagined that *she* would one day be its designated victim. But her supposition was a severe mistake. Caroline Astor had indeed looked directly toward her. Then, when Louisa acknowledged Mrs. Astor, the indignant woman contemptuously turned her head away and ordered her coachman to promptly return to their quarters.

Upon being the victim of such cruelty, Louisa beseeched Randolph, between breathless sobs, to take her back home. Shortly thereafter, she resolved to see her sister, Cassandra, this time refusing to leave her younger sibling's New York brownstone until a convincing explanation was extracted. And so the very next day, still distraught after a restless night's sleep, Louisa paid her sister the unexpected visit.

"I...I'm sorry I had not mentioned anything before, Louisa," Cassandra discreetly began while shutting the sitting room door, "but I...in the absence of any objective proof, I did not know how to explain the reason behind the recent disenchantment from our circle of friends."

"Dearest sister...you mean there is actually a reason for the ill-treatment I have been forced to suffer over the past several months?"

"Oh, Louisa, dear," Cassandra continued while ushering her sister toward a Chippendale chair. "I...at first I wanted to spare your feelings, but...oh," she sighed heavily shrugging delicate shoulders, "it is for your own well being that you find out after all."

"For God's sake, Cassandra," Louisa exclaimed, refusing to sit down. "What in heaven's name are you referring to?"

Cassandra looked Louisa straight in the eyes and placed her long, slender fingers upon her sister's shoulder. "It is your husband, Randolph, darling. He...he is...oh, this is so difficult!" Fidgeting with her wedding ring, Cassandra sat upon a matching chair.

"What...?" Louisa asked, following her sister's cue to be seated.

"Louisa...I did not want to let on at first because it was all speculation...or so I desperately wanted to believe...but...as of late, there has been evidence...rather, reputable sources have it that Randolph, your dear husband, has been seeing other men." Cassandra froze, anticipating her sister's anguish, all the while biting her bottom lip.

Louisa stared blankly. "Seeing other men? What in God's name are you implying, Cassandra?"

"Yes, dear," Cassandra cautiously answered. "He is seeing other men...in the *biblical* sense."

"But of course he sees other men. I...I don't understand...what do you mean, 'in the *biblical* sense?'"

"Louisa," Cassandra sympathetically answered. "He entertains them...in *bed.* He...he has intimate relations with them. Biblically, he would be known as a *sodomite.*"

For one split second, Louisa thought she had misunderstood her sister. Then, realizing the full impact of her words, she sprung from her chair. "You lie!" she screamed while practically throwing herself at her sister. Before Cassandra could utter another word, she raged on. "You...you and Beatrice...both of you! You could never endure what I had become...what you could *never* be! I should have known all along!"

Grabbing her purse, Louisa stomped across the carpet. With trembling lips, she turned toward her sister before exiting the room. "I shall never again set foot upon your threshold until you apologize for these awful rumors and reverse every bit of damage you have done to my dear husband!" But, as she stormed out, she knew in her heart that even the most sincere revocation would not erase the irreversible damage sustained by such abominable accusations.

Ignoring her sister's fervent pleas, Louisa promptly boarded her carriage, ordering the coachman to take her back home. Realizing for the first time that she had been perspiring heavily, she reached inside her purse and took out an Irish linen handkerchief and a painted Chinese fan. It was all so preposterous! Randolph cavorting with men? Indeed! Why, she had never even heard of such rubbish until now. It was a most revolting accusation...ridiculous enough to be conjured up by two jealous sisters. And it hardly made sense at all. Men having intimate relations with each other? Why, how in the world could such things be?!

As the matching grey horses trotted along the heated streets of Gramercy Park, Louisa felt as if every bump and jolt was a mocking testimony to the despicable degradation she had been forced to suffer throughout the last several months...the ice-cold stares, the obvious snubs...and Caroline Astor herself. Of course! It all made sense now. She should have known from the very start, she resolutely concluded while blotting her creased forehead with the lace handkerchief. They were all jealous. Every one of them! Why! During last year's Christmas gala, did not Mrs. Astor herself aspire to be Queen Victoria as she reigned upon her red velvet divan? Surely, it must have infuriated Caroline Astor to have a genuine countess seated beside her, relating regal tidbits of information as tasty as her gaudy hors d'oeuvres! Why, an uppity woman of her disposition would surely welcome any bit of gossip she could claw her nails into! Louisa placed the moist handkerchief inside the purse and vigorously fanned herself. What would she tell Randolph? How would she approach him? Surely, there was not a bit of truth in it. Or was there? Of course not! she chastised herself. Randolph was unreservedly devoted to her. How awful to even entertain the possibility of such absurd accusations! She would make it a point to bring the matter up with him this evening, but only for his sake. As the coach approached the flower-decked steps of her stately residence, Louisa was further determined to help salvage her husband's good name. Her ever faithful Randolph Eugene Governey, the one and only most reputable Earl of Cheshire, certainly had the right to know what shocking rumors people had been spreading about him!

chapter 9

Explanations

Having hardly touched dinner, Louisa begrudgingly asked Randolph to escort her into the parlor prepared by the first floor maid. The room, subtly illuminated by the glow of moonlight embellished by the glimmer of a banquet lamp, provided the most comfort for a warm summer evening. As a tepid breeze slipped through the drawn, screened windows and ruffled its loose, sheer curtains, she seated herself beside her husband, timidly bringing up the dreadful matter which had been gnawing at her since early morning.

"I visited Cassandra today." Eyeing her wedding band, she paused, then looked into the concerned eyes of her husband. "My sister made the most dreadful accusations...they were about you, Randolph. I...I did not believe her, of course, but it does hurt me so!"

"My dear Louisa," Randolph answered, reaching for her hand. "Whatever did she tell you?"

"Oh, Randolph, darling. It is all so bizarre! All day long my head has been spinning and I cannot comprehend it even now."

The earl reached for a snifter of cognac placed upon a parlor table next to two tall water-streaked glasses of pink lemonade. "Go on."

Louisa gazed toward the darkened fireplace and sighed. "She said...she said that you...that you...were...were somehow intimate with other men." The countess quickly looked back at her husband and, without a moment's passing, added, "Mind you, my dear Randolph, I do not believe a word of it!

It is the most terrible lie! I do not know how to cope with such an accusation!"

Disguising any trace of apprehension, Randolph slowly put down the snifter of cognac. He then caressed his wife and gently stroked the warm back of her dress, ever tolerating the heavy scent of her flowery perfume. "There, there. Do not trouble your pretty head about such matters. There has been some grave mistake, of course. But...I cannot imagine how such an unfounded rumor originated."

"Well, I do!" Louisa suddenly retorted, freeing herself from her husband's embrace.

"They are all sick with jealousy! Cassandra and Beatrice could never bear the thought of remaining common wives while their elder sister has achieved the title of 'countess.' And neither could Caroline Astor or any of her snobbish friends, for that matter."

"But it does baffle me yet, Louisa darling," the earl exclaimed while removing a handkerchief from his shirt pocket. "Certainly," he continued while wiping his wife's tear-stained eyes, "if jealousy be the issue, then why an accusation such as that? I have known such men to exist and believe that my mannerisms are, indubitably, a far stretch from those who are prone to practice such wicked behavior. Putting that aside, I have fathered the most handsome son by a most gracious wife. However," Randolph said while shaking his head, "I suppose there are a few of these men who are successful in masquerading their effeminate tendencies."

Louisa sniffled her reddened nose and raised her faint, thin brows. "So, there are such men who cavort with each other, then?"

"Yes, my dear," he answered, handing over the handkerchief. "But, there is no need to be concerned. A lovely lady such as yourself must be spared the ugly details of their detestable lives."

Louisa vigorously blew into the handkerchief. "Oh, but Randolph! This seems far worse than what I had formerly imagined! I cannot bear what others are willing to believe of you!"

"Come, come now," the earl declared, pressing his wife's perspiring hand between his own. "Let us not be distressed by such disagreeable circumstances. Here now," he offered while reaching for a glass of pink lemonade. "This will soothe you."

As the lemonade glazed her parched throat, a new possibility entered Louisa's mind. Handing the unfinished drink over to Randolph and wiping her lips with a linen napkin, she pursued the idea. "Randolph?"

"Yes, darling?" he answered while placing the tall glass upon the parlor table.

"Would it not be possible to leave for England sooner than planned? I do not care that the castle is incomplete. I think I would prefer to live in a hovel if it meant staying away from these contemptible people forever!"

Taking less than a mere moment to consider his wife's welcome proposition, Earl Governey again took Louisa's hand, looked into her questioning eyes, and staged a heavy sigh. "My dear, all is possible...I suppose I can arrange to have the main quarters inhabitable within the next couple of months. But...are you sure, my darling, that this is what you truly wish? You have always insisted on staying in New York until the castle is fully completed."

"Oh, yes, my dear Randolph. I am more certain of it now than ever!"

"Very well, then. It is settled. We shall put our affairs in order and depart for England before the unseasonable weather sets in."

"And father. We shall have to visit him before leaving."

"Of course, my dear. Of course."

"But he shan't know the reason why. There is no point in relating such dreadful gossip to a feeble old man." Louisa hesitated for a moment. "Randolph?"

"Yes, my darling?"

"You do love me, do you not?"

Still caressing his wife's hand, Randolph fondled the ruby and pearl pendant which graced the lace bodice of her silk blouse. "Do you not remember that I presented this token as a symbol of my never-ending love for you?"

She pressed her pouted lips together, then declared, "Yes."

"Well, then," Randolph finalized, letting go of the pendant and kissing his wife's hand. "Trust that I love you all the more now. So much so, that I am willing to do whatever it takes to prevent you from suffering any further anguish. Come now," he declared while rising from his seat. "Let us catch some sleep. It has been a most trying day for you, I am sure. We shall talk about happier times and further plans for our impending departure in the morning."

chapter 10

Settling In

After some months of planning and several unsuccessful attempts by Louisa's sisters to shield her from the earl's unscrupulous conduct, the Governey family, along with a couple of faithful servants, at last set sail across the ice cold waters of the Atlantic Ocean. Having survived the harrowing mid-October voyage, the weary passengers spent yet another full day traveling by train to their half-finished castle estate, northeast of Wales. Although a welcoming committee of local dignitaries had stiltedly greeted them at Cheshire's flag-draped train station amidst scores of curious townspeople, Louisa could not bring herself to appreciate their formal hospitality. Instead, memories of the warm gaiety she had experienced upon arriving in New York as a blissful bride caused her to feel more homesick than ever. Even the staff of newly-hired attendants who dutifully welcomed the aristocratic family upon the great stone steps of the majestic castle could not soothe the uneasiness in the pit of her stomach. If only her father could have come along, Louisa thought, feeling like a lost child as she walked past the castle's iron doors, perhaps it would have made the transition a bit easier. But the elderly man would never have survived the trans-Atlantic voyage let alone the damp, drab English atmosphere she was already beginning to dread. Pressing little Samuel to her bosom for warmth, Louisa sighed while entering the massive hallway. Looking about the cold, echoing space with scaffolds and drop cloths scattered about, the countess wondered if the decision to leave her once-cherished home town was, after all, a wise one; and if she would ever become accustomed to living within these dismal walls.

As autumn's bleak season sluggishly progressed, Louisa's loneliness lingered while the English gardeners prepared the lavish grounds of the Governey estate for the coming winter. To make matters worse, the British custom of rearing children had left her son mainly in the hands of the head nurse and nanny, allowing Louisa little time to enjoy the irretrievable wonders of his childhood. Overly concerned about the toddler's health, Randolph had specifically instructed his servants that the earl apparent be warmly dressed and kept in his room with a robust fire raging at all times. Therefore, little Samuel, somewhat like a common criminal, was forced to take his meals and baths within the confines of the remote nursery, the three daunting Gothic windows being his only gateway to the outside world.

Three weeks before Samuel's first birthday, upon discovering that she had missed witnessing his very first walking steps, the irascible countess, quite out of step herself, dismissed the head nurse for the rest of the day. Seated on an antique divan aside a crackling fire within the yet-to-be decorated nursery and bouncing the delighted boy upon her knees, Louisa sighed, counting her blessings. In spite of the difficult adjustment that had been forced upon her since arriving in Cheshire, she was, indeed, most fortunate. Never had she imagined that a little child could bring so much pleasure into one's life. And not just any child, but the son of an English earl! Perhaps she would have loved a daughter just the same, Louisa contemplated as the fire's warmth seeped through the soles of her high-lace shoes. But in light of her delicate condition, it was of the utmost importance that she had borne a son. Otherwise, the legacy of her husband's estate would have surely withered. Besides, perhaps a little girl would not have been so handsome, Louisa frowned remembering her maidenly days. Although she was fortunate enough to marry the man of her dreams, a daughter may not have had such an advantage.

Louisa lifted the blanketed toddler from her knees, seating him alongside her. Handing Samuel a picture book, she reflected with wonder how much the boy had grown during the past eleven months. Why, she would surely have to tell Wenda, the nanny, to speak to the valet about consulting the tailor again, she decided, noticing the strained button on Samuel's bloomer pants. She smiled while turning her gaze toward the full head of copper hair and long, thick eyelashes. It was obvious that he was becoming more like his father every day. And smart as a whip, too, she proudly contemplated as the curious toddler voraciously browsed through the picture book, attempting to pronounce the names of each whimsical animal. Also, there was definitely something in his mannerism which reminded Louisa of her dear husband. Or was it the inflection in the child's voice? Whatever the reason, he was bound to be every bit as gallant and handsome as the reigning Earl of Cheshire.

After tucking her son in for a nap, Louisa pulled a hand-knit shawl securely about her shoulders and sat upon a worn satin settee situated a few feet away from the stone-carved fireplace. Feeling a slight chill upon distancing herself from the warmth of the hearth's hardy fire, she peered out the tinted Gothic window. Below her, in the midst of a lazy, late morning fog, several men dressed in dungarees raked and gathered piles of leaves which the giant elms had scattered about the plush, rolling lawns. Gazing out at the barren branches stretching across the grey-suited sky, Louisa felt as if she were a throne without its queen. Regal, yet empty. Although glad to be rid of America's meddling society and her traitorous, two-faced twin sisters, Louisa found the English aristocracy to be overly-formal and oddly aloof. Upon attending a recent tea in honor of her son, not one lady had offered to hold the earl apparent, whereas in New York at his christening party, she had feared that her poor child would break in two. Even the British servants, subject to their own strict hierarchy, drained a great deal of the countess' patience. No longer could she speak directly to the chef or the coachman, for instance. If there was a question about meals or if a coach needed to be brought from the carriage house, the head butler was to be consulted first. And God forbid she decide to sleep in, lest the chamber maids have their rigid schedules inconveniently interrupted. Aside from all of this, the castle itself with its vast number of remote, unfinished rooms and grand corridors was unbearably damp and frigid. Although, unlike other ancestral estates, the earl had equipped the manor with the comforts of indoor plumbing, she nevertheless could not grow accustomed to residing there. Compelled to bury herself and little Samuel in blankets and scarves, the countess wondered why she had even bothered to bring with her the extravagant trousseau which New York's discriminating society had, at a more favorable time, cordially appreciated.

Louisa wrapped the heavy shawl tightly about her bodice while the gardeners, having finished raking the last of the leaves, closely monitored their incineration. As the fragile mounds disintegrated under long, transparent ribbons of smoke, she secretly scrutinized one exceptionally brawny worker.

Craving her husband's physical affections more than ever, she caressed her billowy breasts. Although she had formerly accepted Dr. Gruben's counsel of abstinence as a mixed blessing, the passage of time had begat an inconvenient lapse in memory, prompting Louisa, on occasion, to provocatively approach her unreciprocating husband. She sighed as the burly gardener continued his labor. Randolph was strong. Much stronger than she. Randolph's unfailing love had forbidden him from risking her health and that of another child. She could see by the pain in her husband's eyes that the required abstinence was equally difficult, provoking him to resist even the slightest temptation from an innocent kiss. Nonetheless, she surmised, removing her hands from her barren bosom, like Our Savior offering himself on the cross, life often requires immense sacrifices. And, of course, there was little Samuel to consider, she thought, while envisioning her child's enchanting smile and blazing blue eyes. If she must harness her passions despite her husband's enduring charms for any reason, it must first and foremost be for the sake of their son.

As the long winter season finally drew to a close, Louisa had grown somewhat accustomed to her new life as Countess of Cheshire. Having discarded multiple layers of blankets and clothing, she felt as if a great weight had been lifted from her shoulders. No longer burdened with the task of keeping warm, she could now immerse herself in more meaningful activities, particularly the decorating of Cheshire Castle. Also, by shedding the casual mores of American existence while eventually accepting each servant's unyielding station in life, Louisa's time was no longer consumed by the care of young Samuel. Instead of dressing him in picture-perfect outfits and strolling the inquisitive child along the estate's flowering gardens, she now devoted much of her day to choosing wallpaper and thumbing through multiple swatches of upholstery. As her hands had been formerly plagued with unsightly chilblains from the long, cold winter, her fingers now became calloused from the handling of so many catalogs. With most of the masonry and carpentry work nearly finished, she took an immense interest in the final decorating of the nursery, master bedroom, dining room and other rooms specifically designated for entertaining. When given the chance, she would take a day trip to London, visiting two exquisite furniture stores, Maples-Waring and their competitor, Gillow. Furthermore, the Herend china along with a good amount of crystal and sterling shipped from their New York brownstone clashed terribly with the decor of the castle; therefore, choosing additional pieces of household paraphernalia was an absolute necessity.

By the time young Samuel was running about the castle's flowering gardens in his hard-sole leather shoes and being introduced to the King's English under the instruction of a professional tutor, another year had passed, as well as the near completion of Cheshire Castle. With the construction of the west wing in full sight, Louisa, seated upon a painted wicker chair and wearing a modest, bishop sleeve poplin dress, momentarily interrupted her current activity. Wistfully pressing her pointed chin against entwined fingers while resting knobby elbows upon an elegant antique desk, she gazed up at the French doors of the refurbished sunroom. Although its leaded windows were thoroughly clean, a lingering morning fog gave them a cloudy appearance. Beyond their confines, Samuel, free at last from the bondage of his room all winter long and under the strict guidance of his nanny, romped merrily upon the emerald lawn. Contented with the delightful scene, Louisa continued the tedious task of addressing more or less three hundred invitations to a spring gala, scheduled to take place inside the castle's renovated ballroom. Though not particularly skilled in the art of ballroom dancing, the countess realized that hosting such an affair would win her and the earl further prestige within England's aristocratic community. Moreover, although Randolph, already a member of the House of Lords by peerage, had not yet expressed an active interest in British Parliament, perhaps their increasing popularity would eventually urge him to do so. Who knew what the future might bring? she inwardly smiled while sealing another gold-embossed envelope. Hopefully, if her parties were favorably received, the Prince of Wales himself might express the desire to eventually grace them with his presence. It was, in fact, well known that he and his wife, Princess Alexandra of Denmark, did occasionally bestow the favour of their company upon certain chosen members of aristocratic society.

Louisa paused from her task, counting the stack of invitations she had addressed so far. Fifty-two. Perhaps it was best to quit lest her fingers start developing blisters, she surmised, scrutinizing oversized hands. After all, she had saved them from the horrible chilblains afflicting her two winters ago. Determined never to be plagued with such discomfort of the hands and feet again, she had deliberately timed every movement of her rigid daily schedule during those dreary months so as to avoid the long, frigid corridors and heat-deprived areas of Cheshire castle. Of course, Louisa concluded, capping the tip of the fountain pen, she would welcome blisters any day, save not having to resort to using a quill.

Louisa reclined into the wicker chair, waved to her son, and glanced at her wrist watch. It was almost noon. After lunch, she would not be changing into her usual riding outfit. Although it was customary that she and the Earl enjoy a midday equestrian ride, Randolph would have to go it alone this day. Because one of the servant girls had been suspect of promiscuity, Louisa requested her resignation and, consequently, was to interview a potential employee at one o'clock. Of course, back in New York, it was solely a servant's business what she did with her free time. But in England, the British were less tolerant of anything that could cause a scandal. Louisa sighed while envisioning her husband galloping about the English countryside upon Dibbles, his favorite bay-coated Hackney. After almost four years of marriage, she still loved Randolph dearly. And it was ever so hard at times to resist his intimate embraces. Fortunately, though, being steeped in personal, business and social activities helped keep their minds from carnality's temptations.

While gathering up her writing supplies, Louisa mentally reviewed several details of the forthcoming ball. So far, a string ensemble had been hired to play from noon until early morning, a master chef and his gourmet cooks were arriving from France and her gold-laced chiffon gown had been ordered and fitted by Charles F. Worth, the world-renowned Parisian monarch of clothiers. Her one regret was that, without the presence of royalty, it would not be appropriate to wear her diamond tiara. But, as Randolph masterfully explained to his disappointed wife, perhaps they would at last be invited to Buckingham Palace for some grand occasion. Then finally, she could proudly display the stunning hallmark of her esteemed title, "Countess of Cheshire."

Carefully stacking the envelopes into two neat piles, Louisa eyed one on top addressed to Lord and Lady Wellington of Devonshire and paused momentarily, reflecting upon the decision to leave New York nearly two years ago. How utterly miserable she had been then and how happy she was now! Although the adjustment to a foreign country had initially been difficult, she realized in hindsight that abandoning her sisters and the catty New York crowd was the best decision after all. Why she ever endured that vindictive, backbiting town was beyond her! Unveiling a vengeful smile while envisioning the grand ballroom which would easily fit 600 guests, the countess wondered what Mrs. Astor and her high-nosed society would think of her now. Little did she know, Louisa grinned while staring at the invitation in front of her, what favor the malicious woman had bestowed upon the Governey family by spreading such ugly gossip. It was certainly true then, that behind every cloud there is indeed a silver lining!

chapter 11

After the Ball

As Louisa had hopefully anticipated, word was that her recent spring ball of '93 at Cheshire Castle was tantamount to the most lavish affairs frequently hosted by England's aristocratic elite. For several weeks afterwards, the elaborate gala was the talk of the town, elevating Louisa and Randolph Governey's noble name to a most esteemed status. Delighted by such favorable reviews, Louisa eagerly awaited the coming of Easter week. Whereas she had previously looked forward to participating in this holiest of celebrations, its impending arrival on this particular year also promised the opportunity to spend the remainder of spring and part of the summer season in London.

After cheerfully preparing for the long-awaited journey and arriving in the renowned city with her family and a few indispensable servants, Louisa resolutely prepared to uphold her well-earned reputation. Leaving Samuel with his nanny in the royal suite of Brown's Hotel, the countess, accompanied by her husband, the Earl of Cheshire, took every opportunity to display an array of fashionable hats while attending Royal Ascot. More importantly, however, by frequenting a multitude of lavish political receptions on Park Lane, Louisa aspired to learn the procedures necessary to run a successful campaign for her husband's election, hoping that he would someday reach the highest echelons of Parliament. In return, she felt particularly privileged to renew her acquaintance with renowned figureheads such as the Duke of Westminster and the Marquess of Londonderry, both of whom had graced her grand ballroom in Cheshire. But mostly, she yearned for the opportunity to someday engage in conversation with her majesty, Queen Victoria and, especially, the Queen's son, Albert Edward, the Prince of Wales.

Amidst the not-so-common trivia of daily routine, the Governeys spent the following four years creating alliances and bonding relationships with the nobility of England's aristocratic society. Complying with the straight-laced etiquette of attending weddings, christenings, funerals and other formal as well as informal social events and, of course, reciprocating in kind, Louisa's greatest dreams and expectations finally began to materialize. Having recently purchased a newly-renovated manor in London, she eagerly looked forward to hosting lavish political receptions there, greatly enhancing her dreams of seeing her husband ascend the political ladder. Also, as luck would have it, the Duke and Duchess of Devonshire were giving a most coveted costume ball in July of that year, celebrating the 60th anniversary of Queen Victoria's reign.

Louisa let out a wispy sigh while leaning against the wrought-iron gate of Cheshire Castle as she lackadaisically watched her six-year-old son engage in horseback-riding lessons. Just the other morning while attending tea at Lady Bentley's, she had learned another most exhilarating detail about the lavish costume ball. Among the multitude of guests would be Queen Victoria's son, the one and only Albert Edward, Prince of Wales! Also, she reiterated, stealing a peek at her son on horseback, since the Duke and Duchess had graciously attended her most recent yearly spring ball, she and her husband were certain to receive a reciprocal invitation. Louisa's gaze, wandering far into the fog-covered distance, fixed upon the outline of the castle's elaborate west wing. She smiled contentedly, envisioning the flamboyant costume recently ordered from Charles Frederick Worth for that very occasion. After the Parisian clothiers' suggestion that the unconventional, party-loving Prince of Wales would be most amused by an American lady of notable heritage dressed as Betsy Ross, a stunning gown adorned by flounces of red, white and blue satin, along with a genuine pearled lace cap was promptly designed. And last, but certainly not least, the extravagant costume would be appropriately accented by an American flag embellished with 13 five-carat diamond-studded stars.

Continuing to focus upon the west wing of the imposing Governey mansion, Louisa thought of her forthcoming trip to London and the political reception she would give in her newly-refurbished London residence which would surely be attended by prominent Cabinet-level statesmen. And, as acting hostess of the event, she would finally be allowed to proudly display her diamond tiara! Louisa crossed her fingers, reflecting upon her husband's introductory speech which she helped him prepare for the current political arena. Hopefully, Randolph would deliver it with the authority and bravado necessary to convince his peers of being worthy of the confidence and respect required to hold a position in the Foreign Service. Although this prestigious post would require Randolph's frequent absences from the family, it was well worth the sacrifice considering the distinguished honor he would endow upon the Governey name.

Returning her gaze to the reality of the moment, Louisa marveled at how much Samuel had sprouted during the past year. Why, last spring he could barely mount a pony and now he was riding upon a full-grown French Trotter with the grace and posture of a polished horseman! Thank goodness, in that respect he took after his father, the countess sighed, remembering her scheduled personal ballroom dancing lessons with Master Evans. Sorely aware of her awkward gait, she had hired the professional instructor upon anticipating that His Highness, the Prince of Wales, might ask for her hand in a waltz or minuet. Her first lesson was to be the following day shortly after Samuel's fencing exercise.

Although Louisa was initially fearful that an inherent lack of coordination would forever prohibit her less-than-flattering presence from gracing the ballroom floor, the corpulent Master Evans proved to be worth his weight in gold. Three times a week the servants would open the wide, airy doors of the grand ballroom terrace so that the accomplished tutor could comfortably instruct his student in the posturing, meter and eloquence of the dance. Like an athlete in training determined to win the race, Louisa would review her lessons daily to the tinny sound of a gramophone. For hours on end, she would visualize herself in the stunning red, white and blue costume, being incessantly complimented by the most idolized figure of the modern world...Albert Edward, the Prince of Wales. At times her husband would unexpectedly return from a leisurely day of hobnobbing with members of the aristocracy and demonstrate his expertise on the refinements of ballroom dancing. Although Louisa was long accustomed to suppressing sparks of arousing passion, she would nevertheless experience an intense flame of desire as the graceful earl, like a sleek set of sails, guided her across the parquet floor. But on one fateful morning in early May, as if by an undertow in tranquil waters, Louisa was yanked from all hopes and dreams when, instead of the anticipated footman bearing a gold invitation to the Devonshire House Ball, there stood at the castle two stone-faced bailiffs bearing a set of cast iron handcuffs, charging her beloved husband, the Earl of Cheshire, with sodomizing the 13-year-old son of a prominent London banker.

chapter 12

Scandal

Wedged within the medieval town of Chester and surrounded by ancient Roman walls, Cheshire's local jailhouse was like a piece of human cartilage spit out by lions and trampled underfoot. Inhabited mainly through the ages by common thieves and grave-robbers, the two-cell prison nevertheless suffered most of its wretched days enduring prolonged bouts of vacancy. Even its present occupant, Randolph Eugene Governey, the distinguished Earl of Cheshire, could not elevate the ignoble level of the dank dirt floors and black iron bars which hardened all the more its sweaty, grim stone walls.

Randolph Governey's usually tranquil countenance adopted an unsettling scowl as the sound of heavy metal spilled from the guard's keys, signaling the earl's unavoidable confinement. Sitting upon a stained wooden bench while removing his riding jacket, his perspiring face reddened. It was absolutely preposterous that his morning activities had been terminated by such outrageous nonsense! Hopefully, Greeley Fitzpatrick, the family barrister, would soon be there to reverse his detainment. Randolph glared at the crusted, brown-streaked chamber pot in the corner of the solitary cell. What he needed now was a nice, cool bath. But, unlacing his riding boots, he recognized that such possibilities were futile in this god-forsaken place; adaptation was his only recourse.

Randolph rolled up his riding jacket and shoved it against the bench. Using the jacket as a pillow, he positioned himself upon the crude, unyielding surface. With eyes closed and hands propped beneath his head, he envisioned Mr. Fitzpatrick, confident that the barrister would rescue him from another impending scandal. Greeley Fitzpatrick had, after all, helped the Governey family in numerous ways, especially when he, as a man in his early twenties, was charged with similar allegations. The earl frowned while recalling the improprieties of his youth. He should never have gotten involved with that ragamuffin in the first place, he thought, recalling the alluring 17-year-old son of a common tinker from some 20 years past. The pathetic schoolboy would have placed the Governey estate in severe jeopardy, if not for Greeley Fitzpatrick. The sly sharp-horned barrister was one bull of a counselor, convincing the Magistrate that the lad had contrived those salacious charges in the hope of collecting an immense settlement. Strapping the ungrateful lad to a pole and whipping him with a cat of nine tails was hardly punishment enough. That traitorous bastard was a troublemaker if ever there was one, Randolph scornfully concluded recalling his own deceased father. Those allegations had surely caused the former Earl of Cheshire's premature demise and probably would have killed his mother also if typhoid fever had not already claimed her. After averting the ill-fated incident, Randolph vowed that his engagement in further sexual encounters would be solely with distinguished gentlemen who had reached the age of consent. His cautious tactics had been successful for many years, but deep within, he still longed for the taste and texture of pure pubescence. Unable to abstain any longer, he eventually resumed his affairs with underage boys, enticing them with expensive gifts or British pounds. And he had, for the past few years, successfully pursued these juvenile lovers with no dire consequences. Until now! Despite the fact that Jonathan Lewis, the son of a gentry banker, was a willing participant in the alleged affair, the lad was nevertheless only a raw 13 years of age; young and vulnerable enough to evoke the most serious of all charges...the act of forced sodomy.

Wrenched from his short-lived solitude by the sound of iron bars, Randolph instantaneously sat up, taking notice of Greeley Fitzpatrick being escorted into the cell. Not having seen the man for several years, the earl surveyed him silently. Succumbing to the seduction of old age, the dignified barrister was now in need of a walking stick. His once-refined nose resembled a tilted champagne flute, reddened and cracked from years of overuse. What had not changed, however, was his voice. Demanding and strong, it rang out, saluting his client as it grated the bleak stone walls.

"Randolph, my good sir!" he declared, patting the earl on the shoulder. "It is a pleasure to see you again. Though I must say, not under the best of circumstances."

Composing himself in the manner and dignity of an earl, Randolph rose from the bench, planted his stocking feet upon the solid dirt floor and straightened his muscled back, exhibiting a physical superiority which, at the present moment, masked his unfortunate dilemma. "Sir! Fitzpatrick, my dear fellow. Would you believe it for a moment? Imagine my distress at having been treated in such a manner!"

Barrister Fitzpatrick balanced the silver-gilded handle of his mahogany cane against the stone wall and adjusted the vest of his suit, urging Randolph to be seated once again. "This is, indeed, a most serious accusation, my good Randolph," Greeley explained in a more subdued tone while seating himself alongside his client. "As your barrister, I am well prepared to defend your interests, but in return you must first and foremost cooperate with me whole-heartedly. As you know, any information will be held in the strictest of confidence. So," the venerable barrister added with a pause, adjusting his gold-framed spectacles, "what do you have to say for yourself?"

"These charges are preposterous!" Randolph replied. "Why ever should I, an established nobleman, risk my esteemed title and, in turn, trifle with my dear wife and child's impeccable reputations by engaging in such a practice? The menacing rascal who has pressed such unspeakable charges ought to be strung up by his bony ankles and hung from the Tower of London!"

Greeley Fitzpatrick rose from the bench and paced the confined area. Halting silent footsteps, he dropped both hands to his sides. "In all due respect, my dear Randolph, I do not intend to insult you in the least. But I beg of you, do be aware of the gravity of these charges. The Magistrate, I fear, is not the least bit tolerant of such matters. Therefore, if I am not fully able to share in all intimate details, I will not be able to adequately represent you. Pray...is there anything that may have provoked the child to come forth in such a manner? Wholeheartedly, I assure you again that any of your revelations will be held in the strictest confidence."

Still seated upon the bench, Randolph expelled an exasperated breath and leaned against the warm stone wall, supporting his head with locked fingers. "I assure you, sir, I have never forced myself upon an unwilling companion. And...if I had, indeed, engaged in the situation of which I am charged, I assure you that the pleasure would have been mutual."

"Indeed, sir, indeed. But you do understand, Randolph, that in this case, since the plaintiff is underage, the issue of intent is not relevant." Greeley reached for his cane and twisted the round, silver handle which, in an instant, was transformed into a small cup. Then, tilting the hollow of the cane, he poured its contents into the cup. "Drink up, my friend," the barrister invited, offering the cognac to his client. "A fellow of your stature deserves whatever comforts life has to offer."

Leaning forward, Randolph accepted the cup and drank heartily, uncharacteristically wiping his wet lips with the ruffled sleeve of his riding shirt. Allowing the cognac to run its course, he slumped against the crude stone, fixing his eyes upon the opposite wall. "My Lord…Greeley. What have I gotten myself into this time?"

Cautiously, the barrister removed the empty cup from Randolph's limp fingers. "Provided the allegations are true…," he sighed, fixing the cup to the cane, "there are a couple of probabilities…none of which, I am afraid, will be of much consolation at the present moment." Seating himself beside his client while clinching the mahogany cane with both hands, Barrister Fitzpatrick continued. "The best we can hope for in this case is a private agreement…hopefully one which will entice Master Lewis, with his father's acquiescence, to recant this odious offense. I am afraid, however, that such a mutual agreement would most probably demand of you a sizeable portion of your entire estate. Providing that our most relentless Magistrate will find it in his heart to overlook the lad's false allegations."

Randolph folded his arms across his chest, looking into the stern, supportive eyes of his counselor. "Cannot the charges be fully denied, then?"

"Randolph, my man," Greeley compassionately explained, "had the incident involved a young ragamuffin, this conversation would not be worth my breath. But Franklin Lewis, the father of the plaintiff, young Jonathan Lewis, is a most respected member of bourgeois society. A considerable number of aristocrats, including the Duke and Duchess of Manchester, have patronized the prominent banker." The barrister softened his voice while shaking his head. "I am afraid that unless we can persuade the father to convince his son to recant all charges, it will lead to a most unsavory case."

Rising from the bench, Randolph stretched both arms overhead, inadvertently grazing the gold and onyx ring against the jagged ceiling as he contemplated the barrister's words. Immediately making a fist in order to ascertain any damage, Randolph noticed a deep scratch upon the ring's onyx stone. Throwing down both arms in frustration, he wiped his perspiring hands alongside his riding breeches. "Damn it, Greeley! Exactly how much is this going to cost me?"

Clenching false teeth while still seated on the bench, Barrister Greeley Fitzpatrick attempted to shed the best possible light on the disturbing details of the pending agreement. "I do hate to be the bearer of bad tidings, Randolph, but either way, whether young Jonathan agrees to recant the charges or not, I am afraid that this particular indiscretion will cost you no less than a King's ransom." Noticing the unsettling look upon his client's face, he continued. "You see, my good man, the fact that these charges were brought against you gives me every reason to confirm my suspicions that Franklin Lewis, Sr., is in a bit of financial trouble himself. And, at this point, I believe he is willing to seize upon any opportunity which will remedy his unfortunate situation."

"And if Mr. Lewis does not agree to go along with our settlement, what then?"

Fitzpatrick inhaled deeply while noticing the color draining from his client's face. With trembling lips, he responded, "There can be no alternative, Randolph. I will do my utmost to convince young Jonathan and his father that a compromise will be in everyone's best interest. Otherwise...if the man refuses to succumb to reason...or worse yet, if the Magistrate is the unrelenting boulder I fear he may be...then God have mercy!"

chapter 13

Reality

Louisa wrung her hands and whimpered faintly, peering through the window of the second-story master sitting room for any sign of an approaching coach. Straining reddened eyes in order to discern the long driveway shrouded by blossoming dogwoods, she silently wished it were late evening. Then, the countess lamented, perhaps amid pitch darkness she could have imagined that her husband may be arriving at the door of Cheshire Castle any second. It was awful enough that the appalling events of the morning continued to play in her head like a broken gramophone, let alone having to wait so unbearably long for, hopefully, a reasonable explanation.

Louisa's stomach tightened all the more as she once again focused upon the moment of her husband's arrest, as if going over the incident time and time again would somehow make it all go away...Randolph and herself, leisurely entering their home after a pleasant morning equestrian ride...the echoing knock on the castle's front door...both officers curtly shoving Marjorie, the parlor maid, aside before giving anyone a chance to discern what was happening...binding Randolph's wrists together with that awful iron contraption...reciting at the same time those disgusting words...*forced sodomy. Sodomy...Forced.* **Sodomy**. NO! It could not be true! It *must* not be true! With facial muscles taut as a drawn bow, Louisa tried in vain to erase the mocking smile of her sister, Cassandra. *He is seeing other men...in the biblical sense...a sodomite, dear sister. In the biblical sense, he is known as a* *sodomite.* A fresh set of tears streamed down her face. Was it true then? Was it as Cassandra had claimed? Was Randolph a sodomite? Did he, indeed, force himself upon the young lad? Almost gagging at the thought, she pushed herself away from the window seat. How long had she been sitting there? Two hours? Three?

Determined at last to escape from her self-defeating thoughts, Louisa stomped toward the master bed chamber. There must be another explanation, she feverishly reasoned, and it was all a mistake somehow. Somehow. *It was all an obvious mistake.* Entering the master bedroom, she glanced with burning eyes at a depleted glass of wine upon the nightstand, then focused upon the rumpled silk sheets and satin comforter of the canopied bed. Having witnessed Randolph being dragged from their home that morning was the last thing she remembered before regaining consciousness upon the bed, coughing over a box of smelling salts as Elsworth and Marjorie supported her listless body. There was talk of notifying Dr. Boyle, the respected town physician, but she had forbidden it. Instead, she instructed the servants to directly wire the Magistrate's office, imploring him to look into what surely must be an abominable error. Shortly thereafter, Louisa was informed that the respective charges were being upheld. Her husband, the Earl of Cheshire was indeed accused of engaging in the act of forced sodomy and, after consulting with his barrister, would be released on bond when the proper papers were signed and filed accordingly.

Having received this upsetting news, the countess ordered the bewildered servants to leave her be. She insisted upon remaining in her room until the earl's return. As for her son, Samuel, the boy was to continue his day in the usual manner, completely unaware of the tragic events. Recalling that her son had formerly been under the instruction of a private tutor in the new schoolroom of the castle's west wing, Louisa took a deep breath. Thank goodness he was spared the horror of witnessing his own dear father's arrest!

Raising both hands to her bosom, she grasped the ruby and pearl pendant between trembling fingers, gliding her thumbs along the rough inscription which declared Randolph's everlasting love. How could it be true? How could he, a most loving husband and father, be guilty of such disgraceful conduct? Was there any sense to it at all? And what had she, a most loving wife and mother, done to deserve such a fate? Even if Randolph were innocent...he *must* be innocent!...the news of his arrest would surely circulate. How would this alleged shameful incident affect their good name...the sterling reputation she had worked so hard to attain? And what of Randolph's political future? The upcoming ball at Devonshire House? Allowing the pendant to slip between her fingers, Louisa wiped her bloodshot eyes with the back of her hand. In spite of the appalling circumstances, she must compose herself. Surely, there was some kind of mistake! Upon Randolph's arrival, he would certainly need all the help and support she could muster. Whoever was responsible for such unforgiveable accusations would undoubtedly be punished. Slander and defamation of character was a most serious crime, not to be taken lightly. With those thoughts festering in her mind, the countess straightened her back and headed toward the boudoir to freshen up.

After giving her sallow face a thorough scrub, Louisa had barely finished applying toilet ointment when she overheard the faint slamming of a door followed by muffled, low-pitched voices. Randolph! He had come home! Her heart beating wildly, she firmly rubbed the last trace of ointment into the thin, dark circles underneath her sunken eyes. Then, reaching for two round wooden containers, promptly powdered her long, shiny nose and colored pale, quivering lips. She arose from her vanity chair and paused for a split second before grabbing a perfume atomizer, dousing herself with lotus and lavender.

Descending the winding staircase, Louisa took each step with the tenacity of a trapped hornet. Overly-anxious to comfort her disparaged husband as well as hearing his account of this most vile invasion of personal decency, she quickened her pace to another familiar voice and a second set of footsteps. It was the head butler, Ellsworth. He was escorting Randolph up the staircase. Before another thought could cross her mind, Louisa reached the center landing, stopping suddenly, all the while feeling the churning blood in her veins evaporate into the surrounding spring air. Randolph, like a chastised schoolboy, stood mutely before her. With disheveled hair and crumpled, putrid clothing, Louisa would not have recognized him if not for the uniquely handsome features gracing his ashen face. Although she wanted desperately to embrace him, something in his demeanor forbade her to do so. Or was it Ellsworth's presence? Scrutinizing both men, Louisa felt as if she had unintentionally entered a place forbidden to members of the fairer sex...like the smoke-filled poker parlor of a fashionable hotel or, worse yet, the privy of an exclusive men's club. Unable to bear the collective silence and awkward stares a moment longer, she uttered the first word.

"Randolph?"

The earl, remaining motionless, stared wearily into his wife's pleading eyes. "Louisa...I implore you...we shall discuss this matter when I am more suitable to abide in your graceful presence. Ellsworth will assist me in my bath before I indulge in a late afternoon meal. We may converse afterwards." Followed by his faithful servant, Randolph then brushed past his bewildered wife and proceeded up the stairs.

Holding back a flood of tears, Louisa, slowly turned to descend the remaining steps of the grand staircase. Why had Randolph been so curt with her? What had occurred at the prison? Was he, indeed, guilty after all? She pressed her hand against the pit of her stomach. What if...

"Madame?...please..."

Louisa gasped, noticing Marjorie standing at the foot of the staircase.

"May I assist you with anything, ma'am?"

Suppressing a sniffle, Louisa immediately removed her hand from her abdomen. "Marjorie!...I did not know you were...Where is Samuel?"

"He is with Sir William out on the east court...his fencing lesson, ma'am."

Louisa affirmatively shook her head. "Why yes, of course. You may...If you please, Marjorie, my husband and I will take tea in the drawing room after his meal. You may see to that shortly."

"Yes madame. But...what of Master Evans, ma'am? He is due to arrive within the hour."

"Inform Master Evans that I am not in favor of dancing this evening," Louisa stammered. "Have Robert deliver the message immediately."

"Yes, ma'am...immediately."

Impatiently waiting for Marjorie to disappear, Louisa once again pressed her hand against the pit of her stomach, failing to contain subtle sobs before reaching the foot of the stairs and crossing the grand corridor toward Cheshire Castle's main drawing room.

Facing the towering gothic window of the castle's drawing room, she tensely settled upon a tapestry armchair. Previously belonging to Henry VIII, the multicolored chair was presented in 1589 by Queen Elizabeth I to the prevailing Earl of Cheshire as a token of his invaluable counsel during the Virgin Queen's prosperous reign. Although the armchair had, over the centuries, served a number of deserving dignitaries and calmed countless generations of appreciative ancestors, the despondent countess was nevertheless unable to gather much comfort from its broad cushioned seat and wide, embracing wings.

Overlooking the fading afternoon sun which attempted to invade her hostile space, Louisa gazed past the transparent curtains of the gothic window. Eyeing the long, barren approach, she thought of the old wooden bridge which had recently welcomed her husband back home. Traversing a wide, rock-filled stream which flowed several miles through dense woods and vacant meadows, concluding its journey at the mouth of the River Dee, the old wooden bridge was the pivotal point of entry to Cheshire Castle. She sighed, reflecting upon how, just a short while ago in the privacy of her bed chamber, she had anxiously anticipated her husband's return. The wait had been insufferable and yet...now that he had finally arrived home, she felt no relief. Perhaps if he had immediately reassured her somehow...he had not even offered the slightest smile...her anxieties would have subsided. But now, not only had her fears intensified, but yet another gnawing thought continued to torment her. She had been somewhat troubled by the possibility several times before, but invariably refused to entertain it. Now it would not leave her alone. Like the legendary monster of Loch Ness plaguing the highlands of northern Scotland, it was rearing its ugly head, declaring that it was, indeed, authentic. Louisa wrung her perspiring palms. Was it true then? Had Randolph married solely for wealth? Did he never love her, after all? She gazed down at her ruby and pearl necklace. The pendant's gold, inscriptive plate suddenly felt as if it were burning through the silk fabric of her violet dress, singeing her sensitive skin. Clutching the pendant with both hands, she squeezed it with a force that seemed to burst through every vein, hoping to choke the life out of each tormenting thought...wanting so desperately to strangle each treacherous notion. Collapsing into a fetal position, she forced shut her stinging eyes, pressed the pendant to her tear-salted lips and sobbed.

It was not until Louisa heard her name and felt a slight nudge on the shoulder that she realized her brief sleep was broken. Struggling to rise from her curled position, numbly blinking reddened eyes, the countess faintly discerned the figure of Marjorie standing beside her. Next to the maid on a low, medieval table stood a fragrant bouquet of honeysuckle, sweet williams and white roses. Continuing to blink the short nap from her eyes, she also noticed two tea cups, shortcake and blueberry jam, suddenly feeling a familiar stab in the pit of her stomach.

"Madame," the parlor maid most cautiously explained, "Master Governey has nearly finished his meal. As you have requested, ma'am," she acknowledged, nodding toward the silver service placed upon a nearby Queen Anne sideboard, "I have boiled a most soothing peppermint tea and shall serve it whenever you like."

Louisa rubbed her burning eyes and straightened the lap of her dress. Staring at the cake, she recalled that she had not eaten since breakfast. Even so, the morsels set before her were of no consolation. In lieu of her nervous stomach, they may as well have been chiseled from the turrets of Cheshire Castle. "Why yes, of course...the tea," she weakly addressed the maid, conscious of her own sullied appearance. Aligning her lank back along the posterior of the chair, she continued. "You may go now. Inform my husband that I am awaiting his company." Receiving a slight curtsey, Louisa added, "And if you please, Marjorie, I shall tend to the tea myself. It is my fervent wish that the earl and I not be disturbed."

Louisa waited for Marjorie to leave the room before rising from the chair. With undue effort, she staggered toward the tea service and gazed at her reflection on the sterling silver teapot. Scrutinizing pink puffy eyes and tear-stained cheeks, she removed a lacy handkerchief from the pocket of her dress and blotted her face, all the while attempting to console herself. Although her lipstick had faded to a dusty rose, there was little time to tend to it. And what did it matter anyhow? she lamented while stuffing the handkerchief back into her pocket. Perhaps her appearance was of no concern to her husband. Perhaps it had never mattered at all! And how could she have been so stupid believing that a handsome, prominent aristocrat would be so willing to take her for his wife? A plain...no!...*ugly* woman such as she! How could.... Louisa suddenly flinched upon hearing a baritone voice. At the corner of her eye, she recognized a well-defined familiar figure...the man upon whom, over the past several years, she had so readily hinged all hopes and dreams. Within seconds, her troubled face softened as she noticed the earl's remarkably improved demeanor. Dressed to perfection and bearing a compassionate smile, he prompted Louisa to wonder if perhaps her harsh presumptions had been too hasty. Relaxing aching shoulders, she stood silently before her earl, anxious to hear his long-awaited explanation.

"Louisa...my dear, dear Louisa!" he exclaimed while attempting to pry apart his wife's clenched fists. "Please forgive me. How terrible this most wretched ordeal must be for you! To think that I have wallowed in self-pity for having been so unjustly accused with such absurdities, leaving my sweet wife to battle her own unbearable musings! Come," he gestured, entwining his wife's relaxing fingers and seating her aside himself upon an ivory brocaded love seat. "Unfortunately, the information I shall relate to you is most discouraging. But, I trust the love we have shared over the past eight years will sustain us through this crisis. Unfavorable as the consequences seem, I believe that together we will weather the storm."

"But Randolph," Louisa feebly pouted with dry lips and stale breath, "How could this terrible event ever have happened? It is most unlikely, is it not, that an innocent man should be accused twice of the same crime?"

Earl Randolph Governey stared into his wife's dull, glazed eyes, still cupping her hands within his own. "Louisa...my dear beloved wife...how that very question has tormented me so! I understand deeply your profound confusion, for I have endured the same and much, much more. Pray...tell me please if you may, my dearest...how might I explain such inconceivable charges which I, a veritable man in the true sense of the word, cannot fully comprehend?"

Gradually recovering from the shock, Louisa exhaled in curt, quivering breaths. "Are you professing then, my darling, that you have never engaged in such behavior? That all accusations are, indeed, false?"

Releasing his wife's hands, Randolph leaned back against the love seat, resting the tips of his fingers upon an antique side table. "Louisa...to spare myself from the anguish of further humiliation, I am going to say this once and once and for all." Tapping the surface of the rosewood table with his ringed forefinger and pausing after each emphatic word, he declared, "I did not have carnal encounters with that young man...Jonathan Lewis. These allegations are false!" He then vacated his seat and strutted toward the sideboard. "Now. Let us have our tea before discussing this matter any further."

Saddled by guilt at having so unjustly doubted her husband, Louisa interrupted his hospitality by insisting that she serve the tea. "My dear Randolph! Please...you must let me...I beg of you...pardon my most unforgiveable suspicions. I...I...." No longer able to contain herself, she flung both arms around the earl and sobbed, gushing tears rolling down the plaited bosom of his starched shirt.

"There, there," Randolph reassured his repentant wife, reciprocating her passionate embrace. "Do not burden yourself so! There is no harm so great that our love cannot rectify. Be seated, my dearest. I will serve the tea." He retrieved a monogrammed handkerchief from his suspendered pants and tenderly dried Louisa's cheeks. "You look terribly famished, my dear. A piece of cake will do you good."

Allowing her husband to pour the peppermint tea, Louisa, ever grateful for having received his most sincere pardon, obediently reseated herself, lustfully eyeing the shortcake and blueberry jam. Aware of her growling stomach, she promptly prepared both pieces of cake, hungry enough to eat her husband's as well. Watching Randolph pour the tea, Louisa hardly waited for him to be seated before grabbing her plate, devouring the blueberry-topped dessert in three quick forkfuls.

"So, my dear, you were famished after all. Perhaps I should summon Marjorie to replenish your plate."

Louisa reached for the cup and saucer which stood beside her empty dish, realizing that the introduction of further intimate questions would be violated if Marjorie were in their presence. "Excuse me, dear Randolph, for conducting myself in such a manner," she pleaded while balancing the hand-painted china, "but a second portion of cake will be most unnecessary. Although I have not had a bite to eat since breakfast, I am certain that our forthcoming dinner will satisfy my untimely appetite."

"Very well, then," the earl acquiesced. "However, my grief cannot be contained a moment longer over the suffering my dear, sweet wife has endured on my behalf!"

Deeply touched by her husband's profound devotion, Louisa cautiously asked, "What is to become of this terrible incident? And...however could such awful accusations be repeated?"

Randolph leaned against the back of the loveseat, throwing his hands in mid air. "How is it that in a land of prosperity, a multitude of souls still suffers? How can our most gracious and loving God allow a newborn child to leave this world before taking its first breath? I am afraid, my dearest, that this dilemma is equally puzzling. But," he gravely stated while dropping both hands into his lap, "how this terrible rumor originated is the least of my concerns. However unjust these accusations be, I fear they will reap severe repercussions."

"But, Randolph!" Louisa cried, reaching for her husband's clenched fists, "Whatever do you mean? If you are truly innocent, why is it that you cannot contest the charges?"

The earl shook his head while staring into his wife's pleading eyes. "I have spoken to Greeley Fitzpatrick while in my prison cell. He is an excellent barrister who has served the Governey family since my youth. He informs me that the lad's father, Franklin Lewis, Sr., is in serious financial trouble. It is believed that he has pressed charges on behalf of his son in the hope of seizing a sizable portion of my...our estate."

"But Randolph...in defense of your innocence, you must contest the charges no matter what...you must!"

"It is not so simple as that, my love," he sighed. "Mr. Lewis is a prominent, respected banker who has tended to a great number of aristocrats, including the innermost circle of royalty. Forced sodomy...the crime of which I am accused...is a biblical offense worse than murder itself! If I were put on trial and found guilty, I would be thrown into a dungeon to wither away. Those appalling conditions alone would be unbearable to any other person...but the thought of no longer abiding in the presence of my dear wife and child would surely kill me before serving one single second of such an unjust punishment!"

"Then *must* you go to trial?" Louisa exclaimed, her heart palpitating. "Is there no alternative to this horrific situation?"

"Yes, my dear. There is one alternative," Randolph somberly reflected, "One which, I am afraid, offers meager solace."

Louisa squeezed her husband's fists. "What is it then, my dearest?"

Pulling away from his wife, Randolph rose from the loveseat and retrieved the monogrammed handkerchief from his pocket, wiping beads of sweat from his forehead. "There is no easy way to tell you this, Louisa. Our life in Cheshire...as we know it..." Clutching the handkerchief, he slammed his hand against the silver tea tray. "Men are vultures, Louisa! They see the riches we have...the happiness we share...and lick their lips in anticipation of claiming our wealth as their own! Franklin Lewis...the barrister...even the magistrate will insist upon devouring our entire estate before this noose is loosened from my neck!"

Remaining frozen to her seat, Louisa stared at the wavering teapot while vigorously shaking her head. "But Randolph! It cannot be true! Surely there must be some kind of mistake! By the grace of God, we shall...we *must*, transcend this!"

"Louisa," Randolph proclaimed, brandishing the handkerchief while pacing the carpet. "Their decision is final. You must understand. There is nothing more we can do."

"But," she gasped, hand over heart, "What will be the result of this madness? What will become of us?"

Halting his steps, the earl took one deep breath. "I am afraid our only alternative will be...to leave our beloved England. Perhaps...perhaps your dear father will be kind enough to take us in. His recent illness may necessitate a loving daughter's reassuring hand. As far as I can comprehend, this is our only acceptable alternative."

As if desperately trying to piece together a broken Ming vase, the stunned countess was all at once overwhelmed by anguish and frustration. "But...but...our home...our son...our...our trip to London! Randolph! Your political aspirations! The...the Devonshire Ball!" Realizing the full gravity of the situation, Louisa suddenly felt the intrusive, imagined presence of Master Evans breathing down her neck, uncontrollably spinning her about the room in one last desperate attempt to instruct her in the graces of ballroom dancing...in one futile struggle to salvage her dignity.

Waiting for Louisa to collect herself, Randolph, suddenly taken aback, dropped his handkerchief to the floor and rushed to his wife's side in order to support her limp, unconscious body. Securely positioning her head upon a brocaded pillow propped against the arm of the loveseat, he then exited the room, immediately ordering Marjorie to fetch the smelling salts.

chapter 14

Homeward Bound

Numbly kneeling upon the crude bunk of her second-class cabin while gazing through a scratched porthole, Louisa remained mesmerized as the ocean's white-capped waters spontaneously rose and fell, heedlessly disrupting any form of life which may have sought solace upon its glassy black surface. Impervious to the desolate horizon, she sighed while trying to make sense of the tragic events which had taken place during the past few days. Everything had happened with such haste, it was difficult to comprehend the situation even now...though they already had been at sea for nearly four days.

Although Randolph had tried coaxing her into joining him and young Samuel for a walk on the promenade deck of the Cunard steamer in order to escape the gloominess of their cramped cabin, Louisa opted to remain inside. Leaving Cheshire Castle behind with all its abandoned luxuries and no servants to assist her, the countess was left alone to wallow in her sorrow. Upon placing the liquidation of the estate in the hands of Barrister Fitzpatrick, the Governey family, faring no better than the lowliest of peasants, was left virtually penniless. Since the magistrate had refused an out of court settlement, the date for a criminal trial was being arranged. Realizing the strong possibility that his client would be risking a severe life sentence, the barrister provided the means to smuggle the family out of Britain while arranging the distribution of their estate. Thus, having been systematically robbed of practically every conceivable asset, they had promptly left England like common criminals, salvaging whatever valuables they could wear or fit inside their suitcases.

Passively riding the rhythm of each ponderous wave, Louisa was reminded of the Devonshire House Ball and the forever missed opportunity of dancing with the Prince of Wales. She had anticipated that event for weeks on end—the dancing instructions, the Betsy Ross gown...and even though she would not have worn her diamond tiara at the ball, she had looked forward to that particular opportunity only a couple of weeks ago while preparing to host her husband's London political reception. Now the unadmired tiara was packed amongst other precious heirlooms. And the red, white and blue costume would never have the chance to display its American colors in all their splendid glory.

In a futile attempt to forget her troubles, Louisa's thoughts shifted to her father and the childhood home to which she would soon be returning. Perhaps, as Randolph had so tenderly stated, she could assist the old man on the road to recovery. Upon learning that a good deal of his own assets had dried up, Frank Langley suffered from severe heart failure, leaving him in the care of a costly full-time nurse. Perhaps by selling a few of the Governey heirlooms and sparing the expense of a full-time nurse, the family would be better able to make ends meet. Louisa gazed down at her ruby necklace and cupped it within the palm of her hand. No matter how difficult things became, she would hold onto this precious jewel for dear life. Aside from the cherished memories it prompted, the gem was a constant reminder of Randolph's love. When an occasional doubt about her husband's innocence would invade her thoughts, she would grasp the fiery pendant, recalling that wonderful, enchanted winter evening in New York when Randolph had delighted her with his unexpected presence, their intimate chat in the hearth-warmed parlor and afterwards...the way he had so passionately loved her for the very first time.

chapter 15

Adaptation

A rriving as scheduled at the Ellis Island port on a mild, rainy day, the *S. S. British Queen* discharged scores of passengers, most of who were overwhelmed by the prospect of claiming America as their own. Aware of the Statue of Liberty prevailing over New York Harbor, Louisa witnessed a hoard of modestly dressed immigrants being shouted at, pushed, and shoved by customs officers into segregated groups like herds of cattle. Feeling particularly out of place in her impeccably-tailored shirtwaist visiting dress and matching feathered hat, the countess longed more than ever to be back in the country she had called home for the past seven years. Also unlike these common immigrants, the Governey family, already bearing the privileged torch of United States citizenship, avoided the tedious ritual of going through customs. And, dissimilar to these third-class travelers previously subjected to the harsh, impoverished conditions of the steerage quarters, the Governeys were given a cursory medical examination aboard ship, thus circumventing the demeaning process of being poked and prodded by health officials in search of communicable diseases. Boarding a hired carriage large enough to accommodate the weight of their traveling bags, the aristocratic family started toward the train station, passing the smelly, fish-laden docks and crowded markets of lower Manhattan. Arriving at the station in time to buy three tickets for the 1:00 p.m. departure to Philadelphia, the fugitive family promptly boarded the coach and occupied their upholstered seats. Too exhausted to further reflect upon their deplorable situation, the Governeys had little else to do but wait for the deep, shrill sound of the Pennsylvania Railroad's whistle signaling the departure from New York toward their final destination.

Upon arriving at her father's house on Chestnut Street, Louisa and her family were received by one obstinate housemaid and a solemn, sour-faced nurse, the latter of who correctly suspected that the countess might take over the profitable occupation she had been entrusted with during the past six months. As Louisa leaned over to tenderly kiss her father, however, the impudence of the two servants was soon forgotten. In permanent need of a wheelchair, the former oil tycoon looked as if he had been pushing a plow all of his life. Witnessing her father hunched in the chair and bearing a crooked smile amid silver, brittle whiskers, Louisa realized that her husband's assumption had been accurate. Frank Langley was certain to live the rest of his days in need of her continuing, loving care.

Walking through the spacious entrance hall of her father's colonial mansion, Louisa, with Randolph and little Samuel at her side, wearily reacquainted herself with the home she had lived in during her first 31 years. Whereas she had once taken great pride in being the mistress of such an impressive dwelling, it now reminded her of the sudden loss of a kingdom she would never regain. Compared to Cheshire Castle...the Camelot which would never again flourish...the colonial mansion was but a poor imitation of the honor and chivalry her former home in England had evoked. Even her father's formerly gallant, beechwood chairs in the adjoining drawing room were now neglected beyond care. The elegant, sweeping draperies, also ravaged and raped by the sun, were living testimony to the home's alarming negligence. While viewing all of this, Louisa thought of her younger sisters, confident more than ever of their malice and selfishness. After all, she had been living overseas during the past several years, whereas Cassandra and Beatrice were just a simple day's journey away. Louisa frowned; she was not sure whether to be disheartened or grateful. For although it was not pleasing in the least to see her former home as such, the run-down mansion offered plenty of work to keep her mind off present troubles.

Wearing a light cotton dress, Louisa wiped a sweaty brow with the back of her hand while removing an ashtray from the kitchen table, perturbed by her husband's most recently acquired habit. Sitting upon a walnut chair, she opened a sewing box, preparing to mend one of her father's summer shirts. She hesitated for a moment, wondering if the shaded parlor would be more comfortable for such a task, but instantly decided against it since the lack of an electric outlet would not accommodate a fan. As she guided the wind-blown thread through the eye of the needle, she thought of the letters Cassandra and Beatrice had sent. Reluctant to accept even a sincere apology from her siblings, Louisa's conviction of their self-righteousness was confirmed all the more when, upon proposing reconciliation and offering to lend a hand with their father's care, not the slightest admission of wrongdoing toward Randolph was mentioned. While reading of her sisters' wishes to become reacquainted with Samuel as well as lengthy tidings about her young nieces and nephews, the countess became further inflamed by her siblings' boldness, determined more than ever to take upon herself the business of making the best of a poor situation. Louisa sighed while guiding the needle through the linen fabric of her father's shirt. Although he did not know the source of dissension between his daughters, it was most unfortunate that he was nevertheless knowledgeable of their apparent animosity.

While knotting and cutting loose the thread, Louisa was aware that Samuel's arithmetic lesson was nearly over, reflecting on how competent his instructor, Mr. Harning, had proven to be. Although the aristocratic family no longer enjoyed abundant financial resources, the earl and countess, agreeing that Samuel's education took precedence over other boyhood matters, scheduled daily private tutelage with the highly qualified instructor. For Louisa, however, this arrangement provided an additional advantage. Without having to send her son away to school, she was guaranteed the luxury of doting on the child day and night. Especially pleasing to Louisa was her keen observation that the boy, nearly seven years of age, though somewhat reserved, increasingly exhibited his father's natural charm and dashing looks. She wistfully folded the shirt and replaced the mending supplies inside her sewing box. It was nearly mid-afternoon. Randolph, having been out on one of her father's horses, would be coming in soon for some Chamomile tea. The old man, who was taking a short nap in his shaded, ventilated bedroom, would join his daughter and son-in-law in the afternoon refreshment.

Reflecting upon both men in her life, Louisa experienced mixed feelings. Although she was pleased with her father's rehabilitation, Randolph seemed more distant than ever. Refusing to talk about any significant subject for even the shortest length of time, he would often leave the dinner table before Mary, the housemaid, had a chance to clear his dessert plate. After spending many hours in town, sometimes until near dawn, he would return home in an intoxicated state, reeking of cigarette smoke and using the most intolerable, vile language. So disruptive was this habit, that Louisa insisted upon sleeping in separate bedrooms, wishing not to be so rudely disturbed in the middle of the night. Even his ever-compassionate attitude toward her had taken a most ignoble turn. No longer the gallant gentleman she once knew, it seemed that Earl Randolph Governey had forever been altered by the tragic events which had taken place that fateful spring morning in Cheshire. Louisa wiped a trapped tear from her eye. She must not dwell on this unfortunate situation any longer. She would boil the tea and tend to her father. Thank goodness for his dear feeble presence, lest she surely go mad.

chapter 16

An Indispensable Visitor

Bordered by inlaid sidewalks and emerald lawns lined with meticu-lously-trimmed hedges and rows of thriving flower beds, Frank Langley's three-story colonial mansion on Chestnut Street, located between the Schuylkill and Delaware Rivers, rested within the most presti-gious section of Philadelphia. Purchased in 1851 by Louisa's newly-wedded father, the home, built in 1829, had only once turned over its deed of own-ership. Embracing many equally grand homes of reputable proprietorship, the neighborhood attracted a number of vendors, welcomed by servants who were spared an extra trip to the marketplace. Ripened fruits, dairy products and freshly cut flowers were but a few popular items for sale. Beginning as early as April and continuing all summer long, a team of Belgian horses clip-clopped down the street daily, pulling a heavy yellow wagon filled with custom-sized blocks of ice. In October, a similar team would lead another wagon, this time brimming with piles of coal. Although these vendors were welcomed by the residents of Chestnut Street, the purchase of their merchan-dise was never mandatory...quite unlike that of the neighborhood's most dreaded peddler. For as unwelcome as this particular visitor was, his presence not only required the steepest of payments, but demanded it as well...some-times without even the slightest warning. He did not care if his customers were young or old, rich or poor. The *pale rider* was not fastidious in choos-ing his victims. And so it was that on one blustery January morning, her third successive winter on Chestnut Street, Louisa Langley Governey discovered her dear father lying in his bed, cold and lifeless as the snow-covered branches hovering about the shuttered windows of the stately mansion...the deed to which would now change hands for a second time.

On a clear, bright morning at the start of a new century, a solemn horse-drawn hearse waited in front of the snow-swept steps of St. Peter's Episcopal Church, while hundreds of friends and family members gathered inside to bid farewell to the late Frank Lawrence Langley. His eldest daughter, dressed in black, stood silently, listening to the whining pipe organ as she viewed her father's casket before the candle-lit altar, all the while conscious of her sisters and their respective families in the adjacent pew. With her son Samuel standing between herself and the earl, she reflected for a moment upon a happier occasion which took place within the same sanctified walls nearly eleven years ago. Although she had visited the church weekly for Sunday services during the past two-and-a-half years, the sudden memory of that blissful June wedding day seemed to strike her breast like a burning dagger.

Spontaneously dropping to her knees while an echoing soprano began the refrain, "Lord Have Mercy," Louisa was suddenly aware of the bright sun piercing the arched, stained-glass windows, once again becoming conscious of the shadowing presence of both sisters. Although she would previously arrange alternative lodgings for her own family to avoid Cassandra and Beatrice when they traveled from New York to visit their sickly father, now that he had passed, it was impossible to avoid them. Resigning herself to the grim necessity of residing with both families during the mournful days ahead, Louisa's civilities toward her in-laws were contrived and as brief as possible. In spite of Randolph's recently-acquired improprieties, he was, nevertheless, their brother-in-law, undeserving of the reprehensible rumors which had ever since plagued an otherwise promising life.

Although somewhat comforted by a touching and honorable eulogy presented by the presiding parish pastor, Louisa, upon partaking of the Eucharist, felt as if her stomach, having been a solid ball of twine during the past few days, was all at once beginning to unravel. With hardly the time to comprehend her father's death, she had been caught in a whirlwind of arrangements and practicalities, including the sale of an exquisite emerald brooch to fund the funeral. Contacting friends and family had been another exhausting matter, along with hiring additional servants to prepare their home for the many visitors who participated in the wake, viewing Frank Langley for the very last time. Also, after the burial which was to take place at Laurel Hill Cemetery, a repast was planned for as many as 300 people. But now...Louisa was suddenly confronted by her vulnerability as the hard ball of twine continued to unravel. Miraculously managing to return to her seat, she reached toward Randolph for support. Dutifully responding to his wife, the earl caught Louisa firmly by the shoulders, coaxing her to sit down. Leaning her cloaked back against the hard pew while the nauseating smell of incense permeated the surrounding air, she took little solace in her husband's assistance. Although his gesture had demonstrated a certain amount of strength and physical support, he was nevertheless a mere stone pillar, unwilling to provide the genuine love and understanding she so desperately craved.

chapter 17

Inheritance

Upon the settlement of Frank Lawrence Langley's estate, Randolph Governey, Earl of Cheshire, was rather pleased in discovering that, in spite of the old man's recent financial misfortunes, he had been wise enough to arrange a sizeable trust for each of his six grandchildren. Sitting upon a tufted, brown leather sofa next to his bereaved wife and across the room from his in-laws, Randolph listened intently to Walter H. Hammel, Frank Langley's estate lawyer, who adjusted his spectacles while describing the conditions of young Samuel's inheritance. The first half of the trust, Mr. Hammel firmly stated, intended mainly for education, was to be distributed according to the parents' discretion. The last half, payable upon each child's twenty-first birthday, would remain in the trust, continuing to accrue interest. Concerning the remainder of Frank Lawrence Langley's estate, the deceased's assets, comprised of some low-yielding bonds and certificates, would be divided equally between his youngest two daughters. And, since Louisa Beth Governey, his eldest daughter, had provided exceptional and compassionate care for the deceased over the past three years, the colonial mansion with all its cherished possessions was bequeathed solely to her. Upon hearing this most welcome and unexpected announcement, Randolph, noticing the sudden scowls upon the faces of Louisa's sisters, could barely suppress an innermost delight. Responding to the objectionable murmurs of his in-laws, he then graciously announced that being ever appreciative of such a generous endowment, he would, on behalf of his grief-stricken wife, help manage the inherited estate with the utmost prudence and care.

Although Randolph Governey felt somewhat appeased by the small fortune his father-in-law's death had facilitated, Louisa was bereaved beyond consolation. Forced to live in the very home which was now a blatant reminder of the gentle old man, Louisa felt as if the thickest branch of her family tree had snapped beneath both feet, plummeting her into the depths of despair. No longer distracted by the continual care of her loving father, as well as the former demands of her growing child, the family's tragic, humiliating situation continued to choke her feeble mind. Unable to tolerate these tormenting thoughts any longer, she quickly adopted the earl's decrepit habit of excessive drinking. Finding this diversion a wretched substitute for the fleeting, yet blissful comfort she previously found in her husband's loving arms, she soon took to heavy smoking, consuming nearly two dozen Marlboroughs a day.

Remaining powerless to redeem the serenity she so desperately craved, the countess swiftly plummeted into a deep depression. Incessantly plagued by an inexplicable aching of the joints, frequent dizziness and even an occasional fainting spell, Louisa was ultimately diagnosed with the female malady "neurasthenia" and given a daily dosage of opium drops with complete bed rest under the care of a puritanical full-time nurse. The begrudged caregiver, however, would often be compelled to temporarily abandon her eminent position upon Louisa's insistence that she leave the room in order that her precious son, Samuel, be given the opportunity to share some private time with his ailing mother. Smartly dressed in a sailor suit, dark stockings and ankle boots, her obedient, princely boy would be subjected to sit upon a boudoir chair in the secluded smoke-filled bed chamber beside her untouched dinner tray and read a column or two from the tedious pages of a recent periodical. Afterwards, his bedridden mother, flaunting an exquisite ruby and pearl necklace over a white cotton night gown, would instruct Samuel to paint her dry, ashen lips and brush her long, tumbleweed hair. Unnerving as it was for the young boy to follow his mother's wishes, Samuel would nevertheless appease the eccentric commands of the forlorn countess, despite sunken cheeks, turbulent eyes and an extraordinarily large bosom that resembled a pale life jacket keeping her afloat.

Throughout the long, ponderous months, as Samuel's dim blue eyes witnessed his emaciated mother emptying assorted vials of tonic and filling a myriad of blackened ashtrays, the pubescent boy continued to appease the ailing countess, submissively listening to elaborate tales of life among the social elite. With an exuberant, almost crazed look, Louisa would demand her son's undivided attention, once again narrating her story of the Devonshire House ball where, dressed in layers of red, white and blue satin and carrying a flag embellished with 13 diamonds, she danced away the evening with the dashing Prince of Wales.

Ravaged by broken dreams and endless heartaches, Louisa Langley Governey's short-lived existence paralleled a proud ocean carrier in a raging storm which, upon departing from her sister ships, was tossed between two homelands and hurled upon the rocks. Abandoned by her captain, she was plundered by pirates, her sumptuous lounges and elegant ballrooms stripped of all their glory. Now, at the helm of her sickbed, Louisa, at the premature age of 44, was pressed to retire from life's pier, leaving behind a callous husband and apathetic child. Without the anchoring love of her father guiding her like a beacon in the night, Louisa Beth Langley Governey, Countess of Cheshire, on an ordinary day of an insignificant year, finally slipped beneath the merciless waters of death, never to surface again.

chapter 18

Missing

As the long-awaited season of spring endlessly writhed within the stubborn clutches of winter, Randolph and his son, Samuel, greeted several acquaintances and obliging neighbors who entered the colonial mansion to pay their last respects to the late Countess of Cheshire. Laid out in a plain oak coffin, her appearance rekindled by a gifted mortician, Louisa looked more alive than she had during the past two years of her drawn-out illness. With rosy cheeks and a velvet ball gown camouflaging her otherwise sallow body, the countess looked as if she might awaken any moment to partake in a Viennese waltz. Little Samuel was especially amazed with the improved appearance of his deceased mother. Viewing her with both awe and trepidation, he was particularly aware of the ruby necklace resting upon her blushed chest, despite the dazzling diamond tiara carefully pinned upon her coarse, brown hair.

Standing beside his wife's rose-adorned casket amid the reverent whispers and murmurs of a handful of guests, Randolph suppressed a yawn while anticipating the end of another exhausting day. Wearing a most convincing sorrowful face, the earl appreciated the fragrance of freshly-cut flowers in place of the lingering stench of Louisa's sickroom while shaking hands with consoling visitors. Although Louisa's death, compared to her father's, had drawn only a moderate number of guests, a formal funeral was nevertheless necessary, requiring Randolph to be inconvenienced with tedious arrangements. As his deceased wife had done for her father, it had been incumbent upon the earl to contact friends and neighbors, accommodate out-of-town guests including his estranged in-laws and hire two additional servants. Collaborating with the parish pastor in planning the funeral itself was another unavoidable matter. Tempted to glance at his platinum pocket watch, Randolph forced a smile while tolerating the sympathies of yet another colleague of Frank Langley who expressed genuine sorrow while recounting unending memories of the late oil tycoon. As the evening finally came to an end, Randolph breathed a sigh of relief while bidding goodnight to the few out-of-town guests, including his estranged in-laws, who then ascended the stairway of the colonial mansion to catch some sleep before the long, ritualistic funeral the following morning.

As the bleak morning of Louisa's funeral arrived, Earl Randolph Governey was suddenly startled by an abrupt knock on his bedroom door accompanied by the harried voice of his sister-in-law, Cassandra.

"Randolph! Dear brother-in-law! Open the door if you are able. Please!"

Adjusting his cummerbund, Randolph irritably crossed the room in black socks and opened the unlocked door. Cassandra, primly dressed in black, displayed an alarmed look on her flushed, heart-shaped face. "Randolph! The most awful thing has happened! Do you know anything of it? Please say that you do!"

Not having the slightest idea of his sister-in-law's agitation, Randolph instantly shook his head. "For God's sake, woman, whatever are you referring to?"

Cassandra, breathless, placed a hand to her heart. "It's Louisa! Someone has gotten into her casket!"

"Good Lord! Louisa is missing?"

"No...She's there, but...but...they're gone!"

"For Christ's sake, Cassandra," Randolph retorted, grabbing her arm. "Please get hold of yourself. What's gone? You're not making any sense."

"Someone's robbed the casket. Someone's stole her things! The diamonds...rubies, earrings!...everything!..."

"Good Lord!" He started to hyperventilate. "Are you positive?"

"Yes...yes...quite! I went into the parlor this morning to privately pay my last respects and...and...everything's gone!"

"Have you checked with the servants, Cassandra?" Perhaps Mary has taken the matter into her hands, then."

"No, Randolph...I mean...I've asked Mary and she is as puzzled as I! Beatrice too...there is no one else who would have had the authority to remove them!"

Randolph silently cursed while wedging a shoe horn inside his button shoes. Damn! The thought of removing Louisa's jewels before retiring last evening had occurred to him, but being too weary, he had postponed it. Now some goddamn son-of-a-bitch had stolen them!

Practically shoving Cassandra aside, he careened down the staircase while a few half-dressed guests gathered in the upstairs hallway. Aware of his sister-in-law trailing behind, he entered the parlor, never before so eager to view the remains of his departed wife. Upon personally witnessing the violated corpse, he let out a deep, frustrating moan. Without her diamond tiara, ruby pendant and matching earrings, Louisa appeared half naked, looking as if someone had attempted to sweep her hair back into place after removing the precious stones. Her thin, white fingers, no longer adorned by the diamond wedding and engagement rings, lay across her flattened stomach, as if in twisted prayer.

"We must call the police!" the earl demanded, turning toward his sister-in-law. "The house must be searched immediately! Whoever committed this dastardly crime must be detained and punished!"

"But Randolph," Cassandra protested, following her brother-in-law out of the room. "The funeral...the hearse will be arriving shortly to bring Louisa to the church."

"We must attend to this matter immediately!" he argued, entering the library and heading toward the desk telephone. "The longer we wait, the lesser the chance the jewels will be recovered!"

"But Randolph!" Cassandra pleaded. "Louisa's funeral! It's due to take place within the hour! Please, for my dear sister's sake, delay the investigation until afterwards!"

Paying no heed whatsoever to his meddling sister-in-law, Randolph picked up the receiver and asked for the operator. Before he could speak another word, however, Cassandra knocked the telephone from his hand, leaving a muffled voice at the other end.

"I've known it all along!" she shouted as a few out-of-town guests and servants huddled outside the doorway. "All you ever cared about was becoming wealthy at the expense of my dear sister! You don't even have the decency to wait until her body is at rest beneath the ground before resuming your treasure hunt!"

Aware of the curious spectators gathering in the hallway, Randolph cleared his throat and reached for the dangling receiver, gingerly placing it on its cradle. "Forgive me, my dear Cassandra," he pleaded, patting a handkerchief to his forehead, "but you are gravely mistaken. Nothing could be further from the truth. Those precious gifts...they meant the world to my beloved wife. My grief stems only from the knowledge that her dear memory has been outrageously defiled. Come," he gestured, putting on a most solemn face while escorting his sister-in-law from the room. "You are certainly correct. We *must* wait until after dear Louisa's funeral to proceed with this most disturbing matter."

With nothing left to do but surrender to the untimely circumstances, Randolph returned upstairs to finish dressing for the funeral. Grinding his teeth, he adjusted his bow tie. Goddamn it! Chances were that the jewels would never be recovered. Whoever had stolen the valuable pieces would have had plenty of time to conceal them...especially if one of the servants had broken into the parlor the previous evening. As soon as the funeral was over, he would call the police and demand a thorough comb-out of the home. Perhaps they would be recovered after all. They *must* be recovered! Hell! Randolph cursed while shoving an arm into the sleeve of his tuxedo jacket. The diamond tiara alone had to be worth several thousand dollars, not to mention what he could obtain for the diamond rings, ruby pendant and matching earrings. Certainly, there were other ancestral heirlooms he could bank on, but, damn! The price he could have demanded for the stolen jewels! Deciding there was no use further agonizing about the matter, he raised his jutting chin and descended the stairs with the dignity and calm of a gallant widower who had just suffered the loss of his dearly beloved wife.

As the procession of mourners passed through the frost-bitten streets of Philadelphia in their motor cars and carriages, Randolph Governey, seated by his son inside the horse-drawn hearse, stiffly stared at the stately brick buildings and imposing institutions leading toward St. Peter's Episcopal Church. Although the earl's dull blue eyes discerned the patriotic facade of Independence Hall and other impressive architectural landmarks, his mind never deviated from wondering about the identity of the thief. Could it, indeed, be one of the servants? A guest? Perhaps it was the vindictive doings of his estranged in-laws. Continuing to stare out the window of the hearse, he stroked his waxed moustache. No matter how innocent his sister-in-law had appeared, that little trouble-maker was capable of anything. When the police arrived, he would insist that all their belongings...Cassandra's, Beatrice's, their husbands' and children's...be searched immediately. And, of course, he must not rule out any of the guests. No matter how offensive it may be, he would demand that their rooms and possessions be searched also. Of course, he huffed while the solemn vehicle ambled past Washington Square, if one of the servants was responsible, he would never get the damn jewelry back. Although he had instructed Mary, his trusted housekeeper, to closely watch the newly-hired servants as they prepared a repast for the guests, perhaps they were co-conspirators in the matter, bartering the stolen goods at this very moment.

As the grim-faced guests filed into St. Peter's Church, Randolph, all the while yearning for a cognac, lead Samuel into their pew, continuing to scrutinize each mournful soul with a suspicious eye. Although the solemn music of the majestic pipe organ reverberated along the granite walls of the massive church as the service commenced, the only sound Randolph could hear was his own inner voice pondering on the whereabouts of his missing treasure. During the Gospel reading, the strong smell of incense became unbearably nauseating as the possibility of a house guest smuggling the jewels by way of another "mourner" crossed his mind. Surely, it would be most difficult to keep track of every single person who attended the service! Having paid no heed to the pastor's heartfelt eulogy, Randolph was forced to endure the remainder of the funeral mass with excruciating impatience. After the longest conceivable hour of his life, the earl let out a fleeting sigh of relief as the somber procession headed toward Laurel Hill Cemetery where, following a brief prayer service, Louisa was, at long last, lowered into the eternal solitude of her final resting place. Unable to find a moment's rest himself, Earl Randolph Governey, in the supportive company of his fellow mourners, shed genuine tears after all.

chapter 19

Solitude

After several weeks of grieving over the loss of the precious jewels, Randolph no longer pretended to mourn for his recently-buried wife. Eager to move on with his life while anticipating the long-awaited opportunity to entertain male lovers in the privacy of his own home, he promptly sent his 11-year-old son to a boarding school in Cambridge, Massachusetts. While it was the earl's intention to dislodge young Samuel as swiftly as an abscessed tooth, the feeling had been mutual. Delivered at last from the morbid hands of his deceased mother, yet forced to endure his father's drunken behavior, the young earl-apparent eagerly would have enrolled himself in an orphanage. Although Randolph had never laid a hand on his son, Samuel sometimes wondered if that sort of treatment would have been preferable to the impenetrable wall his father had built between them throughout the years. Aside from continually recounting the boy's noble heritage and incessantly demanding prompt obedience, his father was no more approachable than the bronze busts of Thomas Jefferson or John Locke gracing the spacious rooms of the earl's newly-acquired colonial mansion.

Whereas other students shunned their studies at the Bennings Boarding School for Boys, Samuel utilized his time not only to escape from his father, but also to avoid unpleasant memories evoked by his mother's morbidly long-drawn illness and subsequent death. Continuing his education in mathematics, science and languages, Samuel remained withdrawn from the rest of his classmates. And, the summers and holidays offered no diversity. While other students packed their bags in anticipation of returning to their homes, the exemplary student was content to stay behind and bury himself in books. Left in the care of his headmaster and a few dutiful administrators, Samuel was once again destined to live a virtually solitary life within another set of towering, grey stone walls.

chapter 20

Prognosis

Lethargically gazing out the drawing room window at the dirty, half-melted snow lingering upon the white marble steps and barren flower beds, Randolph pressed a hand to his aching head and inspected once more the pale red spots upon his arm. Having felt particularly sluggish with loss of appetite during the past few weeks, he had at first attributed these symptoms to the unavoidable malady of aging. But now, upon discovering this hideous, sprawling rash, he arranged a visit with Dr. Humphrey Donovan, who continued on as the Governey family physician after Louisa's death three years ago. Moving away from the window, the earl refilled a glass of bourbon and lay upon a long-seated armchair across from the fireplace. Although a warm fire burned within the hearth, upon its ivory mantel remained an empty space. A pair of bronze candelabras, a white porcelain clock and two glazed figurines were no longer accompanied by an impressive eighteenth-century silver eagle which Randolph had formerly exchanged for a hefty price.

Continuing to stare out the undraped window while resting his head against the back of the upholstered chair, Randolph shuddered, dreading the worst possible diagnosis. He was, after all, experiencing a number of strange symptoms: a rash which had spread on the palms of his hands and the soles of his feet, aches and pains all over his body and inside his mouth, a signifi-cant loss of hair—even coming out in clumps at times. Could it be that he had incurred some kind of venereal disease? He began fidgeting with the onyx ring upon his swollen forefinger. If so, how serious? God forbid, could it be the sort that caused paralysis or insanity? Either gonorrhea or syphilis—one or the other. Good Lord! Randolph adjusted the hem of his cashmere robe to cover unsightly ankles. Perhaps there was nothing to worry about at all, he reasoned. Besides, there was no use pondering over it a moment longer since the doctor would be arriving shortly; he would find out soon enough.

Alerted by the slamming of an automobile door, Randolph's attention was drawn once more past the rain-stained window. A middle-aged man of slight stature wearing a heavy overcoat and carrying a black bag was walking toward the wet steps, leaving behind a shiny black 1905 Cadillac. Damn! thought Randolph, forcefully rising from his seat. *That sure is a handsome looking vehicle!* Perhaps he should not have been so hasty in purchasing his 1904 Ford Model K. Bloody two-speed gearbox was already giving him problems. Managing to shuffle toward the foyer before the doctor could exacerbate his throbbing head with a piercing knock, he opened the front door.

After the usual salutations, Randolph complimented Dr. Donovan on his excellent choice of a motor car while hanging his coat and hat. Escorting the doctor into the drawing room, he invited the physician to be seated upon a silk floral sofa as he drew the lace curtain. Upon illuminating a brass lamp, Randolph, pleased with his decision to have paid an exorbitant sum for the luxury of electrical lighting throughout the home, took his place beside the doctor.

Refusing a glass of bourbon while tolerating the smell of liquor upon his patient's breath, Dr. Donovan opened the black bag. "How long have you been experiencing these symptoms, Mr. Governey?"

"It has been about three weeks...perhaps a month since I have not been feeling quite like myself. But the rash," he explained while pulling up one sleeve of his robe, "has appeared just recently...within the past couple of days or so..."

"Open your mouth, please," the doctor interrupted, holding a tongue depressor. Noticing a few small ulcers while probing inside his patient's mouth, an overly-concerned look crossed his face. "You say you have been experiencing fatigue and weight loss," he remarked while wrapping the depressor in a piece of paper and tossing it in his bag. He then pressed his hands to each side of Randolph's throat, feeling for swollen glands, his solemn look intensifying while scrutinizing the earl's patchy hair. "Is there a history of baldness in your family?"

Reflecting for a moment, Randolph tried to focus upon the blurring face of Dr. Donovan. "No...Not at all, sir. My father had a most healthy head of hair until his death and...from what I could gather from portraits of my ancestors, there was not a bald one among them."

"Mr. Governey," the doctor questioned while placing a hand to his patient's forehead, "have you noticed any particular sore upon your genitals...even, perhaps...several weeks ago or so? One which may have gradually subsided?"

"No, my good man...I...I cannot say that I have."

"Mmmm...You feel a bit warm." Dr. Donovan removed his hand from Randolph's forehead. "Mr. Governey... It is my responsibility as a physician to ask you a rather personal question. Were you involved in a sexual liaison within the past few months?"

"My good sir," the earl appealed with upturned hands, "I am as warm-blooded a man as any. Louisa...my dearly beloved wife...God rest her soul... has been deceased for nearly three years. It is all I can do at times to ease my most unbearable sorrow."

"Of course," the doctor politely acquiesced. "However...excuse me again for being so forward...but...has there been more than one such liaison?"

Randolph held his breath, silent for a moment, recalling a number of male lovers he had entertained since Louisa's death. "What are you implying, my good doctor? If I have, indeed, contracted a venereal disease, what does it matter if I have had encounters with one woman or 20? It only takes one, does it not?"

"My dear sir...*if* you have contracted a venereal disease, which...I fear to say...is most likely...it would be of kind service to any persons involved to be notified immediately. Not only for their sake, but for all who may happen to come in contact with them. Of course," the doctor added shrugging his shoulders, "this humane gesture is your decision alone. My duty as your physician is to attend solely to *your* needs."

"And what...exactly would those needs be?" Randolph apprehensively asked, not giving a horse's behind about the fate of his former lovers.

There was a transient silence as Dr. Donovan removed a glass bottle of rubbing alcohol from his bag. "My dear Mr. Governey. What would you prefer to hear first? The good news or the bad?"

"Why...the good news, of course," Randolph quickly answered with a glimmer of hope in his eyes, the smell of alcohol permeating the room.

"Very well then," the doctor conceded, pouring some of the disinfectant upon his hands. "The good news is that if you do, indeed, suffer from the disease which I suspect ails you, the symptoms you are experiencing will eventually subside, leading to a latent stage which may last anywhere from as little as three...to as many as 25 years." Reacting to the stone silence of his patient, the physician continued his counsel while wiping both hands with a soft cloth. "The bad news, however, is...following the latent stage...the disease can be quite fatal...affecting almost any organ of the body."

Randolph slumped back into his seat, slapped a hand to his forehead and grabbed his glass of bourbon. "Good Lord, Donovan, what the hell are you saying, for God's sake!? Just what the hell are you saying?"

"Mr. Governey, please remember. My diagnosis is not conclusive. And even if I *am* correct, perhaps at your age of 63, you will escape the final ravages of this disease. Remember...the latent stage of syphilis could last for up to 25 years."

"So that is your prognosis, then...I do, indeed, have...syphilis?"

"As I have said, Mr. Governey, this prognosis is not conclusive. You are always free to seek a second opinion if you like."

"This final stage..." Randolph went on, oblivious to the doctor's previous words, "does it cause a person to lose his mind...go insane?"

"Yes," Dr. Donovan hesitantly replied. "In some circumstances, it...most likely can."

"And what else may I expect from this most ghastly disease?" Randolph asked, stiffened fingers frozen to the glass of bourbon.

Dr. Donovan let out a deep sigh while placing the white cloth and rubbing alcohol in his bag, realizing that his patient would not rest until given a candid answer. "From what I have seen in my 23 years of practice, syphilis can cripple a person...cause blindness...bone deterioration...often it attacks the nervous system and the heart...leading to...ultimate death." Heeding Randolph's silence, he reached into his bag and removed a small vial of pills. "Here. These will ease your discomfort for the meantime. Take one every six hours or so. Please call my office if need be," he stated, clasping the black bag and rising from his seat. "And...I would strongly advise that you not consume any alcohol while taking this medication. If you would kindly direct me to the washroom, then...I shall be on my way."

After escorting Dr. Donovan out the front door, Randolph numbly held onto the bottle of pills and dawdled toward the kitchen while the dreaded diagnosis continued to echo inside his aching ears. *Syphilis...syphilis....* So this is what he had come down with...the tragic disease he had blocked from his mind all these years had finally caught up with him! As he attempted to recall the doctor's overwhelming list of symptoms, his head began to swirl. *Blindness...paralysis...losing one's mind...insanity...*insanity! Good Lord! the earl thought while entering the kitchen, *I feel on the verge of insanity this very moment!* Attempting to collect himself while turning on the light, he removed a handkerchief from his robe pocket and wiped his wet moustache. Walking past the table and chairs, he headed toward a brass-trimmed cupboard to retrieve an empty glass. Perhaps the doctor's prognosis *was* incorrect, he thought. Perhaps he *should* seek a second opinion. But this short-lived attempt to silence his mind was futile. *No.* It was true. He had known it all along. For several weeks now he had suspected it. Suspected it, yet overlooked the gruesome possibility. And wasn't there a small blister on his penis...maybe two...three months ago? *Yes...*he remembered it now. There was nothing left to do but accept the diagnosis and wait the damn thing out. Perhaps he would be a fortunate victim of this deadly disease after all. He was already over 60 years of age. If the symptoms of syphilis did not manifest for another 25 years, chances were that old age would mercifully escort him to the grave instead.

While filling the glass with tap water, Randolph surmised that when his son Samuel graduated from the Bennings Boarding School for Boys, he should consider having him continue his education at a nearby college. This way...God forbid...if the disease should manifest after as little as three years, the boy would at least be there to tend to his personal needs. And *insurance,* the earl thought while seating himself on one of the oak chairs. Although he still hoped for the best outcome of this worst possible disease, the thing he dreaded most was ending up in one of those nightmarish mental asylums. Perhaps, then, when his present symptoms subside, he should look into obtaining proper insurance. But first he would need a clean bill of health from another physician. Or...if that was not possible, he could always bribe his old friend, Dr. Otto Gruben in New York. Having appeased the ugly issue for the moment and giving his estranged son no further thought, Randolph started opening the small vial of pills. Then, the scowl on his face intensifying, he slammed the vial down, rose from his seat and reached inside the liquor cabinet for a bottle of bourbon.

chapter 21

Enticing Propositions

In the spring of 1907, Samuel Randolph Governey graduated with top honors from the Bennings Boarding School for Boys and was immediately accepted to Yale and Harvard. Remaining true to his resolution, however, the earl insisted that Samuel attend a college in Philadelphia. Purposely concealing his son's initial inheritance, most of which had been used to subsidize five full years of the expensive boarding school, the earl offered to provide the 16-year-old lad with a fully-funded college education at the University of Pennsylvania. If Samuel accepted this proposition, his father promised, he would be rewarded with a hearty allowance, the funding of his subsequent graduate education and a special made-to-order Silver Ghost Rolls Royce, one of the very first to roll off Britain's assembly line.

Unaware of the sizeable trust given him by his maternal grandfather and hoping that his father's behavior had mellowed over the years, Samuel hesitantly accepted the earl's offer and returned home that summer. Upon his arrival from Pennsylvania's train station by means of a Nash Rambler taxi, the high school graduate was neither shocked nor delighted to witness his father stooping with his cane in front of the colonial mansion, hair and goatee as white as the stately pillars dwarfing him. By the apathetic look in his father's eyes, the boy, unaware of the earl's grave medical condition or the circumstances which had spawned it, could tell that life here would be no better, and possibly worse, than when he had left for boarding school five summers ago.

Although Samuel had initially looked forward to owning his very own custom-made Rolls, it was only a short time before he realized its true value.

Unable to tolerate his father's boisterous drinking binges any longer, he would often leave through the back of the mansion which led to the horse-less stables. There he would climb into the sleek Silver Ghost, sit upon its tufted black leather seat, turn over its quiet engine, and head into town. As he would feel the warm wind ruffling his hair, fragments of his father's outrage would be swept behind, if only for an hour or so. Upon starting his freshman year at the University of Pennsylvania, Samuel began spending as much time as possible at the college, attending rallies and other school activities which lasted into the evening. Although the boy was by nature a loner, he would, on occasion, help a professor after school hours or attend a militant demonstration such as those championed by the crusading suffragettes. There were times, however, when he was forced to return home early due to the premature parting of a live-in maid. Strapped with extra duties such as cooking dinner and doing the laundry, it sometimes took weeks to find another servant not only suitable for the job, but able to tolerate his drunken father. During those times, Samuel would promptly return home after classes and remain at the mansion for the rest of the evening. There was, of course, one exception to this weary routine...on a warm spring evening just before the termination of his first year at the University. Immediately after the dinner dishes were washed and put away, Samuel Governey had crossed the Schuylkill River to revisit Philadelphia's suffrage headquarters and confront its headmistress, Violet Stimple.

Although the loss of his ability to father an heir to the Governey lineage and the murder of the suffragette had initially shaken Samuel to the depths of his royal core, the horrendous incident eventually empowered him with a renewed sense of entitlement, making him more determined than ever to unearth the mysteries of an ancestry which his father had so successfully kept intact. As far as Samuel could gather, both parents had traveled from England to care for his maternal grandfather after which his mother's burdensome illness made their return impossible. As the earl's drinking habit worsened, he too, was in no condition to reclaim the Cheshire estate. But, in spite of these presumptions, Samuel suspected that something else was amiss. Maybe it was the forlorn look in his father's eyes or the disingenuous smile upon his face as he described their former life in England. Perhaps it was the man's abrupt silence when Samuel would mention the possibility of returning one day. Or maybe it was the boy's own forgotten remnants of a shrouded past he had abandoned at the tender age of six.

In lieu of these vague suspicions, young Samuel vowed that he would one day travel overseas and possibly reclaim the aristocratic throne his father had relinquished. Then, upon taking a wife of his own, he would likewise produce an heir and continue the Governey legacy. But his short-lived ambitions soon withered when, on that fateful day in late October, he had succumbed to Violet Stimple's irresistible charms. Nevertheless, as the passage of time cushioned the sting of a dream departed, Samuel resolved with a greater vengeance to visit his homeland after becoming a financially independent doctor of medicine.

With the patience of a beekeeper and the stratagem of a lion tamer, Samuel Randolph Governey, having survived the next four years living with his elderly drunken father, graduated Summa Cum Laude from the University of Pennsylvania in the spring of 1911. Although Samuel was eligible to attend virtually any medical school in the country, his father, ever apprehensive of the potential ravages of his syphilis, insisted he attend Hahnemann Medical College, located only a few blocks from home. While pointing his cedar cane to the north, objecting to Samuel's interest in other out-of-town schools, he would bellow out that the esteemed institution was the only school he would fund for his nearly 21-year-old son. Still unaware of the rightful inheritance which would be payable upon his 21st birthday, Samuel, believing he had no other means of income, ultimately enrolled in the medical school of his father's choosing after coaxing the old man to dish out two thousand dollars for a brand new brilliant yellow Stutz Bear-Cat roadster.

Although Samuel had initially resisted enrolling in the Hahnemann School of Medicine, he soon found it to be an excellent choice. Unlike the required curriculum at the University of Pennsylvania, he was now able to concentrate solely on his impending vocation. Especially appealing, though completely inexplicable to Samuel, was the opportunity to work on cadavers. Discovering an overwhelming preference to the cutting of human flesh as opposed to that of dead animal carcasses, he soon made up his mind to become a surgeon. Also, encouraged by his professors, he promptly accepted employment at the Philadelphia General Hospital, allowing more time away from his drunken father. If it weren't for having to put up with the ornery old man, Samuel realized, he would have looked forward to his forthcoming years at Hahnemann Medical College with utmost satisfaction.

chapter 22

A Convenient Discovery

After finishing a strenuous evening of internship at Philadelphia General Hospital during his third year of medical college, Samuel noticed something strange as he veered onto Chestnut Street. Whereas the colonial mansion had always displayed an array of lights after sundown, its windows, illuminated only by the headlights of the convertible, were hardly discernable. Immediately entering the stables and parking his Stutz Bearcat alongside the Silver Ghost Rolls and his father's Cadillac, he strode toward the house, entering through the back door. Stepping into the kitchen, he noticed an overwhelming smell of liquor, accompanied by a drawn-out moan. Discerning the shadowy figure of his father, he quickly turned on the light. Amid broken glass, the old man stretched out a blood-stained arm.

"Sam...Samuel! Help me...for God's sake, please! I...I can't move my legs."

Taking extra care to avoid the splinters of glass as well as the potential staining of his white uniform, Samuel stooped down and unbuttoned his father's sleeve to examine the cuts on his arm. Ascertaining that they were not deep enough to warrant immediate attention, he firmly squeezed the earl's stiff legs through bourbon-soaked pants. "Father...can you feel this? Are you experiencing any sensation at all?" he asked, unaware of the syphilis which had just recently begun to manifest.

"No, son. You must get me up off this floor...please!"

"But...I don't think it wise to move you. If you've injured your spine, then...."

"Then don't worry about my fucking spine, goddamn it! My goddamn legs just gave out on me. So move your ass and get me up, will you?"

Kicking aside the broken glass with his shoe, Samuel bent down in an attempt to hoist his father from the wet tile. Unable to lift the old man after a struggle, he finally managed to drag him to a drier spot. "I'll have to call Philadelphia General," he breathlessly stated, releasing his father and approaching the cabinet telephone. "They'll send an ambulance right away."

"No son...you mustn't!" Randolph pleaded, grabbing the cuff of his son's pants. "If you must get me to a hospital, take me to Bellevue in New York. Dr. Gruben is there...he...he knows my medical history."

"For Christ's sake, father," Samuel argued, yanking his leg from the earl's grasp. "How the hell am I going to bring you to New York? I can't even get you off the bloody floor!"

"Damn it, Samuel! Yes...you can," the earl managed to spit out between deep breaths while placing his hand over his heart. "Call a neighbor. That kike across the street. Maybe he can help."

"Are you out of your mind?" Samuel replied, trying to remain calm. "Even if I did manage to get you in the car...at this time of evening, it would take almost three hours to get there!"

"Samuel, please..." Randolph extended his arm toward Samuel, momentarily discouraging him from reaching for the telephone's receiver. "I've got the sift!" Noting his son's startled reaction, he continued. "There's an insurance policy. Dr. Gruben vouched for me. If the company discovers this deception, they...they'll deny the benefits. Samuel, without that insurance money, I'd be left penniless in some nut house. *Institutionalized.* Placed in an insane asylum! Please...don't let this happen to me!"

Samuel slowly turned away from the telephone and stared at his father, trying to comprehend the significance of the confession. So, the old man had syphilis! The most crippling of venereal diseases! Surely obtained by carrying on with a slue of sordid women. It was almost as if the gates of heaven had opened, sending down an answer to his prayers...*if* he were accustomed to saying them. With his father institutionalized, he would be free at last from the drunken geezer's insufferable clutches and, most likely, have sole control of the estate. The entire Governey estate...the colonial mansion, the land, the furnishings and whatever personal possessions left by his father would be his to do with as he pleased. No more compromises...no more demands...no more drinking binges...free to live his life as he chose!

"Sorry, father," he nonchalantly stated while turning toward the telephone, "but I must do what I think best. Since I am already acquainted with the excellent staff at Philadelphia General, my mind will be at rest knowing that my dear father is under the best possible care."

"Samuel! You cannot do this to me...please! If you take me to New York, I...I'll even buy you a new automobile! Just name it, son...what kind would you like?"

Samuel threw his hands up toward the kitchen ceiling. "What kind of car will you buy for me, father? An old broken-down Lanchester? It will be the only thing you can afford, considering the fact you have sold just about every other bloody thing in this house!"

"No...The insurance money. I...I'll use some of the insurance money!" Challenging the venomous look on his son's face, he clenched his fist. "Samuel! If you don't take me to New York, I'll cut you out of my *fucking* will! You'll be left without a *fucking* roof over your goddamn head, you little son-of-a-bitch!"

"You forget, my dear father," Samuel calmly answered with a sinister smile, "I, too, have medical acquaintances. I'm sure my colleagues at Philadelphia General would be more than willing to declare your mental incompetence and have you committed before you even have the chance to touch your precious will...especially upon fearing that one of their bright, promising interns might be left without a penny to his name!"

"Son!" the earl implored for the last time. Please...please! I beg of you! Don't do this to your father. I...I love you!"

Having never heard anything further from the truth, Samuel turned toward the telephone, picked up the receiver and politely asked the operator to connect him with Philadelphia General.

chapter 23

Buried Treasure

With Randolph Governey finally in the care of Dr. Donovan and staff at Philadelphia General, Samuel savored the silence of the colonial mansion while sorting through some papers inside his father's desk. Better to enjoy the peace and quiet while he could, he frowned, recollecting his conversation with Dr. Donovan the evening before. He had, after all, underestimated the physician's generosity. Upon feigning deep regret about the necessity of putting his father in a state-controlled institution, Samuel was offered a full-time summer job at the hospital in order to compensate for his father's demanding medical needs within the comfort of his own home. With the tertiary, final stage of syphilis having been confirmed, there was no telling how long the dreadful disease would linger, Dr. Donovan explained. At present, his father was suffering with *tabes dorsalis*, a nervous disorder causing loss of feeling and movement in the legs. And, although he was not yet exhibiting signs of mental deterioration, by the end of the summer, this aspect of the disease would most likely begin taking its toll. *Nevertheless*, the physician assured Samuel, his loyal intern...even though he would be returning to Hahnemann Medical College in the fall to complete his fourth year of medical school, they could always work out some other arrangement.

Samuel paused a moment from his task to open a shuttered window inside the stuffy library. Maybe it was just as well, he thought, while focusing upon a flowering apple tree, that although his refusal to collaborate with his father's insurance scheme had backfired, his medical expenses had finally been resolved. After all, having the ill-tempered old codger at home under the care of a full-time nurse while he worked at the hospital wasn't such a bad deal. No matter, he concluded upon hearing the screech of a blue jay, he would still make an effort to contact the Viking Insurance Company. Although it was unlikely that any benefits would be paid, perhaps he could at least, under the circumstances, recoup a portion of the premiums.

Returning to the oak desk, Samuel opened another drawer and removed a large manila envelope. Noticing the words *WILL* and *Frank Lawrence Langley*, boldly written across its surface, he promptly unraveled its thin cord. After removing the stack of papers and placing them on the desk, he was especially surprised to see his *own* name addressed on a letter from the Philadelphia Bank & Trust. Unable at first to fully comprehend its contents, Samuel paled while scanning the letter over and over as he came to realize its full significance. Dated November 16, 1911, the message read:

Dear Mr. Samuel Randolph Governey,

This is to inform you that as of November 24th, 1911, the trust which has been established in the name of "Samuel Randolph Governey" and bequeathed by Frank Lawrence Langley will become fully redeemable upon your twenty-first birthday. As appointed trustee of your impending inheritance in the amount of twenty-five thousand dollars (plus accumulated interest), it is our duty and sincere pleasure to assist you in this matter. Please contact myself or any of our delegates for prompt execution of said trust. Your kind response will be readily attended to.

Very truly yours,

Reginald T. Morgan

With heart beating rapidly, Samuel shoved the letter aside and anxious-ly thumbed through his grandfather's Will, locating under *Testamentary Trust* the terms of his rightful inheritance. So it was true, after all! And there was also an initial trust in the same amount which, he was certain that by now, his father had exhausted. Still dumbfounded by the significance of this aston-ishing revelation, a multitude of thoughts and emotions raced through him. But his ultimate reaction after euphoria and anger was that of fear. Twenty-five thousand dollars...redeemable over two years ago! Why the hell had his father kept this from him, he cursed, slapping the letter across the desk. Was the old geezer that determined to keep him under his fucking thumb? "Good God!" he exclaimed while clenching both fists to his temples. Exposing his father to that amount of money was like opening a slaughterhouse to a pack of vultures. Had that double-crossing swindler somehow squandered every penny, then? Without a moment's hesitation, Samuel picked up the desk telephone and, with a jittery index finger, dialed the operator, immediately asking for a connection with Philadelphia Bank & Trust. Rapidly tapping his foot on the hardwood floor while the telephone endlessly rang, he groaned beneath clenched teeth, fearing that perhaps the officers at the bank were on holiday. His apprehension, however, was soon alleviated after an abrupt click on the other end of the line.

"Philadelphia Bank & Trust," a woman's voice sweetly answered. "Where may I direct your call?"

"Reginald Morgan, please," Samuel swallowed, repressing his anxiety.

"One moment, sir. Who may I ask is calling?...one moment, please, Mr. Governey."

After what seemed an eternity, a man's voice on the other end of the line broke the silence. "Good afternoon, Mr. Governey! Reginald Morgan speaking. How may I help you today?"

Using every bit of strength to suppress his trepidation, Samuel weighed each word. "Yes, sir...Mr. Morgan. I am calling to inquire about the trust...the inheritance from my grandfather. I believe I was eligible to claim a...a substantial amount of money upon my twenty-first birthday." Expecting the worst, he braced himself while awaiting the banker's response.

"Why yes, Mr. Governey. As you requested, we have been holding onto that entire trust, in an interest-yielding account, for an indefinite period of time. Would you care to set an appointment for further arrangements? You may come to the bank or I may meet you at your residence, if you so wish."

Samuel let out one long, silent sigh while relaxing his facial muscles. Although it was apparent that his father had fraudulently intervened on his behalf, the money was still there! "Yes, Mr. Morgan. I should like very much to meet with you...as soon as possible, please."

"Very well, then. Will tomorrow do? Sometime around two p.m.?"

"Yes. That would be fine...thank you.... I will be at the bank at precisely two o'clock then. Good day, sir."

Thinking that he should strangle his decrepit father who certainly would have claimed the inheritance were he able to get away with it, Samuel was too elated to entertain such thoughts as he paced across the library floor. Twenty five thousand dollars...with interest! Damn! How should he spend it all? He ground clenched teeth. Since his father seemed destined to remain a boulder upon his back, instead of working at the hospital, he could pay for the old man's care and take that long-awaited vacation to England as well...as soon as the semester was out. That is, if he chose to finish the semester at all. But...*of course* he would finish! There were only three weeks left. Whether he chose to return to Hahnemann in the fall was fully up to him now. Samuel stopped dead in his tracks. Under such fortuitous circumstances, did he even want to complete his medical education? Although certain aspects of the medical profession were, indeed, fascinating, the idea of having to deal with whining patients on a day-to-day basis was somewhat unappealing...even if he decided to pursue a career as a surgeon. Reconsidering his own thoughts upon realizing that the inheritance would not sustain an affluent lifestyle for an indefinite amount of time, he continued his pacing. Perhaps he could finish his medical schooling in Europe. It was, after all, quite possible. But, he would worry about that later. His primary concern was to meet with Mr. Morgan the following day and collect the inheritance. Then, afterwards, he would pay Dr. Donovan the required amount for three full months of his father's home care and personally thank him for his kind offer of a full-time position, tactfully asserting that in lieu of his newly discovered inheritance and the excellent attention he trusts his father will receive, he has decided to take advantage of an urgently-needed summer vacation. With a smile, Samuel put his grandfather's will back in the envelope and dialed the operator once again, this time for a connection to the nearest travel agency.

chapter 24

Holiday

aving taken care of all necessary matters, as well as completing his third year at Hahnemann Medical College, Samuel continued planning his anticipated overseas holiday in June of the year 1914. Although his ultimate goal was England, he envisioned countries he only had the opportunity to read of in geography books and decided to make the most of his summer journey. While attending boarding school, he had studied the required German as well as several of the romantic languages, and so, determined that hiring a translator would be unnecessary. Also, having developed a fondness for fine automobiles along with a remarkable sense of direction, Samuel decided that driving his own motor car while touring each foreign country would be ideal. Shipping his Stutz Bear-Cat or his Rolls overseas would not be practical though, being that the automobiles were respectively three and seven years old. After all, he was ready to move on to another model. And what could be a finer addition to his British and American models than one more European sports car? After researching foreign automobiles, Samuel decided that the chic French "Gregoire," with its four-speed gearbox, superb handling and a speed of up to 50 miles-per-hour would be the ideal vehicle for his excursion. He would have it delivered to Southampton and proudly drive it off the merry docks of England.

Harboring an uncontainable excitement never experienced before, Samuel Randolph Governey, earl apparent of Cheshire, flippantly wished his ailing father farewell as a chauffeur waited to assist with his luggage. Giving not as much as a mere glance toward the stately colonial mansion, he instructed the taxi driver to take him directly to the train depot. Upon arriving, he boarded a Pullman coach; after two of the most amiable hours ever known, Samuel reached New York's Central Station. Promptly hiring another taxi, he departed the noisy, crowded terminal and headed toward the pungent docks of lower Manhattan where, upon boarding the *R.M.S. Olympic*, he set sail for his long-awaited, one-way trip to England.

Under a bright blue Manhattan sky, Samuel leaned on the transatlantic ship's lustrous mahogany rail as scores of onlookers bid their friends and families *bon voyage*. Feeling the mighty engines of the ocean liner pushing him away from the shore, he breathed a final sigh of relief. Now he had the luxury of entertaining his thoughts for nearly a week about disembarking in Southampton, England, where a French agent was scheduled to present him with his new Gregoire roadster. If all went well, he planned to drive to London where he would vacation for a week or two. During that time he would visit Cheshire Castle, tour the City of London, and, if possible, attend the renowned theatre and opera house. In order to be in proper dress for these occasions, he intended to purchase a good amount of tailor-made clothing from nearby boutiques. After his stay in London, he hoped to move on to the 'City of Love,' Paris, then the hub of German culture, Munich, Zurich and, of course, the capital of Austria...Vienna. Then, if circumstances allowed, the Cradle of the Renaissance and the home of Leonardo daVinci, magnificent Italy. From there he would drive his convertible roadster up along the Amalfi Coast into Nice and possibly vacation in Barcelona for a few days. Suntanned, palatably and aesthetically nourished, he would at last return to England and visit the green, lush countryside of Ireland, time permitting.

Samuel grinned as the Statue of Liberty's mighty torch, extinguished by the unrelenting waters of the Atlantic, vanished beneath the horizon. Perhaps he would never return to America. Perhaps after touring Europe, he would reside in England, he surmised, as he viewed each frothy wave slap against the stern of the ship. Yes...attend the University of London. Then, after obtaining his surgeon's license and practicing medicine for a few years, establish his own hospital. And, if fate allowed, he would ultimately reclaim the beloved former estate of his ancestry, Cheshire Castle. Samuel sneered while watching a looming cumulus cloud split in two. For all he cared, his father could rot in an insane asylum. If not for the desire to remain in the good graces of his mentors at Philadelphia General, he already would have had the conniving old man committed. Of course, he smugly reasoned, if he decided not to return to America, there would be no point in continuing to impress his "Old Blockley" colleagues after all.

Feeling a slight chill from the Atlantic's cold wind, Samuel secured his stiff brown hat, placed both hands in the pockets of his alpaca coat and headed toward his luxury cabin. He was looking forward to spending the better part of the week enjoying all the comforts and services the *Olympic* had to offer. Strolling through one of the plush lounges embellished with crystal chandeliers and graced by the music of a concert pianist, the young bachelor vainly returned the coquettish smiles of several escorted maidens. Acquiescing to his conceit, Samuel realized his exceptionally handsome demeanor would easily win the pleasure of their company. But he resolved to refrain from such temptations, lest he be plagued again by the scourge of gonorrhea, or, God forbid, the dreaded syphilis which had condemned his womanizing father to a life of agonizing infirmity.

Remaining true to his resolution, Samuel spent the following days at sea enjoying all the amenities which even the demands of the late King George could not have enhanced. Although occasionally engaging in idle conversation during dinner or four o'clock tea with a companion or two, he kept mostly to himself, preferring the solitude of his splendid room or brisk walks along the ship's polished teakwood decks. During the evening, he would take advantage of a variety of entertainment the *Olympic* provided, ranging from ballroom dancing to vaudeville shows. Nevertheless, as intoxicating as the transatlantic journey was for its guests, Samuel could not wait to disembark from the great ocean liner as he leaned against the mahogany rail one last time, hoping to catch a glimpse of the new French Gregoire which, by previous arrangement, would be waiting for him on the docks of Southampton.

chapter 25

Arrival

Resembling the neck of a cygnet swan, the gold-framed side view mirror gracing the sleek, white fender of the Gregoire roadster reflected the foggy image of the palatial *Olympic*. The great ship was now at rest along the port of Southampton as Samuel adjusted his goggles and drove the new French automobile off the bustling dock toward the City of London. While turning onto the pebbly road leading to his first European destination, the novice traveler smiled as he eyed the bulging Oxford bag lying upon the dark brown leather passenger seat. So far things were going as planned. The five-day voyage across the Atlantic had been more pleasant than expected, given the calmness of the ocean due to early June's tranquil disposition. After the *R.M.S. Olympic's* arrival at Southampton's port, he had disembarked the transatlantic luxury liner, promptly meeting with the French agent who had delivered the convertible roadster from the port of Cherbourg, France across the English Channel. After taking the automobile on a test drive along Southampton's rugged coast, Samuel then closed the deal by paying a hefty fee of twenty-five hundred dollars. His next destination, London, was approximately 80 miles. Samuel removed the neatly folded map from inside the pocket of his lightweight driver's coat and wedged it next to the traveling bag. If all went well, he should reach the "Duke's Hotel" within a couple of hours. Hopefully, before sunset.

Samuel staunchly inhaled the salty fog-filled air, gripping the smooth, black steering wheel of the purring automobile and eyed the gold and onyx ring upon the forefinger of his right hand. In spite of the deep scratch across its stone, of all his father's heirlooms, this was his favorite. Since both of the earl's nurses preferred that their disabled patient be spared potentially harmful belongings, Samuel had guiltlessly packed the ring along with a few of his father's prized regalia, intending to have it sized in London. To his delight, however, a jeweler on the *Olympic* was able to provide the service. Returning his eyes to the road, he wondered how the ring's precious stone had been deeply scratched. It was unfortunate that, although the jeweler had tried to eliminate the imperfection, it was still noticeable. Even so, he would forever cherish it as a memorable symbol of his British heritage.

As Samuel viewed the sun setting over the hazy English countryside midst the wild fuchsia and fragrant yellow cowslip, an immense pride swelled within his British bones as he reflected upon the Governey coat of arms encrusted upon the ring's black stone. He now knew this was where he belonged. Under the dank, grey sky of England, he was as much a part of the green landscape as the black and white half-timbered houses dotting the winding coastline. Whether childhood memories or simply the knowledge of his ancestry had bonded him to this cherished part of the world, Samuel felt like an orphan discovering his long-lost parents. And the traveling itself had, so far, been a most exhilarating experience. It mattered not if he were visiting Europe or the Far East. Samuel knew that from now on, traveling would be as much a part of him as the regimented life which preceded it.

The roadster's new leather interior was soon overwhelmed by the smell of wet steel as it approached the Vauxhall Bridge which spanned the River Thames. Samuel slowed the French automobile while retrieving the map of London and adjusted his silk poplin driving cap. Upon crossing the bridge, he would turn right on Milbank Road, pass Parliament Square, then turn left toward St. James Street. As the Gregoire's spoked wheels clanked their way across the bridge's heavy steel structure, he experienced a slight chill. Instead of declaring the grandeur of London, the heroic figures which adorned the bridge appeared dark and sinister beneath the shadowy sky. Stilted and aloof, they beckoned the unsuspecting foreigner to enter their majestic city, eager to reveal the cryptic secrets which had, for the past 17 years, been buried deep within its permeable soil.

chapter 26

Accommodations

In the flower-filled courtyard of the "Duke's Hotel" a gloved employee proceeded to light the dozen gas lamps encircling the cobblestone drive. An attendant dressed in velvet knickers and a matching cap immediately approached the Gregoire roadster as Samuel drove up to the main entrance of the Edwardian building. Samuel grinned. So far, he was pleased with his choice of accommodations. Peeling off his goggles, he halted the roadster in front of the canopied footpath as the uniformed page, with luggage cart in hand, untied the bags from the rear rack of the French vehicle. Samuel then departed the Gregoire with a bit of reluctance before the attendant gingerly drove the cherished possession into its own designated parking space.

Dusting off the driver's cap, Samuel stepped into the main lobby of the hotel, unbuttoning his long tan driver's coat as the smell of grey worsted suits along with gallant salutations greeted him. Upon being directed to the concierge's desk, he took note of the stunning bronze sculptures and splendid paintings adorning the mahogany-trimmed room. Even the carved wings of each cherub surrounding the marble fireplace were discernable. Samuel smiled inwardly, relaxing his shoulders as he approached the concierge. Judging from the camelhair rugs and padded furniture, he would be assured a good night's rest.

"May I be of assistance sir?" the balding gentleman in coattails wistfully asked, daintily enunciating each syllable while winking his chained monocle back into place.

Clenching the brim of his poplin cap, Samuel recoiled momentarily upon fathoming the concierge's sexual disposition. "Yes, if you please," he answered with a polite nod. "Governey is the name. Samuel Governey. I believe there is a room reserved for me."

Upon hearing his guest's name, the concierge, gripping the monocle and discerning Samuel from the corner of his eye, fumbled through a large leather-bound visitors' book. "Why, yes," he exclaimed as if recovering a long-lost letter. "Master Samuel Governey." Almost instantly, his eyes widened, focusing upon Samuel's ringed forefinger. "Excuse me, sir...Master Governey, but...may you, by the remotest possibility, be the son of Randolph Governey, Earl of Cheshire?"

Completely taken aback, Samuel could not decipher whether he was flattered or insulted upon being recognized by a man of such dubious character. "Why...yes...yes, I am," he answered, ever unaware of his own ailing father's sexual disposition.

"My Lord!" the concierge squealed, suddenly releasing the monocle as it dangled upon the button of his tuxedo. Flicking his wrist, he leaned closer to Samuel. "My initial suspicions were correct then!" With gaping mouth and speckled hands upon flushed cheeks, he continued to gawk. "My, my. Forgive me for being so forward, but the resemblance is absolutely uncanny! For a moment I was misguided by the absence of the mustache, but..." the flowery-scented man paused while studying his guest. "Perhaps not so much the nose, but definitely the mouth. And your eyes...yes, most indubitably...those alluring deep blue eyes!"

"Then I assume that you were acquainted with my father?" Samuel cautiously asked, leaning away from the prying concierge.

"Acquainted? Why, heavens, no!" the gentleman chuckled, barely able to contain his amusement. "I was hardly *acquainted* with him, but," he added with a dreamy look on his satiny face. "I must admit, I did admire him immensely!"

Wishing to be rid of such an offensive specimen of mankind, but hoping to gather more information about his father, Samuel forced a smile. "It is indeed a pleasure, sir, to know how greatly you admired my father. I have, however, taken this English holiday to reacquaint myself with my ancestry. It has been several years since I have experienced the satisfaction of residing in your most gracious country."

The scantly browed concierge immediately placed a hand upon his slender chest. "Master Governey, let me assure you that the pleasure *was* and is, indeed, all mine. If I may be of assistance to you, just beckon your faithful servant, Darnell."

Repulsed by the concierge's forwardness, yet ever curious to discover additional information about his heritage, Samuel continued his inquiry. "Would you be so kind then, sir, to provide directions to Cheshire Castle? Although the residence had been my childhood home, I have not had the opportunity to revisit the estate since traveling to America so many years ago."

Darnell, placing translucent palms upon the desk, gazed sympathetically at his guest. "Why, yes. Such a shame, was it not?"

"What was that, sir?"

"The family's hasty departure. That whole unfortunate incident!"

"Incident?"

Realizing that his guest was not at all aware of the scandal that had swept across England almost two decades ago, Darnell diplomatically diverted to another subject. "My, my! I seem to have departed from my manners! You ask for directions to Cheshire and I begin rambling on. Now, let's see..." The concierge reached under the desk, pulled out a map and unfolded it. He then located the City of London, tracing his finger upward to the left of the map. "The drive is long, but interesting. About 180 miles as the crow flies. If you wish, Master Governey, I shall hire a taxi forthwith in the morning."

"No need, sir," Samuel retorted, still stunned by the concierge's former comment. "My roadster is available and I was looking forward to a pleasant drive through the English countryside."

"Of course!" Darnell graciously acquiesced. "Indeed, it should be a most pleasant drive. Provided, of course, it does not rain. Oh, yes," he quickly added. "I suspect that upon reaching Cheshire, someone will be able to assist you in locating the Castle. If you like, I shall be happy to ring one of the local establishments to inquire about the matter."

"That would be fine," Samuel answered, extremely puzzled over the concierge's abruptness. "But..." Before he could request any further explanation, the capricious gent was already on the telephone. As Samuel waited for the concierge to complete the call, he could not help but wonder about the full implication of the word "incident." And why had he changed the subject so abruptly? What if there had been some awful *incident?* If there was, then for God's sake, whatever could it have been? Although he, himself, found his father's character to be somewhat deficient, what terrible deed could have caused the earl to flee his beloved homeland? Perhaps it was not something his father had done. Perhaps his mother. Or, perhaps there were circumstances completely beyond their control. Something in the order of...Samuel's speculations were suddenly interrupted by the light, cheery voice of Darnell.

"By Jove, my good man! The proprietress at the Green Gaggle Inn is willing to direct you to the Castle upon your arrival in Cheshire. After taking the main road into town, look for the largest building in the square. There will be an overhead board above the Inn, so you shan't miss it," he beamed.

"Thank you," Samuel curtly nodded. "However...you had mentioned something about some sort of *incident*...something to do with my family setting off for America. What were you implying, may I ask?"

Darnell gingerly pressed two middle fingers against closed lips, as if trying to recall his exact words regarding the matter. After a short moment, he curled both fingers toward his pointed chin. "*Incident?* Did I say *incident?*" He let out an amused giggle while flinging his hand. "Excuse me, sir, but I did not mean to *imply* anything at all. All I meant to *convey* was how unfortunate the whole *incident* was...that an aristocratic family such as yours would leave the country with hardly a moment's notice."

"Yes," Samuel acquiesced, still searching for some answers. "It was rather unusual that a family such as ours would leave so soon, was it not?"

Anticipating where the conversation was going, Darnell quickly waved down one of the bellhops. "Higgins...oh, Higgins! Would you kindly guide Master Governey to his room? I believe those are his bags." He then reached inside one of the cubbyholes behind him and handed Samuel his key. "Your suite is on the third floor." Directing his attention toward the gilded elevator's door, he quickly added, "Higgins will escort you to the lift. And...Oh, yes.... If you have not yet eaten, I suggest dining in our fine restaurant. The hotel employs a most excellent French chef!"

Having been reminded that he had not eaten for almost half a day, Samuel shrugged his shoulders and followed the bellhop to his suite. Though disappointed at not having learned more of his family's plight, he was certainly grateful to be rid of the disgusting concierge. Why a prestigious hotel had employed such an eccentric was beyond comprehension. Nevertheless, Samuel thought, exiting the elevator and stepping onto the hallway's green carpet, his growling stomach was certain to appreciate a fine dinner after which he would retire for the evening. Perhaps tomorrow morning someone in Cheshire would be able to provide him with the information he was seeking.

chapter 27

Peculiar Reception

Samuel cautiously slowed down his roadster and scowled as the shrouded afternoon sun revealed another mud puddle obstructing the main road near the center of Warwick. He had been traveling for almost four hours and was only half way toward his destination. At this motor speed, even without stopping for afternoon tea and crumpets, reaching the Green Gaggle Inn before six was an improbability. Perhaps he should have waited another day after all. The unexpected rainstorm which shook the thick, oak-cased windows of the Duke's Hotel during the night seemed to have taken its worst toll here, he concluded, woefully regretting the vehicle's wheels becoming splattered with yet an additional layer of mud. The Gregoire, which had been cleaned and buffed the previous evening by the attentive staff at the Duke's Hotel, would surely need another good washing upon its return. But that wouldn't be possible until tomorrow afternoon. Samuel frowned. He detested the idea of his new stark-white roadster being dirtied up any longer than necessary. If not for the morning London rain, he would have gotten an earlier start, returning to the hotel that evening. There, the attendants would have promptly taken care of the matter. Now, besides having to obtain directions to Cheshire Castle, it would be necessary to secure a room at the Green Gaggle Inn for the night.

Upon reaching a drier stretch of road as the dense morning fog slackened, Samuel revved the Gregoire to a comfortable 30 miles per hour. Driving through the county of Stafford, he couldn't help but notice through mud-caked goggles a handful of gleaners laboring in a wheat field. Wearing veiled hoods to shield their flushed faces from the late afternoon sun, the women, dressed in shabby aprons of coarse sacking, gathered the grain into bundles while the men cut the tall, wispy stalks with long, curved machetes. A group of children, flinging burlap sacks across their shoulders, approached a wooden wagon hitched to a team of work horses. Old and fatigued, the gold-colored mares reminded Samuel of his grandfather's cherished palominos. Although memories of his early youth were hazier than the English sky, he remembered the horses well. Aside from his grandfather's warm sheltering lap, they had been a source of great comfort, allowing the young boy to escape the sadness his parents had carried overseas. Though never truly discovering the source of their sorrow, he nevertheless felt a responsibility to heal it...especially his mother's unhappiness. No longer able to bear the sight of her tears, young Samuel would gain temporary solace by escaping into the stables and stroking the horses' long, silky white manes, all the while vowing that he would do anything to make his mother truly happy again.

As the rays of the late afternoon sun snugly settled upon the passenger seat of the French sports car, Samuel adjusted his cap. He was pleased upon sighting the city walls and entrance gates which beckoned his arrival at the quaint town of Cheshire. Since drier roads had allowed him to accelerate the roadster to 50 miles per hour, he had arrived somewhat sooner than previously anticipated, though probably not early enough for a pre-sunset excursion to Cheshire Castle. Slowing down the convertible while passing through the gates, he noticed the many shops and large gingerbread buildings bordering its narrow streets. As his eyes continued to scan the passing store fronts, he immediately stepped on the brakes. Hanging from one of the large buildings like a jutting chin was a wooden board reading "Green Gaggle Inn."

Grateful that the unpaved road was dry enough so as not to muddy his new alligator shoes, Samuel tossed his goggles upon the dusty passenger seat and exited the Gregoire, frowning at the splattered mess along the white fenders. Spreading a waterproof canopy over the top of the sports car, he warily assessed a few people dining through the Inn's dark, smeared window while two awestruck boys, eyeing his vehicle, whispered to each other. Concluding that the barefoot lads were not accustomed to the privilege of aristocratic visitors in their paltry, uncultured town, Samuel lent them a patronizing smile as he unbuttoned his mud-soiled driving coat and followed the trodden footpath toward the weather-beaten door of the Green Gaggle. Sensing the two small brats at his heels, he then removed his cap, draped the coat over his arm, and entered the log-braced lobby. Surrounded by the smell of cooked cabbage, Samuel immediately noticed a buxom, dark-haired woman of middle age, wearing a white peasant blouse and showing plenty of cleavage. Sitting upon a high wooden chair behind a small, scratched table, she addressed her new patron without so much as looking up from her ledger.

"Can I 'elp you sir?"

"Yes, you may," Samuel answered, wondering if the woman was, in fact, going to detach her nose from the book. "My name is Samuel Governey. I believe a Mr. Darnell Boyle rang from the Dukes Hotel yesterday informing you that I was interested in viewing Cheshire Castle."

No longer preoccupied with the ledger, the innkeeper spontaneously put down her pencil, acknowledging her guest. "Governey, did ya say?" shifting her gaze toward the onyx ring upon his forefinger.

"Why, yes," Samuel responded, wondering if the woman was, indeed, responding to the prestige of his family name. "Will you be able to provide the proper directions? And...," he hesitantly added, "I shall need a room for the night."

"I can give ya directions, if ya like," the woman coldly answered, eyeing the two boys who were eavesdropping by the Inn's entrance, "but we don't 'ave any rooms left."

Perplexed by the woman's abrupt demeanor, Samuel was about to ask if there was anywhere else he might spend the night, when a child's voice broke the awkward silence.

"But mum...there's rooms...we got a few left, we 'ave!"

"'Scuse me, sir," the red-faced proprietress exclaimed while giving her eldest son a dirty look, "Seems I was mistakin' after all. Gets me days mixed up sometimes, I do." Opening a drawer of the table, she grabbed a large iron key. "Room six," she curtly stated, leaving it on the desk. "Up the stairs and on yer right. That'll be five shillings."

Thinking the price a bit steep for such unrefined accommodations, Samuel removed a bill book from the pocket of his gabardine trousers, handing over ten shillings. "And the castle," he added as the impudent woman dropped the correct change into his open palm, "how might I arrive there?"

"I can take 'im!" the child once again interrupted. "I know 'ow ta get there!"

"You ain't takin' the gen'leman nowhere!" the woman snapped.

"But, mum.... 'E'll get lost goin' by 'imself. I can take 'im...let me...please!"

"I said you ain't takin' 'im nowhere!" the woman yelled, glowering at her son. "Now go back outside an' play...you an' Steven. And don't talk to no strangers!" Wiping her forehead with the back of her hand as the boys exited the building, she addressed Samuel once again. "Seein' that it's near sunset, I wouldn't advise goin' now...you'll never find yer way back in the dark. I'll be 'ere first thing in the mornin.' I can give ya' directions then. 'Ave a good evenin.'" Without a bit of hesitation, the woman returned to her ledger, never giving her unwelcome guest the chance to express his insincere gratitude. Turning away from the proprietress, Samuel noticed a pot-bellied janitor, about 20 years his senior, quickly averting his gaze as he continued to sweep the drab, planked floor of the sparsely-furnished lobby. *Damn yokels would be better off minding their own goddamn business,* the earl apparent silently griped, wondering how long the grubby caretaker had been there.

Climbing the rickety wooden stairs to room number six, Samuel regretted that he had not brought along his toilet kit and an extra set of clothing. Upon entering the rustic room, he scowled, realizing he would have to use the chamber pot in the corner. Scornfully eyeing a filthy braided rug, he kicked it underneath the twin bed. Perhaps if it was warm enough during the night, he could do away with the stained comforter also. Walking over to the sullied window set above a small table and chair, he released its rusty latch to let in some fresh air. It was bad enough having to sleep in this hellhole, let alone being nauseated all night by the smell of cooked cabbage. Looking out into an alleyway, he grumbled, wondering how he would stomach that evening's dinner and the next day's breakfast. Retrieving his father's platinum pocket watch, he noted the time. 6:35 p.m. He had best get ready for dinner then.

After squeamishly using the chamber pot, Samuel poured a pitcher of water into a washbowl and rinsed his hands. Refusing to use the ragged towels stashed upon shelving of unpainted timbers, he headed down the dim, narrow hall. Vigorously shaking wet hands, he hoped he would not have to confront the innkeeper again. At least not until asking for directions to Cheshire Castle the following morning. He certainly was being received in peculiar ways since arriving in England, he thought, whisking damp hands along the sides of his trousers. First it was that "Lord Fauntleroy" at the Dukes Hotel and now this one. Whatever in the name of British hospitality had ruffled that wench's haughty feathers anyhow? As Samuel approached the confined stairway, the clamor of tin dinnerware and voices of other guests drifted up the steps while he continued speculating about the innkeeper. She was quite detached until he had mentioned the Governey name. Then discourteous, even a bit hostile upon noticing his father's onyx ring. Perhaps she knew his father and they were somehow on bad terms with each other. It would not surprise him, considering the earl's obstinate nature. Nevertheless, Samuel concluded while descending the creaky steps, as curious as he might be about the Governey legacy, that stone-faced hussy was certainly not the person to confide in.

Reaching the bottom of the stairs, he glanced out the window of the inn, satisfied that his roadster, though still splattered with mud, remained intact. Revolted by the thought of eating mediocre grub with common country folk, he headed toward the smoke-filled dining area. But no sooner had he taken a few steps across the lobby when suddenly he was solicited by a familiar pot-bellied figure dressed in a faded plaid shirt and bib-overall, no longer toting a broom and pail.

"'Scuse me, sir," the handyman asked. "But that young bloke was right, ya know." Seeing that he had Samuel's full attention, the red-bearded caretaker with mustard-colored teeth continued. "You'll sure get lost by yerself goin' to Cheshire Castle. If ya want'a get there, you'd best be takin' someone along. I know the way," he eagerly volunteered. "I'd be ready first thing tomorra' mornin'...whenever ya like."

Wishing to be rid of the meddling hayseed, Samuel politely smiled. "I appreciate your concern, my good man," he nodded. "Good evening, but I prefer to go it alone." Satisfied that the matter had been diplomatically resolved, he strode toward the dimly-lit dining room occupied by beer-guzzling men and gabby women. Amid curious stares, a gradual silence, like a ripple in a brook, pervaded the pub as Samuel ducked beneath the open portal, making his way toward a table bearing a chipped pair of smudged salt and pepper shakers. As a skinny, braided waitress tossed a set of scratched tin dinnerware onto the distressed tabletop, a hare-lipped lad in the corner of the room wearing a stocking cap resumed throwing darts, prompting other patrons to revive their jovial conversation. Grudgingly placing his order for the most palatable dish available, Samuel wondered if his stomach would tolerate the generous portion of cabbage soup, black bread and mug of dark ale until the following morning.

chapter 28

Compelling Offer

Wearing the same gabardine pants and striped silk blend shirt which had been neatly folded from the previous night, Samuel, with coat and cap in hand, once again descended the rickety stairs with the intention of eating a quick breakfast, obtaining directions to Cheshire Castle and promptly departing the Green Gaggle Inn for the last time. Barely reaching the bottom of the steps, however, his plans were momentarily interrupted as he glanced out the window to view his French Gregoire convertible. It was evident before he retired for the evening that his roadster had not been touched, but now it was obvious that someone had intentionally trifled with it. In spite of the fact that it had rained during the night, the canopy which he had carefully spread across the car was rolled up and placed inside the rear compartment. Pushing open the Inn's front door, Samuel rushed outside, viewing with total astonishment the automobile's sparkling white fenders and silver rim tires, no longer caked with layers of dirt and mud. The brown leather seats, dry and spotless, revealed that whoever was behind the well-intentioned deed had carried it out that very morning. Undecided whether he was pleased or annoyed that someone had tampered with his fine French vehicle, Samuel had hardly the time to contemplate the motive behind such a masterful deed before hearing a familiar cockney voice, accompanied by the clatter of a bucket.

"'Hope ya don't mind me takin' the liberty of cleanin' yer car," the red-bearded handyman shouted, walking across the dirt road away from his

121

truck. "Washed the mud off 'er last night and polished 'er fresh this mornin' after the rain let up. Shook the coverin' off fer ya, too, so it's all ready ta goes," he beamed, pausing a few steps from Samuel. "If ya move it up a bit, I can get the bottom o' them tires."

"Thank you, but that will be quite unnecessary," Samuel replied, relieved that the bothersome busybody had not scratched the Gregoire's immaculate finish. "I shall be leaving shortly and they are bound to be muddied again." He reached into his pocket and took out the leather bill book, flicking over one shilling. "Thank you for attending to my vehicle. Good day."

"But sir...if ya please..." the man interrupted. "Like ya say, sir, it'd be a shame ta dirty 'er up again. Me offer still stands. I stands on me offer ta get ya ta Cheshire Castle in me own truck 'fore the hour. Otherwise, there's no tellin' you'd get lost, like that young bloke said. There's lots o' windin' roads beyond the moors...some goin' nowheres. You'll be backtrackin' yer way 'round most o' the journey." The mangy character, seeing that Samuel was not the least bit dissuaded, stared at the impeccable sports car. "There's brambles and branches 'long them narrow roads. She's bound ta get scratched up fer sure. O' course," he added, "'taint nobody's business but yers to do with it as ya damn please."

As much as Samuel disdained being refuted by anyone, let alone this indigent clodhopper, he nevertheless found it impossible to disregard the handyman's final argument. Eyeing the old, run-down wagon that he would be subjected to ride in, he ultimately gave in. "Very well, then. I shall be ready to leave in a half hour."

"Name's Clive," the delighted fellow replied, extending his hand. Seeing that the proud aristocrat had no intention of returning his gesture, he dropped a hairy forearm alongside his bulging waistline. "'Alf an hour then," he subserviently nodded.

Samuel grunted, opening the heavy, weather-beaten door of the Inn. Discerning that this sudden change of plans was in his best interest, the realization that he would not be driving the roadster to the former Governey estate was disheartening. At least he wouldn't have to confront that impudent, stout-bosomed wench for directions, he huffed while ambling toward the dining hall. Upon seating himself next to the window, he could not help but admire the immaculate convertible with its contrasting dark brown interior. Maybe it was just as well leaving it behind, he frowned, picking up a spotted chalkboard menu. It *would* be a damn shame to have it all scratched up. And maybe...just maybe...that Clive fellow would be able to provide him with the missing puzzle to what was now becoming a most perplexing state of affairs.

chapter 29

A Haunting Revelation

With a less-than-hearty serving of boiled eggs and stale bread weighing like a medicine ball inside his stomach, Samuel stepped outside, half-heartedly anticipating his excursion to Cheshire Castle. Although the fog-veiled rays of an orange sunrise seeped through the purple-laced branches of a mulberry tree, the soil beneath his feet was still wet from the previous night's rain. Having already muddied the soles of his alligator shoes from that morning's encounter with Clive, Samuel grumbled as the ill-groomed handyman, standing aside the old motor-driven wagon, waved him down. *Maybe it's just as well I hadn't changed into fresh clothing after all,* he scoffed, eying the rusted-out Winton while crossing the unpaved road.

Paying no attention to the witless babbling of his self-appointed guide, Samuel hoisted himself into the open cab of the Winton, careful not to catch his driver's coat on one of the sharp side rails. Settling upon the ripped passenger seat, he donned his poplin cap. Unsure of whether the vehicle would be traveling fast enough to warrant wearing goggles, he instead slipped the thick-banded eye guards over his arm. Getting a good whiff of the handyman who was positioning himself behind the scratched steering wheel, Samuel winced, realizing he preferred the smell of cooked cabbage after all. Noticing that Clive was wearing the same clothes from the previous day, he wondered how long it had been since the faded red shirt and dingy cotton overall had been washed, not to mention underclothes...that is, if he had any. Or, for that matter, how long it had been since the fellow had taken a bloody bath.

"Twon't take longer than a 'alf hour's time ta get there," Clive explained, hastily making a sign of the cross. He then rubbed something inside the bulging pocket of his flannel shirt while stepping on the clutch and pulling the choke before starting the engine. "'She's slow's a slug, but sturdier than a sow."

As Clive placed his hands back on the steering wheel, exposing his front shirt pocket, Samuel recognized the object he had been fondling as a rabbit's foot. Not only was this stinking stooge uncouth, but superstitious as well. Hopefully, the rusty-haired boor would be able to manage the trip to Cheshire Castle without further inconvenience.

"As I says 'afore," Clive went on while steering the truck along the main gravel road, "Been ta Cheshire Castle plenty o' times, so it's no trouble findin' me way." Prompted by an awkward silence amid the rattling of janitorial supplies in back of the truck, Clive gestured toward a weather-beaten stone building wedged like a forgotten rat trap amidst quaint town shops. "That there's the Chester county jail," he explained. "Hardly used no more 'cept for old drunkards." Receiving no response from his aristocratic guest, he spoke up once again while veering onto a secondary dirt road, leaving the small town behind. "So...ya plannin' on buyin' the castle? Cheshire Castle," he clarified, noticing the questioning look on Samuel's face.

Unsure of whether the nosy janitor was knowledgeable of his family's history, Samuel responded carefully as the Winton chugged along. "Then I assume the estate is not presently occupied?"

"No, sir...why...no it ain't...not in the way *most* folks sees it anyhow!" Clive answered, his yolk-like eyes widening as he rubbed dirt-embedded fingernails along the yellowed rabbit's foot.

Anticipating further explanation, Samuel could not help notice his guide staring open-mouthed at the onyx ring upon his forefinger and suddenly becoming tight-lipped. Discerning Clive's reluctance to continue confiding in him, Samuel offered a friendly smile. "It is quite remarkable, is it not?"

"What be that, sir?" Clive cautiously asked while guiding the rattling Winton through the fog-shrouded countryside.

Samuel raised his forefinger. "The ring," he answered, pretending to admire the precious stone. "It belonged to a man named Randolph Governey...Earl of Cheshire. It is my understanding that the Castle we are about to visit had been in his family for countless generations." Receiving no response from the handyman, he continued his charade. "The auctioneer at Sotheby's assured me that it was authentic."

"You mean that bloke of an earl ain't yer father, now?" Clive answered, opening up like an unclogged funnel.

"Why, heavens no!" Samuel laughed, tolerating the bouncing Winton as it continued to chug along the bumpy road.

"But..." the puzzled handyman exclaimed. "Monica says yer name is Governey, sure as the bloody Queen rules! Says ya checked in by that very name."

Samuel suppressed a sneer, reflecting upon the prying nature of these uncultured country folk who were no better than a bevy of cackling servants. "Monica was correct!" he retorted. "Indeed, my surname *is* Governey. That is how I became interested in purchasing this splendid ring. My family, however, are merely commoners from Scotland. Unfortunately, possessing this precious stone is my one and only link to such privileged royalty."

"Well," Clive answered, scratching through matted hair. "Ya coulda' fooled me, drivin' a crowned motorcar and dressed in them fancy togs. I s'pose that's why yer set on seein' Cheshire Castle, then?"

"Exactly, my good man," Samuel graciously answered as a curve in the road tossed him against the battered door of the truck. "You say the estate is for sale, then?" he added, wondering what the handyman had previously suggested regarding the castle's occupancy.

"Sure it's fer sale," Clive answered in a somewhat ominous tone. "If anybody's willin' ta buy it." Fiddling with the rabbit's foot, he rambled on. "A Paddy family, ya know, them Irish blokes, bought the place a year 'er two ago. Was hardly there in the wink of an eye 'fore they moved out again." Responding to a bump in the road while heading toward a tree-covered path, Clive grabbed the steering wheel with both hands and nervously licked dry lips.

"Was there a specific reason the Irish family decided to leave?"

Clive squeezed the lackluster steering wheel as if holding on for dear life. "Why...yes sir," he answered, warily staring at a looming canopy of mighty elms. "Sure as them branches turn stick-like, come winter."

"Well, what was the problem, then?" Samuel asked, becoming impatient of his companion's habitual dawdling.

Clive's Adam's apple bobbed like a rubber stone dropped into a shallow pond as he forced a swallow. "Place is 'aunted...there's a lady...a ghost...folks 'ave seen 'er! There's music comes first, they say...the dancin' kind. Then, with 'ardly a warnin', it's stark quiet. Then...then comes the awful wailin'. Mostly in the dead o' night. But sometimes...sometimes if ya keep dumb, you can 'ear her cryin' even durin' the day when the sun is hidin' 'neath a shadowin' mist like 'tis now."

Skeptical of Clive's story, Samuel remained silent, realizing that it was common for country folk to indulge in such ridiculous beliefs. Satisfied that he had not driven his Gregoire after all, as several brambles scratched against the surface of the truck, he amusedly listened as the superstitious handyman continued his story.

"Some folks say 'tis the last mistress o' the Castle...the Countess Governey 'erself...risen from 'er American grave...driftin' all the way 'cross the ocean." With knitted brows, Clive released his left hand from the steering wheel and quickly stroked the rabbit's foot. "Saw 'er once me'self, I did!" he declared, clamping his hand back onto the steering wheel before the Winton could veer out of control. "Years ago...shortly 'fore dusk." Clive eased on the gas pedal while turning onto another narrow road, lowering his husky voice to almost a whisper. "First there's this scratchin' sound...thought 'twas a beast in the woods...but then...then I looks far off toward the face o' the castle and there she be! Floatin' ghost-like 'gainst grey stone walls. 'Er long dress draggin' 'cross them wet leafs on the lawn. Carryin' a wavin' flag with stars that spark'd like a swarm o' fireflies. Some folks say when the full moon's high and the wind's quiet, they can hear 'er wailin' all the way down the dirt road. I never 'eard 'er, though...'ope me never will! N*oooo* sir!" Clive emphasized, firmly shaking his head. "Don't blame no one for not wantin' ta lives there no more!"

Startled by the eerie, almost accurate description of his own mother dressed in the very costume she deliriously described countless times while on her deathbed, Samuel felt his blood curdling. Reasoning to himself that the wild imaginations of these country commoners thrived on concocting such absurd stories, he waited for his queasy stomach to calm down. "Your bravery is to be commended, then," he finally remarked, attempting to make light of the situation. "Only a very few would dare risk confronting such a tormented spirit."

"'Fraid I can't takes credit for bein' so brave as ya say, sir," Clive sheepishly answered, gazing through the menacing fog. "If ya don't mind, I'll take ya up ta the ol' wooden bridge. The castle's 'bout a 'alf mile from there. If yer not up ta the walkin', you mights drive the Winton, if ya like. I can wait fer ya 'neath the dogwoods." Receiving no immediate reply, Clive added, "If yer weary of goin' there 'lone, I gots field glasses, back o' the truck. Can sees the castle safe an' sound with 'em."

A bit perturbed with the option of having to either walk a half mile or drive the ramshackle truck once they arrived on the grounds of the former Governey estate, Samuel forced a smile. "That is perfectly alright," he answered, repulsed by the thought of peering through Clive's filthy binocular lenses. "Perhaps a brief walk will do me good."

"Like I says 'afore, yer welcome ta drives the Winton," he offered as the beaten truck continued to chug along.

Somewhat amused at what a country peasant would put himself through for a meager gratuity, Samuel decided to end the nonsensical chatter regarding ghosts, probing instead into something of greater concern. "So, my good man, how is it that you know your way to Cheshire Castle?"

"Well, sir," Clive began, relieved to change the subject, "First I comes to the castle when me gal was bein' a scullery maid for the earl and 'is family." With a mischievous look in his eye, he went on. "Comes summers, Governeys'd go ta London. So me an' Annabelle 'ould make an 'oliday out o' it ourselves...she 'ad a latchkey ta the cookery, so we'd git in the castle from there. Go up to one o' them bed chambers and spend all mornin' 'fore the 'eadmistress come 'round. No one ever know'd we was there...romped all summers long, we did! Yes, sir...ya knows what I means!" Clive boasted while squirming in his seat. "Had it off with the lass all summers long!"

No longer wishing to hear any more disgusting details about the sexual practices of a whoremongering yokel within the cherished walls of his boyhood home, Samuel attempted to sway the conversation to a more positive direction. "So...Clive, my dear fellow," he carefully questioned. "You must have heard a good bit about the earl and his family, then, I assume?"

"I did, sir! That I did, sir!" the janitor nodded, keeping his glaring eyes glued to the winding road. "Ain't no soul in all o' Britain what can match them stories Cheshire Castle has ta tells!"

Unconsciously playing with the driving goggles upon his lap, Samuel proceeded with caution, no longer concerned with the Winton's bumpy ride. "Then tell me, Clive...why is it that the Governey family no longer resides at Cheshire Castle?"

Clive glanced at his distinguished guest for a brief moment, returning his gaze past a thistle-covered grove. "A downright scandal, it was!"

Samuel stretched the band of his goggles. "*Scandal* did you say?"

"Yes, sir, Mr. Governey. A scandal it be...a stirred-up scandal like never 'afore!"

"What was it about?" Samuel implored, thinking for a moment that perhaps his father had indiscreetly committed the unpardonable act of adultery with the wife of a fellow aristocratic or, even worse, a fledgling country wench. "Whomever did it involve?"

"'Twas the earl...Randolph Governey," Clive answered disdainfully. "Gots 'imself in a heap o' trouble, that one did!"

"My good man...whatever are you implying?" Samuel asked, bracing himself with a stiff upper lip.

"Almost got 'imself locked up, fer the rest o' his life, he did! Was one o' them queer sort o' fellas, he was...not likes me! No sir...not likes *us* blokes!"

"Are you saying that my...the *earl* had broken the laws of Great Britain somehow?" Samuel replied, having no idea what the handyman was insinuating.

"Broke ain't the word, Mr. Governey," Clive sarcastically countered. "Done's the most dirtiest act a devil of a bloke can do's. Gots away, though...'im and 'is family...sails to America. God knows whats the bloody fella's up ta now. Should be rottin' in hell, he should! Last I 'eard, he was left widowered. And that bloody countess...ugly as sin, I hear. Married 'er fer a sack o' sterlin's. 'Twas nothin' else she were good for ta him, bein' he never did find the lassies one bit temptin.' No sir, him bein' one o' them bloody blokes thats can nevers finds the lassies temptin'!"

Feeling the medicine ball inside his stomach starting to roll, Samuel caught his breath. "Are you saying that the earl had a...a preference for...for the men?"

"Yer bein' too kind...too kind, Mr. Governey," Clive answered, pulling roughly on the gearshift. "*Preyed* on 'em is more like it! That's what's got 'is blimey arse in a heap o' trouble...was layin' with them young bloody blokes, he was. That he was!"

"Damn it, Clive...*goddamn* it! Are you implying that my father...the *earl* was homosexual?"

Too enthralled by the conversation to have noticed Samuel's slip of the tongue, the handyman ventured on, keeping his eyes on the uneven road ahead. "Sure as me name be Clive," he defiantly stated. "An' that ain't the worst o' it...bad 'nuff he romped 'round with country blokes, let 'lone bein' snared by a banker's son. Brute went an' forced 'imself on the boy...spoilt' the lad like some d'flowerin' melon, he did! Would 'ave gotten hung by 'is bloody toes, the earl would, if only he hadn't sloped off! Had a son o' 'is own too...woulda' been 'bout yer age by now. 'Tis no wonder Monica thought you was 'im. Was 'avin a bloody fit, she was! Claims she hear'd ya roamin' the hall in the dead o' night. Locked up 'er room and bid 'er boys ta sleep with her, she did." Clive paused for a moment, then looked at Samuel. "Say, sir...you's feelin' awright? Ya looks sick as a cat, ya do! Drive got to ya, eh? No need ta worry, then...we'll be there in the wink of an eye!"

Feeling as if he was going to vomit, Samuel immediately exited the silent truck upon arriving at the old wooden bridge, ripping the hem of his coat on the sharp edge of the Winton's door. Paying no attention to the hapless incident, he stumbled toward a patch of underbrush and keeled over, uncontrollably disgorging his breakfast while bracing clammy palms upon the damp soil. Hearing Clive's voice, he glanced over his shoulder to see him offering a wrinkled handkerchief. Without hesitation, he accepted the dingy piece of cloth, purging the acrid wetness from his trembling lips.

"Ya gonna be awright, Mr. Governey?"

With insides still churning, Samuel, staggering from his knees, dropped the handkerchief into the handyman's calloused hands. "Yes...yes...thank you. I...I am afraid that breakfast did not agree with me."

"Are ya still wantin' ta see the castle, then?" Clive asked, stuffing the putrid, rag-like cloth into the pocket of his shabby trousers.

"Yes...yes, indeed I do," Samuel answered, composing himself. "The walk should do me good. Shall I follow the stone path over the bridge, then?"

"Yes, sir. It'll lead ya straight ta the castle. Ya won't miss it...it'll be starin' back at ya like a window from hell!"

Still trembling, Samuel departed from his companion and let out a mournful sigh, stuffing clammy hands inside the pockets of his driving coat as he wandered across the decaying wooden bridge. The merry sound of rushing water beneath his desensitized feet seemed to mock his state of mind. Crestfallen beyond belief, he was glad that Clive had not accompanied him. If ever there was need for solitude, the time was now. Although his initial reaction to this most repulsive aspect of his father's life was that of denial, Samuel instantaneously knew that what Clive had related was as genuine as the onyx ring upon his forefinger. Still unable to completely comprehend the ignoble revelation, he directed his gaze beyond the unkempt lawn of overgrown grass dotted with dandelions, oblivious to the rotting petals of dogwood which littered the stone path. Hoping to get a glimpse of the castle, he was able to discern a looming presence through the thickening fog.

As Samuel focused upon the faint, shadow-like structure, he could not help but recount within his turbulent mind multiple clues, like twisted, windblown puzzle pieces violently hurled upon a teetering canvas. His mother...her untimely illness. His father's unwillingness to revisit England...those drunken stupors, the innkeeper...her icy demeanor. *Governey, did ya say?* The concierge at the Duke's Hotel, his small, red face, magnified a dozen times, leaning over the reception desk, smiling from ear to ear like a cat that had swallowed a rodent. *The pleasure **was and is**, indeed, all mine!* Samuel shuddered, forcefully spitting upon the loose, moss-covered stones which beckoned his way to the castle, paying no attention to a light drizzle irreverently slapping his ashen face. Why had he never seen it before? It was all so obvious now! In spite of the animosity and bitterness he harbored toward his father, he had, nevertheless, overlooked the most abhorrent explanation of all...an act so revolting...so vile...that it had coerced the earl into fleeing his beloved Britain in fear for his very life. And wasn't that just like him? The coward! The despicable bastard! Any common crime would have been scandalous enough, but one of this magnitude! How could he, his own father, have dishonored the Governey name in such a way...defiling the family crest with this hideous, indelible stain? Samuel cursed aloud, slipping upon a wet stone as he approached a massive, wrought-iron gate. Shifting his eyes beyond the rusted barrier, he was overwhelmed by the apparent size of a familiar, yet peculiar, grey stone edifice. Its mighty towers and rigid pinnacles being slowly digested by the flourishing fog, Cheshire Castle seemed to defy any set of footsteps which dare tread upon its ancient premises. Samuel wondered for a moment if the ponderous gate before him was secured, but soon decided that it did not matter. There was no need to go any further.

Slowly turning away from the castle, he trudged across the overgrown lawn toward the rushing stream. Reaching the water's edge, he removed both hands from his pockets, twisting from his forefinger his father's gold and onyx ring. With one quick motion, he flung the heirloom into the rocky stream, his stomach unwinding as the ring, momentarily caught on a clump of brambles, dipped beneath battering raindrops. Wiping the lids of his eyes with the sleeve of his coat, he watched the struggling ring resurface until, as if being reclaimed by some omnipotent force, it was set free and ultimately devoured by the River Dee's surging current. Stealing one last glance over his shoulder before tracing the stone path back to the dirt road, Samuel suddenly froze. In front of the curtain wall of the imposing castle, he had, for an instant, attributed a floating, smoke-like mist to the accumulation of morning fog. In a mere moment, however, his sullen face paled upon realizing he had been mistaken. Although the cloud-like formation was transparent, it reeked of distorted life, spilling from its belly a faint, lamenting moan. Dragging a long, flowing gown and bearing a striped banner that glittered against the drab wall, the translucent figure seemed to purposely approach Samuel until, pausing in front of the castle's west wing, it clutched the hem of the flag to its heaving bosom, then disappeared.

chapter 30

A Welcome Change

As the fading rays of a Barcelona sun sluggishly swept the sand-covered floor of an elaborate bullfighting ring, Samuel Randolph Governey, surrounded by a crowd of apprehensive spectators, suspended the haunting stream of consciousness which had been choking his captive mind during the past few weeks. Like a hunted killer seeking sanctuary in a cloistered monastery, Samuel had, at long last, found refuge in the pompous country of Spain, geographically estranged from the troubles of its neighboring lands. After having unearthed his father's cryptic past on that ill-favored morning in Cheshire, he had sped back to the Duke's Hotel where he packed his bags, paid for services rendered and hastily departed. Still determined to make the best of his European excursion, he then left England, continuing on with his original plans to visit some of the most impressive cities of the world. But no matter how magnificent these countries were, they had not only failed to offer the solace he so desperately sought, but became a sore reminder of the legacy his father had forfeited. The Eiffel Tower taunted him about the grandeur which was no longer his, while the majestic mountains and waterfalls of Switzerland dissembled into dust. In Vienna, the bewitching music of Mozart, Beethoven and Strauss did little but chisel away at his sanity. While viewing the Leaning Tower of Pisa, Samuel could think of nothing else but how his own aristocratic kingdom had toppled over. Even while driving along the Amalfi coast he could not help but entertain thoughts of plunging into the vivid azure sea, ending his father's shameful legacy once and for all.

Samuel took a hardy draw from his Colombian cigar, his deep blue eyes widening in anticipation of a spectacular bullfight as the sound of a trumpet accompanied by crashing cymbals preceded the procession of matadors dressed in colorful, glittering suits. With a majestic air of confidence, the bullfighters proudly stepped about the ring, gracefully swinging their right arms, unrestrained by the heavy red capes covering the left half of their chests. Amidst the music of the band and the cheering of the crowd, Samuel smiled. It was shortly after crossing the Spanish border that he had experienced a certain measure of comfort. Driving his roadster through the open countryside, he was quaintly engrossed by a large expanse of land covered with row upon row of white crosses and tombstones. Soon afterwards, while cruising past saffron-tinged Gothic architecture, its iron-worked balconies sculpted with gargoyles and dragons, Samuel's melancholic mood had lifted considerably. While residing in a private Spanish villa, he had sought out a prestigious bordello, endowed with lavish, baroque-style furnishings and eminent cigar-smoking patrons. More than eager to reaffirm his manhood, he spoke to the Madame of the bordello in her native tongue, strongly expressing the necessity of being provided with female companions possessing a clean bill of health. Desiring to remain in control of every situation, he would request the youngest women available, taking pleasure in dainty, dark-haired senoritas.

Surrounded by hushed spectators, Samuel leaned toward the bullring, holding the corona between his thumb and ringless forefinger, flicking its ashes upon the painted seat as the trumpet sounded, signaling the bull pen to be opened. Inside the arena, a few men, some on foot and some on horseback, awaited the forceful charge of their horned aggressor. Like an escaped prisoner, the bull, goaded by the capes of the matadors, began charging. Samuel held his breath, his heart beating rapidly, recalling with twisted glee the outcome of the last bullfight he had attended. The matador, having executed his moves ever-so-gracefully, was suddenly outwitted by his diabolical opponent, unexpectedly flung into the air and gored by the beast's mighty horns. Before the bull was finally killed and dragged from the ring, it had spilled the blood of a horse, its rider, and two *banderilleros* as well. Never before had Samuel found any one event so exhilarating and, while presently witnessing the picadors piercing the bull's neck and shoulders in an effort to weaken and anger the doomed animal, he had silently hoped for a repeat performance.

Amid mixed reaction from the crowd, Samuel cheered as the *banderilleros*, clutching a decorated, spiked lance in each hand, rushed the bull on foot, piercing its blood-dripping flesh even more. Stepping in like a master of ceremonies, one of the matadors maneuvered his scarlet *muleta* in several graceful sweeps, deluding the exhausted animal until, like a mountain lion claiming his prey, the poised bullfighter unsheathed his shining sword, thrusting it into the nape of the bull's neck. Crashing down in the center of the ring like a one-ton weight, the lifeless animal, stretched out amidst the smell of blood and guts, was further assaulted by the approaching darkness. Reminiscent of an eccentric funeral march, the bull then was hitched to a team of mules and dragged around the ring to the tempo of Latin dance music.

Samuel wiped beads of sweat from his forehead, extinguished the cigar, and folded his arms across his chest. Witnessing three bullfights over the last couple of hours had been exhausting, to say the least. Still, although on this day there were no unusual mishaps, seeing each bull being slain so cunningly had been pleasing enough. Rising from his seat, he followed the murmuring crowd from the arena, contemplating a nearby inn where he anticipated indulging in a hearty portion of veal chops and washing them down with a glass of red Valdepenas wine.

chapter 31

A New Mission

Despite the transitory comforts Samuel enjoyed within his newly discovered sanctuary, external forces were soon to determine a
different course in his life. Whereas the neutral country of Spain
remained immune to the impending conflict which would soon engulf most
of Europe, Samuel was nevertheless destined to become an active participant.
Initially, the headlines of the *Barcelona News* announcing the assassination of
Austria's Archduke Francis Ferdinand and his wife had not concerned him in
the least. However, approximately one month later, upon learning that
Britain had come to the aid of France in her battle against German forces, he
was racked with an unwavering allegiance, prompting him to abandon the
comforting womb of the sunny country in which he had taken refuge over
the past few weeks. Armed with the opportunity to make amends for the
shame his father had bequeathed upon his native land, he packed his bags
once again and steered his Gregoire toward the City of London where, on
August 24, 1914, he enlisted in the British Army or, as the Brits would say,
"took the shilling," destined to serve the next four-and-a-half-years in the
blood-drenched clutches of the Great War.

After enduring three grueling weeks of basic training, Private Samuel
Randolph Governey, equipped with three years of medical schooling, was
immediately promoted to first lieutenant, his primary military detail being
that of administering physicals to incoming recruits. Demonstrating exceptional proficiency while serving in this tedious post, he was promptly

assigned to the infirmary. There, to Samuel's expected satisfaction, his talents as a surgeon proved to be invaluable, particularly after the Battle of the Marne where several British soldiers, having first been treated by the Red Cross in France, were sent back to England. Although a few of these soldiers' medical demands involved no more than a case of trench-foot, many required vigilant care while the more unfortunate were destined to undergo a serious operation or, worse yet, an ill-fated amputation.

Revitalized once more by the prospect of cutting into human flesh, Samuel experienced a renewed sense of purpose. Working for months on end in the infirmary as countless soldiers were delivered from malaria-breeding battlefields and roach-infested trenches, his status as an exceptional surgeon was overwhelmingly reaffirmed. Exhibiting extraordinary skill and dexterity, he was promoted to captain of his division, given his own quarters and granted the additional privilege of working in the forensic unit. Although the task of identifying body parts of slaughtered soldiers was repulsive to the average army surgeon, Samuel not only found this particular duty quite satisfying but reveled in the actual embalming of the corpses before sending them back home in canvas bags. Fascinated by this newly-assigned task, he resolved to learn whatever he could of the mortuary sciences, keeping in the back of his fatigued mind the possibility of a future vocation.

Welcoming the occasional opportunity to discard his surgical gear and leave the strong smell of formaldehyde behind, Samuel would take advantage of his furloughs by vacationing within unscathed territories of the United Kingdom. While troops of "Tommies" were still securing gas masks to avoid the deadly repercussions of mustard gas, Captain Governey would don his driving goggles, looking forward to residing in the meticulously clean boarding houses and fashionable inns into which he had formerly inquired. Safe from the ravages of war and redeemed from the wounds of his father's past, he would contentedly steer his roadster along the peaceful countryside of England and Scotland. And, though civil unrest sporadically stalked the Emerald Isle, crossing into Ireland via St. George's Channel proved to be of no consequence.

Satisfied with his decision to travel alone and especially pleased that his roadster was, at the very least, being spared the littering ashes of a British comrade, Samuel would occasionally contemplate the Silver Ghost Rolls and Stutz Bear-Cat left behind in Philadelphia. Possibly after the war, he would return to America and see to their reconditioning, along with that of the

Gregoire. Or maybe he would remain overseas and have an administrator handle the sale of the Rolls and Stutz. Perhaps, if fortune smiled upon him, his father would be dead by then and the Governey estate would finally be his. Just how much longer the old codger would be hanging on for dear life, one could only guess. Hell! He wasn't even sure of the earl's whereabouts. Perhaps he was rotting away in an insane asylum after all. At any rate, even though communication with his former colleagues at Philadelphia General Hospital had been nonexistent since his induction into the British Army, Mr. Morgan at the Philadelphia Bank & Trust was sure to notify him in the event of his father's demise. Of course, Samuel would sometimes realize with a taste of regret, if he had granted his father's original wish to be taken care of by the unscrupulous Dr. Gruben, there may have been some additional insurance money to pocket.

Continuing to alleviate his overburdened mind from the backlashes of war while on a four-week leave, Samuel, one star-filled evening in the approaching summer of 1917, had just returned from viewing a Scottish drama at the High Street Theatre in Edinburgh, when the concierge at the Fortress Hotel presented him with a telegram. Because of a recent London bombing, he was to report for active duty immediately. Promptly arranging an overnight stay in the industrial city of Birmingham, England, Captain Governey telegrammed his commander that he would be departing forthwith. Anticipating scores of severe casualties, he diligently guided his roadster once again toward the City of London, stopping only for fuel, a bite to eat and his scheduled overnight stop. Arriving at his home base later the next afternoon, however, he was surprised when, upon entering an infirmary overcrowded with wounded soldiers and civilians, he was saluted and informed by a Private medical assistant that Colonel Bharat from the Fifth division was waiting for him inside Samuel's quarters. Making certain that his freshly polished brass buckle had not repositioned itself within the last two minutes, and confident that his shoes were buffed and medals spaced properly over the left pocket of his shirt, Captain Governey smoothed the cover underneath his belt, straightened his shoulders and promptly stepped inside.

Colonel Bharat, a brown-skinned man of small stature, rose from his seat, sharply returned Samuel's salute and invited his comrade to sit behind the small, plain desk surrounded by shelves of neatly arranged medicine bottles. Eyeing the familiar skeleton in the corner of the room, Samuel suddenly felt like a stranger in his own quarters. Although he had convened with several superior officers during the last three years, the present situation was, to say the least, unusual. Never before had any officer awaited his company for such a prolonged period of time and, though certainly aware that few men of Indian heritage were fortunate enough to serve as high-ranking officers in the British military, Samuel had not, as yet, been compelled to act as one's subordinate.

Still standing with hands clasped behind his back, Colonel Bharat spoke in distinct English with an eastern dialect, breaking the awkward silence. "Captain Governey...I hoped not to disturb you so quickly upon your return, but there is a matter of importance I must speak of."

Samuel returned the colonel's smile, wondering how this Indian, clad in British military attire and still wearing a turban, could justify such an untimely intrusion. "There is no need for concern, Colonel Bharat," he graciously answered, opening a drawer on his right. "You are not inconveniencing me in the least." He pulled out a box of Cuban cigars and handed one to his superior officer. Retrieving a Havana for himself, Samuel then closed the cedar box and offered the colonel a light, which was promptly refused. Thinking this a bit strange, he proceeded to ignite his own as the smell of rum tobacco, mingling with that of alcohol, filled the room.

"I understand you were on leave, Captain Governey," the colonel remarked while sitting down, humbly gesturing toward Samuel with the unlit cigar. "I trust your trip was a pleasant one?"

Samuel, puffing his cigar, wished that this Indian officer would disregard the formalities and get to the point of his visit. "Yes, sir. It was quite pleasant at that."

"I see," the colonel answered. "Please...address me by my given name...Tayib. There is no need to be so...*stiff*, as they say?" Placing the cigar in his mouth, he began gnawing at its end.

"Of course...Tayib it is," Samuel said with a slight nod. "And please...address me as Samuel."

Tayib removed the indented cigar from his mouth as the smoke from his companion's Havana snaked toward him like a charmed cobra. "I take it you delight in your travels, Samuel. Perhaps you will one day have the opportunity to visit my homeland of Bangalore," he contemplatively stated. "Tell me, captain. Where did your last leave take you? You do not mind my asking, I hope."

Samuel did mind, but answered anyway. "The usual," he responded, suspending the smoking cigar above a Waterford crystal ashtray. "The outskirts of Britain...Wales...Belfast. I was in Edinburg when I received news of the London bombing."

"I see," Colonel Bharat replied, holding the distorted, wet cigar between his dark fingers. "And had you the opportunity to visit your homeland?"

Samuel tensed his facial muscles, resentful that this Indian, chewing on his cigar like one of their sacred cows, was meddling into his personal life. "America is my homeland, colonel. I have not been there since before the start of the war."

"Of course," Tayib replied. "I am sorry I did not make myself understood. What I mean to ask is, had you the opportunity to visit the homeland of your father?"

"My father, sir?"

"Yes. Your father," Colonel Bharat retorted, twirling his waxed, handlebar moustache while simultaneously holding onto the stagnant cigar. "He was from...*Cheshire*...was he not?"

Having inadvertently inhaled his cigar upon the colonel's unexpected inquiry, Samuel started coughing uncontrollably. Thrusting the Havana into the ashtray, he let out another cough and cleared his throat. "I...the subject of my ancestry is one..." He released a final series of coughs while pressing his palm against the chevron of his military shirt. "One that I do not wish to exhume either alone or with anyone else, sir!"

Colonel Bharat glanced at the human skeletal display in the corner of the room. "There is no reason for you to be disturbed, captain. We all have skeletons in our closets. I assure you that despite your father's ignoble behavior, *your* credibility remains steadfast in my eyes. However...I am not so certain that other officers of my rank would be so understanding of your father's disreputable conduct...should they uncover it. But, I do not think there is need for concern. You have my word as a man of honor, captain, that any knowledge I possess will not travel beyond these walls. Which," the Indian added while rising from his seat, "prompts me to speak of yet another matter."

Suspiciously eyeing Colonel Bharat, Samuel once again reached for his cigar, discovering that it had been snuffed out in a moment's rage. Remaining silent, he cautiously waited for the colonel to resume.

"I find myself in quite a dilemma," Bharat continued, head down, while pacing the floor. "My unmarried daughter is with child...an English soldier,

I suspect." Returning his gaze past the desk, he paused momentarily as Samuel rekindled the Havana. "A situation such as this is considered unforgiveable amongst my people. Such a situation...if it be discovered...would surely bring disgrace upon my family. Fathers in my position have *killed* their daughters. But...despite my loss of face...I cannot do this to my Leya...my first-born." Placing palms together in a prayer-like fashion, his anxious eyes pleaded with Samuel. "I come in good faith, Captain Governey, to ask for your help in terminating the pregnancy of my daughter."

Intrigued by such an unexpected proposition and quite pleased to be holding the trump card, Samuel gingerly placed the lit cigar upon the ashtray and casually exhaled a thick ribbon of smoke. "I should like very much to be of help, Tayib. I think you should be aware, however, that despite my medical background, I have not, as of yet, had the opportunity to rescue certain young ladies from such misfortune. But, my good chap," he remarked, folding his hands upon the desk while leaning forward. "I am more than willing to assist your daughter with all the medical expertise at my disposal."

"And that is precisely what I had in mind, Samuel," Colonel Bharat responded, pointing the flattened cigar toward Samuel while reclaiming his seat. "You see...Dr. Wesley Carvelle...the physician who was to originally perform the operation...was injured during the London bombing. Unable to have use of his right arm, he is most willing to instruct a skilled surgical doctor, such as yourself, of the procedure. You see," Tayib implored, "Time is of the utmost importance. My daughter, Leya, having endured three full moons in such a condition, will no longer be able to conceal her shame. I implore you, Captain Governey. Please say that you are willing to help."

Samuel leaned back on his chair, placed both hands behind his head, and pursed his lips as if in deep contemplation. After several seconds, he rose from his seat, stepped toward the colonel and shook his hand. "Tayib, my good fellow...there is no need to concern yourself any longer. Under the guidance of Dr. Carvelle, I am sure that I shall be able to, indeed, induce a successful miscarriage."

Colonel Bharat returned Samuel's generosity with a grateful smile. "You will not regret this, captain. I shall reward you most kindly. Please," he added while reaching into the pocket of his uniform trousers. "Here is the address of Dr. Carvelle. You may reach him by wire. He awaits your reply."

"Very well, then," Samuel answered. "I shall contact him discreetly, but immediately."

Concluding the gentlemen's agreement with a square-jawed handshake and keen eye contact, Samuel waited for the colonel to leave his office, then strode past scores of makeshift hospital beds toward the infirmary's main station where he wired Dr. Carvelle, informing the compliant abortionist that he would be more than willing to help alleviate Miss Bharat's most unfortunate disposition.

chapter 32

Discreet Extractions

On a grey, quiet June morning in the year 1917, as the Great War stumbled upon scores of amputated limbs, an illusion of peace embracing the battered City of London did little to pacify its neighboring allies. Across the vast continent of Europe, cratered battlefields, like pockmarked faces, were a blatant reminder of the heavy price for unbridled tyranny. On the Eastern front, Russia became further entangled in a web of revolution as Lenin and his Bolsheviks attempted to overthrow the Tsarist regime, fatally crippling an army already demoralized by countless defeats and prolonged combat. On the Western front, despite innovations in the form of lethal mines and British tanks, anti-aircraft guns and high-powered searchlights were still necessary in thwarting the enemy. And, across the great Atlantic, like reams of dollar bills of illusory value destined to roll off the U.S. printing presses, troops of newly-conscripted American soldiers in gleaming leather boots and well-pressed fatigues, unaware of the incomprehensible horrors of battle, prepared to enter the harrowing theater of foreign war for the very first time.

Sprawled upon a thinly cushioned table inside the secluded office of Dr. Wesley Carvelle, a Hindu female, no older than 16 years of age, her bright yellow sari slovenly gathered above her bare belly, lay motionless as a medical captain of the English Army, accustomed to handling mutilated bodies and embalming decomposed corpses, proceeded to abort her twelve-week old fetus. A generous dose of chloroform, having been administered to the unconscious girl a short while ago, still lingered in the cold, shaded room revived by a solitary light bulb.

Unmoved by the angelic expression upon the girl's flawless face, Captain Samuel Randolph Governey, seated upon a crude bench, labored in deep contemplation as Dr. Carvelle wiped beads of sweat from his forehead. Diligently heeding the instructions of the wounded senior physician, whose right arm was restricted by a discolored cast, Samuel cautiously maneuvered a metal curette inside the cervix of the unconscious patient which was already dilated by curved metal rods and scraped the final pieces of embryonic tissue from her uterus. While depositing the bloody remains into a rusted iron wash kettle strewn with shavings of black pubic hair, he felt an overwhelming sense of relief and accomplishment as Dr. Carvelle congratulated him on a task well done. Presuming the delicate operation completed, Samuel prudently removed the metal rods from the cervix. Promptly reaching for a heavy towel to arrest the flow of blood, however, he was suddenly startled upon feeling the tingle of light steel upon his palm. But before looking in the direction of his heavyset mentor, he had already, in one split second, identified the familiar object. Having become initially accustomed to such an indispensible instrument while attending Philadelphia's Hahnemann Medical College, as well as in performing countless operations while currently serving the Armed British Forces, Samuel knew it as well as the back of his hand. Stealing a glance toward the pen-like handle and protruding blade, he extended a perplexed gaze toward the approving doctor.

"Captain Governey...lest we forget, one final procedure is to be executed at the request of her father, Colonel Bharat." Receiving a blank stare from his colleague, the bearded doctor continued. "A circumcision, my good man. A *clitoridectomy,* to be medically precise. Of course, you *have* heard of such an operation, have you not, my good chap?"

Samuel stood mute for a moment, clutching the cold scalpel firmly within his damp palm. He had heard of such a procedure, even touching upon the subject at Hahnemann College, but was of the impression that this primitive practice took place mostly within uncivilized Africa and certain areas of the Middle East. "Why yes, of course," he answered upon realizing that the patient before him, her fawn-like thighs spread apart by stirrups and dripping warm blood onto a muslin cloth did, indeed, originate from one of those very geographic regions.

"Very well, then. Let us get on with it," Dr. Carvelle replied with an eager look in his sharp eyes. "You will have to make an accurate incision deep enough to assure that the entire clitoris is taken, as if you were removing a sebaceous cyst."

Exposing the small, erectile organ located beneath the shaven pubic bone, Samuel readily positioned the cutting edge of the scalpel against the flesh and started to sever the dark pink nub with a firm but delicate motion. Of course, it all made sense now, he contemplated as the edge of his scalpel penetrated deep into the moist skin, loosening the delicate member like a slug emerging from a patch of stagnant red soil. Here was the young, beautiful daughter of a proud Indian British Officer who, by whoring around, had put the honor of her family at risk. It stood to reason that her father, the colonel, would wish to permanently numb her sexual desires in order to prevent the possibility of any such subsequent scandal. No doubt, he would have done the same.

Dr. Wesley Carvelle molded his flabby back along the cross rails of the side chair, repositioned his casted arm against the pocket of his blood-stained surgical coat and reached for the suture. "You are no doubt aware that this procedure is becoming more widely accepted within progressive countries such as Britain, are you not?"

Having dissected the final segment of rigid flesh from its gaping source, Samuel discarded it into the cast iron kettle while simultaneously arresting a fresh flow of blood with some surgical gauze. "No, sir. I cannot say that I am."

"Are you not familiar with Isaac Baker Brown, then...the London obstetrician?"

"No, sir, I cannot say that I am," Samuel repeated, retrieving the curved needle and stiff thread from his mentor's chubby hand.

"It just so happens, my good chap, that I was privileged with the fortunate opportunity of being under Dr. Brown's tutelage at the University of London. As I have mentioned before, Dr. Brown is a renowned London obstetrician and author of a famous publication in which he establishes that treatments such as the one we have just performed are the answer to a variety of feminine weaknesses."

Unsettled by memories of his own mother plagued by such "weaknesses," Samuel's nimble fingers lagged for a moment while utilizing the suture.

"Are you claiming then, Dr. Carvelle, that women with such propensities have indeed been cured?"

Pleased with the chance to elaborate on his expertise regarding feminine ailments, Dr. Carvelle inhaled, taking a deep breath, and shrugged his shoulders. "That is correct, my good man. It has been medically established that a number of women plagued by certain forms of insanity, epilepsy, catalepsy and hysteria have indeed been cured. And since I have had the opportunity and privilege of working with the esteemed Dr. Brown myself, I can personally affirm these claims." Cautiously eyeing Samuel wiping blood-smeared hands upon a clean cotton towel, Carvelle continued. "Of course, our method of female circumcision is much more refined than those commonly practiced in less civilized parts of the world. Why...," he stated unashamedly while gazing between the unconscious legs of Miss Bharat, "had this operation taken place in say...Ethiopia...or Sudan, for instance, not only would the clitoris have been removed, but all external genitalia as well. In fact, these methods are so crude, that they can and do, indeed, contribute to the death of many such natives."

Having finished the tedious task of suturing, and rinsing his hands in a nearby wash basin, Samuel reached for another clean towel. "And, my good doctor, have you ever witnessed first-hand the practices of these so-called 'witch doctors?'"

Delighted with his colleague's interest on the subject, Dr. Carvelle raised his worm-like brows. "Why yes. Indeed. Yes I have." Struggling to conceal his excitement, he continued. "Would you believe, captain...more than once have I had the opportunity to witness the barbaric rituals of these native savages. It is a most incredible sight to behold. Perhaps in the near future you might be willing to accompany me on a so-called medical safari into Sudan...when this bloody war has ended, of course."

As if it were a raw scab, Samuel peeled the surgical gauze from his young patient, examining once again her perfectly-rendered incision. "Yes" he answered, satisfied with the coagulation of blood while applying a final dressing. "I should fancy that very much indeed!"

chapter 33

Rugged Travels

L
ike a lingering fever reaching its peak before breaking, so too, did the Great War stubbornly maintain a powerful hold throughout its final year. From Britain's occupation of Jerusalem in December of 1917 to the surrender of German forces by the eleventh day of the eleventh ensuing month, Captain Samuel Randolph Governey sustained his own feverish pace, meeting the demands of wounded, dead and dying phantom-faced soldiers as well as terminating the unwanted pregnancies of an occasional lieutenant's wife or general's daughter.

Presented with the opportunity to temporarily abandon his laborious duties that final frenzied summer, Samuel departed war-torn London to attend a wedding in Bangalore, India, the beloved homeland of his indebted military colleague, Colonel Tayib Bharat. Treated like royalty for the clandestine favor he had bestowed upon the colonel's eldest daughter and now radiant bride of a prestigious epidemiologist, Samuel was showered with priceless gifts and offered an amount of Middle Eastern cuisine plentiful enough to have burst the belly of the Buddha.

Amused at the thought of the unsuspecting young bridegroom being duped by a tiny blood-filled vessel of sheep's gut which would be shrewdly ruptured upon the "virginal" bed by his already deflowered wife, Samuel salaciously gazed at the blissful bride as the couple exchanged wedding vows, fully aware that other men, himself included, had already trespassed into her most intimate temple. Secretly coveting but unable to share the forbidden fruits of other raven-haired Hindu maidens throughout the following week of eccentric festivities and local customs, Samuel nonetheless departed India anticipating the return to England; despite its lack of exotic females, his beloved homeland would always be, in his unwavering opinion, unsurpassed as the archetype of modern civilization.

Despite Samuel's overwhelming appreciation of contemporary England along with the perpetually prim and proper habits of the British, he was nevertheless ready to once again return overseas in early January, eight weeks following the termination of an insufferable war when, loyal to his promise, Dr. Wesley Carvelle arranged their mutually anticipated excursion into the uncharted bowels of darkest Africa. Forlornly leaving his road-tarnished roadster at the residence of the recuperated Dr. Carvelle, Samuel once again crossed the frigid straits of Dover to the port of Calais, France. Recently endowed with diplomatic passports at an officers' Yuletide gathering in appreciation for having covertly performed personal medical services for high ranking officials, the two dauntless travelers, transporting several heavy trunks of cargo, were able to avoid the encumbering inconvenience of customs, leaving a swarm of envious travelers in their wake. Hardly regretting bypassing Paris, the two men began their long expedition by rail across the barren plains of France. Utilizing the power of their special passports during the next several weeks and switching modes of transportation as one would exchange smiles in the course of a day, the weary travelers, having been detained a short while in Zurich, crossed the snow-covered mountains of Austria before traversing the long, tiresome ridges of Yugoslavian hills. Nearly a week after departing Yugoslavia's Capitol of Zagreb, Samuel, being unaccustomed to such exhausting travel and longing for the comfort and convenience of his French Gregoire roadster, was somewhat encouraged when, after reaching the sunny City of Athens, he and Dr. Carvelle boarded the *Mediterranean Princess*. After checking into their small private cabins, they relaxed for the next three days while enduring a slightly rough, but bearable southward journey down the Sea of Crete and across the restless waters of the Mediterranean Sea.

Upon reaching their next destination situated along the white sandy shores of Alexandria in ancient Egypt, the persevering travelers were once again dismayed when, while suffering through foul, rainy weather, they waited for what seemed an unbearable number of minutes to purchase another set of railway tickets. Satisfied that their heavy cargo had made its way onto the littered, dirt-laden floor of a wooden freight car, the two frenzied Englishmen tolerated the better part of their day aboard an ill-smelling, crowded boxcar which wriggled its way from Upper Egypt to its main destination of Cairo. Having been subjected to inhaling gusts of windblown sand and soot, enduring the intolerable smell of human excrement and suffering a number of other unimaginable indignities, the genteel travelers, too refined to utilize the waste-infested clumps of hay scattered along its walls, disembarked the creaking train. Fumbling their way through a throng of sweaty, rag-garbed passengers in search of the nearest rest hole, Samuel Governey and Wesley Carvelle, sorely tolerating the discomfort of bulging bladders, restlessly anticipated the prospect of resuming their privileged lifestyle inside two pre-booked, first-class cabins of a Nile ferry equipped with fine linens, private baths and staffed with an ample number of indulging servants.

chapter 34

Esteemed Tokens

As the pulsating steam engines of the *River Queen* rolled the sultry ferry down the long wet tongue of the Nile, thrusting its passengers deeper into the paunch of Africa, Samuel savored another Havana while seated at a deck table bearing a depleted teacup and half-eaten crumpet, discarding for the time being all memories of the cold, damp island where he had resided during the past four years. Having left the civilized world amid the joyful bustle of a post-war English Christmas season, he had almost forgotten the pungent smell of nature, the spirited scent of grass and soil surrounded by a vibrant sea. Although in this barbaric crevice of the world, there lingered an earthy scent stronger than he had ever known.

While leisurely digesting the splendor of the Nile, Samuel delayed the typical questions which currently plagued his comrades. Like longtime slaves abruptly tossed into a free society, hoards of weary soldiers had returned to their homes, struggling to revive the scope of their humble existence. But whether amused by fishermen along the muddy banks struggling with gill nets of freshly-trapped perch or observing onboard Islamic crew members genuflecting upon rugs of tattered wool, Samuel purposely delayed the discomfiting direction of his own life, allowing instead the swaying motion of palm trees or the high-pitched call of jackals to appease his mind. And, although aware that his squandered inheritance would not likely last beyond a few years, he had arranged a costly safari expedition in Nairobi with twice the usual number of gun bearers, game drivers, trackers and skinners.

Stretching over the slatted rails of the trudging steamer, Samuel straightened his Panama hat under a sweltering sun as the *River Queen* approached her final destination in the South of Sudan. Having grown weary of the four-week excursion and presently annoyed that his white flannel trousers were being sprayed by the sporadic cough of the verminous Nile, he suddenly smiled upon viewing a distant cluster of dung-domed huts surrounded by an expansive yellow carpet of dense grassland. Yes! It was for this very reason that he had initially embarked upon this arduous journey...to experience the forbidden rituals of these savage jungle dwellers...particularly the intriguing rites of adulthood involving young native virgins.

With the corpulent Dr. Carvelle one step ahead, Samuel followed the erratic pace of several porters pushing carts full of baggage off the steamer's platform. Immediately boarding a litter which was hoisted and followed by two others crammed with provisions, both Englishmen spent the next couple of hours seated between four muscular, naked-cheeked natives enduring yet another staggering ride along a narrow road surrounded by eight-foot grass, a scattering of acacia trees and an occasional hamlet of crude huts. As the four sweat-drenched natives jostled the litter along the hard dirt road, Samuel once again regretted the necessity of leaving his cherished roadster behind. Envisioning the tired, sleek-lined motor car idly parked at Dr. Carvelle's English residence, he resolved to promptly see to its refurbishment upon his return home.

Continuing to bear the insufferable jolts of the litter while heeding the unceasing dissonance of the African jungle, Samuel momentarily wondered if embarking upon this journey had been a wise decision after all. Hopefully, it would be, he consoled himself, wiping beads of perspiration from his forehead with a monogrammed handkerchief. Although Wesley would not go into particulars, as if concealing the contents of a spectacular Christmas gift, he had confidently assured Samuel that their ten-week stay in the village of Mukot was certain to exceed his wildest expectations. But, every time they neared another formation of lopsided huts, Samuel's skepticism mounted. The ugly leaf-entwined dwellings, hardly large enough to shelter a swarm of tsetse flies, made him wince, arousing, for some strange reason, memories of his wretched trip to Cheshire and overnight stay at the Green Gaggle Inn. Hopefully, Samuel brooded, blotting his forehead and swatting yet another mosquito, his visit here would not make him yearn for that repulsive excuse of a boardinghouse.

As the four fatigued litter bearers approached a large clearing at the end of their journey, Samuel, suddenly overwhelmed, stuffed the wet handkerchief inside his satin-lined pocket. Like a vibrant oil painting on a previously dull canvas, the spectacle which now appeared just a few yards ahead seemed nothing short of a royal encampment; the only thing missing being the sound of heralding trumpets.

Situated in the center of the courtyard stood a palatial dwelling, its beaded windows enhanced by brightly-painted geometric designs. Rivaling the height of its kaleidoscopic archway and surrounded by a dozen or so bejeweled, bare-breasted women, was the imposing figure of an ebony-skinned man, his white teeth like polished tiles within a wide, cat-like grin. Garbed in multi-colored silks and an elaborate headdress enhanced with precious stones, the bald-headed chief stood like one of the many carved wooden deities in front of the glorious hut. Grasping a gold-gilded ceremonial staff, the Muslim king reflected a twinkle in his eyes as the 12 litter bearers came to a halt. While the king's loin-clothed attendants unloaded a bounty of baggage and escorted both English visitors from their two-seated litter onto the smooth, sun-baked floor, Samuel made a conscious effort to appear oblivious to the half-naked bevy of raven-haired beauties, the likes of which he had never before encountered in his entire 28 years of a highly privileged, aristocratic life.

Satisfied that the leather and canvas bags had been brought safely inside the Mukotese palace, King Shillu Kar Naim extended a hardy welcome toward his old European friend, Dr. Carvelle and greenhorn visitor, Doctor Governey, then graciously ushered the Englishmen into his aromatically spiced abode. After being seated upon elephant tusk armchairs covered with leopard skins, the Englishmen, continuously fanned by four servants and guarded by fly-swatting natives, were offered an exotic meal on ivory plates and bowls of bone china. As Samuel balanced a dish of crocodile gumbo upon his lap, he stole glimpses of chiseled faces with caramel complexions and tattooed bosoms, enviously contemplating with each tantalizing bite of his Sudanese meal how fortunate the king was to hold at his commanding fingertips such a wondrous array of exquisite females.

After the conclusion of a most enjoyable late afternoon meal, Shillu Kar Naim, still seated upon an intricately carved red velvet throne, clapped king-sized hands, instantaneously dismissing a few of his subservient wives along with the four perspiring fan-bearing servants, ordering a few more male attendants to take their places. As Samuel marveled at the ease with which the king maneuvered his subjects, he was further amazed upon being offered an after-dinner drink of Seagram's gin and tonic, served upon an engraved tray of fine British sterling. Stirring the alcoholic beverage with an emerald swizzle stick, he watched in anticipation while Dr. Carvelle, particularly proficient in the language of Mukot, summoned one of his hired porters to bring over the large canvas bag. Continuing to savor the potent taste of the familiar white man's drink, Samuel remained silent as Wesley Carvelle, with great pomp and ceremony, presented the delighted king with numerous gifts from the western world, most of which Samuel recognized as having been specifically purchased by himself. Unrolling the pieces of velvet cloth from each gift, Carvelle's stubby fingers revealed earthly treasures which seemed to magnify the ornate row of pellet-sized scars that stretched like a spray of bullets across Shillu Kar Naim's high, shiny forehead. Prizes of carnival glass from Florence, Irish crystal goblets, fine Venetian lace, silver coins and amber bracelets. Even the least presumptuous gifts of English snuff and French cologne etched a gleaming, thick-lipped smile upon the king's handsome, bearded face. But, even more pleasing and wondrous than these distinctive tokens was another case containing healing herbs and medical supplies, including cutting instruments such as razor blades, scissors and a wide assortment of machine-sharpened knives. And, last but not least, in their own separate box, a menacing display of highly polished, pearl-handled ceremonial daggers.

Having gratefully acknowledged his final gift of the six engraved British military daggers, King Shillu Kar Naim smugly passed the satin-molded case to his young, wide-eyed attendant, issuing the loin-clothed boy an additional command. Picking up two small wooden boxes within the king's reach, the bushy-haired lad immediately presented them to the Anglo-Saxon guests. Suspecting from the anticipation in Dr. Carvelle's covetous eyes that he was already familiar with the contents of the box, Samuel assumed it to be a special blend of tribal, hand-rolled cigars and placed the lightweight gift upon his lap. Waiting for the proper cue before removing the smooth teak lid, he then discovered another box inside, the outlined relief of an African goddess upon its flat surface, her dart-like nipples pointing from firm, gargantuan breasts. Momentarily distracted from the wooden box by a deep voice spoken in Mukotese, Samuel, suddenly realizing that the king was addressing him, waited for Dr. Carvelle to translate the message.

"By Jove, Sam, my good man, the king wishes you to open the bloody box," Carvelle asserted with a mischievous look in his eyes. "Can't you see that the royal bloke is expressing his heartfelt gratitude for the wondrous gifts we have just bestowed upon him?"

Placing the palm of his right hand upon the lid of the box while wedging his well-groomed thumb underneath, Samuel wondered if the cigars contained within would be to his liking. Expecting a hardy tobacco smell to permeate his nostrils upon opening it, he was, instead, immediately puzzled by its odorless contents. For, although what lay inside the box, indeed seemed to be hand-rolled, they certainly were not cigars or, for that matter, anything associated with tobacco. Contemplating three neat rows of gossamer objects, each one about the size of an American quarter, Samuel remained dumbfounded, guessing, to the best of his ability, that the peculiar material used for such items was somehow fashioned from a sort of thinned-out animal skin. Hoping to be rescued from this awkward situation and trusting that he would, perhaps, capture a clue from his amused audience, he looked up at the smiling king and then turned to the grinning Dr. Carvelle.

"My good man...the king would like to know if you approve of his gift," Wesley Carvelle teased, obviously entertained by the perplexed look upon Samuel's face. "Do you not like it? Or shall I tell him to return it then?"

Somewhat perturbed that his ignorance was being made sport of, Samuel revealed a bashful smile. Being especially careful to avoid offending the bemused king, he then voiced a simple "thank you" in Mukotese, after which he leaned toward Carvelle and spoke in a low whisper. "Damn it, Carvelle! This bloody suspense is killing me. What the devil is it?"

"Why Sam, my good man..." Dr. Carvelle announced in the arrogant manner of a patronizing college professor, "this singular gift just so happens to be a most unique and quite practical one...presented only to a privileged few who are fortunate enough to have stumbled into this uncharted village. Yes, Sam," he affirmed while slapping his colleague on the back, "this gift must not be taken lightly. Consider it a most thoughtful favor...one that may very well save your bloody life."

"What the bloody hell are you talking about, Wesley?" Samuel retorted, quickly erasing the glower from his face upon remembering that the king was still in their presence.

As if about to reveal the clever answer to an impossible riddle, Dr. Carvelle reclined in his elephant tusk armchair while folding both arms.

"*Sheaths*, my good chap. *Prophylactic* sheaths...personally crafted by the villagers of Mukot to protect you from the most dreaded diseases known to man. By presenting this magnanimous gift, the good king is offering the intimate services of any one of his wives for your most carnal pleasures. Yes, dear friend...," Carvelle contemplated while stroking his graying goatee, "unless you wish to remain celibate and endure the King's royal wrath for the duration of your stay, I strongly advise that you accept his most kind and thoughtful gesture."

Completely abashed, Samuel nearly dropped the teak chest from his lap, inadvertently knocking over and shattering on the hard clay floor his crystal glass of gin and tonic. As several male servants came to the rescue, he could not help but weigh the significance of what Dr. Carvelle had just revealed. Recalling a rough ink rendition of one such prophylactic sheath in a Harvard medical journal several years back, numerous thoughts merged simultaneously in his mind, not the least of which was a written description of this uncertified device, warning that although the concept was indeed practical, its dependability remained in question. Of course! Samuel realized as a blur of ebony bodies scurried about with twigged brooms. Why, it all made sense now...incredulous sense! The bloody wealth...the western influence...the provocative, painted women. This pretentious one-level palace situated in the darkest heart of an uncivilized, savage world was nothing short of a thriving African bordello!

Scarcely aware of the scratching sound of glass as the servants continued cleaning up the mishap, Samuel felt like he was suddenly immersed into a deep, hot spring as images of native women filled his mind. There was certainly something irresistible about a brown-eyed, dark-haired female regardless of skin color, he secretly acknowledged, still clutching the open teak box. And to have one or more such firm-bodied women at his beck and call for the next several weeks seemed so unimaginably preposterous! Of course, if what Wesley said was indeed true about the prophylactic sheaths, then...then he had nothing to be concerned about. But what if...what if!? Samuel's thoughts suddenly turned to the image of his deranged father wasting away in some Philadelphia sanatorium along with unforgettable memories of another personal, ill-fated incident which had not only swept away his own virginity but also the vital seeds necessary to continue the enduring growth of a withering family tree.

"No need to worry, Sam," Dr. Carvelle interjected as if reading Samuel's mind. "The sheaths are quite reliable. I believe they are made from the intestines of one of their special breeds of cattle. At any rate, the lovely women of Mukot have trusted them for years and the king himself...well, as you can see, there can hardly be more fitting testimony. Do you not agree?"

Still overwhelmed by the incredible circumstances which had occurred over the last several minutes, Samuel, noticing that the mess around him had been cleaned up, continued to reflect in silence.

"There is no need to be concerned about their proper use, my good chap," Carvelle assured with a wink of an eye. The king's wives, being quite experienced, will be more than willing to assist you. And oh..." he casually added, "to be sure that the glove fits, so to speak, you may request a different size if need be."

Cognizant of an ensuing conversation between Wesley and the royal chief, Samuel silently scoffed, reflecting upon the doctor's words. Although he had been persuaded to utilize the so-called sanitary sheaths, there was no way in hell he was going to let some forward, out-of-place hussy handle *his* privates. If anything, she was going to mind her own damn business and do as *he* pleased. While holding onto that thought, he was once again addressed by his influential colleague.

"I have just asked the king about the possibility of witnessing the circumcisional rites of his young female villagers. He was reluctant at first, claiming that the elderly women who perform such operations would not allow it, but, my good man," he firmly stated with a great deal of certainty, "I have had success in handling such matters before. It will not be very long now before his royal majesty changes his mind."

Almost immediately, Samuel noticed two of Carvelle's hired porters carrying in a long, steel box. Placing it before King Shillu Kar Naim, the natives genuflected then briskly left the room. Samuel stared at the mysterious gift, disregarding the other exquisite items stacked beside the chief. With intense curiosity, he watched while the king, kneeling on a silk-covered cushion, unclasped its heavy lid. As Shillu Kar Naim wedged it open, the pellet-like scars upon his forehead seemed to grow thrice their size. Sneaking a side-view peak, Samuel immediately understood the blissful look upon the king's face. For although he could not see the complete contents, he discerned two long black barrels as well as three smaller, highly-polished, wood-grained stocks. As the king nudged the box around for his audience to view, Samuel was now able to take in the entirety of its contents, immediately understanding why Dr. Carvelle had saved the best for last. For, nestled inside the satin-lined case was, indeed, the grand finale of all gifts. As Samuel eyed two repeating rifles with fixed bayonets, three Smith & Wesson revolvers with leather holsters and an array of cartridge belts, he could not help but believe that these top-notch weapons were, in fact, befitting only a king. No longer doubting that he and his companion would soon be able to witness the taboo ritual which had prompted them to embark on this most intriguing journey, Samuel inwardly chuckled as he watched King Shillu Kar Naim carefully close the lid and summon another servant, ordering him to place the long steel case beside the other gifts.

As dusk transformed the howls of jackals and irritating laughs of hyenas into a redundant, sonorous pitch, the king, wishing to further reward the benevolence of his two European guests, hosted a welcoming ceremony in the center of his Sudanese village. Sitting in a circle on cheetah-skinned chairs to the left of his majesty, Dr. Carvelle and Samuel, both reeking of eucalyptus oil to ward off mosquitoes, nevertheless felt refreshed after having made use of two enameled bathtubs, courtesy of the king. Feigning interest in a conversation between the king and Dr. Carvelle, and waiting for the impending spectacle to begin, Samuel contemplated the leisurely figures of bare-breasted, intricately-tattooed women interspersed among the seated guests. Noticing two of the better-endowed women coyly whispering to each other while glancing in his direction, he felt a bit self-conscious, as if he were judging a beauty pageant, surmising that each of the king's wives must have spent the full remainder of the afternoon indulging in their toiletries hoping to win his intimate companionship. For although the native women had been intriguing enough upon first glance, their feminine attributes were now deliberately exaggerated. Chiseled faces, bathed by the glow of many fires, were heavily anointed in colorful pigments. Thick black eyeliner, complementing plaited hair, framed the sparkling light of anticipation in their ebony eyes. Full persuasive lips, dressed in scarlet, puckered underneath shimmering oils. Glossy thong-style sandals and shiny anklets adorning bony feet completed their attire of flashy jewels and multi-colored silks. But more noticeable than any of these adornments, Samuel observed, was the array of firm, naked breasts. Decorated with luminous rings of white paint, their nipples, intentionally stained a thick crimson, protruded like those of the carved goddess engraved upon the teakwood box.

As the conversation between the king and Dr. Carvelle faded amid the increasing sound of high-pitched babbling, Samuel's attention suddenly shifted toward the figures of two females quietly seated within the circle opposite him. Crossing petite ankles while shyly folding slender hands upon their laps, it was obvious to him that the smaller-framed women, painted and embellished like their chosen sisters, were no older than 12 at most. Uncontrollably aroused by this fascinating prospect, Samuel scrutinized apprehensive yet seductive eyes, once again experiencing an abrupt rise in temperature as he imagined the possibility of savoring either one of these diminutive, glistening-haired goddesses.

Suddenly distracted from his lustful musings by a firm tap on the shoulder and jolted from his seat by the sound of drums, Samuel immediately turned toward his unforeseen intruder and noticed Dr. Carvelle offering a huge clay pot of unfamiliar brew. Interpreting the menacing grin on the doctor's face, Samuel sensed that his private thoughts had again been intruded upon and grabbed the communal pot, quickly placing it to his lips. Disregarding the bitter, potent taste of the sorghum beer, he took two large gulps and passed it on to the servant standing behind him. As the alcoholic brew began to take effect, Samuel dutifully focused his attention on the vigorous, rhythmic dancing of masked, grass-skirted natives. Hypnotized by the steady beat of drums while occasionally indulging in the shared brew, he felt a symbiotic kinship with the towering king as they both witnessed a repertoire of astonishing acts worthy of the one and only P.T. Barnum. Wielding long, phallus-tipped sticks, natives with shaven heads, almost seven feet tall, staged a mock battle choreographed to primitive perfection. Nimble-footed men pranced in the midst of flames high enough to warrant a three-alarm fire. And masked women, every inch of their gleaming, muscular bodies raked by tattoos and scars, with underarm hair down to their multi-pierced navels, performed with their well-endowed partners grotesque contortions obscene enough to make Satan blush.

As a quarter-moon peeked through a transparent mist of scattering clouds, the lull of tight-skinned drums and the sudden dispersing of entertainers signaled to Samuel that the evening's events had come to a close. Drained by weariness, as if the commanding sound of native drums had all the while been the source of his enduring energy, Samuel's body ached for a good night's sleep as he was escorted by one of the king's servants to his private room. Realizing that he had not been granted a mistress for the evening and believing that such a late hour would warrant his seclusion for the remainder of the night, he exhaled a surrendering sigh. Dragging tired feet along the smoke-filled, twig-strewn path in an effort to match the servant's steady gait, Samuel yawned as fatigue overrode his usual concerns about the room's accommodations. Even if it be lacking in space and void of customary furniture, so long as there be a comfortable place to rest his weary head, it would serve his bloody bones well indeed.

Like a magic potion suddenly arousing him from a deep and restless sleep, Samuel's weariness was forgotten the minute he stepped into the majestic ambience of his spacious, eclectic abode. Covered from floor to ceiling with brightly colored Middle Eastern rugs and picturesque Persian tapestries, its otherwise crude framework was enhanced all the more by a canopied bed situated in the room's center, draped in opaque layers of pink silk and surrounded by mounds of sumptuous pillows. Momentarily distracted by the indiscernible language of the servant, Samuel noticed upon following the direction of his slender black finger that the contents of his bags had been unpacked, each category of clothing neatly placed within an ornately-carved, partitioned chest. Annoyed that his pressed starched shirts and white linens had been pawed by a savage's hands, but somewhat relieved at having been spared such a trivial task, his attention was directed toward a mirrored vanity with an assortment of toilet accessories, including the erotically carved teakwood box and a petite ivory wash basin filled to the brim. Pushing aside another layer of silk curtains suspended from the rough, beamed ceiling, the servant revealed a porcelain bathtub three-quarters filled, over which hung an array of thick, colorful towels. As Samuel watched the attendant submerge his hand into the soap bubbles to demonstrate the water's comfortable temperature, he followed suit, also noticing the meticulously clean chamber pot in the corner, elegantly covered by an ivory-embossed lid.

Ringing a shiny gold bell, the servant, finally identifying himself as Kamin, handed the ornament to Samuel, gesturing toward the curtained entrance that he would be available in the adjacent room. Having exuberantly expressed his willingness to serve, Kamin, with a hint of anticipation in his charcoal eyes, deeply bowed, pushed aside the flowing silk curtains and disappeared. Deliberately placing the polished bell on the table and looking forward to a warm bath, Samuel strode toward the chest to retrieve his nightwear when suddenly he halted, noticing at the corner of his eye a suspicious sight in the center of the room. Squinting his eyes, he changed direction, ambling toward the bed. Moving a bit closer, he detected a wild, sweet scent, all the while discerning through long silk multi-layered curtains a faint shadow, hardly noticeable except for its slight undulation. A subtle rustling sound, which Samuel had formerly attributed to a gentle breeze, seemed to accompany the swaying mirage. Unsure of whether the excessive consumption of sorghum beer was still dulling his good senses, he groped the pink silk in an effort to locate an opening. Impatiently turning to the side of the bed, he noticed the smooth layers of fabric slowly surrendering as the wild scent, becoming stronger, engulfed the room. Upon parting the silk, Samuel, unexpectedly overwhelmed by a most unusual sight, impulsively let go again, doubting for a second whether what he had just seen was indeed real. Feeling a bit disconcerted, yet tremendously intrigued, he parted the curtain once again, finally feasting upon the spectacle which seductively lay before him. Acquiescing to his gaze with pubescent, apprehensive eyes were not one, but *two* lithe, unclad females whom Samuel quickly identified as the youngsters he had coveted at the start of the evening's festivities. Succumbing to the urgency of his most carnal cravings and forgetting about the lesser comforts of a soothing bath, he promptly kneeled onto the bed and, focusing his attention on one of the young girls, reached for her budding, painted breasts, welcoming the fortuitous opportunity not only to avoid the king's wrath, but to demonstrate his sincere appreciation for Shillu's most kind and generous hospitality.

chapter 35

Intriguing Ritual

Having gratefully savored the largess of King Shillu Kar Naim over the last several days, Samuel was ultimately presented with the long-awaited opportunity to attend the ritualistic ceremony which initially spawned his journey into Africa. Informed by King Shillu that an adolescent girl in a nearby village was being prepared for her initiation into womanhood, he promptly abandoned the solitary comfort of his rumpled, perfumed bed the next morning, setting out in the pre-dawn chill with Dr. Carvelle. As the two-seated litter once again jostled over the dry dirt road, Samuel ignored its discomfiting drive, tingling, instead, with the prospect of witnessing the most drastic form of sexual mutilation imaginable—that which Dr. Carvelle had, in the past, repeatedly referred to as *pharaonic* circumcision. Having just recently enjoyed the carnal favors of women who had been subject to these very rites, Samuel grinned, recalling the flat, wide scars between the legs of his mistresses. Now he looked forward to viewing and perhaps, with a bit of persuasiveness, *performing* this operation which was so primitive, that the use of broken glass, acacia thorns, and catgut were as commonplace as the scalpel was in the civilized world. Upon approaching the ceremonial site, Samuel was once again overwhelmed with anticipation while reaching inside the pocket of his field pants, feeling its contents. Still secretly coveting the opportunity to participate in this barbaric procedure, despite the oppositional sentiment of King Kar Naim, he had brought along his old, but favorite penknife recently sharpened for this special occasion by a whetter in London. Feverishly fondling its smooth, white pearl handle, his thoughts immediately turned to a distant but unforgettable place in time. Though slightly scratched from being kicked under a crude desk by an insolent suffragette over a decade ago, its fine tempered-steel blade had, fortuitously, remained intact.

As the incisive rays of a rising red African sun sliced their way through flowing, emerald robes of towering vegetation, warming the faces of its eager English visitors, the four enervated natives placed the litter at the edge of a small clearing and were promptly but stoically greeted by a bellowing, decrepit old woman. Naked from the waist up, and donning a long, single strand of gnarled hair upon a scab-covered head which stretched down to bare, twisted feet, the sharp-toothed hag indignantly assessed her two unwelcome guests. Dismissing the wary litter-bearers with a thunderous clap of her leathery mottled hands, she then commanded the Englishmen to follow. Wedged between the dwarfish black sorceress and Dr. Carvelle, Samuel, urged by the guttural cries of a rustling jungle, pulled on his panama hat while guardedly treading a snake-infested path hindered by gnat-filled grass and thorny overgrown leaves. Forced to focus upon the woman's contorted back, he was left to envision two sagging breasts hanging like a pair of shriveled, mismatched eggplants. Thankful that the festering eyesore had, at the very least, the civility to be wearing an ankle length, tiger-skin skirt, Samuel found himself unconcerned at having arrived empty-handed. Previously wishing that he had brought along a persuasive token, he now realized, by the woman's obstinate disposition, the futility of such a gesture.

Detecting high-pitched, female voices beyond the obstructing foliage, Samuel remained cramped between the odious guide and Dr. Carvelle, soon arriving at a larger clearing occupied by an assembly of native women. As a chorus of dark, suspicious eyes gazed one by one upon the two white male guests, a hushed silence permeated the unpretentious ceremonial ground which was guarded solely by a small, crackling fire. Feeling extremely uncomfortable and self-conscious at being the object of such adverse attention, Samuel observed halfheartedly that, though certainly not as attractive as the King's wives, the middle-aged matrons, all with a full head of tightly-braided hair, were certainly tolerable in appearance. As the unwilling guide addressed the dozen or so bare-breasted females, Samuel's uneasiness turned to avid anticipation upon noticing a young child covered from the neck down in animal skins. No older than eight years of age and distinguished from the rest of the crowd by a long strand of matted hair similar to that of the old matriarch, the terrified girl, clenching tiny fists, stood between four intimidating women. Pried from his musings by the strict barks of the Draconian empress, Samuel obediently sat down upon the cool earth alongside Dr. Carvelle, all the while scrutinizing several crude surgical instruments situated next to a blood-stained pelt and a clay basin of water, as well as a more familiar piece of cutlery. Lying among a pair of old scissors, two sharpened stones, a large piece of broken glass, a peeled lemon and what appeared to be a wad of cow dung, was a dagger with a handle so polished and a blade so sharp, Samuel instantly recognized it as English tempered steel, a gift that had proudly been presented to his majesty upon the day of their arrival in Mukot.

As the risen sun at last provided the solemn gathering with adequate lighting, Samuel heard the low murmur of chanting voices and the synchronized clapping of numerous hands, realizing that, although the initiation ceremony would not be celebrated with drums and festive dancing, it had, indeed, commenced. Anxiously anticipating what lay ahead, he watched as the trembling, wide-eyed child, being pulled from her place, left a trail of urine along shallow furrows formed by tiny bare heels. Unmoved by the child's obvious distress, the matriarch picked up the pair of scissors and waited until the four stone-faced women compelled the whimpering child to sit upon the blood-stained pelt. Gripping the scissors with hooked fingers, she stooped over her victim's head and swiftly snipped off the long strand of hair, leaving whisker-like roots upon her shaven head. As though conducting an execution by means of a black noose, she twisted the hair loosely around the child's neck while reciting something in Mukotese. Retrieving the tempered steel dagger from the ground, the witch doctor ordered her chanting assistants to hoist the young virgin to her feet, then placed the tip of the blade to the midriff of the girl's simple garment. As the razor-edged dagger sparkled in the early morning sun, the matriarch carefully guided it lengthwise in a firm but delicate manner, past the child's heaving belly all the way to the bottom of her dress, splitting the fabric in two. Placing the dagger back on the ground, she stood rigidly as the four women, still chanting along with the others, pushed the panic-crazed child onto the pelt, struggling to stretch her into an operable position. Panting heavily while the old woman exposed her from the belly down, the hyperventilating child, noticeably void of the slightest trace of pubic hair, watched in horror as misshapen fingers reached over to seize one of the sharpened stones.

Keenly aware of the child's chattering teeth, parched lips and twisted torso, Samuel sat, petrified. Realizing that the incessant chanting and clapping had grown louder in an attempt to drown out the pleading screams of the captive child, he watched with fascination as the old woman dug the finely-honed stone into the jewel of her maidenhood, contributing yet another splatter of blood onto the worn, stained pelt. Quickly working now with taut, nimble fingers as the struggling legs of her victim fell limp, the matriarch grabbed a piece of the broken glass and proceeded to sever the remaining external genitalia, cutting through each segment of labia as if it were an unpalatable piece of fat stubbornly attached to a choice cut of beef. Tossing the long, wet pieces of skin into the hissing fire, she then inserted a sliver of wood into the child's vaginal opening and, reaching for an acacia thorn attached to a string of catgut, began suturing her mutilated genitalia. Finally, completing the sacred ritual, she saturated the butchered area with citric juice and sealed the gaping wound with larvae-infested cow dung. Purging her hands of virgin blood in the basin of water, she then doused the flourishing fire as one of her cohorts, having removed the long strand of hair from the unconscious child's neck, bound frail, unresponsive ankles.

Averting his attention to the child's drooling tongue and wrenched mouth, Samuel, rather disappointed that the festivities has passed so quickly, watched the four women hoist the flaccid body from the blood-soaked pelt and, with a sudden cessation of chanting, carry her in a procession-like manner down the traveled path. Realizing that his tailbone was a bit raw from sitting upon the hard earth for nearly an hour, he remained in place until the silent promenade, ultimately culminated by the hobbling of the old matriarch, had vacated the smoke-filled ceremonial ground.

Certain that he and Dr. Carvelle were quite alone, Samuel rose to his feet, brushing a cluster of dirt from the seat of his sweated pants. Giving the body a good, long stretch as his companion did the same, he wholeheartedly expressed his gratitude to Wesley Carvelle for the opportunity to witness such a unique and rarely attended surgical procedure. Pompously expounding specific aspects of the barbaric rite of passage, the doctor then informed Samuel that four guides would be arriving shortly as escorts to the king's village. Sweeping a wet strand of copper hair beneath his rumpled panama hat, Samuel began contemplating a cool, soothing bath, when something upon the ground suddenly caught his attention, stimulating within his mind a final glimpse of the decrepit old matriarch. As if carefully replaying a silent movie, he envisioned the hunchbacked woman hobbling away from the ceremonial site, clutching the rolled-up, blood-stained pelt. Formerly assuming that the old sorceress' bulging pelt contained all of her surgical implements, he now realized that he had been terribly mistaken. For, while noticing that the clay water basin was absent from the trampled ceremonial ground, it was also evident that she had either purposely or unintentionally left many other items behind, not the least of which was the British tempered-steel dagger. Riveting his gaze upon the commemorative dagger which, despite its ignoble setting, glistened like a crown jewel reflecting the late morning sun, Samuel pondered if he should, perhaps, reclaim it. Reassured by Dr. Carvelle that it had been purposely discarded since only virginal instruments were used when performing such rituals, Samuel approached the ceremonial site, cautiously picking up the dagger. Admiring its long, tapered blade as a virtuoso would a genuine Stradivarius, he noted, with a glimmer in his eyes, that a good polishing was sure to restore its pristine appearance. Feeling a bit of remorse upon the realization that it had merely been used to split the martyred child's garment, he walked over to the surrounding brush, plucked a few large leaves from an overgrown sumac shrub and firmly twisted them around the blade. As heavy footsteps and sonorous voices signaled the arrival of the litter bearers, he clutched the tightly-wrapped dagger with sweaty palms and turned to join his jovial companion. Passing the ceremonial site, however, he suddenly paused, then abruptly turned around and retraced his steps. Standing directly upon the spot formerly occupied by the old matriarch, next to which a half-circle of mud oozed from a wet, dormant pile of sticks, he contemplated the remaining surgical tools. Deliberately removing his panama hat, he stooped down, momentarily laying the leaf-sheathed dagger beside him. Careful not to cut himself, he gathered the broken glass along with the sharpened stones and, one by one, deposited them inside the crown of his hat, all the while captivated that each jagged edge had been smeared a bright, uneven red.

chapter 36

A Different Hunt

L
ike the round, warm belly of a spotted leopard satiated by the harvest
of a thriving jungle, Samuel Randolph Governey felt quite content
while bidding his majesty, King Shillu Kar Naim and his bevy of wives
farewell after a most intriguing adventure in the munificent village of Mukot.
Taking his place beside Wesley Carvelle under a vacillating May morning sky
while boarding the standard mode of transportation that would lead them
once again to the muddy banks of the White Nile, Samuel watched as eight
more servants, lagging behind, struggled to balance the contents of two additional litters. Keenly eyeing these personal belongings to ensure they would
not tumble from their unstable platform, Samuel removed from his jostling
pocket a gold-plated matchbox and lit a quivering African leaf cigar as smiling, colorfully garbed natives faded into the distant landscape. Looking
forward to another peaceful journey upon the "River Queen" as the robust
smell of tobacco enhanced the intoxicating air, he inhaled the hearty
Mukotese cigar, silently hoping that after witnessing two circumcisional rites
and sampling the exotic charms of a select number of the Muslim king's most
compliant wives, his voracious desires would be furthermore enhanced during his upcoming four-week hunting safari on that favorite "big game" turf
of former warmongering president, Teddy Roosevelt: the unpredictable,
rugged terrain of southwestern Kenya.

It was not until Samuel caught his first glimpse of the *River Queen* as the
litter bearers cleared a high, thick stretch of reeds bordering a bug-filled

swamp, that the realization of having left behind the hospitable village of Mukot evoked in him a nostalgic sigh. Patiently waiting for its passengers by the narrow, moss-covered loading dock, the steam ferry not only seemed less glamorous than he had remembered, but significantly smaller. Resolving with determination to revisit the captivating village on another journey, Samuel exited the stationary litter and extinguished the butt of his cigar with the heel of his foot upon the slippery dock. Then, kicking the remnants of his Mukotese smoke into the murky waters of the Nile, he directed the white-shirted servants to handle with care the wide-ranging assortment of provisions he and Dr. Carvelle had brought from England to accommodate what he certainly hoped would be another exhilarating adventure.

As the churning paddlewheels of the *River Queen* once again transported the two European travelers along the southern banks of the abounding Nile, Samuel gradually tucked away memories of Mukot like a dream soon forgotten. With the overwhelming excitement of a school boy starting summer recess, he instead focused during the next few days upon the well-planned African safari, prearranged for departure at the popular trading center of Nairobi. Inspired by the elusive manner of a tough-skinned crocodile or the resonating roar of a jungle lion six miles away, Samuel enthusiastically entertained the prospect of hunting powerful beasts, mentally noting with accelerated breathing, that the biggest and best kill of all would be a full-fledged male lion. Perhaps a man-eater at that. To overcome such a "king of the jungle" would surely be the ultimate challenge! And its intimidating, regal appearance would be most impressive within the polished antechamber of an English Tudor mansion or, better yet, its fanged, feline head mounted over an imposing fireplace or upon an oak-stained library wall.

Arriving at the northern tributary of Lake Victoria after being absorbed by the poetry and prose of John Milton and Edgar Allen Poe for the better part of his journey, Samuel disembarked the dutiful ferry for the last time, having formerly arranged with Dr. Carvelle an alternate route back to England by way of the Indian Ocean. Using their British diplomatic passports, the two privileged travelers, protected from an unrelenting rain by hooded "London Fog" trench coats, boarded a steaming railroad train from Uganda. Making a conscious effort to overlook the boxcar's rough interior, Samuel was further perturbed at being squeezed between the hefty Dr. Carvelle and a fellow from Manitoba whom he had so far managed to avoid while on the steam ferry. Intermittently gazing through a dust-encrusted, mud-streaked window at an expanse of wooded savanna, he nevertheless tactfully tolerated the ruddy Canadian's nosy inquiries about their mutual safari. Although he was previously informed by Dr. Carvelle that the safari would consist of a party of 12, he now questioned the prudence of such an arrangement. After all, the prospect of having to associate with the likes of nine more fully-armed, inebriated strangers was not a pleasant scenario considering his preference for a smaller, more intimate party. About to take advantage of a lag in the conversation by pretending to nap, Samuel felt a firm tap on the shoulder. Looking into the face of another gent of slight stature with horn-rimmed glasses and a prissy voice, he listened as the intruder excused himself, explaining that since he had overheard in conversation that Samuel would be joining them on the expedition and since it was going to be his first time out, that perhaps he would find it advantageous to study the hunter's manual he had brought along. Politely thanking the obtrusive passenger, Samuel accepted the frayed, leather-bound handbook, realizing that perhaps he would now attain a bit of solitude while giving the impression of being immersed in details ranging from ammunition for rifles to grass-grazing zebras. Having thus successfully avoided further involvement with the human species, he nonetheless found the manual to be quite informative, spending the first few hours of nearly a full day's journey between thumb-worn illustrative pages while the so-called "Lunatic Express" traveled across the treacherous terrain leading into Kenya. After picking at a meager meal consisting of rye bread and canned ham, Samuel at last settled down for the night on the upper berth of the small compartment shared with Dr. Carvelle. More disturbed by his companion's snoring than the train's continuous rattling, he was finally lured into a deep slumber, reassured by the knowledge that the next evening would find him settled at camp and in possession of his own private quarters.

Having arrived the following morning at their designated post to pick up their supplies and join with a few dozen porters, gun boys, cooks and professional guides, Samuel Governey and Wesley Carvelle were informally acquainted with the remaining entourage of hunting companions over a brief but stout meal. Advised by the head guide that they commence their 30-mile journey immediately to take advantage of favorable weather conditions, they then set out on horseback into the vast, open scrubland southeast of Nairobi. With snow-capped Mt. Kilimanjaro providing a breathtaking backdrop,

Samuel manipulated both reins of his long-necked Basuto with the expertise of a skilled equestrian, trailing a caravan of wagons bearing 15 tents and an enormous amount of provisions.

As his tall, agile body bounced to the steady canter of the well-trained horse, it seemed to Samuel only yesterday that he had mounted Taffy, his favorite French trotter, outside the perpetually maintained stables of Cheshire Castle. Reflecting upon the delight of having finally outgrown his spotted Shetland pony, he reminisced about eagerly anticipating another daily lesson from his personal instructor, Mr. Hubbarth. With aspirations of soon being able to match his father's long, galloping strides, Samuel would obediently assume proper English posture upon the horse's custom-built saddle. Gingerly heeding the resourceful commands of the kind horse master, he particularly enjoyed demonstrating his commendable jumping skills.

But, like a child prodigy unexpectedly stripped of the budding gift of genius, he was abruptly torn from his beloved home, leaving the cherished trotter behind. And although his grandfather had permitted, and even encouraged, Samuel to exercise his prized palominos after the lad's involuntary move to America, he had found the opportunity less than motivating. No longer inspired by the exemplary horsemanship of his apathetic father, his passion for horses gradually shifted toward a more current and practical mode of transportation. Though unable to jump over hurdles or canter its way around unforeseen obstacles, the modern motor car with its own horse-power engine and speeds of up to 60 miles per hour was, to say the least, the utmost substitute.

Jolted back to the present by the rearing of his horse, Samuel thought he caught a glimpse of a sluggish scorpion inching its way underneath the rotted ruins of a petrified log. Wincing, he hoped his twelve-square foot safari tent was secure enough to prevent such venomous creatures from crossing the threshold of his confines. Always demanding the best accommodations possible, he had insisted on purchasing the heavy canvas shelter through a reputable outdoor supply company while in England. Large enough to fit his extra-long, superior-quality sleeping cot as well as a few folding chairs and numerous duffle bags overflowing with clothing and other necessities common to the gentry class, the duck tent was guaranteed to outperform its most sterling competitors. Of course, Samuel reflected, focusing upon a herd of wildebeest lazing about a waterhole, though accommodations in this God-forsaken land were the best to be expected, he nevertheless craved bathing in a tub with a running faucet or tugging upon the chain of a flushable privy.

As the filtered early afternoon sun continued to penetrate each spoked, rolling wheel of the caravan, Samuel's spirits were lifted when noticing a herd of distant gazelle grazing near a cluster of dense, brown bushes. The graceful, reddish-brown antelopes, their lyre-shaped horns extending toward the whitened rooftops of Mt. Kenya, prompted Samuel to realize that, within a short time, he would be hunting the likes of such beasts. With a noticeable smile upon his shaded face, he let go of one of the reins and took a swig from his water flask. Hopefully, he would finish out the expedition with a magnificent collection of African trophies.

Dropping the leashed canteen alongside the bronze, gleaming flank of the Basuto, Samuel's marble blue eyes glistened like the sharp, pearled skin of a water snake. With a little luck and a great amount of marksmanship on his part, he would take down his lion. Lord of all beasts! Reflecting upon this possibility, Samuel wondered if it might not be wise to purchase his own residence upon returning to England. Despite the fact that his remaining inheritance would be a bit tight for such an acquisition, he certainly could not expect to reside in less than fashionable hotels the remainder of his life. Even though Dr. Carvelle had kindly offered to store for him the skins of any wild game that had been hunted, he would surely be eager to display the trophies in a home of his own. That is, Samuel surmised, unable to ignore a giraffe gliding across the open plain, if he decided to pursue the purchase of a permanent estate in England. Returning to America was, of course, always an option, although by neglecting to keep in touch with his colleagues at Philadelphia General, especially regarding his father's care, he may have burned that particular bridge. Nevertheless, hopefully, in that possible future event, his less than endearing father would be long dead and eternally entombed, forevermore. And even if the case prove otherwise, it would be of little or no concern to him whatsoever. The decrepit, wanton and sexually perverted old beast would not have to know that his less than prodigal son had returned and with his excellent credentials, he could always secure a position elsewhere. Samuel grunted. If his father *was* alive, whatever remained of his diseased mind would not be enough for any type of cognitive discernment, let alone the recognition of his one and only heir.

Finding himself in a grim, reflective mood, Samuel wondered about his father's colonial mansion in Philadelphia. Was the old whoremonger still the rightful owner? Had the doctors at Philadelphia General taken the conniving goat under their wing? Maybe the mansion had to be sold to fund his long-term medical care. Perhaps being terminally ill and mentally incompetent had rendered him penniless, leaving him to wither away in a public asylum. Or, perhaps the best case scenario would be that he conveniently died about the same time his liquid assets were drained, leaving his estate intact and in probate, awaiting the return of legal heirs. In that fortuitous event, the only barrier to acquiring the estate would be mere formalities. Unless that double-crossing scoundrel made good on his promise to cut him out of the will. And what in the world had become of his beloved motor cars, the Silver Ghost Rolls and his Stutz Bear-Cat? He was, after all, the rightful owner. Hopefully, he pondered with a sinking heart, his father had not extended his revenge in that regard. Although he had, on occasion, wondered about the custom-designed graduation present as well as the newer American sports car, both given as a bribe by the old man, there was nothing much he could do about it. Nevertheless, Samuel decided, as the herd of gazelle with large lustrous eyes, heeding the approaching caravan, scurried into the nearby brush, he would inquire about these matters upon returning to England. Yes! That is exactly what he would do—contact Mr. Morgan by wireless at the Philadelphia Bank & Trust. The reliable bank assistant would be able to accommodate his inquiries regarding the present status of his father's health and the Governey estate in general.

chapter 37

Carnivorous Acquaintances

As a succulent tangerine sun set over the semi-arid lowlands of Kenya, a scattering of porters, having arrived at their destination after eight hours of rugged travel, prepared portable boilers for supper while others set up tents and stocked piles of wood for the evening's campfire. Purging themselves of African dust from a long day's journey at the bank of a rapidly-running stream, Samuel Governey and Dr. Wesley Carvelle looked forward to a hot meal, all the while engrossed in a discussion regarding their hunting strategy for the weeks ahead. Ordering one of the heavily armed porters to retrieve clean clothing hung over low branches of an acacia tree, the two pale-bellied Englishmen briskly toweled their privates and dressed before heading once again toward camp.

Having feasted on a meal of freshly hunted antelope, various greens with pre-packed rice, and an indigenous assortment of fruit, Samuel remained seated beside Dr. Carvelle and a few other guests upon a folding chair, experiencing an almost hypnotic state of being as the long ribbon of smoke from his recently lit Havana mingled with the sparks of the flaming campfire. Drinking in the buzz of conversation and occasional laughter emanating from his fellow expeditionists, he reclined against the back of his seat, crossed his legs, and gazed at the black sky swarming with stars, deeply inhaling the mountain-scented air. Cognizant that the campfire provided a safety net between him and numerous flesh-eating predators, he basked in the contemplation that tomorrow morning, with the help of an experienced guide, he would be tracking his first big trophy. Would it be a zebra? An impala? Although conquering a magnificent lion was his ultimate goal, he realized that dropping such an animal required the hand of a more experienced hunter. Hopefully, Samuel surmised while gazing at the Milky Way smeared across the sky and puffing on his cigar, by the time he recouped the shooting reflexes acquired as a private-in-training for the English Army, he would be more than well-prepared to graduate from the tamest creatures of the jungle to the most ruthless beasts reigning at the top of the food chain.

Continuing to revel in the solace of deep meditation, Samuel's musings were abruptly suspended by a prissy, yet familiar voice.

"By Jove, old chap! So this is your first time 'round, you say?"

Samuel, a bit put off at suddenly being torn from his peaceful solitude, stared blankly while recognizing his intruder. It was the slight English gentleman from whom he had borrowed the hunter's manual on the train headed for Nairobi. "Yes...yes, quite so," he answered, annoyed at being drawn into another circle of inconsequential chatter, having just recovered from a distasteful conversation with the Eskimo-faced Canadian and his buck-toothed wife over supper. If he were to engage in a safari again, he would make bloody sure it was a private affair.

Realizing that his distinguished, newly found companion required more prompting, the small-framed gentleman with the large lips and trim moustache continued. "I'm afraid we haven't introduced ourselves properly," he apologized to Samuel and Dr. Carvelle before nudging a tall, slender woman with piercing green eyes and platinum blonde hair. "Name is Rupert. Rupert Hines. And this is my lovely wife, Mimi."

As the small circle of guests exchanged greetings and salutations, Samuel, resenting the fact that weak-kneed females were allowed to participate in such vigorous expeditions, extinguished his cigar into the soft, brown earth, all the while contemplating the middle-aged woman nonsensically donned in hunting apparel. Why, a saber-tooth tiger would split her in half! And as far as the Eskimo-faced Canadian's wife, a mere cheetah would devour her in two gulps, buck teeth and all.

Dr. Carvelle slapped a mosquito from his face and joined in on the conversation. "Is this *your* first time 'round then, my good chap and dear lady?"

"Why heavens, no!" Rupert replied in an almost indignant manner. "My dear Mimi and I have encountered quite a few expeditions. As a matter of fact, this is our eleventh, having just stopped off at the Congo. One more and we'll have a dozen under our belt, I say! Isn't that right, luv?"

Casually re-crossing long, booted legs while tearing her gaze from Samuel, Mimi Hines dispensed a tolerant smile toward her spouse. "My hubby is an avid hunter, Dr. Carvelle. Sometimes his enthusiasm is a bit severe."

"Mimi is much too modest," Rupert enthusiastically retorted, pushing the bridge of his horn-rimmed glasses to the top of his vertical nose. "Why, gentlemen...I'm not drawing the long bow here...but just hand her a blazing double-barrel shotgun and she could hunt down a mammoth-sized lion with the best of blokes!"

"My hubby regards me too highly," Mimi rebutted, coquettishly returning her gaze toward Samuel. "One would think it a bit ridiculous that a woman of my slight stature could possibly outmatch the likes of such strapping gentlemen as yourselves. Shouldn't you agree?"

Impressed by Mimi's witticism despite her gender, Samuel uncoiled a bit, allowing himself to engage once again in harmless chatter. Besides, the fair-skinned wench had an alluring look about her, even though she was a blonde. "It is my personal belief, Mrs. Hines, that gentle-natured women would do best to stay behind and out of harm's way."

Mimi released a seductive laugh. "Well, I wouldn't go *that* far, Samuel. Missing out on all this fun would be a darn, bloody shame, now wouldn't it doctor?" Receiving a forced smile from Samuel, she brushed from her unblemished forehead a wisp of shoulder-length hair. "Why, in just a week or so, we shall be leaving you fine chaps to pursue a particularly ferocious man-eating lion. Isn't that so, Ruppie dear?"

Rupert Hines, a bit perturbed that his wife had literally let the cat out of the bag, gave his new acquaintances an apologetic look. "Yes, quite so, indeed," he answered like a stalking iguana, nodding his small, rounded head. "By a small stroke of luck, we happened to overhear a conversation between one of our guides and a native villager while in Nairobi. I *do* comprehend and speak Swahili fluently," he firmly established. "Seems the nearby village is being bullied by a man-eating lion. They've tried to capture this bloody beast, by Jove, but the brute keeps slipping away...not being adept at using firearms in that particular village, these savages don't stand a chance in hell, I say!"

"Is it a very *old* lion, then?" Dr. Carvelle asked, thinking that unless he applied some eucalyptus oil to keep the mosquitoes away, he would be eaten alive himself.

"Now that's the remarkable situation," Rupert Hines replied in a more serious tone while leaning forward in his seat. "You would think so, now wouldn't you? Being that a lion in fit form is likely to avoid humans. But..." he paused, pressing two fingers against his cleft chin, "from what I could gather, the wretched beast, being trapped by a circle of indigenous hunters, not only eluded their spears, but ripped the forearm right off one of the unfortunate natives before escaping. Since getting a mouthful of human blood...well, by Jove...that seems to explain it, one would think."

"So your implication is that you are going into the village, then, to capture the lion yourself?" asked Samuel, wondering if the man was fool enough to take his wife along.

"Why certainly!" Hines boasted. "Mimi, too, of course. We make a splendid team! Why, so far, we've bagged *seven* lions...not to mention over a dozen tigers as well as a *stupendous* number of less lethal game!"

Dr. Carvelle interrupted, ignoring the mosquitoes for the time being. "I don't suppose there would be the remotest possibility you should require two good Englishmen to buttress your efforts, then?"

Before her husband could mutter another word, Mimi chimed in. "Why, that would be splendid!" Turning her attention to Samuel, she flaunted long, spidery lashes. "Won't you please say you'll join us!"

"I am afraid that would be out of the question," Samuel answered, "being that there is only one man-eating lion and four of us. Why, I would do best to stay here and bag my own game, however less exciting that may be."

"I think that is a reasonable decision, my good chap," Rupert promptly added. "Being that we shall, most likely, be gone three nights at maximum, you really *would* do best to stay in camp. And...," he contemplated, grinning ear to ear, "I really *do* anticipate bagging the beast *before* the third week 'round...when the moon's at full face."

Having no recourse, Dr. Carvelle rose from his seat, scratching his reddened face. "I do declare...I shall be eaten alive after all if I don't get away from these goddamned bloody mosquitoes! If you'll excuse me then, I should like to retire for the evening." Extending his hand toward the mismatched couple, he bid them goodnight, gathered his folding chair and proceeded to walk a short distance to his tent, after which the remaining two gentlemen stood, ready to do the same. Announcing to her husband that she would join him shortly after savoring the mysterious African night with its clamor of foreboding sounds, Mimi remained in place as both men departed her company, whereupon she waited for Rupert to enter and close the flap of their nearby tent. Then, like a white-maned lion stalking her prey, she retraced Samuel's footsteps to the opposite end of the camp.

"Samuel..." Mimi panted, determined to catch his attention before he disappeared inside his own canvas quarters.

Promptly recognizing the woman's voice, Samuel released the tent flap and made an about face, awaiting a reason for such an imposition.

"Samuel..." Mimi repeated, smiling sweetly, "please reconsider your decision. We would so much *love* having you along!"

Samuel leaned his chair against the side of the tent and let out an exasperated sigh. "I am sorry, Mrs. Hines," he civilly responded, "but I have quite made up my mind. In lieu of the fact that such a prized man-eating lion would be the target of *any* hunter, I do not think it wise, lest the hunted end up being one of *us*."

"Samuel...Sam..." Mimi cooed, her cascading breasts barely grazing the ivory buttons of his silk safari shirt. "Suppose, then...just *suppose*...that this was not the case." Slowly tracing a long, polished nail down the seamed placket of his shirt, she continued. "I mean...suppose that you and I were the only two people on this particular hunt. Perhaps *then*, would you change your mind?"

Striving to remain civil, Samuel stolidly stood his ground. "I am afraid, *then*, Mrs. Hines, that in such a case, the existing dilemma would, nevertheless, be *enhanced*. You see..." he continued, arresting her roaming finger with a strong grip of his hand, "it is difficult enough competing with my *male* colleagues, let alone a member of the *fairer* sex...especially one so lovely as yourself."

Encouraged by Samuel's flattering words and blatant gesture, Mimi elevated her lank body while digging the toes of her hunting boots into the soft, cool earth, barely pressing her lips to his. "Well then, Sam...Suppose I allowed you alone the opportunity of bagging the lion. Would you agree then?"

Mustering all the patience he could while tolerating her hot breath upon his face, Samuel firmly placed the palms of his hands on top of each unbending shoulder, gently positioning his pursuer back in place. "In that case, then, I would be a fool to decline such an opportunity, would I not?"

Interpreting Samuel's aversion toward her as reluctance to take advantage of another man's wife, Mimi was all the more encouraged by the challenge of the chase. "Well, then, Sam," she purred, clasping his forearms with sturdy fingers as he lowered them from her shoulders, "perhaps I may be able to arrange something for you after all." Gazing into his eyes, she slowly released her grip, then abruptly turned around and swiftly walked away.

chapter 38

Change of Venue

Attributing Mimi Hines' distasteful tete -a-tete to the pathetic aspirations of a discontented hussy in heat, Samuel continued without the slightest change of plans for the next three weeks. Awakened each morning by a scorching tropical sun, he would attend to personal hygiene, don his hunting clothes and join the group for breakfast. Then, securing his pith helmet and making sure that his polished boots were tightly fastened, he would set out with Wesley Carvelle and a couple of guides to hunt big game along the vast plains of the Kenyan lowlands. Undaunted by his initial failure to successfully use his sniper rifle, even at point blank range, Samuel realized he was merely out of practice, soon reacquainting himself with the shooting tactics and mechanisms he had learned as a private in boot camp. Toward the end of the week, he had killed three buffalo, two impala, and one rhino, the latter shot at a range of over two hundred meters. Coming within a hair's length of bagging a magnificent leopard, the longing to capture his lion had not only resurfaced, but erupted like an active volcano as he witnessed Rupert and Mimi Hines preparing to claim the coveted man-eater. Although Mimi's unwavering attention and seductive stares only made him crave the young, passive brunettes he had enjoyed in numerous European bordellos, he realized that he would, nevertheless, welcome the opportunity to accompany her on this particular safari should he, indeed, be awarded the privilege of taking down the lion himself. And while still believing that the private conversation previously held between them was pure nonsense, he would sometimes catch himself wondering just what the impudent Mimi Hines had in mind.

Having been awakened one wet morning by the haunting refrain of a black-beaked shrike amid the smell of bacon and coffee, Samuel, dressed in hunting gear, tarried in deep contemplation while brushing his thick, coppery hair. Gazing into the full-sized mirror set atop a makeshift washstand accommodating a Gillette safety razor and several toiletries, he imagined the anticipation of his hunting rivals. Tomorrow they would be departing for the big kill. It was all that four-eyed braggart had been talking of lately, flaunting the prospect in front of everyone like a cold-hearted warden dangling a prime rib of steak in the faces of starving convicts. He would be glad when the mismatched duo were finally gone, Samuel grimaced, reaching for the unstarched shirt a servant had hung upon a bamboo rack the evening before. With a bit of luck, the lion would be more elusive than expected, prolonging their absence all the more. *Or,* Samuel surmised with a trace of venom in his flint-blue eyes, perhaps the lion would be awarded the rare opportunity of feasting upon an authentic English meal.

Satisfied that he was presentable enough to join his companions for breakfast, Samuel checked the cartridges in his belt, grabbed his headgear and proceeded to peel open the canvas flap when he was halted by an excruciating scream emanating from the opposite end of camp. Looking in the direction of what seemed to be the sound of a man in wrenching pain, he noticed several servants scurrying frantically toward Rupert and Mimi Hines' tent. Having initially intended to head straight for the cook's tent, Samuel was suddenly compelled by the moans, quickening his pace instead toward the source of the commotion. Catching up with other anxious guests, he discerned from their confused conjectures that Rupert Hines had most likely been the victim of a scorpion's sting. Boldly announcing that he was a doctor of medicine, Samuel pushed his way through the crowd and into the canvas shelter. There, surrounded by servants and seated upon one of two cots, was Rupert Hines, half dressed, with one booted foot on the ground. The other bare foot, grossly swollen and held upright by one of the guides, was being closely scrutinized by a seemingly distressed Mimi Hines seated on the edge of the cot, wearing a pale satin dressing gown which, unbuttoned below the neckline, exposed the contours of her sensuously sloping breasts.

"It's all my fault! I *know* it is! Oh, dear, how *could* I have let this happen!" she cried, staring at the swollen red foot while noticing Samuel from the corner of her eye. "I should have known better, but...but when I saw his boot had fallen from the dresser, I...I didn't think it had been on the ground very long. I should have checked it, regardless! Now look what I've done! Oh, my poor, poor Rupert!" she declared, fervently clasping her husband's sweaty hand.

"God-damned bloody tent!" Rupert wailed. "I knew the flap on that bloody door wasn't secure enough. Someone's going to bloody pay for this, he damn well is!"

Addressing Mrs. Hines in Swahili, the attentive guide gently handed over Rupert's foot and departed the tent, indicating that he would return shortly.

"He said he was going for the medical kit," she explained to Samuel who had, by now, taken the servant's place.

Scrutinizing the swollen foot firmly held by Mimi, Samuel let out a concerned sigh. "There is nothing much that medicine will do any more than *time* will at this stage. I have treated acute swelling of this nature during the war. I am afraid this nasty sting will render your husband incapacitated for at least a week."

"Incapacitated?" Rupert panicked. "This won't do me in, will it now?"

"There is no need for alarm, sir," Samuel calmly stated while setting aside his rifle and headgear. "According to the medical journals, fatalities from such stings are quite uncommon in adults. The worst you may expect will be some very unpleasant side-effects. But," he continued, taking Rupert's foot into his own hands, "in the meantime, I can only alleviate your discomfort, with your permission, of course."

"But the hunt! We...Mimi and I are leaving tomorr...!"

"I am afraid you will be in no condition for a hunt," Samuel retorted, capriciously eyeing Mimi. "By morning the physical manifestations will have taken their full course. It is most likely that the foot should be lanced to ease the swelling, leaving you quite unable to travel." Distracted by the reappearance of the guide who was now toting what resembled a large shoe box, Samuel stepped aside to allow the surrogate medicine man access to his patient.

"But..." Rupert choked, feeling a bit faint while paying no attention to the herbal medicine the guide was applying to the stinging sole of his throbbing foot. "You claim to be a bloody doctor...isn't there any goddamn thing you can do, then? Hell...throw a pint of gin down my bloody throat at least, goddamn it!"

"Darling," Mimi tenderly interrupted, coaxing her husband to lie on a pillow, "You heard what Doctor Governey suggested. These things take time. Perhaps...," she sighed while rapidly patting his perspiring forehead with a perfumed handkerchief, "perhaps we shall have to delay the hunt until you are quite well again."

"But," Rupert contested, his voice weakening. "The full moon...it won't last, damn it! And chances to bag that bloody lion might be lost forever!"

"Now, now. Don't fret so! You're only going to make matters worse. I know just how badly you want that lion and I *do* feel absolutely awful about this. Why...why I must admit that I, too, had counted on adding that spectacular beast to our marvelous collection. And what an absolutely fantastic specimen it would be! Unless...," she paused before biting her bottom lip. "Unless...oh dear, my darling Rupert! Why don't I go after it myself, then? I mean...it would still be *ours,* of course. Yes! That *would* be the best decision, I think. You know that under the right circumstances I shall be able to pull it off...don't you, my sweet?"

Feeling quite nauseated as the guide wrapped a piece of gauze around his foot, Rupert felt his faculties diminishing. "You...Mimi...alone? What...What bloody...bloody non...sense..."

"Oh my dear, *dear* Rupie! You need not concern yourself with *my* well being! I shall be quite alright, I shall! Why, after all, I shan't be *entirely* by myself. Why...our guides, Zabar and Tibuk will be coming along, not to mention the skinners and porters, and...and...perhaps...perhaps if it will make you feel better, darling, I am sure Doctor *Governey* would be willing to escort me. Can I depend on you, Doctor Governey? Would you be willing to accompany a damsel in distress, then?"

Receiving no immediate reply from the genuine object of her affection, Mimi innocently shrugged, her platinum blonde hair softly stroking sheer-covered shoulders. "Oh, dear! Where in the *world* have I placed my manners? Of course, I wouldn't *dream* of taking you away from camp, Doctor Governey, without some sort of compensation. And I *do* realize that it would be *quite* unethical to offer a man of your stature any sort of monetary reimbursement. So...what if I agree that our first night of the hunt in Zadari be yours alone? If, through fortune, you happen to bag the lion then, in all fairness, his head shall belong to you. If not, then...in all fairness again...I shall have my shot at him. One day yours, two days mine. We shall continue the pattern until the beast is destroyed. I think that is fair and quite ample, considering that Rupert and I have, after all, arranged this extraordinary hunt. May I count on your presence, then?"

Somewhat taken aback, Samuel paused a moment while weighing the disadvantage of Mimi's proposal. After all, it would probably take more than one or two days to track the lion, thereby increasing his opponent's odds. And being isolated in the foreboding African jungle with no more compensation than a blonde nymphomaniac and a few savage servants would be most unpleasant, to say the least. "I appreciate your generosity, Mrs. Hines," he smiled, "but I think it would be in my best interest to decline your offer, given the fact that I am not quite prepared to undertake such a challenging quest. Perhaps I shall be of greater service to your ailing husband should I remain here," he added, observing the shivering man.

"Your haggling is quite deplorable, Samuel," Mimi countered, paying no appreciable attention to Rupert while clasping her tanned, freckled hands. "Very well, then. Honors even. One day shall be yours and one day shall be mine. Do we have a gentleman's agreement then?"

Quite satisfied that the cricket field had been leveled by the insolent blonde, Samuel stood mute for a prolonged moment, feigning deep contemplation. "It is obvious to me that this expedition means a great deal to you, Mrs. Hines. Very well, then," he firmly stated, collecting his rifle and headgear. "I suppose I shall be able to muster myself for such an endeavor. And concerning your husband's care, I am most positive that Dr. Carvelle is more than amply equipped to look after him if need be. In the meantime, my dear madame, I shall fetch something to ease his discomfort." Having vouchsafed the agreement, Samuel once again made his way through the curious pack after authoritatively exiting the tent, leaving Mimi and her vomiting husband behind.

chapter 39

Danger

Having provided Rupert Hines with an ample supply of medication to treat a merciless amount of unpleasant symptoms, Samuel spent most of the remainder of the day preparing for the 30-mile expedition to the primitive village of Zadari. Not wishing to spend even a single night without suitable shelter, he had shunned Mimi's suggestion that, should the villagers fail to offer fitting accommodations, both should be content to get along inside a small tent furnished only with a couple of bedrolls. Accordingly, the following morning, after ordering a few servants to disassemble his oversized tent and store it inside one of the covered wagons along with an abundance of personal items and supplies, Samuel claimed his seat beside the horse master guide. Observing a sky which seemed saturated by a vat of spilt milk, he ignited the tip of his Cohiba as the wheels began to roll. Eyeing a giraffe gracefully traversing the wet lowlands, he then exhaled a stream of smoke, appeased that Mimi and the designated servants, completing the small caravan, were following separately on horseback.

Originally having set out from camp in good spirits with the understanding that he would have first crack at the prized king of beasts, Samuel's hopes were brutally dampened when, arriving within a few miles of the remote village of Zadari, they were caught in a torrential rainstorm. Unable to take refuge within the crammed, covered wagon, Samuel and the rest of the disgruntled safari had no recourse but to carry on. Forced to waste precious time avoiding a myriad of mud holes and uprooting sinking wagon wheels, he experienced grave misgivings about having embarked on such an expedition. Intermittently wincing from the angry glares and brutish profanities of his drenched fellow travelers as they attempted to rescue one of the horses from a near-crippling fall, he yearned once more to escape behind the leather-bound wheel of his French Gregoire roadster, comfortably cruising along the paved, dry streets of merry old London. Finally approaching the primitive, rain-soaked village of Zadari with wet, mud-besmeared clothing after a grueling five hours of travel, Samuel was on the verge of total exasperation, realizing that his chance of bagging the man-eater that particular evening was zero to none. Even with the assistance of the seasoned trackers, he speculated, scowling at subsiding rain clouds, any paw marks the beast would have made were sure to have been washed away, giving Mimi an unsporting advantage under the light of the morrow's full moon.

Located south of Nairobi just a few miles short of the Nyiri Desert, the tiny village of Zadari, sandwiched between Mount Kenya and the mighty Kilimanjaro, appeared like a scrawny mountain goat in comparison to the thriving village of Mukot. In the not-too-distant past, Samuel's first impression of King Shillu Kar Naim's prosperous village had surpassed his wildest expectations. But now, the impoverished village of Zadari only served to intensity his foul mood. Scoffing all the more as his freshly polished leather grain boots were sucked deeper into the mud, he gave the wretched village another hard stare. Not only were the thatched, palm huts dwarfed, crooked and drab, but there was not one person in sight to offer salutations. And the forecourt was so miserly, it would barely accommodate an outhouse, let alone his king-size tent. *Bloody mother of hell,* Samuel thought, recalling the pleasant surroundings he had left behind at camp while swatting blood-sucking flies from his face with a damp, tattered sleeve. If it weren't for the truly majestic Mount Kilimanjaro gracing the village, the cluster of dwellings before him would be as bleak as a plague-infested town in the aftermath of a fleeting fire.

Aware of the puzzled expressions on the perspiring faces of the enervated guides, Samuel, silently shunning the presence of Mimi Hines clinging to his side, cautiously followed the armed attendants into the ominous village square. Although he had not yet become fully acquainted with the Swahili language, it did not take him long to ascertain their deep concern regarding the unexplained absence of village life. Whereas early morning chores would have already been long completed, the lack of even one naked child and his bare-breasted mother frolicking in the shade of the mid afternoon sun was completely inexplicable if not a bit unnerving. Cautiously strolling further into the silence of the village, it became apparent that every door of each hut had been securely fastened, the only apparent sign of life being a brittle shutter here and there kept slightly ajar to insure ventilation for any possible inhabitants.

Unexpectedly distracted by the drawn-out mooing of a domesticated cow, the small entourage, unaware that a few villagers had timidly started to open their flimsy barricaded doors, began tracking the source of the distant bovine. Upon reaching a clearing bordered by rows of palm trees, the small party noticed an extremely thick handmade circular thorn fence invading the grassless setting. Beside it stood what seemed to be a carved wooden deity, the head of which resembled half serpent and half boar. To Samuel's befuddlement, at its charred base were the smoldering ashes and skeletal remains of a small, four-legged animal. As Samuel and his self-appointed female friend pondered the significance of such a macabre spectacle, the apprehensive guides, all too familiar with the towering fence or, in native parlance, *boma*, recognized the sacrificial carcass as a final, desperate attempt by the superstitious Zadarians to regain control of their village. Suspiciously shifting his gaze from the consummated offering to the ugly barbed barricade, Samuel marveled as to why the native villagers might have taken such extraordinary precautions to keep their livestock so confined. Or, he aptly surmised while peeking through the interlocking brambles of the *boma* at the measly array of penned-in animals, why they had taken such drastic measures to protect them.

Still entranced by the imposing thorny fence, Samuel's thoughts were once again severed by an unfamiliar, high-pitched voice, the lyrical language of which was unintelligible. Instinctively turning around, he noticed an impish figure of a man wearing a skirt of camel skin and guarded by three other slender-boned compatriots. Carrying a gnarled staff, he hastily approached one of Samuel's guides. The worried look upon his face was softened by horizontal lines of white paint which spared him from blending into the surrounding landscape. Rapidly reiterating his words in native tongue, his frantic pleas were simultaneously translated to Swahili, whereupon Mimi took absolute pleasure in relating to Samuel the village's tragic fate.

Apparently, the native was chief of the village, burdened with the protection of his people in the wake of the man-eating demon which, just that very morning, had murderously attacked one of the young village girls. Although, during the last couple of weeks and within only a few meters of the village, the phantom beast had managed to maul to death an elderly native as well as prime livestock, it was only toward evening that the ruthless lion dared to show his blood-smeared mane. But now, in the stunning light of day, while the stripling child was gathering dry sticks at the bottom of a nearby hill with a dozen or so companions, the carnivorous beast had, without warning, emerged from the hollow of a crag and pounced upon the unsuspecting victim, stealing her away from the rest of the clan. Feverishly attempting to save their little sister, a few brave girls began hurtling rocks and stones with all their might, all the while screaming and shouting in hopes of forcing the beast to release their playmate. By a stroke of fortune, fate, or the hand of providence, the chief explained, one of the sharper rocks struck the lion *directly* in the eye, causing the stunned animal to drop his measly quarry back onto the hill, where the tiny morsel rolled into the outstretched arms of her horrified companions. Continuing to shout for help, the frightened girls swiftly carried their injured sister back to the village where she now remains, suffering from deep claw gashes and a multitude of lacerations. Although Wabena, barely skin and bone, had been spared the misfortune of becoming the unmerciful beast's paltry appetizer, it was feared that because of her serious injuries, she would not survive the vicious attack after all. Consequently, the terrified villagers had locked themselves in their brittle huts and most likely would remain there for days, hoping that the demon lion would be slain by a just hand.

Requesting to see the semi-conscious Wabena, Doctor Governey and his comrades were cordially accompanied by the chief to one of the rickety huts. Shouting something in the Zadari language while rapping at the shuttered door with his gnarled staff, the chief was respectfully greeted by a man several years younger than himself. With only a sliver of dusty light escaping through the open door, Samuel, stealing a glimpse of the darkened room, instantly sensed the terrified mood of the rest of its inhabitants. As if anxiously awaiting the commencement of a firing squad, three Zadari children, also dressed in camel skins, stood stiffly against a wall, one of the boys fidgeting with a rope-like bracelet around his bony wrist. On the opposite side of the crudely furnished room, a woman sat upon the hard dirt floor. Her lower lip, grossly stretched by a clay plate, her torso draped in similar sand-colored skins which exposed a single breast, rocked her blanketed daughter in a steady, rhythmic motion. The mangled girl, around ten years of age, her pierced, slightly swollen lower lip temporarily free of a sharpened dowel, remained in a zombie-like state, the sole expression of life being the occasional blinking of coffee-colored eyes which gazed fixedly upon a stone container filled with stagnant, blood-tainted water.

Allowing only an interpreter guide inside the small hut while one of the servants fetched his medical bag, Samuel followed the village chief into the center of the stuffy abode, carefully avoiding its low, rough ceiling. The cleansing smell of the recent rain suddenly turned sour as it lingered inside hidden crevices of the hut's thatched walls and roof. Gently nudging a warped shutter to let in more light, Samuel focused on what appeared at first to be a thick, uneven band of dye along the girl's black, gnarled hair. As the hazy sun forced its way into the room, however, he quickly ascertained that the reddish hue was none other than a streak of blood oozing from deep-seated claw marks. He kneeled upon the hard dirt floor while the child's mother assisted in carefully peeling the blanket from her wounds, noticing that the festering lacerations, originating from the scalp, extended to the nape of her neck. Ordering his guide to tell one of the villagers to bring in some fresh water and a supply of clean rags, Samuel proceeded to inspect two prominent slashes which ran vertically from the base of her dimpled chin. Fortuitously having missed the jugular vein of the neck, they cut across the surface of her developing left breast and abruptly ended at the waist an inch or two above her hip. Inquiring as to the absence of puncture marks, he was informed that the girl had been extremely lucky in that respect, having been saved from the lion's canine teeth by the loose clothing, the remains of which had eventually been removed from her pubescent body by caring hands.

Despite the fact that the blanket around Wabena's hips was loose and void of blood seepage, making it obvious that her wounds were solely contained above the waist, Samuel was nevertheless compelled to continue the examination. Keenly aware of no apparent suspicion from the mother and only a tremulous flinching from the surrendering patient, he parted the tattered hem of the blanket, fully exposing the unmarred area below her navel. Straining to compose himself, Samuel fixed his gaze upon traces of gossamer pubic hair and shadowy legs which seemed much too long for a girl of only ten years. Mesmerized by several dark pink, jagged rope-like scars originating from the center of the vaginal area, he felt his own blood coursing at the recollection of the first circumcision he had performed on the daughter of a

Hindu colonel, coupled with visions of similar ceremonial practices under the auspices of his majesty, King Shillu Kar Naim.

As two more servants entered the hut, one carrying a medical bag and the other a questionable container of water, Samuel's thoughts once again veered to the critical task at hand. Unsnapping the latch of the black leather case, he reached inside and pulled from its orderly contents a roll of fresh gauze and an eight-ounce bottle of the standard disinfectant, permanganate of potash. Snatching from a servant's clenched fist a torn rag instantly recognized by its pattern as that of one of the guide's shirts, he reluctantly dipped it into the unboiled water and proceeded to cleanse the child's wounds, paying special attention to those showing even the slightest hint of infection. Alternately applying the yellow medication with the gauze, he was again smitten when, exceptionally forgiving of the disfigurement of Wabena's lower lip, he savored her black cherubic features and glistening swan-like neck. Unquestionably the injured child was an untamed bloody savage at best, Samuel cynically surmised while gently tracing a few light scratches along her finely-chiseled cheekbone. However, one could easily gather that *had* she been seized from this native jungle and delivered into the resourceful hands of any European Madame, she would undoubtedly turn the most defunct house of ill-repute into a far more profitable establishment, indeed!

Having treated and dressed Wabena's wounds, Samuel, with cracking knees, stiffly rose from the floor. Annoyed at having to brush the dirt from his mud-caked trousers, he handed the medical bag back to his servant and asked to speak with one of the trackers. Responding to the servant's gesture to follow him before Mimi had the chance to intervene, he strode back through the courtyard and down the wide muddy path where the restrained horses, snorting and brushing their hoofs along the supple earth, remained near the caravan. A bit startled by the servant's sudden exasperation, Samuel immediately noticed Tibuk, one of the trackers, stripped of his white field shirt and with rifle in hand, dozing at the foot of a mango tree. The agitated servant, vindictively kicking the lazy tracker with the battered toe of his hunting boot, all the while screaming Swahili obscenities, was suddenly appeased as Tibuk jumped from his cozy repose like a locust on hot gravel.

"I beg your pardon, sir Governey. I must have dozed off for a time. But I most assuredly would have sensed the presence of a lion," the flustered tracker explained in his most succinct English while adjusting the strap of the rifle slung over bare, massive shoulders.

Momentarily presuming that the indolent African was but the hapless prototype of his primal ancestors, Samuel was in no mood even for the most formal of apologies. "At ease...never bloody mind that," he sternly replied. Desiring to remain in the good graces of the bungling buffoon, he patronizingly slapped his upper arm, establishing firm eye contact. "Tibuk, my good man...tell me...what is your professional opinion regarding this treacherous man-eater? Do you suppose, judging from circumstances surrounding the half-eaten child, that we may have a good lead in rendering the bloody beast his just desserts, then?"

"Most indubitably, sir Governey...I do suppose that may be so," the tracker replied, emboldened by Samuel's sudden change of disposition. "As I see it sir," Tibuk continued, gazing beyond a stretch of brown grassland while ominously pointing the barrel of his rifle toward a range of tree-covered hills, "that is where the lion first appeared. Far off at the rock's ledge before creeping out and pouncing on that group of children."

Somewhat more respectful of the guide's military demeanor and disregarding the breathtaking view of Mount Kilimanjaro, Samuel fixed his eyes upon the rocky ridge. Perhaps, he speculated, extending his gaze toward the dense, wet foliage, in spite of the heavy rainstorm early that afternoon, it was still possible to track the beast within his thickly sheltered territory. "If the lion is still stalking the outskirts of the village then, my good chap, what are the odds that we might track him down by nightfall?"

"Sir...I would not recommend that course of action," Tibuk answered, snapping back to attention while slinging his rifle over his shoulders. "Penetrating the underbrush, that is. Day tracking is a dangerous sport in itself, not to mention the perils of tracking by night. And a wounded lion at that! A lion knows his jungle like his mate knows her cubs. We would certainly be inviting disaster in that case. Most likely," Tibuk warned while angling bushy brows, "*we* would be the hunted...giving ourselves away by human scent and he in return baring only his fangs before the attack!"

Weighing the wisdom of Tibuk's words, Samuel realized that in his eagerness to capture the lion, he had foolhardily overlooked the obvious dangers. "Tell me then, my good chap," he persevered, determined not to pass up his first chance at killing the lion, "what is the likelihood that we could lure the beast out of the underbrush...into the clearing where I could get off one unobstructed shot?"

"Yes sir..." Tibuk replied, poking two fingers underneath the gun strap to scratch his hairy chest. "It has certainly been done before. When a lion is forced to abandon its kill, it will sooner or later always return to claim it. The way I see it, sir Governey, the lion assumes the little girl is dead. Its animal instinct will bring it back near the spot of the ambush, aiming to depart the underbrush and reclaim the girl before the hyenas do. Only this time, there will be nothing to feast upon since the villagers have locked all their children away."

"So, Tibuk...," Samuel questioned, his eyes focusing once again upon the long, barren outcropping of the cliff, "are you implying, then, that if we stand watch all night, there is a good bloody possibility that this beast of the jungle will emerge upon that very spot, again?"

"I have witnessed it before. Yes sir! Only...," Tibuk reflected for a second while scrunching up his face like a slab of cracked marble. "However, I am certain that only the scent of human blood and raw flesh will lure him back for sure."

"Good God, Tibuk...are you implying that one of the villagers would have to risk himself, then?"

Bemused by the white English doctor's lack of reasoning, Tibuk released an exasperated sigh. "No, sir, Doctor Governey. Not even a primitive villager would be willing to participate in such a scheme. I am merely suggesting that we tie an animal to one of those trees just before the clearing. We can use Wabena's blood-stained garment to smear the animal's sweaty hide, leaving her scent behind. The hungry lion will most likely pounce upon the animal, allowing for a most favorable target."

"And do you think the villagers would be willing to sacrifice one of their livestock, then?" Samuel asked, recalling the sorry display of penned-up animals within the crudely-constructed *boma*.

"Why, yes sir. Most assuredly. No less willing than I had been in offering the shirt off my back. These natives are so overwrought with fear that it would not surprise me should they hand over the most prized of their livestock."

"I see," Samuel reflected, clasping the palms of his hands. "So, Tibuk, old chap, let us say we tie a cow to one of the baobab trees at the foot of the hill. That being done, when do you think our beastly friend would be most likely to show up for dinner?"

"Judging from former experience, sir, a lion which has been struck so unsuspectingly, would most likely linger until dusk before reappearing...instinctively wary, of course, at being so vulnerable under the light of day." Tibuk hesitated while biting sharply into his broad lower lip. "We must take into consideration that the moon will be nearly full tonight. Perhaps this will be enough to intimidate our ferocious friend from showing his courage after all."

Contemplating the tracker's logical deduction, Samuel nonetheless was hopeful that perhaps the man-eater would be so desperate for a meal, it would after all be willing to risk its very life. "So, Tibuk, my good man...if I should, indeed, decide to give it a go after all, how do you suggest we proceed at bagging this vicious devil?"

Tibuk stretched his thick neck and scanned a cluster of trees above the tall grass at the north end of the clearing. "That tree...over there," he decided, pointing a steady finger. "I can secure a platform for you upon its branches with some rope from the wagon. Then, if the beast should appear after all, you will undoubtedly have your best view of him. But we had better make haste if we wish to position the bait before sunset."

"Very well, then," Samuel stated, tossing Tibuk a gold coin. "We mustn't tarry lest we miss our four o'clock tea. What are we waiting for?" Immediately turning on his heels, he hurried down the muddied path, his delighted servant striding closely behind.

chapter 40

The Hunt

As the pale orange light of a setting sun sank behind the majestic peaks of Mt. Kilimanjaro, Samuel sat perched ten meters above ground upon a planked platform and adjusted the scope's cross hairs on his modified sniper rifle. Camouflaged by foot-long leaves of a mango tree, he watched as Tibuk rubbed Wabena's blood-stained garment into the sweaty hide of a domestic cow after securing it to an isolated baobab tree about 40 meters away. Feeling the icy breath of Mt. Kilimanjaro ruffling the long sleeves of his lightweight shirt, he wondered if perhaps he should have dressed more appropriately. There was no telling how long this bloody show would take, he frowned, longing for the warm cashmere jacket he had left back at camp. And returning to the wagon to rummage through his belongings now that he was well situated would prove to be quite foolish. Nevertheless, he sighed, he was on the right lines; according to Tibuk's hypothesis, his human scent was disguised by the stronger fragrance of bird-pecked mangos. And the increasing wind, dropping into the valley, would continue gathering the scent of Wabena's blood, wafting it up to the ledge and into the underbrush where the lion's belly churned with hunger.

Continuing to watch Tibuk tie the blood-covered camel skin onto the cow with a strand of hemp, Samuel contemplated the submissiveness of the unsuspecting animal, bringing to mind a similar situation he had witnessed several times in a Spanish bullring nearly five years earlier. Though certainly not as complacent as this brown spotted cow, the belligerent bull, goaded by a skillful matador in brightly colored costume, was equally unaware of its inescapable doom. And even though the destiny of this trusting cow was less than certain, Samuel pondered, wondering if the lion would indeed fall for the trap; at least the horned beasts of the arena confronted the matador's sword and their ultimate death nobly on a glorious battlefield.

Tightening a knotted rope around the thick trunk of the baobab, Tibuk signaled to Samuel, then ran across the dampened brown grass to join him. Panting at the foot of the mango tree with a rifle dangling across his bare chest, the determined tracker attempted to persuade Samuel to allow him to remain, declaring that if Samuel did, indeed, shoot the lion, he would quickly notify the other guides. But, emphatically stating that he wished to be free of all distractions, Samuel answered that if he did come top, he would fire three successive shots and the entire village could help carry off the beast. Well-assured by a standby military issue rifle conveniently positioned to his right on the makeshift platform, Samuel watched as Tibuk, dejectedly hanging his head, started toward the village. Turning his attention once more in the direction of the barren rocky ledge, he observed the shrinking hue of the powerful landscape and the increasing darkness of the neighboring jungle while feeling the secure weight of the sniper rifle in his lap. Now, finally, the chance of a lifetime was here, he exhaled, stroking its long, oiled barrel. Would he be able to come up trumps? If the lion suddenly emerged from the underbrush to the edge of the ledge, would a full-moon, long-range shot allow a kill on the spot, striking the man-eating beast in the chest or the head before it even had a chance to pounce upon the cow? Or would he miss altogether and instead scare the bloody beast away, forfeiting his chances considerably, allowing Mimi the next opportunity to capture her prize? With this vexing thought in mind, Samuel pressed the butt of the rifle to his shoulder and set its sights upon the draped cow which, contentedly chewing its cud, reclined upon the stiffening grass. Satisfied that his recently purchased weapon was in good order, he released the safety, once again laying the rifle to rest against his thumping heart.

As the fading countenance of Mt. Kilimanjaro witnessed over its snow-capped shoulders another perpetual sunset, Samuel readjusted his seat upon the makeshift platform while bracing himself against the trunk of the mango tree and involuntarily shivered, feeling a cool gust of wind upon his spine. Momentarily arrested by the sacred view of wide, sweeping slopes which loomed like soaring eagles above the grass-covered hills and grey, jutting cliffs, a most peculiar feeling overwhelmed him. Something familiar, yet indefinable. Connected to his childhood, yet closer in time. As if he were gazing at an object inside a looking glass, only to realize that it did not reflect anything within its sphere. Quickly turning his attention downward in the direction of the leashed cow, he noticed that the brown grass, no longer bogged by wetness, was rustling about. As the steady swaying of the grass contributed to his sense of uneasiness, Samuel gripped the stock of his rifle and focused his attention upon the reposing cow. Although this was the fattest cow the village had to offer, it still looked rather famished, as if its sagging skin were the result of tolerating the weight of several days' stress. And how could it be that a creature in such danger appear so calm, he contemplated while whisking a stray mosquito from his face—that a creature in such danger could be so oblivious to what awaited her? It seemed that this cow could very well be the unfortunate victim of cannibals, unknowingly confined in a pot of lukewarm water. Like the rustling grass, the water would soon erupt and bubble forth, adding to its buoyancy intolerable temperatures which no living creature could endure.

Surprised to notice the intensity of a virtual full moon hovering above the rocky cliffs, Samuel once again focused upon his intended task. Would this random match work? So far, everything was progressing according to plan, he noted, amazed that the moon had, indeed, illuminated the night. Unlike the warming rays of the sun, however, its mournful glow seemed only to magnify the north wind's briskness. Rubbing his hands together, as if squatting before a blazing bonfire, he regretted, once more, the absence of his cashmere jacket or, at least, not having taken time to retrieve his favorite knitted jersey from the wagon. In any event, he must forget his discomfort and soldier on, remembering the crucial task at hand. Why, at any moment, the lion might appear quite unexpectedly, so he must be prepared at a split second's notice to take aim and fire. Adjusting the well-balanced sniper rifle to the ready, Samuel, experiencing the numbing effects of the rigid platform, repositioned his back against the trunk of the mango tree. Peering downward past the slumbering cow and onto the jagged cliff where the man-eating lion might appear, he realized that he had hardly given a thought to the particulars of this hunted beast. Not that it mattered a great deal, but surely it would be quite awesome to display a magnificent, out-of-the-ordinary specimen of muscles, claws and teeth packed into three meters of a man-eating machine. And, hopefully, one bursting with a full, healthy mane at that, he speculated, recalling the graphic photographs he had seen in the hunter's manual while on the train from Uganda.

Reflecting upon the long, canine teeth and sharp, hooked claws, Samuel began to feel a tightening of his nervous system as a terrifying thought occurred to him. What if the bloody, blasted beast should backtrack and attack before he had a chance to get off a shot? Had Tibuk made sure that the platform was set high enough? he wondered while gazing at the rustling grass 10 meters below. According to the guidebook, he calculated, while focusing once again upon the rocky ledge, it would only take the lion six or seven leaps at best to cross the grassy plain. Calling to mind the loud, intimidating roars he had heard several times echoing across spacious plateaus and piercing through dense, vibrant jungles, he wondered if he had not been too hasty in dismissing his ever-resourceful tracker. With hardly a chance to consider this notion, Samuel, all of a sudden and without warning, felt every nerve in his body surge through his goose-bumped skin as the repercussion of a loud, abrupt *thud* hung in the air like a condemned man dropping off the gallows. Surely this was it! he quaked as the horrifying, cave-like image of a wide-open jaw exposing two projecting rows of canine teeth impinged his frazzled mind. The undetected bloody lion had emerged from the shadows and was about to devour him instantly! Nearly falling from his leafy sanctuary, Samuel clutched onto a nearby branch while desperately attempting to regain his footing, all the while certain that he could hear the cunning creature's heavy breathing. Scraping the soles of his boots against the trunk of the tree as broken leaves and pieces of shaved bark tumbled down, he struggled against the tug of gravity, frantically scrambling back onto the platform as quickly as his legs would allow. Unaware of the facial abrasions he had just suffered, Samuel braced scraped palms upon the supporting surface. Breathing rapidly and sitting motionless, he scanned the surroundings. Nothing had changed, he eventually concluded, as his reeling mind took in the peaceful landscape. Momentarily, he was off the boil. Even the brown spotted cow, bathed in the moon's bright light, continued its slumber.

Feeling somewhat like an escaped canary upon his lofty perch, yet still confused as to the absence of even a vervet monkey, he began assessing the startling incident with a clearer mind. Something had indeed made a sudden noise, but it was not his dreaded lion. Of that he was sure. He groaned suddenly while gazing down. Damn bloody mango! So that had been the true culprit all along, he lamented while eyeing the innocent-looking piece of yellow-red fruit nestled atop dried grass and rotted leaves. Feeling rather foolish from almost having been knocked to the ground by an inanimate object, but heartened by the fact that his reserve military-issue rifle had not been dislodged from its position, Samuel straightened his sore back and brushed the dirt from his torn trousers. Carefully lifting the strap of the sniper rifle over his head, he laid the weapon upon his lap and began inspecting it for damage. Immediately noticing a fresh nick upon the polished, walnut stock, he grimaced. Resolving never again to let his fears get the best of him, he resolutely checked the safety, along with the steel barrel and trigger, as well as the scope's alignment. Satisfied at last that his weapon was in good order and still at the ready, he braced himself in the proper offensive position as the steady north wind proceeded to assail his stiff, perspiring body with its dampening chill.

Straining tired eyes in a futile attempt to decipher the position of the intricate hands upon his Oris Big Crown wristwatch, he realized that even the light of a full moon was not enough to penetrate the broad leaves of the mango tree. At any rate, it was probably close to midnight. Feeling somewhat envious of his hunting companions who, despite primitive accommodations, were probably fast asleep upon their warm cots, Samuel momentarily entertained the idea of abandoning the discomfiting mission on the chance that Mimi's luck would run dry the next day. Then, as a result of taking the proper measures to track the lion, he would be further prepared to hunt the beast down. After all, he silently complained while readjusting his cramped posture, he had been seated upon this most uncomfortable platform for more than five hours, bones aching from the intolerable chill, and still there was no sign of his bloody prize. But Samuel had hardly enough time to reconsider this option before quickly dismissing it. For the thought of some arrogant female, a blonde one at that, besting him at his own game, was more than he could bear. Like it or not, he resolved while retrieving a monogrammed handkerchief and wiping his runny nose, he would sit this one out with the stamina of a British tank.

Stretching forward to better view the likely location of his impending target, Samuel was overtaken by a strange sense of lightheadedness and leaned into the trunk of the mango tree. What was it about this God-forsaken land that made him feel so vulnerable? This feeling...a similar sensation he had experienced earlier that evening...was not the result of any mere physical ailment. Rather, it was something tied into his thought process. The surrounding landscape...the mountains...the blowing grass...all oddly reminiscent of something. Something from his past. Not as a white-bearded gentleman reflecting upon his former years with fondness, but rather like a condemned prisoner confined in a dank, dark dungeon. It was sinister...claustrophobic, this feeling.

Attempting to pull himself together, Samuel shifted his rifle, wishing that he had brought along one of his quality cigars. Not only would it have helped ease his mind, but perhaps the smoke would have taken away some of the chill. It was so goddamned cold! And what of the sudden silence? he observed with chattering teeth. The stillness in the air seemed to have increased one hundred fold. If not for the sound of chirping crickets, the silence would be horrifying. Under the eerie light of the full moon, looking down into the valley, his attention was drawn to the leashed cow. No longer lying on the grass, it was standing on all fours, not tranquil and passive, but swaying sporadically. Something was wrong. *Very* wrong. Aware of his uncontrollable shivering, Samuel, as if striving to ward off a paralytic dream, forced himself to look upward toward the rocky ledge. Half expecting to discover the emerging lion, yet, in the depth of his bowels, anxiously anticipating the presence of another being, he suddenly recoiled, knocking the spare military-issue rifle from the platform, sending it plummeting to the moist earth. Continuing to stare ahead as if in a hypnotic trance, he remained motionless, wondering...hoping that perhaps the long tedious hours of waiting for the man-eater to emerge had caused him to slip into a dreadful nightmare. For what paraded before him upon the bordered ledge, dwarfed by the shadows of Mt. Kilimanjaro, was not the conquerable beast he was currently pursuing. Though certainly ample in size and moving with the ease of the most cunning jungle creature, its lank, fragile form was undeniably human. A mournful-looking figure dressed in a ball gown, distinguished beyond doubt by the striped flag it so grievously carried. A ghostly shadow drifting listlessly against a curtain wall. And Mount Kilimanjaro! Rapidly squinting disbelieving eyes, Samuel gasped aloud. Its sweeping slopes were no longer there...replaced instead by the massive, grey stone of Cheshire Castle! And the snow-covered peaks were not peaks at all, but majestic, winding turrets! Determined to escape from this ghoulish dilemma, Samuel quickly shifted his gaze downward, hoping that the solid, stable earth would hurl him into reality. Focusing full attention on the brown, rustling grass, it seemed that he would, for a moment, gather his wits together when, as if under the spell of a commanding wizard, the fluttering turf began swirling like a mighty whirlpool, instantaneously abandoning its solid form. Before he could fathom what was happening, he was in the midst of a swollen, raging river...a familiar yet antagonistic entity rising beneath him. With gaping mouth, he watched as a clump of brambles rushed by, clutching within its prickly claws a gold and onyx ring. Stupefied, he remained motionless as the raging river with its surging current swept past the castle, surrounding it with inescapable force. Compelled once again to look toward the grey stone wall, Samuel observed the translucent figure beckoning him. Casting aside the starred and striped flag upon the parapet walk, it stretched forth bony arms and, with a piteous come-hither look in its hollow eye sockets, pressed skin-less palms against heaving breasts. Without further hesitation, Samuel groped for his rifle and brought it to his shoulder. Placing his right eye against the scope, he instantly focused upon the cross hairs and, aiming at the eerie phantom, pulled the trigger and fired.

As a sudden burst of pressure dramatically disbands an airtight bag, Samuel discovered himself once again amongst a peaceful setting. With ears still ringing from the discharged rifle, he dumbfoundedly looked about. Surely, he concluded, a sudden, deep sleep must have overwhelmed his good senses, whereby he had fallen into some cruel, outlandish nightmare. Gratefully observing the steady grass which covered the valley below, he smiled upon noticing the brown spotted cow resting peacefully. And Mt. Kilimanjaro. It was still there...standing as it always had for endless ages. Breathing more controllably now, Samuel detected a burning smell from the muzzle of his rifle and ran cold fingers along the smooth, warm barrel. So he fired it. He *actually* fired it! Recalling the inexplicable apparition which had provoked his reaction, he immediately glanced toward the rocky ledge. Expecting to find it unoccupied, he was compelled to blink...then blink again. For beneath the moon's ominous scarlet glare, the premature morning exposed an object not formerly there. Although the flagging tail looked somewhat like a bony arm, and the long, flowing mane could, indeed, be mistaken for a woman's gown, it was, for certain, *not* the ghostly figure con-jured in his sleep. With heart palpitating rapidly, Samuel's only fear was that he had *never* awakened and was, indeed, *still* dreaming. For what listlessly lay sprawled across the blood-stained ledge just 40 or so meters ahead was truly a wonder to behold! With eyes sparkling from such an exhilarating vision, he confirmed the unlatched safety of his rifle, aimed in the air, and triumphantly fired three successive shots.

chapter 41

After the Kill

It was not until a dozen or so natives arrived with search lanterns, gathering vines and cutting down two stout saplings with which to haul the lion off, that Samuel realized the situation at hand was, indeed, a real one. After watching six villagers barely roll what was most likely 500 pounds of carcass upon the makeshift stretcher, Samuel felt like a revered god as he was lifted upon the shoulders of several natives and escorted back to the village. Victoriously greeting Mimi who stood by the torch-lit entrance and acknowledging her less-than-sincere congratulations, Samuel was then led into one of the huts where a warm bath and fresh sleepwear awaited him. Assured that his well-earned prize would be skinned immediately by expert hands and informed that a hot meal would soon be at his disposal, he wearily disrobed, unable to shake the most minute images of the hunt from his mind, hoping that his aching body, with the aid of a good cigar, would finally lull him into a deep and restful sleep.

Reclining atop a straw bed covered by animal skins while half-consciously shielding specks of sunlight from refurbished eyes, Samuel let out a deep, slow sigh. Further aroused by a gentle, steady breeze upon his rested body and calling to mind the circumstances which led to his present comfort, he slowly opened his eyes, discerning the blurred, perspiring form standing aside the bed. Samuel was not given one moment to address the boy when, with feathery fan in hand and bowing profusely, the lad quickly turned around and exited the musty hut. Temporarily amused by such queer behavior,

Samuel pushed back the sleeve of his nightshirt, bringing his wristwatch into focus. Finding the circling second hand, he adjusted his focus once more. Could it be? he wondered. Had he actually slept for that long? Propping himself up on one elbow, he looked around the room. The pelt-covered mud floor and crudely-constructed walls were certainly not that of England's Duke's hotel, nor one of King Shillu's accommodating chambers, for that matter. But, Samuel grinned, sitting up with outstretched arms, it had been comfortable enough to allow him a good 12 hours sleep.

Anxious to savor the magnificent sight of his skinned lion, Samuel stooped over a filled stone basin after having made use of a small chamber pot, suddenly realizing there was no available change of the accustomed fresh clothing. Being especially fastidious not to soil his woolen socks and wondering what had happened to his previous day's apparel, he stepped onto a large pelt while heeding the hut's low ceiling. Amid a potpourri of faint, native voices originating from outside, he eyed a smaller animal hide situated near the closed, unbalanced door and prepared to reach for it. His cautious strategy, however, was quickly interrupted by the sudden shaking of the thatched door heralding high-pitched whispers amid the deep, clear voice of Tibuk. Bidding his callers to enter, Samuel instantly noticed the prankish grin upon the tracker's face.

"Sir Governey," began Tibuk, his coarse black hair grazing the rough ceiling as he towered like a dapper nobleman over the chief of the village and several accompanying elders. "It is my esteemed honor to introduce his highness, Balakuda, who is here to extend his personal gratitude for saving his village. He wishes to know, doctor, if you have rested well."

Samuel could not help but notice that although the impish chief still carried his grotesquely-gnarled staff of authority, he was regally adorned in a woven headdress and wearing matching bangles of painted, polished stones. "Yes. Thank you, my good man. I have rested very well, indeed," Samuel curtly answered, wishing to skirt the usual courtesies and instead, discover the whereabouts of his belongings. "I must apologize, however, for my unbefitting appearance," he added while scratching a large bug bite. "It seems as if my afternoon apparel has been misplaced, and I am afraid that my other possessions have been left in the wagon."

"Allow me to assure you, Doctor Governey, that there is no need to worry," Tibuk interjected. Turning aside to address the accompanying villagers in their native tongue, the amused tracker evoked several high-pitched chuckles. "Continue to follow me, sir, and you will discover soon enough what has become of your belongings."

Immediately pointing his staff toward the village's main road, Chief Balakuda commanded his subjects to follow, with Tibuk and Samuel at his side. Treading past sack-like beds and camel-skin clothing left beneath the sanitizing rays of an afternoon sun, Samuel, irritated by the ludicrousness of parading about town in his stocking feet and undergarments, pondered the reason for such ridiculous excitement. Noticing the reverent gazes of breast-feeding women with pancake-sized plates stretching lower lips, and the admiring stares of naked, skinny children who quietly paused amid a game of sticks and stones, his thoughts shifted toward the young girl he had previously doctored.

"Tibuk," he asked while sweeping beads of sweat from his reddened forehead, "Would you happen to know the condition of the young lady I treated yesterday? Is she getting along quite well, then?"

"I believe so, doctor," Tibuk answered, slowing his gait a bit. "I have not heard anything to lead us to believe otherwise, so I assume she is coming along quite well."

Satisfied with Tibuk's report while momentarily appreciating the attributes of modern medicine, Samuel's thoughts once again turned to the absurdity of the present situation. Here he was, Samuel Randolph Governey, former Lieutenant and doctor of the British Army and son of an English earl, being regarded as royalty for having saved an African village from the claws and fangs of a man-eating lion, parading about the streets wearing the most improper attire imaginable, not to mention a pair of perfectly good socks which, beyond doubt, had certainly met their ruin.

As the meandering dirt road exposed a row of motionless palm trees reminiscent of the path he and his party had followed the previous day when they had stumbled upon the thorned *boma*, Samuel's mouth began to water from the smell of roasted meat. Slowing down a bit despite Tibuk's hasty footsteps, he noticed that under the shade of several palm trees and a few meters from a couple of newly-erected tents stood a portable stove, manned by a two male natives. The three trackers and skinners as well as Mimi, informed Tibuk, were indulging in an afternoon meal consisting of lion meat, boiled yams and sun-dried llama strips. Realizing that he hadn't eaten for more than half a day while tactfully disregarding Mimi who gestured toward him with a piece of mango pie, Samuel became puzzled when Tibuk instructed his famished hero to carry on as the persevering procession of natives still followed. It was not very long, however, before arriving at the same clearing where the *boma* had been, that he finally paused alongside his many admirers, standing speechless. For in place of the ugly thorned fence stood his private spacious tent, its door flap held open by a grinning native and seemingly furnished with every personal item previously crammed within the covered wagon. And if that were not enough, a wooden bathtub was being filled by the water jugs of three Zadarian women. Further prompted by Tibuk to gaze toward the far corner of the tent, Samuel focused his attention upon the butchered carcass of the man-eater harmlessly sprawled along an unfurnished area of the floor. Though stripped of its muscle-driven flesh and gouged of its keen, carnivorous eyes, the imposing skinned trophy with its golden mane and canine teeth seemed to impart an even more sinister, unearthly appearance.

"Doctor Governey, sir...if you will allow me to interrupt for a moment," Tibuk broke in, noticing Samuel's preoccupation with the blood-stained carcass. "If it should please you, sir, as soon as we arrive back at camp, I can arrange to have it taken to a taxidermist. There is one located near the supply depot in Kenya. You can reclaim it on your way back to England, then."

"Yes...yes, that would be bloody convenient," Samuel replied, secretly preferring that one of the servants would carry out this duty promptly. Reflecting upon the unpleasant fact that he would be sharing the night with such a ghoulish companion, his wary mood was soon interrupted by a familiar flowery scent and a voice more abrasive to his ears than the perpetual whining of a female hyena.

"Congratulations once again, Doctor Governey," Mimi declared, grazing her loosely bridled breasts against his sunburned forearm. "I must confess, I was not prepared to be outclassed at my own game so quickly. But..." she paused, searching sea blue eyes, "I suppose I shall find a way to somehow make it worth my while."

"Doctor Governey...sir...excuse me, may I please beg your pardon once again," a deep voice interrupted before Samuel could fully digest the true implication of Mimi's forwardness. "Chief Balakuda would be most delighted if you should agree to stay on for a time...perhaps a fortnight. His people wish to arrange a celebration in your honor...as hero of their village."

"Oh, yes!" Mimi interjected, firmly gripping Samuel's upper arm with both hands. "We simply must! It would be most rude to refuse, and after all...a native celebration would be quite the diversion, don't you agree?"

Inwardly swelling with pride, Samuel, considering his company's departure for civilization in one week's time, observed the anticipation in Tibuk's eyes and looked over at the smiling chief. "A fortnight of revelry is out of the question, but a few more days will not alter our plans in the least. Communicate to the chief, Tibuk, that I and my companions would be most honored to participate in celebrating the rebirth of their village."

Responding to the apparent compliance of his village's esteemed white hero, the chief motioned toward the tent's unoccupied interior after which Samuel stepped inside, resolving to privately tend to his personal grooming as promptly as possible, anticipating the promised celebration as well as the immediate afternoon's long-overdue meal of freshly-cooked game.

chapter 42

Resuming the Chase

Clean-shaven, well-groomed and fully nourished, Samuel was the epitome of an English country gentleman while seated upon his canvas-backed chair. With his own silver cutlery, he had sliced through and eaten the tough, bloody-rare lion steak, personally butchered by Tibuk. Having complemented the exotic picnic with a glass of Chateau Lafite-Rothschild and the inhalation of his favorite cigar, he was at last fully prepared to spend the remainder of the afternoon indulging in the hospitality of the regally attired Chief Balakuda and several others solely clad in netted, hook-bearing belts. Brandishing hunting spears and toting leather-lined sacks, the entourage of hunters, led by Chief Balakuda, proceeded to escort Samuel and the rest of their visitors, including the "moon-haired female," through the liberated village. Remembering the abandoned surroundings he had initially encountered upon his arrival, Samuel's burgeoning ego was further inflated upon eventually observing an assemblage of babbling females. No longer overshadowed by fear of the stalking lion, the cheerful natives, casually attending to their children, gathered within the shade of olden trees, hammering snakeskin sandal straps, molding decorative pottery and kneading rye-based dough in preparation for the evening's meal.

The well-equipped Zadarians, bidding the moon-haired female to stay behind, guided the hunting party toward the underbrush. Paying no attention to Mimi's distant protests, Samuel adjusted his safari hat and followed the relentless hunters. Unable to avoid an unusual amount of worm-infested elephant dung along the wide open path, he was amazed at how the natives, feet barely shielded by flat strips of straw, maneuvered themselves around the large, firm droppings. He was grateful, though, for having invested in a pair of sturdy, puncture-proof duck boots, thus preventing the parasitic worms from burrowing into his toes and multiplying inside his body. Stepping into another pungent pile of dung upon reaching a dense stretch of tropical wilderness, Samuel wondered for a brief moment how Mimi's husband, Rupert Hines, was getting along. As the natives slashed their way through bristly stems of overgrown foliage strewn with insects, a slight smirk crossed his sweat-beaded face upon realizing that the boastful bloke was undoubtedly still wallowing in misery. Despite the highly qualified medical care he was sure to receive from Dr. Carvelle, the unpleasant effects of the scorpion's sting were sure to last for at least another three to five days. And what would Rupert's reaction be upon discovering that the opportunity to bag the lion had been missed forever? That the man-eater was, instead, the trophy of the doctor who had so graciously accompanied his darling Mimi? Suddenly distracted by a stream of urine sent down from a hooting chimpanzee atop a saeple tree, Samuel quickly darted aside to evade the unwelcome shower, cursing beneath his breath upon realizing that he had been the chimp's prime target. No longer appeased that the lingering smell of eucalyptus oil emanating from beneath his urine-stained hunting pants and long-sleeved shirt would shield him from the foul afflictions of jungle life, his sense of well-being was further assaulted while treading past a row of thick-trunked, chatter-filled trees. Unaware that the chief had spotted a herd of zebra crossing the open, grassy plain, causing him to whisper commands of attack which suddenly halted the steps of his subjects, Samuel was inadvertently thrust against the hook-covered sash of an attentive native. Not owning even a scant moment to express displeasure about his torn trousers and smarting thigh, he suddenly felt as if he were caught in the eye of a hurricane. Witnessing the hunched, agile bodies of the natives, his vexation turned to fascination as the fleet-footed hunters, stealthy as cheetahs and graceful as gazelles, advanced through the surrounding jungle, gradually forming a wide semi-circle. Encouraged that the migrating animals had not yet detected their scents, the hunters, wielding well-balanced spears, suddenly sprung upon the unsuspecting herd, instantaneously tightening the human ring. Allowing all but one whinnying victim to escape, the whooping natives then goaded the frantic zebra until, driven to the brink of desperation, the animal lunged toward one of its adversaries. In what seemed to be only a fraction of a second, Samuel, watching from a safe distance, remained mesmerized as the tip of the hunter's two-meter spear pierced through the vital organs of the animal. No longer doubting what would be served for supper that evening, he continued to observe the delighted team as they retrieved ropes from their woven sacks and cut down young saplings, anticipating the hauling away of the blood-streaked zebra.

Assuming that the successful slaying of the zebra concluded that afternoon's eye-opening expedition, Samuel was somewhat perplexed as Chief Balakuda pressed further north. Gradually departing from the noisy, mosquito-infested jungle, the band of men, patiently crossing the Kenyan highlands, dragged their fresh kill behind them and headed toward a rushing stream surrounded by steep, vacant cliffs and giant nest-bearing cypress trees. Reminding Samuel of a troop of boy scouts led by a proficient scoutmaster, the natives, upon reaching the wide, shallow stream, carefully laid the slain zebra along the cool, sandy bank. Vigilantly guarding his people's exotic supper from the scavenging beaks of hungry ravens, the chief then raised his gnarled staff. Responding to the silent gesture, the hunters reached inside their leather-lined bags, retrieving, then attaching to their pointed spears long, tough pieces of thread resembling the catgut used by the Mukotese during rites of circumcision. Unexpectedly diverted from that alluring recollection by Chief Balakuda's invitation to rest upon a smooth, dry rock, Samuel saw that Tibuk and his personal entourage, having removed their shirts and boots, were cooling themselves by the edge of the creek.

Samuel took a swig of warm water from his canteen, wiping sweat from his face, then bent over to unlace his boots. A sharp stinging sensation reminded him of the hook which had pierced his thigh just before the zebra kill. There was a dry, red stain upon the ripped trousers. Assured with the knowledge that five more remained in his possession to last him during the course of the expedition, he retrieved his pearl-handled jackknife and cut through the urine-spotted duck pants to determine the extent of his wound. Running the tips of his fingers along the scabbed abrasion and satisfied that the hook had not burrowed too deeply into the skin, he nevertheless resolved to treat the wound with some permanganate of potash upon his return to the village. Tucking the folded jackknife into his back pocket, he wondered how the pubescent child who had been attacked by his lion was getting along. Although he had repeatedly inquired about the timid young virgin during lunch and had been assured that her condition was improving greatly, it seemed as if there was a strange reluctance to have her re-examined. It certainly did not seem that the villagers mistrusted him. On the contrary, they seemed overwhelmed with gratitude for having Wabena's life so unexpectedly spared. And to amplify this most puzzling situation, Samuel briefly pondered, watching a fisherman pull his struggling catch from the river, there was definitely something mysterious about the approaching celebration in three days' time in honor of his heroism. Of course, it was perfectly understandable that these uncivilized souls would be so greatly inclined to pay him homage, but it certainly seemed, from the glint in their devilish eyes, that there was more to this whole bloody situation than they were letting on.

Attempting once again to loosen the laces of his hot, sticky boots, Samuel's thoughts, as if frozen in time, remained fixated on Wabena's diminutive, virginal body. If she was, indeed, convalescing as quickly as the natives recounted, it would serve his curiosity well to see for himself the results of his medical expertise. After all, this *was* one of the benefits of his profession, was it not? To witness the recovery of a mortally-wounded patient who, without such medical intervention, would surely cease to exist? Slipping off a boot, he recalled the extent of the young girl's wounds and how her critical condition had made him question the plausibility of her recovery. But, he concluded, envisioning sutured lacerations spontaneously clotting beneath layers of blood-stained gauze, judging from the overt indebtedness of these simple savages, he had once again retained his irrefutable reputation while practicing what was surely considered to be one of life's noblest professions.

Bringing to mind fawn-like eyes and chestnut hair, Samuel began unbuttoning the cuffs of his shirt. Although he was, indeed, interested in the child's recovery, there was definitely something more intriguing...no, rather *stimulating* about the thought of re-examining her. Certainly it was not the abnormal augmentation of her lower lip, which would, over a lifetime, expand to gross proportions under the forced pressure of a graduated series of cake-sized plates. To intentionally mar the countenance of such ideal symmetry may be customary for these jungle barbarians, Samuel surmised while pivoting the ivory button of his second cuff, but to a civilized Englishman, it was undeniably sacrilegious. *However,* he concluded, in spite of this peculiar imperfection, he did not find her overall appearance remotely repulsive. On the contrary, this apparent susceptibility to the mores of her untamed peers made her all the more alluring, subsequently magnifying her youthful, inno-cent nature.

Anticipating the opportunity to alleviate his perspiring body from an abrupt rise in temperature, Samuel stared toward the river at his frolicking, bare-chested companions and began to unfasten the top button of his col-lared shirt. Perhaps in due time he would be permitted to check in on his young patient's progress. After all, any inflammatory cuts along with the existing stitches would best be cleaned and removed by the agile hands of an experienced doctor. Pondering this possibility, he envisioned the frightened child, flinching in response to his firm, imposing touch. Yes! It certainly was compelling to have at his absolute mercy a female so young...and one so vul-nerable! Recalling moist, supple skin and dark, scant pubic hair, Samuel, feeling smothered by the intense tropical heat, hastily unfastened the remain-ing buttons and peeled off his shirt. Finally removing his sun-baked hat while anticipating a refreshing dip in the nearby stream, he stiffly rose from his solid seat. No sooner had he stood up, however, before hearing once again the high-pitched voice of Chief Balakuda. Responding to its beckoning tone, Samuel gazed straight ahead to see that the Zadarians, along with Tibuk's entourage, had gathered their supplies and clothing, and were heading back from the river. Realizing that he had dallied too long, he glanced at his avia-tor's watch and, disappointedly plucking his shirt from the rock, blotted his sweaty face. It was time to push along. It would be near sundown before arriving back at the village. Unbefitting for late afternoon tea after all. It would serve him bloody well, then, after another two-hour hike beneath the blistering sun, to indulge in a cool, relaxing bath.

chapter 43

Illusion

It was not long after Samuel returned to the village of Zadari that a pleasant bath, laced with his own supply of violet ammonia, was prepared by a brimming handful of spritely native women. Treating the cut upon his leg with the permanganate of potash, he soaked his fatigued, bug-bitten body in the restorative water of the oval wooden tub. Wishing to banish the drone of voices outside his tent, he closed his eyes, retaining the forceful image of his skinned lion, much too prized for a throw rug upon a dirt floor. He reflected on how remarkable it had been that only yesterday, bagging this prized trophy of trophies was but a mere aspiration. And now, as sure as soaking in this poor excuse for a bathtub, not only had he successfully vanquished the ferocious man-eater, but captured the interminable devotion of these superstitious natives as well. Remarkable! By any measure of a man, he was a bloody goddamn hero! Presumptuous, maybe, but perhaps even a god—straight from the pages of Rudyard Kipling. Leaning back against the slatted tub, he pondered upon the19th-century novel's protagonist, Officer Daniel Dravot, who, accompanied by his thieving companion, Peachey Carnehan, conspired to obtain riches from a remote region in Afghanistan. By some freakish stroke of luck, Daniel was suddenly regarded by the natives as a revered deity…much like himself, Samuel mused, except in the kingdom of Zadri, he wasn't really a perceived god, but rather a revered white man lion-slayer. Reveling in this thought as the therapeutic bath continued to soothe his weary bones, Samuel's mind drifted toward the outcome of Daniel and

Peachey's deceptive scheme. Unexpectedly bitten upon the neck by his young, frightened bride amidst a throng of savage celebrants, Daniel's true human nature was suddenly revealed by the spilling of his blood. Then, attempting to escape the wrathful natives, the two British soldiers were ultimately captured. While Peachey was crucified and left for dead, Daniel, forced upon a rope bridge, demonstrated his mortal nature once and for all by plummeting into the ravenous gorge below. Dreadfully sad it was for those two Englishmen, Samuel contemplated, basking in the thought of his triumphant victory over the king of the jungle, but for him and Dr. Carvelle, fate had indeed treated them bloody well.

Adjusting his cramped body, Samuel was comforted by the knowledge that his own revered status had not been the result of some intentional deception, but rather of a heroic feat. In his case, there was no reason for the natives to turn on him. Perhaps, he fancied, if accommodations in this barbaric land were more agreeable, he would welcome the opportunity to reign as their king and likewise acquire a virgin bride. Then that "moon-haired" Mimi would really have something to pout about. He recalled the look on her face as the procession of villagers, flaunting the slain lion, carried Samuel upon their shoulders while entering the village gates. Perhaps it would be worth taking a bride just to be rid of the bothersome wench. Deciding that he had forfeited enough of his precious time ruminating about his former female rival, Samuel rose from the tub, grabbed a monogrammed towel and leisurely dried himself, preparing to dress for the evening's meal.

As Samuel had so woefully suspected, no sooner had he emerged from the tent when he noticed the albino presence of Mimi Hines gliding toward him like a snowy avalanche induced by sultry weather. Refusing to acknowledge her clinging skirt and partially unbuttoned satin blouse, he responded to her trite comments and annoying inquiries in as curt a manner as civil politeness would allow. He then gave full attention to one of the guides who, up until now, had been hesitant to interrupt their conversation. Informing Samuel that a special place of honor beside Chief Balakuda had been pre-arranged for the evening's meal, the reverent guide then escorted him and his high-heeled damsel along a smooth dirt road bordering an assemblage of palm huts. As the progressive smell of freshly roasted meat and steamed greens wriggled its way through the dry, scalding heat, snuffing out the arresting scent of Mimi's perfume, both guests were led down an unfamiliar path at the end of which, to their surprise, stood a large clearing, part of which simulated a glamorized mess hall. Graciously acknowledging Chief Balakuda who was seated between four fan-bearing boys, Samuel noted that the primitive dining room was quite civilized; the cleared jungle area consisted of rows of sturdy log benches paralleling tables dressed with colorful animal hides, upon which were placed a variety of pottery. Surrounded by several lit torches to ward off mosquitoes and shielded by a massive awning consisting of interwoven ferns and elongated leaves, Samuel guessed that, in light of the accommodations and a mammoth stone hearth attended to by a number of Zadarian women, the entire village would be sharing in the evening's lavish banquet.

Ordering Mimi to wait at the back of the dining area, the dutiful guide directed Samuel to be seated next to the chief. Experiencing the refreshing breeze of ostrich feathers upon his perspiring neck, Samuel had barely a chance to greet the village's proud leader when a servant, bearing a horn-like instrument larger than his toga-covered torso, released a low-pitched shrill loud enough to excite a stampede of forest elephants. Reminiscent of the regimented routine he was forced to partake in during his bygone days of boarding school, Samuel watched the villagers file in one by one, first the men occupying the rows closest to himself and the chief, followed by a smaller number of women with children. Surmising that the remainder of the females were designated to serve the feast while at the same time wondering how they would manage to consume a meal wearing such hideous lip plates, Samuel glanced at Mimi who, judging by the indignant look on her heat-flushed face, was not the least bit happy to have been placed, for the second time that day, in such a discriminatory situation.

Reflecting upon the quiet manners, efficient servitude, and abundant resources of the Zadarian natives, Samuel held a wide-rimmed bowl in both hands, taking in one last portion of wild game soup, concocted from the meat of his coveted lion. Complimenting Chief Balakuda on such pungent, yet delectable cuisine, he then accepted a generous chunk of lightly-seared zebra steak, flavored with a variety of indigenous herbs, alongside the largest catch of fresh lake salmon from that afternoon's resourceful hunt. Feeling the strain of the excursion starting to take its toll while finishing off another clay cup of fermented berries, he hoped the zebra steak was not as tough as the lion he had feasted upon that afternoon. Attempting to pierce the bush meat with a small, spear-like utensil, he inwardly grimaced, deciding that it would best serve his weary body to miss out on the exotic dish and sample the alternate entree instead. Staring down at the cooked fish which seemed to gaze back with dulled, bulging eyes, Samuel recalled the circumstances under which it had been caught, along with his intention to join the guides in a brief lakeside frolic to escape the oppressive heat. Remembering the pubescent young maiden he had doctored, he momentarily abandoned the wild game feast and warily looked once again into the crowd of women who, a short while ago, had removed their lip plates, taking advantage of the suggestive shape to accommodate their meal. Forced to observe lower lips barely grazing glistening throats like stretched pieces of putty, he cringed while searching rows of females for the black cherubic face of one particular virgin. Depending on how quickly Wabena recovered from the lion's claws, perhaps she might be able to share in the banquet after all, he hoped. And although the child's otherwise perfectly formed lower lip had already been marred in preparation for the eventual plates, she would, nonetheless, be spared such extreme consequences until reaching a more mature age.

Concluding that his young patient was not among the prattling females, Samuel returned to his meal, severing the dull-eyed fish head, then carefully cutting it open and removing the spine intact. Digging into the soft, sweet flesh while occasionally removing a stray bone, he resumed the feast. Unable to shake the image of the whimpering young virgin, he dejectedly assumed that she had been left behind in the care of her mother. Whether the rest of her family was there, he did not know. Having so intently focused on caring for the girl the day before, he had not taken enough notice of her mother, father and siblings to recognize them now. Nevertheless, the thought of the diminutive, ebony-skinned, chocolate-haired princess continued to drug his mind like an elusive, unforgettable dream.

Aware of the provocative stares and highly suggestive glances Mimi Hines was posting his way throughout the duration of the feast, Samuel nevertheless finished his meal in a polite and civil manner, leaving a large portion of the leathery zebra shank untouched. Praised by the chief and his elders throughout the evening for the bravery he exhibited in hunting and dispatching the terror of their village, he detected once more an air of secret anticipation when the mention of the prized, brown-spotted cow was accompanied by mischievous winks. And, to Samuel's satisfaction, Tibuk, acting as interpreter, assured him that the girl he had doctored was, indeed, recovering remarkably, with the possibility of engaging normal activities within a day or two. Whereupon Samuel suggested that perhaps he should take another look at the young patient himself, the chief quickly objected, stating that the village's hero had toiled enough the past two days and that, perhaps, an earlier retirement would serve him well. With that stated, Chief Balakuda sharply clapped his hands, signaling the horn blower to raise another loud blast, announcing that the evening's feast had finally come to an end.

As the scattering crowd of Zadarian men left their women to the mundane toils of non-warrior tasks, Samuel, no longer disconcerted about the intimidating presence of the blood-stained lion pelt, looked forward to returning to the private ambiance of his amply furnished tent for a good night's rest. Graciously thanking the chief, with the help of Tibuk, for the extraordinary cuisine and wonderful hospitality amidst the sound of scraping stoneware, he stepped out from under the canopied eating area into the domed vastness of a star-filled evening. As if a colossal hand had suddenly unleashed a room abounding with wildlife, a myriad of jungle sounds, formerly snuffed out by the mirthful conversation and uninhibited laughter of dining natives, was instantly rekindled. Experiencing the lingering effects of the wild berry wine, Samuel staggered a bit as one of the torch-bearing natives guided him and the rest of their guests, along with Mimi Hines, toward their sleeping quarters. Determined to discourage the platinum blonde's alluring presence should she continue to pursue him, Samuel made known his agenda for the evening, verbally reiterating the exhausting zebra hunt he had so relentlessly engaged in just a few hours ago. Certain that he would not have survived an elaborate, all-night spectacle reminiscent of King Shillu Kar Naim's munificent village of Mukot, he was grateful that the evening had ended early. And the last thing he desired, Samuel reflected while tediously maintaining a steady gait along the tidy dirt path, was to entertain the lovelorn whims of some blonde-haired, man-stalking over-ripe tease who, despite her flagrant cordiality, most assuredly still smarted from the long-gone opportunity of bagging the most coveted prize of the jungle.

Having finally stepped inside the wide perimeters of his private tent, Samuel placed a lighted match to the wick of his kerosene lantern, instantly transforming shadowy objects into discernable treasures. Impatiently aware of the torch-bearing guide still suspending the door flap, he signaled the native to be on his way. Wearily, he teetered toward a corrugated box containing his nightwear, careful not to trample upon the freshly skinned lion pelt. Too fatigued to take notice of the sharp, yellow fangs and blood-ringed eye sockets which had intimidated him that very afternoon, he sat upon the tightly made camp bed and began unbuttoning the collar of his silk shirt when, unexpectedly, every nerve in his body was awakened by a bold, flowery fragrance reminiscent of some of the finest bordellos in Western Europe.

"Samuel, darling!" the all-too-familiar voice whispered between a crack in the flap of the tent, pried open by long white fingers capped with crimson polish.

Finding it hard to believe that this blonde-bristled siren had the audacity to disturb him after being so specifically informed of his wishes for an early night, Samuel grunted while bracing himself upon the extra-long cot. "Bloody well...what is it, then?"

"May I come in, please?"

"I...I am not dressed. I am about to retire, you see."

"In that case, luv, I can wait. Just let me know when you're decent."

Detecting a slight giggle in her voice, Samuel indignantly rose from the bed and stepped closer to the entrance of the tent. "Listen here, my dear Mrs. Hines...it's been a rather exhausting day and I am much too weary to entertain good company. Now, if you would please be kind enough to be on your way..."

"Really, Samuel! After all we have gone through, Mrs. *Hines*, is it still? Honestly, Samuel darling! We have been acquainted with each other for nearly a month. Where in heavens name are your manners? I find your sentiment toward me quite inconsiderate. And if being poor company is what you fear, why not allow me to be the judge of that? Shall I find you the least bit boring, I shall leave immediately."

Before having the chance to respond, Samuel remained standing as the tent flap parted, revealing the silhouette of a tall, agile woman with sheer, clingy clothing revealing every slender curve of her willowy body, her long, shapely legs and painted toenails accentuated by a pair of reptile skin heels. As she stepped toward the light of the kerosene lantern, he could not help but notice that she had intentionally removed her brassiere, the buttons of her satin blouse undone to the point of barely bracing the pink pointed nipples of her white, cascading breasts. As if being taunted by the strings of a masochistic puppeteer, his gaze spontaneously hastened toward the center of her paper-thin skirt, his blue eyes fixed upon a heart shaped silhouette discreetly shrouded by an enticing tuft of platinum blonde. But before he could fathom the full eroticism of such a mesmerizing discovery, the spell was irreversibly broken upon the sound of Mimi's reproachful voice.

"Why, Samuel, you naughty boy...shame on you! My, my...your manners are truly abominable this evening! And so illusive! Why...you've not undressed at all! You've merely unbuttoned the collar stud of your shirt!"

Suddenly feeling like a young lad on the verge of being caught peering through the keyhole of a women's dressing room, Samuel was at a loss for words, remaining all the more vulnerable to Mimi's advances.

"Perhaps you need a bit of help," she teased, brushing her sharp, brightly polished fingernails along the taut flesh of his collarbone.

"Mrs. Hines...*Mimi*," Samuel cringed, unable to avoid inhaling the heavy scent of her perfume as she began unbuttoning the rest of his shirt. "I really do not think it proper to..."

"Now, now Samuel, luv, there is no need for such concern. Addressing me by my first name wasn't so difficult either, was it?" Hardly able to contain her delight upon noticing the apparent bulge at the front of his khaki trousers, she purposely slid her left hand along his upper thigh. "See how easily things fall into place?"

"But...," Samuel blurted, instinctively pulling back. "Your dear Rupert...how would he react should he see us like this?!"

"Really, Sam...You can be quite whimsical at times!" Mimi laughed, stepping forward to undo the shirt button directly above his waistline. "Why, heavens! We are in the remotest region on earth and you are fretting over how my poor Rupert will react?"

"Mrs. Hines...please," he protested as Mimi slipped his leather belt through a loop band. "You are, after all, a married woman and I..."

"Oh, spare me, Sam! Do you honestly think that a ninny like Rupert could possibly satisfy any woman, let alone myself? And as far as being a *married* woman, I find it quite challenging to break the rules now and then. Besides," she added, eagerly unbinding the waistband of his trousers, "I find that men are their friskiest after a successful hunt. And I am never one to miss out on a good kill!"

Feeling as if he had just ingested a potent aphrodisiac while desperately attempting to remind himself of the loathing he felt for this impudent woman, Samuel was further mystified by a deluge of conflicting emotions welling up inside him. Nervously aware of the unavoidable force which surged between his thighs like a fitful stallion, he impulsively shut his eyes, arresting beads of perspiration within tanned, wrinkled temples. Dreadfully sensing a lump in his throat which seemed to be growing almost as quickly as the irrefutable vigor of his manhood, an unavoidable swarm of boyhood images began flashing before him. A dark, smoke-filled room. The shadowy figure of a forbidden female presence.... In silent desperation, Samuel gathered all the will power he could muster, wresting from his assaulted mind a more congenial memory, yet still forever repugnant...a shapely brunette defiantly brandishing a suffragette banner. An old printing house. An ink-stained floor cloaked by a scarlet blanket. Violet Stimple in a reclining position, her corset deliberately loosened, unabashedly exposing lily white breasts and the promise of pert, wanton nipples. The explicit curve of her torso as she seductively peeled away her bloomers. His heated response...and fateful surrender.

As Mimi's determined hands began groping through his britches, Samuel's mind immediately departed the confines of the old publishing house, along with Violet's unremitting ghost, once again entering that dark, smoke-filled room of his childhood. A room he was compelled to visit a countless number of times, reeking of liquor, burnt ashes and antiseptic, along with trays of dried-up, foul-smelling food. And the massive iron bed. A sickly woman—her coarse, brown hair blackened by the absence of care and adequate light. Her emaciated body made all the more unsightly by the imposing presence of a diamond tiara and ruby pendant....

Feeling as though he was about to suffocate when Mimi's wandering hands cupped the firm, naked flesh of his privates, Samuel urgently inhaled, forcing himself to focus upon the slain lion, hoping that its powerful appearance would shake him from the soiled remnants of his unforgettable past. No longer intimidated by its unearthly presence, he now welcomed the sight of genuine, ferocious teeth made all the more explosive by a robust, golden mane and bright, wickedly-gleaming eyes that seemed to be staring right through him. Realizing the significance of this last observation, Samuel impulsively recoiled as a sudden flow of stomach acid saturated his gut. The eyes! Those bloody carnivorous eyes! The lion, which had, just that very morning, been gouged of its fierce, menacing eyes was not only somehow intact again, but the bloody thing, having regained its sight was staring straight at him! Painfully mindful of this terrifying revelation, Samuel stood motionless, witnessing the beast slowly rising from the floor, its coarse golden mane sweeping through the air like wings of a monster eagle, its hovering hide regenerated by muscle and flesh which instantly flourished beneath the invincible creature, enlarging it to twice its original size. And it was alive! Petrified by horror as the animal violently lashed its tufted, snake-like tail, brandished its long, sharp claws and spread open its salivating, fang-lined jaws, Samuel could stand it no longer. Breaking away from his motionless state, he gave the attacking beast a vicious kick with the heel of his boot, causing the injured animal to let out a peculiar, piercing scream. Watching in amazement as the lion instantly shrunk back onto the tent floor reverting to a lifeless hide, Samuel was suddenly distracted by a softer, whimpering sound. And now, Mimi was no longer standing before him; she, too, was sprawled across the floor! Her sheer skirt, drenched by the water basin which had been dislodged along with the makeshift washstand, clung halfway up her milk-white thighs, the ripped satin blouse exposing heaving, disheveled breasts. Wiping a trickle of blood from her swollen lips with the back of her hand, she gave Samuel a long, hard glare.

"You demented bastard you!" she finally blurted, propping herself onto her knees while vehemently adjusting the sopping wet skirt. "You goddamn crazy bastard!"

Dumbfounded by the harmless animal pelt lying next to the incensed woman, it was now obvious to Samuel that he had been under some phantasmagorical illusion, whereby Mimi had been the unfortunate victim. Wishing desperately to apologize, but at a complete loss for words while remaining defenseless fodder for Mimi's verbal attacks, he extended his hand in an effort to help her to her feet.

"God damn it! Get your hands off me, you bloody bastard!" she screamed, attempting to push him away. Samuel backed off as Mimi teetered to her feet, securing her exposed, spurned nipples by pulling together the wide open front of her torn, soiled blouse. Glancing at the lion pelt, she scowled back at Samuel with flashing green eyes. "So!...now I know that *this* isn't the only ruthless beast left in the jungle!" Having spit out her fury, she withdrew her pointing finger, collected her strewn shoes, pivoted on bare feet and stormed from the tent.

Samuel cautiously parted the tent flap, suddenly concerned that the hysterical woman may have attracted the questioning attention of his fellow comrades. Unaware of her undergarments lying outside the tent wall, he eyed Mimi beneath the accommodating light of a complete full moon as she tripped her way across the open grounds toward her secluded quarters. Unable to detect another solitary soul while attentive to an unusual abundance of nocturnal sounds, he sighed. Remaining quite shaken, he released the flap, ambled over to his camp bed and sat down. In an attempt to make sense of his preposterous behavior, he stared at the menacing lion skin. Everything was intact. Just as it had been that very afternoon. The blood-stained hide...bone-like teeth and claws...the gouged eyes. Everything. Except for the splattered mud upon its stiff fur coat caused by the spilled water basin, not one millimeter of the butchered beast was out of place.

Pressing both hands to his temples, he struggled to make sense of it all. The entire situation seemed so bloody, goddamn real. He was positive had he not reacted quickly, the man-eater would have devoured him whole. And Mimi too. But it *wasn't* real. He had imagined every bit of it. Just like the previous evening when he had shot the bloody goddamned thing. *Unless...*Samuel suddenly straightened his back and felt his clammy forehead. Perhaps he had gotten a touch of jungle fever, resulting in some hallucinatory reaction. Considering the invasion of so many mosquitoes, it was quite reasonable. It was the only sensible explanation. Of course! And, most likely, the extreme volatility of recent events had prevented the conscious awareness of any fever, though he *had* been experiencing disparities in temperature. The chilling cold of last evening...his sudden dizziness...the recurring episodes of insufferable heat and uncontrollable perspiration as he presently experienced. Perhaps these were not the result of the surrounding climate, but a reaction to his own internal temperature. And his long, drawn-out slumber into the early afternoon. Hell! Never before in his whole life had he remembered sleeping for 12 straight hours! Yes. It was the only feasible prognosis, he concluded while rising from the cot to retrieve his medical bag. While on this bloody expedition, he had inevitably contracted a case of malaria. And how ironic! He had just participated in a recent worldwide war, barely escaping the ravages of an influenza epidemic dropped upon Western Europe by American soldiers like an artillery shell filled with deadly shrapnel. *Nevertheless,* Samuel pondered, surrendering a frail sigh, hopefully after ingesting the proper amount of quinine, the problem would be resolved once and for all. Although he might experience some unpleasant side effects from the bitter medication, they were sure to be less troublesome than the alarming symptoms he was now forced to endure.

Fetching the medical bag which he had placed upon a canteen of cutlery, Samuel retrieved the bottle of quinine and, with the aid of a small measuring cup, swallowed the prescribed amount of medication. Still wincing from the aftertaste of the bitter drug, he capped the bottle and placed it inside the bag. Realizing he had no water left with which to rinse the measuring cup, he set it aside and strode toward the lion skin. Being careful to avoid the small mud puddle seeping beneath it, he dragged the hide to where it would dry, then tidied up by standing the makeshift washstand upright, and placed upon it the empty water basin. It was by a large stroke of luck, he mused, eyeing the kerosene lamp, that it, too, hadn't been knocked over during the fracas. Would have caught the whole bloody place on fire! Retrieving his Italian leather belt which Mimi had passionately removed and tossed to the ground, he wondered if he should offer the contentious woman an explanation. Carefully draping the belt over a small wooden rack, he began to think it best to keep things mum. As trying as the whole ordeal had been, it may very well have turned into a serendipitous event after all, he reasoned while pulling off his trousers. If Mimi's anger lingered on, he would be free of her presence once and for all. And as far as the debauching of his sterling reputation, she was unlikely to publicly accuse him of assaulting her, considering the fact that she, a married woman, had willfully entered his tent during such ungodly hours.

Satisfied that his living quarters were once again all shipshape and Bristol fashion, Samuel pulled a nightshirt over his head and shuddered as his thoughts returned once more to the hallucinatory vision of the slaughtered lion. If the situation had, in fact, reflected reality, there would have been no bloody way for him to escape. He would, indeed, have been eaten alive, clothing and all. Reflecting upon the awesome power of the mighty beast, he marveled at the realization that he, a trained amateur at best, had truly accomplished such a heroic task. Pulling back the cover of his cot, he recalled what Tibuk had related to him about the taxidermist in Kenya. Perhaps, he brooded, while glancing once more at the intimidating hide, he would not have the whole thing reconstructed after all. Maybe he would arrange to have the head preserved by itself, and the hide, separately maintained, could eventually be used as a decorative rug or wall hanging. Then, upon returning to England, if his financial status was secure enough, he could purchase an estate and display them regally.

Settling back down upon the cot, Samuel longed to experience once again the often unappreciated blessings of civilization. It seemed like an eternity since he had been gone, he sighed, recalling carefree excursions behind the wheel of his Gregoire along smooth, unobstructed roads while taking in the sweet, heavenly smell of wildflowers and salty ocean air. Feeling somewhat melancholic as images of prestigious hotels, expensive boutiques and fanciful theaters enticed his troubled mind, he consoled himself with the thought that in a couple weeks' time after their brief visit to Zanzibar followed by one final holiday in Bombay, he and Dr. Carvelle would be heading back to their beloved homeland. *Of course*, he contemplated, perking up a bit, he was bound to enjoy his status as hero of the village during the next few days. That in itself should make staying in this god-forsaken land for a bloody tad longer worth his while. Lethargically rising from the cot to extinguish the flame of the kerosene lantern, he wondered once again what shenanigans the natives had up their sleeves regarding the ceremony to be held in his honor. He would find out soon enough, indeed, he concluded, reaching for a sterling silver snuffer. Holding the elongated device up to the lamp's flame while eyeing the lion from the corner of his eye, he paused for a second. He placed the snuffer down, stepped over to the camp bed, removed an extra blanket at its foot and spread it over the damp pelt. Then, finally extinguishing the flame, he reclined upon the cot and, pulling the remaining covers up to his neck, fell fast asleep.

chapter 44

Relaxation

Casually stretched upon a hammock suspended between two sheltering palms and balancing upon his lap the literary writings of Henry James while enjoying a Cuban cigar, Samuel sensed an unusual excitement in the late morning June air. A number of natives, along with trackers and skinners, strode back and forth to load the wagon, temporarily situated at the edge of the tent site. Tomorrow at daybreak, he would leave this amicable village and head for camp to pack up for his ultimate destination, London. Most anxious to once again enjoy the benefits of a civilized society, he regretted agreeing to a return trip by way of the Indian Ocean with a tentative sojourn in Bombay. Although there had been time enough to experience Bangalore a year ago for the wedding feast of Colonel Bharat's beloved daughter, he had also wished to tour Britain's Far East Empire more extensively when given the opportunity. But presently, he simply was not receptive to the idea. Just contemplating the arduous journey by steamboat and railway cars compelled him to the wishful sprouting of his own set of wings, he sighed, enviously eying a soaring heron. *Nevertheless*, in order to facilitate the first transition of travel with a minimum of difficulty, the guides had suggested loading the wagon before daybreak tomorrow. Having been careful to identify only the items he absolutely would not need within the next 20 hours, along with a few souvenirs in remembrance of his visit, he was, nonetheless, happy to comply with such an arrangement, looking forward not only to the next morning's departure, but the widely anticipated celebration to be held that very evening in his honor.

Carefully setting the leather-bound book within reach upon a tree stump next to a Dewar's flask of pre-boiled water and his smoking cigar, Samuel reclined deeper into the hammock, cradled his hands behind his head, and closed his eyes, meditating on the past days' events. Despite a bout with jungle fever at the start of his visit, events were proceeding quite reasonably. Although the quinine did, indeed, produce the adverse effects of nausea and dizziness, he was quite recovered, but, most importantly, had experienced no further hallucinations. And as far as Mimi Hines was concerned, the bloody wench had certainly wasted no time diverting her wounded pride as well as her lustful appetite. Gathering from a number of inappropriate liaisons within her private tent, coupled with the wide, boyish grin plastered upon Tibuk's gleaming face over the past several days, there was certainly no longer any reason to be concerned that the scorned woman would utter even one solitary word about their calamitous encounter.

Feeling a gentle breeze fluttering the coppery locks of his wind-dried hair, Samuel discerned that in a short while, the men of the village would be starting out on their daily afternoon hunt. They were probably reluctant to request his participation, he surmised, considering the fact that he had declined their invitation to join them during the past three days. But, in spite of their encouraging pleas, he had politely refused, explaining that in light of his delicate health, it was best for him to stay behind and rest. Consequently, the disappointed natives, respecting his wishes but ever grateful to their conquering hero, catered to him all the more, eager to fulfill every wish his heart desired, yet remaining totally secretive regarding any details about the forthcoming evening's extraordinary celebration.

Opening his eyes, Samuel reached for his cigar and placed it to his lips, glad that by tomorrow he would be on his way. Being waited on hand and foot had been pleasant, indeed, but he was growing quite bored with it all. Surely, he had plenty of books to keep him company, but there were only so many stories one could read in a day's time. If only he had brought along more medical manuals, he reflected while releasing a puff of smoke. Distanced from his practice for nearly half a year now, he was beginning to miss the more challenging aspects of his work. Witnessing the circumcision of two young maidens in the village of Mukot had been exhilarating, to say the least. And treating Wabena had been most rewarding. But now he longed to return to a civilization where one could utilize the most modern of medical techniques. To feel within his fingers the weighted precision of the sharpest surgical tools, whether performing a complicated amputation, a simple abortion or, for that matter, embalming a corpse. However, having felt the need before departing England to disengage himself from such a demanding profession, he had packaged only one basic handbook, specifically for survival purposes. And any such literature that Dr. Carvelle might have brought along would be back at the camp. *Nevertheless,* he concluded while staring at the elongated leaves of the towering palm, he would walk the streets of London soon enough and, in light of his impeccable credentials, easily procure any medical position he desired.

Having had his fill of the depleted Havana and noticing a less than usual number of villagers preparing for their daily hunt, Samuel extinguished the stub upon the tree stump and reached for his canteen. Here was another reason to return to civilization, he mused, swallowing the tepid water. He would give anything just to savor the sensation of some plain chilled water. Continuing to watch the small group of villagers assemble together in their hooked, netted belts, he rationalized that had it not been for such an exhausting hike and the possibility of further mishaps, the likes of which he had experienced his second day there, he may have agreed to join them after all. He wondered what breed of wild animal would become prey today and ultimately challenge his discriminating palate this evening. Hopefully, it would be of a gentler variety. One that would not place such a strain upon his golden molars. Nevertheless, he sighed, there would be the standard fish and rye he could resort to for the fifth consecutive night. Pondering further upon such details, Samuel once again closed his eyes, anticipating the upcoming banquet to be held in his honor.

chapter 45

A Hero's Celebration

As pleated blankets of transparent clouds stretched across a fading full moon and starless sky, the uncharted village of Zadari stood ablaze with rows of torches bordering a long dirt road which introduced a promenade of seductively-swaying flames, their brilliant spheres of light encircling the festive communal area as well as an adjacent clearing.

Donned in a ceremonial robe of dyed animal skins and seated beside Chief Balakuda on a pillow stuffed with the plumage of peacocks, Samuel savored an unusually sweet smell of roasted meat while anticipating the long-awaited ceremony to be held in his honor. Although he had no doubt that the natives would prepare a special feast celebrating his heroism, he certainly had underestimated their enthusiasm. Scrutinizing the throng of natives with painted faces, their fully sheathed bodies adorned by polished stones and carved animal bones, he inwardly beamed, realizing that he may as well have been back in England attending the coronation of King George. Enjoying a refreshing breeze provided by four fan-bearing servants, he also felt a tinge of remorse over his imminent departure the following morning. For the past day or two he had been on the verge of impatience while contemplating his journey home. But now, in the midst of such gay hospitality and obvious reverence, he was convinced that remaining another week or two would have suited his fancy bloody well. Nevertheless, he conceded, arrangements had already been made and the best he could hope for was to return again when afforded the opportunity.

Continuing to peruse the lavishly dressed natives who proceeded to occupy their seats, Samuel's eyes shifted toward the rear of the canopied dining area as his patient, Wabena was brought to mind. It was, indeed, a strange phenomenon that he had not been allowed to further assist in the child's recovery. Although he had inquired of her from time to time, even insisting that her deep lacerations be re-examined for infection, the natives had been adamant, insisting that Wabena was recovering remarkably. Yet, he frowned while gazing at the lip-stretched faces of several adolescent females, Wabena had not been present during any of the gatherings or festivities. He shrugged his shoulders. Perhaps the natives were merely overly cautious, waiting until the child was completely recovered before allowing her to rejoin the tribe. Or, perhaps her absence was due to some silly superstition. Regardless, he reasoned, the matter was certainly out of his hands, so it was no use dwelling upon it.

As Samuel unfolded his personal monogrammed napkin, he scanned the dirt clearing lined with a few animal skins and canvas-backed chairs, in the center of which stood a curtained, wooden booth reminiscent of a miniature theatre. Leaning along one side of the booth lay a couple of concealed oblong items wrapped in animal hides. Contemplating their contents and wondering if, perhaps, they were intended gifts, his musings were suddenly suspended as he noticed three fully garbed female natives bearing large platters laden with food. Expecting the subservient women to wait on Chief Balakuda first and foremost, Samuel was surprised when the largest piece of roasted meat was placed upon his personal English china. Intensely honored by the magnanimity of this gesture, yet wary that the chief would be deeply offended lest he finish every bite of the tough bush meat, Samuel grit his teeth. Further perplexed by Chief Balakuda's command to sample the meat despite the royal leader's own barren clay plate, he cautiously picked up his sterling fork and placed it to the meat's surface. Preparing to bear down on the roasted slab forcefully, he was suddenly amazed to notice that the prongs of the fork sank into the plump portion of flesh with hardly the least bit of effort. Glancing aside, he could not help but notice the wide grins upon the faces of the chief and his entourage, apparent as the ceremonial lines of white paint on each hollow cheek. Bolstered by this display of unexpected enthusiasm, Samuel lifted his knife and began slicing the tender game, noticing with ever-increasing fascination that the meat, which had been browned to a crisp on its outer side, was of a medium, almost rare, texture within. Finally coming to the realization that this succulent entree was no ordinary wild game or, indeed, no wild game at all, Samuel placed the carved portion to his salivating mouth, anticipating its sweet, familiar taste. Yes! he concluded, reveling in the sublime, delicate flavor. But, of course! How utterly oblivious of its scent he had been all along! And how soon one forgets! This presumed "bush meat," which he had just moments ago been so wary of consuming, was no other than a prime filet of beef!

Demonstrating his utmost approval with a smile and nodding head as the three women began attending to the chief and the surrounding guests, Samuel suddenly shuddered. The cow! The brown-spotted cow! So this is what had become of her! Chewing more slowly now, he envisioned the bovine mammal lolling among the small assortment of goats, chickens and other domesticated animals within the unthorned animal pen. Had he not noticed how much plumper she had become since the night she was tied to the baobab tree? Of course he had, initially attributing her burgeoning health to the good fortune of a village which had reaped the benefits of being newly liberated from the demonic claws of the vanquished lion. But now...upon fully comprehending the true significance of her thriving condition, it all made the most absolute, logical sense! Instantly disregarding the animal's docile disposition and surrendering manner, Samuel resolutely swallowed the tender morsel of beef. Then, tactfully declining a side of fresh fish, he pierced his fork into the oozing portion of rare meat and sliced away.

With the sweet taste of roasted beef and French wine lingering upon his lips, Samuel graciously acknowledged the servants as they adjusted his attire and seated him next to Chief Balakuda upon one of the canvas-backed chairs in preparation of the continuing celebration. Lighting his usual Havana cigar, he observed the male guests and villagers forming a human circle around the clearing. The more prestigious guests filled the remaining chairs and strategically placed animal hides while others, cross-legged, seated themselves upon the soft, cool earth. Delighted that the rich, full-bodied essence of his cigar was enhanced all the more by the most civilized meal he had experienced since entering such a savage world, he gazed at the stage-like contraption and sheathed objects in the center of the clearing, wondering what sort of entertainment the Zadarians had planned for the evening. He certainly could not imagine that these gentle-natured people would present anything even remotely resembling the escapades he had recently witnessed in Shillu Kar Naim's munificent village of Mukot. Hopefully, though, the villagers would be able to arouse his attention long enough to overcome the natural drowsiness induced by a hearty meal and a bottle of fine wine.

Not at all concerned with Mimi's obvious disapproval of seating arrangements despite her being the only female honored with an animal hide to sit upon, Samuel's curiosity increased as the last of the women and children, huddling behind the circle of men, settled into place. Alerted by the sudden stance and bellowing voice of Chief Balakuda heralding the commencement of the ceremony, he discreetly positioned his cigar upon a handmade tray fastened to the arm of his chair and listened to Tibuk's translation of Balakuda's speech. Inwardly beaming with pride, Samuel reposed in an unassuming countenance as the chief sang the praises of his honored guest's remarkable manhood, as well as recounting the village's jubilation over the slaughter of the demon man-eater at the hands of such a valiant and providential white man from beyond the mighty mountains of the north. Although the chief's tribute lasted much longer than any of the countless sermons Samuel had been subjected to under the domes of Gothic cathedrals attended in his boyhood, he nonetheless remained remarkably alert despite the wine and hearty supper. And, albeit he had only learned a mere pittance of the Zadarian language during his last few days of pleasurable captivity, he was certain that had he not been allowed the benefit of an interpreter, he would have enjoyed, as well as understood, the contents of Balakuda's speech no less.

Upon reclaiming his seat of honor, Chief Balakuda raised his gnarled staff. Wasting no time in resuming the pleasure of his Havana, Samuel watched as three natives rose from the ground, two disappearing behind the bamboo booth while the other pulled apart the makeshift curtain of animal hides. As soon as the miniature stage was revealed, Samuel could see an artificial background of tall mountains and two distinct trees and could hear the loud vocalization of one of the concealed villagers. Immediately following, a large voodoo-like doll appeared, propped by a sturdy twig and carrying what seemed to be a small, whittled rifle. At this point Samuel realized that a puppet show, reenacting his encounter with the man-eating lion had begun. Slightly amused, he leaned back into his soft canvas seat, inhaled his cigar and watched as a smaller Tibuk-like, black-faced doll mimicked the tying down of a brown spotted cow to one of the trees. Impressed by the agility with which the natives animated this over-simplified form of entertainment, Samuel's mind wandered back to the days of his childhood when Sandra, his nanny, would accompany him on country outings during the warm summer months and occasionally stumble upon a Punch and Judy show. The color-ful marionettes, unlike the crudely made puppets cavorting before him now, evoked a bellyful of laughs from children and adults alike, as Punch, the humpbacked, hook-nosed wife beater, along with Toby the dog, Baby, the Doctor, the Negro Servant and the Devil all contributed to a simple, yet mis-chievous plot. Of course, Samuel silently noted while watching the doll-like Tibuk exiting the primitive stage, as a child viewing the slapstick mari-onettes, he could not quite understand what all the nonsense was about. Absolute poppycock! However, he concluded upon hearing the high-pitched tones of the Zadarian puppeteers escalating to a menacing roar, these well-meaning natives could learn a lesson or two from the English masters, indeed. Focusing his attention once again upon the performance at hand, Samuel inhaled his cigar as a flaxen-hued four-legged figure, sporting a mane full of yellow grass suddenly sprung from behind the larger of the two moun-tain peaks. Giving the audience hardly the chance to gather the appropriate theatrical tension, an unexpected thud, brought on by the obvious slapping of the bamboo stage, sent the sorry-looking lion tumbling over the mountain and into the stiff, stuffed arms of his slayer; instantaneously, the natives, caught up in the dreaded memory of their formerly terrorized village explod-ed into a crescendo of cheers and laughter.

Patiently scrutinizing the pride-filled puppeteers, Samuel's interest peaked once again as they exchanged places with two other male natives who proceeded to unwrap the blanketed objects. He immediately identified them as primitive musical instruments, one being a zither consisting of indigenous wood and what appeared to be thin bands of palm leaves, the other a wind-pipe, most likely fashioned from the horns of an antelope or gazelle. After waiting for a hush to fall over the natives, the two musicians, one standing and one kneeling behind the zither, began to manipulate their prized instru-ments, instantly drowning out the faint, hypnotic flood of distant jungle sounds. Attempting to appear as attentive as the rest of the listeners while the stiffly postured duet played on, Samuel suppressed a yawn. Although the primitive melody delivered an undertone of gaiety, it was nevertheless tran-quil and melancholic. Retrieving his cigar in the hope of conquering an oncoming case of lethargy, he regretfully remembered the fine movie houses he had left behind in Europe. Under the skilled genius of French directors, these orchestral-accompanied films starring such gifted thespians as Sarah Bernhardt and Max Dearly were certainly an improvement over the nonsensical vaudeville shows and nickelodeons he occasionally tolerated while living in Philadelphia. Nevertheless, those tawdry nickelodeons with their cheap, twanging upright pianos had served their purpose, allowing him to momentarily escape from the miserable company of his drunken father.

Having beckoned the subjugated Earl of Cheshire to the forefront of his mind, Samuel wondered once again how the decrepit old goat was getting along. Still suffering the ravages of syphilis, undoubtedly; unless the unrelenting disease had finally gotten the best of him, placing him ten feet underground. In that case, then, whatever remained of the estate, if indeed anything, should be rightfully his, he reiterated, visualizing the sparsely furnished, yet opulent colonial mansion complimented by none other than his long-cherished Silver Ghost Rolls Royce and Stutz Bear-Cat roadster. And in the event that his bloody father *was* still alive, the degenerative venereal disease may have, over the past few years, rendered him so mentally incapacitated that it would be necessary to step in as guardian, not only to his father, but the estate as well. Of course, Samuel frowned, there was a good possibility that much, if not all, of his grandfather's legacy had been devoured by medical bills and administrative costs. On the other hand, there was still a sporting chance that, due to his father's possible premature death or other unforeseen circumstances, a good portion of the inheritance remained unscathed. In that fortuitous event, acquiring his own estate in London or elsewhere would be far more attainable. *Yes*, Samuel reaffirmed, savoring the robust flavor of his Havana. That would be his priority upon re-entering civilization. Inquiring as to the condition of his father, that perverted old lecher.

Determined to steer his thoughts from the recurring recollections of his father, Samuel forced himself to focus once more upon the anesthetizing rhythm of the zither and wind-pipe. Granted, the measly ensemble of musicians and their accompanying instruments was certainly no symphonic orchestra, but *if* the primitive noise could, from here on in, keep his mind off his father, it would serve him bloody well, indeed. Making a conscious effort to hang on to his cigar as he exhaled another rivulet of smoke, he glanced at Chief Balakuda to his left, amazed that the old wide-eyed tribal leader had not only remained awake, but was swaying, like a king cobra, to the monotonous rhythm of the primeval lullaby. Nevertheless, his faith in the sensibilities of mankind was soon restored upon noticing that Tibuk, seated to his right, had fallen fast asleep, despite the ability to remain upright like a tautly-strung marionette. Momentarily wondering whether it was worth fighting the urge to do likewise, Samuel's concerns were promptly halted by the intrusion of external stimuli. What had initially alerted him to such an abrupt distraction, he could not discern. Was it the sudden way in which Tibuk had opened his eyes? Or was it the steady, dominant rhythm and powerful urgent beat that only one particular musical instrument was capable of delivering? And it was not one, but several of them. All emitting the same exuberant din. Like the changing of the guard at Buckingham Palace, yet much more emphatic. A seductive, compelling sound. Focusing now toward the direction of the exhilarating pulse, Samuel noticed that a half dozen drummers were ceremoniously dancing along the torch-lined path. Behind the invigorated celebrants trailed a decorative, curtained litter supported by four male servants who, unlike their fully dressed counterparts had barely concealed their nakedness with tinted stone loincloths and adornments of antelope toe bones. Hardly given the opportunity to fully ascertain the purpose of such an extraordinary ritual, Samuel braced himself as the drumming ceased and Chief Balakuda majestically rose from his canvas throne. In response to their leader's authoritative staff and curt command, the litter bearers immediately lowered the stubby-legged vehicle to the ground, whereupon another tribesman, inexplicably resembling his long-missed, lion-ravaged patient, stepped beside the litter and spread apart the camel skin curtains.

It was not necessary for Samuel to be aware of the crowd's laudatory gasps or Chief Balakuda's explanation to realize the significance of the exquisite vision so reverently presented before him. The wild berry wine and hearty filet of beef which, just a short while ago, had almost lulled him into an inescapable stupor seemed suddenly to be a most powerful stimulant, forcing his heart to accelerate to an unceasing, rapid beat. Unable to avert his gaze from the Zadarian people's obvious token of indebtedness, Samuel remained mute while Balakuda, in his usual falsetto voice, continued his speech which, despite the language barrier, was virtually discernable through gesture and inflection. Drinking in the cherubic features and bejeweled nakedness of such an extravagant human token, Samuel's gaze was that of an expert beholding a Renoir masterpiece, assessing corner to corner each exquisite brush stroke of a scantily-beaded skirt exposing youthful legs decorated with intricately-sketched flowers, and fingers and toes painted a vivid, orange-red. Fervently feasting upon accentuated eyes, unbridled lips and scarcely budding, painted nipples, Samuel's rapture became momentarily arrested. For majestically poised upon Wabena's cloud of loosely braided hair was an oversized ivory crown beset with raw, precious stones. Firmly held in place by a bright, beaded turban, the imperial ornament overshadowed a pound sterling-sized non-faceted ruby pendant hanging against a black canvas of subtly defined cleavage. As if confronting a beggar amidst a crowd of fashionable party guests, Samuel's ruminations evoked bygone memories of his sickly mother obsessively recounting her storybook rendition of an aristocratic, diamond-laden crown and wearily whispering endless tales of personal liaisons with His Highness, the Prince of Wales. And how could he forget the mystery of the countess' ruby and pearl necklace, that which was so abruptly snatched, along with the valuable tiara the morning of her funeral? He could still envision his distraught father, frantically careening down the winding steps of the colonial mansion, agonizing over the pillaged corpse and arguing with his Aunt Cassandra about the necessity for an immediate investigation. However, morbidly spellbinding as these recollections were, the deep, forceful voice of Tibuk immediately delivered Samuel back to the primitive ceremony at hand.

"The honorable highness, Balakuda, once again extends his most heartfelt gratitude to Doctor Samuel Governey for liberating his besieged village from the ravages of the demon lion," Tibuk translated while bowing toward the chief. "Consequently, Chief Balakuda presents to you, Samuel Governey, the most sacred and prized gift his kingdom has to offer—the virginity of this lovely young maiden. It was *her* perilous plight which determined the irreversible fate of the slain demon lion and *so*," he offered, glancing at the chief while extending a hand toward the motionless child, "it is understandably appropriate that his majesty, Chief Balakuda, along with Wabena's most respected father, bestows upon you her untarnished virtue."

Mustering full strength to restrain the slightest symptom of his abounding gratitude, Samuel tactfully smiled, lest he appear too eager to acquiesce to such a prize.

"Doctor Governey, sir...if I may," Tibuk, ending the translation, interjected, "allow me to ease any discomfort you may feel regarding the apparent youthfulness of the girl. It is an ancient tradition...yes...and under circumstances such as this, even *customary* to seal the good fortune of a village with a sacrificial offering...in this particular situation, the virginity of Wabena. Consider this the highest of compliments, Doctor Governey, for the Zadarian people offer their possessions to the gods sparingly...in supplication as well as thanksgiving, and it is a rare occurrence, indeed, that any tribe exercise such customs on behalf of mere mortals. I strongly advise you, then, sir, if I may," he cautioned, warily noticing the apparent impatience of Chief Balakuda, "that you ensure the loss of the girl's virginity by spilling the mark of her innocence. An unsoiled fleece has been placed inside your tent to confirm the consummation of this most sacred union. Again, sir...Doctor Governey, it is extremely important that you respect this most profound custom. The consequences of offending his majesty, Chief Balakuda, along with the Zadarian people are not those, I am certain, you would wish to provoke."

Inadvertently dropping the stub of his cigar, Samuel slowly rose from his seat and broke his curbed silence. "Relay to Chief Balakuda that I am deeply humbled by his magnanimous and benevolent gesture. However...however troublesome it may be for an English gentleman to concede to such an otherwise impious arrangement, I owe my allegiance to the chief and his honorable village and will, accordingly, undertake this solemn duty with the utmost care and vigilance."

Acknowledging Samuel's acceptance, Chief Balakuda raised his gnarled staff and stabbed it into the earth, whereupon Wabena's father escorted his reluctant daughter from the decorated litter, presenting her to Samuel. Then, slipping a scarlet band of woven palm fibers from his forearm, he positioned it around her neck, completely enveloping the blood-hued ruby pendant. Firmly shaking his tear-stained daughter to compliance, he stepped away, allowing the litter bearers to elevate her from the ground and place her petite body back inside the primitive carriage. With an authoritative double-clap of Chief Balakuda's hands, the four fan-bearing servants, immediately reminding Samuel of that first sweet taste of victory, hoisted their celebrated hero upon sturdy shoulders and escorted him in procession behind the curtained litter as the invigorated drummers, now accompanied by mirthful chanting, proceeded in the direction of his private tent.

If not for the lion skin spread across the damp earth floor, Samuel would not have believed he had entered his own personal quarters. Carrying Wabena within his unstrained arms, all other senses momentarily ceased to exist, except a flourishing clarity of vision aided by a circling mass of flickering candles. Scanning the oversized tent which had been stripped of nearly all its possessions, Samuel contemplated in disbelief the proficient ingenuity of the Zadarian people. Barely mindful that his camp bed had been removed, his wondering eyes imbibed a swollen, pelt-covered mattress, blanketed by an untainted fleece and canopied by rows of stringed, polished stones suspended from a frame of slender boughs. Alongside the bed stood several phallic-shaped jars, which, from the strong, sweet scent of coconut and sandalwood, he assumed to be filled with aphrodisiacs of herbs and oils. Gazing beyond this focal setting, he noticed two colorful, mosaic water basins filled to the brim atop an unfamiliar carved wooden stand, laden with soaps and fresh swatches of fleece. Finally recognizing the mirrored dressing table replete with the accustomed toiletries and the brimming wooden bathtub in its usual place, he was cognizant once more of the excited whispers emanating from the surrounding, tightly packed congregation. Aware of Wabena's bare thighs against his forearm and her jeweled, ivory crown digging through the shoulder of his silk shirt, he turned to face the small crowd which had followed him inside, anticipating an affirmative gesture to place his temporary bride upon the virginal bed. Heeding the eager nods of the multitude and outstretched arms of one of the litter bearers, Samuel strode toward the bed and, making his way through the stone-beaded curtain, gingerly placed his ebony princess atop the snowy white fleece. Recovering from his stooped position, he had hardly an opportunity to look over his shoulder before noticing that the gathering of natives were departing the tent as quickly as they had entered, stepping away from the sound of Wabena's quick, heavy breathing amidst the fading tinkle of swaying curtains.

Feeling as though he were in the middle of a staring match with a defenseless, cornered kitten, Samuel's eyes remained fixed upon the child as both of his feet remained firmly planted upon the ground. Did he dare move? Did he dare speak? If so, how would this affect his apprehensive young bride? Convinced that her irregular breathing was, indeed, becoming more prominent with every passing second, he felt a powerful inclination to reach out and subdue her. Not for her sake, but for his own. Ever since having the fortuitous opportunity of entering her musty, cramped abode and nursing her back to health, he had waited for this moment. Yes! It was all so apparent now. Perhaps he had not been so willing to fully acknowledge his desires owing to the delicacy of her youth, but it was true. He had wanted her from the very first moment he touched her. And how often had he fantasized about her? Even ravished her in his dreams? But this was not a dream. It was real. Dropped right into his lap like manna from the heavens! Cautiously observing Wabena's painted fingernails digging into the thick, white fleece as she guardedly eyed the erotic, sweet-smelling jars, Samuel wondered what

was ruminating inside her impressionable mind. Could she possibly understand what was expected of her? Had her mother schooled her chaste young
daughter as to the intimate details involved in pleasing a man? Had she sat
the fledgling child upon her lap, cupping tiny fingers within her own, carefully enumerating the unskilled maiden's carnal duties? Perhaps she had
instructed Wabena to anoint herself or *himself*, for that matter, with the herbs
and oils confined inside the sealed jars. Perhaps that and even more. But
regardless of any such tutelage, it was obviously all for naught. Considering
the wary look in Wabena's eyes along with her rigid demeanor, it was clear
that this pubescent virgin bride had no intention of offering her affections.
And, for that matter, it was all the more fine and dandy with him! The last
thing he desired was some half-naked sprout steering his sails. If there were
lessons to be taught, *he* would be the master and a most satiated one, indeed!

Temporarily indifferent to the blood-stained lion pelt against the canvas
wall, Samuel parted the beaded curtain, setting his eyes upon Wabena's red
ceremonial collar which extended beyond her lower neck, concealing tense,
stripling breasts. That tightly woven monstrosity was some sort of nonsensical custom, he was sure of it. But now, as her lord and master, he would
unshackle it immediately! Having no desire to verbally communicate with
the child in any way whatsoever, he remained quiet. Leaning over bare, slender shoulders, he had hardly begun to separate the back of the collar before
hesitating a moment. Although, as a doctor of medicine, he had previously
given Wabena a thorough examination, he had not taken notice of the soft,
black traces of hair upon the nape of her neck which, most likely due to the
child's apparent anxiety, presently seemed to be standing on end. Up until
now, he had not been the least bit concerned about any problems the current
situation might entail. Not only had the child's virginity spared him the fear
of contracting a venereal disease, but his former bout with gonorrhea, rendering him infertile, insured that he would not be mingling life-giving seeds
of British aristocracy with primal African blood. Nevertheless, at this very
moment, witnessing Wabena's frenzied breathing, he felt a sense of danger.
Could it be that she would not hesitate to lash out at him in some way? Bite
him on the neck as the Afghan bride, Roxanne, had done with Officer Daniel
Dravot? Immediately bracing himself while removing Wabena's collar,
Samuel regarded the consequences of such a savage act should it, indeed,
occur. Despite a transient sting and blood-letting puncture which a bit of
boric acid would certainly cure, there was no reason to fear that the Zadarian

people would seek revenge upon discovering his mortality. Taking into consideration that there were no witnesses aside from his bride, he reassured himself that he had never given the natives any impression that he represented anything more than the noblest form of humanity. *So,* Samuel concluded while tossing the collar upon the dirt floor, it was best to take his chances with the bite-sized tart after all, lest *he* be harshly penalized for *hindering* the shedding of blood!

Expecting to at last reclaim a closer vision of Wabena's berry-painted nipples, Samuel instead was hurled into a poignant awareness of his own afflicted childhood. As if under a deep trance, he disregarded Wabena's nakedness altogether and focused upon a certain unavoidable object. A singular adornment which made her rose-tinted nipples pale in comparison—a primitive jewel which not only emphasized the present, but ushered him into a menacing distant past. The ominous ruby stone, attached to a beaded cord, hung loosely about the child's neck. This was another ritualistic practice, he was sure of it, but one he could not treat so flippantly this time. Compelled now to glance at the slain lion despite a deep reluctance to do so, Samuel was no longer conscious of Wabena's heavy panting amidst his own sporadic breathing. Entranced by blood-smeared eye sockets and yellow-spotted, dagger-like teeth, he began to feel a sense of uncontrollable panic when suddenly he reached into his pocket, pulling from it his ever-present pearl-handled jackknife. Grasping Wabena's necklace, he cut through its cord and flung the pendant aside, whereupon the cringing child recoiled upon the virginal bed as the silk turban, which held the bejeweled crown in place, fell from her tilted head. With feet firmly entrenched, Samuel released a few remaining stifled breaths before withdrawing his attention from the child's unfettered head of black, braided hair. Apathetic to Wabena's trepidation and uncompromising position, he fingered the tip of his belt, methodically assessing the acquired trophy. Ever grateful that her trembling lower lip displayed only a mere trace of ritualistic barbarism, Samuel noticed that although the light scratches upon her cheekbone had disappeared, the deep lacerations on her quivering chin were subtly camouflaged by a tasteful display of Zadarian artistry. Retracting the tip of his leather belt from its brass buckle, he was cognizant that the slashes across Wabena's developing left breast had likewise been masked by a sampling of decorative tattoo-like sketches. Savoring the sight of enhanced, adorned nipples, he directed his gaze downward past Wabena's navel toward flawless calves, barely concealed by her disheveled beaded skirt.

Continuing to mentally assess the most secret regions of her chaste body, Samuel recalled the jagged pink scars so obviously acquired during a tribal rite which would, from there on in, ensure her everlasting apathy toward carnal pleasures. With this rousing realization in mind, he defiantly stared at his prized lion. Then, with nothing further to dread, he allowed his gabardine trousers to fall to the floor and hastily unfastened his silk underdrawers, liberating, at last, the carnal repercussions of his famished mind.

Carnivorously eyeing Wabena as she shielded her torso with muscle-tensed arms, he knelt upon the spotless white fleece, hungering to examine once again the irrevocable consequence of the child's barbaric circumcision. Mindful of her resistance, however, and not wishing to be caught off guard lest she attempt to assault him, Samuel, instead, positioned himself over her partially naked pelvis and grabbed hold of her bare shoulder, pushing her down upon the grass-stuffed mattress. Paying no heed to the black-stained tears rolling down her tightly closed eyes, he cupped his free hand over the child's painted lips to muffle the whimpering as mucus from her mouth and nose dampened his palm. Savoring the sight of her heaving, budding breasts, he basked in the imagery of jagged female flesh as he managed to wedge both kneecaps between clenched thighs, forcing his way past loose strands of beaded skirting. Feeling as if he were on an inflatable raft skirmishing rough, exhilarating waters, a sense of euphoria bubbled up inside as his engorged manhood fought its way past layers of tough scar tissue. All the more encouraged to subdue his rightful bride as her perspiring body struggled beneath the weight of his unrelenting grip, he was further inspired by a sensation he had never before experienced during intercourse. A tight, unyielding presence. A curiosity he had heard of many times over in medical school, but particularly in man-to-man conversations regarding penetration of the female sex. Yes! There must be no doubt about it! He was, indeed, experiencing the characteristic of a true virgin! Feverishly motivated by this predictable, yet startling reality, Samuel forced himself inside her, resolving to break the stubborn barrier which presently prevented the scale of urgency to shift toward ecstasy. But, to his dismay, Wabena's shield had not budged. Was it, in fact, her inexperience or her continuing stubbornness? His self contained temper on the verge of eruption, he grit his teeth and thrust forward once more with full force, this time successfully accomplishing his quest.

Briefly startled by the sudden spasm and stifled scream of his now deflowered bride, Samuel instinctively backed away. But this reflexive reaction lasted only an instant. Resuming his former position before Wabena had the chance to scurry from beneath him, he shoved her back onto the fleece stained with virginal blood, determined more than ever to take advantage of the prize he had so rightfully earned. Then, completely surrendering to his most carnal cravings, he repeatedly bore down into her. Harnessing a force much stronger than had ever been gathered by any harlot or his own eager hand, he instantaneously spilled his poisoned seeds, releasing a primal scream capable of penetrating the remotest region of any African jungle. Immediately collapsing upon the wilted torso of his conquered bride, Samuel allowed his expended body to rest a short while until the inevitable withdrawal. Receiving such a cue with a bit of reluctance, he let out a muffled sigh and rolled back upon the dampened fleece, particularly careful not to soil himself with the unfamiliar oddity of virginal blood. Then, with hardly a glance in Wabena's direction, he succumbed to a slumber as deep and gratifying as he had recently experienced after delivering his slain lion to the forever indebted villagers of Zadari.

chapter 46

Unexpected Tidings

As if the last traces of regret about departing the kingdom of Zadari had been crushed beneath the rolling wagon wheels of the mud-encrusted caravan, Samuel smiled while decapitating the tip of another cigar with his pearl-handled jackknife. Scrutinizing the blade's unusually drab appearance beneath the damp, canopied sky, he was not the least bit discouraged, anticipating the opportunity to once again prove its veracity by slicing it through a single page of newspaper; preferably, that of the *London Times*. Gingerly folding the knife and placing it inside his pocket, he then retrieved his sterling matchbox and kindled the cigar. Surrounded by the distant silhouette of majestic mountain peaks and shadowy cliffs, he adjusted his posture aside the horse master guide, grateful that his padded seat cushioned him from the distressing bumps and jolts of a long day's journey. Diverting his attention from the colorless Kenyan terrain, Samuel brought to mind the events of that final morning spent in the village of Zadari. Having been awoken by the jovial sound of bustling natives and the smell of seared meat, he noticed that Wabena, no longer lying beside him, sat breast-huddled and tight-kneed in the corner of the tent, eyeing him intensely, without uttering a sound. Somewhat amused by the girl's curious behavior, he reached for a lap robe to drape over his naked body while pushing aside a patchwork quilt of animal skins. But, no sooner had he climbed out of the grass-stuffed bed when Wabena, like a startled field mouse, skirted across the room and quickly exited the tent. Without hesitation, a handful of female natives scurried inside and, nodding profusely toward him, stripped the blood-stained fleece from the bed, whereupon another group of Zadarian women appeared, eager to tend to his morning bath.

Yes, Samuel reflected, fastidiously adjusting his Panama hat as the over-loaded wagon continued across the tree-scattered grassland. The Zadarians were certainly a peculiar lot. Although they had appropriately treated him as royalty, and ceremoniously sent him on his way, he was nevertheless looking forward to once again fraternizing among his civilized comrades back at the main camp. Upon abandoning his companions less than a week ago, he had welcomed the opportunity to leave behind Dr. Wesley Carvelle and Rupert Hines, among others, but now, especially in light of his marvelous achievement, he would surely be the envy of everyone there. And poor Mimi! How would her dear husband, Rupert, react upon discovering that his calculating wife practically handed the coveted lion over to a mere acquaintance? Appeased at the thought of his vanquished blonde nemesis trailing behind upon one of seven Basuto horses, Samuel indulged in his cigar, releasing another mouthful of smoke. As the pungent puff lingered in the dank, late morning air, he could almost see, like characters upon a cinema screen, everyone's surprised reactions. Since they would likely be arriving shortly before nightfall, taking into account the usual late afternoon pause for high tea, there would be several campfires burning. Perhaps one or two of the guides from camp would first become aware of their presence and alert the rest of the company which would promptly abandon all tasks at hand to scramble and greet them. He could imagine his delighted comrades nearing the caravan—Rupert hurriedly limping alongside the ruddy, buck-toothed Canadians, while others, like Wesley Carvelle and a few sluggish natives would choose a more casual approach. There would even be someone on horseback...on horseback? Samuel squinted. Then squinted again. Good Lord! There actually *was* someone on horseback...materializing beyond the smoke-filled air...growing in the midst of a distant swirling of dust. Samuel felt his heart racing along with the phantom equestrian's silent, urgent stride. He was not sure who the rider was or the nature of the intruder's quest, but his back stiffened as he sensed the spooking of the Basuto horses, accompanied by the rousing shouts of the wagon master. Reaching for his loaded rifle, Samuel lost his balance, almost tumbling from his seat as the wagon practically came to a bone-breaking halt. Almost instantly, the meager brigade of trackers and guides encircled the caravan with firearms in hand, dispatching a clanking of gun metal into the tranquil Nairobian air. But no sooner had Samuel's band of natives brandished their machetes and rifles, when the singular approaching bandit, sporting a dusty blue uniform along with a deflated saddlebag draped over the flank of his sweating horse, offered with upraised hand a surrendering gesture.

Immediately slackening their defensive posture as the Swahili-speaking officer dismantled his horse, the guides and trackers, chattering in indiscernible unison, concluded their brief discussion, then motioned toward Tibuk.

"Doctor Governey, sir." Tibuk began translating as the stranger reached into his weather-worn saddlebag. "This telegraph courier brings to you an urgent message. He has been directed this way by our fellow comrades back at camp."

Upon being presented a wax-sealed square of correspondence, Samuel curtly nodded. Uneasily aware of a sudden silence, he opened the message. Whatever it was, he did not know. If his travel arrangements back to England were being altered, Dr. Carvelle would surely have taken care of the matter. Perhaps the message was from a fellow army officer regarding some sort of unfinished business, or perchance, one of the resident lieutenants, weakened by a horrific bout of the influenza epidemic, had finally turned up his bloody toes. Or perhaps...perhaps....

With clenched fingers, Samuel stared at the bold black words upon the shaking page.

19 June 1919

Dr. Samuel Governey
Kenya Post Circuit
Nairobi, Kenya, Africa

Philadelphia Bank & Trust
210 Independence Street
Philadelphia, Pennsylvania

REGRET TO INFORM DR. SAMUEL GOVERNEY OF
THE DEMISE OF HIS FATHER, RANDOLPH EUGENE
GOVERNEY. IT IS IMPERATIVE YOUR PRESENCE BE
ACKNOWLEDGED IN PROBATE COURT JULY 14, 1919
TO CONTEST ALL CLAIMS TO SAID ESTATE.

With deepest sympathy and regards,
Reginald T. Morgan

So the bloody old sod had finally come through! Samuel silently reveled while staring at the sweat-stained page. That filthy son of a bitch had finally paid his dues! And there was surely something in it for his dear son after all, regardless of his empty threats! But, in an instant, Samuel's eyes darted back to the specified date in the message. JULY 14. He was to be in probate court by the 14th of July to contest all other claims to his father's estate. Why, that was hardly more than a fortnight! There was no bloody way he would make it by then. And since he and Dr. Carvelle were not scheduled to sail across the Indian Ocean from the port of Zanzibar for three more days, it would take the better of six weeks, at the least, to reach England alone, provided, of course, that he and Wesley Carvelle cancel their plans to traverse Bombay. Still clutching the telegram, he grit his teeth, aware that Tibuk, along with the other natives, awaited his response. He would somehow have to contact Mr. Morgan at the Philadelphia Bank and Trust requesting a procedural court extension. Would it be possible to send a telegraph from Zanzibar before crossing the Indian Ocean? And, if so, what if the response should be delayed before they set sail? He would never know until, perhaps, arriving in India whether or not the court had granted his request. Maybe it would be more prudent to decline the time-consuming trip by way of the Indian Ocean and take the more expedient train to Cairo instead. It was, indeed, a shorter route! Still unlikely to guarantee a timely arrival, but well worth running the rule over. He could telegraph the bank from Nairobi or Uganda and follow up in Cairo, if necessary. Yes—it was the only chance to claim what was rightfully his, he concluded, feverishly envisioning the Silver Ghost Rolls and Stutz Bear-Cat sheltered within the quaint stables of the vacant colonial mansion. Attempting to blink watery eyes into existence, Samuel broke his gaze from the damp, yellow paper and, looking up with a remorseful face, prepared to relate to his patient companions the sorrowful news of his father's demise.

chapter 47

Foreign Proposition

n a public tavern on the banks of the River Nile overlooking the mighty
pyramids of Giza, Samuel Randolph Governey choked a cup of black tea
with the palms of his sweating hands while Wesley Carvelle remained contentedly entertained by the hypnotic swaying of an Egyptian belly-dancer.
Although under a different set of circumstances Samuel may have found the
sable-haired entertainer and her accompanying Arabian musician somewhat
amusing, he presently was in no mood to appreciate this bare-footed woman
who most certainly was well into her middle twenties. Unlike cultured ladies
reminiscent of his early childhood, sweeping spacious marble floors with
flowing layers of satin and lace, this poor excuse of a dancer looked more like
an advertisement for dime store drapery purchased with the fabricated gold
coins upon her hips and arms which jangled like a roomful of malfunction-
ing cash registers. Seeking some reprieve from this distasteful display of
eurhythmics, Samuel turned toward a windowless seating area, scrutinizing a
German soldier in dusty aviator attire who, after lunching on ground lamb
and fried potatoes, had settled against the long brittle back of an unvarnished
chair, sucking the life from a cigarette plucked out of a near-empty package
of Lucky Strikes. What the hell was a bloody scar-faced Kraut doing with a
package of American-brand cigarettes and a fifth of Russian vodka? Samuel
scowled, tapping his sorely neglected fingernails against the table's hard surface. And why wasn't he wearing civilian clothes? The war was over, wasn't it?
Then why didn't the bastard just get on with his bloody goddamned life? As

his personal predicament weighed on his brain like a pair of mud-soaked army boots, Samuel's eyes wandered to a clerk inside an adjoining room which served as a telegraph office. It had been almost three hours since relaying his message to Mr. Morgan at the Philadelphia Bank and after checking on its status every ten minutes or so, it seemed most uncertain that a response would be forthcoming any time soon. Upon reaching for his shirt pocket, Samuel suddenly made a conscious effort to stop the impulsive gesture; his mouth felt like an overstuffed humidor. Wincing, he turned toward the filmy, scratched window set within the long stone wall of the men's tavern, reflecting upon the foul luck he had encountered in Africa. Unable to communicate with the civilized world while stranded in Nairobi due to an unmanned telegraph office, his subsequent attempts were also crippled in Uganda because of an abrupt electrical storm. Wary of wasting more precious time, he and Dr. Carvelle decided to immediately undergo the nauseating train ride to Cairo—and now this! Fuming with disgust, he found himself gazing past two complacent camels roped to a sagging palm, discerning beyond the desolate sand hills the faint outlines of distant pyramids. Though obviously remote, he suddenly felt their intrusion, struck by the peculiar thought that though this be the second time traversing this ancient city, he had yet to fully witness the most magnificent of the world's seven wonders. Continuing to focus upon the miniature white shadows, he experienced an uneasy sense of inferiority upon realizing that his own presence was but a grain of sand compared to the vast desert of time these archaic structures had endured. To be virtually eternal! How could anything be grander? It was a revelation he had never before experienced and, until now, one which had never proclaimed such emphatic significance.

Thrown again into his crude surroundings by what seemed to be an invasion of silence, Samuel was suddenly aware, by the buzzing of two overhead electrical fans, that the perspiring belly dancer, along with the spirited accompanist, had temporarily halted her solicitations. As if purposely attempting to avoid the adulations of his smitten traveling companion, he excused himself from Dr. Carvelle's presence and sauntered a few steps toward the telegraph office. Painfully aware of the clerk's inability to comprehend more than a few civilized words, let alone the King's English, he once again captured the Egyptian's attention with a contrived cough, which was sluggishly acknowledged with a mere shrug of the shoulders. No longer able to contain his patience, Samuel began raising his voice, verbalizing in his

Majesty's English the importance of receiving a timely reply and demanding that the message be re-submitted. But no sooner had he perceived that he had failed utterly to communicate with the inept clerk, when he was startled by a heavily-accented voice and a firm tap on the shoulder. Spinning on his heels almost immediately, Samuel found himself face to face with the German aviator who, discharging a few broken phrases of English through a layer of vodka-laden breath, made it emphatically clear that he was likely in a position to be of assistance. Inviting Samuel to be seated at his table, the German pulled out a chair for his British guest, and stooped to retrieve a mail bag, withdrawing from one of its side pockets a large, tattered map.

Eyeing the rough outline of the Mediterranean regions, Samuel experienced a glimmer of hope while noticing a lucrative gleam in the German's lashless eyes. Though still somewhat wary of the aviator's ability to mitigate his present dilemma or, even more, his own willingness to adopt the inevitable solution, he felt that a request for a procedural court extension may not be necessary after all. Accepting the Ace's benevolent, yet crass gesture of hospitality by occupying the offered chair, Samuel expressed his gratitude in the German tongue before proceeding in English.

"Allow me to introduce myself," Samuel said with a firm handshake. "Doctor Samuel Governey, former captain of the British Army. Third Division."

"Likevise, Captain," the German answered, puffing up his uniformed, decorated chest. "My name is Hans. Major Hans Pfifer. Former adversary of the allied forces, yet...as fate vould have it, presently facilitating the needs of those who have risen to the status of my fellow comrades. Come..." he asserted, loosening his grip and snapping his fingers for a waiter. "Share a glass of vodka vile ve discuss this forthcoming venture. After all, under my commission, ve shall be spending a great many hours together."

Samuel cautiously eyed the major as he commanded the waiter to fetch a glass, taking an instant dislike to the arrogant fellow. Yes, he fervently desired to reach England and book a transatlantic cruise for America before the week was out, but for this overgrown rendition of the Red Baron to readily assume that he, Doctor Samuel Governey, captain of the British Army, would, without a doubt, accept the services of a pompous piece of war residue, he was quite over the edge. And furthermore, he surmised, observing that the scar along the German's cheekbone had appeared to double in size...perhaps traveling by air was not his cup of tea. Yes, indeed, he quivered as Hans proceeded to further spread open the deeply creased map. Although he had faced a multitude of tribulations during the past several years while serving as a doctor in the British Army and...by the grace of God...had successfully hunted down the fiercest of beasts in the wilds of Africa...he was, after all, familiar with these newfangled flying contraptions solely from *terra firma*. And though the hawk-necked fighter pilot certainly appeared competent enough to handle such a mission, could he be relied on to soberly navigate through treacherous Mediterranean skies?

"As I see it," the German major barked, breaking Samuel's train of thought, "the surest vay to reach the British Isles vould be to follow a direct route over the Mediterranean Sea to the Isle of Crete. Upon refueling and a night's rest," he pointed out, stabbing the map with claw-like fingers, "ve shall continue on to Catania, Sicilia; then, Florenzia, Frankfurt and," with one resolute stab of the fingers, "our final destination...London. You vill find my fee is quite reasonable, Captain Governey," Major Pfeiffer added, pausing for a moment as the waiter placed a short, wide glass upon the table and removed some dirty dinnerware. The major then continued, filling Samuel's glass with the Russian vodka. "Considering the maintenance on my 'Rottweiler' and the fuel required for such a great distance," he mentally calculated, gritting squared, chalky teeth, "1500 German marks vich vould amount to...485 British pounds. Yes!" Hans declared, offering Samuel the smudged glass of Smirnoff, "485 British pounds. That is my price. You vill take it or leave it," he bluntly stated, pounding his fist into the table, then resolutely folding the coffee-stained map. "I do not haggle like the Jews, Captain Governey, so if you vill, please make your decision immediately and spare my valuable time."

Somewhat taken aback by the outrageous fee, yet disinclined to divulge his feelings on the matter, Samuel, emphatically aware that the bottle of Smirnoff had been repeatedly contaminated by the major's impudent lips, took a curt drink from the glass and swiftly set it back upon the table. Though deeming the German's aversion to dickering rather admirable, he was not fond of being pressured into making such a hasty decision. After all, even though the exorbitant fee surely was affordable, he was still quite uncertain about the whole bloody prospect of spending hours on end in a most constrictive space, smothered in stifling aviator gear, scads of meters above the bloody earth in God knows what sort of hazardous weather. And what about Dr. Carvelle? Samuel silently questioned, glancing over at his traveling companion who was, by now, dozing off, open-mouthed in his creaking chair. Surely, there would be no room for an extra passenger on the two-seated bi-plane. He would have to go the remainder of the journey on his own, likewise accompanying all of their belongings. But before Samuel could further weigh the viable venture, the major broke in.

"I can assure you, Captain Governey, that my piloting skills far exceed excellence. As an expert under the command of Kaiser Vilhelm the Second, I have been awarded several medals of honor in aerial combat under the most appalling conditions. Surely, if I possess the capacity to accomplish such wartime feats, I can certainly achieve the rudimentary task of navigating my 'Rottweiler' on a routine trip across our heavens."

Guardedly sizing up the German major one final time as he took another boorish swig from the fifth of Russian vodka, Samuel glanced at his own filled glass and then over to Wesley Carvelle who was still fast asleep. Politely excusing himself and informing the major that he would return shortly, he then returned to his original table, leaned over the dozing doctor and, with a gentle shake and the sound of his name, awakened him.

chapter 48

First Flight

Sitting atop a jiggling mailbag in the cockpit of a Junker 802 J.I., flying at an altitude of 700 feet and a speed of 90 miles per hour, Samuel Governey welcomed the sight of land gradually spreading beneath wide silver wings. The world's first all-metal biplane, having so far successfully executed her mission, crossed the English Channel and was now heading toward London. Disdainfully neglecting a converted canteen urinal while plagued by an aching back and wind-burned face, Samuel tried to relax amid the deafening vibration of the biplane's Benz engine and propeller blades, attempting to make the last leg of the horrendous journey as comfortable as possible despite days of being subjugated to the shackles of hell. With the taste of hot oil forever assailing his palate, he cocked back his helmeted head despite a crackling sore neck and closed his goggle-encased eyes. It was fortunate, he acknowledged, recalling a half dozen or so discarded vomit-filled bags, that when first starting off, he had not imagined the true extent of such an endeavor. Otherwise, he may have rejected Major's Hans Pfeiffer's offer and foregone the opportunity to claim the remainder of his father's estate. Granted, the novelty of traveling from one destination to the next without the aid of land or sea did leave one in a merry pin, particularly during take-off. But, like a young lad initially enamored with a bonny schoolmarm, he was soon disillusioned by the Rottweiler's stern, cantankerous disposition. And he should have known better than to trust a Kraut, he grimaced, further regretting that his voluntary confinement had made it nearly impossible to enjoy any of his Cuban cigars. The cunning son-of-a-bitch was not only earning a handsome fee from a civilian passenger, but making double the amount delivering bags of bloody mail in the process, hardly leaving his fellow passenger enough room for the smallest of traveling bags. And then the traitorous bastard makes a paid holiday out of the well-timed deal by cavorting with his mates in Frankfurt! Attempting to ease a crick in his neck, he felt satisfied about the decision to considerably trim an otherwise handsome gratuity; he would have abandoned the journey altogether after the first 1,000 kilometers, he huffed, had it not been for a taste of civilization on the Island of Crete, where, after a quick jaunt to a Tobacconist's shop and a wine merchant, he indulged in a hearty meal, a good night's rest and engaging dreams about a Silver Ghost Rolls and Stutz Bear-Cat.

Having curbed his temper for the meantime, Samuel's musings veered to the French Gregoire he had left behind at Dr. Carvelle's private abode just outside the city of London. He had reluctantly authorized one of the neighbor gents to give the war-torn roadster a brief spin every week or so to keep it up and running so there should be no problem with it. Nevertheless, perhaps she may still need a bit of coaxing upon his return, he thought, envisioning himself behind the lackluster steering wheel while gingerly starting her well-used engine. In any case, he concluded, shifting his weight upon the lumpy mailbag, whatever her condition, he was growing forever impatient to experience the luxury of traveling from place to place without consistently encountering the brutal bombardment of elements—whether they be natural or man-made.

Eagerly anticipating the Junker's arrival in London, Samuel recalled his decision to promptly contact a local travel agency and schedule a first-class cabin on a luxury ocean liner, facilitating a serene passage to America. Of course, he also would inquire into the possibility of shipping the roadster overseas so that he needn't be concerned for hours on end with filthy taxis and their nosey drivers. It had, indeed, crossed his mind to make all the necessary traveling arrangements from Florence or Frankfurt, but skeptical of the competency of these lesser Europeans, concluded it best to wait it out for two or three days. After all, he still had a good fortnight to play with. But first and foremost upon his arrival in London, he would nevertheless engage a taxi to Dr. Wesley Carvelle's in nearby Brentford. There he would bathe and change into some decent clothing and then, hopefully, get the roadster going for a drive to the Crown Travel Agency in Richmond. And perhaps he would visit his old barracks before the day was out. Attempting to relieve a cramp in his lower right leg, he wondered how Dr. Carvelle was getting along. Was he managing the baggage alright? Had he even crossed the Mediterranean? Hopefully, his cherished lion would withstand the long journey. He was glad of his decision not to have the priceless trophy reconstructed after all. Otherwise, the oversized parcel may have been too large and fragile for transport. Nevertheless, it was fortunate that Dr. Carvelle was willing to part ways. Coincidentally, he had seemed a bit relieved at the prospect of traveling at his own leisure. Of course, Samuel simpered, with all that extra body weight to drag about, he would not be surprised if the good doctor decided, with every opportunity, to plop down in whatever quarters he was assigned, breaking the self-imposed stalemate only to eat his supper or visit the latrine.

Ever aware of his own needling bladder, Samuel stretched against the side of the biplane, cocked his head and peered down. They had set out bright and early in the morning, as usual, and the weather had likewise been favorable, but now a misty, overcast sky enveloped what appeared to be miles of multicolored patchwork interspersed among long stretches of vivid green. Instantaneously recognizing the all-too-familiar phenomenon as London fog, his heart skipped a beat. Never in all the years spent in Britain had he ever welcomed this perpetual manifestation! Gazing through the creeping vapor at tiny tilled fields awakened by the dogged rays of a mid-afternoon sun, he grew increasingly impatient, guessing his exact location. Perhaps they were flying over the countryside of Canterbury or, could it be that they were already nearing Chatham? It was impossible to tell. Recognizing the futility of harping upon such a silly guessing game, Samuel repositioned himself within the cockpit and shut his eyes, concluding that there was nothing much else to do but wait for the Rottweiler to take its final bite.

No sooner had he settled in like a caged animal succumbing to the acute commands of a forceful master, then Samuel was suddenly startled by the newly acquired feeling of falling through space. Flinging his eyes wide open while once again enduring the unpleasant popping of the ears, he wrenched his lean torso over the edge of the cockpit as the biplane began its descent. Observing a drastic change in the landscape, he was struck powerless in curbing the widest grin ever to cross his countenance. For directly below him, where just a few minutes ago lay miles of cultivated farmland, there suddenly appeared, like a magician's transformation, the ancient River Thames, snaking its way along rows of shingled rooftops bordering tree-lined streets.

His heart pumping with anticipation, he identified, like flies on a bull's tail, an occasional automobile or horse-drawn carriage moving at a snail's pace. Fixating sea-blue eyes upon the genuine cinematic spectacle, Samuel's jaw dropped as the biplane, taking a sudden turn, hovered above lush gardens and cupola-capped cathedrals until briefly, after bypassing Kensington Palace, the Tower of London and the famous landmark tower of Big Ben, prepared itself for one final harrowing landing.

chapter 49

Sentimental Reunion

Leaning forward upon the flaked leather interior of a British taxicab, Samuel reached into the pocket of his oil-speckled safari trousers, pulled out a gold, initialed money clip and tipped the driver generously, grateful that the elderly hireling had recognized his place and minded his own business. Grabbing his overstuffed traveling bag, he stepped off the corrugated sideboard of the boxy black vehicle and onto a familiar cobblestone walkway, catching his breath as the sound of the taxi's tired engine ambled on its way. Looking straight ahead toward Dr. Wesley Carvelle's modest estate while blotting beads of sweat from his heated forehead, a lump of nostalgia arrested his throat. He had managed so far: he had endured the half-hour drive without the least bit of mawkish emotion. But now, the fangs of sentimentality began gnawing at his bones, castigating him for abandoning a place so near and dear to his heart. Feeling as if the ground beneath him was giving way, Samuel proceeded to walk toward an old refurbished barn situated just 20 yards or so from Dr. Carvelle's Tudor style home. As his battered hunting boots sank into the moist, resilient grass, his eyes remained fixed upon the barn's wide, latched door. Stepping more resolutely now while nearing it, he felt the perspiration trickling down his breastbone, then clinging to his yellowed cotton shirt, but became oblivious to the irritating sensation as his humid fingers, nimble as a prolific spinner's, finally reached out to unfasten the bulky, rusted clamp. Like a loving father about to awaken his son from a restful nap, he carefully pulled open the heavy door, conjuring a slow, steady creak. Having barely exposed the contents of the barn's hidden treasure to the stunning brightness of the midday sun, he could already discern within the shadowy walls a pair of brass-encased headlights attached to a white cylindrical frame. With one final shove of the wooden door, the French Gregoire, which he had backed into the painted barn over six months ago was once again revealed in all its naked splendor.

Somewhat breathless, Samuel stared at the roadster in reverent silence. It was as if he were confronting an aging mistress. Though still remarkably appealing, the dependable sports car which had abundantly shared her endless charms during the past several years seemed to have lost her youthful glow. Placing the traveling bag upon the barn's dirt floor, he reached into his trousers, pulled out his bill book and wedged from the secret pocket alongside his pearl-handled jackknife, the roadster's ignition key. Overstepping the generous sideboard of the topless vehicle, he slipped inside and sat down, restlessly fondling the enameled steering wheel. With an eager hand he inserted the key into the ignition, stepped on the clutch and held his breath. A sluggish clatter resounded as he turned the key and, for an extended moment, Samuel's hopes sank like a set of tires in a mud-filled ditch. Reverting the key to its starting position, he once again turned over the engine, all the while coaxing the stubborn vehicle with urgent, persuasive pleas. As the roadster continued to display no apparent change in temperament, Samuel nearly surrendered the prospect of indulging in a brief jaunt about the outskirts of London when, as if having been resuscitated by a physician's persevering strokes, she let out a brief cough, followed by a prolonged, escalating roar. Ecstatically maneuvering the stick shift into first gear, Samuel slowly released the clutch while stepping on the gas pedal, rolling the humming vehicle onto Wesley Carvelle's thriving green lawn.

Extremely satisfied that his Gregoire was in secure operating condition, Samuel once again stepped on the clutch and brought the vehicle to a halt. Immediately exiting the doorless roadster, he backed away, viewing his cherished possession with full benefit of broad daylight. Revealing an erratic frown, he nearly choked under a sudden spell of endearment. How bloody good it was to be back! And how, until this very moment, had he not realized the full measure of his homesickness. Resisting the urge to jump back inside the idle convertible and cruise the countryside until sunset, he began instead to slowly pace alongside the roadster, assessing its condition. Yes, he sighed, shaking his head, observing the fine scratches along its sleek, white body. Four long years of war-torn roads and six months of virtual stagnation had surely taken its toll. And patches of discoloration on the brown suede seats certainly revealed its endless hours of faithful service. Walking toward the front of the roadster, he extended his hand, caressing the brass frames around the front grill and headlights. A good polish was in order. And the tires. They would need replacing again. Feeling a twinge of guilt at the prospect of trading her in for a new model, Samuel nevertheless entertained the idea for a moment. Owning a new motor car *would* be jolly pleasant. Perhaps something a bit more modest this time around. Like the American-made Stanley or the sportier Wood Mobilette. And since he was on his way to the states, it would, indeed, be the ideal time to purchase either automobile. But, suddenly questioning the velocity of the Stanley while bringing to mind the boxier style of the Mobilette, he furrowed his sun-bleached brows. Maybe he should hold off until his financial situation was more concrete. After all, the money he had inherited from his grandfather had dwindled considerably over the last six months. And although he was the rightful heir to his father's American estate, there was no guarantee of capital ample enough to ensure an aristocratic lifestyle until he secured lucrative employment, let alone the funds to purchase a spanking new vehicle. Of course, on the other hand, he reasoned, blotting his wrinkled forehead with a damp handkerchief, if he should discover that his father's estate was, indeed, the golden egg, he would not only purchase another motor car, but pay on the nail for a skilled technician to refurbish the Gregoire. Regardless, he resolved, he would carry on his plan to ship the roadster overseas and let the hands of fate orchestrate her eventual tune.

Impatient to take the roadster for a test drive, Samuel glanced at his wrist watch, disappointed by how quickly the time had passed. Looking toward the side entrance of the Tudor, he squinted, briefly focusing upon the shriveled Christmas wreath hanging from the weather-beaten door. Then, after stepping back into the barn to retrieve his traveling bag, he walked toward the private residence, anticipating a refreshing shower and a clean change of clothing before his impending visit to the Crown Travel Agency.

chapter 50

A Slight Delay

Surmising that heaven itself could not match the exhilarating experience of maneuvering the French Gregoire down a cobblestone road lined with orderly street signs and flower filled storefronts of a recovering, post-war town, Samuel came to a temporary halt, allowing a bobby on horseback to cross to the other side of the avenue. Basking in supple Italian calfskin shoes pressed against the clutch and brake pedal, an unerring grin crossed his sun-tanned face as he reflected upon the ability of finely woven, smartly styled fabric meticulously outfitted upon a gentleman's virile physique to elevate one's sagging spirits. Still able to smell the clean fragrance of English oatmeal soap emanating from his freshly showered body and perfumed pomade dressing upon his coppery, wind-teased hair, he reflected upon the array of suits and casual wear which Dr. Carvelle had allowed him to store in his home after being dismissed from the English Armed Forces. It was jolly good of him to offer his assistance in that respect, he thought, forcing the convertible into first gear as the trotting thoroughbred and its jack-booted rider cleared the road. Since he had no residence of his own for the time being, it was bloody convenient to have a place in which to abide and keep his cherished possessions, as well as those forthcoming from the African expedition.

Steering the roadster onto Kent road, Samuel slowed down a bit as he approached his destination, his attention arrested by a young fellow on a step ladder adjusting a newly fashioned signboard. Deeming it unnecessary to read the obstructed sign, he parked the Gregoire in front of the travel agency which he had visited several times while planning his long-past journey to India. Re-positioning his haircloth hat and tugging upon his peaked-lapel jacket, he then exited the Gregoire, smoothing the wrinkles from his cuffed, silk-woven trousers. Satisfied with his appearance, he once again directed his gaze toward the shop, observing the dutiful apprentice descending the ladder. Despite the bold black lettering identifying the Crown Travel Agency, his attention was immediately drawn to the billboard's focal point, majestically carved within the crest-shaped sign. Instantly severing his gaze from the ivory crown beset with ruby-like stones, he instinctively paused for a moment to catch his breath. Then, acknowledging the young lad's courteous salutation, he forged straight ahead, opened the brass-trimmed door, and walked inside.

Stepping upon a Louis XV Savonniere carpet, Samuel removed his hat and ambled inside the reception area which was solely occupied by the cheerful trill of a warbler wafting through a partially open, curtained window. Eyeing a Regency sideboard replete with a full tea service and an assortment of finger sandwiches, jellies, and butter scones, he seated himself upon a colorful sofa adjacent to a tulipwood desk which supported an Emerson typewriter, a candlestick telephone, and other clerical items. With hardly a chance to comprehend the congenial memories invoked by such familiar surroundings, Samuel was suddenly distracted by a nasal voice which he recognized as belonging to Miss Audrey Farnsworth.

"Greetings, Captain Governey, greetings!" heralded a woman of slender bosom, impeccably dressed in a black-buttoned business suit, extending unadorned, pencil-like fingers. "How handsome you look in your civilian clothes. But it's been too long. Much too long, indeed!"

"It most certainly has, my dear Miss Farnsworth," Samuel replied, standing at once while bending over to kiss the woman's liver-spotted hand, filling his nostrils with the scent of cold cream.

"Pray tell, Captain Governey," the proprietress blushed, flattening together the palms of her hands. "What have you been about this past year? Or has father time, indeed, denied me of your most gracious presence even longer than I had supposed?"

"My dear Miss Farnsworth," he answered, noting that despite tightly-laced shoes and dark silk stockings, rising hemlines were, nevertheless, becoming much too absurd. "To be precise, I have retired myself from your most exquisite company for nearly one year, since the time I had arranged to attend the wedding of Colonel Bharat's daughter in India," he said, briefly waving his haircloth hat. "Then, approximately six months ago, shortly following the culmination of the war, I had the most unique opportunity of embarking upon an excursion down the River Nile followed by a pre-arranged safari in Nairobi. But," Samuel straightforwardly rectified, hastily pointing his ringless forefinger, "all accommodations had been scheduled by my good colleague, Dr. Wesley Carvelle who, despite my repeated pleas to utilize your most wise and informative guidance, was nevertheless determined to employ his accustomed means of counsel."

Audrey Farnsworth tenderly placed her hand upon Samuel's squared, tailored shoulder and shook her stiffly coifed head. "My dear Captain Governey...there is no need for apologies. As a devoted agent of the travel industry, I quite well comprehend the inevitability of such unavoidable circumstances. Now then," she resolutely stated, turning toward the bountiful sideboard and reaching for a globular teapot, "enough said about these unpalatable formalities. Indulge yourself in a cup of tea. A slice of Battenberg cake, perhaps?"

"Yes. That would be most delightful, indeed," Samuel replied, observing the dutiful dowager preparing his tea exactly to his liking, thinking it a bloody shame that most women who chose to occupy themselves in any particular line of business were destined to remain spinsters.

"And you must sample some of these high tea sandwiches," Miss Farnsworth insisted, scooping the triangular-shaped fare onto a flowery, gilt-edged plate.

Samuel recalled the greasy frankfurter and dry roll he had scoffed down on the biplane. "Please. That would be so kind of you."

Carefully setting the refreshments atop the upmost corner of the desk, Miss Farnsworth, still standing, invited Samuel to sit upon a corresponding padded tulipwood armchair, then proceeded to pour a cup of tea for herself. "So, Captain Governey, I take it that traveling agrees with you, seeing that you have just returned from a most expeditious journey and are once again well-equipped to utilize my services. Or," she jested with a teasing wink and snorting laugh, "do you relish my companionship with such undying magnitude?"

"My dear, dear Miss Farnsworth," Samuel answered, replacing his cup and saucer upon the desk while reaching for the plate of sandwiches, "you are undoubtedly a most gracious and obliging lady, and I am confident that I would enjoy the pleasure of your company under even the most appalling of situations, yet, I must admit, as recent, unpredictable circumstances have dictated, I find myself in dire need of booking a round-trip cruise to America."

"Well!" Audrey Farnsworth exclaimed, placing her own cup and saucer opposite Samuel before clapping her hands. "I should have suspected as much. Very well, then," she added, studiously taking her place behind the desk. "I am most delighted to be at your service! Let's see...," she rambled, donning a pair of rimless spectacles and opening a ledger. "A regal suite on Cunard's *Mauretania* would be ideal for you. She departs from Liverpool, but if you do not mind traveling the required distance, it will be an experience of a lifetime and surely one you will never regret!"

Recalling his disastrous journey to Cheshire and reluctant to follow the same wretched route once again in the Gregoire, Samuel swallowed the last bite of his sandwich before replying. "Are there no departures from Southampton then?"

Why yes, of course...," Miss Farnsworth, disillusioned by Samuel's unexpected rebuff, prudently responded, ceasing to comb through the page at hand and turning to another section of the ledger. "If you so prefer, I can book you with the White Star line." Pursing thin lips while running her finger down a neatly penned page, she then paused. "There are some first-class staterooms available on her majesty's ship, the *Britannic* as soon as the second of August. I shall reserve a place for you immediately if you so wish."

Hastily setting his teacup back on its saucer, Samuel tensed his back and leaned forward. "Forgive me, Miss Farnsworth, but I am afraid I have failed to articulate the urgency of my situation. I must arrive in America no later than July 14th, although I would prefer to arrive even sooner if at all possible."

"Oh dear! I am afraid this may present a problem," she stated, looking up at Samuel, knitting pencil-lined brows. "As of this morning, all first-class accommodations have been booked for the month of July. Why...if you had made the same request last year, I would have easily accommodated you, but now that the war has ended, people have been most eager to take advantage of our luxury cruises. Even second-class accommodations are difficult to come by, but, if you would like, I could inquire into the possibility of any cancellations."

"And the *Mauretania*?" Samuel responded, letting out a sigh of resignation. "Is she not available, then?"

"I am afraid not, Captain Governey. The *Mauretania* is the most popular ship afloat nowadays. I doubt she even has a *third*-class cabin available. However...," Miss Farnsworth hesitated, clicking the tips of her enameled fingernails, "there is a Blue Star line of ships which departs from Liverpool. Although I do not normally deal with that particular company, I will be most happy to inquire into the status of their schedule. Mind you, however, that their accommodations, though certainly adequate, undermine the excellent standards to which you are accustomed."

Remaining silent for a moment, Samuel set his tepid cup of tea on the desk and donned a persuasive smile. "My dear, dear Miss Farnsworth...is there not anything you can arrange for me? You see," he forlornly whispered, "I have just been informed of my dear father's death and I must see to it that he be given a decent and proper burial."

"Why, Captain Governey! I am so sorry to hear of your recent loss!" she remarked while setting down her teacup. "Under the circumstances, I can surely understand your desire to reach America in the briefest possible time. However...your most unfortunate dilemma only serves to foster the deep regret I already feel regarding my inability to accommodate your needs. I shall, however, be most persistent about inquiring as to any cancellations."

Suddenly realizing that the opened window had not been sufficient enough to ventilate the shading room, Samuel removed a fresh handkerchief from his pocket and briskly wiped his sweating forehead. "Is there not anything at all you can do, then? If it is a matter of money..."

"Why good heavens, no, Captain Governey! Money is of no consequence! I assure you that if it were within my power to accommodate your wishes, I should not accept a farthing more for rendering my most loyal assistance!"

Attempting to contain his exasperation, Samuel focused upon his untouched piece of Battenberg cake, recognizing that given the chance to contract with the appropriate party, anything could be purchased for the right price. "Excuse me, my dear Miss Farnsworth," he apologized while rising from his seat, "but I did not mean to imply that you would in any way compromise your most honorable integrity. On the contrary, I sincerely appreciate your generous offer to look further into the matter and trust that you will do whatever possible to secure for me the best available accommodations. Until then," he said while reaching into his bill book for a calling card, "given the lateness of the hour and the fact that there is nothing to be done until morning, I shall be on my way. You may reach me at this number. Good day and God save!" Upon giving Audrey Farnsworth the customary kiss on the hand, Samuel departed her company and stepped out into the enveloping dusk, determined that, first thing in the morning, he would look into taking his business elsewhere.

chapter 51

Abrupt Correspondence

An exceptionally bright morning sun, unhindered by the usual veil of fog, flooded through the front door window and into the untended vestibule of Dr. Wesley Carvelle's residence as Samuel sprinted down the main staircase. His stomach growling in anticipation of a professionally cooked breakfast of curried eggs, creamed codfish on toast and sectioned grapefruit, he was suddenly distracted by several diversely sized envelopes littering the lackluster parquet floor. Immediately identifying the scattered obstacles as postal correspondence which had been deposited through the mail chute of the entrance way door, he bent over to gather them up, wondering how long they had been lying there. Having previously used the back stairwell yesterday, he had neglected to check the anterior of the house. Conscious of a dusty chestnut console which lined the papered wall of the tastefully furnished foyer and contemplating that Dr. Carvelle would be well off to arrange for a good housecleaning soon after his return from the Mediterranean, he was about to place the letters atop the Chippendale when his attention was suddenly drawn to his own name handwritten in familiar penmanship which, in accordance with the return address, he immediately recognized as belonging to his former commanding officer, Major General Evan T. Briggs. Placing the rest of the correspondence down, he located a letter opener within one of the console drawers and sliced through the envelope's earmarked seal. Then, eagerly unfolding its contents, his eyes focused below the notable letterhead:

June 16, 1919

"Greetings, Captain Governey and welcome back to our beloved homeland! I trust your journey was more pleasant than not, but, of primary importance, allow me to offer my most sincere condolences on the death of your dear father, Randolph Eugene Governey. It was upon the inquiry of Mr. Reginald T. Morgan from the Philadelphia Bank & Trust that I learned of your unfortunate loss. Please forgive me if my disclosure of your whereabouts was indiscreet; however, I determined it of the utmost urgency that you be notified under such circumstances. On a more uplifting note, I hope you are well inclined to pay me a visit at our barracks as I am in possession of a letter which was entrusted to me by your most devoted comrade, Colonel Tayib Bharat, who likewise has asked me to forward his condolences and assures me that he is presently in a position to offer you a most favorable proposition which, in your bereaved state of mind, you may wish to decline. However, I suspect, at the risk of overstepping my bounds, that this proposition may well be worth your serious consideration. Consequently, I look forward to enjoying your good company once again. You shall most likely find me stationed within my usual quarters or undertaking my customary rounds about the infirmary.
Very sincerely yours, Evan T. Briggs."

No longer intent on curing his morning hunger pangs, Samuel refolded the letter and placed it back in the envelope. A proposition? Colonel Tayib Bharat had a proposition to offer? As far as he was concerned, the calculating turban-top was back in India where he rightfully belonged. So whatever, in the name of heaven, could this mean? Another pregnant daughter, perhaps?! No...It was preposterous. Whatever did he have up his bloody sleeve, then? Perhaps a promising medical position? In India? Samuel tapped the edge of the envelope against his pulsing wrist. They would have to drag him onto a boxcar and then strap him inside one of their filthy infirmaries before that occurred. *If* that was, indeed, what the colonel intended to propose. But what if it was not? Perhaps it was something he hadn't thought of. Something that may be well worth looking into. After all, Major Briggs was certainly advocating the suggestion. And although the major general had a tendency to be dogmatic, he did, nevertheless, respect the old soldier's opinion. Furthermore, simple curiosity was beginning to get the better of him. *Yes,*

Samuel concluded, stuffing the folded envelope inside the inner pocket of his waist seam coat. He would visit the barracks straight after breakfast and then proceed with his plan to locate a more obliging travel service. Repositioning his Moroccan leather belt, he gazed into a mahogany-framed mirror, then straightened his dotted necktie and adjusted his chocolate-colored Derby. After smoothing out his flawlessly creased pants, he unlocked the front door, stepped onto the arched porch and started on his way.

chapter 52

General Reunion

U neasily aware of the grey clouds forming above him while recalling the discouraging forecast predicted by a barometer inside the prestigious restaurant he had just patronized, Samuel stared for a moment at the rear compartment of the Gregoire. Having discovered no trace of General Briggs inside the officer's private quarters where he was now parked, his only other option was to either go through the trouble of covering the open roadster with the canvas cloth and take the short walk to the infirmary, or parking the vehicle in front of the infirmary where he could keep an eye on it. Deciding upon the latter option, he once again jumped inside the roadster and drove the short yet equally nostalgic distance.

Feeling a bit of a trespasser in his civilian clothes, Samuel removed his hat, took a deep breath and pried open the creaky wooden door which led to the small entranceway of the multi-windowed infirmary. Immediately stricken by the all-too-familiar smell of alcohol mingling with the stench of dried blood and warm sweat, he was suddenly taken aback by two long rows of beds which, with the exception of those nearer to the doorway, were occupied by a strange breed of wounded soldiers. Focusing his attention upon a rotund Red Cross nurse in the process of sponge bathing her patient, he pondered the reason for such a busy ward when, in fact, the war was over and the infirmary virtually should have been empty. Looking away from the preoccupied caregiver, he glanced toward a set of doors at the other end of the ward and wondered if perhaps Major General Briggs was engaged in the operating room. Proceeding to walk straight ahead, his echoing steps were suddenly interrupted by a bold, boyish voice accosting him from the rear.

"Ya lookin' for the big cheese, kiddo?"

Defensively spinning around, Samuel found himself face to face with a grinning lad in a body cast, obviously American and no more than 18 years old, supported by a pair of crutches, with stained bandages covering all of his forehead and most of one cheek. "I beg your pardon, young man," Samuel retorted, his rankled mood softening upon observing the intoxicated fellow's contracted pupils.

"Major General Briggs, sir! He just went in the operatin' room," the lad offered, awkwardly removing one arm from the crutch and pointing toward the end of the hall, nearly toppling over. "'Cept no one's bein' cut on today. I'll go get him for ya!"

"That will be quite unnecessary," Samuel quickly responded, positioning his hand on the boy's shoulder to catch his fall. "I know my way perfectly well around here. I shall address the major general myself. Thank you, private."

"But I know right where he is! Really! Everything's jake. The walk will do me dandy! Lookie here," the young soldier insisted, hobbling over to the foot of his bed and pointing to a rumpled newspaper. "Get a read on the news while yer waitin'. Sit your can down—I'll be back before ya can say 'Jack Robinson'!"

Being deprived of the opportunity for further objection, Samuel was left with no recourse but to watch the convalescing doughboy scamper down the corridor. *Methylmorphine,* he mused as the patient struggled to open one of the heavy double doors. *Briggs must have given him the optimum dosage. Keep a fellow on that and he'll do just about any bloody favor you damn well please.* Somewhat amused upon witnessing the dexterous maneuvers the lad had utilized in order to achieve such a trying goal, Samuel once again turned toward the disheveled bed. Maybe he *would* take a gander at the London Times while waiting for the general. After all, he did intend to inquire into other travel agencies and perhaps he could locate one in the advertising section. But he'd be damned if he, a former captain of the British Army, was going to sit at the foot of that pompous Yank's bed. Spotting a short-legged bench below one of the open windows and satisfied that the weather was holding out, he grabbed the paper, approached the bench, laid down his hat and seated himself. *Hmmf!* he grunted, crossing an extended leg while eyeing an arresting photograph of several American women marching in a victory parade. Those insufferable wenches got the bloody vote after all! And it was the only one-upmanship America had over Britain until now! Samuel abruptly turned the page in search of a plausible travel representative. But no sooner had he begun the task when he was alerted by the sound of echoing footsteps and clopping crutches.

"Over there, sir!"

Looking up from the *London Times* and spontaneously coming to attention, Samuel recognized Major General Briggs at the end of the corridor, a beaming grin across his stone-cheeked face, approaching in a medical tunic alongside his impulsive patient.

"Captain Samuel Governey, my good man! I was hoping it was you...yet I did not expect you to arrive so soon. What a bloody pleasure it is to see you again!"

Still standing at attention, Samuel waited until the general extended his hands before replying. "Likewise...likewise, major general! It has been much too long, indeed, sir!"

"Much...much too long, my good man!" Briggs echoed while consummating the firm, resolute handshake. "But first, allow me to express my regret upon having learned of your father's death. I do hope you received the letter I deposited in Wesley Carvelle's post-box."

"Yes indeed, major general!" Samuel answered as the American soldier boy hobbled over to the nearest open window. "I appreciate the time you have taken to inform me of such matters."

"Colonel Bharat's communiqué is still in my office," the general explained, animating his grey, bristled moustache. "I would have deposited it in Carvelle's post-box as well, but since it was specifically entrusted to me, I felt quite responsible for it. And furthermore, by deliberately securing the letter upon my person, I realized that the likelihood of meeting once again with my dear old comrade before he left for America would be substantially increased! You *are*, my good chap, intending to travel overseas, are you not?"

"Yes, by all means, major general. That is, if I am ultimately successful in securing a cabin. Unfortunately, I was informed yesterday that travel has become an extremely popular pastime and, consequently, I am afraid our magnificent ocean liners have all been accounted for."

"Every bloody goddamn cabin?" Briggs rebutted, thrusting his crumpled face forward like a charging British tank.

"Indeed, major general! Every bloody suitable accommodation," Samuel answered, trying not to flinch from Briggs' Listerine breath. "My travel representative has informed me, however, that I would be notified of any cancellations. But," he interrupted wishing to change the distressing subject, "enough of that! Tell me, major general, if you please...for I cannot sustain my curiosity a minute longer...are you quite cognizant then of the contents of Colonel Bharat's letter?"

"To some extent," Briggs answered. "Colonel Bharat...you know the old chap still resides in India...had enclosed a separate letter for me along with your own, explaining that his son-in-law...that epidemiologist, I think...seems to have an interest in offering you a position at the hospital he's recently been commissioned to serve."

"In India?"

Major General Briggs raised his calloused hands and shook his balding head. "No, no...of course not, my good man. I'm afraid I've given you the wrong impression. The son-in-law is in America. As you might remember, he was commissioned there when the dreadful flu epidemic broke out in the fall. As I have it, he serves at a veterans' hospital...Detroit General, I believe. And then, of course, upon being aware that your dear father had passed and assuming that you would be heading out overseas, well...as word gets around, it seems that they could use a good physician or two such as yourself, Sam. And, as you surely must know, I am forever at the ready to offer my comrade-at-arms my highest recommendation. "

Samuel stood quietly for a moment. Although it might be in his best interest to look into the proposition, he had, after all, hoped to make England his permanent residence. "The proposal is indeed enticing...and one that could indubitably be promising. But, my dear major general, you may not be aware of this, but the industrial city of Detroit is quite a distance from my hometown of Philadelphia. And I never intended to travel such a way...that is, if I am able, God willing, to procure a passage across the Atlantic after all."

"Naw...that's horsefeathers!" an intrusive, yet newly familiar voice rang in. "You can take the rail. My cousin, Dan, rode it last summer and was back in a blink! Say...that your motor buggy out there? Bet she can take the drive in two days if you really cranked her!"

Reluctant to offer the asinine Yank the satisfaction of a civilized response after the lad had so rudely listened in on their private conversation, Samuel stood indignantly, allowing the major general to proceed.

"Yes, Zach, it certainly is!" affirmed Briggs with a hearty chuckle. "Sam...I want you to meet Private Zachary Dorkins. Zachary, my dear boy...former captain and most esteemed doctor, Samuel Governey. And to confirm what a small world we do, indeed, live in," he expounded, patting the grinning lad on the shoulder, "would you believe, Sam, that Private Dorkins is, himself, from the city of Detroit? Zach is a member of the 339th Infantry," he added, noticing the inquisitive look on Samuel's face. "Were you not aware of the fact that the 339th Infantry joined our French and Canadian allies in Archangel, Russia to thwart the revolution? The distinguished infantry served under the command of our own British Major General, Frederick Poole, but has recently been dispatched back home, except for these brave unfortunate souls," he explained, gesturing toward the occupied hospital beds. "Samuel you were no doubt wondering why the infirmary was so popular these days, were you not?"

"Yes, Major General. I did, indeed, find it rather perplexing," Samuel affirmed, experiencing a bizarre respect for these wretched soldiers who had, without question, confronted the red devil himself countless times while tramping across miles of desolate terrain in unbearably cold temperatures, all for the sake of an undoubtedly disputable crusade.

"I was one o' the lucky ones, I guess," Zach broke in, leaning on his crutches. "Lots o' my fightin' buddies didn't make it. But, then again, if we was back in Michigan, we might not o' made it at all. That flu you was talkin' about claimed lots o' folks back there too. Got a uncle owns a funeral parlor an' nobody knows better n' him. That bastard got lots o' business, that year. Should see that damn place. Looks like one o' them southern plantation homes. Ya know, big white pillars to boot! Be real ritzy-titzy if it weren't a funeral home. On the main drag o' Grosse Pointe. Ever hear of it? Just one spit and a stone toss away from Detroit. Few miles or so from the big city. *Millenbach's* the name. Fancy ass name. Millenbach Funeral Parlor. Worked there myself a couple o' summers...ya know, cleanin' up after them dead bodies and all. Uncle wants to sell it, though. Guess the old bastard made too much dough or just can't handle them stiffs no more. Say...how fast does that motor buggy run anyhow?"

Reminding himself that the jabbering lad was still under the influence of a powerful narcotic while sorely aware that the major general was infamously known to harbor a soft spot for his patients, Samuel adopted a more tolerable stance. "Well my young man, on a good day I have been known to coax her up to 60 miles in an hour, but I am afraid she may not be up to such a brisk pace as of late. She is in the most dire need of tuning."

"Were you intending then to ship her overseas with you?" Briggs interjected.

"Yes I should like that. That is, if I am destined to make the journey at all."

Major General Briggs flattened his wrinkled lips and began stroking his moustache. "I have an idea, Sam. Mind you...it's a bit far-fetched, but I think that it may, indeed, be the answer to your present dilemma. I say old chap...be kind enough to accompany me into my private office, and we shall discuss the matter in detail over a calming cup of black currant tea," he invited, unfastening his medical tunic and throwing it over his arm. "I shall attend to matters here later."

Retrieving his hat which he had left upon the short-legged bench, Samuel brusquely bid farewell to Private Zachary Dorkins and started walking with the major general toward the entranceway when he once again was disrupted by the outspoken soldier.

"Take her to one o' them places near the Ford plant!"

"Excuse me, young man?"

"Yer motor buggy. Take her to one o' them big cheeses out there. They'll fix her up swell!"

Acknowledging the young lad's advice with curt acquiescence, Samuel then followed Major General Briggs outside, thinking it the most sensible piece of information the insolent soldier had offered thus far.

chapter 53

A Novel Approach

With Colonel Bharat's letter in hand, Samuel glanced out the window of the major general's private office as a spontaneous burst of rain bombarded the canvas covering he had just spread over the roadster. Reassured that the large canopy had been properly secured and thinking the Gregoire was in need of a good wash anyhow, he began to read the letter while the major general prepared tea in the adjoining kitchen. Painfully sifting through Colonel Bharat's exotic scribbling, he discovered that the letter not only confirmed what Major General Briggs had related, but included a detailed map to the location of Detroit General Hospital and an extended invitation to the home address of his daughter and son-in-law, Mr. and Mrs. Daksha Khamal. But perhaps the most engaging aspect of the letter was the implication that had it not been for the skillfully performed abortion at the hands of his most faithful comrade, Doctor Samuel Governey, Colonel Bharat would not be anticipating, with overwhelming joy, the approaching birth of his first grandchild.

Abruptly rising from his seat to give General Briggs a hand, Samuel thanked him for the aromatic black currant tea and placed his fine china cup and saucer on the edge of the mahogany desk.

"Sorry it took so long, old chap," the elderly soldier apologized, "but being that it's a fresh pot, I wanted to allow it ample time to steep. Here..." he added while lifting from the desk a lacquered oak humidor, "May I offer you a Cuban cigar directly from Havana?" Removing two exquisitely rolled cigars from the box, he sliced off both tips with an engraved guillotine cutter and handed one to Samuel, assisting him with a light.

Gratefully acknowledging the major general's kindness once again, Samuel gave the hand-rolled cigar a manly draw, relishing its rich, esoteric flavor. Noticing that the rain was letting up, he then returned to his seat, anticipating that after a productive conversation with his superior officer, he might depart the office with the assurance that his travel arrangements had been vouchsafed.

"Have you found Colonel Bharat's letter satisfactory, then?" Briggs inquired while placing an iron ashtray within the proximity of them both.

"Yes, quite assuredly," Samuel answered. "The information you had related to me was included in the letter, along with a few other significant details...addresses, telephone numbers...that sort of thing."

"Splendid!" the major general replied. "Which leads me to my case in point. How receptive are you of air transportation?"

"I beg your pardon, major general?" Samuel blurted, nearly dropping his cigar upon the ashtray.

Briggs placed his cup back on its saucer after indulging in a hearty sip. "*You know*, my dear chap," he quipped, "traveling by *air* as opposed to land or sea."

Deciding that his own cup of tea could wait, Samuel sat mute. To have experienced travel by air across the Mediterranean was certainly hellish enough, but to suggest a trip across the mighty and treacherous Atlantic was absolutely preposterous! And furthermore, as related to him by Hans Pfifer, there was, quite recently, only one ship in existence so far, a Vickers biplane manned by two British pilots, which had successfully endured such a mind-boggling journey. "Major general...I cannot believe what you are implying! Are you pulling my leg, old chap?" Uneasily discerning the major general's tight-lipped smugness, he added, "And even if such a journey were, indeed, possible, I would not be the least bit fond of the idea. You see...in order to return so quickly to England, I was, indeed, compelled to undergo a most horrendous flight upon a German Junker piloted by a most odious German pilot...an experience I vowed never to repeat for the remainder of my natural bloody life!"

Somewhat amused by the thought of his genteel comrade tramping a ride with a German aviator, Briggs suppressed a chuckle with a contrived cough. "No need for concern, Sam! What I have in mind is not nearly as shocking. As a matter of fact, I can think of no other form of transportation which provides such tranquil passage. Specifically speaking, the royal air force has developed an airship called a dirigible...more precisely, the R34...which is scheduled to depart from East Fortune on her maiden transatlantic voyage mid-week next. She was successfully tested in June, undergoing a 54-hour endurance voyage, so you see, Sam, my good man," he explained tapping the ashes from his cigar into the iron tray, "we are quite confident that our crew will be as safe as a babe in his mother's arms. I am acquainted with the captain personally and am quite sure, that, given your untimely situation, he may be well inclined to augment his flight personnel by including an experienced surgeon and veteran on board."

With a slight tremor running through his fingers, Samuel reached for his tea, sipped pensively, and placed it back down. He was indeed familiar with these mammoth airships, having first encountered their ominous presence as they hovered over London dropping a slew of lethal bombs from black, protruding bellies. "My dear general...is it quite true, then? The middle of next week you say?"

"Indeed, Sam...Indeed, yes. I shall have one of my subordinates notify you as soon as I relate our conversation to Captain Scott."

His thigh and calf muscles invigorated, Samuel instantly stood up and leaned across the desk, initiating a heartfelt handshake. "Very well, then, major general, and thank you! Thank you most kindly, indeed! I trust, then that my fate is once again in your most benevolent hands!"

chapter 54

Ocean Crossing

With the R34 scheduled to depart East Fortune, Scotland during the foggy morning hours of July 2, 1919, Doctor Samuel Randolph Governey was attired in a durable regulation flying suit, equipped with parachute, harness, and life saving collar. With every bit of awe and apprehension a crewman would experience upon initially entering the watertight hull of a dreadnought battleship, he then boarded one of four gondolas suspended from the airship. Having arrived five days prior to the R34's transatlantic departure had allowed him ample time to ship his roadster overseas on the first available freight boat, after which he endured an extensive training program, along with a crew of 30 military and non-military personnel. Although Samuel had become acquainted with his new lodgings as well as the inner workings of the mighty airship several times during the detailed and often exhausting orientation, the actuality of her being coaxed out of her shed by 700 ground crew members and majestically rising into the misty night sky was nevertheless overwhelming.

Bracing himself against one of the ship's railings as the turntable of an Oxford gramophone reverberated strains of jazz, Samuel soon discovered he had nothing to fear when suddenly realizing, from the fading shouts below, that the airship's ascent had already attained the height of a staggering 1300 feet. Pushing aside a lightweight curtain while futilely attempting to detect the ship's momentum through the early morning darkness, he momentarily considered reclining upon one of the available hammocks on board, but still finding himself in a rather restless mood, decided instead to slump into his stationery chair and close his bloodshot eyes, valuing the fact that between his scheduled watches, there would be plenty of time for relaxation. As the R34 wafted its way over Rosyth and Glasgow, he surrendered to a deep slumber, only to learn from the heckling of other crew members the following morning that, not only had he slept throughout the historic, yet uneventful night, but had entertained the crew with a most amusing case of somnambulism. He had slowly risen from his seat, they recounted, and proceeded to walk the full 50-foot length of the gondola, just stopping short at its far end. Then, towering over one of riggers who was fast asleep upon a hammock, began stroking the bloke's balding head, eventually "groping for a good feel," as they put it, beneath the dormant fellow's blanket. For his unconscious efforts, Samuel received in return a mere shifting of body weight. Standing motionless for a fraction of a moment, he then moved to his next target, a fully cognizant chap, seated at one of the dining room tables who was completely engrossed in a girlie publication while nursing a teacup full of Irish whiskey. Playing along with his catatonic companion, this assistant engineer allowed Samuel to continue the peculiar ritual amid the whoops and hollers of several cohorts until the roguish fellow began to fondle the oblivious doctor below the waist, producing an agitated look on Samuel's face, causing him to momentarily pause before moving to the next available victim. This jolly quest continued for a good half hour, he was informed, until after accosting several more of his fellow comrades, he suddenly changed direction and meandered back to his own seat where he continued to repose in slumber.

Questioning the credibility of such a bizarre account and doubting himself capable of such outlandish behavior, Samuel nevertheless vowed that from then on, he would only shut his eyes while cradled within the handwoven comfort of one of the ship's sixteen hammocks. Tending to the numbness in his shoulder, he trusted that if the preposterous account was indeed true, the pivotal duties involved in navigating the R34 toward its destination of Long Island, New York would eradicate the embarrassing situation from the crew's voyeuristic minds.

As the flying dirigible, trailed by two warships, the Renown and Tiger, propelled its way across the tranquil Atlantic, Major G.H. Scott, after navigating her through two electrostatic-inducing cloud layers, was faced with another annoying dilemma when, while retaining the airship within a layer of fog to avoid overheating on the gas bags, two stowaways were discovered on board. The first trespasser, immediately identified as William Ballantyne, had been one of several crew members left behind to make room on board for the other 30. Resentful of being denied passage on the record-setting voyage, particularly when that same privilege had been granted to the rookie Doctor Governey, the determined telegrapher had hidden himself in a cramped, gaseous section of the ship which was, ultimately, the cause of his eventual surrender. The second stowaway, having been less bothered by the cramped conditions than the nauseous gas, was, conversely, well-received, not only because she had been smuggled onto the ship against her will but previously had been deemed mascot of the now delighted crew—a small furry kitten known by everyone, including the captain, as "Whoopsie." Having no choice but to keep Mr. Ballantyne on board until the R34 set foot on American soil, Major Scott and Brigadier General E.M. Maitland determined that after the marginally gas-poisoned interloper had been attended to by Doctor Samuel Governey, he would serve the remainder of his waking time working in the galley as well as hand-pumping petrol into the tanks of the now overloaded ship. After force-ingesting a small dosage of Ipecac to induce vomiting and drinking plenty of water provided from one of several reservoirs, the contrite Mr. Ballantyne was soon well again and free to attend to his new responsibilities, proving Samuel to be a most proficient physician after all, worthy of the privileged status recently granted him.

Having grown accustomed to the crew's waning mockery over his alleged bout of sleepwalking while endlessly tolerating the incessant, annoying company of the ever-stalking furball, Whoopsie, Samuel's patience was once again put to the test the following evening as the skipping needle of the gramophone and Whoopsie's deep-throated murmurs signaled the onslaught of an approaching storm. With all five engines at full power, the dauntless dirigible prepared for the battle with the elements by nosing herself directly into brutal southeasterly winds. As the frantic crew attempted to stabilize the airship throughout the night while it was tossed to and fro like a toy balloon, Samuel, securely belted to his seat, found himself clinging to one of the hand rails, instinctively uttering a simple prayer he had learned as a child, yet quickly reverted to his own agnostic ways at the very first sign of the ship's stabilization.

Fortuitously earning another notch on his medical belt upon doctoring one of the riggers' fractured arms as well as treating various cuts and bruises other crewmen had suffered during the harrowing night, Samuel breathed a sigh of relief after partaking in the first nutritious, yet unpalatable meal of the day. Wearily sipping a cup of tea while resting on one of the hammocks, he witnessed a morning so translucent as to reveal not only a mountain-like iceberg thousands of feet below, but, like ducks in a pond, subsequent smaller bergs and surrounding pack ice. Later on, however, after waking from a four-hour nap, a heavy fog signaling their flight over Newfoundland accompanied disconcerted mumbles among the crew that there may not be enough fuel left to reach their intended destination without stopping due to continuing headwinds as they flew along the northern Canadian coastline toward Nova Scotia. But after the liquid ballast was released, allowing the dirigible to be successfully lowered to 800 feet for the remainder of the journey to escape the unrelenting winds, Samuel, at long last, was able to repose in undisturbed comfort, eventually enjoying an excellent view of lush, green shorelines, the welcoming sounds of abounding wildlife and the fresh, pungent smell of the towering pine trees of North America.

With only 140 gallons of fuel remaining on board after four demanding days of an unprecedented flight, Samuel began making himself viably presentable as the dirigible's destination of Mineola, New York was well within reach. Joining the other crew members as they peered down at a swarm of cheering spectators surrounding a huge grandstand occupied by local and national dignitaries in full formal dress, Samuel also stared in awe at scores of motorcars blanketing Roosevelt Field, wondering if the Gregoire had arrived and was, in fact, waiting for him inside a storehouse near the crowded docks of Manhattan. As the R34 continued to circle overhead, Samuel helped Special Duties Major J.E.M. Pritchard don a parachute, after which the senior officer drifted to the ground, thus becoming the first man to arrive in America by air from the first dirigible ever to complete a transatlantic voyage. Extremely proud of being counted among the passengers associated with such a historic event, Samuel impatiently waited for the airship to finally land as Major Pritchard directed the swarming ground crew. Stepping onto the ramp and into line with his own comrades-in-flight, Samuel then exited the resilient craft, overwhelmed by tributary salutes, waving flags and triumphant music.

Pre-scheduled to remain in the United States for three full days before her journey back to Scotland, the British airship faithfully abided at her landing site as her venerated attendants indulged in a fanciful, speech-filled luncheon. Soon afterwards, they were escorted by several shiny black Packards to their own private chambers inside the Bellevue hotel where they rested and showered before participating in a string of commemorative functions and festive galas scheduled for the duration of their stay. Fervently basking in unbridled praises and laudatory rhetoric offered by pompous celebrities and backslapping politicians, Samuel was reminded of his recent experience in the village of Zadari, yet filled with gratitude that this time he was most fortunate to be in the good company of New York's civilized, fashionable elite. But as with all happy occasions, the celebrations reached a dynamic conclusion when the now famous R34, gassed to capacity and loaded with provisions, was launched from Mineola, New York near midnight on July 10th for her return trip to Scotland, leaving Doctor Samuel Governey in his solitude amid a cheering crowd of street and rooftop dwellers. Illuminated by searchlights, she majestically rose into the cool, windy sky and began heading eastward. Finally, during late morning, when the crowds were dispersed and she was far over the Atlantic well on the way to her motherland, Samuel was joyously driving through the hilly country roads of New Jersey in his beloved Gregoire, anticipating, with newly found optimism toward the land of his birth, a most promising stay in the city of brotherly love, Philadelphia.

chapter 55

Coming Home

When, as a young lad, Samuel Governey attended the Bennings Boarding School for Boys in Cambridge, Massachusetts, it was a yearly tradition for some of the braver students to introduce newcomers by accompanying them on a ritualistic dare. During the first full moon of October, these intrepid souls, along with their underlings, having staged a convincing pretense of peaceful slumber, would rise from their wobbly, disheveled beds. Then, without the merest whisper, they would gather some warm clothing, tiptoe along the dark, creaking hallway and down the back staircase off the main kitchen before entering the adjacent wine cellar. After filling three large flasks to the brim with red wine from one of the many large oak barrels, they each took turns wriggling through the cellar window before scampering across the freshly raked lawn. Breathlessly crossing a desolate road bordering a heavily wooded thicket, they would head straightforward past skeletal, wind-teased branches and scratchy, scented pines until arriving at a fenced-in clearing which revealed row upon row of eerie gravestones illuminated by a vibrant moon. Taking turns hoisting each other over the barbed wire, the experienced seniors then instructed their freshmen classmates to choose a comfortable spot where they would camp until all the aged wine was fully consumed. Finally, after relieving their bloated bladders by "christening" the graves of their choice, the staggering greenhorns, guided by their inebriated brothers, would split their sides all the way back to the dormitory, plop headlong onto their beds, and drift into a deep sleep, only to be awakened the next morning by the startling shrill of a brass bell amid the painful awareness of a battering headache.

Casting aside these nostalgic memories evoked from the mixed emotions of excitement and trepidation experienced while nearing his father's colonial mansion, Samuel decelerated while approaching a stagnant line of traffic along Walnut Street. He was so close now, he could almost smell the freshly mowed lawn and hear the excited twittering of blue jays that frequented the backyard apple trees. Gradually applying the brake pedal and clutch, Samuel geared down with his perspiring palm, bringing the Gregoire to a full halt. Damn! Maybe he should have followed his original plan of registering at a hotel before making this impulsive decision, he fumed, noting that a stalled cleaner used to scrub the granite block street was the cause of the traffic standstill. And why did the road have to be so goddamn bloody narrow? It was hardly possible to pass a gent on a bicycle, let alone the filthy exhaust-spewing Model T directly in front of him!

Squirming in his seat, Samuel scanned an array of buildings enveloping the predominant Hall of Independence—a bank, several offices and a few unfamiliar new shops. Despite his growing impatience, the fact that the city had flourished considerably during his four-year absence did not elude him. And in all probability, would he be correct in assuming that many alterations had taken place on Chestnut Street as well? Would the stately colonial mansion still stand as regally as he had remembered it? Or...heaven forbid...what if for some reason it wasn't there at all? *No*, he quickly concluded, blotting beads of sweat from the strained wrinkles of his forehead. Such an improbability was out of the question. But what if...what if...? Samuel shut his eyes, unleashing a faint groan while stuffing the monogrammed handkerchief inside the pocket of his summer sport coat. It was the same haunting question he had ceaselessly reiterated since reclaiming his Gregoire and driving it all the way to Pennsylvania. What if, for some reason, the mansion had no longer belonged to his father prior to his death? Or, remaining true to his threat, the vindictive sexual degenerate had willed the entire estate to some gold-digging lover along with the Silver Ghost Rolls and Stutz Bear-Cat? The odds were, indeed, very possible and quite probable. Especially if the old man's syphilis had not deteriorated his mental faculties to the point of forgetting that his thoughtless son had actually deserted him. Maybe it would have best suited his needs to be more civil with his father by corresponding occasionally. Perhaps a cheery holiday letter or two. But it obviously was too late for regrets. His everlasting spite for the cantankerous old goat had gotten the bloody best of him and he would be forced to accept whatever consequence fate had in store. *Of course*, Samuel reasoned, attempting to calm his churning stomach, there must be something worthwhile waiting in the wings. Mr. Morgan, the executor of his father's will, would not have interrupted a perfectly exhilarating holiday in Africa with a telegram advising him to travel all the way across the Mediterranean, half a continent and the treacherous Atlantic if it were not absolutely imperative. Surely, he was letting his imagination overwhelm him. Perhaps there was nothing at all to worry about since the mansion, along with the Silver Ghost Rolls and Stutz Bear-Cat was, indeed, waiting to be claimed by "his truly," Samuel Randolph Governey, the rightful heir.

Feeling another bout of anxiety as the tight line of cars, headed by the reactivated street scrubber, began to loosen like a prodded caterpillar, Samuel shifted gears once again, visualizing the short route he would follow from here on in. After proceeding past 13th Street, he would turn right at Broad Street and then make an immediate left onto Chestnut. This maneuvering would allow him to avoid Rittenhouse Square with all of its nauseating memories of that incorrigible suffragette Violet Stimple, who had not only condemned him to a lifetime of infertility, but provoked her own untimely demise by struggling against his reproaches, he recalled, maintaining a vice grip on the leather steering wheel. Far better to avoid such odious memories by driving along a quieter, wider road. Taking his final cue from behind the sputtering Model T as it began creeping forward, Samuel gently released the clutch, loosened his white knuckles from the steering wheel and started on his way.

The first thing Samuel could not help but notice while turning onto Chestnut Street was the sight of even more buildings. Not the customary Philadelphian upper-class homes, but tall brick commercial buildings. And they were sprouting from the spacious backyard grounds of the formerly accordant residential neighborhood like overgrown beanstalks—a repetition of what he had increasingly witnessed while proceeding along Walnut Street. An absolute abomination! An audacious invasion by greedy capitalists which would surely bring about the ultimate ruin of an otherwise aesthetically tailored, private and peaceful community! But now, while steering along the uncongested straightaway, his indignation was suddenly transformed into utter dismay as his father's abode became increasingly apparent. A blood-red sun, setting over the Schuylkill River, seemed to smother the colonial mansion in a curtain of scarlet—as well as the taller, partially constructed building sitting on what was formerly the backyard, eradicating the stable which had housed his Silver Ghost Rolls and Stutz Bearcat.

Notwithstanding a couple of residents lighting their gas lamps and the melodious tones of a mother beckoning her children to supper, Samuel noticed no other signs of life about his father's white-columned mansion except that its impeccable maintenance required constant human care. Unable to quell the bitter lump in his throat or dismiss the permanently extinct garage from his racing mind, he coasted the roadster all the way up the paved asphalt driveway, past the painstakingly manicured lawn and blossoming geraniums, numbly bringing the purring automobile to a gradual halt. With a stupefied look upon his reddened face, Samuel sat frozen to his seat as he studied the half-erected commercial building where his Rolls and Bear-Cat should have been. It was as if both automobiles had been sucked up the shaft of the bloody monstrosity's chimney, vanishing into oblivion. Sensing that his head was about to implode, Samuel forcefully swallowed, scanning both the colonial mansion and its towering guillotine-like abductor. It was true. Bloody goddamn true, then! His deceased father's property to which he, Samuel Randolph Governey, was the rightful heir, had been split in half like an expendable piece of drainpipe and sold right under his unsuspecting nose! And his two cherished motorcars! Gone like pieces of ash caught in an abrupt whirlwind! Samuel's forearm struck the side of the Gregoire, activating the assailing shriek of the Klaxon horn. Further agitated by the blunder, he disengaged the motor, slumped into his seat, and let out a guttural moan. Now and forever more, there was no bloody reason ever to enter the premises of his childhood home, he lamented, envisioning the house key he had carefully tucked away in his bill book. And even if he should, indeed, try to use the key, any new proprietor with the least amount of horse sense would surely have commissioned the services of a good locksmith. Of course, he could approach the front door and knock. But what bit of good would that do? Even if he could extract information from the current resident, the home was obviously sold; furthermore, it would be quite rude to disturb a respectable family during supper hour...if, indeed, anyone should be home at all. But...goddamn it! he fumed, feeling his blood reaching a boiling point once again. Why had Mr. Morgan, the executor of the estate, advised him to return? There must be some rational answer to this distorted puzzle! However, the sun was setting and the day had dwindled, so it was definitely too late to contact him. He would call first thing in the morning, though, and demand an explanation for this outrageous breach of trust! However, before Samuel could calm himself down by reiterating his plans for the remainder of the evening, he was alerted by the soft scraping of unsteady footsteps approaching the rear of the roadster. With one swift turn of the head, he locked eyes with a stout, elderly gentleman dressed in fine daywear and slippered feet, bearing a cautious but adoring smile.

"Lookin' for someone sonny?" the stranger inquired in a diluted Georgian accent, exposing uneven teeth coated with moist tobacco.

Inwardly cursing the consequences of accidentally setting off the Klaxon horn, Samuel forced a half smile of his own. "Please excuse me, my good sir, but I am afraid there has been a terrible oversight. You see," he stuttered, initially intending to proclaim that he had arrived at the wrong house, but realizing there may be more to gain by divulging the simple truth. "You see...perhaps you can help me sir...allow me to introduce myself," he finally asserted, sharing in a convincing handshake. "Samuel Governey...Doctor Samuel Governey is my name." He then allowed the rosy-cheeked fellow to introduce himself, but politely declined his offer to pursue the conversation inside. "I beg your pardon once again for disturbing your evening, Mr. Hogan, but it seems that I find myself in quite a predicament. You see, I have literally traveled thousands of miles across two seas and a continent to return to my dear father's estate which is obviously your home now. In God's almighty name, I had no idea that it had been sold without my knowledge or consent and...well...as you might imagine, I am, indeed quite shocked beyond belief to find it otherwise occupied, let alone adjacent to that brick monolith which was once my backyard."

Stretching a pair of thick forearms in front of his barreled chest, Mr. Hogan twitched his bulbous nose and forcefully sucked in a hearty helping of sultry Philadelphian air. "Yep...indeed so," he replied, shaking an artificially adorned head. "Indeed so. Sam Governey, is it?" Mr. Hogan reaffirmed in a gruff voice, eager to change the subject. "Sorry to hear of your pop, son. Although I didn't know the gent personally, I was told by Reggie Morgan at the Philly Bank that he'd been quite ill. Yep...sorry to hear of his passing. So...you say you just arrived here then?"

"Yes sir...indeed I have," Samuel complied, leaning his elbow on the top door jamb of his bug-splattered convertible, somewhat annoyed that this unsophisticated backwoods man with stale tobacco breath was trivializing his cataclysmic predicament. "I have not had the occasion to meet with Mr. Morgan as of yet and so decided to visit my father's home...where I personally resided for a number of memorable years." Swallowing his pent-up frustration, Samuel continued, still wishing to humor the potentially useful fellow. "I must say, however,...putting aside the terrible circumstance I presently find myself in, it is obvious that you have, indeed, attended to the upkeep of my former residence jolly well."

"Why thanks, Sammy boy. It needed scads of work, but damn it!... I did nab the home at a fair price," Hogan blurted, a glint of satisfaction illuminating owlish eyes. Sure you wouldn't like to come inside and see what we've done? The wife won't mind. Stay for supper, maybe?"

"Thank you kindly, Mr. Hogan, but...I am afraid I must decline your generous offer," Samuel politely replied, his aristocratic ears still stinging from the mindless assault on his proper Christian name. "You see, my good man," he hastily fabricated while glancing at his wristwatch, "I am scheduled to arrive at my hotel within the hour. However, before I depart, would you be so kind as to tell me when it was that you so fortuitously acquired my father's estate?"

"Well, I'll tell ya sonny. Happened in 1917. Two years ago this month, would ya believe it! That damn monstrosity behind my house over there wasn't even begun yet. Rumor has it, gonna be some fancy-dancy coat factory. Yep, sure as sugar! Knew I took my chances though, seein' the lot was split when I bought it. Don't regret it a bit, though, Sammy boy. Still think...no...I know it...got a hellava damn good deal!"

"And the stable?" Samuel inquired, anxiety frightfully engulfing him once again. "The large stable in the back...before the building was erected...was it still there when you moved in?"

"Yes siree!" Mr. Hogan promptly confirmed, placing both hands upon his hips while gazing toward the lofty factory. "Sure was, as a matter of fact. But gone now...and just as well, too. Thing was beginnin' ta be a real eyesore. Shingles fallin' off, rottin' wood, an' broken windows all over...not a rat in sight, though. Varmints probably wanted nothin' ta do with the place. Yep...The company tore the thing down in the fall right 'fore they started buildin' the place."

"Yes...yes, Mr. Hogan. I do understand...but...but do you happen to know if there was anything left inside the stables...an automobile or two, perhaps?"

"Nope. Can't say that I can," Mr. Hogan replied, looking Samuel straight in the eyes. "Weren't none of my business, goin' noseying around the place. Anyhow, I got better things ta do than gettin' myself in trouble for trespassin'." Noticing his agitated gestures and a look of near panic surfacing on Samuel's virtually drained face, Hogan softened his abrasive voice. "Sorry I can't be of any more help, Sammy boy. Perhaps Reggie Morgan...he's the guy who sold me the place...you know, that Philly banker...maybe he can answer some of your questions."

"Yes, perhaps," Samuel sighed, no longer perturbed by the undiplomatic butchering of his given name. "I suppose I shall be on my way, then, Mr. Hogan," he added with a faint tip of his poplin cap. "Thank you very kindly, all the same."

Acknowledging the beaming homeowner's farewell with a half-hearted wave-off, Samuel engaged the headlights of the Gregoire and backed it down the long drive. Reaching the narrow street, he then sluggishly headed toward the main thoroughfare, dreading a restless night's sleep, yet consoled by the thought of a prestigious hotel, a good cigar, and a fine bottle of wine. However, with hardly any time to mentally retrace his former route, Samuel's reflections were suddenly interrupted by an ear-piercing, feisty whistle. Instinctively glancing in his rearview mirror while breaking to a stop, he impatiently waited for the breathless Mr. Hogan to catch up.

"Dang it, Sammy...almost forgot!" Hogan blurted, opening the door to the Gregoire with tobacco-stained fingers and squeezing inside. "Seems my wife's got somethin' for you. Looks like someone come around the other day lookin' for you. Hold on there buddy...just turn around and pull up the drive a bit."

Suppressing his anger at the uncouth intrusion of his beloved Gregoire, Samuel now regretted the decision to visit his father's estate altogether. It was most likely nothing but some nuisance of a salesman, he surmised, fidgeting in his seat while Mr. Hogan rolled out of the Gregoire and headed for the front door. One of those double-tongued charlatans selling bibles or some such thing. There certainly was no one in this town whom he had any interest in seeing, aside from who now seemed to be his double-crossing banker, Reginald Morgan—let alone this worthless swine, Samuel sulked, unable to overlook the depressed passenger seat while waiting for the man to reappear. Nothing but a waste of time, he griped, irritably eyeing his wristwatch again. Starting to seriously entertain the idea of departing without notice, his unmannerly musings were all of a sudden diverted by the sight of Hogan limping down the mansion's white marble steps, clenching a small rectangular object between his thumb and forefinger.

"Here it is Sammy boy...yessiree, by golly, I got it!" Mr. Hogan announced, gasping for air while holding onto his lopsided toupee, handing the printed calling card to Samuel. "God, I'm sure glad I remembered! The wife said it was important. Woulda' been mighty mad if I forgot. Said this person come to the door—a relation or something lookin' for ya. Had somethin' belonging to ya. Looked mighty desperate, Wilma said...that's my wife's name, you know...Wilma. Anyhow, hope this helps ya out, Sammy. Sorry about not knowin' anymore about them automobiles. That's a mighty fine one ya got right there, though. Yep...mighty fine...mighty *spittin'* fine!"

Disregarding the bumbling oaf's long-winded ramblings, Samuel focused instead on the fancy, scrolled-written calling card, immediately recognizing the name from his boyhood...a person who had not played a significant part in his life and to which he presently attached no importance. He scowled inwardly, preferring the intrusion of an anonymous salesman after all. Politely thanking Hogan for the trouble, Samuel stuffed the calling card inside his jacket pocket, shifted the Gregoire into reverse and backed down the smooth asphalted driveway.

chapter 56

Fruitful Conference

Reginald Morgan burst through the glossy oak door of his private conference room, frantically catching his leather folder as it slipped from jittery fingers. "Please, please accept my sincerest apologies, Samuel! I am so sorry to have kept you waiting—I was just about to step out for an appointment, but fortunately, my secretary informed me of your presence just before leaving," the bank administrator explained, brushing a strand of unruly hair from his silver-framed eyeglasses. "Consequently, I instructed her to reschedule that meeting to allow ample time to converse with you." Aware of Samuel's seething anger, Morgan cautiously placed the brown leather folder on a long mahogany table and began pulling out a copy of Randolph Eugene Governey's Last Will and Testament. "I understand you paid a visit to your father's estate last evening." Further prompted by Samuel's assenting glower, he quickly resumed. "I'm so sorry you had to find out this way, Samuel, but if you allow me to explain, I think you will come to realize that there was no other choice than to resolve things the way we did. So, my good friend...where shall we begin? Ask any question...any question whatsoever!" the middle-aged attorney appealed, brushing the lapel of his pinstripe suit before removing a Parker fountain pen and taking a seat across from his client.

Samuel squinted through burning eyes and took a deep breath, glancing over a half empty cup of tea. Attempting to blink away an escalating headache, he contemplated his flustered attorney as the counselor positioned his eyeglasses upon the table and wiped the sweat from the bridge of his concave nose. It was peculiar, even laughable, that at the very moment when he should be solely concerned about his future welfare—incensed by the manner in which things were handled—that the uppermost thought in his mind was how much this bank executive reminded him of Rupert Hines. It wasn't Morgan's mannerisms by any stretch of the imagination, because Mimi's dear hubby was not nearly as animated. But, put Morgan—this inept, two-faced banker—in safari gear, knock him down a few inches, and he could easily pass for the unsuspicious dupe's long-lost brother!

"Samuel...I could see that you're quite upset," Morgan said, breaking a silence made even more conspicuous by the tap tap tap of the Parker fountain pen against his thumbnail. "Hopefully, what I am about to relate to you will at least generate a better understanding of these unfavorable circumstances. Mind you Samuel...as you well know, your father was not the most flexible person to reason with," the lawyer added, pointing the pen at his speechless client in a dart-like manner. "I do realize your father's illness had taken a considerable toll on him and that he was under excessive stress...but... he was, after all, of sound mind, you do understand, when he authorized the sale of the property as well as making his wishes known. Unfortunately, by the time your dear father expired, most of his liquid assets were drained and those that were left...well...Samuel, I don't know what went on between you and your father," he hesitated, obsessively twisting the pen's removable cap, "but...but what few assets remained were willed to a person who now resides in the town of Steubenville, Ohio. Finley Pennyfeather is the party's name. You don't happen to know him, do you?"

Beginning to feel the delirium of a sleepless night starting to wear off, Samuel slumped further into the leather chair and vented a scornful grunt. *Goddamn it!* Of course he didn't know anyone by the name of Finley 'what's his feather,' but he had a damn good idea of who he might be—most probably one of his father's former bloody lovers, that's who! Adamantly shaking his reeling head, he finally spoke up. "No, sir! Indeed not, Mr. Morgan. I know of no one bearing such an asinine name!"

Reginald Morgan quickly gathered up his glasses and slipped them on. "Well, nonetheless, it doesn't really matter," the disconcerted lawyer replied while retrieving the fountain pen, relieved that his client had finally spoken up. "Considering that the will is definitely a valid one and the beneficiary in question does, indeed, exist, there should be no reason that the presiding judge would strike the document down, although God knows...being responsible for the welfare of my own two sons...I was compelled, though unsuccessfully, to try to persuade your father to do otherwise."

Like an unexpected rush of air invading a stale, vacuous cavern, Samuel's mind flowed with a renewed sense of clarity. Stretching back his aching shoulders, he released a scornful laugh, envisioning an elusive Silver Ghost Rolls and Stutz Bear-Cat maniacally circling the oval stucco ceiling above him in an endless, unavailing race. "So...Mr. Morgan...are you telling me that there is *nothing?* Absolutely *nothing?* Nothing whatsoever left for me of my father's goddamn bloody fortune?! Then *why!*" Samuel thundered, pounding his fist on the table. "*Why* in the name of God almighty was I lured over here like some money-grabbing whore? Do you not realize, Mr. Morgan...do you not realize the travesty of this situation? This detestable mockery of filial devotion?!"

Momentarily regretting his previous desire to have Samuel break the silence, Reginald Morgan stiffened his tingling back, rapping the non-business end of his Parker pen against the gold metal clasp of the legal folder. "Samuel...please...but if you will only hear what I have to say...please, first of all, let me assure you that, despite your father's incomprehensible decision, all is far from lost." Resolutely discarding the pen from his fingers, he cautiously eyed his scorned client as the gold-trimmed writing device rolled off the folder's leather binding and onto the polished table top. "As incapable as I was in persuading your intractable father to bequeath a portion of the remainder of his estate to you, I *was,* nevertheless, able to convince him to consign what was already rightfully yours...as a measure of precaution, you understand...particularly since the Rolls and Bear-Cat were still registered in his name. I know," he continued, decisively striking the edge of his palm upon the title page of the will's parchment, "that as your father's sole and only heir, you were hoping...and deservedly so, I might add...to inherit the total remainder of his estate, but...if I may offer my ever-so-humble opinion, that magnificent Silver Ghost Rolls and that splendid American-made Bear-Cat are worth far more in equity than what you may have otherwise received."

Resisting the impulse to leap from his seat, vault across the table, and embrace the sharp-witted counselor, Samuel pushed his palms together, words falling from his dry tongue like tokens from a slot machine. "My good man...are my ears deceiving me or am I hearing you correctly? You say you are currently in possession of my two precious automobiles? Both of them?"

he questioned, leaning halfway across the table, grabbing Morgan's fragile wrist. "My one-and-only Silver Ghost Rolls Royce *and* my inimitable Stutz Bear-Cat?"

Though grimacing from Samuel's vice-like grip, the attorney took full delight from his client's astonished reaction. "Why yes, certainly Sam!"

"And what of their condition, Mr. Morgan?" he exclaimed loosening his fingers a bit. "Will I still find them in pristine condition?"

Reginald Morgan shrugged his shoulders and raised a virtually invisible brow. "Considering that no one has operated them in years, not bad...not bad at all, in my opinion, although I suppose a good refurbishing would boost their value considerably. If I were you, Samuel, I would certainly look into it." Morgan wriggled his smarting wrist from Samuel's python-like grip and rose from the table. "But why take my word for it when you can judge for yourself? Both of your precious possessions are safely sheltered in a garage...near the railroad station on Market Street. You know, Samuel, I really don't have the time to escort you presently, but, if you would like for me to accompany you later, perhaps tomorrow, if my schedule permits or, if not, the day after then. Nevertheless," he reassured, massaging his smarting wrist, "there is no need for concern. Believe me, your automobiles are secure...locked up safe and sound. And Samuel, be mindful of the fact that although the expense is minimal, there is a written stipulation in the will which covers this trite financial arrangement." Morgan reseated himself and rested the length of his forearms on the table. "So...are there any other questions you would like to explore with me at this time? Or shall I have my secretary make arrangements for the both of us to pay a visit near Philadelphia Station?"

Still wallowing in the knowledge that he would soon be reunited with the Rolls Royce and Bear-Cat despite an underlying disappointment that there would be no further fortune to anticipate, Samuel wriggled his tired back and contemplated Morgan for an extended moment, realizing that, due to his own presumptuous impatience, he had failed to ask several pertinent questions. "Mr. Morgan," he began, straightening his necktie, "I beg your pardon for what must appear in your eyes to be ungentlemanly and inexcusable behavior on my part, but I beg you to understand the undue distress I most recently suffered upon discovering that my father's entire estate had indeed been sold...my home which, despite the usual familial squabbles, evoked many fond memories. Well...it is a poor excuse, but perhaps one you could find in your heart to forgive. That unpleasant matter being settled," he hastily added while quickly clearing his parched throat, "it seems I have over-looked some basic, yet important facts concerning not only my dear father's estate, but the dire circumstances regarding what must have been, to say the very least, an extremely lonely and painful death."

Discerning Samuel's less-than-sincere effort to exonerate himself, Reginald Morgan nevertheless empathized with his 29-year-old client, recall-ing the inexcusable attempt his villainous father had made to conceal the inheritance the young man had received from his maternal grandfather over eight years ago. "Samuel..." he began, tapping the butt of the Parker pen upon the glossy tabletop, "being in this business for over 25 years, I have had my share of experience with people who were, like your father, forced to face their own mortality. Some, who previously had their Last Will and Testaments drawn up, wished to revise the legal document, whereas others needed the guidance of a good counselor to arrange, for the first time, the distribution of their assets. And, despite the overwhelming mental strain they undoubtedly endured, most handled the situation quite responsibly," Morgan explained, waving his pen around like a maestro's baton. "Your father, however...your father...whatever the reason...faced the brutal reality of his illness in a more rebellious manner. As I mentioned before, Samuel, I don't know what transpired between the two of you and it is certainly none of my concern, but your father's initial request upon being confronted with his illness was to irrevocably omit you, his only heir, from the will, after which he proceeded to jeopardize the entire estate by making extremely poor choices which, had he not been diagnosed as mentally competent, would have convinced myself and others that the dementia of syphilis had, indeed, taken its final toll."

Samuel sat stone-faced, temporarily oblivious to Morgan's continued rambling, the vision of his father sprawled upon the kitchen floor amidst broken glass and spilled bourbon. He remembered the fear in his father's eyes as he threatened to pick up the telephone receiver to call Philadelphia General, knowing full well the consequence of revealing the deception which the pathetic old man perpetrated against the insurance company. Had not Dr. Gruben given him a full bill of health, no insurance company would have underwritten him. But now he felt a sharp sting of regret, not so much for the former Dr. Gruben who subsequently lost his medical license, and his father who reaped the tribulations for his personal indiscretions, but primarily for himself and the bloody bridges that he burned. Out of sheer spite, he had betrayed and deserted his father altogether, leaving him to his fate while he selfishly cruised the Atlantic to England, continuing his five-year odyssey through the Great War and his exotic African adventures. He had been like a foolish schoolboy who, having crossed the superintendent, had gotten expelled, losing the respect of his fellow classmates as well. Samuel continued in his trance-like state, picturing the huge white hospital building of Philadelphia General set inside thick, whitewashed walls which could have, under alternate circumstances, offered him a substantial means of income. It was at that moment that he realized more than ever, that deserting his father in such a callous manner had finally come back to haunt him. Suddenly aware, however, that Morgan was attempting to regain his attention by blatantly tapping the pen upon the desk, Samuel shook himself into the present, his eyes focusing upon the attorney's exasperated face. Responding to Morgan's look of concern, Samuel swallowed his pride, along with another sip of tea and continued to listen in a calm and courteous demeanor.

"Samuel," Mr. Morgan expounded, leaning toward his client, "it was as if your father was determined to squander every last cent of the estate before he died. Granted, the high-quality nursing care he insisted upon was a legitimate expense—I'll personally vouch for that, but other behavioral traits...why, if I had perceived for one minute that he was deriving the least bit of genuine pleasure from his eccentricity, I would have found his actions more acceptable, but...and please excuse me if I am out of step...it seemed that the more he squandered, the more insufferable he became." Morgan paused for a long moment, lightly tapping the pen against his two bottom teeth, then continued. "For instance...he would sell certain pieces of home furnishings and then use the proceeds to purchase highly speculative stocks or, even worse, hire a bookie to bet on a horse with the most unwinnable odds! Eventually compelled by his degenerating condition, he sold the mansion and its adjoining property, using a portion of the proceeds to finance his care at Seven Hills, an upscale sanitarium in Manhattan, where he remained until his death."

"Which was?..." Samuel broke in, his question immediately being curtailed by a timid knock at the door, followed by the cheery voice of Mr. Morgan's personal secretary, Barbara, carrying a tray of fresh tea and coffee. After the smartly-tailored woman placed the tray before them and refilled their cups, she left the gentlemen to their business. But the secretary was no sooner out the door when Mr. Morgan rose from his seat and stepped over to an unadorned cabinet, pulling out a bottle of Beefeater's gin.

"Care to spruce up your tea?" he inquired, uncapping the half-filled bottle while pouring a liberal amount into his cup of coffee. "May as well enjoy it while we can, Samuel, although God knows there have been plenty of rumors running rampant about bootleggers providing the stuff once prohibition takes effect next year."

Samuel immediately placed his hand over the teacup, politely declining Mr. Morgan's offer. Aside from wishing not to pollute a perfectly good cup of tea, he never was one to indulge in hard liquor, although he found an occasional glass of fine wine to be most tolerable. And as far as being concerned about the inevitable Volstead Act of prohibition which would take place on the 16th of January, he realized that Mr. Morgan's conjecture was correct. Since arriving in England less than two weeks ago, he had heard plenty of small talk about the ineffectiveness of such puritanical legislative nonsense which would undoubtedly result in illegal bootlegging, underground smuggling and all of its adverse ramifications, enabling nationwide availability after all. Still unsatisfied about the circumstances surrounding his father's death, Samuel diverted the subject-at-hand as Mr. Morgan returned the liquor to its respective hiding place and reseated himself across from his client. "So, Mr. Morgan, as you were saying...precisely when *was* the exact date of my father's demise?"

Staring into his client's unperturbed eyes, Reginald Morgan puckered moistened lips, replaced his coffee cup upon its china saucer, then thumbed through the tail end of the legal document. "I believe...I believe it was toward the end of May. Yes...that was it...May 29th," he resolutely confirmed with a blunt rap of his pen upon the will's final page. "Just a few days short of his 78th birthday," he added, shaking his head in disbelief. "It is indeed difficult to fathom that a man in his condition...or anyone, for that matter...would live such an exceptionally long life! Nonetheless, it was his heart which ultimately failed him. Although he had already been declared legally insane several months beforehand, that was the final, conclusive diagnosis," Mr. Morgan verified, placing the will on top of the leather folder and pushing the document aside, allowing ample room to lean upon the table. "I was notified by his physician, Dr. William Cobb, that I, acting as his executor, was responsible for the prompt arrangement of his funeral with all of its financial responsibilities. As I mentioned before, Samuel," the attorney went on, rolling the Parker pen back and forth upon the desk's slippery surface, "your father was eccentric, to say the least. The elaborate service spelled out in his Last Will and Testament which demanded a full chorus for high mass, a room full of floral arrangements, and a solid brass coffin with ornate trimmings, nearly drained the remainder of his estate. And that didn't even include the exorbitant mausoleum he had pre-purchased on prime cemetery property. To be forthright with you, Samuel, I am not so certain that in lieu of outstanding gambling debts or promissory notes which may show up in probate, Mr. Pennyfeather will be left with anything at all. So!..." the satisfied lawyer declared, glancing at his pocket watch before slapping together the palms of his hands, "that is it in a nutshell. Have you any further questions, or shall I have Barbara arrange with you a convenient time for reclaiming those two fine automobiles?

"Oh yes...yes, Mr. Morgan," Samuel answered putting down his teacup, still attempting to digest the ludicrous, yet credible account of his father's escapades as Mr. Morgan finished consuming his cup of coffee. "Yes, indeed...I am most anxious to be reunited with my motor cars as soon as possible."

"Very well, then...very well," Morgan serenely smiled. Then, rising from his seat, he placed the will back inside the brown leather folder. "If you will let Barbara, my secretary, know of your whereabouts, she will contact you first thing tomorrow morning."

Taking Reginald Morgan's cue to leave the room, Samuel recalled the attorney's comment about refurbishing the automobiles, along with the sweeping realization that he was virtually penniless. Adding to this revelation, it occurred to him that perhaps, instead of staying in Philadelphia any longer, he, should, after all, take a serious "stab" at "riding the rail" to Michigan, as that morphine-addicted American soldier at the London infirmary had suggested. Once there, he could investigate that promising position at Detroit General Hospital and, perhaps...perhaps, despite his aversion toward his former army colleague, Colonel Tayib Bharat, he would work for the Arab son-in-law, the epidemiologist, until he was financially on his feet again. After all, at this stage of the game, Samuel surmised, continuing to follow Morgan to the door, what did he have to lose? "Mr. Morgan..." he asked as the attorney, with pen securely pocketed, held the clasped folder loosely to his side. "Is it still quite necessary for me to show up in probate at all, then...considering that there is nothing more to gain from my father's estate? Aside from the automobiles, that is."

"Why certainly, son. It is imperative that you appear in court for that very reason," Mr. Morgan emphasized, closing in on Samuel with warm liquored breath, aspiring to extend the litigation for its maximum financial gain. "But the proceedings are a mere formality. Once they have been concluded," he said, giving Samuel a reassuring pat on the back, "you will have the complete legal satisfaction of truly possessing those exquisite automobiles!"

"Mr. Morgan?" Samuel asked as they both neared the door.

"Yes, Samuel?"

"Being that my father was so determined to exclude me from his will, how was it that you persuaded him to sign the motor cars over to me after all?"

Reginald Morgan hesitated for a moment, affectionately eyeing his client with a bit of caution. Pursing gin-coated lips, he recalled the insolence with which Eugene Randolph Governey truncated his personal pleas that he should, under no circumstances, sever Samuel, his only son and heir, from the will. In one last desperate attempt, Morgan had threatened to turn the contemptuous beast over to the authorities for concealing the lad's rightful inheritance bequeathed by his maternal grandfather—unless he legitimately relinquished the two automobiles. But Morgan would never forget the homicidal glare which oozed from Randolph's diabolical eyes as the outwitted scoundrel scratched his name upon the revised legal document, as if signing with his own syphilitic blood. Releasing a slight shudder, he stared into Samuel's congenial blue eyes. Recalling the question regarding his father's abdication of the Silver Ghost Rolls and Stutz Bear-Cat, he extended his palm and grasped his client's hand with firm sincerity. "I have my ways, son...I do have my ways."

Feeling a genuine camaraderie toward his newly found mentor, Samuel walked outside the conference room, impatiently looking forward to being, at last, reunited with his Silver Ghost Rolls and Stutz Bear-Cat, yet particularly eager to introduce both of them, along with the Gregoire, to the promising streets of a city renowned for its unsurpassed expertise in the automotive industry. A city of sprawling factories, Great Lakes shipping and merchant barons, pregnant with residents of every race and nation, extending its abundant arms to anyone willing to pry them open. An exemplary symbol of freedom and opportunity, invariably earning the prestigious reputation of "motor capital of the world." And, as Samuel would soon discover, one which offered, with the flip of a coin, either a bustling metropolis or tranquil suburbs. From the moment he had made up his mind, Samuel could not help but aspire to be part of this thriving city, the crown jewel of the Midwest; and from the moment the Pennsylvania railway car had crossed the Ohio-Michigan border, he realized that, like a butterfly shedding its cocoon and sprouting a pair of glorious wings, his life would somehow, in some way, be transformed in a manner he had never before imagined.

chapter 57

Sunday Drive

Freshly bathed, ambrosially scented and dapperly dressed in the latest fashion courtesy of Joseph Hudson Clothiers, Doctor Samuel Randolph Governey steered his sleek French Gregoire convertible beside a streetcar track on Mack Avenue, anticipating a Sunday afternoon dinner at the home of Dr. and Mrs. Daksha Khamal, son-in-law and pregnant daughter of the forever-indebted Colonel Tayib Bharat. Bringing the professionally waxed roadster to an accelerating speed along the relatively quiet road, Samuel grimaced under the glaring sun and adjusted his green-tinted glasses. Although his idea of spending an enjoyable Sunday in Michigan's most vivacious city was not that of sharing a meal and conversation with virtual strangers, let alone those of a substantially lower social class, it was, indeed, in his best interest to do so. After all, according to the way fate was guiding him, he would most likely be employed by the end of the month, depending upon the decision of Detroit General Hospital's Board of Directors, of which his dinner host was an influential member. Financially backed by automobile tycoon Henry Ford, the prestigious veteran's hospital was much more impressive than Samuel had previously imagined. His countenance softened as he recalled the personal tour he was given of the newly built institution just two days prior, its spacious wards and operating rooms equipped with the latest surgical innovations. Although a starting salary was not quoted as of yet, he reasoned that the salary implied for the position of assistant head surgeon was substantial enough to insure an advance down payment on the estate of his choosing. And, because the recent influenza epidemic had claimed some of the hospital's finest physicians, including several top-notch surgeons, the aspiring position had practically fallen into his financially depleted lap.

Upon noticing an approaching curbside Gulf Oil filling station to his left, Samuel's thoughts veered toward his arrival in the "Motor City." It was nearly a week ago that the shrill whistle of the Pennsylvania railway preceded the introduction to a burly stump of a man, "Ross the Boss," owner of Nubuck's parts and accessories shop, after which this roughneck character coaxed the Silver Ghost Rolls and Stutz Bear-Cat from a crowded boxcar and in the direction of Brush Street. "Ross the Boss" had promised the delivery of both motor cars in less than two weeks. Feeling the hot, humid air slapping his stiff-collared neck as he continued along Mack Avenue, Samuel envisioned a team of automobile technicians restoring leather interiors and rubbing out visible scratches. If everything was up to snuff, he would have the Gregoire refurbished also. And, to double his fortune, the proprietor of the Pontchartrain Hotel had agreed to allow him the rental of two additional parking spaces within the lavish inn's garage. Of course, if lady luck continued to walk by his side, he pined, finally passing the Gulf Oil gas pump, he could purchase a mansion of his own with enough acreage to support a three-story warehouse if he so wished. And, quite naturally, he would ship the remainder of his belongings from Dr. Carvelle's home in London. He need not have inherited his father's money after all, he scowled. Somehow, some way, either legitimately or by highway robbery, he, Samuel Randolph Governey, compelled to leave England and his respectful title, "Earl of Cheshire," not to mention the loss of the Philadelphian estate due to his father's insane extravagances, would nevertheless overcome these aforementioned curses and triumph once again. He could taste it as much as the bloody Michigan humidity! And all's the better to have earned it himself, not to be constantly reminded of his father, that old backstabbing whoremonger!

Passing an import liquor store on the deserted corner of Bewick Street, Samuel was pleased he had purchased a bottle of Cabernet Sauvignon the previous day at one of the specialty shops along Woodward Avenue. He would have been completely out of luck had he made a last minute attempt to purchase a bottle of wine, being that all retail businesses were closed on this so-called "Lord's Day." And perhaps his dinner host would be inclined to present the French libation with the main entree, thus delivering his most discriminating palate from the sour-tasting bilimbi or bland rice wines these Indians were so accustomed to serving. Retaining the vivid image of down-town's Woodward Avenue, Samuel recollected some of the numerous shops he had patronized along Detroit's most flourishing thoroughfare during the past several days amidst towering landmarks, churches, grandiose parks and jubilant fountains—department stores, hat shops, jewelers, even a tea room and many more tobacconists than he could ever have hoped to frequent in Philadelphia or London. Bringing to mind the stout-bellied proprietor of the Peninsular Cigar store, he recalled the "Miss Detroit," the current addition to his smoking collection, which he had presently enjoyed before setting out. And was it not the height of extravagance to indulge in this newly found lux-ury while occupying a plush velvet seat in the gentlemen's section of the Detroit Opera House during their premiere production of Puccini's *LaBoeheme?* Whether he had enjoyed that particular event more so than the therapeutic massage and cabinet bath he had experienced earlier that after-noon at the YMCA was surely most difficult to determine!

Continuing his drive, Samuel noticed a small group of children in front of a roller-skating rink eating ice-cream cones. This reminded him of "Sanders," the sweet shop he had discovered on the corner of Michigan and Woodward featuring an ice-cream soda made with Detroit's own Vernor's—the finest ginger ale he had ever tasted. And their tantalizing chocolate! Never before in all of his 29 years had he sampled such a divine array of confec-tionaries! But, at this very moment, he would prefer a tall glass of Vernor's straight up, he concluded, licking dry lips. Aware of the unavoidable perspi-ration on the underarms of his newly purchased Antonio Rinaldi suit, he peered at an overcast sky. He had experienced a few unpleasant bouts of humidity while in England, but here in Detroit, particularly on this day, it was almost unbearable. Temperatures were climbing into the high 80s and the newspapers were predicting no relief. Hopefully, the Khamal home was well ventilated by several ample-sized electric fans or, in the very least, well-stocked with plenty of ice.

Anticipating a black-lettered traffic sign adjacent to a Catholic church about 50 feet ahead, Samuel released the clutch and stepped on the brakes, temporarily distracted by some shouting and cheering. Immediately shifting his gaze toward an open field, he noticed an assembly of young black men engaged in a game of baseball. Gradually coming to a complete halt while reflecting upon the prevailing situation, he experienced a twinge of gratitude.

It was just yesterday that the *Detroit Times* featured a front-page article about a recent outbreak of race disturbances in major cities—the latest still continuing in Chicago—resulting in several Caucasian deaths. Of course, some Negroes were killed and lynched as well, but most likely because they couldn't refrain from keeping their savage tempers under control. But so far, he sighed, as he began to accelerate, noticing that one of the baseball players had paused to admire the French Gregoire, this epidemic of Negro brutality had not infected Detroit—nor his beloved Philadelphia, for that matter.

Somewhat intimidated by the attention his presence was generating, Samuel proceeded past St. Bernard's church, recalling how his elderly grandfather, being wheeled inside the colonial mansion by his mother some 20 or so years ago, expounded on a similar disruption in Wilmington, North Carolina. And what about those scandalous incidents which took place in Atlanta during his senior year at Bennings Boarding School? It was all that the students and their headmasters could talk about, particularly those who had sisters and mothers living in the south. Why, with all the rapes going on, white women were reluctant to travel unchaperoned even within a few blocks of their own homes. Envisioning his recent African expedition, Samuel grimaced as he recalled the muscular guide, Tibuk, his black skin glistening with sweat upon emerging from the blonde-haired Mimi's tent. Hopefully, the Negroid population of Detroit knew well enough to stay in their own neighborhoods and keep to themselves. It was unfortunate enough that he had to contend with the likes of brown-skinned turban tops such as Daksha Khamal and the doctor's father-in-law, Colonel Tayib Bharat, let alone be employed as one of their underlings!

As the faint sound of an approaching streetcar neared an obsolete stamping plant below Conner Avenue, Samuel surmised that a good number of citizens were probably spending the day at a nearby beach or frolicking on Lake St. Clair. Maybe they had taken a short excursion to Belle Isle, the recreational island located on the Detroit River between Michigan and neighboring Canada. Perhaps he would make it a point to visit there within the coming week. In fact, if it were not for the irresistible allure of downtown Detroit, he would have done so already.

As the virtually vacant streetcar passed by, Samuel decided he had best start paying attention to the road signs, lest he bypass his destination. Gazing toward a busy Italian eatery with a large glass-fronted window that read "Russo's Restaurant—Give Our Spaghetti a Twirl," he strained to decipher the looming sign at the end of the long block of businesses closed for the day. Continuing to maneuver the Gregoire, he read the sign—Alter Road. That particular main street had been accentuated on his roadmap along with the exclusive "Outer Drive" which, according to the map on his knees, was only a mile or two away. Cautiously returning his eyes to the road again while removing one hand from the steering wheel, he repositioned his tie and then scrounged inside his jacket for an Altoid. Not only would the strong English mint help neutralize any staleness of breath, but might help relieve whatever intestinal discomfort he may experience upon ingesting what he anticipated to be an exceedingly spicy Indian meal. Fidgeting with the square tin container, he decided it would be best to pull over. Although he had been delighted to discover that these mints were now for sale in the United States, the tin was more difficult to open than the small cardboard box which formerly accommodated them. Intentionally avoiding a large puddle purposely created by a gushing fire hydrant to accommodate a small group of bare-footed children, Samuel decided to drive another block or two. He just recently had his convertible roadster professionally cleaned and polished and would be *damned* if these unrestrained sopping wet kids were going to splash water all over his custom leather seats.

Taking advantage of the first available strip of dry pavement, Samuel raised his right hand to signal a maneuver, then veered to a sudden stop. But before he had a chance to open the tin of mints, he had inadvertently forgotten about them. He was not sure whether it was the scroll-lettered sign at the front of the prominent establishment or the mammoth white-bricked Georgian-style building itself which first arrested his attention. All he could perceive at that moment was that it was staring at him like a Yankee general straight out of the Civil War. An image of a young man bound in freshly wrapped bandages and hobbling on uneven crutches suddenly came to mind. He could still hear the American soldier's country-like drawl as he bragged about his eccentric uncle's indispensible profession. "Millenbach's the name—Millenbach Funeral Parlor! What a fancy ass place—for a funeral home, that is! You know the old man wants ta sell it. Guess the lucky old bastard made too much dough. Can't handle them stiffs no more...." Samuel pushed his back into the soft contours of the leather seat and removed his sunglasses, the pupils of his eyes taking in the full panorama of the revelation before him. *Well now.* So this was the renowned Millenbach Funeral Parlor— the one that half-crazed private was raving about! But, as blabbermouthy as the lad was, he nevertheless managed to underestimate the bloody place. Why—it must accommodate at least a half dozen viewing rooms! Noticing a few motor cars parked in the adjacent lot as a Ford Runabout rambled its way in, Samuel tossed his glasses next to his straw hat on the passenger seat, wondering if the funeral home was still up for sale. But didn't the young soldier mention it was located just on the outskirts of Detroit? What was the name of the town he cited? "Grand" something or other? But wasn't *this* Detroit? Of course it was, he noted, tapping the map with his ringless forefinger while spotting the street sign for Outer Drive just ahead. And it *had* to be the same funeral parlor. How many funeral parlors called Millenbach would there be in an area, let alone one as pretentious as this—especially since the very idea of displaying a corpse in other than one's own home is a virtually novel practice? *Pitiful fellow,* he reflected, finally reaching inside his jacket pocket for that elusive tin of Altoids. *So saturated with narcotics, that kid didn't know what the bloody hell he was talking about.*

Prying the small container open with professionally manicured fingernails, Samuel wondered what it would be like acting as the proprietor of such a prestigious establishment. *Now that's an intriguing consideration,* he grinned, recalling with satisfaction the gruesome procedures required to embalm a cadaver, particularly that of cutting into a main artery and draining the corpse of its life blood...although, he acknowledged, the monotonous task of massaging the limbs to prevent rigor mortis was always an unpleasant pre-requisite. *Of course,* he acknowledged, his grin slowly tightening, he would not be embalming battle-fallen soldiers. And he wouldn't be packing any corpses into cheap shipping coffins. His new clientele would require the utmost attention for suitable presentations. *In fact,* he conceded, gingerly placing the small white mint on the tip of his pointed pink tongue, half of his clients would most likely be female. And, of course, some of them would be very young...perhaps even in that most enticing state of pubescence. *Yes!* he practically murmured under the facade of a low, foreboding hum. *Very young, indeed!*

Realizing that these lingering thoughts might cause him to be late for his dinner engagement, Samuel stuffed the tin of English mints back into his pocket before replacing the sunglasses, dabbed his perspiring forehead, and proceeded on his way. Upon making a left turn on Outer Drive, he could not help but be impressed by the elegant homes bordering the two-lane street. Not nearly as ostentatious as the funeral parlor he had just come across, of course, but finer than any home he imagined any Indian doctor to own. Slowing the convertible down a bit, he focused his gaze beyond a rotating lawn sprinkler to decipher the address of a Williamsburg colonial encircled by bright red geraniums. Making the determination that Dr. Khamal's home would be situated on the same side of the street, he concluded that it was bound to be at least another two or three blocks down the road. No longer preoccupied by his first impression of these stately homes, his thoughts drifted back to Millenbach's Funeral Parlor. Was the place indeed for sale? Would it be possible for him to successfully operate such a business? And what about the physician's post he was hoping to win? Perhaps he would not be offered the promising medical position, after all. Then, as a last resort, would he consider looking into such an atypical occupation—that of being an undertaker? Momentarily distracted by a perspiring young couple on a bicycle built for two, Samuel returned their friendly salutation and continued to drive forward, his mind immediately slipping back to the subject which presently engulfed him. What about income? And what kind of profit would such a funeral home reap? Perhaps Mr. Millenbach was trying to transact the current real estate sale because of insufficient income necessary to maintain the establishment. Maybe, Samuel speculated, tensing his wrists against the steering wheel, the recent American income tax amendment could most probably have strained the business just enough to push it over the financial precipice. Or *are* there enough prestigious clientele in this affluent suburb to finance the funeral home, regardless? After all, he reminisced, easing his foot off the accelerator while sinking further back into his sun-drenched seat, that wounded soldier back at the British infirmary *had* mentioned that his uncle…this Millenbach…was making too much money there. But what did that drugged-up kid know anyhow? And what does the concept of wealth mean to a youngster in such a delirious state? Probably just enough money to afford a common man's Model T. But yet…perhaps the lad was correct. Maybe his uncle was but another simple soul who did, indeed, earn more money than he knew what to do with. Perhaps the wealthiest of families had, indeed, contributed to the success of the Millenbach funeral home. And wasn't a business of that nature practically guaranteed? After all, as Benjamin Franklin once stated, nothing in this world is certain but death and taxes. *And finally,* he reasoned with an icy glint in his shaded, blue eyes, if he should acquire the funeral home, he would have no one to answer to but himself.

Neglecting to pay further attention to his present surroundings, Samuel unconsciously slowed the Gregoire to an unaccustomed sluggish speed. How much would such a venture cost, he began calculating. Since he had been so unjustly robbed of his rightful inheritance by his father's squandering, he most likely would not be able to afford the required good faith payment, let alone the substantial monthly funding required by the bank to perpetuate ownership of the funeral home. In reality, he probably could not even afford the least expensive home on the bloody street he was currently navigating, for that matter. After all, there was scarcely fifteen hundred dollars left in his personal bank account. Perhaps he could borrow more money? But what collateral would he have to offer? His three motor vehicles? Would that be enough? Hell! he thought, remembering that he had nearly lost the first two automobiles. Better some bloody luck than none at all! Of course, life would have been simpler were he related to a rich uncle like that young hillbilly private!

Samuel suddenly brought the Gregoire to an immediate halt, then paused for a moment, pressing his thumb to his chin. True, he did not have a rich uncle, but perhaps if he played his cards well, he may have the next best thing...that is, if he should decide to pursue the enticing venture! A potential benefactor played on his mind along with the image of a flush-faced Mr. Hogan darting down the long driveway of the colonial mansion, handing over to him a calling card bearing the name of a familiar, yet distant figure from his childhood. Yes! By Jove! he perked, mumbling the name so elegantly scripted upon the visiting card. First thing tomorrow morning he would inquire into the availability of the funeral parlor. And if things looked favorable, he would pursue the possibility of that potential loan. Perhaps his afternoon dinner hosts, the Khamals, might offer more insight into the funeral home's possible procurement. Of course, he would not let on about his deep personal interest in the establishment. Not presently, anyhow. He would bring the matter up casually, as if asking for another cup of tea. *Now,* he chided, slapping his trouser pocket, what the bloody hell had he done with that calling card? Had he inadvertently discarded it? What was that bloody address again? Firmly resolving to track down his plausible benefactor, regardless of whether or not he could retrieve the engraved card, Samuel pulled on the Gregoire's manual choke, started the engine and turned the roadster around, noticing that he had unintentionally bypassed his destination.

chapter 58

Divulged Secrets

Balancing a plate of unfinished hors'deurves with one hand and chilled lemonade with the other, Samuel was suddenly rushed out of a lavishly furnished living room and into the main dining area by his flustered hostess, Leya Khamal. Samuel's arrival at the Khamal's Tudor-style home nearly a half hour ago had been awkward enough when Leya's doting husband, Daksha, assuming that the two had never met, had formally introduced them. And being rescued by her loving spouse from the self-imposed chores of the kitchen to engage in a few minutes of pre-dinner conversation had been obviously uncomfortable for her, particularly when her husband, Daksha, boasted about the high opinion his dear father-in-law had of Doctor Samuel Governey. But now, after having endured a brief discussion on the peculiarities of American culture and the decadence of its women, it was certainly no mystery to Samuel why Leya Khamal could no longer retain her graceful composure especially when her husband had just cajoled Samuel to affirm his good fortune in possessing such a virtuous and dutiful wife.

"You must excuse my dear wife, Leya, Doctor Governey," Daksha pleaded while accompanying his only guest to the dinner table, placing Samuel's dish of marinated shrimp and cheese-stuffed vegetable balls upon the bright scarlet tablecloth. He turned to Samuel, stating that his wife was a bit nervous and had not been quite herself for the past few days. "It has been difficult for my dear wife, Samuel, this being her first time with child. Particularly with these hot and humid Detroit summers. And then...at a moment's notice, our otherwise reliable housekeeper informed Leya that she will be unable to attend to us this afternoon, leaving my poor wife to labor about the kitchen herself, consequently depriving us of her undivided companionship."

Seating himself upon a red ivory-framed chair as his pregnant hostess scurried back into the shelter of her kitchen, Samuel could not help but recollect the partially covered body of Leya as he performed an abortion followed by the intriguing clitoridectomy. Unaware of Daksha's adoring gaze toward his wife, he envisioned Leya's long brown legs as she lay sprawled across Dr. Carvelle's operating table aside an iron wash kettle containing her dismembered fetus, along with the remains of her surgically removed clitoris. But that was back in England when the 16-year-old had been impregnated by an American soldier, making it advisable to protect her honor with these surreptitious procedures, both vouchsafed by Leya's father, thus insuring her sacred bond with Dr. Daksha Khamal, her oblivious future husband.

Samuel's reminisces were suddenly terminated as his eye caught Daksha Khamal seating himself at the head of the table. "It is all we could do to keep the house comfortable," the bearded, turban-coifed host exclaimed, pointing to closed venetian blinds and electric fans hovering over large blocks of melting ice. "Samuel, my friend...you know it is a great misfortune that we cannot take residence on the shores of Lake St. Clair, even though Jefferson Avenue is quite nearby. Then we would not need these ice blocks and fans to keep ourselves cool. But," he sighed, shrugging broad shoulders, "being of Indian origin, we are forbidden, as you may well know, to reside in the City of Grosse Pointe."

Grosse Pointe! So *that* was the name of the city that Millenbach's nephew, Zach, was babbling about back at the infirmary. *Then Mack Avenue must somehow be the dividing line between Grosse Pointe and Detroit.* "Dr. Khamal, do you really mean to say that an internationally certified physician such as yourself is denied access to this place you call 'Grosse Pointe' merely because of your ancestral heritage?"

"That is absolutely correct. Yes, it is most unfortunate, but irrefutably true. However, Doctor Governey," Daksha grinned, exposing large white teeth while reaching for his lukewarm drink, "I suppose, that you, yourself, being of pure English extraction and, of course, Caucasian, would experience no difficulty in securing a home in Grosse Pointe if you so desired. In fact, despite my own family's exclusion from that splendid neighborhood, I would nevertheless recommend that you look into the probability of acquiring an estate in that community should you decide to reside here in Michigan after all, being that the city has a great deal to offer for men of your particular stature." Daksha rolled his large expressive eyes with a look of yearning and drank from his tall colorful glass. He then placed the finished drink upon the table and slowly rotated it like a painted carousel. "You know, Samuel, there are even private clubs for boating, if your heart should so desire. There are also golf facilities, tennis courts, stables and arenas for horse riding and polo games. Is that not a favorite sport of your people? Polo?"

"Why...yes, Daksha," Samuel replied, replacing his own half-melted concoction upon the linen tablecloth, wishing instead for the Cabernet Sauvignon he had brought along, or, in the very least, a chilled glass of Darjeeling tea. "I've dabbled with the game somewhat at my University. But, as of late, I've been out of practice. However, I suppose I could recover my passion for it with a bit of serious rehearsing. Nevertheless...despite all of the advantages of living in Grosse Pointe, it would most certainly be quite a shame to suffer the deprivation of venerable neighbors such as yourself and your lovely wife, Leya. But please, my dear chap, Daksha, bend my ear a bit more and enlighten me with further details regarding this reprehensible custom. Is it true, then, that others would be denied residence in Grosse Pointe merely because of their ethnic predisposition?" Samuel could not help but focus upon Daksha's dark Indian skin before blurting out. "The Negro population, for example?"

Dr. Khamal let out a high-pitched chuckle. "Why yes, yes, of course! *Particularly* the Negroes, Doctor Governey. Why...we have been most fortunate to keep our own neighborhood free from them, so you see, Doctor Governey, a most...how do they say...picky?...community as Grosse Pointe would be certain to guard their lily-white district as well!"

Samuel patronized Daksha's self-satisfied grin, somewhat amused at having been so casually reminded that, in spite of their inferiority, the Indian people did, indeed, maintain their own societal preferences, even to the extent of perpetuating a caste system within the Indian race—not to mention their ridiculous belief in an afterlife that could transfigure any one of their lowly kind into some sort of four-legged animal or even a blood-sucking insect. But, pushing aside those unappetizing thoughts, he became further intrigued by the possibility of, sometime in the near future, residing in such a judicious city. About to inquire further of Grosse Pointe's logistics, he was suddenly distracted by the figure of Leya bearing a pewter tray containing three painted bowls of cucumber salad and a tinted carafe filled to the brim. Samuel aspired with widened eyes, hoping the carafe contained the Cabernet Sauvignon he had brought along.

"Ah! Leya my darling...you are such a lovely little flower!" the proud father-to-be exclaimed.

Promptly acknowledging the submissive hostess once again, Samuel kept his own opinion to himself, thinking that, in reality, she rather resembled a prized pumpkin. Adorned in a bright orange sari, her bulging belly replaced the shapely figure which, just two years prior, several layers of silk had failed to conceal; her dark stem of hair, draped by a transparent veil, complemented the dot in the center of an otherwise unblemished forehead.

Daksha's hairy arms supported clasped hands, his countenance beaming as he further addressed his wife. "My dear Leya...while you were busy in the kitchen, we were discussing the unbearable weather and the possibility of Doctor Governey taking residence in Grosse Pointe should he stay, since temperatures are more pleasant and similar to that of our city of Bangalore. Would you not agree, my dear?"

As bangles on swelled wrists jingled under the willowy sway of a thick gold necklace, Leya placed the pewter tray upon a marble-top sideboard and forced a modest smile, casting doe-like eyes downward. Keeping her answer curt as she had frequently done all afternoon, she coyly replied in a maidenly voice. "Yes...I suppose he should."

"You see, Doctor Governey...even my beloved Leya agrees!" Daksha gloated, clapping his goblet-sized hands before raising them into the muggy air. "Come," he invited, rising from his seat and retrieving the carafe while Leya served the abundant salads. "Let us enjoy the delightful meal she has prepared for us!"

As Dr. Khamal poured the wine into their respective glasses, Samuel maintained an appeasing stature, despite his disappointment. As long as the libation had remained in the tinted carafe, its true color was impossible to predict, but now, having been released from the rose-colored container, it had naturally transformed into the pale yellow of a typical Indian rice wine. He should have suspected as much. Ever since stepping foot into the Khamal residence and being asked to remove his two-tone spectator shoes for the sake of their plush white carpeting, every trace of American civilization had disappeared. And why did every bloody inch of this Indian home have to be so ostentatious! He may as well have stumbled into the pith of a painter's palette. Even the colors of the rainbow paled in comparison. Bright, vivid remnants of every hue nearly overwhelmed his optic perceptions, from the royal blues and emerald greens of rich wall tapestries to the regal violets, shimmery golds, and lavish reds of ornate brocade upholstery. It was inexcusable enough that he was forced to tolerate such gaudiness, but the omnipresent odor of curry along with the annoying smell of lingering incense, wherever it was coming from, was starting to give him a headache. As Daksha finished pouring the wine, Samuel concluded that it was just as well he had not served the expensive French bottle. Aside from the incorrect use of Hock glasses which were fashioned exclusively for German and Alsace wines, they were tinted a garish rose color—certain to spoil the brilliant garnet of the fine Cabernet Sauvignon. In any event, he would discreetly grin and bear whatever else his gauche host had to offer and then be on his way, but not without first inquiring about the Millenbach Funeral Home.

It was during the main course of lamb and potato curry that Samuel found an opportunity to mention the subject which preoccupied his mind. After sampling a small mouthful of some dreaded vegetable which had been forced upon his plate, he was surprised to find himself piercing a different spiced delicacy once more with his sterling fork in anticipation of another serving. "I must say—this is the most delicious cabbage I have ever tasted! I must admit that I have never cared for it before—*despised* it actually—but this...this is absolutely *divine!*" Encouraged by the grateful acknowledgement of his host and hostess, he continued. "I suppose my averse distaste to cabbage had been previously formulated by people who, unlike you, my dear Leya, had not yet mastered the art of preparing it. And, I must say, in all my travels during the past several years, I have, to my dismay, come across some witless characters. *In fact,*" he emphasized, cutting into the ginger-spiced cabbage, "one young man in particular crosses my mind this very instant. Actually, I was reminded of this simpleton while driving here this afternoon. The most amazing thing!" He leaned forward a bit, gently placing his knife upon the blue gilded rim of the Spode dinner plate. "While briefly visiting my old infirmary in England shortly after that horrific war, I came across this boyish soldier—a most peculiar lad—who claimed that his uncle was the proprietor of a funeral home in, would you believe, *of all places*, Grosse Pointe. 'Millenbach Funeral Home' was the…" In a sudden, panic-stricken instant, Samuel recoiled from his seat, realizing that his hostess had inexplicably tipped over her wine glass upon hearing the name "Millenbach." Ever so grateful that his acute reflexes had successfully prevented the splashing wine from sullying his custom-tailored Italian suit and silk necktie, he noted that it was quite a different matter for his pregnant hostess whose saturated belly was unmercifully transformed into a dilating sphere of henna.

As Leya frantically blotted her drenched sari, her husband attended to the red linen tablecloth, all the while showering Samuel with unending apologies. "Doctor Governey…please, sit down, my good friend and continue with your meal. We are quite fine. I am only thankful that my wife's mishap has not ruined your own handsome garments. It is a good sign you have such athletic reflexes; as well you should for a promising young surgeon, yes?"

Realizing that the conversation would take a different course unless he purposely diverted it, Samuel offered an unassuming smile and reseated himself. Noticing that the stain on Leya's sari was a shade lighter, he watched as his flustered hostess waited for her husband to regain his composure and reseat himself before following his lead. "I hope that my mention of the name 'Millenbach' did not startle you for some unknown reason, my dear Mrs. Khamal. My intention was merely to relate the coincidental circumstance of encountering a funeral home by that very name described to me while in England."

An impetuous blush pervaded Leya's taut cheeks as she struggled to give a reply, but all efforts were in vain as her husband interjected on her behalf. "*By Jove*, Doctor Governey! No, no…Good heavens no! You are most certainly mistaken!" he replied at the top of his strained voice, strangling a wine-dampened napkin with wet fingers. Ultimately succumbing to the skeptical look in Samuel's keen blue eyes, he fell into an unmanageable stutter. "It is only that…well…well…you see…there has been a very un…unfortunate cir…circumstance which happened." There was a forced pause—an obvious attempt to regain equilibrium. "A beautiful flower of an Indian woman has been the victim of a most tragic accident." Controlling his words carefully, he continued. "Doctor Governey, that poor young woman drowned in her swimming pool and is now laid out for viewing at the Millenbach Funeral Home. This young woman was not only a close acquaintance of our family, but a mere child…barely 14 years of age. It was a most unfortunate stroke of fate. An incident too unbearable for ordinary sentiment!"

"My dear Daksha and Leya," Samuel offered with prayerful hands after an interminably awkward silence. He then removed a pristine handkerchief from his breast pocket and pressed it to his nose. "Please accept my sincerest condolences regarding your dear friend," he said, still convinced by the horror in Leya's eyes that there was much more to the incident than had been related. "But Daksha, my good man, please be kind enough to tell me...and please excuse my curiosity if it seems inappropriate. Since having the good fortune of becoming acquainted with your dear father and somewhat cognizant of Indian customs, it very much surprises me that this bereaved family should agree to employ the services of a Western funeral parlor rather than display the precious body of their beautiful daughter in the sanctity of their own home...not that there is anything improper with the situation, mind you," he innocently shrugged. "I only suppose that this is a genuine testament to the credibility of the Millenbach Funeral establishment, is it not?"

Realizing that his tenacious guest was not about to relinquish the agonizing subject, Daksha sighed in resignation as Samuel swallowed another piece of lamb. Perhaps it was appropriate to relate the whole bloody episode. After all, if Doctor Samuel Governey was to become a trusted colleague, it was best to be forthright about the matter, lest he find out through other channels. "You are quite correct, my dear Doctor Governey and very perceptive, may I add. Yes, it is true that the Hindu people regard death to be a most sacred matter. But we also regard our people's behavior in this life to be of utmost importance, for it is through our actions that we will eventually become one with Brahman, the supreme soul." Completely ignoring his cold, half-eaten mutton, Daksha pushed his plate away. "It only stands to reason, then, that we expect the most honorable behavior from our children, particularly our wives and daughters who have a solemn duty to remain the principal guardians of their virtue. However..." Daksha contorted his lips like a little Indian boy excusing himself for accidentally stepping on a bug. "Occasionally our people forget that we now live in America and the societal values differ greatly. What is sometimes tolerated in India can be considered a most serious crime in the United States. I am being forthright and honest with you, Doctor Governey, because you are one of my dearest and closest American friends." Daksha lowered his voice along with bulbous eyes. "The unpleasant truth is that this particular young woman was discovered by her all-trusting father in the arms of a man exchanging the most intimate mutual caresses." He let out a dragon-like bluster, shaking his sweating head, all the while envisioning the young Indian suitor fondling the bare breasts of his now-deceased lover. "Doctor Governey...I implore you...what is a father in such a predicament to do? Of course, you can imagine the rage and shame one must feel upon finding his daughter in such an uncompromising position, *particularly* with a stranger of a lower caste. And the untimely death due to drowning probably would have all passed as a mere tragic accident...had it not been for a neighbor who had witnessed the entire, unfortunate incident."

Scarcely aware that a piece of barely masticated lamb lay dormant on his speechless tongue, Samuel realized why Leya was suffering from an acute bout of neurosis. Had it not been for her dear, compassionate father, she too, would most likely have succumbed to a fate similar to that of her recently drowned companion. And to exacerbate matters, it was apparent that her overtly condemning husband, an affluent epidemiologist upon whom she fully depended, had no bloody idea that his own "virtuous" beloved wife had been guilty of much more than an isolated rendezvous with a man of inferior Indian heritage. If the incident in question were grounds for murder by drowning as Daksha had seemingly supported, then it would not be difficult to imagine what punishment Leya's husband would dole out to an Indian woman impregnated by an American soldier, let alone deliberately undergoing a surgical abortion. More conscious than ever of the castigation and wrath Leya must fear should her husband ever discover this shocking truth, Samuel swallowed the last morsel of lamb and promptly put down his fork, acutely aware, yet not particularly moved, by the innocent pretense in Leya's eyes desperately pleading for Samuel's oath of eternal secrecy. "Are you *telling* me, Dr. Khamal, that this young lady's father was so enraged by the actions of his daughter...his own beloved flesh and blood...so as to *deliberately* and *premeditatedly* murder her by drowning?"

"That is correct, Samuel," Daksha nodded, retaining his confidant's attention as if pressing a pointed dagger to his freshly-shaven chin. "But you must understand, my dear Doctor Governey, in your mind as well as in the minds of your Western colleagues, this young maiden's father has committed the unthinkable. However, in *our* eyes, it is the *daughter* who is guilty of the more grievous offense. By defiling herself in such a manner...in such an *impudent* manner, this particular young woman had disgraced her family beyond ordinary Western comprehension." Offering a transcendent smile, he reached for his wife's dampened hand. "You see, Samuel, by transgressing the sacred laws of our people, she unquestionably consented to her own demise."

He then lifted Leya's frail hand from the table. "Why Samuel, you must agree...she may as well have slit her own wrists and spilled her own despoiled blood!" Continuing to caress his wife's fidgety hand, Daksha gently laid it back on the table, shaking his head in deep regret. "It would have, indeed, been better for all involved had she never been born. So you see, my good man...by crossing the sacred boundaries of Hindu law, she was predestined to have chosen her own death sentence."

More than ever aware of the laborious whirring of the electric fans, Samuel mournfully, and for the very last time, laid his knife and fork to rest across his empty plate. Wiping his mouth with a linen napkin, he was about to break the uneasy silence by praising his host and hostess on a superbly-prepared meal. But before he could speak up, Daksha suddenly stood, both hands firmly planted on the table, and, with the back of his legs, pushed away his chair. "And so, my dear friend...that is *why* funeral arrangements are as such!"

Turning toward the marble-top sideboard, he pulled open a drawer and drew out a cigar box. "The home is still being investigated by the police and the family thought it best for visitation to take place at Millenbach's. Of course," he added, offering Samuel his pick of the Cuban cigars, "after the visitation, the family can resume the customary cremation ritual. So, you see, Doctor Governey," he concluded, lighting Samuel's cigar with one hand while lovingly extending the other toward his troubled wife, "it is no mystery why my beautiful bride is so distressed by this terrible situation. It is, indeed, a great responsibility to become a parent. A most burdensome responsibility, indeed. But perhaps Brahman shall look favorably upon Leya and myself and deliver to us a family of all boys. Then we will truly be blessed...yes?"

Appreciating a brief break from the conversation while savoring the rich, earthy flavor of the cigar, Samuel glanced pitilessly toward the teary-eyed mother-to-be, fathoming the futility of Daksha's attempt to console her. It was crystal clear now why Daksha Khamal, forever ignorant of his wife's tainted past, was initially reluctant to reveal the drowning incident. The apparent murder of the child was, on the surface, surely a great discredit to his people. And it was indeed ironic and somewhat amusing that by merely misinterpreting his curiosity about the Millenbach Funeral Home, Daksha had been compelled to unveil a covert, chilling secret which, up until now, was meant to be discussed solely within his own ethnic circle. However, Samuel discerned, despite the Khamals' menial place in society, he suddenly felt a peculiar affinity with Daksha along with an unequivocal admiration toward his astute sense of justice.

Realizing the inappropriateness of pressing his initial inquiry any further, Samuel graciously accepted an invitation into the drawing room, feeling as if a casual excursion had been delayed by an unexpected, yet exhilarating rain-storm. Consequently, he would finish out the afternoon as swiftly as proper etiquette permitted. Then, with a refreshing cold shower in mind, he would return to the Hotel Pontchartrain, take two aspirin for his growing headache, retire to bed and call the undertaker in the morning.

chapter 59

Visitation

The first thing Samuel noticed as he stepped from the elevator and into the dimly lit basement corridor of the Millenbach Funeral Home was the obvious change of temperature accompanied by a steady, audible vibration. Although it was only mid-morning, he had already felt the approaching heat of day creeping through his freshly showered pores nearly an hour ago as he requested a valet to retrieve the Gregoire from the garage of the Pontchartrain Hotel. And even his drive amid newly constructed mansions alongside the breezy waters of Lake St. Clair had decreed another unbearably humid day. But now, as Samuel was escorted by Mr. Millenbach toward the embalming room, he felt as if he were inside a moderately controlled icebox, verifying the presence of one of those newfangled air-cooling devices he had currently read about in the *London Times*. Grasping the generous brim of his straw boater hat, he observed the wide grin on the undertaker's pink, sagging face as they walked through an adjoining doorway, whereupon Mr. Millenbach activated the overhead carbon arc lighting, converting the previously indiscernible room into a plethora of the most up-to-date clinical equipment Samuel had ever laid eyes upon. It was obvious that, after entering the building's spacious lobby, the funeral director had been more than eager to usher him through the main floor with its multiple viewing rooms, powder rooms, and plush sitting areas, neglecting to offer so much as a cup of tea. However, at this particular juncture, the aging man's overwhelming pride seemed to rival that of an exuberant father distributing exotic cigars on behalf of a newborn son.

"*So*, Doctor Governey...," Millenbach asked in a raspy Midwestern drawl followed by a repressed emphysemic cough. "What do you think of this new technology of mine? You won't find this in any other funeral parlor, no sir!"

With increasing bewilderment as to how such an extraordinary establishment had fallen into the hands of someone so blatantly unrefined, Samuel glanced around the ultramodern embalming room as Millenbach cleared the remaining phlegm from his throat, poignantly aware that the price of the pretentious mortuary had just increased by threefold. Directly in the center of the room, situated upon the antiseptically clean tile, was a long, glaring metal table. A ceramic bathtub, a deep-seated sink and what he assumed to be a sizeable refrigerator were positioned against the far wall. Near the embalming table stood a tall cabinet with wide drawers—probably containing linens, syringes, and other essentials, he surmised. Shifting his gaze to the other side of the room, he noticed three rows of shelving containing empty glass bottles and small wooden barrels. The familiar smell of formaldehyde emanating from the barrels was hardly noticeable, though, since he had already grown accustomed to the pungent odor halfway through his private tour as it clung to Ed Millenbach's black tailored suit. As Samuel squinted at the smeared identification labels glued to a wooden cosmetic chest, he was once again addressed by the mortician's wheezing voice.

"Got the air cooler goin' down here," he gratefully declared looking around the room while pocketing his phlegm-filled handkerchief. "Got it on the main floor too, but for some danged reason, it stopped workin' up there yesterday. There's a separate unit on the top floor where me and the wife live," he explained, pointing his crooked index finger toward the cement block ceiling. "Thank the Lord that's workin'...makes sleepin' a lot more bearable." Millenbach folded his arms across his emaciated chest. "Got a fella from the company comin' round ta fix it tomorra', though. Yep! Then it'll be good as new again. And get a load of that, won't you?" Millenbach suddenly exclaimed, obviously eager to change the subject at hand. "It's the latest ice freezing machine they make," he gloated, walking across the room and unlocking a nearly seven foot tall freezer door, then pointing at large cubes of solid ice. "No more havin' the ice man gettin' in my way to restock it every coupla' days." He then closed the metal door and gestured toward the long porcelain bathtub. "Yep! At times when I can't get to a body right-aways, I just pack the tub fulla cold, hard ice. Unlike them other morticians who don't have no choice but ta use their customers' bathtubs in the middle of the night or embalm them cadavers right smack dab on the kitchen table. No sir! Anyway, havin' plenty of ice on hand sure spares me lots o' time and trouble and that terrible stink o' death, and it keeps the stiffs nice and fresh. My wife Hildy can attest to that," he affirmed, nodding his virtually bald head toward the cosmetic chest. "She pretties 'em up for me. Does a fine good job too." Millenbach sniffed and rubbed his rawboned nose with the back of his liver-spotted hand. "Nobody fixes hairdos and makeup better'n my Hildy. No sir! She really gussies em up!"

Samuel broodingly retained his silence. Millenbach had just exhumed an important matter to which he had not, as of yet, given much thought. If he *did* happen to procure the funeral home after all, he would, without a doubt, find it necessary to hire someone with experience in mortuary cosmetology. Granted, he did possess the basic skills of properly embalming cadavers, but styling the hair, applying a suitable shade of lipstick and bringing out a rosy tint in the cheeks had not been a prerequisite when shipping soldiers back home to the states in plywood coffins.

"Lightin's good too!" Samuel heard Millenbach declare as the funeral director waved his hand toward the ceiling's tubular lights. "Brighter n' most. Use em' way over in Hollywood ta make them motion pictures, they do. When I heard about it, I figured *what the hell!* If them lights are good enough to help pretty up the likes of that clown of a fella' Charlie Chaplin and that sweet little Mary Pickford on the big screen, they're certainly good enough for prettyin' up dead bodies for layin' in a casket!"

Samuel intentionally brought his mind back to the moment, realizing that he had not paid attention to what Mr. Millenbach was saying. Something about Mary Pickford in a casket. His thoughts had drifted to a more practical place, pondering the unlikelihood of obtaining the funds for such an elaborate establishment, no matter what the source. A look of concern crossed his face as he envisioned the familiar name inscribed on the gold-embossed calling card which the current owner of the Philadelphia mansion was so insistent on giving him. Perhaps he could offer Reginald Morgan his three motor cars as collateral for a loan as well. But even if he could obtain the required down payment, would the funeral home draw enough income to sustain his monthly notes, let alone his privileged lifestyle? With a sinking heart, he straightened his shoulders, switched the straw hat to his other hand, and confronted the elderly mortician whose cracking grin and bloodshot eyes begged for a complimentary response. "Please excuse me, my dear Mr. Millenbach. I hope you don't find my inquisitiveness to be out of order and I am certainly more than impressed with your management of this fine funeral home...a funeral home which, I am certain, must be one of the most technologically advanced in existence. However, I had never suspected that the vocation of undertaking...a most noble profession, indeed... would reap profits in such abundance as to warrant the extravagance of your modern physical furnishings. Have my presumptions been incorrect, then, or am I unaware of an additional wellspring of compensation?"

With an illuminated look in his otherwise lackluster eyes, Ed Millenbach pursed his pale lips and quickly cleared his throat. "Why I'll be damned if you aren't one smart fella, Doctor Governey! You certainly got all yer marbles in one jar, ya do. That's something I've intended ta discuss in my office, back upstairs. But first," the old undertaker went on, fumbling inside the lining of his well-pressed suit, accidentally spilling a package of Camel cigarettes, "there's somethin' else I want ta show ya down here." Laboriously stooping over to retrieve the cigarettes before Samuel had the chance to intervene, Millenbach mumbled something about his aching arthritis, stiffly stood back up and offered Samuel a smoke. "Yep...one smart fella ya are," he replied to his guest's polite refusal. Placing the butt of the cigarette to crusty lips, he stashed the pack of Camels back inside his pocket, then fished for a book of matches. "It's a mighty damn nasty habit, it is," he sputtered, scratching a match to light up. "Try ta limit myself ta three o' these here coffin sticks a day now." He paused from his ramblings to take a deep drag, then continued. "But it's mighty damn hard. Was smokin' up ta three *packs* a day, would ya believe? My honey, Hildy, keeps beggin' me ta stop altogether," he went on, disclosing a smudged, gold pocket watch. "Don't have ta worry about her smellin' the tobacca' smoke, though, no sir! Havin' ta work with formaldehyde's a damn good blessing in disguise." Millenbach made a quick sign of the cross and gestured toward the wooden barrels. "That stuff's strong 'nuff ta cover a multitude of sins! A *multitude* of 'em, yes sir!" Suddenly plagued with another bout of emphysemic hacking, he promptly took care of the matter, then released the watch's swing ring. "We'd better get goin' if ya want to see whatever else I've got to show ya. This way.

"Now this here's somethin' you won't see in any other funeral home, either," Millenbach remarked as they entered a fully equipped, yet simply furnished kitchen area. Moving toward one of several checkered, cloth-covered tables, he leaned over a long wooden bench, tapping his cigarette against the edge of a red tin ashtray. "Thought o' the idea myself," he declared, nodding affirmatively, then taking another draw from the Camel. "It's for my patrons ta use if they want to. *You* know...after the funeral and all, they can come down here for a gatherin'. The ladies can prepare any kind o' food that they bring along," he defined, pointing to the modern, cast-iron Mayflower oven. "Ya know, my people really appreciate it...'specially during the hot summer months like this. Yes siree!" he grinned, exposing yellow teeth while depositing more ashes in the tin tray. "Folks wanna settle down for a good meal in comfort. They ain't gonna get that in their own homes, no sir. So long as Millenbach's got an air coolin' machine. Only other place they can go ta cool off is one of them fancy movie theatres, and that ain't no place for gettin' together after burying a loved one, you bettcha!" Millenbach indulged in one last drag before snuffing out what was left of the Camel. "Good for business too, sure as shootin', damn it! But enough o' that," he gasped, unfurling another handkerchief from his pocket to clear his phlegm-plugged throat before wiping puckered lips. "Just one more thing I wanna show ya, doc. Follow me...come on here."

Leading Samuel toward a sparsely stocked open pantry area, Millenbach delved inside another pocket, retrieving a brass ring bearing several keys. Pausing in front of a heavy oak door adjacent to the pantry, he selected the longest key and inserted it into the ominous-looking lock, slowly releasing the dead bolt. With considerable effort, he rotated the braided brass knob and pulled the protesting door open, thanking Samuel for his assistance.

Even before the cumbersome door was fully open, there was no doubt whatsoever as to what lurked behind it, since it had taken only the slightest crack to detect its contents. Nevertheless, if Samuel had suffered from blindness or loss of hearing, it would have mattered not. His keen sense of smell was the only faculty required to unveil the shrouded mystery. Inhaling the emanating fruity, familiar scent as Millenbach activated a dim lantern, Samuel remained as still as a young lad with his nose pressed against the window of a penny candy emporium. Finding it difficult to believe that a man like Millenbach would own such an exquisite collection, he gazed at the array of bottles before him, each slightly angled in its own separate tile cubbyhole. Granted, the distinguishing label on some of the bottles divulged that these were of a common, frugal sort. But, on the other hand, he mused, mindful of the cruder smell of fermented grapes permeating a large brass-hooped barrel, the old man *had* managed to collect some exceptionally rare vintage wines, indeed! Speculating that a dusty, cobwebbed bottle of 'Chateau Latour' was probably from the turn of the century, he peeled his gaze from the smooth, green bottle upon hearing, once more, the scratchy voice of the undertaker.

"Yes, sir," Millenbach declared, smacking ghostly lips while pocketing his keys, "every kind of wine you can think of. Merlots, Burgundy...all kinds of 'em. Got 'em from all over—Germany, France...Italy...you name it!" Withdrawing swollen hands from his creased trousers, he pulled a straw-encased bottle of Tuscan wine from a crowded shelf. "Like Chianti? Go ahead...take it!" he insisted, thrusting the bottle toward Samuel. "I've got lots of Italian wines...give 'em to all my clients. Sicilian mostly, but Italian just the same. Yep!" he boasted, returning one hand to his pocket, jostling and jingling his keys, "Do it for all kinds o' ethnic folks, ya know. Boosts up the business considerable. There's Hock for the Germans and other Italian wines like that Barolo over there. Lots o' people seem ta like that sherry...that's from Spain, ya know, doc, even though we don't get much Spaniards here like they do down south. Got some English wine too," he pointed with a wink. "Don't seem to be gettin' rid of much o' that, though. Of course, you can never go wrong with a bottle of the French. I save the real good ones for the wealthy folk. Pays off in the long run, it sure does! Nope," he sniffed, "I ain't seen no one turn down a good bottle o' French wine yet...except for the Irish," he clarified, wrinkling his nose. "Always keep a few bottles o' beer on hand for that group...usually Pabst or Stroh's...they ain't fussy. They'll drink any, long as it foams. As for me," he emphasized, gesturing toward the oak barrel, "that's my fav'rite right there. Got a buddy down in Indiana makes his own dago red, then sends it along every year or so. Here ya are." He reached for a dusty wine glass, filling it from the spout of the oak cask. Then, noticing that Samuel's hands were already occupied, he snatched the straw hat and stretched on tiptoe, plopping it on his guest's head. "Try some."

So that was it, Samuel contemplated, hesitantly accepting the questionable vintage. It was now quite obvious that Millenbach was a native of Indiana. He struggled not to grimace while sampling the crude Port, then quickly swallowed. "Yes, very good. Very good indeed," he commented, wiping his lips with the tip of his tongue in an effort to appease a forever assaulted palate. "Indiana, did you say?"

"Yes, sir, that's correct. *Spurgeon*, Indiana. Down in Pike County. Right near the Kentucky border. That's where I originally come from. Owned a furniture store there some years back. That's how I first got into this business, selling caskets and all—though I never owned a funer'l home 'til now. Folks in Pike County show their love 'uns in their own homes. As folks still did 'round here 'til I showed up," he clarified, folding his arms across his starched white shirt. "But fate sure has a funny way o' turnin' things around. Nope...ain't makin' furniture no more," he said, clearing his throat. "Or caskets, for that matter, doc. Order all my caskets from Owosso now, right here in Michigan. Reggie Vincent, the guy I sold my old furniture shop to, was sellin' em to me when I first started here, but they don't make no *fancy* caskets down there." Millenbach removed one of the crumpled handkerchiefs from his pocket. "Too many rich folks in this here area. Yep...old Reggie wasn't too happy about it, but ya got ta give yer customers what they want," he emphasized, snapping the kerchief to attention and waving it around like a surrendering flag before arresting it with both hands. "Ain't no casket too good for some o' these folks right here in Grosse Pointe. No siree! None o' them snotty, high-falootin' uppities livin' in those ritzy mansions o' theirs are gonna settle their loved ones in a common timberwood casket for all eternity." Millenbach paused for a moment to gob more spit into the handkerchief. "Do you know, Doctor Governey, that Owosso supplied caskets to two of our own American presidents? William McKinley and Benjamin Harrison. Yes, sir...rumor has it that Owosso's the largest casket maker in the nation. Maybe even the world. I'd have ta be crazy ta give up the chance of dealin' with them, 'specially since the location's so convenient and all."

Seizing the opportunity to slip a word in edgewise, Samuel quickly spoke up, still coveting in his mind's eye the opulent mansions he had ogled on his way to the funeral home, radiating royalty amid fluted pillars, magisterial statuary and acre upon acre of freshly manicured lawns. "So, my good man, would I be correct in assuming that your earnings from the furniture business allowed you to purchase such a fine facility here?"

"That rinky dink shop of mine? Why...hell no! My damn furniture business had nothin' to do with it. Was draggin' me further into my own grave, if anything...excuse the pun. Like I says, got a damn lucky break that turned things 'round for me. But that's somethin' we can chew over back upstairs in my office," he said, noting from the time on his pocket watch that he hadn't another moment to spare if he were to promptly greet his bereaved clients due to arrive within the hour. The undertaker then motioned for Samuel to follow him, seized his guest's unfinished glass of wine, placed it on one of the cloth-covered tables, and escorted him back into the elevator leading to the main floor.

chapter 60

Gauche Negotiations

In comparison with most of the other rooms comprising the funeral home, Millenbach's front office located on the main floor was not only of moderate size, but simply furnished as well. Even the grandfather clock peeking out from the corner was not at all imposing. Just enough to give the impression of sincere sympathy and humble servitude, Samuel thought as he stepped into the shaded, air-fanned room. He then surrendered his straw hat and bottle of Chianti to Millenbach. Upon hearing a soft-spoken voice greeting both himself and his host, Samuel turned around to see a snowy-haired, spectacled woman carrying an unadorned silver teapot. She demurely excused herself, hunched over two delicately painted china cups previously set upon the office desk and began filling the stuffy den with the aroma of black licorice. A dead ringer for a Mrs. Kriss Kringle if there ever was one, Samuel entertained, envisioning the stout, aproned woman in a red, fur-trimmed coat and hat, secretly wishing that this particular image could conjure up a blast of cold, invigorating air. He responded with a gallant nod as Millenbach beamingly introduced her as his wife, Hildy. Samuel then waited for Mrs. Millenbach to place the silver teapot upon a wooden server before taking her wrinkled hand and anointing it with a tender kiss. He then responded to her husband's invitation to be seated across from the desk as the missus departed the room, after which Samuel sank into a leather club chair, blocking from his mind the less-than-appetizing encounter with Millenbach's better half.

"So, Doctor Governey," the funeral director sniffed, leaning into his swivel chair, momentarily ignoring his steaming cup of tea. "No use beatin' around the bush. This is the part o' sellin' I'm not too fond of. Never did care much for makin' business deals. 'Specially between friends of kin," he explained, recalling the kind words Samuel had shared about his nephew, Zach, still recuperating in a British infirmary from his deployment to Russia. An unwarranted intervention, Millenbach thought to himself, and a damn disgrace to the U.S. Army, forced to be commanded by a British general, but, damn it, there was no use fretting about it. President Wilson had made a decision and there was no fightin' fair with Uncle Sam. 'Specially since it was against the law to gripe about any of his wars. But, what was done was done and the sooner Zach was well enough to come home again, all the better. "Yep," Ed Millenbach proclaimed, crinkling a leaky nose while scratching an elbow through the sleeves of his black suit, "I'm grateful that the boy's healin' well. Damn good boy, that one is. Spent two full summers workin' for me here. Helped back in Indiana, too. Hildy says she wants ta throw a welcome home gatherin' for the lad, bein' that he's been an orphan and don't have folks of his own ta do it. But that depends whether or not we've moved ta Florida by then. That's where we're goin' once I sell the place," he said, tugging open a desk drawer and removing a neatly ironed handkerchief. "Do ya know, Doctor Governey, that use ta be nothin' but swampland over there, but they've developed it considerable since, and the weather's nice and warm all year round. That's where we get most of our oranges from...takes less than a week ta ship em by rail. Even in the wintertime, yes sir!" he proclaimed, finally shutting the stubborn drawer. "That's when my emphysema really starts ta act up...in the wintertime. Almost died last winter, I did," he said, oblivious to the melodic chimes of the grandfather clock ringing out the half hour. "Anyhow, my doc says Florida's the best place ta be for a man in my condition. Kinda lookin' forward to it, damn it. Don't misunderstand me, doc. Bein' a funeral director's a hellava good occupation, but there comes a time when a man's got to retire. So...Doctor Governey," Millenbach concluded, raising the spotless white handkerchief toward his dripping nostrils, "do you have any questions about my place before we start talkin' business? Oh, yes...and another thing," he added, stopping the kerchief mid-nose, "sorry I didn't show you the upstairs, but was afraid I was runnin' out o' time seein' that my guests are arrivin' soon. Figured we can discuss the finances now. Then, if ya like, Hildy can show you the rest after we're done, seein' that you probably won't be makin' up yer mind right away, anyhow." He paused to clear his nose, then continued. "There's our livin' quarters up there along with the casket room and one more extra viewin' room. In fact, got a dead one up there for viewin' right now...that's what my guests are comin' for. Folks usually like their loved ones laid out on the main floor, but seein' that the air coolin' machine ain't workin' down here, I suggested the upstairs room. Lot more comf'trable, 'specially on a muggy summer day like this. *But...,*" he emphasized, "like I was tellin' ya before...the problem will be fixed real soon. So, doc," he said, turning over the monogrammed handkerchief to its unsullied side, "Is there anything else you'd like ta know before we begin?"

Ever so grateful that Ed Millenbach's incessant yapping had been interrupted by his emphysemic hacking, Samuel took another drink from his teacup, entirely convinced that the all-annoying gift of gab, as evidenced between uncle and nephew, was indeed, an inherited trait. Furthermore, he ruminated, placing the cup upon its saucer, although he did have several questions in mind, he was not about to further waste his precious time in this hotbox of a room, squirming through another montage of the mortician's ramblings in an attempt to gain a simple answer. Unless, of course, by some small miracle he was absolutely certain that the funeral home was well within his financial grasp. If that be the case, Millenbach could talk his ear off for all he cared, and then depart for Florida with his blessings. Keeping a watchful eye on the undertaker as he finished clearing his throat and shoved the handkerchief inside an already overstuffed pocket, Samuel seized the opportunity to speak up. "My dear Mr. Millenbach," he began in a compassionate tone while repositioning a tingling foot, "first and foremost, let me extend my most sincere concern for your continued good health. And do be assured, my dear friend, that, as your doctor has predicted, your condition shall most certainly improve considerably upon your relocation to our sunshine state of Florida, its therapeutic powers having been repeatedly confirmed in a large number of medical journals." Acknowledging the funeral director's gratification for his extended wishes, Samuel quickly recaptured the discussion. "Be that as it may, my good man, I do think it best, for your own sake, that you not be unnecessarily burdened with further inquiries regarding the funeral home until we are reasonably certain that I can afford to purchase your fine establishment. So, by all means," he continued with a bit of trepidation, "for your sake as well as my own, what exactly *is* the cost of the Millenbach Funeral Home?"

Releasing a curt sigh, Millenbach pulled at his lower lip, then dropped his loose fist upon the lackluster oak desk. "You *do* understand, Doctor Governey, that I've put a consid'rable amount of money into the place, so my price is gonna be substant'lly higher than any old run o' the mill fun'ral home." Attempting to detect the least bit of understanding from his prospective buyer, he nervously continued. "Well, yes, uh...ya understand, doctor, that I don't expect to get back all I put in, o' course," he specified, suspending both hands in mid-air. "I do realize that I'll be takin' a loss, considerin' I've added lots more niceties than the average funeral director might care ta pay for. *But...*," he suddenly interjected, slapping both hands together, "lucky for you, I'm not yet beholdin' to any sales agent. Yes, sir, Doctor Sam, my good friend, lucky for you! That means if ya want ta buy the home, I can pass the c'mmission charge in your favor! Ain't that a coincidence now?" he beamed, his hazel eyes unleashing a circus barker's gleam. "I was just about ta contact the real estate agent this very afternoon ta make a deal with 'im when lo and behold, you call from right out o' the blue. Like a sign from heaven, it was," he exclaimed, making another sign of the cross. "Yes, sir! Been draggin' my heels long enough about sellin'. Really hate ta see the place go, I do. That's why it's takin' me so long ta get goin.' Don't bother my dear Hildy as much. She's lookin' forward ta the change, but me..." he emphasized with a firm shake of his perspiring head and another sniff of the nose, "gonna miss it like a jackrabbit without his hole, I cert'inly am."

No longer able to tolerate Ed Millenbach's colloquial babbling, Samuel took a deep breath and finally broke through the one-sided conversation. "My dear Mr. Millenbach...I do understand your reluctance to depart from this outstanding establishment into which you have obviously poured your heart and soul. And let me assure you," he added, now virtually convinced from the undertaker's guarded demeanor that the price of the funeral home was well beyond his reach, "if I am fortunate enough to acquire the home, I shall, indeed, do my best to be deemed worthy of owning it. However, I fear that it is getting rather late and I understand you are expecting some clients soon, so please, do inform me of the price you wish to acquire for your establishment before we exhaust every last minute of an otherwise fruitful morning."

Reacting as if he were struck by a falling boulder, Millenbach wrenched backward, opened the inside of his jacket and pulled out his pocket watch. With a concerned look on his face, he quickly shoved it back inside and leaned forward, placing his forearms on the desk in a businesslike manner. "What it comes down to is this, Doctor Governey. Havin' built the place myself some five years ago, give or take a few months, I've poured just about thirty-thousand inta' it altogether. But I'm willin' ta let it go for twenty-five grand. Now, mind you," he added, noticing the resigned look on Samuel's face, "the price isn't set in stone. If ya think the askin' price is too steep, I'm still willin' ta negotiate, providin' I don't get any other bites in the next coupla' months. But, then again, if I don't sell it by the first of October, I'll have to settle for what I can get, seein' that the cold weather will be settin' in and I best be on my way ta Miami. If ya care ta think it over, you're welcome to do so. I'll even hold off on signin' with the agent ta give ya time. *And*, I'll give ya as much as two full weeks ta think it over. You can give me yer answer then. Of course, if ya decide ta purchase the home, I wouldn't expect ya ta pay it off all at once. I'm a reasonable man, Doctor Governey. We could work out a payment plan that suits your likin' and is good for the banker. Would that be agree'ble to ya?"

Sensing that lady fate herself was engaging in a hearty last laugh, Samuel tightened his jaw to conceal an unavoidable pout. Twenty-five thousand dollars was a ridiculous sum for a funeral home, indeed, but, nevertheless, a price he should have expected for one so elaborately equipped with the latest up-to-date conveniences. And how ironic it was that Ed Millenbach had quoted the very amount he, himself, had reaped from his grandfather's will well over eight years ago. He could almost feel the stinging hand of providence suddenly appearing out of nowhere to administer one swift slap on the rear for exhausting the generous gift in such an eccentric manner, he pondered, as fleeting images of luxury cruises, lavish hotels and African adventures raced through his mind. Poignantly aware, however, that Mr. Millenbach was awaiting a response, he erased these bittersweet reflections with one impulsive pull upon his necktie. "My dear Mr. Millenbach," he replied, nearly choking on his words, "I am sincerely sorry for having expended so much of your precious time, but *twenty-five thousand dollars* is...I am afraid...quite out of range for a gentleman in my financial position. Unless, of course," he hesitated, somberly envisioning the unoccupied viewing rooms on the main floor, "unless the business of undertaking proves to be so profitable as to allow for myself an adequate living even after the monthly bank note is paid."

With forearms still anchored to the surface of the desk, Ed Millenbach's calculating eyes shifted as he squirmed in his oversized seat, evoking from it an abrasive rubbing sound. "Well, now, Doctor Governey," he began at a slower pace, but in a more definitive tone, "That depends on a slew o'circumstances, it does. Why...just a few months ago with the influenza an' all when people were droppin' like flies, had so much business ta handle, had ta get outside help. Worked day and night, too, me and Hildy did. Was a lot o' strain, but handlin' all them bodies sure brung in the cold hard cash. Made quadruple the amount in that there period, yes sir! Could o' paid a bank note five times over, I coulda, with plenty left over ta spare!" Like a shrewd miser caught in the act of revering each of his cherished gold coins, Millenbach immediately unglued his elbows from the desk and straightened his back against the tufted chair, placing both hands upon his hips. "O' course, Doctor Governey, 'twas a sad time for so many...young 'uns too," he emphasized with his signature sign of the cross. "Most in their middle *a*-dult years, but more yung 'uns than I'd ever care ta bury again. Boys an' girls both...lots of 'em barely on the verge o' *a*-dulthood. Lots o' families did a heap o' grievin', they did, yes sir. It's a double-edge sword sometimes this here business is. But every profession's got their downfall, I suppose, Doctor Governey. Yep...every good-standin,' legit'mate profession does." Somewhat unnerved by the bizarre expression in Samuel's eyes at the mention of the stricken children, yet choosing to interpret it as a sign of agitated impatience, Millenbach quickly continued. "Now I ain't gonna lie to ya, Doctor Governey...I coulda showed ya the books for that dismal period o' time an' led ya on about how prosp'rous the business is, but I'm an honest, God-fearin' man, yes I am. So I'm gonna be truthful with ya," he added with an astute nod of the head while thrusting forward and jabbing both elbows onto the desk. "Bein' an undertaker ain't the most pros'prous occupation, but it's a rewardin' one as ya well know...you havin' had some experience durin' the war an' all. And durin' the slow periods, it don't fetch a whole lot o' income at times. *But,*" he specified, shaking a finger, "one can make a mighty good livin' dependin' on his person'l wants and needs. I s'pose I'd be safe ta say that you'd have a guar'nteed daily income at least as much as any hard-pressed fella workin' on Henry Ford's pr'duction line, yes sir. An' let me tell ya, five buck a day ain't no chicken feed, no siree. Ya don't see many o' them fellas complainin', no sir, ya sure don't!"

Ignoring the fact that his foot was practically numb, Samuel had a peculiar inclination to reach over and grab the crusty embalmer by his stiffly collared neck. Why, it was infuriating enough that for the past half hour he had been forced to listen to accounts of the old geezer's medical ailments, not to mention suffering through each gag-inducing display of mucus expulsion. Samuel winced, averting his eyes as the funeral director once again started clearing his phlegm-filled gullet. And a most unnecessary account of the world-renowned influenza epidemic—an obvious attempt by the cunning mortician to sway his decision—had been tasteless to say the least, although the mention of pubescent female corpses had made the report somewhat more tolerable. But now, in one last-ditch effort to clinch the sale of the funeral home, the ungracious weasel adds insult to injury by exalting Henry Ford's highly acclaimed five-dollar daily wage, albeit commendable for a mere industrial worker who, along with a henpecking wife and a couple of unruly tykes is content to reside in a modestly priced home at best. He, however, was Samuel Randolph Governey, a privileged highborn who, despite his father's despicable behavior, forever bore the ancestral crest of aristocratic bluebloods dating back to the earliest British Barons and English Earls. The rightful heir to his father's title certainly deserved much better. *Furthermore,* he continued to deliberate as the funeral director spit another gob of phlegm into the handkerchief, how in the bloody hell did Millenbach expect him to pay off the mortgage while earning such a meager wage? Why, at that rate— including interest on the loan, provided he could even obtain one—he would be up to his bloody elbows in dire debt for the next 25 years. Samuel's body tensed as he folded his arms across his chest while looking out into the spacious lobby at the spiraling grand staircase. *Accordingly,* he'd be an old man in his middle fifties, still living on the upper floor of a business like some common immigrant instead of residing in the Victorian mansion of his dreams. And how in the devil's name, he seethed, had Millenbach succeeded in transforming what should have been a modestly sized and simply furnished funeral home into a cadavers' vaudeville? But before Samuel had the opportunity to continue his speculations, his exasperation was compounded when Millenbach, having finally finished his repulsive throat-purging ritual, had not only interrupted Samuel's intense train of thought, but seemed, by some sort of clairvoyant flair, to invade his innermost private musings as well.

"Now I know what yer thinkin', Doctor Governey," the sniffling mortician declared, directing the handkerchief toward his pocket before abruptly tossing it into a hidden corner of the room, "yer wonderin' how in the world I fancied up this place earnin' a wage not much higher than that Henry Ford fella's five dollars a day. Well, I'll tell ya," he continued, nudging his chair into a slight swivel while clenching his hands around its thick arms, "*Luck.* Plain ol' sure-as-shootin', high-as-the-hills luck. Would ya believe it, doc?" he asked, bringing the chair to a halt by placing his foot on the side of the desk. "One summer's day about six years back or so, some spruced-up fellas come ta my home and says there's oil on my property and offer me a heap o' money ta sell my land. I near fell over when they told me how much I'd get for it. Well," he declared, releasing his grasp from the chair as he placed both hands on his hip pockets, "I'd a been a fool's gold idiot not ta take 'em up on the offer. So, in less than six weeks, it was a done deal. Always heard about how all them rich folks livin' in this here area would order their caskets from Owosso, so I figured I'd build the finest goddamn funeral home anyone ever laid eyes upon, yes sir! Like the sayin' goes, 'build it and they shall come,' yes sir, Doctor Governey! So that's just what I did. Built the biggest, best funeral home this side o' heaven, I did." With a wistful look upon his face, Ed Millenbach paused and relaxed both arms on his thighs, ever disappointed that, all things considered, the Millenbach Funeral Home had not yet attracted the adequate number of patrons necessary for a thriving business. "Only thing is, Doctor Governey, like I was sayin' before, probably won't be gettin' back all I put into it. But, like I was also sayin,' ya gotta remember what I said about savin' on the commission. If ya make up yer mind before I get hold o' the real estate agent, that whole percentage is in yer lap. And I won't steal a penny of it, no sir. The full thing'll be yours. I figure it'll amount to at least 15 hundred, it will, if ya include the attorney fees. And oh yeah," he offered as an afterthought with a quick bob of the head, "ya know that wine cellar I showed ya downstairs? It's all yours—the whole kit'n kaboodle of it. And there's some pretty expensive stuff down there, I'm tellin' ya. Why, I bet if ya were ta sell it all, you'd get at least a couple more grand out of the deal. I ain't pullin' your leg, doc. Ask any wine dealer about it, they'd tell ya the same thing. An' I wouldn't be handin' it to anybody, no siree! Yer special on my list cause o' my nephew Zach. Any friend of Zach's is a friend o' mine so the sayin' goes, and any friend o' mine deserves extra special attention with a dollop o'honey on top, I always say. *Besides...,*" he added pointing to the bottle of Chianti resting beneath a coat rack bearing Samuel's straw hat, "ya got ta remember, doc, the Fed'ral Goverment'l be springin' that damn prohibition law on us come the beginnin' o' next year. Won't be able ta buy no more wine after that, no sir! So if ya *do* end up buyin' this here funeral home, you'll be sure ta have plenty o' bottles ta keep yer customers happy. So what d'ya think, doc?" Millenbach concluded, slapping the top of the desk. "Like I said before, though, ya ain't gotta give yer answer right away, but I'd like ta know if you're at least considerin' it."

Eyeing Millenbach over an empty cup of tea as the undertaker began to drink from his own lukewarm cup, Samuel stretched both legs and sank further back into the low-seated chair, maneuvering his numbed foot into a slow, soothing wriggle. There was certainly no doubt about it, he thought, pressing two middle fingers upon tightly pursed lips. Even though this shark of a funeral director had failed to fast-talk him into purchasing the funeral home, there certainly was no doubt that Ed Millenbach was one of the most manipulative salesmen he had ever encountered. Why, just place him in the circus ring with P.T. Barnum and it would be quite an exhilarating contest indeed! And forget about all the money he had raked in from his *crude* oil. The lucky bastard could be selling *snake* oil and making millions.

Subconsciously taking advantage of a small window of silence as Millenbach placed the cup back on its saucer, scooped up a linen napkin and wiped his glistening lips, Samuel resumed his previous contemplations, half-amused, yet slightly annoyed with the flawed logic the tenacious mortician had utilized in the futile attempt to sell his precious piece of real estate. First of all, he rationalized as he watched Millenbach clumsily wipe some spilled tea from the desk, as far as any savings on the commission, if he could afford to purchase the funeral home for twenty-five grand, sacrificing another thousand or so would hardly put a dent in his mortgage. On that same erroneous note, if there ever *were* a good reason to purchase the funeral parlor before two weeks' time, it would be because the archaic codger could very well croak before any deal is consummated and the property goes off the market altogether. And regarding the acquisition of the cherished wine collection, if he *had* decided to purchase the funeral home, he would not have agreed to any transaction before insisting upon the inclusion of the rare vintage wine.

As Ed Millenbach yanked another freshly laundered handkerchief from the desk drawer, Samuel's foremost thoughts were suddenly diverted by an engaging revelation. Was it possible that the funeral home had never attained its full potential because the well-heeled residents of Grosse Pointe were offended by Millenbach's uncouth demeanor? Perhaps, Samuel contemplated as the mortician began coughing up another mouthful of phlegm, if he *were* able to somehow secure the required loan, he could turn the place around—lure more customers with his debonair appearance and English charm. After all, if the people of Grosse Pointe were, indeed, as sophisticated as everyone affirmed, it was no wonder that they might naturally be repulsed by the mortician's inferior breeding and boorish mannerisms. *But what the bloody hell,* he silently cursed, chastising himself for entertaining such a distant possibility. Aside from the fact that it would be quite risky to gamble on such mere speculation, he was still as financially strapped as some poor son-of-a-bitch doomed to dish out double alimony. And even if Millenbach acquiesced to lowering the asking price, how much debt could he afford? Fifteen...definitely not. Twelve thousand? Completely out of the question. It was beyond all possibility to afford even *half* of what he was looking for. He should have seen the writing on the wall before wasting Ed Millenbach's time as well as his own. But, then again, he had been irresistibly captivated by the funeral home's seductive appearance, its pretentious white pillars and Georgian architecture enticing him much like an elaborate cathedral beckons its parishioners. *So,* Samuel concluded, particularly attentive to the look of anticipation on Millenbach's face as the mortician gave his dripping nostrils one final wipe. He would, like a gracious loser in a mismatched polo tournament, cordially shake hands with his long-suffering host and be on his way, accepting as his consolation prize the position of assistant head surgeon at Detroit General Hospital. *However,* in order to avoid further confrontation with Ed Millenbach, he would not presently divulge his plan, but instead inform the unsuspecting fellow of his intention to think matters through.

"My dear Mr. Millenbach," he began in a patronizing tone, "You do present an extremely tempting offer. However, before I commit myself to such an enterprising venture, I must consult with my banker to see if I am, indeed, qualified for the loan. You do understand?" But before Samuel could rise from his seat and bid his heartened host adieu, Hildy suddenly appeared at the doorway, informing her husband that his bereaved guests were likely to arrive within minutes. Without further hesitation, Ed Millenbach thanked Samuel for his kind consideration, offering a generous handshake. Then, following through on his promise to show Samuel the upper floor of the funeral home, he asked his obliging wife to escort their respectful guest up the spiraling grand staircase.

chapter 61

Heavenly Vision

Partially due to the aid of an electric fan, but mostly because of the anxiety he experienced regarding potential ownership of the Millenbach Funeral Home, Samuel had paid no attention to how uncomfortably stuffy it was while in Millenbach's cubbyhole of an office. But now, as he approached the last few steps of the plush blue carpeted stairway, he could feel, like a cool hand on hot sweaty knees, a gradual drop in temperature generated from a fully functional air cooling unit. At least he would be delivered from another unbearably hot muggy day for a few more moments, he scowled, envisioning the dark brown leather seats of his French Gregoire convertible baking under the hazy summer sun. He should have put the top back up to save the upholstery from further deterioration, he chided, recalling that, in his haste, he had neglected to do so. Of course, he reasoned, unenthusiastically following Hildy's waddling, yet reverent footsteps down the hallway leading to the occupied viewing room, he *was* planning to have the war-torn convertible refurbished as soon as Nubuck's repair shop returned his Silver Ghost Rolls and Stutz Bearcat. Then, after all three reconditioned vehicles were again in his possession, he would be sure to pamper them as if he had driven them straight out of the showroom.

As an acute decline in temperature had verified Samuel's arrival on the second floor, so did the bursting fragrance of flowers disclose his proximity to the solitary viewing parlor. When Mrs. Millenbach paused at the entrance, identifying the room with a solemn whisper, Samuel courteously nodded, deliberately inhaling the fresh, sweet air—a welcome change not only from the stuffy office, but also from the artificial scent of cold cream the old woman was wearing. Politely complying with Hildy's invitation to enter, Samuel's first impression was that the parlor was not as spacious as those he had seen on the first floor, though just as sumptuously decorated. However, this thought had not lingered in his mind but a moment before his eyes were drawn toward the opposite end of the room, focusing upon the object of the parlor's sole purpose. Like a character from the pages of Grimm's fairy tales, a young maiden, barely 14 years of age, lay dormant in a rosewood casket; a single lamp above her placid face illuminated a translucent complexion accentuated by pale crimson lips, brunette hair and arched eyebrows framing thickly lashed eyes immersed in perpetual sleep. In what appeared to be one miraculous instant, Samuel felt as if his own dearly departed soul was suddenly hovering above the deceased child, bestowing upon her youthful image a clarity and beauty no mere mortal could perceive. And although he sensed that Hildy Millenbach was verbally explaining the tragic circumstances leading to the untimely death of the young Indian girl, her otherwise clear, deliberate voice sounded, in Samuel's transcendent state of mind, slow and indiscernible as if being smothered by a tightly held pillow. Even the abundant display of floral arrangements, now in full view, did not impress him as his anesthetized body seemed to be spontaneously lured by some dark, unfathomable spirit. Visions from Sunday's dinner at the Khamal residence flashed before him along with the poignant echoes and inflections of their voices—the flustered Leya inadvertently spilling wine upon her pregnant lap; her overly apologetic husband, Daksha, offering every excuse in the book to avoid what he sincerely believed to be the cause of his wife's apparent distress. "A beautiful flower of an Indian woman...barely touching upon her 14th birthday...drowned in her swimming pool." *Drowned.* The word blazed in his memory like a reignited torch. "Discovered by her father...exchanging intimate caresses...my dear Doctor Governey...what is a father to do?" *Murdered.* So this was she! Samuel marveled, numbly drifting toward the rosewood casket. Now, before him lay the young Indian girl who was the victim of that "unfortunate accident." And to think that he had hardly given her a second thought...until now...that is, until now....

Samuel's legs felt heavy, yet weightless as he struggled to steady himself against a polished brass balustrade which shielded the corpse from being touched by unwanted hands. And adding to his frustration, the cold, ponderous railing acted as an impregnable wall between them. Altogether aware of a painted cedar jewelry box and stuffed doll placed by her side, Samuel flinched. For over an hour this Indian maiden had hovered above his concern with worldly affairs, unbeknownst to him as he conversed with that decrepit old man downstairs. She had reposed in eternal peace above the very mortician who had had the pleasure of caring for her...undressing her...possessing her yielding body for countless hours. Feverishly gazing upon an angelic, gold-dusted face and fragile body dressed in layers of white silk chiffon, Samuel felt an agonizing stab of jealously as he envisioned Ed Millenbach's leathery hands engaged in the common practice of massaging her limbs to prevent the otherwise-fated rigor mortis of the body. What earthly riches he would trade—his classic French Gregoire...the jaunty Stutz Bear-Cat and yes!...the Silver Ghost Rolls, his very first love. He would surrender each and every one of these cherished automobiles, if only to possess this exquisite body through such ultimate means of intimacy! Samuel nearly gasped, imagining his own hands forcefully kneading the smooth, cocoa-colored flesh of the child's arms...running the palms of his hands along the length of her legs...fondling her lithe calves...caressing impeccable, supple thighs. His grasp of the balustrade immediately tightened, as if strangling the neck of a newborn babe. Continuing to ogle her motionless body, he contemplated that there may likely be a smooth pink scar discreetly obscured in the pubic area to confirm the certainty of a professional circumcision. With quick, heavy breaths, he reflected on the similar operation performed upon Daksha Khamal's wife, Leya, as well as those of a primitive nature he had witnessed during his two-month holiday in the village of Mukot. *It is of no matter*, he meditated, his salivating tongue moistening dry lips; whether performed with broken glass, sharpened stones, or a physician's scalpel, the nature of that tantalizing beast—that most resourceful and ingenious medical procedure—would be so gratifying to perform once again...so bloody stimulating, that no amount of compensation could ever match its execution!

Scarcely aware of the dampness upon the brass railing caused by the sweating of his trembling hands, Samuel perused the child's perfectly formed torso, affixing his eyes, at last, to her delicate, fledgling breasts. Initially discouraged that the garland of flowers placed around her neck was hindering any trace of attentive, pert nipples, he nevertheless imparted a rebuking shrug. Under present circumstances, the otherwise rosy peaks of her breasts were sure to display manifestations of dormancy, regardless of the fact that in lieu of a pre-arranged cremation, the body had not been subjected to the usual embalming process. *Of course*, he mused, continuing to mentally strip away each oppressive layer of the white silk funeral gown, had *he* the opportunity to properly prepare her for viewing...to take possession of her naked body...to feel her arms and legs yielding under his strong, commanding strokes, then—*and only then*—would he have had the occasion of cupping the pubescent flesh of each budding breast within the crux of his hands...squeezing them...stirring them...churning them in one firm, circular motion...ever-so-slowly migrating the tips of his fingers toward those pliable pink nipples and ultimately molding them as if they were delectable morsels of jellied candy...resurrecting them like unsuspecting tulips restlessly sprouting beneath the fleeting warm breath of an unpromised spring.

Like a viable fetus ruthlessly ripped from the life-giving walls of its mother's womb, Samuel, startled by his elderly escort's bellowing whisper, suddenly stumbled from the unshakable balustrade, almost knocking over an incense-filled lamp placed near the feet of the deceased. Swiftly grabbing the stem of the lamp's fluted pedestal while Hildy Millenbach prevented the glass dome from crashing onto the decorative carpet, his initial inclination to offer a prompt apology was instantaneously curtailed, his exasperation magnified, by the skeptical look in Hildy's wide and fearful eyes. Horrified at the realization that he may have crossed an irreversible line—that his most private, lascivious desires may have finally been exposed, he nevertheless offered a sympathetic smile and crossed his hands over his heart. "My dear Mrs. Millenbach...I beseech your forgiveness, but...I find such a situation most disturbing and difficult to comprehend." Piously glancing at the deceased Indian girl, he emulated Ed Millenbach's sign of the cross, then dismissed an invisible tear with the side of his ringless forefinger. "Such a poor, unfortunate child! Why...in God's divine, merciful name...how difficult it must have been for you and your husband to prepare such a young body. But...I must say...that under such tragic circumstances, the two of you...your own compassionate self as well as your dear, benevolent husband have certainly exceeded the pinnacle of expectations! Why...in the blessed name of our sweet Jesus, she looks like an angel...an angel straight from the clouds of heaven. Such a tragedy, however," he reiterated, remorsefully shaking his head. "A most difficult, senseless tragedy, indeed."

Feeling a bit awkward and somewhat ashamed for misjudging the kind and honorable Doctor Samuel Governey, Hildy Millenbach offered a sheepish smile and clasped Samuel's hand within her own. "Now, now, Doctor Governey...there's no need to fret," she softly whispered. "But please...we have to go. I'm afraid the poor gal's family will be up to see her any minute now. Besides...there's still some rooms up here to show ya if you'd be so kind to follow me."

Unable to steal one last glimpse of the reposing corpse, but ever so satisfied that he had successfully appealed to the woman's inherent sense of empathy and pride, Samuel, hearing the soft cries and loud whispers of bereaved guests approaching the bottom of the staircase, immediately followed Hildy's quickened footsteps out into the long, open hallway and into the casket room. But by the time Mrs. Millenbach had shut the door behind them and began describing the origin, quality and price of each unoccupied, satin-lined coffin, his mind, still obsessed by images of the deceased Indian child, already was eternally sealed. No matter what was required, he firmly resolved, whether it be squeezing shards of silver from jagged rocks or nuggets of gold from the most treacherous mines, he *would* find a way to purchase the Millenbach Funeral Home. And, *yes*, he promised himself, smiling nonchalantly as Hildy's description of coffin displays fell on deafened ears, he would engage in nothing short of incessant begging, excessive borrowing or grand larceny if the situation demanded. *Of course*, he reasoned, feigning fascination with the array of caskets, since choosing the last option would most likely land him in the penitentiary, he would be all the wiser to consider instead the other two possibilities, no matter how distasteful the first alternative may be.

Resolutely embracing that final notion, Samuel trailed Hildy Millenbach through another doorway leading into the main living quarters, all the while determined that upon returning to the Pontchartrain Hotel, he would search for the calling card given to him by Mr. Hogan almost three weeks ago or, if need be, contact a telephone operator in New York for information on the inscribed name, Beatrice Martin, long-lost aunt from his childhood and estranged sister of his dearly deceased mother. Why in the devil's name she wished to contact him in the first place, he could not fathom. But, presently it was not of any consequence. From what he could recall, she was rich...*sinfully* rich. Surely wealthy enough to help an otherwise devoted nephew—one who had been forced into alienating himself from his mother's family by a controlling, relentless father; a depraved father who had squandered every last bit of his inheritance, leaving hardly a penny for his loyal and loving son. Yes, by Jove, that is exactly how he would approach the situation. Appeal to the old lady's inherent sense of empathy—as successfully as he had done with Hildy Millenbach. Then, upon his return to Michigan, strike an agreeable bargain with Ed Millenbach. *A splendid plan, indeed!* Congratulating himself, Samuel harnessed an irresistible urge to snap his fingers. Hopefully, if all went well and before the summer neared its end, he would become a permanent resident of the City of Grosse Pointe and newly respected proprietor of the Millenbach Funeral Home.

chapter 62

Prudent Strategy

If there are, indeed, two faces to every town, then New York City on any given Monday during the sultry month of August in the post-war year of 1919 was certainly no exception. On Manhattan's Lower East side, rows of overflowing clotheslines hanging across narrow, littered alleyways alerted the casual passerby of scores of immigrants dwelling in noisy, overcrowded tenement houses. Corroded fire-escapes, serving as children's playgrounds, were crude reminders of the destitution his fellow foreigners had endured in their beloved homelands and their courageous decision to become newly sworn citizens of an unfamiliar yet promising country. As the unyielding bridge of time had yet to span another decade before the inception of an ever-increasing welfare state, it was the general rule of thumb that these noble families would be further compelled to fend for themselves. Like freshly-planted trees thirsting in dry climates, forced to drive roots deeply underground for life-sustaining water, so too, were many a backbone strengthened through strenuous labor and incessant determination in the likely hope that the fruit of future generations would thrive and flourish. Contrary to the struggles of their impoverished Lower East Side neighbors, however, the inhabitants of New York's Upper Crust had already reaped the benefits of their hard-working forefathers, many of these ancestors respectably pegged as "Knickerbockers" because of the knee-length trousers worn by early Dutch settlers. Having been dedicated to the everlasting virtues of diligent labor, instilled discipline and genteel civility, their elite empire prospered and multiplied, producing sons of bankers, grandsons of lawyers and great-grandsons of mercantile businessmen. Resourceful wives managed active households and assisted local charities while well-bred, chaperoned daughters attended social gatherings and debutante parties in the hope of securing upstanding husbands and four-story brownstones of their own near prestigious Central Park.

Appreciating a brief reprieve from Michigan's unrelenting humidity, yet ever so grateful that the peaceful, tree-lined streets along Lexington Avenue offered him temporary shelter from an oppressive New York sun, Samuel Randolph Governey, noticing the distinctive winged shutters which graced the third approaching brownstone, veered his restored but road-sullied Stutz Bear-Cat toward the curb and engaged its handbrake. Since the restoration of the bright yellow sports car had taken a few more days than expected, he had purposely postponed his jaunt to New York. Not only did this short delay give him an opportunity to become one with the Bear-Cat during the 600 mile trip, but since the American automobile was more dated and less ostentatious than his French Gregoire, he had decided that it was the better choice if he wished to convince a certain elderly auntie of his unseemly financial situation. Better yet, he had declined the opportunity to have the sports car professionally washed by the hotel's garage attendants upon his arrival in New York, realizing that nothing could devalue the appearance of an otherwise classic automobile as much as the dust and grime accumulated from even the smoothest of paved roads. Similarly, he had patronized a secondhand men's shop on the seedier side of Detroit's Bagley Avenue, choosing an out-of-season dark tweed walking suit, supplemented by slightly-scuffed, manure-colored shoes and a cockeyed cloth hat a half size too small. He wouldn't think of skimping on the flowers, however. The abundant bouquet of pink & orange carnations, purple asters and black-eyed susans he had just purchased at the Waldorf-Astoria's exclusive flower shop may not have been as expensive as the dozen long-stemmed roses a more affluent nephew might present, but they would, nevertheless, demonstrate how grateful he was for the opportunity to be reunited with his beloved, long-missed auntie.

Pausing for a brief moment before turning off the automobile's ignition, Samuel smiled as he rested his eyes upon the Bear-Cat's doghouse-shaped hood which hovered over its finely tuned engine. He had been too weary upon last evening's arrival at the Waldorf to appreciate her dependable road endurance during the 14-hour drive from downtown Detroit. Having journeyed through several states while reaching speeds in excess of 75 miles-per-hour, the Stutz had performed with hardly a burp. And the air-compressed tires, the latest in Harvey Firestone's reputable inventory, had remained intact without one single incident of failure. Leaning forward to disengage the four-cylinder T-head engine, Samuel could detect the discernable scent of saddle soap before quickly sinking back into the black bucket seat to nurse a sore arm. Despite all the modern amenities which had been added to the sports vehicle, she still required strenuous steering and provided a noticeably stiff ride. She behaved like an unruly woman, he frowned, rubbing sore muscles through the heavy tweed sleeves of his second-hand suit. Somewhat like the ungovernable Katherine in Shakespeare's *Taming of the Shrew*, or perhaps even more fittingly, like that best-be-forgotten incorrigible vixen, Violet Stimple. Instantaneously sensing a sharp, hot sting behind reddened cheekbones, Samuel stroked the long, curving arm of the automobile's tufted leather seat. Aside from the seething anger those dreaded memories evoked, he felt a genuine pang of regret. He had not intended to compare his Stutz Bear-Cat to a creature as vile as Miss Stimple, but, like an angry lover in the heat of passion, had unjustifiably done so. *No*, he resolved, tenderly gazing at the American sports car's artfully crafted chassis. She was nothing like that gonorrhea-ridden hussy. Best to leave those odious recollections buried beneath the muddy bed of the Schuylkill River beside her fleshless bones where they belonged, lest he insult his beloved Bear-Cat any further. And although his newly refurbished sports car was presently a bit unruly, he would, like Katherine's Petruchio, eventually conquer her every last shortcoming. But first, Samuel reminded himself while shifting his gaze toward the shuttered brownstone, he had an important mission to accomplish. One which, if successfully executed, would not only change the course of his life, but grant him the opportunity to realize his ultimate dream. Without so much as a second thought, Samuel seized the bouquet of flowers from the passenger seat, stomped upon the running board and, abandoning the Bear-Cat like a mistress scorned, embraced the promising sidewalk of Lexington Avenue.

Upon smoothing the last remaining wrinkle from his brown cuffed pants, Samuel ascended the paved walkway abutting the residence of Mrs. Leonard Martin and took a deep, cleansing breath. Despite the fact that he had traveled hundreds of miles to see his estranged Aunt Beatrice, he was puzzled more now of her intentions than before conversing with her on the telephone. Initially assuming that she had only wished to extend her condolences regarding his father, he had been prepared to implore his aunt's permission for a familial visit. However, she had not only suggested the same, but practically insisted upon it. And although she had originally responded with delight, her voice sounded rather guarded and the conversation unusually hurried. Additionally, she had given him implicit instructions to arrive either shortly after nine o'clock in the morning or, in the event that he should be running late, to delay their engagement until after the twelve o'clock luncheon hour. In truth, by the time their discourse was completed, he hadn't even known the status of his Uncle Leonard, the successful estate lawyer, or if he was still alive and well at that. However, a disturbing possibility *had* occurred to him. What if, for some god-forsaken reason, his aunt had run into financial difficulties of her own? Perhaps she hoped that he might be in a position to bail her out on the speculation that his father may have left behind a substantial inheritance. But Samuel had quickly dismissed this possibility, preferring, instead, to believe that, despite prior disputes in the family—the details of which were unbeknownst to himself—his aging aunt had been touched by the passing of her brother-in-law and wished to make amends with her eldest sister's only child. Samuel subdued the urge to gag while approaching the steps of the grey-painted brownstone. Whatever the reason, he would commence with his original plan. He would be truthful about his wish to purchase the funeral home; after all, aside from the unpleasantries associated with administering to the deceased, being an undertaker *was* a respectable profession. However, he would not reveal the entire cost of the Millenbach Funeral Home lest she think him a bloody, bumbling fool. The remaining amount could be obtained by exaggerating his need for living expenses, not the least of which would include a modest residence of his own. And, of course, he would continue to play the charming pauper. *So*, he paused, practically crossing his fingers with his free hand while waiting behind the imposing oak door, *hopefully*, if fortune was smiling upon him, he would ultimately win the heart—and most importantly, the pocketbook—of his dearly beloved and long-missed Auntie Beatrice.

chapter 63

Tearful Reunion

I f not for the stylish, flounced garden dress and bow-trimmed satin pumps which so charmingly befitted his Aunt Beatrice's delicate figure and shapely ankles, Samuel would have been compelled to query the possibility of being mystically escorted into his childhood past. From the moment she had punctually opened the door, he was amazed to discover that instead of the matronly, silver-haired woman he had previously anticipated, his mother's younger sister still appeared youthful and vibrant, as if she had emerged from the pages of *Ladies Home Journal,* enticing him to purchase the latest Hoover sweeping machine or Maytag's newest motor-driven, easy-release wringer-washer.

Exceedingly grateful that his hands were much too occupied to reciprocate his tearful aunt's impulsive hug, Samuel promptly surrendered the flowers along with his cockeyed cloth hat and, stepping away from the dimly lit foyer, obediently followed the overwrought woman into the drawing room. Sensing a bit of apprehension as her free hand reached for a crystal vase set upon a gilded console, he compliantly sat upon a beechwood, needle-point armchair as she excused herself and hurried into the kitchen. Aware of the sound of clinking glass and running water, Samuel glanced about the shaded room, purposely assessing the value of what appeared to be an exquisite combination of turn-of-the-century French and English furniture, not the least of which was a Hamilton upright piano, its intricately carved mahogany surface apparently custom-designed by a time-honored master of cabinetry. Aside from the fact that a personal servant was nowhere in sight, it certainly did not appear that Aunt Beatrice was currently in the midst of financial turmoil by any means. Every available nook and cranny of the cozy parlor was still amply provided for, he confirmed, remembering with a slight scowl how his syphilitic father, in a desperate attempt to support his impious spending habits, had turned his grandfather's lavish Georgian-style home into a practically vacant storage vault. Even Aunt Beatrice's mantle pieces were intact, including a porcelain-paneled brass clock with *fleur-de-lis* hands displaying her requested visiting time of half past nine. As a matter of fact, the only thing out of place, Samuel observed, was a Macy's hatbox indiscriminately forgotten upon a cherrywood drop front desk.

Hearing a bit of rustling from the kitchen as his aunt arranged the flowers, Samuel glanced at a small gallery of framed photographs set upon a French provincial demi-lune table. A wedding portrait, evidently of Aunt Beatrice and Uncle Leonard, commanded the center of attention, while a half-dozen other photos sweetly captured ribbon-haired, rosy-cheeked additions to their flourishing family tree. But one photograph in particular, obviously taken several years before any of the others, was of special interest to Samuel. Framed by embossed silver plate, his own dearly departed mother was once again alive and thriving amidst the hugs of her younger twin sisters. Up until now he had nearly forgotten about his Aunt Cassandra, wondering for a moment if she had also experienced the privilege of drinking from that same fountain of youth which had rendered her fraternal twin sister, well into her 50th year, to appear no older than a handsome, middle-aged woman of 35. As far as his own piteous mother was concerned, however, it was just as well that she had passed on before her time. Having been no beauty queen by society's standards and taking into account her incurable depressive tendencies, the relentless forces of gravity caused by inevitable aging surely would have weighed all the more upon her unpalatable countenance, throwing the Countess of Cheshire into a downward spiral which not even her precious Prince of Wales at the Devonshire Ball could have danced away. *But*, Samuel chided, attempting to shrug off the distasteful images of his bed-ridden mother, these unsavory memories were best left dead and buried also, lest he be thrown into an irreparable depression himself.

Alerted by a melodic voice announcing that a pot of coffee as well as hot water for tea had been readied upon the stove, Samuel straightened his shoulders and flashed a generous smile as Aunt Beatrice appeared with the vase of flowers in one hand and a tray of assorted *petits fours* within the other. Quickly springing from his seat, Samuel snatched the dish of miniature iced cakes and placed them on a mahogany butler's tray situated within arm's reach of his chair. Having carefully balanced the fragrant flowers upon the gilded console with nimble, nail-painted fingers, Aunt Beatrice excused herself once again, then promptly stepped back into the kitchen, this time returning with the hot water and coffee she had promised. Placing the two pots upon a buffet sideboard while delightedly answering inquiries about her daughters and elementary-school grandchildren, Aunt Beatrice withdrew a tin of Earl Grey tea from a rosewood caddy, sincerely thanking Samuel as he helped set the fine china and sterling silverware alongside the assorted cakes. A bit disappointed that his tea had not been conventionally steeped, he nonetheless politely concealed his disapproval as his aunt poured the steaming water into his empty cup, sorely aware of the leaf-filled muslin bag; although he generally appreciated the wealth of progress and convenience which the free market of America provided, there were just some things in life which should never be compromised under any circumstances.

After pouring a cup of strongly brewed coffee for herself, Beatrice Martin swaddled the teapot with a butterfly motif tea cozy, then set both pots upon the sideboard, all the while scrutinizing her last-minute efforts. Presently satisfied that everything appeared to be in order for the time being, yet suddenly overwhelmed by an uncomfortable flash of heat normally afflicting ladies of late middle-age, she activated an electric fan discreetly situated in the room's far corner. Removing an embroidered handkerchief from her dress pocket, Beatrice daintily dabbed her slender, lace-vested bosom, gracefully spread the back skirt of her rose-patterned dress and sat opposite her long-lost nephew. Attempting to conceal the jittery nerves and queasy stomach she had experienced that morning since awakening to the touch of her husband Leonard's tender kiss, she took a deep uneven breath, initiating the anticipated conversation. "So, Samuel, my dear nephew! 'Tis quite enough boasting on my part. Do please tell me...how have *you* been faring these past many years? Has life been favoring you kindly?"

Appreciating the forceful breeze of the electric fan while still contemplating the actual cause of his aunt's apparent distress, Samuel could not help but further scrutinize her pleasing countenance as he released the string of his tea bag, allowing the green dusty leaves to idly soak. Though still appearing younger than her true years, the brighter light of the drawing room's crystal chandelier revealed several slight wrinkles along the edges of willowy, wide-set hazel eyes. A heart-shaped face of translucent complexion complemented blush-colored lips and a slightly tipped nose while curled, cropped hair appeared three shades lighter than the darker auburn he had remembered as a young boy — a sure sign of the artificial tinting used to mask natural gray-ing, available to women who patronized the more exclusive downtown beauty salons. Eager to shove aside these trivial observations and address the real purpose of his visit, he realized that he would nonetheless be compelled, like a gentleman engaged in a binding courtship, to pursue matters delicate-ly, all the while participating in tedious, yet necessary small talk.

"My dear Aunt Beatrice...how kind of you to inquire and how generous of you to invite me into your lovely abode for a heart-to-heart visit," he began, gallantly kissing her jasmine-scented hand adorned by an exquisitely set emerald-cut diamond ring. "I must say that I have been awaiting this long-overdue visit ever since our telephone conversation. But before I reply to your inquiries," he went on, gradually releasing the satiny hand, "please allow me to compliment you on your most stunning appearance. I trust that Uncle Leonard has been half as fortunate concerning his own good health and welfare?"

At the mention of her husband's name, Beatrice Martin anxiously glanced at the brass mantle clock. Reaching for a pair of silver tongs, she plucked a sugar cube from a *Limoges* bowl and dropped it into her coffee. "Your Uncle Leonard is doing very well, the good Lord willing," she remarked much too confidently. "He still manages to walk to the courthouse daily...weather permitting...and though I've tried to persuade him otherwise, he nevertheless insists on handling more than his share of litigation," she explained over-stirring the coffee. "I know I am being self-indulgent and should be grateful that he has been appointed district court judge for the past 18 years...not to mention our marriage of nearly 34,...but your Uncle Leonard is, after all, approaching his 68th year." As Samuel took his first sip of tea, she immediately stopped stirring, removed the silver spoon, and dropped it upon her saucer. "Oh, I am so sorry, my dear Samuel...would you care for some cream or sugar?"

Gently repositioning his teacup on its saucer, Samuel offered his aunt a forgiving, yet appreciative smile. As any Englishman worth his weight in pound sterling well knew, it was never proper to offer cream instead of milk for one's tea, which should be poured into the cup beforehand. However, although he, unlike the average Englishman, preferred to drink his tea forthright, perhaps a touch of cream might make the harsh taste of the Earl Grey...caused by excessive tannin from the teabag's dusty leaves...a bit more tolerable. With an affirmative response, he congratulated Aunt Beatrice on behalf of her husband's esteemed promotion while she poured the cream. It was quite obvious now, in light of her queer behavior, why his jittery aunt had been so particular about Samuel's visit at a specific time; being that her husband, the Honorable Leonard Martin, promptly arrives at the courthouse by 9:00 a.m. and punctually takes a noon lunch break at home, she was purposely avoiding a chance meeting between the two of them, though for whatever reason, he did not yet know.

"So, my dear, dear nephew; I beseech you," Beatrice implored while setting down the Lenox creamer. "Please refrain me from further sharing my mind, lest I appear uncivil when, in truth, it is yourself I wish to learn more about. Pray, tell me...have you the privilege of being engaged in a pleasing occupation? Is there, perchance, a fortunate young maiden with whom you are willing to share your good company?"

Sorely aware that there was nothing this side of heaven which could doctor his cup of Earl Grey tea, Samuel welcomed the opportunity to delay its consumption by taking the utmost advantage of his aunt's prying inquiries. "Why yes...yes my dear Aunt Beatrice," he began, fabricating a wistful face. "There is, indeed, a young lady I wish to pursue in courtship. However," he cautiously proceeded, carefully pulling the saturated tea bag from his cup and placing it upon his saucer, "I fear she will be tempted by another before my financial position dictates the appropriate means necessary to support a wife and family. In regard to my occupation, however, it is most unfortunate that merely one year before I was due to graduate from medical school, I was persuaded, out of sole allegiance to my father's native country, to join the British Army, thereby forfeiting my chance of obtaining a certified medical diploma. And though I still have the opportunity to complete my education," he fabricated, balancing his teacup in mid-air, "I am afraid that...that my dear Edith's father will not allow such a long period of time to elapse before his daughter is formally engaged and properly married."

"But surely, Samuel," Aunt Beatrice interjected, daintily plucking a pink-laced *petit four* from its doily-covered plate, "an elegant, well-bred gentleman such as yourself should be able to persuade any respectable father to consent to his daughter's hand in marriage."

"It would seem to be reasonable, Aunt Beatrice," Samuel replied, attempting to conceal the natural grimace provoked by a second swallow of warm tea. "However, as I have heretofore implied, there is another gentleman who is competing for Edith's affections and who, I may add, exerts an extremely favorable impression upon Mis...Mis...ter Grey...my darling Edith's respectable but overly solicitous father. Yet, it is understandably so," he expounded, emulating Aunt Beatrice's gesture, hoping that the sweetness of the cake's icing would counter the lingering, bitter taste on his tongue. "The gentleman in question...my rival for Edith's hand...though not in the medical profession by any means...is extremely well-established and runs his own profitable business in the fur trade. So you see, my dear Aunt Beatrice, although I suspect there would otherwise be an opportunity to win Mr. Grey's...as well as Edith's affections...my adverse financial situation seems to predict that quite the opposite is true."

"But Samuel, my dear," Beatrice replied, carefully blotting her painted lips with a linen napkin, "have you spoken with Mr. Grey? Is he, indeed, aware of your potential vocation as a skilled physician? Perhaps if you..."

"It is of no use, Aunt Beatrice," he interrupted, savoring the sweetness in his mouth as he reached for his aunt's brightly manicured fingers. "I have learned from other sources that Mr. Grey is most eager to marry off his daughter, being that she is already well past the prime and proper age of 16. And, being that I am a reasonable man myself, this notion is not difficult to comprehend. Surely, if I were fortunate enough to have a daughter of my own," he continued, alluding to the framed photographs upon the French Provencal table, "my sentiments would be exactly the same. Though..." he added with a look of tenderness in his eyes, "I would gladly accept Edith's hand in marriage be she 16 or 60!"

Beatrice released a tender sigh and patted her nephew on the back of his hand. "Well, well...don't give up, my dear, Samuel. One never knows how these matters sometime manage to iron themselves out. I am sure that there is a special purpose assigned to you by our compassionate and benevolent Lord."

"Indeed, my dear aunt, I do realize that it should well be so. However, I must admit that my faith has been shaken as of late, particularly in lieu of the fact that a seemingly God-given opportunity has recently departed from my grasp due to my paltry finances. I doubt you are aware," Samuel remarked with downcast eyes, "that my father had squandered every last penny of the family inheritance so that upon his death, hardly a pittance was left to be had."

Beatrice took it upon herself to squeeze both of Samuel's hands in an attempt to console her discouraged nephew. "But...Samuel, my dear, dear boy, there was a trust set up by your grandfather Langley...a trust in the amount of two separate installments of twenty-five thousand dollars. Please forgive me for intruding into your personal affairs, but I am aware of this benevolent gesture only because the same abundant gift was bequeathed to my own three daughters as well as your Aunt Cassandra's two beloved children, Thomas James and Monica Clare."

Indifferent to the long-forgotten fact that he had five existing cousins, let alone the recollection of their proper Christian names, Samuel nevertheless took a lengthy moment to reply, allowing his sacrificial, saintly smile to ripen like some forbidden fruit forgotten upon the vine. "Your memory serves you kindly, my dear Aunt Beatrice," he began, concealing both her hands beneath his own, "for it is indeed true, as you recall, that I was fortunate enough to receive the same generous gift from my dearly departed and most revered grandfather...may the dear Lord rest his soul. However," he stipulated, raising his lowered head as well as his whispering voice, "it was even *more* fortunate for my own dearly departed father that I had been given such a fine inheritance. You see, my dear aunt...I do not know if you were cognizant of my father's unspeakable malady...that of having contracted a disease much too contemptible to be mentioned in the company of ladies." He slid his hands back toward himself, clasping the palms, tensely entwining his fingers near his chin. "The good Lord knows I tried mightily to keep him comfortable, but when the dreadful disease manifested itself into complete and irreversible paralysis, I had no recourse but to entrust his care to the best nursing facility in our state of Pennsylvania. Being that shortly after my dear mother's death, the first half of my inheritance had been spent mainly on an expensive boarding school, I used most of the remainder to finance his exceptional, yet prolonged care." Pausing to subdue a well-fabricated constriction of the throat, he then continued. "When my suffering father finally did pass on to his final reward...which I sincerely believe that our forgiving Lord in all his mercy and kindness had granted him...I wished to provide the finest funeral any devoted son could imagine. Unfortunately..." he cautiously stated, casting eyes downward once again, "even though the war was officially over, I was still in the service of Her Majesty at the time...attending to the multitude of injured soldiers left behind in a British infirmary. Consequently, I could, under no circumstances, desert my post to attend my dear father's funeral. But," Samuel followed through, unsure as to whether his aunt had, perchance, personally attended his father's elaborate, self-orchestrated funeral, "I trust it went well since the gentleman I commissioned to oversee the arrangements is a very scrupulous and upright confidant of mine."

Experiencing a flash of guilt and a tinge of regret amplified by the whirring of the electric fan, Beatrice leaned back into her chair, retrieving the embroidered handkerchief from her dress pocket. She wished to assure her nephew that the funeral was, after all, fit for a king, particularly since it was apparent that, despite Randolph's dire shortcomings, Samuel had surely developed a loving bond with his father. But the truth of the matter was, although she wished to attend the funeral...and for disparate reasons...she had restrained from doing so lest her husband become suspicious. Leonard would surely have wondered why she desired to pay respects to a brother-in-law and nephew, both of whom had estranged themselves from her dear sister's family. "My dearest Samuel," she implored, pressing the dampened cloth to her delicate cleavage as if blotting away a medley of sins, "I am thoroughly assured of your success in securing the finest funeral for your dearly departed father, but must admit that I am somewhat chagrined at having passed up the opportunity to attend. You see," she pleadingly explained, gently replacing the handkerchief and attempting to smooth the wrinkles from her skirt, "when you were just a lad, there was a misunderstanding between your parents and myself...as well as your Aunt Cassandra," she explained, carefully choosing her words, wondering all the while if Samuel was aware of his father's homosexual misgivings. "And unfortunately...," she went on, gravitating slightly forward, hugging the teacup with moist hands, "words were spoken and accusations exchanged that could never be reversed. Although...although there were genuine attempts on both my part and Aunt Cassandra's to resolve them. Still, words can build impenetrable walls." She lapsed into a momentary silence, remembering the dreadful afternoon Cassandra had called on her, relating the unpleasant details of her attempt at explaining to Louisa the gravity of Randolph's intimate relationships with other men. But she could never erase from her vivid memory the spiteful look on Louisa's flaring countenance...the enraged words spilling from her stammering lips when, the very next day, she herself had gone to Louisa's Park Avenue home in a barren effort to curtail her denial and win her trust.

Further prompted by the empathetic look in her nephew's baby blue eyes, Beatrice at last spoke up.

"Samuel...I loved your mother. Even now, there is not a single passing day that I do not reminisce of her. And I have thought of you often through these many years as well. The good Lord knows," she choked, impulsively reaching for his clasped hands, "after your mother's passing, I tried in vain to keep in touch with you, but your father would have no part of me. Believe me, Samuel...I would have taken you into my heart and raised you as my own flesh and blood, if called to do so. After all, you were my dear sister Louisa's only child. I assure you, my sweet," she implored, pushing against the sturdy tendons of his hand, "although I have forever entombed within my soul the unhappy memory of that distressing confrontation, whatever words *were* spoken, were offered out of pure love and tendered with the most genuine of intentions." Relaxing her grip, her voice softened. "I only pray that you will find it within your own heart, my dear child, to forgive a well-intentioned aunt who, after several attempts to restore familial harmony, had abandoned all probability of reconciliation. It was for this reason and only this reason, Samuel, that I neglected to attend your father's funeral. Being estranged for so many years had rendered that impenetrable wall impossible to climb."

Samuel pursed his lips into razor thinness. Having a bloody good idea that the undisclosed altercation had everything to do with his father's twisted sexual trysts, he didn't give a tinker's damn whether or not his melodramatic aunt had attended the philandering bastard's funeral. The devil only knew he would have made that same rational decision himself—even if he hadn't been thousands of miles removed. And thank God she *hadn't* taken him in after his mother's death; he would rather have spent the remainder of his days in that despicable boarding school than be raised by this sanctimonious aunt and a pestering trio of fancy-pants cousins. Why, if she were any more righteous, there would be an "impenetrable" *halo* hovering above her sugar-coated head, let alone some metaphorical wall. Nevertheless, Samuel resolved, noting his aunt's fleeting glimpse toward the *fleur-de-lis* mantle clock, better to get the conversation back on track before *Mr.* sanctimony was due to arrive home for lunch. The only thing more intolerable than having to endure such a gibberish-filled morning would be the necessity of departing without having the chance of addressing his intended purpose. Leaning forward, Samuel reclaimed his aunt's fidgeting hands. "My dear, dear, Aunt

Beatrice. Please...there is no need to extend yourself. If anyone should fathom the depths of misunderstanding, it should surely be myself. Why...I have been to hell and back, having faithfully served as captain of my division in the British Army during the past several years. And after attending to a distressing number of wounded soldiers, along with the most sorrowful task of preparing the deceased for their long journey home, I have learned that life is, indeed, too fleeting to harbor any kind of animosities. Consequently," he explained with a gentle squeeze, "I find it necessary to offer apologies on behalf of *my* obstinate parents for the obvious distress you have been forced to endure in return for your loving, yet futile attempt to reconcile. So let us be in concurrence, Aunt Beatrice," he declared in a cheery tone, "to let bygones be bygones and be ever grateful to our most judicious Lord that we have been reunited at last!"

Aunt Beatrice felt as if every nerve in her body was suddenly melted by a burst of sunshine. How fortunate to have such a wise, understanding nephew and how *unfortunate* it was that fate had kept them apart all these years! Despite the contempt she held for her brother-in-law, Randolph, she now realized that his decision to send Samuel to a reputable boarding school had not, after all, been so fruitless. Certainly, Samuel's admirable demeanor had nothing in common with his insidious father. It would be a bright day in Hades before Randolph would have so honorably served his fellow men in a war which surely must have been a living purgatory, if ever there were such a place. And how nobly resourceful that, aside from attending the wounded, her nephew was of such a sound mind and strength of character, enabling him to prepare the bodies of the bravely deceased! But Beatrice's smile soon slipped into uncertainty as she recalled the true purpose of her extending Samuel an invitation to visit and wondered, when morning turned to noon and all was said and done, if his present affection toward her would turn to animosity. Nevertheless, she resolved, she must reveal her hidden agenda before her husband, Leonard, arrived for lunch, but only after buffering her nephew's unnecessary apology with a flattering, yet sincere compliment. "Samuel...my dear boy. I am so very proud of you! And I know your Uncle Leonard would foster similar sentiments! Why, it behooves me to imagine the hardships you must have endured and the bravery you displayed while assisting our fellow allies during such a prolonged and certainly agonizing war. As long as I shall live, I shall never live up to the worthiness you have demonstrated or the countless sacrifices you have endured!"

Taking full advantage of the direction in which he had steered the conversation, Samuel seized the opportunity with a modest smile. "Please, my dear, *dear* Aunt Beatrice...while I certainly appreciate your sincere support, I am afraid that I do not deserve such abundant acclaim. Yes, it is true that I have surrendered four years of my life for the good of my fellow man. However, it was but a miniscule sacrifice in return for the many blessings I have encountered during my own lifetime. And as agonizing as the trenches of war had proven to be, I must admit there were certain aspects of my duty which I found most gratifying, particularly those which would further prepare me for my intended station in life."

"Of course, my dear nephew, but you are much too modest," Beatrice reaffirmed with a patronizing pat on the wrist. "Being presented with the opportunity of reinforcing your knowledge in the medical field must have certainly been beneficial. But...nevertheless, had you forgone your military duties and completed your studies, you would, in all likelihood, have secured the medical diploma so necessary in winning the hand of your beloved Edith."

"Yes, dear aunt, it does seem to be so," Samuel stated, pushing aside his long-forgotten cup of tea while declining another, "but as I have heretofore mentioned, the good Lord seems to have rewarded my faithful service with yet another promising opportunity...the only obstacle being that a considerable amount of expenditure is required in order to obtain this profitable business. But even so, I have not completely disregarded this presently unattainable prospect, for I have often found throughout my journey in life that when the good Lord closes one door, he often opens another."

"Yes...yes, that is indeed so," Beatrice beamed. "But please, dear Samuel...if you would care to inform me of this possible venture, perhaps I could be of some assistance." Pausing a moment while biting into her lower lip, she continued. "I do, after all, have a small account put aside for a rainy day which may, perhaps, facilitate matters for you."

"My dear Aunt Beatrice," Samuel smiled, questioning all the while his aunt's estimation of 'small account,' "how generous of you to extend such a kind offer. However, you are undoubtedly unaware that the reputable business of funeral directing...the vocation for which my duty in the British Army has well prepared me...has recently taken a most unexpected turn which would require the purchase of a separate facility for displaying, as well as preparing, my deceased clients. Consequently, to *insure* the success of this evolving vocation, it is imperative that I purchase a building not merely functional for such purposes, but that which will offer beauty and comfort, thus serving as a most welcoming harbor before loved ones are lowered to their final resting place."

Beatrice gave Samuel a questioning stare. Although, since her own father's death nearly 20 years ago, she had been fortunate enough to escape the sorrow of burying another intimate relative, she had, nevertheless, been obligated to attend several funeral services regarding her husband's business acquaintances. And as it were, indeed, accurate that some of the more prosperous families chose to utilize these so-called funeral parlors which appeared proper enough, it would be a crying shame that her nephew be compelled to cast aside the more respectable vocation of physician for which he seemed to have been destined. "So...Samuel...are you acknowledging that you are relinquishing every aspiration of obtaining a physician's license?"

"Please, Aunt Beatrice," Samuel began, entwining her hands within his own, "if you will understand...I am not, by any means, sacrificing one vocation to realize another. Although I have been intensely trained in the medical profession, I have also gathered invaluable experience in the mortuary sciences for which I have developed a particular ability. And it is not only the vocation itself which attracts me. I also find consoling the bereaved during such a crucial interval in their lives to be extremely gratifying, particularly since losing my own father," he explained with a reverent bow. "So you must understand, dear aunt, that although my father's death was certainly a tribulation, I firmly believe that this cross was accorded to me for a purpose—so that I could truly empathize with my patrons and feel their pain and sorrow as if it were my very own."

Beatrice offered her nephew a reverent smile. Though his undying devotion for her late brother-in-law was certainly undeserved, there was no doubt in her mind that if and when the time came to be reassured at such a difficult time, Samuel was indeed the kind of person with whom she would feel most comfortable. Surely, his serene disposition and compassion for the bereaved was a gift endowed by God himself...a gift which she had no right to censure. "Then you *shall* have my full support, dear nephew!" she exclaimed, tearing both hands from Samuel's loosened grip and spanking them daintily into her lap. "If you truly believe that the profession of undertaking is your calling, then so be it. Pray...tell me, then...how did you happen to stumble across this opportunity and...if you don't mind my interfering, what is the purchasing cost of such a venture?"

Suppressing a delighted smile, Samuel straightened his back and gazed into his aunt's curious eyes. He had snared her surely as he had used Wabena's blood-stained garment to lure his lion; except this time, the chase had been virtually effortless. And, hopefully, this gentler feline would likewise deliver the goods. "How kind of you to take a sincere interest in my ordinary affairs, Aunt Beatrice," he said, handing over his cup and saucer as she proceeded to stack the china. "The funeral parlor which has captured my interest is located in Grosse Pointe, Michigan—a small community just within miles of Detroit. I happened to stumble upon it while visiting some colleagues of mine. It's quite an impressive place and one that is well-designed with all the latest furnishings and equipment necessary to remain the lucrative business that it is." Samuel gave his lips a final wipe before placing the linen napkin atop his aunt's. "The present owners are quite elderly and in need of retirement. A bit pricey, in my opinion, but you must understand, my dear Aunt Beatrice, that I do not take such business ventures lightly. Even though a less expensive funeral home would be more within my means, I do have an obligation toward my future wife and family to invest in a business which will reap a substantial profit for years to come. And it is my estimation that the Millenbach Funeral Home, presently being offered at the *very* reasonable price of fifteen thousand dollars, will surpass its weight in gold in less than a generation. So as you can see, dear aunt, unless I can find the means to finance this promising opportunity as well as securing a loan to sustain personal living expenses...including the purchase of a modest abode...I am afraid I shall find it necessary to inform Mr. Millenbach that he must eliminate my name from his list of potential buyers."

For an extended moment, Beatrice contemplated her nephew with a heavy heart. She had hoped to be of financial assistance, but *fifteen thousand dollars!* And this costly amount did not even include living expenses which he was in dire need of, considering the shabby attire he was presently obliged to wear and the run-down automobile which, by the grace of God, delivered him here. *No.* The price was far more than she could comfortably afford without her husband's knowledge. Perhaps one thousand or two, but *fifteen* or more was definitely out of the question. Perchance her nephew could borrow the money from a Bank & Loan or arrange for an alternate payment method. "My dear, dear Samuel...how I wish I could help you...and...as modest as my savings are, I would forfeit my personal banking account, if necessary...but I am afraid that present circumstances would not allow me to lend the amount you require. But please, do not give up, my dear," she implored, exploring the look of discouragement on Samuel's face. "Perhaps there is some other avenue you can pursue. Have you yet consulted with an officer of a savings & loan? Or, persuaded the seller to consider a more facilitating method of payment?"

Samuel sucked the flesh behind his lower lip. He had the bull by the horns and wasn't about to surrender now. And he'd be bloody damned to hell if he had neglected to properly clean his beloved Stutz Bear-Cat and put on this raggedy monkey suit for nothing. "Yes, Aunt Beatrice, I have, indeed looked into these matters, but to no avail. Mr. and Mrs. Millenbach, the proprietors of the funeral parlor, are most anxious to purchase a considerable amount of property in the state of Florida, and thus unwilling to accept anything short of sound payment. I have also spoken with my banker, Mr. Morgan, who assures me that his establishment would be most willing to lend me the money provided I possess the necessary collateral to guarantee payment. Unfortunately," he went on, compressing controlled fists, "although I know in my heart of hearts that the possibility of the funeral parlor's foreclosure...should I acquire it...is next to none, I nevertheless have hardly a pittance left to my name, either in liquid assets *or* material belongings as collateral. Perhaps..." Samuel pleaded, softening his voice and cupping his hands, "perhaps your faithful husband, Uncle Leonard, would be so kind as to offer me some advice concerning this life-altering venture?"

Reacting as if Samuel had made a request tantamount to her engaging in an extra-marital affair, Beatrice instantaneously turned her attention toward the mantle clock, knocking her knee against the table leg, causing the butler's tray to wobble and the color to drain from her face. "Oh no! Dear, dear Lord...my good God!" she exclaimed, trembling as she helped Samuel steady the table. "Uncle Leonard couldn't possibly be bothered...I mean, of course..." she fumbled, pressing both hands against her well-defined clavicle, "he couldn't...he doesn't...." Her heart-shaped mouth slipped into paralysis as random, infantile syllables attempted to squeeze their way through. But then, almost as quickly as her unsettled disposition had surfaced, every muscle in her flushed face seemed to slacken, giving way to hopeful, widened eyes and a beckoning, yet apprehensive sigh. "Samuel..." she began, pushing a hairpin back into place while rising from her chair, "I believe I may have a solution for your compelling predicament. I know that you may think less of me for it," she explained, making her way toward the cherrywood desk, "but what I am about to reveal will clarify the reason for your presence here." Having finished her outburst, Beatrice reached for the oversized Macy's hatbox which Samuel had noticed upon his arrival. After seating him upon a turn-of-the-century French Provincial loveseat, she carefully placed the large, weighted box between them. "Please be at liberty," she nodded. "Open it. The contents belong to you."

Becoming extremely weary of playing games, Samuel lifted the circular, faded lid. Probably a few sentimental objects his mother had left in her sister's care, he bitterly surmised. But why, in God's almighty name, his Aunt Beatrice would attach so much importance to a few antiquated items was beyond his comprehension. Unless?... Samuel's heart began to race as the tips of his fingers felt hardened points beneath carefully wrapped tissue. Like a slain corpse submerged under water and suddenly released from its binding chains, long-forgotten memories bobbed to the surface of Samuel's mind as he envisioned his partially dressed father on the morning of his mother's funeral darting down the long winding stairway of the Philadelphia mansion like a crazed lunatic, lamenting the apparent theft of his deceased wife's priceless jewels and cursing the demise of a grave robber who hadn't the decency to wait until the corpse was freshly buried before raiding the dead. Ushered back to the present moment by Aunt Beatrice's encouraging voice, he began unraveling the seemingly endless roll of tissue, oblivious to the fact that he was scattering the thin paper all over his aunt's Azerbaijan camelhair rug. "It was your mother's," he could hear her declare as his eyes remained glued to the unshrouded object, its weight resembling that of a fine surgeon's scalpel...its brilliance like that of a freshly-honed blade.

Samuel continued to stroke trembling fingers along the curved platinum setting and every peak and hollow of the familiar, distinguished heirloom, wondering with each lingering caress the number of diamonds it contained and its ultimate cumulative value. Why, every one of the bloody stones—not including the rock-sized diamond set in the center— had to be at least two carats each! And there must be no less than *fifty* of them altogether, he nearly gasped. Certainly, he was no connoisseur of precious gems, but his best guess was that they would reap a profit exceeding twice the amount he sought!

"I know, dear Samuel, that I owe you an explanation as to how your mother's tiara had fallen into my hands," Beatrice tormentingly stated, "but before you make any harsh judgment on my account, please...allow me to reassure you that I never intended to retain the jewels for myself. On the contrary, I always sustained the best of intentions for their eventual return to you, having been my dear sister's only child. Mind you, my dear nephew," she expounded, rotating her diamond wedding ring, "regardless of all my motives, I am still profoundly ashamed by the thievery I was compelled to engage in...but you must understand, Samuel, it was mainly for your mother's sake. I knew how dearly she coveted her personal jewelry and I was afraid...*terrified* that if left in your father's hands, he would have viewed the precious stones merely as a means to further engage in the flagrant lifestyle to which he was so accustomed. Surely, you must understand, dear Samuel, that I could not bear the thought of my sister's treasures falling into the clutches of some avaricious pawnbroker to sustain your father's unorthodox behavior. Why...if there be any earthly power capable of resurrecting Louisa from her grave, it would surely have been such a diabolical transaction!"

Beatrice's last few words provoked Samuel to loosen his gaze from the diamond tiara, reawakening eerie apparitions of his mother's haunting spirit pacing about the moonlit gates of Cheshire Castle, then prowling upon a rocky ledge bordering the Kenyan jungle in the form of a predatory lion. Of course, he rationalized, staring into his aunt's teary eyes, those were vulnerable times and circumstances were such that even the most dauntless of men would, most likely, have been privy to such delusions.

"I know my dear nephew," Aunt Beatrice sniffled, misreading Samuel's contemplative stare, "that you certainly must wonder how I had managed to perform such an unseemly deed...particularly since at the time of your mother's funeral wake, there were so many guests scurrying about the Langley mansion. Well...the truth of the matter is," she explained, reclaiming her wrinkled handkerchief and gracefully blowing her nose, "I waited until very early in the morning...when everyone...including your Aunt Cassandra and your father...were still fast asleep. You see, Samuel...I was able to sneak into the viewing room to which I had been entrusted a key and remove your mother's tiara along with her ruby pendant and matching earrings. Then," she added, wringing the limp handkerchief, "I concealed the valuables within my cloak and carried them out to the stable. There was a hiding place there...when your mother and I were children...Cassandra too...we would hide little trinkets behind a loosened rafter within the loft. Apparently, your mother had remembered these little games also, for when I removed the rafter to store the precious items I had seized, there was already a small crate filled to the brim—boxes of jewelry, most of which she had inherited from your grandmother Langley, that Louisa had been compelled to hide. And although this surprising revelation somewhat confirmed the fact that I was following the proper course of action, I have, nevertheless, continued to keep this secret to myself...even directly lying to my own dear sister, Cassandra, when confronted about the theft. Why, the only time I've ever deceived my darling Leonard has been over this matter...the first time being the morning of our departure from the mansion...I...I purposely left some of my clothing behind in order to fit the jewels in my traveling bag. Afterwards, I told Leonard I had forgotten them and he was good enough to retrieve them for me during his next business venture in Philadelphia. Soon after our return home," she stated, casting solemn eyes downward, "to insure that the jewels would remain in safe keeping, I insisted on contacting a locksmith, telling Leonard that I had learned in the beauty salon that a burglar had found his way into another lady's home and stolen most of her and her husband's valu-ables. And then..." she emphasized, rolling her eyes toward the heavens, "then when you returned my telephone call, I was compelled to concoct some silly story about a salesman trying to peddle house wares. And...although Leonard said he never heard of anything so absurdly rude, he, nevertheless, believed me. So...as you can see, dear nephew, although I have been forced to choose between the lesser of two evils, the gravity of what I have done has surely caused me a great many years of anguish. I only pray that you will find it in your compassionate heart to forgive an aunt whose less-than-honorable actions were carried through with purely the best of intentions!"

Samuel mustered all the will power necessary to maintain a serious face. Forgive her? *Forgive* her??? Why...he wanted to collapse upon his luck-laden knees and kiss all ten of her remarkably-preserved toes! And mind-boggling as it seemed, was it *indeed* true that more jewels remained stored inside the hat box? Wallowing in utter ecstasy, yet experiencing a dread-filled shudder as he mentally envisioned the ruby pendant and matching earrings, Samuel purposely altered his focus. What were the *other* treasures Aunt Beatrice had just mentioned? Valuable heirlooms belonging to his maternal grandmother, did she say???

"Go ahead and see for yourself, if you wish," Beatrice instructed, nodding toward the circular box. "But we must hurry. Leonard is due to arrive for lunch within the hour. I assure you that *everything* is there...*every* valuable item down to the last cameo brooch...including a few pieces which belonged to your grandfather," she emphasized, gently pulling the diamond tiara from Samuel's fingers. "I have not...nor would I *ever* have retained even a single hatpin for myself, may the good Lord strike me dead!" Heartened by her nephew's intense interest in the contents of the Macy's box, she began gathering the discarded tissue. "Perhaps you shall propose to your beloved Edith after all," she cried, swiftly rewrapping the sparkling tiara. "With all of these valuables to declare as collateral, I am sure that you shall procure any loan you may request."

Samuel nearly chuckled as he proceeded to open several of the velvet-lined jewelry boxes, ignoring his aunt's description of each piece's sentimental value. *Collateral,* his bloody ass! He was going to sell every last piece of his mother's precious mementos and convert them into a big fat bank account. But he wouldn't allow the newly-discovered treasure to fall into the hands of some common pawnbroker, as his father had done when pillaging the colonial mansion. After all, he had presently taken up residence in Detroit, one of the nation's most prosperous cities. Surely, there were some reputable jewelers who could advise him regarding the appraisal and sale of each item, *particularly* the diamond tiara, he grinned, closing the lid on an eighteen-carat gold barrette and reaching for another box. If he departed from the City of New York within the hour and drove non-stop, he would, most likely, arrive in the nation's automotive capital shortly after midnight. Then, after an honest attempt at a good night's rest, he'd secure a safe-deposit box at the People's Savings Bank on Griswold Street, he noted, lusting after an emerald-studded Christmas tree pin.

"The ruby and pearl necklace along with the matching earrings are in the large green case," Aunt Beatrice hurriedly pointed out. "I am sure you will recognize these pieces...particularly the ruby pendant. I don't believe that a day ever passed without your mother wearing it."

Samuel once again felt his stomach tighten. He had better be on his way before Uncle Leonard returned, he rationalized, attempting to rid his mind of the nauseating images of his sickly mother flaunting the blood-red pendant between the pronounced cleavage of her sagging breasts—calling to him...beckoning him. Gesturing with spindly, web-like fingers. *Besides,* he impetuously concluded, disregarding the green velvet box, he had no reason to mistrust his gullible aunt and was certain everything was intact. "Thank you kindly, dear aunt. Thank you kindly for everything!" he declared, wiping beads of perspiration from his forehead with the back of his hand while rising from the tapestry loveseat, "but I am afraid it is getting rather late and I hope to return to Detroit before midnight. And rest assured, dear Aunt Beatrice...you have no reason to regret what you have done, for you are surely a saint in my eyes! I shall forever treasure these items and hold them dear to my heart...as shall my beloved Edith who should surely accept my hand in marriage now!"

Beatrice felt a soft flutter in her heart and looked into her nephew's gem-blue eyes, gently placing the wrapped tiara with the other valuable items, then assisted Samuel with closing the hatbox. "How I dread to see you go!" she cried, teary-eyed. "Perhaps...perhaps in the near future you can call on us another day...both myself *and* Uncle Leonard. You can make believe it's a surprise visit." Her hazel eyes sparkled nearly as much as the diamond tiara. "And you can even bring Edith along too...you can declare that since your father is no longer alive, you have been yearning to reconcile and wish to share your happiness with us. Then, perhaps Uncle Leonard and I can plan a wonderful reunion where all can assemble with the rest of the family...Aunt Cassandra and Uncle Stephen's too!"

Samuel clasped Beatrice's hands within his own. "My dear Aunt Beatrice...that is truly a most considerate proposal. But...I cannot help to think that such a gesture may be rather dangerous, particularly if I wish to present Edith with these precious heirlooms. Why...she may desire to wear my dear mother's magnificent necklace or stunning earrings during one such visit...or mention them in conversation, which may surely unlock the doors of suspicion." Wary of his aunt's impending rebuttal, he gave her hands a gentle squeeze. "*You* may be willing to risk that chance, Aunt Beatrice, but... although I again assure you that your well-intentioned deed was more than justified, I am afraid that a man of Uncle Leonard's honorable stature may never absolve the act of thievery under any circumstance. Aunt Beatrice..." he whispered, his eyes a convincing blue, "I could never forgive myself if I should, in any way, be the cause of discord between the marriage of yourself and Uncle Leonard. Now!" he proclaimed, pulling his hands away from her grasp, then tapping her dimpled chin, "Let us always treasure in our hearts the memory of this visit. I know I shall," he declared, lifting the hatbox from the loveseat, "but perhaps the good Lord will find a way for us to be reunited again after all. If not in this world, then certainly in the next!"

With heavy, lingering steps, Beatrice accompanied Samuel toward the darkish foyer. "Oh Samuel, my dear nephew! How shall I ever know how you are faring?" She opened the closet door, reaching toward the top shelf. "You know, Samuel, I cannot very well subscribe to a *Detroit* newspaper. Why...how would I explain my sudden interest in such a publication to Leonard? I must confess," she said, retrieving his cockeyed cloth hat, "that not too many years ago while you resided in Philadelphia with your father, I would now and then stumble upon a newspaper release in the *Pennsylvania Evening Post* regarding momentous occasions of your life...such as your graduation with honors from the University of Pennsylvania and ultimate acceptance into the Hahnemann School of Medicine. How proud I was of your accomplishments, Samuel! And oh..." she added, tenderly holding onto the hat's lopsided rim, "I shall never forget the lovely article written at the time your father presented you with that *exquisite* Silver Ghost Rolls. It's such a shame that you no longer own it," she assumed, envisioning the seemingly run-down Bear-Cat. "I believe the featured article was written because that particular Rolls Royce was the first of its kind ever manufactured. I must admit, sometimes when Leonard was obliged to travel to Philadelphia, I would purposely accompany him and then hire a taxi during business hours to drive by the Langley home. On one particular occasion, I was fortunate enough to capture a glimpse of you returning home in that magnificent silver automobile. At other times, I would instruct the taxi driver to park down the street until..." She paused, remembering the time she witnessed, from the back seat of the taxi, her brother-in-law, Randolph, escort one of his male lovers from the house. "Until I could obtain visual evidence that you were, indeed, still living there. Then...then one day, to my astonishment, I noticed your father's name in the obituaries. But...by that time, it was too late. It had been quite a while since my last visit and the home had already been sold. That is when I presented my calling card to the new owner, hoping there would be a remote possibility that he would find an opportunity to place it in your hands."

Samuel lent his aunt a patronizing smile. He didn't care a pauper's penny about her clandestine escapades. All he knew was that his arms were beginning to ache under the weight of the clumsy hatbox and the sooner he could place the recovered jewels into his Bear-Cat, the sooner he would arrive in

Detroit and get on with the business of finding a buyer. "Aunt Beatrice," he soothingly declared, somewhat perturbed with her tenacious grasp upon his second-hand hat, "if I were granted one wish, I would choose to spend another hour or two with you so that I might enjoy more of such pleasant reminiscing. However...I am afraid that if I tarry any longer, Uncle Leonard will surely discover my whereabouts. So, my dearest aunt, if you would please place my hat upon this box, I shall be on my way. May the good Lord be with you and bless you always!"

Like a weightless blanket around disencumbered shoulders, Samuel could feel his Aunt Beatrice's heavy-hearted presence as he turned his back on the tidy brownstone and stepped into the piercing sunlight. How fortunate that devious circumstances had required his early departure, he sighed, gingerly placing the Macy's hatbox upon the Bear-Cat's unshaded black leather passenger seat. Hopefully, the distant gathering clouds ahead would linger as he proceeded westwardly, preventing the sun's rays from further gnawing the restored interior of his beloved roadster. Ever aware of his aunt's abiding presence upon the top step of the best-be-forgotten brownstone, he walked around the rear of the Stutz, offered her an affirmative nod and, placing his hat upon his head, positioned himself behind the newly-replaced steering wheel. With a shortage of funds no longer an obstacle, he realized, sensing the sun-induced heat on the back of his thighs, he was now able to provide the best possible upkeep for all *three* of his restored automobiles, including the permanent procurement of adequate shelter. No longer preoccupied with the pretense of 'loving nephew,' Samuel felt an ecstatic well of euphoria bubbling up the length of his spine. Given a year or two, it would no longer be necessary to contract with an outside source for the safe storage of his cherished Bear-Cat, French Gregoire, and Silver Ghost Rolls. He was rich...oil-gushing rich! Rich enough to build the biggest Tudor mansion the City of Grosse Pointe has ever laid eyes upon! And, along with it, a garage spacious enough to house a whole *fleet* of automobiles if he bloody well pleased! After securely replacing the box of jewels on the passenger side floor, Samuel bore down on the clutch, started the ignition and released the parking brake. Trusting that his new set of Firestone tires would guide him safely and swiftly back to Detroit, his thoughts shifted once again to the Millenbach Funeral Home with its tall white pillars and plush viewing rooms, appropriate enough for presenting the most alluring of meticulously-prepared corpses. As if unleashing a thousand demons, the Bear-Cat's idling engine continued to churn as he visualized the young, lily-robed Indian maiden in sweet repose upon the perfumed pillows of the rosewood casket. Suddenly propelled back into the present at the sight of a shiny black Cadillac rambling by, alerting him to the fact that the Honorable Leonard Martin was due to arrive within a quarter of the hour, Samuel promptly shifted the Stutz into first gear. Bidding one curt nod of a goodbye as Aunt Beatrice wiped another tear from her rouge-smeared cheek, he nimbly loosened his tie and proceeded down Lexington Avenue. Feeling a deep sense of gratification as the corner of his eye focused upon the Macy's hatbox, his mouth flared into a triumphant grin. No matter what his time of arrival at the Pontchartrain Hotel, he firmly resolved, he would offer the valet a generous tip, instructing him to see to it that the Bear-Cat was properly cleaned and gassed up by morning. Then, he would hurry the hatbox up to his private suite, double-bolt the door, recline upon the four poster feather bed and, savoring images of the funeral home's cellar stocked with the promised, yet soon-to-be illegal vintage wine, light up a congratulatory cigar.

part 2

Eleanor

chapter 64

Reflections

Quite satisfied that his two-toned Oxfords were properly cleaned and buffed and the polishing supplies neatly stored within the utility room of the luxurious kitchen, Samuel eyed the marquis-shaped sapphire ring he had previously set upon the window sill. It had been nearly 13 years, he fondly reminisced, reaching for a brick-sized cake of lye soap. Thirteen years since he had consulted with Mr. Rose, the Detroit jeweler, who had wisely advised him about the sale of his valuable inheritance. Samuel's eyes glazed over, nearly matching the color of the ring's deep blue stone as he lathered his hands, the bar of soap darkening from the washed-out shoe polish. It seemed like only yesterday when he had entered Rose Jeweler's, situated at the bottom rung of a four-story warehouse, tucked between a news depot and dry goods store. He could still hear the falsetto, 'old world' voice of Mr. Rose crescendo into unrestrained elation as he held a jeweler's loupe to his tortoise shell spectacles and studied each diamond of the bejeweled tiara as if he were a miner panning for gold.

"Superrrior quality...exzellent color...fine...very fine!" he exclaimed, casting aside the loupe, yet keeping both eyes glued to the ten-carat, oval centerpiece, flanked on each side by 21 nearly flawless diamonds. Carefully repositioning the tiara upon a black velvet cloth while momentarily disregarding the remaining unappraised heirlooms which Samuel had brought along, the old Jewish master cautiously looked toward the front of the unoccupied shop, then back at Samuel. His Eastern Ashkenazic eyes appeared twice their size as he peered through the thick lenses of his glasses. A look of refrain...then anticipation...crossed his face like an obstetrician about to inform his patient of impending motherhood. "Doctor Governey...I have not ever seen such a vunderful display of vhite diamonds in all my years as a jeweler. If you only vish to know zee value of zeese many pieces," he explained, gesturing toward the Macy's hatbox, "zen perhaps for an insignificant fee I shall offer you an estimated figure. But let me assure, you, Doctor Governey, zat if you vill allow me, I can find zee best buyer for you who vill give you zee best price available, particularrrly for zis extremely valuable tiara. Be assurred, Doctor Governey, zat zere are several vays of how ve can approach zis. I suppose..." he added with a sigh and a pendulum-like rocking of his yamaka-clad head, "zat zese diamonds can be removed from zere settings individually. But I vould not recommend it. *Not yet,* at least. Such sentimental piezes such as zis have been known to vin a heavy profit if vun finds an eager buyer. But I do not szink zat Detroit is zee best place for zis. I szink...I szink zat zee City of New York vould be best. And, vith your blessings, I vould be more zen happy to make zee trip over zere...vithout an *additional* charge, of course. You may accompany me, by all means. I vouldn't szink of doing it any ozer vay. Of course, ve are likely to spend a veek or two zere to obtain zee best price. I know zis may seem a bit of an inconvenience, but...trrrust me, Doctor Governey...zee sale of such exquisite heirlooms should not be handled in a frivolous manner!"

All the more miffed that the cathedral window overlooking his garden was in want of a good cleaning, Samuel continued to lather his hands with the lye soap, remembering his initial gut reaction to Mr. Rose's suggestion. Having just returned from his Aunt Beatrice's New York brownstone while anticipating the prompt purchase of the Millenbach Funeral Home, there was no bloody way in hell he was going to retrace his tracks back east and then waste another couple weeks of his precious time. Particularly with some pushy old Jew who rolled his r's while spitting out saliva and emphasized his t's to the point of unbearable annoyance! Why...he'd best go back to England and let one of the reputable auction houses...Christie's or Sotheby's, for instance...handle the sale of his mother's priceless possessions. After all, these auction houses *did* have a sterling reputation for attracting the world's most affluent collectors eager to pay an extravagant sum for authentic heirlooms, whether a full tea service once owned by the Empress of Russia or an original oil painting commissioned by the British Royal Family. But that option, too, at least for the meantime, was surely out of the question.

As Samuel rinsed the blue-grey lather from his hands, he recalled how he briefly considered Mr. Rose's suggestion of removing the diamonds from their settings and selling each one individually...that is, until the crusty jeweler, as if having read Samuel's mind, spoke up one more time. "Zhere is vun more suggestion I could make forrr you, Doctor Governey, if you care to know. Zhere is an auction at zee Hotel Cadillac zee Monday from next...just down zee street a little vay from here. I cannot say for sure zat zis might be good to do, but you never know how zees zings sometimes vork out. If I vere in your shoes, I vould consider trying zis. I know zee man who you can talk to. My righteous colleague, Harry, is his name...Harry Malovsky." He reached for a pencil and paper and scribbled down a note. "You tell him Reuben sent you...Reuben Rose. And if you vant to do it zis vay, you tell Harry to start zee bid for zee tiara at vun hundred fifty zousand dollars. Anyzing less vould be highvay rrrobbery. And also...if you vish...I can appraise zee rest of zee items for you to auction off as vell!"

Unequivocally thrilled with the likelihood that a certain item in his mother's cherished collection should reap thrice as much currency as initially imagined, Samuel decided to forego the jeweler's final suggestion. After all, the remainder of his mother's jewels would only appreciate and yield even more capital once he *did* have the opportunity to return to England. Nevertheless, he immediately contacted Harry Malovsky who, to guarantee himself an extra commission of five "big ones," proposed to feature the "resplendent" tiara on the auction block at a starting bid of $155,000.00. Having engaged in a gentlemen's agreement with Mr. Millenbach that the money for the funeral home would be paid in cold hard cash within the next two weeks, Samuel then found himself in prime position to sit back and enjoy the sportive spectacle of sophisticated, urbane men dressed up to the nines, battling with numbered paddles in the hope of outbidding their competitors. And, to Samuel's utmost delight, two automobile moguls, whose highly-impressionable wives had taken a fancy to the exquisite, bedazzling tiara once belonging to a Countess of "profoundly respected royal heritage" had, like a couple of white knights on a quest for their ladies fair, vehemently crossed swords. As a result, the price of the desired heirloom was elevated to over one-and-a-half times its initial suggested value, reaping a grand total after-tax, post-commission sale of $173,240.00. With a wide-open grin and check in hand, Samuel immediately deposited his windfall into a personal savings account, authorizing the first withdrawal of such funds to be made payable to Mr. Edmund G. Millenbach, Jr. Eagerly awaiting full possession of the funeral home come October, he received an additional bonus when Ed Millenbach was critically stricken with one final bout of emphysema, ultimately becoming Samuel's very first client. Consequently, Ed Millenbach's bereaved widow Hildegard, having no more reason to resettle in unfamiliar swamp-filled Floridian territory, agreed to remain as Samuel's personal assistant, along with her orphaned nephew, Zachary Dorkins, the morphine-dependent American private with whom Samuel had first become acquainted at Major General Briggs' London-based infirmary.

Staunchly aware that his primary obligation as an unseasoned owner of a prestigious funeral establishment would be to master and promote the business, Samuel delayed the construction of his English Tudor mansion. However, he secured for such future purpose an imposing parcel of land overlooking the wide-stretching waters of Lake Saint Clair. Realizing the importance of an invaluable mentor, he had acquiesced to Hildy Millenbach's request that she continue dwelling within the upstairs living quarters of the funeral home. Meanwhile, Samuel and Hildy's nephew, Zachary, who was appointed to play the dual role of apprentice-in-training and domestic servant, temporarily rented the only available nearby two-bedroom cottage. Most eager to promote his prospective business and to inform the Grosse Pointe community of the funeral home's new ownership, Samuel commissioned a local artist to design a tasteful stained-glass sign illuminated by incandescent lighting. To increase the opportunity of luring the patronage of bereaved parents who had surrendered their pubescent daughters to the eternal arms of death, he purchased a string of advertisements in the *Detroit Free Press* and ordered several hundred brochures from a local print shop extolling the compassionate care and exceptional attention that only the *Governey Funeral Home* could provide. Extremely impressed by Doctor Samuel Governey's refined British demeanor and aristocratic mannerisms, residents from neighboring communities as well as those from far-reaching cities experienced newly-found consolation by surrendering their deceased loved ones into his endearing hands.

To Samuel's ever-recurring disappointment, however, the anticipated quota of dearly-departed young maidens left much to be desired. But, as unfulfilled desires often lead to alternate paths, it was not long before he stumbled upon "Madame Charlotte's Chalet," a suburban brothel blessed with the excellent reputation of remaining "clean," due to the Madame's insistence that every customer's genitalia be examined and bathed before enjoying the many charms and talents her girls were so capable of offering. Likewise, her seductive flock of women, concerned about the possibility of inadvertent pregnancy, yet eager to pull the last silver dollar from the bulging bill books of highly-esteemed patrons ranging from liquor law enforcement officials to venerated clergy, were happy to forego the usual prophylactic sheaths in order to insure the sexual enjoyment of these loyal customers. Instead, they were properly schooled by their Madame in the use of contraceptive devices be they cervical caps, vaginal suppositories, or vinegar douches. And, as so often happens when the forces of nature are uncooperative regardless of prudent planning, Doctor Samuel Governey, Madame Charlotte's' solely-appointed patron physician, was always ready to provide the appropriate means necessary to eliminate any biological inconvenience, if not for profit, then for the immense satisfaction he derived from sucking the embryonic life from another fertile womb— whether the 'not-to-be' mother was a common prostitute or...as word tends to travel...a high-class socialite. As an additional bonus, in return for the proficient abortions and occasional medicines, particularly the eventual introduction of a penicillin used to remedy the affliction of numerous social diseases, Madame Charlotte was forever ready and willing to bestow upon Samuel the pleasure of bedding the youngest newcomer of her establishment. And, if lady luck were indeed on his side, the procurement of a delicately-formed, dark-haired, acquiescent virgin...for a few gold 20-dollar double eagles...would occasionally drift into his appreciative grasp.

As the span of three more years propelled Samuel into another unexpected windfall, he began to insist that his girls be elegantly dressed from head to toe. Consequently, every one of the Madame's personally-handpicked harlots were provided a complimentary wardrobe consisting of the latest exquisitely-tailored fashions and low-cut ball gowns unaffordable to many a proper lady, giving Madame Charlotte's Chalet the unequivocal reputation of being "the most respectable whorehouse this side of bootleg paradise."

As the rum-running, gangster-busting decade of the "roaring 20's" was well underway and the outstanding reputation of the *Governey Funeral Home* became more eminently known, Samuel, further provoked by the failing health of Hildy Millenbach, was compelled to contact the University of Minnesota, one of the very few learning institutions in the United States offering instruction in the mortuary sciences. Having procured one of their finest graduates, he then assumed a voluntary leave of absence from the duty of embalming the dead, freeing himself to entice and console prospective customers while intermittently superintending the construction of his long-awaited English Tudor mansion. But there were certain exceptions to Samuel's agenda, the most prevalent being that only he himself be allowed to handle the delicate matter of "personally attending to the children," citing a promise he habitually would make to their bereaved parents, although this vow often left him with the lesser-fulfilling responsibility of embalming young males in order to avoid even one fleeting ounce of suspicion. And, be that as it may, such a promise sometimes burdened him with the task of battling bitter cold and biting winds in the dead of night while traveling from his two-bedroom cottage to the *Governey Funeral Home* in order to accept a freshly-deceased body. However, every trip was well worth the inconvenience when he found himself in sole possession of a delicately-boned, angelic-like pubescent female; lifeless, yet still warm from the blood which, just hours ago, had flowed within her virginal veins.

Whereupon administering abortions empowered Samuel with a sort of impenetrable armor, embalming a freshly-deceased young maiden was tantamount to feasting on the rarest of gourmet meals. Amid the soft, hushed murmur of diffused lighting, Samuel would begin his secret ritual by placing the limp, naked child into the long porcelain bathtub filled with relatively hot water in order to help maintain a tepid body temperature. Then, using a bar of pure-scented soap, he would carefully cleanse every curve and orifice, especially aware of the intact clitoris and labia so typical of the Western female. After gently positioning her upon an adjacent towel-encased embalming table, he would reach for a dull, black metal box noticeably scratched around its rusty, gold-plated fastener. Upon retrieving a stick of red lip color from the wide array of mortuary cosmetics, he'd enhance the nipples of the child's breasts, thus simulating one of the many titillating customs he had initially witnessed in the African village of Mukot. And to further insure that his desires be fulfilled, he would, like a sudden eclipse descending upon an unsuspecting moon, enshroud the deceased maiden's hair with a black silk scarf if her locks were not of a pleasing color.

A bit disappointed that, due to the rapid decomposition rate of deceased bodies, he was forever prohibited from using the slower-performing circumcisional stones and broken glass brought over from Africa, Samuel would instead set his sights upon a freshly-honed scalpel. Sensing a fragile trembling within, but with eager, steady hands, he'd firmly grip each pliable wad of tissue and, with the other hand, maneuver the blade in a sawing motion, brisk enough to ensure a superb castration, yet sluggish enough to savor the extraordinary moment. Then, regretfully foregoing the use of catgut to suture the mutilated genitalia, he would follow the engaging procedure with a quicker cauterization to deter any bothersome bleeding. More determined than ever to fully possess the genitally-mutilated corpse, he would then savor the stroking of the child's body to relieve any signs of *rigor mortis,* commencing with the arms and legs and culminating with an upward kneading and twisting of each cosmetically-ripened nipple. Then, as if augmenting the grand finale of some compelling operatic production, he would fully disrobe and mount the lifeless body like a lion in heat, grinding his pelvis into the unresponsive lap of his victim, conjuring enough life within his loins to resurrect the both of them.

Being certain to expend no additional time lest the body begin displaying visible signs of decay, Samuel would, with the ease of donning a liturgical vestment, quickly slip on a full-length medical smock and, abutting the embalming table to the soap-ringed tub, slit open an artery and vein in the groin of the corpse, allowing the blood to drain before replacing it with the required amount of formaldehyde. After inserting a large-bore needle into the belly to pump out waste and any remaining blood, the pungent-smelling, crimson-colored fluid would again be infused to give the little corpse a healthy life-like pallor. Finally, recalling the professional training he had acquired from his dearly-departed predecessor, Edmund G.Millenbach and his dedicated wife, Hildegard, Samuel would tenderly administer the final cosmetic touches upon the deceased child, transforming contorted lips into an angelic smile and sunken eyes into undefiled vessels of heavenly, peaceful slumber.

chapter 65

Momentous Moments

Reassured that the last trace of bluish grey lather from his freshly polished shoes was rinsed from his hands, Samuel shook the excess water into the kitchen sink, ready to replace, on his barren forefinger, the marquis-shaped sapphire ring. Although he held no reservations regarding the disposal of his mother's diamond tiara, he was pleased to have followed his own inclination about waiting for a more opportune time to sell the remainder of his chance-acquired fortune. In light of the fact that fortuitous circumstances had rendered such an action unnecessary and those very jewels, particularly his mother's ruby pendant, had been safely hidden for the past decade inside a mahogany bureau, his maternal grandfather's sapphire ring could have easily, under a different state of affairs, found its way into another gentleman's jewelry chest. Though certainly not as ostentatious as his own father's gold and onyx ring forever cast beneath the rolling waters of the River Dee, Frank Langley's sapphire stone could not only reap quadruple the price, but possessed the elegance and sophistication expected from an esteemed funeral director and prospective candidate for mayor of Grosse Pointe—a position which would surely help him profit from alternate forms of illegal activities now that the lucrative business of bootlegging would soon be put to an end. Yes, Samuel affirmed while reaching for a linen towel. Although his intention of returning to his beloved England to auction the remainder of his mother's jewelry had never been fulfilled, it mattered not. For the past 13 years, Lady Liberty's torch had been dimmed by compassionate, society-reforming citizens, determined to cure the brunt of humanity's ills by forcefully thwarting the manufacture, sale and transport of all alcoholic beverages, ensuring for himself a rewarding opportunity greater than any he had ever imagined—rendering the acquisition of the Langley inheritance as merely the tip of a nation-shattering iceberg.

Samuel's short-lived grin transformed into a scowl as he began wiping his wet hands. The towel was already soiled. *Bloody bastard!* he cursed under his breath, alluding to Zachary, his recently deceased personal servant and housekeeper. *How in the devil's name he ever managed to get hold of that bottle of poisoned liquor I'll never know.* Compelled to dry his hands upon a scant corner of the white linen, he was further perturbed that the front of his undershirt was forever sticking to his chest. Upon entering the kitchen nearly an hour ago, he had released the shades and opened the etched glass windows when the ceiling fan failed, but the humidity was transforming the fresh lake air into a saturated teabag. It was during these exceptionally hot, humid days that he regretted postponing the installation of a high maintenance air cooling machine within the English Tudor, relying instead upon Lake St. Clair's steadfast breezes to sustain him through another Michigan summer. *At least he could have gotten the ceiling fan fixed before passing on,* he silently complained while testing the stubborn device one more time. The plank-shaped blades whirled about slowly, then gathered more speed, finally transforming into one circular motion. As the descending draft attempted to appease him, he refolded the linen towel, then ran his fingers through damp locks of amber-tinted hair. *A world of good that bloody fan will do now.* Resigning himself to the fact that a good part of his morning had been whittled away, he resolved to go upstairs and shower after drinking a glass of chilled water. Thanks to this modern convenience, he thought, while opening the porcelain door of his newly-acquired Frigidaire, at least there was no longer an annoying drip pan or large blocks of ice to fool with.

Having poured the water from a half-filled crystal decanter, Samuel quenched his thirst while gazing through the kitchen's screened cathedral window which overlooked the west side of a lavish garden. A sparrow's cheerful chirp originating from the rear of the mansion accompanied the din of crudely crafted wind chimes as he surveyed his privately owned paradise, its plush green lawn and masterfully planted foliage presently endangered from want of a reliable gardener. Reminiscent of Elizabethan England, the garden stretched around the back of the mansion into an expansive plot of land which housed a collector's Eden. Among the English ivy and marigolds bordering the garden's distant boundary wall, a palatial stone gazebo from the mountainous region of Switzerland majestically displayed long, fluted columns and wide-winged Griffins. At the garden's center, stretching branches of a giant elm softly shaded a painted rod iron bench imported from Marseille. Within its delicate reach, a winding pond adorned with water lilies bordered a flowering Italian trellis. Proudly standing within the pond's center, a statue of a young goddess shamelessly presented every feature of her Grecian splendor. But away from the heart of the bountiful garden, closer to the rear of the mansion in clear sight of the kitchen and guest bedrooms, stood Samuel's most prized possession. Crafted by his own skillful hands, the memento consisted of a six foot high phallus-tipped spear supporting a wooden plate of pancake size from which random objects used in African circumcisional ceremonies dangled beneath multiple strands of intestinal gut. And although the actual employment of these irregular pieces of broken glass, scissors, blades and razors was geographically impractical, the memories they invoked when nudged by a moderate lake breeze were even sweeter than the initial excursion behind the sleek, polished wheel of another newly-acquired automobile.

Setting his glass of water upon the marble counter, Samuel turned toward the breakfast room, refocusing his gaze upon a distant brick structure crowned by a mushroomed cupola and laced with terra cotta tiles which would have easily accommodated a splendid team of horses attended to by loyal servants, its ample courtyard awaiting the hourly recess to witness an engaging game of racquets. However, since the mere thought of inept servants groveling at his feet and cackling maids snooping about would for a moment prompt Samuel to consider retreating to a single thatch hut, the only attendant to occupy the spacious upstairs quarters of the two-story building had been his trained servant, Zachary Dorkins. Aside from his abiding loyalty and remarkable efficiency, Zachary's punctuality was unsurpassed. As sure as the rooster crows at the break of dawn, there was no need for Samuel to rely upon the latest *Gruen* "doctor's watch" to affirm that breakfast was served on time; Zachary's daily need for morphine was certain to usurp even the most reliable of *Big Ben* alarm clocks. Waking promptly at 6:00 a.m., the young American veteran, still suffering from shrapnel wounds, would be down the steps in ten minutes time, eager for his injection of pain killer and ready to prepare the first meal of the day as he sprinted across the brick flooring, past stained oak walls and nine fluted cherrywood pillars, providing each of Samuel's twelve classic automobiles, purchased and traded like shiny new marbles, with its own private accessible stall. A set of four cast iron radiators continuously warmed the cherished collection during Lake St. Clair's brutal winters and a Mobil oil gasoline pump kept each tank filled to capacity, rendering them far better fed than the much-too-frequent roadside beggar.

Turning his back toward the breakfast room, Samuel indulged in a second gulp of chilled water while a fox squirrel, scampering about the garden's west side, became the center of attention. As the frisky animal scurried around the stout clay belly of a Sudd pot, Samuel suddenly wondered how his elderly colleague and fellow traveler, Dr. Wesley Carvelle, was getting along. Due to Samuel's sudden departure from his initial visit to Africa upon learning of his father's death, Dr. Carvelle had temporarily retained the Sudd pot, as well as Samuel's other cherished belongings—particularly the preserved head of his magnificent lion—within his private London residence. Then, in-between two subsequent journeys with him, shortly after the Tudor mansion was completed, Samuel provided Dr. Carvelle with a ticket to and from the United States on the luxury cruise ship, *Maurentania* to spend a good part of the summer in Grosse Pointe and to personally see to it that every single item, down to the last hay-cushioned crate, was returned from overseas unharmed. In remittance for his valued time and mindful vigilance, Samuel had treated his good friend to all the finer things the city had to offer, not the least of which were many complementary visits to Madame Charlotte's bordello. Dr. Carvelle had returned one more time since then, shortly before the great stock market crash of 1929 nearly three Octobers ago, this time bearing gifts from his own extended travels and once again enjoying Samuel's gracious hospitality—whether it be participating in polo matches at the Grosse Pointe Hunt Lodge, indulging in the invigorating sport of sailing at the recently built Yacht Association or patronizing the Lochmoor Country Club while trying his amateur hand at the increasingly popular game of golf.

Having finished his tall glass of water, Samuel began refilling the crystal decanter from the tap while noticing the fidgety squirrel running circles around a pedestaled gazing globe, bringing to mind his deceased servant, Zachary. It was only a few feet away from the silver Chinese sphere that he had discovered that lifeless addicted body, his stiffened pink fingers clutching the thick neck of a broken bottle of illegal whiskey; its remaining contents, along with a stream of vomit, discoloring the healthy, green hue of Samuel's lawn. But despite the inconvenience his otherwise loyal servant's death had caused, Samuel couldn't help but feel a twinge of gratitude toward Ed and Hildy Millenbach's capricious nephew, considering the fact that, due to Zachary's quick wit, enough leverage had been provided to insure Samuel's partnership in yet another business which would not only exceed the worth of his mother's heirloom jewels multiple times over, but also make the profits from the funeral home seem like merely a handful of beans from a charity-sponsored soup line.

chapter 66

Just Rewards

It was during his second full summer as sole proprietor of the *Governey Funeral Home* that Samuel first became acquainted with Tony 'The Tank' Terillo, ringleader and prevailing brains of the 'Bocci Boys,' an Italian mob with illegal bootlegging operations encompassing Detroit's lower east side. From the moment the self-assured immigrant had entered the funeral home to make arrangements for his mother's funeral, Samuel instinctively knew that Tony Terillo, still spouting broken English with a native Sicilian accent, had not come into sudden wealth by pushing cartfuls of fruit and vegetables. Dressed to the nines in his European pinstripe suit, imported shoes and silk tie adorned with a full carat diamond pin, 'Tony T' flagrantly flashed a bullet-sized diamond ring while explaining to Samuel the intention of sending his younger brother, Angelo, back to the quaint Sicilian town of Terrasini in order to insure the expedient passage of his father's formerly entombed body to the United States. His dearly departed parents could then be placed aside each other within an impending family crypt of chapel size encompassing a 12-plot stretch of land at Detroit's prestigious Elmwood Cemetery. For the funeral itself, Tony specified, he wanted "nuttin' but da best" for his dear mother, Lucia, including a polished bronze casket with pure gold plated handles, a duplicate of which was to be ordered for his *"patri caru,"* Roberto Paulo Terillo.

Initially pleased that the extravagant Italian funeral had progressed with nary an obstacle and sensing an unusual dexterity in his arthritic-prone fingers while recounting his stack of 20-dollar bills, Samuel's blissful state of mind was suddenly interrupted by a sharp-knuckled knock and choirboy voice which, as far as Samuel was concerned, could correspond to only one living creature in all of this Darwinian universe.

"Sir! Doctor Governey sir! Please! Somethin's balled up downstairs sir! In the eatin' room! Hurry on down...we gotta' help. Get a wiggle on! "

Steeped in the awareness that his slang-slinging servant, Zachary, was bound to get excited over a nickel candy bar, Samuel ignored the lad's unrefined pleas and proceeded to count his hard-earned wages. Immensely satisfied that every bit of currency was there, he retrieved a set of keys from his jacket pocket, opened the top drawer of his desk and safely stashed the tightly banded wad before opening his office door.

Appearing as if he had just witnessed the sinking of the *Titanic*, the flush-cheeked lad, a billow of perspiration covering his freckled nose, wasted no time in showing his unruffled boss the unfolding calamity. Taking to his heels like 'Tarzan of the Apes' he rushed Samuel toward the elevator, all the while mumbling something about a mishap among the mourners in the eating room. Up until that very moment, Samuel had nearly forgotten about the Terillo family's presence in the hospitality room located in the air-conditioned basement of the funeral home. Initially unreceptive to Samuel's suggestion that they utilize his fully furnished kitchen for their post-funeral luncheon, Tony with his two brothers and their wives, bedecked in black from head to toe, had reconsidered their decision upon realizing that hosting the solemn affair within any of their own homes, with no relief from summer's relentless heat and humidity, would only enhance their already unbearable grief. Consequently, promptly after the burial, adhering to Sicilian tradition, the parched family had returned to the funeral home with platters full of stuffed *brucioluni*, sacks of hand rolled pasta, jars of canned tomatoes and spiced olives and cheeses, all of which became deliciously apparent as the doors of the elevator began to slowly reopen.

One might expect the sweet aroma of Italian cooking to be accompanied by the merry sound of a mandolin. Instead, Samuel's senses were accosted by broken glass being swept up amid the beautiful Italian language being butchered by those engaging in a crude and frenzied Sicilian dialect. Upon reaching the source of the auditory confusion, Samuel's annoyance suddenly quickened into bewildered animosity. For among the clamor of a roomful of adults and children waiting for their meal to be cooked, the trio of brothers was directing the cleanup of what appeared to be a straw-encased bottle of Ruffino Chianti from his personal cherished wine collection. Sensing an immediate tightening of the neck, Samuel pulled at his dotted silk tie, resisting the urge to yank it off and strangle the first available guest, all the while questioning how in the world these boors had violated the sacred cellar, drinking one of his coveted red wines. Yes, it was certainly true that, in lieu of Michigan's poorly enforced prohibition law, he had *initially* reinstated Ed Millenbach's custom of providing a few complimentary bottles of table wine for patrons who chose to utilize the dining facility. However, since the recent legislation of national prohibition during the past year had invoked the iron fist of the federal government, he realized that it would be in his best interest to terminate this welcoming gesture, resolving instead to personally indulge in the consumption of his finest wines in self-imposed solitude. *How then*, Samuel fumed while beads of perspiration, as from a loosened spigot, trickled down his forehead. How in the devil's bloody name had the Terillo family discovered his forbidden collection of vintage wines? Had he, by some odd chance, forgotten to lock the bloody door of his private cellar? But, in an instant, as if crushed by the sharp blow of a temperance leader's axe, his exasperation dissipated into confusion followed by sheer relief when an anonymous guest, having discovered Samuel's presence, began quickly clearing the table of a dozen or so bottles of wine along with an assortment of hard liquor. For in that one chaotic instant, Samuel suddenly realized that the broken Chianti along with the other bottles of alcohol, could not have been retrieved from his wine cellar after all; instead, his prior suspicions that the Terillo family had most probably been profiting from the illegal liquor trade was indeed reinforced.

Except for the bubbling of boiling water and the gurgling of spaghetti sauce amid the soft whimper of a nursing baby, the room became ominously hushed until Tony, after giving his younger brother, Angelo, a patronizing pat on the back, strutted toward Samuel with a wide open grin.

"*Scusi, Dutturi* Governey," he implored, raising a bejeweled hand to Samuel's shoulder. "We so sorry we mess uppa yo floor. But...you no worry!" he quickly interjected, gesturing toward his two sisters-in-law, both kneeling upon the dark green linoleum while sweeping broken glass onto a cardboard lid with the aid of a wine-stained towel. "We clean up *prestu!*"

Detecting a nervous laugh, Samuel suddenly found himself tracking Tony's deliberate footsteps into the darkened hallway, speculating all too well the reason for the sudden diversion. As far as he was concerned, this pug-faced dago didn't have a thing to worry about; his suspected bootlegging shenanigans were as safely concealed as the locked cellar. He didn't care a flapper's feather what sort of illegal activities his clients might have decided to engage in. Giving the clean-shaven, fat-lipped Sicilian his undivided attention, he acknowledged Mr. Terillo's keen ingenuity and sinister courage.

"*Dutturi* Governey..." the burly-browed immigrant pleaded, his eyes black as soot and hairy hands folded into one boulder-sized fist. "You my friend, no? I giva you anyting. Anyting you like. You lika fancy car? I giva you one! You justa name it...Forda...Buicka...Bentaley...I giva you the bigga Bentaley, eh? You justa name. Whata color you like, huh? I order for you!" Responding to Samuel's tactful declination, the robust racketeer, like a lover about to bestow his first kiss, leaned even closer until Samuel could feel the revolver at his groin and smell the garlic through his pores. "You don'ta see notting!" Terillo insisted in a forceful tone. "If anybody ask, or snoopa 'round, you tella dem you don't know a notting! Da cops, dey come-a by, you don't knowa notting! *Capisci?*"

Unable to back away from the ironclad pressure of Tony's gunmetal leather shoe pressed upon his toe, Samuel gulped down a charming smile. "Mr. Terillo...if you will please be assured...as I am most honored and grateful for your loyal patronage, my allegiance rests solely with you and your loving family. And please be further assured," he breathlessly squirmed, continuing to wonder when the stone-faced Sicilian would release the crushing weight from his foot, "I do possess the remarkable ability to disassociate myself from matters which are not of my concern. And I would not hesitate for even a minute to exercise that propensity, *particularly* during an interrogation by a posse of law enforcement officials, should that remote possibility ever happen to be realized."

Like a disengaged cylinder from the barrel of a Colt revolver, Tony's jaw dropped from the rigid corners of his mouth as he released his foot from Samuel's freshly polished calfskins. Even though he couldn't comprehend most of what this *gentilomu* was saying, he could not have been more stunned if Father Rubino, the presiding priest at his mother's funeral, had suddenly leaped from the pulpit and gave him a swift kick in the *cugiuni!* But, on the other hand, despite an indistinguishable chemical odor masked by cologne, there was something about this funeral director that was reassuring...it was like walking along the Sicilian countryside, having a heart-to-heart talk with his dearly departed *papa*. And as far as his concerns about this Governey *uomu* spillin' the *vinu*, he couldn't put his finger on it, but was sure that far from being some two-faced *Americanu*, this dignified beanpole had the real potential to become a true *cumpare*.

Like an all powerful *capo di tutti capi*, gracefully abdicating his blood-begotten throne, Tony 'The Tank' Terillo stepped away from his potential confidant with an affirmative nod of the head, bearing in mind that this upstanding undertaker, whom he had prematurely misjudged just a few minutes ago, had also somehow earned the title of "doctor"—a title which might just come in handy at a time when making an emergency visit to a local hospital would prove far too risky. "S*cusi, Dutturi* Governey," he said, extending his hand in a conciliatory manner. "I sorry I steppa onna your clean shoes. I someatimes getta...how do you say in English...jumpa the boat! I tella you what," Terillo chuckled, matching Samuel's solid grip, "I buya you a branda new Bentaley, eh? And I don'ta taka no for the answer. You justa tella me what color and I get. Notting but da besta for my friend, eh? The *meggiu* besta!" Tony paused a moment, inconspicuously glancing at Samuel's scuffed shoe. "What siza you taka? In-a shoes, I mean...I getta you a new pair too. The besta kind! The besta kind aroun'!"

Ever so much the wiser, Samuel consummated the hearty handshake with another firm grip of his unoccupied hand. Despite his proper English upbringing, this certainly was not the time to simulate appropriate behavior as outlined in *Beadle's Dime Book of Etiquette*. And though he had always been taught from the time he was a young lad that it was a mere matter of courtesy to initially decline an overtly generous gratuity, he also knew quite well that this pompous immigrant from the indigent island of Sicily had surely developed his own habit of playing by a completely different set of rules. *Besides*, he envisioned, rewetting dry lips, if he *was* after all required to participate in this new game, he may as well go for the full match. "My dear Mr. Terillo...how very kind of you to offer such generous gifts. But, as you may have very well noticed," he explained, temporarily glancing downward, "I do have a rather large foot, rendering it quite necessary to have most of my shoes purposely built. However, it is quite fortunate that my relatively tall stature has never precluded my enjoyment of the most exquisite of pre-fabricated vehicles...in particular, the fine British archetype which you have heretofore mentioned. Perhaps," he cautiously stated, loosening his grip while wearily envisioning the shiny black hearse he had been obliged to drive for the past two years, "perhaps a *cheery* shade would be in order, then." Detecting a bit of confusion on Tony's face, he released his hands to draw an imaginary "X" on the front of his new *amico's* suit jacket. "*Any* color will be most appreciative, my good friend. Any color but black. ***No nero.***"

Exactly one week later, almost to the hour, Samuel was once again subject to the excitable demands of his servant, Zachary, pounding on his office door, proclaiming that a representative had just delivered the "bee's knees"—one of the most "hotsy totsy" auto cars he had ever laid eyes on. Sustaining a brisk pace while following the limping heels of the panting boy, Samuel found it necessary to catch his own breath as he stepped through the front door of the funeral home and out onto the brick-paved drive drenched by a marveling sun. He remained speechless as a driver in a smartly dressed uniform stepped out of the running vehicle, handed over a voucher for him to sign and asked if a telephone was available to arrange for his return to the dealer. Complying without question, Samuel then perused the automobile in all of its royal blue splendor. From the elegantly long chassis to the hooded spoked wheels, the three-litre model Bentley convertible was obviously one of the first to be assembled and surely like no other. As he stepped closer to inspect its interior, the astonished look on Samuel's face instantly changed to a wide open grin when immediately noticing another unconventional gift placed beneath the chrome steering wheel atop the pearl-toned driver seat...one of the finest pair of black leather calfskin shoes he had ever seen, graced on the inside by the insignia of renowned Italian designer *Giuseppe Santoni* scribbled above the indicated shoe size of '12-1/2 M.'

chapter 67

A Binding Pact

I n the late autumn of 1921, an increasing number of Michigan residents listened to startling reports of bootlegging and random killings broadcast by *Detroit News* Station WBL through their radio receiving sets. It was during that same pivotal year, nearly four months after their initial meeting, that Samuel was once again contacted by his lifelong friend, Tony 'The Tank' Terillo. It had been nearly 11 years ago, Samuel recalled, capping the crystal decanter of water while ambling toward the Frigidaire. He remembered that moment as vividly as the sparkle of the sapphire ring he had just replaced upon his finger—as *vividly* as the headlines which had appeared in the newspaper that same morning so many years past: **"Fire Assists Feds In 'War on Booze.' Warehouse Destroyed."** When Samuel opened the door of the Frigidaire, a refreshing blast of cold air struck his face as it had that brisk November evening after the funeral parlor's closing when he had rushed from the second floor viewing room to answer the call of an unexpected guest. Though dressed in a double-breasted overcoat, his face obscured by a mink storm collar and matching hat, Samuel instinctively knew by the visitor's olive-shaped eyes and exceptional girth that another lucrative proposition, most probably regarding the illegal running of liquor, was about to cross his ever-so-opportune path. Without hesitation then, he ushered the beseeching man inside, politely acknowledging Mr. Terillo's needless introduction.

"I so sorry I disturba you tonight, *Dutturi* Governey," Tony began, stripping the fur collar from his weather-beaten cheeks. "But I hava someting

moltu importante to discussa with you...*moltu importante*...ifa you please."
Without voicing another word, he was escorted into Samuel's office, emphatically declining a glass of *vino Barolo.* Ignoring a second offer to hang his
coat, Tony tossed it over the back of a brown leather chair, slumped his lead-
en body into another and retrieved a Havana from his host's fully stocked
cigar box. "Please...*pi' piaciri*...letta me begin bya tella you, *dutturi*, that me
anda my brothers, Gieuseppe and Angelo, tink-a you as our besta *Americanu*
friend." After preparing the cigar for a light and drawing in a prodigious
amount of tobacco smoke, he continued. "And letta me be sure to tella you,
that ifa there is anyting you needa or wanta from us," he embellished with a
swift motion of his free hand, "it's as gooda as done...*finitu!*" Casually engaging in the robust flavor of the Havana, he complimented his host on the
excellent choice of cigars, then with a pair of incendiary eyes gave Samuel one
long, contemplative stare. "My gooda friend...that'sa why I come-a here
tonight." Leaning forward, Terillo pressed his hand to his chest. "I-a know
inna my heart that you woulda do the same for me. Anda I know, that what
I about to aska you is a bigga *favuri,* but believea you me...ifa you do thisa
for me anda my brothers, you never be sorry. Gieuseppe, Angelo anda myself
willa be *sempri gratu.* So whatta you say*, Dutturi Governey?* Willa you do a
speciali favuri for me anda *me famigghia?"*

Samuel leaned into his tufted leather chair, temporarily disregarding his
guest's indulgent slaughter of the English language. Rubbing a thumb along
the length of his lit Perfecto, he secretly admired Tony's bullet-sized diamond
ring. At the moment, he did not know exactly what this bullheaded Sicilian
had up his impeccably tailored sleeve, but although the funeral establishment
was doing fairly well and he was, indeed, planning to utilize the remainder
of his mother's fortune to finance the eventual construction of his Victorian
mansion, he instinctively knew this was one opportunity he should most
prudently consider. After all, he surmised, recalling accounts in newspapers
and magazines of barrels of Canadian liquor crossing the accessible waters of
the Detroit River and Lake St. Clair...after all, hadn't he himself, on many an
occasion, entertained the notion of participating in the most profitable venture the Congress of the United States had ever afforded mankind? Of
course, being involved with the likes of the Terillo family would entail defi-
nite risks...the worst scenario, aside from incarceration, being that the funeral
home would be gravely jeopardized. But then again, he determined, scrutinizing the intimidating bulge at the hip of Terillo's wool trousers, did he truly
have a choice?

"My dear Mr. Terillo," he finally answered, gingerly positioning his ash-crowned cigar upon a silver tray. "Once more, please allow me to express my deepest gratitude for your most sincere kindness. Your past generosity will forever be appreciated and I am deeply honored that you consider me a true friend and confidant. Therefore, my dear *amico*, I shall be happy to assist you if it, indeed, be within my ability to do so." Before Samuel could fully comprehend the true significance of his words, he found himself slumped over the desk as Tony grabbed him by the shoulders and heartily kissed him upon both cheeks, sealing the amorous gesture with one firm smack on the lips. Initially worried that the unrestrained Sicilian might burn the fabric of his suit jacket with his molting cigar, Samuel was instead relieved when the spontaneous ritual soon ended without incident, though the moisture from Tony's lips, still cool from the November air and forever reeking with basil and garlic, remained upon his own. Resisting the temptation to pull out a handkerchief and scour his face, he responded to his new partner's suggestion that they finally break open the sequestered *Barolo* after all which was quickly retreived from inside an unassuming liquor cabinet. Then, setting the appropriate glasses and coasters on his polished oak desk, he awaited Tony's forthcoming machinations.

Smugly reseated upon the leather chair with smoking cigar still in hand, Tony tossed one leg over the other, stretched his thick neck and began scratching the bristles beneath his rounded chin. "Before I tella you whatta we need, you musta understand that what I tella you does notta leave your lips fora nobody. You musta keepa this the *megghiu segretu*. You don'ta trusta nobody...*capisci?* Detecting an eager compliance in Samuel's steel-blue eyes, he proceeded. "I don'ta know ifa you reada the papers thisa morning, butta we hava a *grossu problemu*, my brothers anda me. And asa you already shoulda know, thisa *problemu* is abouta some shipaments we hada stored away inna the warehouse thata was burna down lasta night. *In ogni modu*," he emphasized with a shrug of the shoulders and one bushy eyebrow shifting toward the ceiling, "we hava some mora shipaments coming inna tomorrow early inna the morning anda nowherea to put. I tella *me famigghia* thatta you a gooda friend and willa help. I canna see when we wasa downa stairs for the lunch for the *funerali di mia matri*, thata you have a lotsa room," he quickly explained, attempting to squelch any potential excuse on the part of his host. "Anda you no worry abouta getta caught," he assured, wagging his large-knuckled index finger. "Me anda Giuseppe anda Angelo knowa lotta the cops...they look outta for us. But I don'ta think no cops is gonna tink to look in a *funerali* place lika this. Anda if it *wasa* to happen thatta the Fedsa finda out, they gonna do notting to you. Firsta time just a *piccolo* slap onna the hands. But don'ta you evena worry 'boutta that. Itta no gonna happen. *Allora!*" Terillo exclaimed, rising from his seat as Samuel handed him the wine, whereupon he toasted his *cumpare* with a hearty *Salute!* "What you thinka my besta *buon amicu?* We make a gooda planna...no?"

Welcoming the sweet taste of the *Barolo* upon his violated lips, Samuel reseated himself at the desk, meticulously placed his wine glass upon one of the coasters and leaned forward with hands entwined. Momentarily considering the possibility of utilizing the Italian he had learned as a schoolboy in order to deter Tony's consistent carnage of the King's English, he ultimately vetoed the notion. Even if it were possible to recall enough of the Italian language to carry the remainder of the conversation, it was much too late in the game to risk any insult which may arise from such a self-serving gesture. "My dear Mr. Terillo...I am most honored that you have taken me into your confidence and I cannot emphasize enough my desire to aid you in your time of need. However," he added, pondering the fact that, as of yet, there had been no guarantee of fair compensation, "there may be some profound complications which I shall be required to manage...and manage them I shall. But notwithstanding the distraction from my livelihood that this venture will obviously demand, it will require a great deal of ingenuity on my behalf to insure that my employees, particularly Mrs. Millenbach who presently shares her living quarters here, does not jeopardize this most crucial endeavor." Surveying the Havana limply hanging at the edge of Terillo's mouth, he gave a moment's pause to rephrase his statement. "I am happy to help you, my dear friend, but it will be more work for me to do my job and make sure that *your* job remains a secret. Can you tell me then, my dear *amico*, what will be in this agreement for me?"

As if a vacuum tube had suddenly been activated inside his head, Tony flashed an ear-to-ear smile, miraculously keeping the wine from sloshing out of his tottering glass. "*Bonu bonu!* he exclaimed, extracting the cigar from his fish-shaped lips while exposing a set of widely spaced teeth. "I understanda now. Ofa course, *Dutturi* Governey, I woulda notta aska you this *favuri* without me givva you somethinga back. *Allora!*" he spewed, shoving Samuel's cigar aside while crushing the butt of his own upon the inundated tray. "How aboutta I maka you a deal, eh? I tella you what...I giva you fiva percent of everytinga we makea froma the hooch. Anda I tella you," he clarified with joined finger and shaking wrist, "thatta isa notting to laugha at. Fiva percent willa getta you *tanti sordi.* You notta gonna get fiva percent froma nobody—notta even ifa you work alla the day and alla the night inna thisa place. Anda please," he asserted, sinking back into the chair, "no mora Mr. Terillo. You calla me Tony, eh? Lika my *megghiu amicu!*"

Contemplating Tony's offer amidst a lingering haze of smoke, Samuel knew that, no matter how underhanded his guest may otherwise be, he indeed spoke the truth now. Recalling newspaper articles and verbal accounts of bootleggers making well over five million dollars a year, he quickly calculated that his five percent take could bring in a handsome $2,000.00 a month—almost as much as he had reaped during his first full *year* of business—providing, of course, that Tony and his brothers continue utilizing the funeral home as their designated storage depot. But *then, again,* he reconsidered, rubbing his hands together as if igniting a fire, conspiring with the Terillo brothers would surely make for a risky trade. "How *molto gentile* of you... *Tony,*" he finally spurted, the name practically strapped upon his tongue. "I do agree that five percent *is* a good amount. However," he continued, bearing in mind Terillo's limited comprehension of English, "as you have already agreed that my funeral home *is* the best place to hide your goods and considering that I can help your business grow by giving to you more good ideas, I think that maybe *15* percent might be a fairer wage. But...no matter what you decide," he guardedly stated, I assure you, my good *amico,* that you shall find no one more able or trustworthy than I to help manage such a dangerous trade if you so wish."

Continuing to slouch in his seat like a satiated emperor, his half-filled glass of wine forever threatening to stain Samuel's Bakshaish ivory carpet at any given moment, Tony pinched his upper chin with his free hand and ground his teeth as if munching on an uncooked piece of mostaciolli. "*Dutturi* Governey...you putta me in a harda spot. I already talka to my brothers anda they had a harda time to even giva you the five percent I justa offer. And you musta remember too...my brothers anda me hava all the family to taka care anda the *cugini* to pay." After forming a fist and kneading his lips, he continued. "I don'ta know if you realize how mucha five percent canna make for you, *Dutturi* Governey, but...I tella you what. Ifa I canna show my brothers how mucha you canna do for us, I willa try for thema to agree to giva you *tenna* percent. So...my besta *Americanu* friend. What you say, eh? Can I plan for the shipament to come to thisa place someatimes early inna the morning justa before sunrise? We bringa the goods at the backa door. So...whata you say? *E' un buon affare?*...do we make a gooda deal?"

As the grandfather clock continued to ring in the 11th hour, Samuel contemplated the prudence of spending the remainder of the night on the unforgiving hallway sofa instead of his cozy featherbed back at the cottage, lest he miss an earlier than expected delivery. Provided he did not receive an unforeseen call requiring him to promptly embalm another departed soul, everything should run as smoothly as each meticulously woven thread on Mr. Terillo's silk brocade tie. Of course, if the inevitable should occur, he would telephone the cottage, instructing Zachary to come straightaway and mind the rear entrance while he finished preparing the corpse downstairs. At this point in time, there certainly was no reason to alert Mrs. Millenbach who would be sound asleep in her upstairs quarters. Furthermore, since visitation hours did not commence until early in the afternoon, nothing short of the funeral home itself catching fire should retard the advancement of the Terillo brothers' scheme. "My good man... *Tony*, my dear friend," Samuel finally answered, still keeping his cohort's confined knowledge of English in mind while rising from his seat and stepping around the desk. "I shall look forward to your next visit as well as the agreement of your brothers regarding my possible ten percent. Perhaps as time goes on," he explained extending his right hand, "I will prove myself helpful enough to earn a growing respect in your eyes and in the eyes of your two brothers."

Disregarding the spare coaster upon Samuel's desk, Tony immediately rose from his seat, pushed his empty wine glass along the desk's unprotected surface and consummated the illicit transaction with another triple kiss, firm handshake and memorable pat on Samuel's back. After buttoning his coat, he then allowed his new partner in crime to escort him to the front door. "Thanka you once again, *Dutturi* Governey. You don'ta know how mucha this means to my brothers anda me. Anda please..." he paused, securing his mink hat, "don'ta you worry abouta nobody nosying around. Ifa any cops or anybody aska any questions abouta the shipaments, you tella them you needa more supplies for the funeral home causa business is good, no? Nobody gonna know any different to see a lotta wooden crates comin' in the backa door. *Capisci? Allora...tutto beni, Dutturi* Governey...*bonu sira,*" Tony curtly remarked, stepping out onto the elongated porch dusted by the season's first sprinkling of snow. But before he could turn his back to make his way through the teasing flurry, he was momentarily delayed upon hearing one final request.

"My dear, dear *amico...Tony...*," Samuel emphasized. "Again...please rest assured that you and your brothers have placed this most delicate matter into the best of hands. I guarantee that you will not regret your decision to include me in such an important venture. But, please...if I may be so bold, I have but one more favor to ask...*un altro favuri*," he asserted through a devilish grin, sensing the suspicious apprehension in his departing visitor's eyes. "In all fairness, I must insist that since you prefer to be addressed by your given Christian name, that you, yourself, do likewise with me. Therefore, my dear friend, you shall stop addressing me as *Doctor Governey*." Then, as if the frigid night air had bound his tongue in a fleeting sheet of ice, he paused in contemplation, once more extending his hand toward Tony, amazing even himself with the ease in which he uttered his next few words. "Henceforth," he finalized, his warm breath materializing into the late autumn darkness, "you shall address me as *Sam.*"

chapter 68

Lucrative Commerce

I t didn't take but a fortnight for Samuel to realize that he would at last be able to abandon his temporary sleeping arrangement at the funeral parlor and once again return to the two-bedroom cottage and his own comfortable bed, ready to reawaken promptly at the stroke of 5:00 a.m. on random days via secretly coded telephone calls. Allowing himself 40 minutes for a morning constitution as well as administering Zachary's initial dose of morphine, Samuel, content with the knowledge that his Silver Rolls, Stutz Bearcat, and French Gregoire were safely confined in a nearby rented garage, would drive his royal blue Bentley back to the funeral home to oversee the delivery of the Terillo brothers' bootleg liquor. As surely as a plethora of sound frequently whirled from the grooved disc of a Berliner gramophone, so too did wooden crates of various sizes arrive at the back door of the *Governey Funeral Home*. Before the yawning sun had even the slightest opportunity to suspect any unlawful activity, a couple of Tony Terillo's several cousins, aided by Samuel and his schooled servant Zachary, were already inside unloading the Canadian contraband into a vacant spare cellar. Soon after the stock was sorted and accounted for, a fleet of hearses would discreetly depart the funeral home one-by-one, their final destinations being local blind pigs and waterfront speakeasies as well as specialty shops which sold directly to their customers, not the least of which included mom & pop grocery and confectionary stores.

As the alluring province of Ontario, Canada, continued its illicit love affair with the surrendering shores of Michigan's Lake St. Clair, whereby scores of offspring in increasing numbers blatantly indulged in the ingestion of bootleg liquor, the Terillo brothers came to realize the indispensability of their resourceful *dutturi amicu*. While men and women smuggled an abundance of booze across the Canadian border in unsuspecting vessels including resealed egg shells and hollowed-out loaves of bread, and school children occasionally drank from bottles of moonshine obtained from their parents' private stills, Samuel would sometimes seek repose from the tedious duties of undertaker by concocting a few ingenious ideas of his own. When the Terillo brothers finally caught and "popped" the rat responsible for the incineration of their only warehouse, Samuel arranged for the body and any thereafter to be conveniently disposed of in an affiliated crematorium. On a more harmless note, he took the liberty of investigating a Canadian law which allowed drinking in that country's residential homes, yet prevented Ontario distilleries from directly selling their wares. Augmenting the previous deal with the Terillo brothers which eventually increased his five percent take and ultimately gave birth to his desired 15 percent share of the business, Samuel, taking advantage of a loophole in Canadian law, volunteered to personally obtain orders from Windsor customers at his funeral home address. Then, as smoothly as a shot of Haitian rum is guzzled down the throat of a shameless hoofer, one of Tony's cousins would deliver the checks to each participating distillery, allowing them to finally deliver their goods, thus earning a handsome commission for "Sam" and his increasingly devoted partners in crime. But although the convenient arrangement was somewhat short-lived due to a change in Ontario importation laws, there were more clever opportunities to receive the abundant blessings of the enterprising 'Bocci Boys.'

When one of Samuel's bereaved clients happened to mention that he was "twice grief- stricken" due to the extensive loss of revenue suffered from the sole manufacture of soft drinks at his former brewery, Samuel initiated plans for an underwater pipeline connected to a Windsor distillery, eagerly assembled by the hardworking Terillo cousins and explicitly directed by their *capo cuscinu*, Tony. And, when Detroit's ruthless Jews of the 'Purple Gang' threatened to "bump off" the Terillo brothers unless they handed over a hefty percentage of their profits, Samuel intervened and prevented mutual bloodshed by arranging a gentlemen's agreement which motivated the Jews to "lay off the doc's docks." The very least of this deal granted the Purple Gang unlimited funeral services and 24-hour access to the crematorium for the disposal of their slain opponents. *Dutturi* Governey also promised to personally attend to any medical attention the Purple Gang or members of their family might require, as well as providing unlimited narcotics and an occasional abortion for any witless molls they may have "knocked up."

Despite Samuel's sheer ingenuity at nullifying the bloodthirsty quarrels between the Jews and the Sicilians, there was one particular incident shortly after the completion of his English Tudor that earned him the greatest respect in the eyes of the Terillo brothers. At a time when cocktail parties were more popular than silk pajamas and cops collected bribes faster than a bullet-ducking speedboat, Doctor Samuel Randolph Governey once again flexed his cerebral muscles, sparing his reckless Sicilians a one-way trip to the slammer. Surely as Babe Ruth was slugging his way into the hearts of New York Yankee fans, President Hoover was stepping up to the plate, determined to place law and order back into jazz-infused nightclubs and blood-splattered streets. So, consequently, while federal agents in Chicago hunted down notorious gangsters like Capone and "Bugsy" Moran with a feverish pitch, another police raid was occurring at, of all places, a prominent funeral home in the genteel town of Grosse Pointe, Michigan.

chapter 69

Narrow Escape

Having placed the filled decanter of water inside the Frigidaire, Samuel's mind returned to the grave inconvenience his servant Zachary's death had been causing him the last several days. *Perhaps it is a small price to pay after all,* he thought, acknowledging that if not for the nearly 15-year survival of the Volstead Act, he would have been subject to a substantially less affluent existence. Casually glimpsing his dark suit jacket and straw hat still spread over the kitchen chair, he sauntered toward the butcher block where his freshly polished two-toned shoes still sat atop the newspaper. Immediately eyeing a "Dick Tracy" comic strip, he was reminded of the unexpected raid by federal agents at his funeral home on that unforgettable day of early April, 1926. While lifting his shoes from the paper, he tried to recall what had first alerted him to the assault. Was it the stomping of hard-soled boots? The crash of a candelabra? The distressing cries of an elderly woman? Nevertheless, Samuel concluded while clearing the butcher block of the colored funnies, it was Zachary whom he mostly remembered, running down the basement corridor like a whiskey-filled jalopy on an ice-covered lake, gibbering something completely incomprehensible, yet all the while reciting "jeepers creepers!" As the brawny shoulders of Tony's two cousins suddenly froze, bringing the first several boxes of that morning's smuggled liquor to a temporary halt, Samuel instantaneously realized that the hurried stomping originating from upstairs hadn't been Zachary practicing the *'Lindy Hop'* and the cries of Hildy Millenbach weren't the result of her accidentally breaking one of her master's cherished possessions. *Rather*, Samuel recalled as he tossed the crinkled funnies into the wastebasket, he had instinctively known, as a mother prudently discerns the cries of her infant child, that the frantic pitch in Zachary's voice and the wild look in his eyes were *not* due to the fact that the *Ringling Brothers Circus* had just arrived in town.

"We're bein' copped! The Feds! ...just busted smack through the fucking back door!" Then, screaming at Terillo's two cousins, he exclaimed, "Peppino cut out with the rest o' the loot, but...quick...we guys gotta cheese it outta here or we're duck soup! Up the elevator ta the casket room...load the rest o' the shit in there...in the caskets and get the fuck outta here...it's our only chance!"

Without the slightest hesitation, Samuel realized that Zachary was right on the button. With the Feds fresh on their heels and bound to be tramping down the basement stairs any second now, there was no time to deposit the contraband liquor inside the distant cellar. Their only chance was to roll the two dollies into the adjacent elevator, take them straight to the second floor and unload the contents of the wooden crates, along with the two cousins, into the first few available caskets. But just as soon as Zachary rushed the men into the elevator, Samuel changed his mind, issuing further instruction and insisting that the thug closest to Zachary in stature—the one with the baby face—remain behind. As Zachary and the rest of the convoy safely made their way to the second floor, Samuel hurried the smoothly shaven palooka into the embalming room, imploring him to lie still upon the stainless steel table as he administered a dose of calcium bromide to calm him down. Then, quickly throwing a white sheet over the body, he hastened toward a nearby cabinet.

Professionally poised alongside the embalming table as the unnerving thud of footsteps and slamming doors loomed closer, Samuel took a deep breath while filling in the pudgy chops of the blonde-wigged accomplice with crimson lipstick, all the while imploring the 'cadaver' to lie perfectly still. Having barely completed the task, his diffused concentration was abruptly seized as the door to the embalming room was kicked open, causing him to inadvertently misguide the crimson tube of lipstick down the square jaw of his motionless subject. His alligator shoes practically glued to the tile floor, Samuel found himself face to face with a Smith & Wesson revolver, backed by the menacing black barrel of a Tommy gun. Staring at the two federal agents as though completely surprised, he dropped the lipstick to the floor and held both hands halfway up in surrender, waiting for one of the agents to address him.

"Doctor Samuel Governey?" the skinny one with the hooked nose blurted. "Yer under arrest for violation of the Volstead Act." Then, with a swift nod toward his sour-pussed partner holding the Tommy gun, he buried the Smith & Wesson inside his greasy overcoat and fished out a pair of handcuffs. But before the stubbly-faced sergeant was provided the opportunity of consummating the arrest, he became distracted by the aristocratic demeanor of his intended captive.

"My dear gentlemen..." Samuel began, in a tone of utter disbelief while staring with widened eyes. "I do not know the reason for such an intrusion, but I am certain there has been some grave error on your part or, in the very least, a gross misunderstanding. So please...I implore you...before you bind my hands like a common criminal, first and foremost be assured, as you can clearly see," he indicated with a nod toward the crimson-jawed henchman, "that I am a respectable undertaker managing a most demanding business, holding nothing but the highest regard for the laws of this land...the land of my birth. So again, I implore you," he continued, returning his attention to the dangling handcuffs, "if you shall be so kind as to provide me with an explanation for such an unwarranted intrusion, I assure you that I shall be able to clear my good name to your utmost satisfaction."

Agent Lenny Reinholt guardedly stuffed the handcuffs back into his overcoat and retrieved the revolver, instructing his junior deputy to relax his grip on the Tommy gun. *Goddamn* this man was good! In all his 22 years of service, he'd never encountered such a smooth-talking son-of-a-bitching bullshitter! Doggone dapper too—even in that white kimono he was wearing. Why...dress any one of Chicago's thugs in a tail coat and top hat and he still couldn't hold a candle to this stud. *But, just maybe...*Reinholt reluctantly considered, squinting baggy eyes while continuing to size up the peculiar suspect...was it possible that this doc was really on the up and up? That the anonymous tip at the bureau last week was nothing but a hoax? God knows this wouldn't be the first time he'd been involved in giving someone a bum rap. After all, unless his boys still shaking down the top floor come up with something fast, it will all be just mere speculation. And from what he had gathered from the doc's background, there was no previous criminal record. But if he was all that innocent, Reinholt frowned, what was in them boxes that were bein' delivered at the back door the last few weeks? He'd been so positive that he was onto somethin' that he could practically smell the bust. But then again, he deduced, cringing before the unsavory countenance of the cadaver, why would a fella still be playin' around with dead people if he was able to make a truckload of dough by just smuggling booze? Nope, there were just too many *t*'s to cross and *i*'s to dot. But he, Agent Lenny Reinholt, sure as hell would get to the bottom of this, he resolved, yanking the brim of his cap and issuing a loud snort before finally speaking up. "O.k. doc...if you insist...we'll play it your way, then. Are you denyin' the charge that you've been engagin' in the illegal importation and sale of hard liquor? Does the name *Terillo* ring a bell?"

Releasing an audible sigh, Samuel shook his head as if utterly flabbergasted and turned the palms of his hands upwards, all the while hoping against hope that his fabricated cadaver continue the charade. "Gentlemen...once again I proclaim my innocence! As you can readily see, I have a reputable business to uphold and an unyielding commitment toward my bereaved patrons. And as for the name...the name... *Terillo*...I don't believe I have had the privilege of ministering to any such family as of yet."

Reassured that his junior deputy was again in full control of the Tommy gun, Reinholt tucked away his Smith & Wesson once more, pulled from his coat a folded document and flaunted it in front of Samuel's face. "I've a search warrant here. Gives me the right ta search every nook and cranny of this place, anywhere I damn well please. So doc, you're tellin' me you ain't got nothin' to hide? I got men combin' the upstairs this very minute, so it'd make it a lot easier on all of us, not ta mention sparin' a lot less damage to this joint if you'd just come clean and tell me where you're hidin' the hooch!"

Ever so grateful that a secret passageway to the locked cellar had been installed and thankful of his recent decision to move his personal wine collection into the newly constructed Victorian mansion, Samuel started to reach inside his own pocket but immediately ceased upon realizing that the long black barrel of a Thompson submachine gun was still pointed straight at his chest. "Then be my guests, gentlemen. And feel free to roam my funeral establishment if you must. I shall personally escort you if you wish, but, then again, I do understand that gentlemen in your position prefer to make yourselves at home. I only ask one favor of you," he cautiously proceeded, though anxiously wondering how his own boys upstairs were coming along. "If you would be so kind as to allow me the opportunity to retrieve my set of keys, it may spare you the trouble of inflicting any additional damage and hasten your search, lest my bereaved guests arrive this afternoon to find their loved ones in the midst of further turmoil."

Feeling a bit warm under the collar, Sergeant Reinholt shoved the search warrant back inside his coat pocket, wondering all the while if Samuel was as sincere as he appeared or if the clever doctor was still continuing to pull his leg. *Regardless*, the perspiring agent resolved, he still had another card to play and hoped it came out being an ace instead of a fucking joker. "I may just take you up on that, doc, but before I do, I'm hopin' you could answer another question that's been pesterin' me."

"And what, may I ask, would that question be?" Samuel responded, continuing to exude the model of innocence.

"Me an' my men been scoutin' this area for some time now," he began, skeptically ogling the motionless corpse with a new set of private eyes. "We noticed you have shipments of crates bein' delivered here every now an' then—most o' them in hearses. Tell me, doc," he boldly stated, moving one step closer to the peculiar cadaver. "What's in them cases anyway and where in the hell did them two delivery men disappear the minute we got here?"

"My dear sergeant!" Samuel emphasized, attempting to divert Reinholt's attention from the cosmetically altered decoy. "I am operating a funeral parlor here and, as you will no doubt notice while continuing your hunt upstairs, there are several bodies in a given day which must be attended to! Why...if you care to look around this very room, you will see that there are a number of supplies which must be replenished daily in order to prepare my many deceased patrons. How I decide to transport such supplies reflects my rather overly cautious nature, as I wish to insure that the quantity and type of each order be examined and then delivered by the reliable hands of my own experienced assistants. May I reiterate, my good sergeant," he continued, relieved that he had temporarily averted his captor's attention from the fraudulent corpse, "that I am a respected mortician in this Grosse Pointe community—one whom many a citizen relies upon for comfort and service at perhaps the most crucial and painful time of life." Well satisfied that the deputy had again relaxed his hold upon the Tommy gun, he entwined his fingers in supplication. "I do not think that it would bode well for my patrons to learn that federal agents of their own reputable government had entered the *Governey Funeral Home* uninvited, wrongly accusing a devoted undertaker of engaging in sinful and unscrupulous behavior. So! My most sincere advice to you, gentlemen, is to promptly depart these four walls before any further scandal ensues. Then...and only then...you may rest assured of my promise to overlook the good pleasure of your company this morning."

Upon suddenly realizing that he had momentarily dropped his guard, Reinholt immediately retrieved his revolver while reprimanding his junior officer, ordering the embarrassed deputy to remain circumspect no matter what the situation. "That's all fine and dandy, doc," he said, inching closer to the blonde-wigged cadaver as if struggling to decipher a foreign menu, "but that still leaves one question dangling in the wind. We spotted two of your men bringin' some goods inta this place before we came through and now all of a sudden, they're nowhere in sight. Now..." he threatened, continuing to scrutinize the peculiar corpse, "if you fess up, I'll try ta convince the attorney general to go light on you and your boys. Otherwise," the agent emphasized with an overdrawn snort, "if you insist on playin' this game of hide and seek, the only winner'll be the jail warden who'll see to it that yer sorry asses are put behind bars. So...what do you say, doc? Pay now with peanuts or with big bucks later?"

Samuel could feel the heat from the agent's smoky grey eyes as the detective allowed him a moment to collect his thoughts. Whether the impudent little beast was bluffing or not, spilling the beans was completely out of the question. Aside from the integrity of the funeral home being in jeopardy, the Terillo brothers, previously having been "slapped on the hand" for serious crimes involving gambling and prostitution, might not be so fortunate this time. Not to mention blowing the perfect cover for their bootlegging business. But this hard-ass dick had it all wrong. This wasn't a game of hide and seek. It was a ruthless game of tug-of-war and he intended to emerge the victor. "Very well, then," Samuel finally conceded with an air of impatience. "If you are so convinced of my involvement in the violation of federal laws, perhaps you shan't believe it when I tell you that the very men of whom you speak have made their way up the elevator just minutes ago to deliver several vases of flowers. After all, my good gentlemen," he boldly stated, glancing down at the living corpse, "in case you have not yet noticed, this *is* a funeral home!"

Aware that his clammy fingers were beginning to slacken around the handle of the revolver, Reinholt tightened his grip and let out a high-pitched snicker. "Now ain't that the sorriest goddamn excuse I've heard all mornin'! Flowers, bullshit! You tellin' me there were *flowers* bein' brought in them boxes? If you get me to believe that line of crap, you may as well tell me that this missy bitch here ain't really dead—or *is* she?"

"I beg your pardon!" Samuel immediately interjected. "Search warrant or not...I refuse to tolerate such disrespectful behavior toward the deceased! Why...," Samuel scolded the agent while tenderly adjusting the white layered sheet, "it just so happens that those very flowers were indeed shipped in boxes due to their delicate nature. You see..." he somberly explained, borrowing the name of a female client reposed in an upstairs coffin, "Here lies Mrs. Pembrooke...a devoted wife, mother, and upstanding member of this community...who actually had childhood roots in Northeastern Africa. Consequently, it was her dying wish that, during funeral services, she be surrounded by the flowers of her youth. And if you know anything at all about flowers, my good sir, it certainly would not seem strange to you that freshly cut *Alstromeria* and *Delphiniums* arriving from Nairobi demand the best possible protection from every foreign element. But then again," Samuel stated, shrugging his shoulders, relieved to see that he had once more diverted Reinholt's attention from the fabricated corpse, "I do understand your blindness to such matters, given your most prestigious position in the federal armed forces of our beloved country. After all," he said, gesturing toward the agent with the Tommy gun, "gentlemen in your position have much more important things to attend to than investigating the trivialities of a simple funeral parlor. Which prompts me to ask, my good sirs, if I may be so bold, how in the name of Providence did your esteemed agency specifically choose this unlikely establishment as a target for your commendable battle against the apparent evils of alcohol?"

Feeling somewhat foolish and a bit sacrilegious while using both hands to steady his revolver, Reinholt clung to the scant possibility that his captive undertaker was still the lord of all con men; like Jack Dempsey backed into the corner of a ring, the disillusioned agent searched his mind for the one counterpunch that would bring Doctor Governey to his knees. But, try as he might, there was nothing left to get his hooks into. Damn! No matter how the son-of-a-bitch was cross-examined, he kept bouncing right back. And just when it seems his goose is cooked, he comes out smelling like a rose! Was the doc really genuine after all, then? As much as he hated to admit it, maybe this straight-laced gravedigger actually *was* "the real McCoy." Reinholt scrunched his lips toward the side of his face. Something still wasn't kosher. But you couldn't just arrest someone 'cause ya feel like your guts were crawling. And it'd be no use ta take him up on the offer to use his set of keys. If the doc really *was* a con man, he was a goddamn genius—probably another fuckin' Houdini! But...where in the hell were those two delivery men anyway? he silently cursed, skeptically gazing once again upon the unseemly stiff. If everyone in this carcass factory were innocent, then why in the hell hadn't his dicks turned 'em over by now? Did they have something to hide after all? Suddenly, the wary detective widened his eyes, then squinted. The corpse...did he really see a flicker in the eyelids? Could it be that his prior suspicions were correct after all? Was this *corpse* really for real or just a plain phony bein' one of the doc's bootleggers in disguise? He might not know much about the funeral business, he quivered, but he'd sure been around the block enough to know that it was too late in the game for any rigor mortis. Reinholt squinted again, miffed by the fact that his own 48-year-old eyes weren't all that reliable anymore, still clutching the Smith & Wesson with both hands and knees bent in a military stance. And it sure didn't look as if the stiff were breathing. Or *was* it? Was he so desperate to justify his suspicions that his imagination was starting to take over? It was hard to tell, but it sure seemed...hell! He might be jumping the gun, but...what's the worst that would happen if he just stepped up to the body and pulled off the goddamn sheet? This Mrs. Pembrooke here...if she *were* Mrs. Pembrooke...would she come back from her fucking grave to haunt him? With a haughty glimmer in his eyes, Reinholt glanced at Samuel, released his left hand from the revolver, ordered his deputy to stay on guard with the machine gun, and stepped forward, reaching toward the white sheet. Before getting the chance to even brush the edge of the stainless steel table, however, he found his free hand in Samuel's clutches, though still gripping the Smith & Wesson with the other, his trigger finger on the ready. But in hardly a moment's time, Samuel unexpectedly released his crippling grip while staring straight ahead, prompting Reinholt to spin around with the revolver still aimed at the distracted undertaker when, instead of the discharge of bullets, a chorus of familiar, protesting voices permeated the room.

"Hey Sarge!" a bullfrog-faced officer gloated, holding Zachary and Tony's moustached cousin in arms, "we didn't find nothin' else, but those boxes these two wise guys brung in were already empty before they tried makin' their way back down the stairs." The cocky agent paused for a second, rolled his eyes and crinkled his face. "Would you believe it?...says they were deliverin' flowers, of all the dumb-ass excuses! Oh...and by the way," he added a bit more sheepishly, extending a vigilant glimpse toward Samuel, "Donny's still upstairs. One of the workers, I guess...an old lady...had a heart attack or somethin'. The ambulance is on its way."

"I don't know what's goin' on, Doctor Governey, sir," Zachary blurted, concealing his remorse upon the possible death of his dear aunt, "but we were just goin' about our business after unloadin' the flowers when these guys came in and arrested us. We didn't do nothin' wrong...really!"

Feeling a lump in his throat upon realizing that his distressed servant, Zachary, was nevertheless carrying out frantic last-minute instructions so impeccably, Samuel, for the first time in his life, longed to reach out and hug Hildy's drug-dependent nephew. "You must allow me to personally attend to the woman upstairs!" he vehemently ordered Reinholt. "Mrs. Millenbach is a dear friend who has been in my employ for seven years." Stepping around the embalming table, he pushed his way past Reinholt, but stopped in his tracks when he felt the cold steel of the Tommy gun pressed against his spine.

"Won't do ya no good, doc," one last officer appearing at the door boldly announced. "Seems she's already dead as a doornail! Don't think nothin's gonna help her now."

"Drop the gun!" Agent Reinholt ordered the militant deputy who was still holding Zachary and Tony's cousin at the point of a revolver. Then, with beet-reddened face and an unfamiliar humility in his voice, he added, "I believe there's been an awful mistake, gentlemen." Turning exclusively toward his former captive, he nodded his head and touched the brim of his cap, painfully aware of the corpse in the process of cosmetic preparation which he had nearly violated. "I don't know how in the hell it was that we got tipped off to your place, Doctor Governey, but it seems someone's played a practical joke on all of us. I can assure you, though, if it be in my power, I'll hang the bastards responsible for this fuck up! In the meantime," he affirmed, allowing Samuel to hasten toward the door, "you can be sure that no federal agents will be botherin' ya anymore. And..." he yelled to the good doctor before Samuel dashed up the stairs, "I know it don't mean much after all ya been through here, but...sorry for your loss!"

chapter 70

Unexpected Caller

With polished shoes, jacket and straw hat in hand, Samuel discerned the eerie sound of the handcrafted wind chimes, prompting him to steal one last glimpse of the discolored grass aside the Chinese gazing globe where he had unexpectedly discovered Zachary's lifeless body nearly two weeks ago. "Sorry for my loss, indeed!" he thought, recalling the prohibition agent's biting sentiment on the tragic, yet conveniently timed death of Hildy Millenbach. If it were not necessary to be personally involved in a cumbersome, drawn-out court case, he would have pressed charges against those federal bastards! Nevertheless, he huffed, little had he suspected that just six years later, he would prematurely lose another member of his invaluable staff. And all because J. Edgar Hoover and his professionally trained feds were on a mission to save their "feeble-minded" citizens from the perils of unadulterated liquor!

Climbing the nearest staircase from the kitchen in anticipation of his shower, Samuel moved with slow deliberate steps, all the while sliding his hand along the oak banister, realizing it was the least he could do to salvage it from the accumulation of more than a week's worth of dust. Upon reaching the second floor, he ambled down the balconied hallway overlooking the grand ballroom, continuing to ponder the likelihood of obtaining a suitable servant to replace Zachary before his mayoral campaign was in full bloom. Samuel winced. Although elections wouldn't be held until November of the following year and a gentleman in his financial position certainly had no need to raise money for the campaign, there would still be the necessary elbow-rubbing and lengthy speeches to win over prospective voters, he thought, bringing to mind the current bedlam surrounding President Herbert Hoover and Governor Franklin Roosevelt on the heels of this year's presidential election. He detested the idea of having to socialize at boring receptions and wasting valuable time making door-to-door visits, but with the presiding mayor about to resign and an upstanding family man threatening to take his place, it was all he could do to insure that any future illicit operations continue unimpeded, remaining secretive.

Making his way down another corridor that accommodated seven guest bedrooms, Samuel felt a transitory sense of remorse while passing the third floor staircase leading to the servants' quarters. Irritating as the sorry bastard had been, he would never find another servant as competent as Zachary. Not only in the domestic arena, but in the occasional assistance of undertaking when the funeral business became overwhelming. And even though the almighty dollar would surely attract a willing servant, how was he to discreetly instruct such a novice in the preparation of the downstairs operating room for each clandestine abortion or the proper disposal of the fetus afterwards? Let alone the overseeing of bootlegging shipments when he happened to be out of town. *Damn it!* Samuel cursed under quickening breaths while approaching the chamber door of his master suite. He felt like a black knight bested at his own game.

Upon entering the magnificent bedroom suite majestically embellished with baroque furnishings, Samuel's eyebrows burrowed deep into his forehead. Due to an unexpected telephone call long before the break of dawn from Mr. Atkinson, his hired embalmer, requesting immediate assistance in the cosmetology of a disfigured corpse, he had neglected to fix his bed. And, worse yet, he was running out of clean sheets. The brocade satin comforter and matching pillows lay at the foot of the oversized bed alongside crumpled linen sheets, while three more disorderly pillows devalued its gilt bronze headboard.

Quickly deciding that his shower would have to wait in light of such disagreeable circumstances, Samuel walked into a birch closet, positioning the shoes and articles of clothing in their designated places. Then, upon activating the room's main overhead fan, he retrieved the last set of laundered sheets and proceeded to make the bed. As the rhythmic motor of the ornamental fan attempted to cool the master chamber which was sorely oppressed by the late morning heat, he entertained the thought of retreating once again upon the smooth, thick mattress of feathery down. Fairly unaccustomed to rising so early in the morning, there lingered upon his perspiring brow a weary nature that even his usual cup of Devonshire tea had not been able to remedy. But although he had arranged with Mr. Atkinson to intercede for him during unavoidable absences, and this same young fellow had certainly kept customers subdued for several weeks while he was revisiting the abounding treasures of Africa, jumping back into bed at this time of day without even so much as a simple cold seemed rather improper.

Maneuvering the edge of the satin sheet to form a neat hospital corner, Samuel pondered his string of bad luck regarding the variety of corpses that, as of late, had inundated the funeral home. Either shriveled old matrons dying from natural causes or witless young men mangled by the jaws of mechanical equipment, he grunted, thinking of the disfigured body he had just labored over during the wee morning hours. Why...it had been ever-so-long since he had experienced the arousing pleasure of embalming an enticing young maiden. Releasing a frustrating sigh, his mind became immersed with the thought of little Helen Cain, the 11-year-old daughter of a shoemaker who, while sail boating with some friends along the Detroit River on Decoration Day, was caught between the crossfire of two opposing bootleggers defending their territory. Prompted by immediate news reports about the unfortunate incident, he had paid a heartwarming visit to the bereaved parents. Before any concerned neighbors were given the opportunity to help raise money toward a proper burial for the impoverished child, he had already graced the cramped, rented flat with his congenial presence, offering full funeral services without charge, complete with flowers and open casket, thus sparing the bereaved parents from succumbing to the more affordable process of cremation forbidden by their Catholic faith. Instead, Mr. and Mrs. Cain had beheld their daughter as never before, sheathed in pink organdy and matching hair ribbons, shaded eyes padded to lifelike perfection and tiny pink mouth in a dreamlike smile. Her family and friends said she looked just like an angel. Like a heavenly angel fast asleep.

Shortly thereafter, Samuel's "magnanimous" gesture was trumpeted by local newspapers and radio bulletins, gathering widespread applause from an otherwise jaded and horrified community. His eyes beamed a deep sinister blue. Not only had that shrewd investment drawn more business for the funeral home and allowed his good name to be publicized well in advance of next year's mayoral election but, even more importantly, it awarded him with an exquisite pubescent female who had satisfied his voracious desires far better than the most compliant harlot at Madame Charlotte's bordello. *Another hat off to the Feds,* he grinned while stroking the comforter to smooth out the last few wrinkles.

After carefully arranging the tasseled pillows at the headboard of the completed bed, Samuel removed his navy serge trousers and calfskin belt, slid them onto the bottom rung of his valet, then peeled off his dampened shirt, commending himself on having the sense enough to have purchased a whole rack full of custom-fitted attire from the local tailor as well as an ample supply of underthings, saving him multiple trips to the launderer. Draping the shirt above his trousers, he then began walking toward the bathroom in his stocking feet when his delayed shower was interrupted yet another time. His first inclination upon hearing the melodious sound of the front doorbell was to ignore it, allowing Zachary to take care of the distracting matter, but returning to his senses, he realized that such an expectation was no longer possible. *Damn!* He would either have to ignore it completely or answer the bloody door himself.

The breeze from the electric fan attempted to ruffle his hair as he stumbled toward the wide bedroom window along the front of the mansion. Drawing one of several shades, he peered below. The long brick drive was empty. There were no motor cars or vendors trucks, and the looming cornice over the doorway obstructed his view. He thought of opening the window and calling out, but remembered he was hardly presentable. Stretching his neck even further, he struggled to discover his caller, but there was no sign of anyone. Maybe he hadn't heard the doorbell after all. Perhaps in his haste to shower, he had mistakenly heard the chime of the grandfather clock in the entrance hall. Glancing at his wrist, he noted the time. A quarter past the ninth hour. Sergeant McCallister, the only visitor expected today, wasn't scheduled to collect his hush money until five o'clock that afternoon. Samuel stared out the window one more time. *False alarm,* he concluded, glancing further down the road. A partially finished home, its construction halted as a result of the current depression, lingered close to the tranquil shore of Lake St. Clair like a misplaced vagabond imploring a neighboring three-year-old Grosse Pointe Yacht Association to grant it safe harbor. He contemplated the Italian-style building with its soaring tower, envisioning the many fine yachts, each one furnished with its own private slip. It did seem a rather bloody shame, he thought, having firsthand access to one of the nation's most prestigious lakes and not possessing even so much as a sailboat. But, unfortunately, he acknowledged with a shrug of his brow, being a boat owner would require an additional eight more hours in his already busy day. Of course, if he *should* ever decide to step away from his present demanding ventures, he would certainly be the dashing owner of the most luxurious yacht the club had ever laid eyes upon, navigated by his own personal captain and crew.

Having spent enough precious time on extraneous aspirations, Samuel's preoccupation shifted toward the faint outline of a deceptively barren Canadian shore subdued by a sweeping canopy of bluish haze overlooking the lapping waters of Lake St. Clair. Paying close attention to an outrigger weaving its way through more leisurely watercraft while heading southward, he envisioned the scores of distilleries it would soon be approaching and wondered if its crew had more than a mere excursion in mind. An impulsive smile curled his lips as he reflected upon the myriad scores of cargo ships which had traversed these very waters, facilitating the operation of a phenomenal empire which rivaled the automobile industry, also granting him equal ownership with the Terillo brothers in a string of swanky nightclubs throughout the bustling City of Detroit and its newly settled neighboring towns. Gazing back upon the skeletal home, he experienced a pinch of compassion. Yes, he certainly had been a fortuitous soul, but clever enough to keep his hard-earned money out of harm's way. Unlike other men who had poured all of their savings into precarious banks, he at least had the sense to hide any uninvested currency in a private safe beneath a seemingly impermeable wall of the abortion room. The medical facility, originally located in the funeral home but afterwards installed in the basement of the Tudor mansion at the suggestion of the Terillo brothers, had not only been a more comfortable location for his pregnant subjects, but had proven to be the most convenient place for storing an excess amount of cold hard cash. *Yes*, Samuel confessed, still eying the abandoned structure while recalling the unusual increase in business he had been experiencing at the funeral parlor over the past several years. If scores of former millionaires weren't leaping from tall buildings while others, as well as young innocent females, were being sprayed with bullets, people were moonshining themselves into the grave. Life was good and worthwhile after all!

A loud, clear ring originating from the downstairs entrance hall interrupted Samuel's train of thought. *Damn*, he cursed, the annoyance in his eyes practically penetrating the looming cornice. *There **is** someone at the front door after all. Who in God's bloody name is it!?* Quickly donning his satin robe and hard-soled slippers from the closet, he turned off the fan, grabbed his dirty clothing from the valet stand and, starting down the hall, removed a set of keys from his pants pocket before depositing the clothing inside a laundry chute. Spiraling his way down the poorly lit staircase, he could hear the doorbell echo even louder, replacing Zachary's usual clamor of lunchtime pots and pans and "Myrt and Marge" spilling from the Silvertone radio. Lingering on the stairs for a brief moment, a feeling of loneliness swept over him like an unexpected cobweb, but he brushed it away as quickly as it had appeared, choosing to concentrate instead on the possible motive of his unknown visitor. Whoever it was traveled by foot, he gathered, recalling the empty driveway he noticed while in his bedroom suite. It certainly wasn't a vendor attempting to sell some useless wares or a member of the Purple Gang or even one of his own beloved 'Bocci Boys' seeking emergency medical assistance. *After all,* he acknowledged while crossing the sunless foyer, recalling that ghastly day just several months ago when he had labored over a bullet wound in Giuseppe Terillo's chest, barely saving the unconscious brother's life; in such a dire situation, it was always mandatory to use the rear entrance.

Pausing at the front door to gaze through the peephole, Samuel's narrow nostrils flared. *A presumptuous lass indeed!* he observed upon seeing a woman with a traveling bag in hand. *And besides,* he seethed, determined not to answer the door, *I specifically instructed the employment agency that I wished to interview only potential servants of the **male** gender.* With that annoying observation under foot, Samuel began scrutinizing his visitor with a more curious eye. *This one is crazier than that old tosspot who smelled of moonshine whiskey,* he winced, bearing in mind the female applicant who had attempted to smuggle everything but his gold molars into her oversized handbag. *The outside temperature is hot enough to melt the bloody solder from my copper gutters and she's wearing a long coat that could accommodate both her and the fat lady at a circus sideshow!* Still uncertain as to whether he should answer the door, Samuel watched as his visitor reached for the doorbell, attempting to discern the woman's age while the sound of Westminster chimes once again reverberated throughout the hall. It was difficult to tell, he pondered, straining to look under her large-brimmed hat. From what he could gather, this determined caller could be as young as 12 or as old as 40. And why was she constantly looking over her shoulder? Furthermore, how had she arrived here? It was unlikely that someone had transported the woman and then departed before seeing her safely inside, he reasoned, continuing to survey his mystery guest as she began utilizing the door's heavy brass knocker. Had this person taken the Grosse Pointe motorbus then? Even so, he calculated, envisioning the heavily garbed woman crossing the intersection of Moross Road and Kercheval Avenue, she would surely have risked a heat stroke walking another half-mile to get here. Nevertheless, he sighed as the resplendent melody of the Westminster chimes gave way to the battering echo of brass upon wood, he supposed that anyone with that much persistence at least deserved the opportunity to explain herself. Moreover, in order to avoid any unnecessary small talk, he would take her directly into his personal library and ask all pertinent questions there.

Impatiently reaching for the dead bolt, Samuel slid it aside, released the lock and opened the door, inadvertently hearing the woman pleading out loud. But although it was quite obvious to Samuel that this aspiring housekeeper was altogether embarrassed that the peculiar habit of speaking to herself had been so unexpectedly disclosed, he instead took advantage of her prompt recomposure, awaiting the wide brim of her dingy straw hat to be swept away from the face as she looked upward to address him.

chapter 71

Confusion

Receiving no immediate response from an apologetic introduction, Eleanor Ann Snyder stood stiff as a picket and cleared her parched throat before addressing the strange man in the fancy housecoat once again. "I hope this ain't the wrong address, sir," she anxiously stated, pressing the worn leather traveling bag against her midriff. Being that she'd left the raincoat unbuttoned, it was all she could think of to keep it from suddenly opening and exposing the burlap sack which hung about her waist. "I'm looking for a doctor...Doctor Governey. This *is* the right address, ain't it? 16 Pennington Avenue?"

In an effort to appear polite despite the bothersome intrusion, Samuel invited the caller inside while continuing to secretly assess her. It was still somewhat difficult to pinpoint an age, he frowned as she practically tiptoed inside the foyer; the straw hat had now fallen past her eyebrows and she was making no effort to reposition it. But, taking into account her puerile demeanor, vibrant cheeks and unobtrusive nose, there was no longer the possibility, aside from her incompatible gender, that he could even *consider* her being the experienced housekeeper and servant his daily life demanded. Nevertheless, Samuel resolved, he had invited the little woman inside and it was better for the both of them that he get this matter over with as quickly as possible.

Being ever so careful not to stumble, lest she release any demons which may be lingering above the doorway, Eleanor, still in awe of the palatial hall and winding staircase illuminated by a magnificent chandelier, softly stepped right foot first onto the lustrous marble threshold. Under a different set of circumstances, she thought, such a clumsy happening could be reversed by a mere snap of the fingers, but then she'd have to let go of the traveling bag and her coat might open up. She could avoid any mishap altogether if she were a giant, but her smaller than average feet needed to take several steps before she could cross the threshold entirely. As Samuel's embossed satin robe flapped about stocking-sheathed ankles while she followed him through the foyer, Eleanor hoped the good doctor wasn't too upset upon being inconvenienced, or offended that she hadn't allowed him to take the traveling bag. But, feeling a bit more at ease upon flawlessly matching his quickened pace while moving past the staircase banister, her composure was tested once more when she was compelled to decline another kind gesture.

"Would you care for a drink, Miss Snyder? A glass of iced water or a Vernor's, perhaps?" Samuel offered, intending to bring the young lady into the kitchen with him as he prepared the drink, determined that no stranger should be left alone again in his study to steal whatever she bloody well pleased.

Sorely regretting the neglect to remove the burlap sack hanging from her waist and hide it between the doctor's neatly trimmed bushes before ringing the doorbell, Eleanor, wishing she had at least done likewise with the obstructive straw hat, pressed the traveling bag closer to her belly while moving along the decorated corridor. Even though a tall glass of ginger ale was just the thing needed to make her thirst go away, she painfully realized she would have to let go of the cumbersome bag to accept it. *Besides*, she reasoned, aware that her snug cotton slip and wide-brimmed hat were practically saturated with perspiration, Daddy always told her that saying *no* when a grownup offered something was the polite thing to do. "No thank you, Doctor Governey, sir. I...I just wanna get this over with quick as possible, if you don't mind...sir."

"Very well, my dear," Samuel answered, somewhat perturbed by his uncultured guest's persistent stubbornness. "If you will, please...continue to follow me, then."

Despite her overwhelming discomfort, Eleanor couldn't help but glance in every direction as Doctor Governey led her further down the hall. Never before had she seen a house so grand! Not even at the picture shows. Why...the shiny mirrored cabinet sitting among the fancy cloth chairs and padded walls was probably worth more than every single piece of furniture above the dirty old filling station back home.

"This way, Miss Snyder," Samuel stated, directing her past a Renoir and into another room. Upon entering the magnificent parlor, Eleanor felt the traveling bag drop halfway to her knees. If it weren't for all the grand furnishings and decorative items displayed beneath the high sloped ceiling and stained glass windows, it would surely have seemed like she'd just entered a cathedral. It almost felt naughty to step upon the colorful, patterned rug which covered the whole wide room, particularly since the bottoms of her walking shoes were still soiled from the two-hour journey. But, encouraged by the doctor's steady pace, she tightened her grip on the handle of the bag and proceeded on through, a pair of wandering eyes, dark as black strap molasses, coveting each delectable artifact.

As Samuel led Eleanor through the formal dining room and into the main library, she felt as if she were flying on a magic carpet, visiting one remarkable destination after another. Even at the Wilmington Library back in Ohio, she had never seen so many books in her whole life. And brand new too with pretty leather bindings! And the bookshelves...without one single scratch and all polished up...were way higher than those at the library. Why...the average person would need a stepladder to reach most of them. But, she concluded, being that Doctor Governey was so tall was probably the reason she didn't see a ladder...unless he wanted a book on the very top shelf. Then, maybe he just pulled out a chair from that long, fat-legged table.

Nearly bumping into her host as he paused at the far end of the library, Eleanor felt compelled to cover her nose, yet resisted the temptation, realizing she would have to let go of the traveling bag. Something smelled unearthly, she grimaced, spontaneously stepping backwards. She had smelled it a little when first arriving and thought it had something to do with the house, like some kind of strong cleaning powder. But now, she realized, waiting for Samuel to sort through his keys in order to unlock another door, the peculiar odor was definitely coming from the doctor. It smelled something like medicine. But not like any medicines in the operatin' room at the Cottage Hospital, she noted, cautiously breathing inward, attempting to distinguish the unrecognizable odor. She didn't mind *those* smells so much. But her preoccupation with the yet-to-be identified formaldehyde was immediately forgotten as Samuel finally opened the door to his private study, unleashing an array of potent, yet enticing terrestrial scents.

Timidly stepping into the study, Eleanor felt as if her magic carpet had arrived at another continent. The room wasn't large like the others, she quickly noticed, but cluttered with a lot more objects. *Old* objects. Like the ones in the *National Geographics* that her favorite teacher, Mrs. Brodeur, had in the two-room Wilmington schoolhouse. Even all the painted masks nailed to the far wall behind the big desk looked like they just come fresh out of those pages. And there was hair on them too...and places cut out for the eyes. As the doctor beckoned her to follow him into the study, Eleanor continued to stare at the mask-covered wall, remembering what she had learned in geography class about wild natives who ate people. *Cannibals*, she remembered Mrs. Brodeur calling them. Feeling a sudden shiver along her spine, she hesitated to follow the invitation to make herself comfortable in a big black leather chair, wondering all the while if the natives who wore those masks ever ate people.

"If you would care to hand me your coat, Miss Snyder, I shall hang it for you," Samuel forcefully smiled, nodding his head toward a coat rack while turning on the light of a Tiffany desk lamp.

For a lingering moment, Eleanor pressed the traveling bag closer to her tummy, then cautiously sat upon the edge of the black leather chair as an eerie glow from the stained glass shade flooded the room. Being extra careful to keep the front of her coat intact, she placed the traveling bag on the planked wood floor. "Thank you for offering, sir, but I'll keep my coat on. You can take my hat, though," she eagerly volunteered, removing the oversized obstacle and handing it over.

Graciously accepting the perspiration-stained hat from the slender hands of his obstinate guest, Samuel was suddenly struck by her unhindered face. It hadn't been apparent before she had removed the straw hat, but now, accentuated by the incandescent light of the Tiffany lamp, he could see it more clearly. It wasn't her delicate lips or button-sized nose which had arrested his attention. And certainly not the olive tone of her impeccable complexion. Instead, he realized, perusing matted hair, exposed forehead and expressive eyebrows, this absolute stranger who, by his estimation now appeared to be somewhere around the age of 17, reminded him of a particular acquaintance from his best-be-forgotten past. *Of course*, he marveled, momentarily bewitched by raven hair and eyes so overwhelming that he could crawl inside of them and be lost forever. Now it was quite obvious that this unfamiliar visitor was reminiscent of no other than that incorrigible suffragette, Violet Stimple, who had indelibly altered his life nearly a quarter of a century ago. *However,* despite this unpalatable memory, Miss Snyder's unassuming manner and overall virtuous countenance was nothing like that of his former nemesis. *And furthermore,* he concluded, knuckles whitening while compressing the brim of her stained straw hat, unlike the pile of bones picked clean by scavenger fish which roamed the murky waters of the Schuylkill River, this young woman seated before him...this Eleanor Snyder who had appeared unannounced at his doorstep a mere few minutes ago...was still alive and vibrant, hoping to obtain a position as housekeeper—a position which she had as much chance of securing as the possibility of hell freezing over.

Misinterpreting Samuel's penetrating glare to be that of annoyance provoked by her refusal to surrender the camel colored coat, Eleanor finally spoke up. "It's really not worth the bother to hang it up, sir." Tiny beads of perspiration bridged the two soft peaks of her upper lip. "It's nowhere near as hot as it seems. See? The lining's all torn out," she explained, grasping the corner of the bottom seam and turning it over to prove her words.

"Very well then," Samuel immediately replied as if snapping out of a trance, nervously positioning the hat upon the coat rack. "Let us discontinue these futile formalities and proceed with business, shall we?"

Still concerned that she may have insulted the distinguished doctor, Eleanor's eyes remained glued to Samuel as he crossed in front of her and seated himself behind his desk without the merest glance in her direction. She warily watched as he slid open a drawer and took out a cigar humidor. Eleanor didn't know what the humidor was, but despite being twice as big, noted that it looked something like the recipe box her mama used to stash away in a cupboard when they still had their farm in Ohio. Feeling a pang of regret upon being reminded of happier days, she focused more intently on the doctor's fastidious behavior, trying hard to forget the disturbing circumstances which compelled her to quickly pack her traveling bag and catch an early bus out of Dearborn. Though somewhat distracted as he removed the longest cigar she had ever seen, snipping its tip with some sort of cutter, her mind began wandering over to the dirty old filling station back home and all the unpleasant memories that went with it. Her throat felt all the more parched as Doctor Governey braced the cigar between vanishing lips and thumbed a golden lighter, its flickering flame distorting every remaining feature except the striking glare of his icy blue eyes. Feeling somewhat nauseous, she forcefully swallowed, attempting to ward off the discomfort kindled by the mingling of tobacco and formaldehyde. But unsettling memories continued to haunt her. All the more aware of her parched throat, she struggled to ignore the tremor which had been clawing at her insides all day long. Up until this moment, she'd been able to block out the reason for such a hasty retreat; worrying about getting to the doctor's house had occupied her mind a great deal. But now, sitting in this creepy room, painful images of that morning's awful experience were beginning to sneak up on her. *No,* she silently scolded amid threatening tears as the doctor removed a pearl-handled jackknife from his desk drawer and began slitting open some mail. She had done alright so far and wasn't going to let anything get her goat. It had taken a bushel-full of willpower to block things from her mind and goddarn if she was going to give in now!

Defiantly clutching the arms of the leather chair, Eleanor looked away from Doctor Governey. Perhaps by counting the objects in the room, her mind wouldn't stray. Like the times she'd drive with Daddy into the city and count all the horses along the way. Except, instead of horses, there was a bunch of the doctor's old belongings. And heaven knew...the doctor surely had collected enough trinkets to keep her occupied for hours, if need be. Forcefully inhaling quivering breaths, Eleanor attached herself to the first available object toward the corner of the desk and began counting. A large magnifying glass...*that's one.* A carved wooden box...*that's two.* Pivoting her body clockwise, she gazed downward. A big globe of the world that would spin if she pushed it...*three*...a couple of tall clay statues that looked like her six-year-old cousin in Tuscaloosa made...*four...no...**five**.* A stone elephant on a marble pedestal...*six.* Spontaneously gazing upward, she began scanning the wall to the right, becoming all the more absorbed with the leather hides nailed to it, realizing she hadn't noticed them when first entering the room. There were three of them. The first was just a dark brown color...the plainest, but the biggest. *Let's see...that would make seven*...the second hide was a lighter brown with black spots...maybe it belonged to a leopard...*number eight*...and the third...the third...all white except for what looked like a smear of dried blood in its middle.... But before she could even begin to imagine the significance of the stained, ivory-hued fleece, something at the corner of her eye...something with a majestic presence...demanded her attention—coercing her to scoot forward in her seat and pivot the chair toward the back wall. In one remarkable moment, all of Eleanor's sordid memories were suddenly squelched as if swallowed by the regal fireplace which loomed beneath the imposing predator.

Remaining spellbound, Eleanor continued to gaze upward, her gypsy eyes glued to the entrancing, all-powerful presence. Feeling as trivial as a one-winged gnat, she began shrinking into the big black chair, further scrutinizing the petrified object, certain that it had, at one time or another, seethed with life while reigning over every imaginable wild creature in some distant African jungle. Captivated by a bounteous mane which clung like crushed straw around a ferocious face, she contemplated the flattened, mud-ballish nose and fierce mouth, its yellow canine teeth appearing eager to sink into her body and rip her apart at any given second. But, despite every other threatening feature, it was the lion's penetrating eyes, slanted and beady, which spooked her the most. It didn't even matter that they were most like-ly made of glass...not one *iota* of a difference. They were probing straight through her...forever stalking...hexing the trespasser in its closely guarded kingdom. Impulsively, Eleanor began cracking her knuckles—a trick she had learned as a young child to scare away evil spirits. She wanted to look away, but didn't dare now, lest the savage beast attack her from behind. Mrs. Brodeur had once said that a lion will suddenly pounce upon a passing ani-mal, knocking it senseless, then dig its claws into the flesh and finish it off by stabbing it through the neck with its sharp teeth. Or sometimes a group of male lions would roar, causing their prey to scatter so they'd be easier to attack.

With no more knuckles to crack, Eleanor felt helplessly paralyzed...like the times she lay stiff as a board in her bed, unable to awaken from a dream-like state. Lending no apparent regard to the sound of papers shuffling in the background or to the immediate silence which followed, she continued giv-ing her undivided attention to the mounted lion's head. Then...suddenly...without the slightest warning...Eleanor's thoughts were shattered like shards of glass reeling inside her skull. A ferocious roar had unexpectedly ravaged the quiet room; the beast had come alive! Frantically jumping out of the chair, she wanted to run, but her knees were too weak. She wanted to scream, but each silent attempt was no match for the lion's overpowering breath as slapping locks of hair blinded her line of vision. In one redeeming second, however, upon recognizing a familiar voice asking if she were feeling alright, Eleanor realized that the loud roar wasn't coming from the lion after all, and the assaulting locks of hair were none other than her own. Shifting full attention toward the mechanical device which had made her heart spin faster than a pinwheel in a hurricane, she inhaled deeply, still standing, all the while feeling her insides unraveling. Momentarily unconcerned with the disapproving look on the doctor's face, she instead contemplated with softening eyes, the circulating, caged metal "animal" standing obediently in place—its roaring, whirling blades delivering an overwhelming breeze throughout the previously stuffy library.

Aware that he had startled his guest by activating the noisy fan, Samuel was nevertheless unsympathetic toward her apparent alarm. Contemptuously eying the little conspirator standing off guard with coat halfway open, he now understood why she had been so reluctant to remove it in the first place: a thick rope around her waist secured a burlap sack. And though presently empty, the sack was large enough to accommodate a small tea service. Before Eleanor could even spit out a token explanation, his commanding voice transcended the clatter of the fan. "Miss Snyder...I am sorry to have wasted your precious time, but I do *not* believe this arrangement is going to work for either of us. If you will be so kind, then...please allow me to escort you to the door."

Eleanor remained standing before Samuel as if the mismatched laces of her dusty shoes were pinned to the floor, realizing, in one regretful instant, that the unbuttoned panels of the trench coat had parted open, exposing the burlap sack. Not knowing what to say as her dismissive host strode toward the coat rack and reached for the straw hat, her rosy cheeks felt hotter than when she had come down with the scarlet fever. She initially had tried to avoid an awkward explanation by keeping the sack hidden from sight and certainly didn't expect the doctor to react so abruptly should he discover it. But now, she trembled, realizing that Doctor Governey was gazing upon the burlap sack with disdainful eyes as he practically shoved the hat into her hands. Determined to immediately settle the misunderstanding and win back his good graces, she finally spoke up in a tone short of hollering, yet discernable enough to override the clamor of the electric fan. "Please sir...Doctor Governey, sir...I know it looks like I was gonna steal from you, but I wasn't! Really! Please, sir...you gotta believe me. This bag here...it...I didn't have time to pack some more stuff in it before leavin'...I was gonna, but then I'da missed the bus," she pleaded, remaining hopeful as Samuel seemed to at least consider the contrived explanation. "I had ta leave behind some of my things. The clock in my room stopped so I thought I had more time...until the church bells rung. Then I knew I had ta go or else have ta wait another forty minutes for another bus." Eleanor continued holding onto the limp brim of the straw hat as if it were a wet mop, still wary of the doctor's disapproving glare. "I didn't have time ta take off the sack...I just grabbed the travelin' bag and scooted outa there really fast...barely made it too. Scout's honor!" she declared, raising her right hand. "I...I just had ta leave Dearborn quick as I could," she implored, fighting back tears. "I just couldn't stay a minute more!"

Allowing the flustered soul to rattle on, Samuel wondered whether there was an ounce of truth to her cockeyed explanation. She certainly sounded convincing enough, but then again, it wasn't unusual for a snake to try and wiggle its way out of a hole. Nevertheless, he concluded, feeling somewhat uneasy as a stream of tears slithered down his guest's sun-baked cheeks, her questionable sincerity was no longer relevant. Since it was apparent that the aspiring applicant would never measure up to his demanding criteria, it was time that he discontinue this sorry charade and let the blubbering lass be on her way. His only regret at the moment was having allowed the situation to get this far out of hand. "Miss Snyder...please, my dear. I am afraid that this arrangement will work out for neither of us. Perhaps there is another employer who will be able to utilize your services."

Eleanor stared blankly at the rankled doctor as he picked up her traveling bag, suddenly realizing that the confusion surrounding the burlap sack was not the only misunderstanding to clear up. "Who could use *my* services, sir?" she questioned with a curt sniffle.

Supposing that Eleanor was stalling for time, Samuel strived to remain patient, his restless fingers still compressing the worn handle of the traveling bag. "That is correct, Miss Snyder. I am sorry to have squandered your precious time, but when I contracted with the Ellis Employment Agency, my expectations were that I be provided with a more *experienced* housekeeper. Preferably of the *male* gender. However...," he continued with a sympathetic smile, "if you remain persistent, I am certain that another household will be more than willing to utilize your good services." Receiving no immediate response aside from a delicate mouth drawn open like a loose ribbon, Samuel placed the traveling bag back upon the floor and gestured toward his circular dial desk phone. "If you would like, I shall fetch a taxi for you."

Before the good doctor had another chance to further misread her intentions, Eleanor dropped the hat to her side, hoping that the impromptu visit had not been in vain after all. "But sir...Doctor Governey, sir...I didn't come here for a job. I...I'm here to use *your* services, sir."

"I beg your pardon, my dear...but...*really*...are you, indeed, saying that you did not arrive here with the intention of obtaining a position as domestic servant?"

"*No* sir!" Eleanor quickly rebutted, reaching for the arm of the black chair with her idle hand in an attempt to steady herself. "I have no mind to be a housemaid...I'll be headin' outta here shortly. I had an appointment with you last week, but you cancelled it. Don't you remember? My mamma...*Lucinda Snyder*... called and made it for me. At least that's what she said. But then she said you cancelled it and would call back. But it's been a week and we haven't heard anything. *Please*, Doctor Governey," Eleanor implored, casting remorseful eyes toward her belly, all the while fearing she would faint from thirst unless she reclaimed her seat, "you can't send me away now...not until you give me the operation. I just gotta leave town quick as possible, but can't do all that travelin' with the baby still inside!"

Samuel walked over to the noisy fan and turned it off, insisting that the distraught young woman reseat herself. It had been a long, grueling week, indeed, he reflected as the blades of the fan began to subside, blanketing his ears with a warm, welcoming silence. The sudden death of Zachary and all the unforeseeable inconveniences that went along with it had certainly taken its toll. And though he initially had the presence of mind to cancel a certain appointment made by a Mrs. Lucinda Snyder on behalf of her pregnant daughter, he had nevertheless forgotten to reschedule it. And now, because of his neglect, this same daughter, quite alone and obviously desperate, had appeared at a most inopportune time, hoping once and for all to obtain the prearranged abortion. Reproachfully tightening the sash of his satin robe, Samuel strode over to a window, unhooking its shutter and cranking open the pane, having faith that the procedure would be a quick one, free of complications. As a gentle breeze of warm air accompanied by the peeping of sparrows began to fill the room, he reseated himself upon the desk chair, mentally noting that after taking care of this delicate matter, he would thumb through his appointment ledger, lest he overlook any other impending engagements. "You must forgive my indiscretion, Miss Snyder," he began with an endearing smile, "but I have been obliged to manage some critical, yet unexpected details these past couple of weeks. Nevertheless...," he continued, tapping his slow-burning cigar upon the edge of a silver tray to dislodge the growing ashes, "I am now in a position to resume my customary duties and shall be most happy to assist you. However...before we begin, I need to ask a few pertinent questions."

Still longing for a drink of ginger ale, yet relieved to be off her aching feet, Eleanor peeled the cotton twill coat away from her threadbare blouse and faded plaid skirt, draping it over the back of the chair. Aware of the burlap sack which hung about her waist, but no longer concerned about the questions it might raise, she patiently watched Samuel as he indulged in the robust flavor of the Havana, happy that the window had been let open to lessen the smell which was nauseating her. The doctor looked much better in the light, she observed, even though now she could see a few more wrinkles around his eyes. And for an older man, his hair still had a nice yellow-brown color to it. He was clean cut too...not all bristly faced like Jimmy Ray. Eleanor cringed. For a few tranquil minutes, she'd been able to keep her mind off her mama's younger boyfriend, yet no matter how hard she tried, the disgusting bastard always seemed to find a way to creep back into her thoughts. But the worst part would soon be over, she rationalized, lifting both feet off the floor, then scooting further onto the chair's leather seat while Samuel placed his cigar upon the silver ashtray and removed a small calendar, pen, and pad of paper from the desk's top middle drawer. Hopefully, it wouldn't take too long for her to recover after the abortion and she'd soon be on her way to California.

Casually looking up from his desk, Samuel's train of thought was suddenly interrupted as he inadvertently fumbled the fountain pen, recovering the writing implement before it dropped onto the desk's leather-framed blotter. With hardly a thought given to Eleanor's coat sloppily thrown over the back of the tufted chair, his eyes became fixed upon the composed patient. A stream of smoke from the resting cigar lazily slinked in the girl's direction, encircling a tattered blouse which, despite the noble intention of guarding the young lady's virtue, had nevertheless failed miserably. Likewise moist with perspiration, the camisole underneath her blouse was not at all disinclined to reveal an exquisite pair of rounded breasts which could have easily adorned a pubescent female, nipples hinting a subtle shade of pink, practically bursting through the gossamer fabric. In a genuine effort to repossess a professional state of mind, he redirected his gaze to the desk, reaching for a leather bound notebook. Quite satisfied that the fountain pen was secured in his grasp, he then opened the notebook to the first available blank page, took a deep breath, cleared his throat, and, without a mere glance in Eleanor's direction, proceeded to speak. "So...my dear...let us begin with the simplest questions first, shall we? What is your age and weight, if I may so kindly ask?"

"Well, sir...," Eleanor guardedly began, wondering if the doctor had actually been staring at her bosom or if she was just still all worked up about Jimmy Ray, "the last time I got weighed was at the Clinton County fair when I had a chance to win a prize on account of a fella guessing it," she said with a serious look in her eyes. "It was a real *tall* scale too. Even taller than *you.*" For a brief moment, she remained silent, recalling the day Jimmy Ray treated her and Mama to the yearly June carnival before they started shackin' up. He was all dressed up in his Sunday proper trying to impress not only Mama, but her as well...she could tell even then by that sick, pig-like look in his eyes. "'Cept I didn't win the prize cause even though he didn't guess the right weight, he still guessed it close ta five pounds," she explained, determined for the umpteenth time to get her mind off Jimmy Ray. "That was the rule," she pouted, affirmatively nodding her head. "If the fella guessed within five pounds, then he won. But I *almost* won," she defiantly added, curling pallid lips into a kewpie doll smile. "Said I was 90 pounds and I weighed in at 95." Eleanor paused with a reflective look in her eyes. "But...that was over two years ago and I ain't weighed myself since, so...I'm sorry, Doctor Governey...I really don't know how much I weigh now...particularly since becomin' pregnant an' all."

Lending Eleanor a conciliatory smile, Samuel promptly returned his straying eyes to the notebook, its blank page still awaiting an initial scrawl of information. "That is perfectly acceptable, Miss Snyder," he assured the contrite patient, scribbling down the estimated weight, thinking it about average for a woman of around 17 years of age. "In that case, you may weigh yourself upon *my* scale when you are ready. In any event," he continued, looking up from the desk and offering a smile as he retrieved his cigar and relit it, "surely, you do know your age, do you not? Or do we need to consult a carny employee for that matter too?"

Initially wondering why the doctor had asked her weight if he *already* had a scale, and feeling a bit foolish, Eleanor bit into her lower lip. There she was, running at the mouth again. Maybe she shouldn't have gone on talking about the carnival when the doctor just wanted a simple answer. Hopefully, though, he was just being friendly and wasn't annoyed by it. Her mama always said she could talk someone's ear off and by the looks of the doctor's ears, he couldn't afford to lose even a fraction of an inch more. "Oh no... I mean *yes*, sir...there's no need ta guess about my age. I'm *14*...but I'll be 14-and-a-*half* come September. My birthday's in March...March twenty-third...same day as Joan Crawford's."

Samuel felt as if a piece of tea leaf had suddenly stuck in his throat. So, by Jove, it was true *indeed!* This young peasant princess, whom he'd been sorely misreading during the entirety of her visit, was indubitably pubescent after all! Trying to remain politely inconspicuous as budding nipples bursting through gossamer fabric blissfully assaulted his line of vision, he finally shifted his eyes toward the calendar which lay in front of him, noticing that the Havana, dangling limply between his fingers, had burnt a hole halfway through the blotter. With hardly a thought given toward the mishap, he placed the smothered cigar back upon the silver tray and whisked away the littering ashes, all the while aware that the star-struck girl was still rambling on about several movies featuring her mutual birthday idol. Taking full advantage of his guest's loquacious disposition, Samuel began to calculate the possibility of becoming a bona fide beneficiary of the youngster's unfortunate predicament. Up until now, his abortion record had been surgically flawless, with not even a single patient suffering so much as a hemorrhage. But records were made to be broken, he contemplated, quietly unfolding the cover page of the 1932 calendar. By purposely botching this particular abortion, he could appease two of his favorite pastimes in the same day—killing both birds with one stone, so to speak. And though it was quite obvious that this young lass was no vestal virgin, the mere thought of taking full possession of the little chatterbox *post mortem* was, nevertheless, extremely tantalizing. But before Samuel could further entertain the prevailing fantasy, he was obliged to look up from the calendar and straight into the inquiring eyes of his oblivious patient.

"...Doctor Governey, sir? Did you know she's just come out with another movie? It's called *Grand Hotel.* Greta Garbo and John Barrymore are in it too!"

Feeling as if an angel of God had suddenly delivered him from the gates of hell, Samuel affirmatively answered the adoring fan, nevertheless retaining his prior ruminations. Though there was no longer a servant to worry about, it was preposterous, really, to think he could actually commit such a definitive deed in secret, he contemplated, steadying the pen in preparation for the next question. Even if he managed to quickly dispose of the body, there would be loose ends followed by an investigation. In fact, it was her own mother who had arranged the original appointment and would surely know of her daughter's intention to seek his services. And what about any number of witnesses who may have seen her in this vicinity or while walking here? *No...*It was completely out of the question...totally untenable. Even if the deed *was* exposed and he happened to find a lawyer shrewd enough to deliver him from life imprisonment, his sterling reputation in this Great Lakes community as funeral director, doctor, and philanthropist...all that he worked toward attaining during the past 13 years...would corrode as quickly as his pearl-handled jackknife submerged in acid, he pondered, eyeing the cherished knife atop his mail. In such a case, he may as well throw his aspirations of becoming Mayor of this exclusive City of Grosse Pointe down the sewer. And never mind that, according to Michigan law, he'd escape execution. The Terillo brothers, tolerant of anything short of child molestation, would likely take care of him in their own *Sicilian* way. *Yes*, he finally concluded with a quick swallow. Risking everything he had acquired was obviously much too dear, even for this splendid specimen whom fate had placed at his mercy. With an abrupt clearing of the throat, Samuel once again spoke up, congenially reiterating that he was not only aware of Miss Crawford's latest film, but had intended to immediately view it when his busy schedule allowed. Then, reaching for the magnifying glass, he proffered another smile. "Now, my dear Miss Snyder...would you be kind enough to try and remember the exact date of your final menstrual period?"

Thinking that the doctor's flawless set of teeth resembled a freshly washed picket fence, Eleanor sat in silence for a moment before wrinkling her nose. The only *minstrels* she was aware of were the singing and dancing colored folk in the first talking movies and the *Amos & Andy* radio show. "My *what* sir?"

"Your *menstrual* period," Samuel tolerantly emphasized. "I must know approximately how far along you are in the pregnancy."

"Oh...*yes*, sir..," she finally answered, realizing that although she knew a good share of medical talk, she'd just gotten her words mixed up, not being familiar with them all. "You mean...the last time I had the monthly sickness?"

Samuel tightened his grip upon the magnifying glass. "Yes, my dear. The last time you had your monthly sickness. Now when would that be?"

Eleanor shrunk back into her seat and began fidgeting with the rope attached to the burlap sack. The doctor was annoyed with her. She could feel it as sure as the wind was stirring up outside. The last thing he wanted to be bothered with this morning was some surprising caller coming to his door asking for an abortion...especially some stupid young girl who didn't even know what a *menstrual* period was. And *gosh darn* if she kept track of her sick days! She'd only started having them a few months ago and wasn't used to keepin' an account of 'em like her mama did by puttin' little "x's" on the Pabst beer calendar. And...what was that noise? That awful noise? she wondered, hearing the scratching and scraping of the hand-crafted wind chimes. It was giving her the goose pimples. Suddenly deciding that the sooner she answer the doctor's questions, the sooner she'd be out of there, Eleanor elevated pointy elbows while twisting the rope around her middle finger. "Well...uh...I'm not *exactly* sure the last time I had the monthly...the last time my period...my *menstrual* period come. But it musta' been when I last helped Jimmy Ray with replacin' the muffler on Mr. Buxby's Chevy before he went on vacation." She stopped twisting the rope and ran moist hands in the soft fold of her lap. "I remember, cause just when I was shinin' the flashlight so he could see what he was doin,' I fell against the jack on account of I had the most awful cramp the way I do when I first have the...when I first be startin' my *menstrual* periods." Wringing her hands now, she continued. "The Chevy come crashin' down before we knew it...almost tore Jimmy Ray's arm right off its socket." She pouted her lips and knitted her brows. "I wish it would have! Jimmy Ray give me hell for dentin' the fender. Thought he was gonna whip me somethin' awful, 'cept Mr. Buxby tells him it's o.k. Tells him it's just a *jack*-cident...'cept Jimmy Ray didn't think that was so funny neither."

Forever waiting to calculate the approximate date of conception, Samuel kept his upright posture intact, all the while feigning interest in his patient's lengthy recollection. He didn't give a pauper's penny about her untimely female episodes at some bloody family service station or who the hell this scoundrel, Jimmy Ray, was. The only thing which interested him at the moment was any indication that her anecdote had finally reached its climax, allowing him to speak up before she could get another word in edgewise. "Yes...that's all very well, indeed, my dear. However, let us return to the original question, shall we Miss Snyder? Now...is it, indeed, possible for you to recall the exact day Mr. Buxby brought his Chevrolet in for repair?"

Eleanor scrunched her face and squeezed eyes shut, opening them in an instant. "Well, sir...it was...it must've been sometime early June cause I remember thinkin' how people were gettin' ready to go on summer vacation and bein' such a cold spring and all, the morning glories I planted hadn't even sprouted yet..." She was about to tell him how good she was at tending to flowers, but instead began wondering why the doctor was using a magnifying glass to see the numbers on his calendar when he could just put on a pair of spectacles...especially when Woolworth's was having their big summer sale. But before another syllable could spill from her thirsting lips, she decided not to question him about it after all, concentrating instead on the sudden solemnity in the doctor's stormy blue eyes.

Perusing the minuscule numbers of the 1932 calendar, Samuel attempted to quell an insistent scowl. Given that the morning's events had certainly proven to be disappointing, it should be of no great surprise, then, that the little harlot was, most likely, not even seven weeks along in the pregnancy. And given the fact that his day had been so unexpectedly and rudely interrupted, he was hoping to at least be awarded the pleasure of aborting a fetus no less than two or three months developed. *All the later the better*...when each evolving feature of its tiny body, tactfully torn from the safety of the womb, would be that much more discernable. *But then, again,* he frowned, suspending the magnifying glass over the month of June, maybe he was just wasting his bloody time. Considering his bout of ill luck today, it was quite possible that Miss Snyder *wasn't* being plagued with an unwanted pregnancy. After all, it was not so uncommon for such a young lass to undergo irregular menstrual cycles. And it certainly would not be the first time he was confronted with a false alarm of that very nature. Setting the magnifying glass back upon the desk, he released a feeble sigh, once again directing his gaze toward the apprehensive guest. "What symptoms have you been experiencing, Miss Snyder?"

Despite the uneasy feeling in her tired bones, Eleanor immediately perked up, dropping both hands upon her lap. She knew what the word *symptom* meant, having heard it from other doctors plenty of times. Now, maybe Doctor Governey wouldn't think she was so stupid. "Yes, sir! I been havin' plenty of *symptoms,* Doctor Governey. Well...I mean...not *too* many symptoms, but one o' them is feeling like I'm gonna throw up sometimes...mostly in the early morning. I tend to get tired more, too. And then," she continued, the moistened rope from the burlap sack loosening around her middle finger, "I don't seem to get no headaches anymore. I used to get 'em a lot, but it's been a long while now since I got any."

"Tell me, Miss Snyder. Is there any possibility that your menstrual period has merely been delayed...that you are not, indeed, pregnant after all?"

"Oh no, sir...Doctor Governey, sir. I know I ain't showin' yet, but even my mama said I had all the symptoms. She even had a dream the night...the night after..." Eleanor caught herself, not wanting to dredge up the sordid episode which led to her pregnancy. "She even dreamed that Jimmy Ra...my mama's boyfriend...died. And when you dream someone dies, it means one o' your kinfolk is gonna be with child real soon."

Inwardly dismissing the superstitious dream as plain nonsense, Samuel was nevertheless further convinced of the authenticity of his patient's pregnancy. Notwithstanding her apparent symptoms, any mother willing to attest to her own daughter's illegitimate pregnancy would most likely be unerring, particularly one who had originally requested the abortion in the first place. Therefore, he would not dwell upon the subject any longer but, rather, make the final confirmation while in the operating room. *However,* he determined, somewhat disenchanted that the thin fabric of the blouse was nearly dry, there were still a few additional questions to ask. Maintaining his professional demeanor, then, he allowed his congenial voice to temper the room's incessant gloom. "Is this your first pregnancy, my dear?"

Eleanor stared at Samuel for a moment, considering the question unusual since she was barely 14 years of age. "Why...*yes,* sir. Of *course,* sir." She lowered her head for a moment, wondering what he must be thinking. It was bad enough having conceived against her own will, let alone the good doctor believing she was some kind of loose-kneed Jezebel. "It wasn't of my own doing, you know. I was forced into it. *Really,* I *was!* But...but I'm hopin' that someday I'll marry proper...if anyone'll have me...and then I won't have to...and then I can keep all my babies!" Her bottom lip quivered as the next words cowered forth. "Doctor Governey? If I have this abortion...I'll still be able to have more babies, won't I?"

Samuel leaned slightly forward, palms downward, fingers entwined upon the desk, reflecting upon the many occasions he had been obliged to play the role of compassionate psychologist. It was burdensome enough consoling clients on the death of their loved ones, let alone offering words of solace to some despondent woman who had chosen to annihilate her own flesh and blood. But then again, the venerable vocation of funeral director had certainly prepared him for unpalatable times such as these. "Now, now, my dear Miss Snyder. I see no reason why you would not be able to conceive another child if you so wished. Having an abortion is no different than experiencing a simple miscarriage. And..." he nonchalantly recited with a short shrug of the shoulders, "as medical records so accurately demonstrate, there happens to be an abundance of women who, after undergoing this particular procedure, are indeed able to reap the full benefits of motherhood several times thereafter...providing she be of average health which I trust that you are, am I not correct?"

Suddenly realizing that this was the doctor's way of asking the next question, Eleanor broke a brief silence, allowing the rope to slide off her middle finger. "Well, sir...I reckon I am. My daddy always said that I was strong as an ox." A sudden sadness spanned pensive eyes. "That was the time I caught the scarlet fever. Only...I got better, but then...but then my daddy went and caught it." Fondling the rope between her thumb and forefinger, she nearly whispered. "I just wish he'd been as strong as me."

"So, Miss Snyder," Samuel interjected, hoping to avoid the unpleasantness of listening to another soap opera account of his patient's hackneyed family. "I presume you are not presently taking any medications and, of course..." he facetiously added, "I assume that you do not ingest any tobacco products or engage in the imbibition of alcoholic beverages."

Eleanor forgot about her father for the moment. She knew what *medications* were and thought the word *engage* to be used improperly, but didn't recognize the word *imbibition*, though she could tell from the sentence that it had something to do with heavy drinking. "Oh no, sir!" she promptly retorted, conveniently dismissing her one and only taste of Jack Daniels whiskey when Jimmy Ray and Mama were in a drunken stupor. "I ain't never had even one *sip* o' white lightning." She remembered a tattered poster nailed to an old hitching post by the Wilmington general store with a picture of some angry looking women on it and the large print beneath it which said, *'Lips That Touch Liquor Shall Not Touch Ours.'* "And I ain't never done any *smoking* neither!" she immediately emphasized, hoping that the doctor would start thinking more kindly of her.

"That is quite commendable, Miss Snyder. Then I can safely presume that you are not presently under the influence of any medications as well?"

Eleanor was quick to respond, realizing she had gotten so caught up about the drinking and smoking, she'd neglected to answer the doctor's prior question. "No sir...not *presently*. And I don't know of taking badly to any *anesthetics* neither," she proudly stated, realizing that would be the doctor's next logical question.

Samuel raised an eyebrow. "And have you eaten anything within the last few hours?"

"No, sir...I just stuck a piece of cornbread in my coat pocket for later, but didn't eat anything, knowin' you ain't supposed to *ingest* any food before an operation. Anyhow..." she scooted forward upon the chair to avoid further damage to the smuggled provision banded in brown paper. "I was in such a hurry ta get here, I didn't have time for any kind o' meal." She remembered the ginger ale previously offered and though, still sore of thirst, was glad she hadn't accepted. "I haven't had a thing to drink neither...even though I'm really thirsty."

"Now, Miss Snyder," Samuel interjected, disregarding his patient's obvious begging, "as I already assured you, the operation is a relatively simple one. And though the ideal period for performing such a procedure is anytime after the first eight weeks of gestation," he went on, positioning the pad of paper in front of him, "I see no major problem, being that you are nearing that very stage of development. However, I will need for you to provide me with the name and telephone number of a person I may contact just in case there are any complications...only as a *precaution* you understand. Perhaps I may reach your mother at home?"

Her parched throat tightening, Eleanor felt the color draining from her cheeks. "But...I...I can't! I mean...I can't...I didn't...I don't want anyone to know I'm here!"

Samuel dropped the pen back on his desk and shoved it aside, sliding the pad of paper along with it. "Are you saying, my dear, that *no one* knows of your presence here this morning?"

Eleanor felt something turning inside her stomach and it had nothing to do with the baby. The way the doctor's eyes appeared to darken suddenly, it seemed he was disturbed about what she just said. Yet...there was something else...something frightening about the way he was looking at her. And that creepy scratching sound coming from outside was starting up again. She grasped the rope, mangling it around her finger. "No, sir...I...but...I just couldn't let anyone know I was here...especially Jimmy Ray. That's why I went and ran away in the first place!"

Samuel let out a brief, forceful cough. "So...*Miss Snyder*...are you, *indeed*, telling me that since you have run away from your home, there is absolutely *no one* who is aware of your presence here ?"

Eleanor began cracking her knuckles. She hadn't realized that the doctor would be so disapproving of what she'd done. And she wished he would stop calling her *Miss Snyder*. Maybe if she explained why she *had* to run away, he'd be more understanding. "No, sir...I mean, yes, sir...that's *correct* sir! But...please don't make me go back! I just had to do it...really I did! I just couldn't stand knowin' that if I didn't get away soon, Jimmy Ray would...would...*rape* me again!"

Despite a feeling of euphoria bubbling up inside, Samuel remained as still as the lion's head forever lurking above its library jungle. "Is Jimmy Ray the father of your baby?"

"Yes, sir," Eleanor answered, eyes welling up with tears. "But he don't care a hound's tooth about it. And my mama...my mama can't wait 'til I'm rid of it!"

"*Miss Snyder*...," Samuel proceeded, fully aware of his ability to buy off any threat of incrimination regarding his dispensing of abortions, if need be, "since it is very important that this operation remain a secret for *obvious* reasons, I must be absolutely certain that no one be in the position to testify against me. So...is there even the *slightest* chance that anyone else might suspect the reason for your visit here this morning? Perhaps someone on the bus with whom you held a conversation or one of the neighbors along the way?"

Eleanor quickly let go of the rope. "Oh no, sir...I don't think there's *any* chance o' that," she declared, eager to ease the doctor's concern, being that abortion was illegal and all. "I made sure I didn't talk to anybody...even wore my hat all the way here, bein' that I didn't want anyone ta recognize me, lest my whereabouts got back ta Mama and Jimmy Ray. Anyhow," she added, brushing a stray hair from her tear-streaked cheek, "there weren't anyone around here ta talk to either, seein' there ain't many houses and half of 'em not even bein' finished anyway."

Samuel began rubbing his hands together as if attempting to expunge a stubborn stain of blood. "Well, then, *Miss Snyder*...since it appears we are not in any danger of being discovered, I see no reason for further delay. In the meantime, you may leave your things here." Disregarding the magnifying glass and depleted cigar, he gathered the calendar along with the pad and fountain pen, placing the items back into the desk drawer. A dull thud echoed through the room as he closed it, emulating the final closing of a coffin.

Eleanor felt her legs going limp as the doctor rose from his seat. Although she'd been in the room for what had to be nearly half an hour, everything was happening all too fast. And Doctor Governey hadn't even asked for any money yet, she considered, envisioning the wad of dollar bills she had snatched from Jimmy Ray's trousers. Keenly aware of her rapid pulse and heavy breathing, her eyes caught hold of the pearl-handled jackknife at the far left corner of the desk as the doctor repositioned the magnifying glass. A gust of wind swept through the room, reactivating the wind chimes. It seemed to resonate even louder as he picked up the silver ashtray, disposing its contents into an adjacent wastebasket. She shivered. The sound reminded her of a woman in pain...like a woman on the verge of childbirth, but much worse. Suddenly, overwrought with a concern for her own comfort, she opened her mouth, doubting for a fraction of a second if her words would make it out. "Doctor Governey...will...will the operation hurt?"

"There is no need to worry, my dear," he responded, fastidiously placing the ashtray back upon the desk. "I guarantee that *you* won't feel a thing. I will make sure you are adequately sedated."

Eleanor knew what the word *sedated* meant, but didn't feel so smug about it anymore. "And the baby too...it won't be hurtin' either, will it?"

"Now, *Miss Snyder*," Samuel answered, retrieving a handkerchief from his robe pocket, attempting to alleviate the cigar burn on the blotter's cardboard surface, "tell me, my dear...how could something no larger than your thumbnail possess the capacity to feel?"

Glancing down upon an unadorned nail which was grown a fraction of an inch past her thumb, Eleanor thought of the carpenter ant she killed the other day, writhing in pain until she finally ended its misery. "Will it be quick, then?"

"Quick enough, *my dear.*"

"But...will...will it take very long for me to *recover?*" she asked in one last attempt to stall the inevitable, rubbing perspiring hands along the dampened fabric clinging to her thighs. "There's a storm comin' through and I want to be on my way before it starts."

"Why, *Miss Snyder*...I don't think there is *any* need to worry about an upcoming storm," Samuel asserted, placing the neatly folded handkerchief back inside his robe pocket. "It's a rather *delightful* day!"

"Oh...but there *is* one comin'," she quickly disputed. "The frogs were croakin' ever so loud at the Miller's pond earlier this morning, and when I was walking to your place, a line of crows was sittin' on the telephone wire. But it wasn't that they were just *sittin'* there," she explained wide-eyed. "They were hollerin' something awful too. So, you see, Doctor Governey," she continued, searching for another knuckle to crack, "there *is* gonna be a storm tonight, and it's gonna be a bad one. It may not come through 'til late, but... just the same...I'd like to leave fairly early...if I can."

"Very well, then, *Miss Snyder*," Samuel said, turning toward the open window, "in that case, we'd best hurry things along then, mustn't we?"

Eleanor could already feel the baby dropping from her womb as the doctor strode toward the window and reached for its latch. A wave of hysteria started to sweep over her as if the coming storm had already begun. She wanted to run, but her legs wouldn't let her. They were telling her something, she thought...letting her know she just *had* to go through with the abortion before moving on to Hollywood. It would be hard enough convincing some director to get her into the talking pictures *without* a baby growing inside. But before her internal storm could release another rumble of thunder, Eleanor watched in bewilderment as the doctor nearly poked his head through the screen, uttering some words Mama once washed her mouth out for saying. Then, swirling around in a flash, he ordered her to stay put as he ran past the desk and out the door like a frenzied bolt of lightning.

chapter 72

Intrusion

All the more irate from being cursed with a pair of slippers which refused to keep up with his forceful stride, Samuel dashed through the main library and toward the nearest back entrance off the kitchen. It was all he could do to spare his garden from further damage, he angrily mumbled, particularly since he no longer had within his employ a resourceful servant to remedy such a distressing situation. Propelling his way into the immaculate kitchen, he brushed against one of the cherrywood chairs, pushing it out of place before heading through the breakfast room. Unlatching the patio door, he stepped out onto the furnished veranda, veering to his right, toward an abundant row of fully bloomed hibiscus. Whatever in the devil's bloody name had possessed some mangy mutt to sneak into his back garden, let alone obliterate one of his favorite flowering perennials was, at the moment, too outrageous to comprehend! Promptly spotting the menacing black pup at a close distance digging further into the rooted soil, Samuel released a punitive scream, inciting the loosely leashed canine to suddenly cease its vandalizing venture and aimlessly dart about the overgrown grass, evading its pursuer's numerous attempts to chase it away. But before Samuel was given ample time to accomplish the insurmountable task, another ambulatory object caught his eye as it eased up the driveway, purring like a sun-warmed kitten and stopping just short of the closed, wrought iron gate.

In a futile attempt to maintain all the dignity he could muster, Samuel disregarded his prior preoccupation and readjusted the sash of his satin robe as he walked over to the heavy gate, all the while ready to apologize for his unsightly appearance. It was disconcerting enough that Sergeant McCallister had stopped by at this precise moment to return the automobile he had borrowed for his niece's wedding, he inwardly grumbled while sporting a flashing smile, but the sergeant's partner also was waiting behind in the patrol car. After pulling the gate open to allow the candy apple red Duesenberg access to the back driveway, he promptly greeted Sergeant McCallister who avoided stepping upon the automobile's corrugated running board, choosing instead to slide along the caramel colored seat and leap out onto the paved brick drive.

"Top o' the mornin' to ya' Sam!" Clancy McCallister answered while tipping his hat. "Hope I didn't catch ya' at a bad time, now!"

Samuel quickly glanced toward the direction of the assaulted hibiscus and then to his left, concluding that the frisky pup had retreated through one of the many gaps in the wrought iron fence. "I was about to go upstairs and take my shower," he explained, throwing both hands up in exasperation, "when I couldn't help but notice a bloody dog digging up my flowers!"

"Ya mean that little bastard there?" the sergeant replied, stretching widened lips into a roguish grin which practically reached his reddish, pork chop sideburns.

Immediately turning around to see to what his comrade was referring, Samuel's jaw dropped upon spotting a chagrined Eleanor standing beside a dwarf spruce with the restless pup in her arms. Compressing lips so tightly until he could feel the blood draining into his throat, he returned his attention to the sergeant, trying to remain as calm as the barren breeze of Lake St. Clair. "Why, yes, indeed, Clancy old sport!" he exclaimed, feigning sheer satisfaction while cursing under his breath at the disobedient duo. "The truth of the matter is, the young lady over there appeared unannounced at my doorstep a short while ago in search of a housekeeping position. It seems there was quite a misunderstanding with the employment agency as I *specifically* requested a male servant to replace Zachary...may the good Lord rest his soul. *Nevertheless*, I shall be happy to dismiss her promptly, lest the day escape before allowing me the indulgence of that refreshing shower!"

Clancy McCallister offered Samuel an obsequious nod. His first impression upon sighting the lass was that perhaps some sort of tryst had been going on between them. But Samuel's explanation, along with the fact that the lass *did* appear quite destitute, was as easy to swallow as a flagon of bootleg beer.

Stepping quickly forward, the sergeant gave Samuel a solid pat on the back. "I guess I'd best be on my way then. I was just gonna leave the Duesy out on the drive for ya and then return this afternoon on my own," he clarified, anticipating his weekly hush money while awkwardly glancing toward his partner still waiting behind the wheel of the squad car. "Woulda' delivered her even sooner, but wanted ta have her all cleaned up for ya. Took her over ta Vito's," he boasted, with a gleam in his emerald eyes. "Ya know...that new automobile laundry them Italian boys opened up on Mack Avenue just a few blocks down from yer funeral home. Best automobile laundry around if you're askin' my opinion. Even polished up all the brass on her too. Looks better than new, she does!"

As if an amber traffic light had warned him to proceed with caution, Samuel quickly disregarded the erratic events of that morning, choosing instead to inspect the newest addition to his ambulatory harem. When lending out the special edition Duesenberg, it had not occurred to him that his sergeant buddy would personally take it upon himself to have it scrubbed, realizing that Zachary was no longer available to care for the matter. Driving skeptical eyes over each alluring groove and curve of the 1931 Model SJ while unable to detect the slightest scratch, Samuel's cynical scowl became practically nonexistent as he scanned a spotless leather canopy and rows of cylinder valves shining like stacks of newly minted silver dollars. Yes...there was no doubt about it, he concluded as Clancy McCallister rattled on about the many compliments he received at his niece's wedding regarding one of Samuel's most recently acquired prized vehicles. The magnificently detailed automobile was surely a testament to the fact that laying bricks, selling fruits and vegetables and being involved in organized crime were not the only occupations these immigrant dagos excelled in. Perhaps now he needn't hesitate to take more of his motor cars out for a spin since the problem of having them cleaned had been so conveniently resolved. But with hardly a moment to reflect upon this welcome revelation, Clancy McCallister's concerned demeanor alerted him to yet another inescapable quandary.

"Ya know, Sam," he began, resting his arm upon Samuel's shoulder, trying not to wince at the smell of formaldehyde, "I think it be only fair ta tell ya that while at the wedding, I struck up a conversation with a young fella who works for Mr. Spangler at the bank who'll be runnin' his mayoral campaign next year." He lowered his voice, making sure the conversation would not be overheard. "As much as I hate ta be the bearer of bad news, it seems that...seems there's an ugly rumor goin' around about ya *preferrin' the boys*, if ya know what I mean." Worried about any future losses he personally might incur should Samuel forfeit the election, McCallister slapped the palm of his hand against his benefactor's back and looked straight into an attentive pair of shocking blue eyes. "Now, Sam, my good friend...I think it be my duty ta let ya know that this ain't the first time I've heard such blather, though never before so *hatefully* delivered and, *anyhow...*" he instantly clarified, wondering if there was any ounce of truth to the matter while rolling his eyes toward the sparsely clouded heavens, "Damn it ta hell...I swore ta him in the name of Jesus, Mary and Joseph that it was nothin' but a sack o' blarney!"

Samuel took two deliberate steps backwards, allowing a good arm's length between himself and the officer's suspicions. "And as you rightly should have, *by Jove!*" he immediately emphasized, his chest becoming all the more prominent as he pulled back straightened shoulders, forcefully placing fists to hips. "If my very life should hinge on such outrageous accusations, I should have nothing to worry about, being that I am as much interested in the ladies as any other red-blooded Englishman!" he boasted, impetuously glancing in Eleanor's direction, aware of the fact that he had just been robbed of one of life's most memorable experiences. "And whatever, in the devil's *bloody* name, do you mean about having *before* witnessed such atrocious accusations?"

Convinced that he had agitated the blood in Samuel's money-grubbing veins as surely as if he were stirring a pot of Mulligan stew, Clancy McCallister softened his voice a bit, attempting to cool down the flaring disposition of his longtime partner-in-crime. "Sam, my good fella...now there's no need to be alarmed as of yet, but...ya have ta take inta account that given yer way of life...never bein' married and especially livin' with a male servant all these years...folks might naturally suspect the worst." Upon noticing the young female visitor wandering out of auditory range, he resumed his normal tone of voice. "All I'm sayin' Sam, is since such misgivins' have already been brewin', that son-of-a-bitch Spangler is in prime position ta put the final nail in yer coffin, so ta speak, 'specially since the deputy I was talkin' ta swore up and down on his own grave that the whole damn town would be certain o' yer fancies before that bastard Spangler was through with ya."

Samuel's shoulders began slumping forward as he considered such a malignant attack, realizing that being accused of such deviant behavior was a dilemma he would not be able to buy his way out of this time. Of course...he *could* arrange for Tony and his brothers to bump off the bloody son-of-a-bitch and shut his tattling trap for good. "So...Clancy, my good man...are you, indeed, telling me that my campaign is going well, provided we can arrest the malicious gossip being promulgated by this so-called representative of Mr. Spangler?"

Immediately sensing the degree of malice in Samuel's eyes, Clancy leaned forward despite the lingering formaldehyde on his unbathed body. "Why, heavens ta Betsy, no!" he answered, his hot whiskey breath singeing Samuel's cheekbone. "Sam...I know what you're thinkin'...but there ain't no one you're gonna get rid of that won't be replaced by another. Besides...the match is lit." McCallister hesitated for a moment before proceeding any further. "Ya know, Sam...when ya got yer own dago boys suspectin' yer queer, you can bet yer ass that Spangler is gonna grab yer balls and hang onta them any which way he can!"

Samuel staggered backwards alongside the Duesenberg. "However...what do you mean...my *own* boys are suspicious of my...my *personal* preferences?"

Pleased that he had elicited the response he was hoping for, Sergeant McCallister tilted his head and scrunched his face like a ripened cabbage. "Now I don't mean ta stir up no trouble, mind ya, but like I said, I've even heard from time ta time some *nasty* speculatin' on the part o' yer buddies, the Terillo boys." Before Samuel could protest, the hefty sergeant continued. "I'm only tellin' ya what I been hearin', Sam...At times when yer not around at the pool halls and poker games ta vouch fer yerself." McCallister pushed the knobby palms of his hands forward as if stopping heavy traffic. "Now...the only reason I'm mentionin' this is ta get ya ta understand that the shit's been hittin' the fan and we'd better find a way ta shut it off fast before there's nothin' left ta do about it."

Nudging perpetually scrubbed teeth against his lower lip, Samuel folded both arms to his chest. "Clancy, my good man...do you think it would be in my best interest, then, under such grossly misunderstood circumstances, to seriously consider hiring a servant of the *female* gender...at least until the election is final?"

McCallister swiftly removed his cap, brushing a perspiring forehead with the back of his hand. "Hiring that sweet little tart over there might be a good place ta start, but let's face it, Sam. She ain't no way gonna match the skills of yer manservant, Zach." Sizing up Samuel while repositioning the crumpled cap, he then continued. "Take it for what it's worth, Sam...If yer willin' ta hear a few advising words…" Grabbing the brim of his cap once again, he then gave it a good slap on the knee. "Goddamn it, Sam…For the love o' Saint Pete, save yer sorry ass and get yerself a good wife! Why…look at ya! Yer as handsome a devil as any good lass'd hope for…aside from the fact that ya got bags o' money ta lure her in." Before Samuel could object, McCallister held the cap to his chest as if paying his respect to a fallen soldier. "Now…I hope you're listenin' and listenin' well cause this ain't no laughin' matter, Sam. Yer opponent…that bastard spreadin' all that shit about you… has got everything goin' for him…'specially a wife and three little wee ones…all that's needed ta get the votes in this God-fearin' town." Despite noticing that Samuel was beginning to squirm, the sergeant placed the cap back on his head, making sure not to break the momentum. "This is the month of *August*, Samuel…that means we've got well over a year before elections come next November. If we keep on our toes, there's plenty o' time ta get ya hitched…maybe ta even get ya' goin' on one of yer *own* little wee ones. Then, nobody'd be able to accuse ya of things ya ain't in no way or manner guilty of. Now, Sam my good man…I've got ta tell ya, that there ain't nothin' better than a good woman. Why, my own dear bride, Maureen, has been a blessin' to an old son-of-a-bitch like me since I married her 19 years ago…bore me five handsome babies, all growin' up now. And I can't begin ta tell ya what good housekeepin' a proper wife'll do. Of course," he added, his eyes scanning the vast rear of the mansion, "you'd be best ta hire some outside help too…maybe a team o' gals who'll come in once every week or two…'specially if the Mrs. is busy taking care o' the little ones. Anyhow, you'll be sure ta get good home-cooked meals every day. That is…if ya go ahead and marry the right lass." Sporting a mischievous grin, McCallister stepped forward and slapped Samuel on the upper arm, knocking the stupefied look off his face. "I know a few decent lasses who'd be happy ta have ya. Nice Irish gals too. Pretty as a bed o' roses in full bloom, they are. Ya just give me the word and I'll get the ball rollin' for ya. *Otherwise*," he emphasized, sliding an index finger across his own throat, "I'm afraid ya got more chance o' findin' that pot o' gold at the end o' the rainbow than bein' elected mayor o' *this* town." Having gotten the matter spoken of once and for all, McCallister removed his hand from Samuel's shoulder, reached for his cap and tipped it. "Well, Sam, my good fella, I'd best be goin' now. Keep in mind what we've talked over and I'll be back again at me regular time this afternoon!"

Samuel lingered a few feet ahead of the Duesenberg, bidding his confidant goodbye as he watched McCallister saunter down the driveway and climb into the passenger seat of the squad car. He should have known such disconcerting speculations were going to rear their ugly heads, he silently seethed, while waving off the two police officers. Over the past several years, such unethical backstabbing among political opponents was becoming absolutely despicable with hardly a thought given to slandering a man's good name. Feeling as if the oppressive morning heat was melting the pomade right off his freshly barbered hair, Samuel cringed at the thought of being accused of such disgraceful conduct. It was offensive enough that his own father had engaged in those same odious activities and heaven forbid should *that* truth ever be discovered! But *for now*, he reflected, waiting for the squad car to drive out of sight, his primary concern was how to maintain his own sterling reputation. Samuel retreated a few steps backward as the policemen made their way down Pennington Avenue, all the while picturing the family portrait of his rival gracing the main interior wall at Detroit Savings Bank, a monumental institution forever thriving within the heart of the motor city despite current economic hardships. Proudly sitting upon a velveteen armchair with wife and children surrounding him, William G. Spangler seemed more apt to be elected president of the United States then mayor of a quaint suburban Grosse Pointe town.

Somberly pivoting toward the Duesenberg in anticipation of returning it to the garage, he gave thought to his own personal situation. It was understandable that such rumors had the ability to grow long legs given his solitary lifestyle. In this conventional town, his unmarried status was just the ammunition people needed to fill their minds with idle, vicious gossip. Furthermore, regardless of what Clancy McCallister was proposing, he hadn't the slightest intention of marrying. It would be distressing enough having to endure the inept assistance of a female servant, let alone entering into the holy state of matrimony with some gold-digging, freckle-faced Paddy...particularly one that was destined to be childless, compliments of that licentious hussy, Violet Stimple, he sneered, realizing that he would never escape the slain suffragette's bedeviling ghost. Having hardly a chance to ponder any alternative action he might take to protect himself from subsequent slander, Samuel's thoughts were instantly arrested by a familiar female form standing near the far end of the mansion, inspecting his surviving hibiscus while containing the rambunctious pup within her determined grasp.

Immediately delaying the reinstatement of the Duesenberg to its designated stall, he stood mute for several prolonged seconds while scrutinizing the preoccupied lass, realizing he was no longer angered by her unanticipated appearance. It was as if the superstitious girl had cleverly cast a spell in his direction, he mused, admiring ringlets of loosely bound hair cascading down the back of her blouse like thickened trails of pure crude oil. And though he could not hear her bubbly voice, Samuel knew she was speaking to herself by the deliberate movement of celestially curved lips. Somewhat startled by an unexpected solidarity welling up inside while admiring a delightful grin which spread like wildfire across a field of silken corn, he waited for Eleanor to gaze back at him, only to be entranced by a pair of nomadic eyes he would have recognized a mile away. And, as she eagerly made her way toward him, practically skipping across the sun-drenched lawn, he realized that, although pursuing his original covetous plan was no longer a remote possibility, he still had some unfinished business to take care of.

chapter 73

A Change of Mind

"Your hibiscus are just fine, sir...I checked every one of them!" Eleanor stopped abruptly, a look of absolute delight accentuating flushed cheeks. "My dog, Makara, started digging by the flowers, but I checked the roots too and they're still strong as a bull's horns!"

Samuel sternly contemplated his newest patient for another extended moment before speaking, realizing for the first time that it was *she* who was, indeed, the owner of the vandalizing pup still wriggling within her arms. "You'll have to find a way to contain your dog, Miss Snyder, if you still wish to proceed with the operation."

Suddenly conscious of Samuel's disapproving stare, Eleanor reflected the imploring look in Makara's puppy dog eyes. "I'm sorry about her gettin' away like that, Doctor Governey. I...I did my best to keep her tied up ta one of the bushes out front, but it looks like she chewed through the rope and got away!"

Samuel eyed the makeshift harness, noticing that it matched the rope still tied around his visitor's tiny, unswelled waist. "Are you meaning to tell me, Miss Snyder, that you were able to contain your dog on such a long journey without a proper leash?"

"Yes sir," she answered, her agile body twisting as the pup repeatedly attempted to jump from her arms. "I never did get around to buyin' her a *proper* one, so the best I could do was make one out of the tattered rope Jimmy Ray had hangin' around the fillin' station." She shifted her eyes toward the pup. "Guess it just wasn't strong enough ta hold her once we got here, though."

"Well, then..." Samuel curtly stated, nevertheless impressed by the girl's apparent strength as the unruly pup remained within her grasp, "I suppose we have a problem, Miss Snyder. Unless you can find a way to contain your dog, I am afraid we shall have to postpone the operation."

"Oh, no...Please, sir...please!" she begged, her eyes widening like two hoisted sails. "If you let her come inside with us, I promise she'll be good. There's still a little rope left that'll tie onto something. Pleeease, Doctor Governey, sir," she cried, glancing down at the undisciplined pup. "Please don't send me back home!"

Struggling to retain his composure, Samuel clamped his lips together and forcefully inhaled. Although he was still willing to perform the abortion, there was no way in bloody hell he was going to let a mangy mutt inside his pristine mansion. "I am sorry, Miss Snyder, but I have no place in my home to accommodate such a lively pet and I certainly cannot keep my eye on her while taking care of you. So...unless you have an alternative suggestion, I fear there is no other option."

Appearing as if she were suddenly inspired by an apocalyptic vision, Eleanor flashed a hopeful smile. "Doctor Governey? I think...I think..." She hesitated for a moment before proceeding, disregarding an overwhelming sense of thirst. "I do have a way, sir...to *contain* Makara, I mean. I did it before bringin' her over here so she'd be quiet on the bus...bein' that pets aren't allowed on them. You see...I had to sneak her on, but before I could do that I...I put her in this sack here," she said glancing down at the burlap bag, her voice becoming weaker and her speech a bit sluggish. "I know I told you otherwise, but didn't want to get myself into trouble. But now...anyway, I have some *ether* that I gave her to sedate her with, sir. I could use it again...if I *have* to, I suppose."

With mouth agape, Samuel stood mute, wondering if perhaps his auditory capacity had somehow been impaired. Never mind that the little schemer had somehow gotten hold of the powerful anesthetic, but possessing the ability to administer it was an indispensable skill he had not even entrusted over the past 13 years to his clinically trained servant, Zachary. "You sedated the dog *yourself?*"

"Yes, sir. I learned how to do it at the Cottage Hospital where I work in the operatin' room," she struggled to spill out, being careful not to reveal how she had stolen the ether from the medical supply room.

"You *actually* worked in the operating room there?"

Continuing to feel faint from the late morning heat, Eleanor wished the doctor would stop asking her so many questions and let her bring Makara inside so she could at least sit down. "Yes, sir...I...I work with Dr. Blake, sir," she listlessly answered with shallow breaths. "He's the doctor who...who...told my mama about yoooou...."

With hardly a moment to spare before Eleanor could collapse upon the paved brick drive, Samuel swooped forward to catch her, unconcerned that the opportunistic mutt had escaped its owner's embrace. As she lay motionless within his arms, he darted toward the furnished veranda to obtain access to the kitchen, remembering all the while the telephone conversation between himself and Eleanor's mother. Yes, it was true, he acknowledged, stumbling past terra-cotta planters and cast iron chairs, that Mrs. Snyder had mentioned one of his many colleagues, Dr. Blake, as a reliable reference. But he had no idea that her daughter had actually worked for the fastidious surgeon. Upon reaching the kitchen entrance, he glanced at the unconscious girl, her lifeless face as pale as a misty moon. Without sparing even a second's time to reflect upon her beauty, he flung open the glass beveled door, practically ignoring the scampering pup which scooted ahead of him onto the cool limestone tiles. Perhaps he should have been more attentive to her susceptibility to dehydration, he scoffed while heading toward a cabinet to retrieve the smelling salts. The city of Dearborn is, after all, quite a distance from Grosse Pointe and the unfortunate lass hadn't anything to drink since the start of her journey. Of course, he *was* taking into consideration the impending abortion, but still...he, Samuel Randolph Governey, being a bona fide doctor of medical science, should certainly have been more responsive to her symptoms. Having managed to obtain the smelling salts within his restricted grasp, he strode over to the kitchen table and, taking advantage of the chair he had pushed out of the way while first heading out into the backyard, tenderly positioned Eleanor onto its cushioned seat while maneuvering another chair with his leg in order to elevate her feet. Remaining within inches of the swooned patient, lest she keel over, he twisted open the jar of smelling salts and held it beneath her nostrils.

The first thing Eleanor noticed upon awakening was the intense look of fatherly concern upon Doctor Governey's face and his reassurance that he would return quickly with a tall, cold glass of water. It was sure a good thing he was there to catch her when she fainted, she thought, watching him from the corner of her eye...although she was still feeling mighty weak. And she was glad he didn't seem angry anymore about the hibiscus or Makara. But... Eleanor suddenly felt compelled to roll off the chair and search for her dog before noticing the curious pup sniffing about the mahogany cabinets. Disclosing a wistful smile, she allowed herself to relax, all the more appreciative of the good doctor for letting Makara inside the house after all. Continuing to regain her composure, she was awestruck as she watched Samuel retrieving a crystal decanter of water from the Frigidaire, fascinated by the refrigerator's capacity and spotless white interior. She hadn't even known that such a large icebox existed, she marveled, as he closed the door and walked toward the kitchen cupboards. She'd only seen such iceboxes in her mama's *Good Housekeeping* magazines and even then they didn't seem half as big as this one.

While Samuel reached for a glass from the china cabinet and started to fill it, Eleanor's eyes began to wander, her impressionable mind consuming one newfangled appliance after the other...the unscratched porcelain sink with its long, sleek faucet...the golden colored stove set upon curving legs with glossy black burners and a full set of shiny gold pots and pans hanging on a giant rack above it...even one of them toasters you can brown your bread in. And the window itself, she mused, her eyes traveling upward past the polished Italian marble counters and toward the cathedral ceiling. Its domed shape reminded her of the ones she'd seen in the big city churches. Refocusing her gaze downward, Eleanor felt secure in realizing that the kitchen, as well as the adjoining breakfast room, wasn't cluttered up with a bunch of objects like the doctor had in his office, though there were still several gadgets she didn't recognize and even so, they weren't at all old or spooky. Even the tile floor was allowed to breathe, not being covered up by one kind of rug or another like those throughout most of the other rooms.

Attempting to moisten chapped lips as Samuel set the decanter of water upon the silk embroidered tablecloth, Eleanor leaned forward to take a sip from the glass he held, minding the doctor's orders to drink slowly. The water tasted extra good, she noticed, as it trickled from the crystal glass down her parched throat. Not at all like the grayish well water back home. And it didn't have anything to do with her being so thirsty, either. Removing her lips from the rim of the glass to catch her breath, she thanked the good doctor, assuring him that she'd be alright sitting up on her own. Unexpectedly, yet pleasantly intrigued by his compassionate touch, she then allowed him to help lower her legs and position herself at the table, all the while hoping that the centerpiece of fresh calla lilies would eventually help mask the strong medicine smell forever lingering upon his satin robe. But after he left the table for a moment to try turning on the ceiling fan and get his own water glass, she was somewhat spared when, upon his return, he seated himself at the head of the table a couple of chairs away.

Trusting that his patient was well on the road to recovery, Samuel could feel his chin spontaneously quivering. Within the past few fleeting minutes, the reason for Miss Eleanor Snyder's visit was beginning to take on an entire new meaning. It hadn't occurred to him, really, as he had rushed her into the kitchen to retrieve the smelling salts, or even when she stirred back to life, awakening within him a rather unfamiliar jubilant sensation. Instead, the intrusive yet welcoming ideas he was presently experiencing, encouraged by Clancy McCallister's admonitions of crippling gossip, began creeping through his mind the minute he went to get her the glass of water. And, what had begun merely as a passing notion was now evolving into an enticing lorry-load of possibilities. Painfully conscious of having to eventually accommodate the snooping pup and thereby humor his recovering guest who sat in unusual silence as if awaiting the first question on a final school examination, Samuel reached for the decanter of water and began pouring its contents into his own glass. Although it may be too soon to jump to conclusions, he fervently considered, this promising lass who had inconveniently interrupted his morning schedule, may have, after all, entered his life under the most serendipitous of circumstances! For, if it was, indeed, true that she was Bill Blake's assistant, not only would this pretty little nurse prove to be of valuable service in the operating room, but, taking into account her apparent knowledge of floriculture and perhaps other housekeeping duties...was it really possible, then? *Particularly* considering the most advantageous factor being that she was *already* pregnant with a child he could never, under any circumstances, have sired? So maybe...just *maybe*...this 14-year-old ingenue...this Miss Eleanor Snyder, whose life he had almost snuffed out of existence nearly an hour ago, was predestined to become the wife of an aristocratic citizen and future first lady of the exclusive City of Grosse Pointe, *Mrs. Samuel Randolph Governey!*

Immediately springing to his feet while pulling the decanter away from his glass as the water began overflowing upon the scarlet tablecloth, Samuel begged Eleanor's pardon for being so clumsy before carrying both items back to the sink, returning at once with the last remaining, yet slightly soiled, kitchen towel. Promptly setting the vase of calla lilies out of harm's way, he then began blotting the spilled water only to be interrupted by Eleanor's self-assured voice.

"I don't think that's gonna do much good, Doctor Governey...that water's gonna leave a ring on the fabric, seein' that it's such a fine silk and all. You'd be best ta wash it right away or at least soak it for a while." Attributing Samuel's intense preoccupation to his ignorance about caring for such domestic matters, she quickly spoke up again. "I can go over ta the sink and soak it for you if you'd like...I'm feelin' *much* better now."

Upon realizing that his hospitable guest was skilled in the tedious task of laundering, Samuel's sober look transformed into a gentle smile as he returned his attention toward Eleanor, pleased to see that her face had, indeed, regained its natural, vibrant sheen. "Why...thank you very kindly, my dear, but there is no reason to go through the trouble," he assured her, envisioning the many other tablecloths which were stacked in his linen closet, sent to him from India as gifts of gratitude from Tayib Bharat, the father of his very first abortion patient. "It is only a tablecloth after all...such things can easily be replaced."

Eleanor stared at the large wet splotch upon the embroidered cloth which reinforced her superstition of the upcoming rainstorm, amazed that the doctor was being so calm about the mishap. Once, after seeing the talking picture, *Anna Christie*, she had snuck into Mama's room, putting on her best silk dress while pretending to be Greta Garbo asking for a whiskey at the bar and ended up spilling a Hires Root Beer all over it. When Mama found out, she not only got a whipping, but was forced to kneel on a cheese grater until her knees began to bleed. Nevertheless, despite the wealthy doctor's composure, she couldn't help but offer some additional advice. "You'd better wipe the table underneath, Doctor Governey, sir...or it'll get water-stained too."

Feeling slightly foolish, Samuel sported a boyish grin. He wasn't accustomed to cleaning such messes; in fact, he wasn't accustomed to being so *clumsy*. But, the young girl was certainly correct. Though he could easily sacrifice one of his many tablecloths, having to go through the trouble of purchasing another kitchen table would be nothing but a waste of time. Without saying another word, he picked up the vase of calla lilies along with Eleanor's glass of water, carefully positioning them on a nearby counter. But, before he could return to finish the task, Eleanor was already standing there, the bundle of silk within her arms as she attempted to wipe the table with the wet towel.

"Do you have another *dry* towel, Doctor Governey? This one's just too wet ta finish wipin' the table with."

Trying his best to ignore the straying mutt who had just wandered into the breakfast room, Samuel retrieved the soiled laundry from Eleanor, respectfully declaring her as his guest and ordering her to sit down while he took care of the matter. "I am afraid I have run out of clean towels for the moment, Miss Snyder," he explained, stooping over the table while using a dry portion of the silk to whisk away the remaining beads of water. "My former servant, Zachary, would always keep a fresh supply for me in the kitchen, so I did not realize that my stock was running so low. Nevertheless, there is a Chinese laundry on Mack Avenue which I occasionally frequent under exceptional circumstances...*and* I believe they may be able to restore our pretty silk tablecloth also. I shall make it a point to go there as soon as I am able."

Eleanor pondered over the doctor's words as she watched him place the bundle of soiled laundry in a corner and saunter toward the kitchen cabinets. In the first place, as much as she would have loved to own such a fine piece of silk, it seemed odd that he should talk about the tablecloth as if it belonged to *both* of them. Secondly, even if the China-men were able to get the stain out, it would probably cost a heap of money. She remembered her best friend, Phyllis, back in Ohio, saying how her pappy once brought one of his shirts to a storefront laundry and was charged a whole 50 cents for it! Maybe when she became a rich movie star, *she* wouldn't have to wash her clothes anymore, she hoped, as Samuel retrieved a couple of coasters and proceeded toward the table. She wondered for a moment what her long lost friend was doing now; she wondered if the Chinese actress, Anna May Wong, still did *her* own laundry.

As the grandfather clock in the vestibule struck 12 noon, Samuel placed the refilled glasses upon the silver coasters and reclaimed his seat at the unadorned cherrywood table, eager to learn more about Eleanor's clinical experience with his widely-respected colleague, Dr. Blake, a renowned, strict disciplinarian, uncompromising in medical practice. "So, my dear, *dear* Miss Snyder..." he affectionately began, maintaining his usual physical distance while bracing himself for another lengthy account, "May I inquire how long you have been employed with Dr. Blake?"

Feeling somewhat guilty for not showing up at work and wondering what Dr. Blake must be thinking of her, Eleanor tightened her lips and focused her eyes toward an intangible horizon, the way she always did when preparing to remember every detail of a non-rhetorical question. "Well...I...it all began, Doctor Governey...sir, when Daddy got sick two years back with the scarlet fever. Dr. Stevens...he was our family doctor at the time..." she continued to explain, momentarily calmed by the compassionate look in Samuel's warm blue eyes, "well...like I was saying...Dr. Stevens put him in the county hospital back in Wilmington and me and Mama would be goin' ta visit him and sometimes she'd even let me stay through the night too, but *she* couldn't stay 'cause of all the farm chores, sayin' she was willin' ta do my own chores for me so *I* could stay with Daddy."

Eleanor experienced a brief moment of resentment upon recollecting the *real* reason why her mama had been so accommodating. "Anyhow...," she quickly continued, "the very first time I went to the hospital, I seen a sign in the waiting room that said, 'Orderlies Needed.' Well, Doctor Governey...I didn't know what *orderlies* were, so I asked Mama and she said they were somethin' like nurses that helped out with the patients. Then she had an idea that maybe *I* might like ta take the job. And she was right...only...well..." Eleanor sulked while pressing her spine against the back of her chair, lowering her eyes. "She only wanted me ta be an orderly so she could carry on with Jimmy Ray in Daddy's bedroom without me bein' around, thinkin' I was stupid enough not to know. But I still wanted ta work at the hospital...and I liked it far better than helpin' out at the farm," she explained, perking up again, "even though I had ta clean up the smelly bedpans and change the dirty linen. But it sure beat pitchin' manure and sloppin' the hogs. And I even got paid for it too...even though Mama took most o' the money for Jimmy Ray's whiskey and cigarettes. Anyhow...Dr. Gillis...he was the doctor in charge of the county hospital...one day he comes over and tells me ta go with him in the operatin' room on account of some o' the nurses come down with the fever." She paused for a moment, remembering how the virus had eventually taken her daddy. "After that one day of helpin' him, I got the chance ta' work more and more in the operatin' room and even got a pay raise." Eleanor moistened her lips and squinted her dark brown eyes, suddenly realizing that despite all her yapping, she probably still hadn't answered the doctor's original question.

Eager to sweep aside the tormenting reminder of his sickly mother's appalling addictions during his own discordant childhood, Samuel took full advantage of the short intermission offered him by his guest while eliciting a patronizing smile. "That is quite a story, my dear and very commendable and generous of you to share it with me. But, would you be kind enough to elaborate...how is it that you entered into Dr. *Blake's* employment at the Cottage Hospital?"

Feeling somewhat embarrassed, yet pleased to be delivered from her lapse in memory, Eleanor released an apologetic gasp. "Oh...yes...well...it was all because Mama and Jimmy Ray wanted ta move up ta Michigan. Ya see, Doctor Governey...after my daddy died, Mama went ahead and sold the farm, so Jimmy Ray talks her into investin' the money into a fillin' station up here. I really didn't want ta leave Wilmington and especially stop workin' for Dr. Gillis, so he let Dr. Blake know about me and Dr. Blake says that if I'm willin' ta travel from Dearborn to Grosse Pointe durin' the week, I could come work for him then." She waited for Samuel to swallow another drink of water. "That's how I knew how ta get here, Doctor Governey...bein' already familiar with Grosse Pointe and all, I knew how the busses would be runnin' and which ones ta take. Otherwise, I might have gotten lost like the time I went over..."

"So, I understand, Miss Snyder," Samuel quickly interjected at the risk of appearing ungracious. "You have been working as Dr. Blake's assistant, then, for a year or so now?" Allowing Eleanor to answer in the affirmative without her slipping in another word, he prudently resumed his interrogation. "Tell me, then, Miss Snyder...if I may so kindly inquire...what sort of duties are you accustomed to performing in the operating room?"

Requiring hardly a fraction of a second to respond, she straightened her back against the kitchen chair, folding both hands within the lap of her skirt. "Yes, sir...first of all, I make sure all the medical equipment is sterilized and set up." Eleanor took another several minutes to describe in minuscule detail the procedure used for sterilization as well as the preparation and sedation of the patient. "Then," she continued, "when the operation is goin' on, I make sure I hand Dr. Blake all the right instruments. I know every surgical instrument by name, too...bovie, abdominal clamp, Simpson forceps, retractor...all Dr. Blake has to do is name it and it's there for him quicker than a blue jay on a June bug." As she began to describe in detail the time she had saved a patient from permanently becoming a human receptacle for a stray surgical sponge, her story was suddenly interrupted as Makara, having finished her investigation of the breakfast room, trotted toward Samuel, only to recoil at his slippered feet while letting out a disapproving whimper.

"I must apologize, my dear Miss Snyder," he quickly intervened, eager to remain within the good graces of his loquacious guest. "I am afraid that Makara's acute sense of smell has been terribly compromised. You see...," he explained, reluctant to reveal for the time being, his primary vocation as funeral director, "I am in the process of developing a substance which will terminate the weeds on my lawn without jeopardizing the vitality of the encompassing grass. But...as you can very well discern," Samuel gestured, alluding to his indecorous attire, "I had nary the opportunity to indulge in my daily shower and thus rid myself of its pungent odor before experiencing the pleasure of your unexpected company!"

Eleanor could feel herself blushing as she struggled to keep an eye on Makara at the far end of the table, making sure the pup didn't wander out into the hallway. Although she wasn't familiar with some of the big words the doctor was using, she still knew what he was saying and could tell by the way he pronounced them that he was pleased as Punch with her. It was a good thing, too, she had mentioned Dr. Blake, being that he seemed quite taken by her working in his operatin' room. Continuing to bask in the heartfelt admiration of such an ingenious doctor, Eleanor wondered for a moment how this gent would look once he got rid of the weed killing smell and was all dressed up. But before she could further imagine how handsome he'd be in a tailored Sunday suit or realize how long she'd been staring at him without even uttering a single word, Makara returned from the opposite end of the table, sniffing and whining at her impoverished feet. Somewhat relieved to be delivered from her peculiar feelings toward the doctor, Eleanor quickly leaned over, lifting the pup from limestone floor. "I...I think Makara is hungry...or...or thirsty, maybe."

Concealing the displeasure of having to confront such an unpalatable matter, Samuel feigned genuine approval toward the intrusive canine with a succinct nod of the head. "Well, then, in that case, my dear, your little Makara is certainly in luck. I just happen to have a ham in the Frigidaire which has been begging for some good company," he stated while pulling himself away from the table. "And you, Miss Snyder?" he offered, walking toward the glamorized icebox, "Would you also care to share a portion with us?"

Eleanor could feel her taste buds coming alive as she watched the doctor reach into the Frigidaire and pull out a large brown package. She was surprised, at first, that he had asked if she wanted some of the ham, being that she was about to have an operation, but then figured he was just being polite. It sure looked good, though, she thought as he placed it upon the butcher block and started to unwrap it. She hadn't tasted a good ham since Daddy slaughtered one of their prize hogs for Easter Sunday supper the same spring he caught the scarlet fever. Trying her best to ignore the sweet smell which prompted Makara to swiftly depart the solace of her company and scurry toward the butcher block, Eleanor finally answered the doctor, bearing in mind that a ham so fine must have come from a pig that was slaughtered on a rising moon. "No sir...I mean...I sure would *like* to have some, but..." She stopped for a moment, suddenly startled. "You *do* still have time to give me the abortion, don't you?"

Leaving the unwrapped ham upon the butcher block, Samuel went over to the china cabinet, removing two dishes and a bowl. "Why, yes, my dear," he answered, opening the silverware drawer. "Having enough time to conduct the operation is certainly no obstacle. And I have every intention to accommodate your wishes. However," he hesitantly added, suppressing a short-lived scowl upon realizing that the only clean napkins available were composed of paper, "I am quite concerned about your intention to travel immediately afterwards without an escort...in case any complications should arise." Placing some silverware and the paper napkins near the kitchen sink, Samuel began filling the bowl with water. "If you would like, you and Makara are most welcome to stay here with me...and there is certainly no reason for the operation to be immediately performed," he clarified, leaning over to place the bowl upon the floor. "As a matter of fact, if you would be willing to wait a few more days, or better yet, a week or so, your body would be more amenable to such a radical procedure."

As Makara greedily lapped up the water, Eleanor gave serious thought to the doctor's proposal. Although the possibility of complications from the surgery had crossed her mind since taking refuge in a neighboring shed early that morning, she didn't see the point of dwelling on it, being that she needed to get far away from Jimmy Ray as fast as her legs would carry her. But Doctor Governey was right. There was a chance she might need time to recover, and in that case, her only choice would be delaying her trip to California. But that would be the *only* reason she'd stay a little while longer in Grosse Pointe. *Of course*, she determined while Samuel stretched toward a high shelf to withdraw a serving platter, those two police officers that came here a little while ago were likely to remember her if Jimmy Ray went ahead and reported she was missing. So, in spite of what the doctor was advising about waiting another week or so, getting the abortion over with as quick as possible so she could soon be on her way was, really, still the best decision. "Thank you very kindly, sir," she answered as Samuel reached into a long, sectioned drawer, "and it's nice of you to offer for me to stay if I must...but I'd *still* like ta have the operation today."

Seemingly unruffled by the tenacity of his unrefined guest, Samuel retrieved his largest butcher knife, its wide blade shielded in brown paper. "Forgive me, please, my dear, for being so concerned for your safety, but even under the *best* of circumstances, it is still quite dangerous for a young lady...particularly an *attractive* lass such as yourself...to be moving about without an escort. And, as your doctor, I would strongly advise you against traveling any distance unaccompanied after a procedure of this nature...all by *yourself*," he added, noting the look of concern on Eleanor's face.

Despite the doctor's compliment about her being so pretty, Eleanor felt a familiar stab of fear as he strode toward the butcher block. Sure, she was scared about traveling all alone. Why, just the other day over the breadboard radio she heard about a young woman down in Alabama who'd not only been murdered, but raped and cut into little pieces. But she just *had* to take that chance, she thought while Samuel positioned the serving platter in front of himself upon the butcher block. And maybe traveling over to California wouldn't be so dangerous. People went to Hollywood to make something of themselves...not to murder or hurt other people. Eleanor breathed deeply as Samuel began unraveling some string from the butcher knife's brown paper wrapper. At times like this, it was always helpful to think of happy things, she resolved. Like becoming a glamorous screen star who'd be wearing fancy dresses made of the finest fabrics and riding in shiny new auto cars like Doctor Governey's Duesenberg. Even living in a big mansion like this one. She'd go to all the famous dancing parties with rows of tables filled with all kinds of fresh-cooked meats and fancy cakes. And there'd be enough left over to feed Makara and her whole litter of pups if she happened to bear any when fully growed. Experiencing a sudden pang of guilt about planning to take the life of her own child, Eleanor shifted her attention toward the pup which was seated upon its hind legs, awaiting her very first taste of tender baked pork. Somewhat comforted by Makara's presence, Eleanor reassured herself that everything would turn out fine and she would be making the best decision. Besides, like the doctor said, she'd *still* be able to have more babies when the right time came. And as far as her journey to California being safe, Makara would surely protect her from any harm. After all, she was no ordinary dog. But before she could daydream any further, her fantasies were interrupted by her hospitable host.

"Are you not afraid, then, my dear, to venture out on your own?" Samuel repeated, the cutting edge of the butcher knife gleaming as he held onto its riveted black handle. "I do not intend to alarm you, but there are many deranged souls wandering about who would not hesitate to take advantage of a young, defenseless girl in the most appalling of ways. And it does not even matter if your destination be as close as Ohio or as far as Chicago," he chided, uncertain of where the little fugitive intended to escape. "So please, my dear Eleanor...I beg of you to reconsider my offer...I shall not be able to sleep at night knowing that you, having been entrusted to my care, are traveling through some strange town all alone and quite unprotected...particularly after undergoing an operation which may leave you in a most vulnerable state of mind."

Now, not feeling so certain about her traveling plans anymore, Eleanor squirmed in the rigid chair, unable to tear her gaze from the butcher knife. Yes, it was true that her final destination was Hollywood, but, as Doctor Governey just reminded her, she'd still have to stop in Chicago to switch trains. Eleanor began fidgeting with the rope still hanging from her waist, recalling how her daddy always spoke ill about the City of Chicago, saying how dangerous and sinful it was...especially after that Bugsy guy killed all those gangsters on Saint Valentine's day a couple years back. But those were *gangsters* killing each other. *Evil* men fighting over cases of smuggled hooch. And heaven knows she had no intention whatsoever of getting mixed up in *that* kind of dangerous goings-on. "I'm sorry, Doctor Governey, but...I'll be alright, really," she answered, twisting the stretched rope. "And I really won't be all alone after all. I have Makara to protect me. I know she don't look like much of a watchdog, but really, she *is*," she insisted, recalling that it was Makara who had alerted her to Jimmy Ray's sexual advances that very early morning, allowing her to retrieve the baseball bat under her bed and knock the drunken bastard out cold. "So you see, Doctor Governey, there's *really* no need to fret about me. I'll be alright...*I promise!*"

Remaining poised despite ever-growing discouragement, Samuel nearly let out a spontaneous snicker, realizing that, regardless of the confidence the young lass placed in the seemingly inept canine, she hadn't the slightest idea of how grateful she actually *should* be, owing to the fact that it was this same prankish pup which had inadvertently saved her from a fate beyond death that very morning. "As you wish, my good lady," he exclaimed while slicing through the choice pink meat of the ham. "We shall proceed with the operation in a little while, then. I certainly hope you do not think it unmannerly that Makara and I take in a bit of nourishment beforehand, though, being that it is already past noon. But I shall be sure to save you some...that is, if you are not feeling *too* indisposed from the surgery afterwards."

Upon realizing that the moment of her operation was finally at hand, Eleanor's stomach began to tighten. Delicious as the ham looked and good as it smelled, her eyes focused only on one particular object, ever so sharp and more precise than any she'd seen in a butcher's market. As the doctor sliced off another thin piece of ham, she wondered what type of surgical instruments he would use while performing the abortion. It seemed strange she didn't know, considering how she'd assisted in all sorts of operations...amputations, tonsillectomies, and an occasional childbirth. There was even that man who got caught up inside a gristmill, she clearly recollected. It was hard to believe that the unconscious farmer, soaked in blood, was still alive. She'd never seen Dr. Gillis so frantic, but after working on him for hours, was finally able to pull him through. Afterwards, they flew his mangled body to St. Louis on a monoplane for a special operation just so he could pee straight. Eleanor grimaced as Samuel rewrapped the ham and returned it to the Frigidaire, leaving the fat-smeared knife upon the butcher block. Although she had attended to all kinds of operations, she never before helped with an abortion...most likely because they were illegal. Paying no attention to Makara as the hungry pup practically adhered to the heels of Samuel's slippers, Eleanor grappled the contorted rope as she pictured herself unconsciously lying upon the long rigid operating table, her naked body covered merely by a thin white sheet, legs spread apart with both feet secured by metal stirrups. Would the doctor use a cervical dilator? Simpson forceps? Clamps? Would it be necessary to use a scalpel? And how would the baby be dispelled? Would it come out in one small clump or in tiny pieces? *Still,* she inwardly acknowledged, in spite of her curiosity, she really didn't want to know.

Eleanor's darkened mood intensified as her speculations were accompanied by a strange melodious sound struggling to make its way inside an open kitchen window. It was the same sound she heard from Doctor Governey's library earlier, she realized, recoiling from the memory. The same awful scratching sound that was going on before the doctor noticed that Makara was digging up his flowers. Feeling overwhelmed by August's unrelenting humidity, she glanced toward the ceiling, wishing that the motionless fan would suddenly activate and whisk away all her fears. Unconsciously letting go of the rope, she started cracking her knuckles, following Samuel's every move as he walked over to the breakfast room closet and returned with soap flakes in hand before filling the sink with sudsy water and leaving the butcher knife to soak. She hoped she wouldn't experience any problems after the abortion, especially seeing that it was past midday now. Otherwise, she would have no choice but to stay overnight. Or, worse yet, she envisioned while spontaneously grasping the tall glass of water, she'd miss boarding the next evening train to Chicago and end up sitting for hours inside Michigan Central's waiting room...unless she was desperate enough to fork over a whole eight dollars at a nearby hotel.

With ham-ladened serving plate securely in hand, Samuel gathered the remaining dishes and silverware from the kitchen counter, carefully balancing them on his way to the table before setting everything down. Retrieving one of the china dishes, he placed upon it a couple slices of ham, then cut them into smaller portions. Impatiently anticipating the disengagement of the pesky pup forever clinging to his feet, he promptly brought the plate near the butcher block, placing it upon the floor aside the small bowl of partially consumed water. Delighted that the dog had been so willing to depart his good company, yet annoyed that he hadn't one crude dish in the house to save his fine Lenox dinnerware from the stinking wet tongue of a scruffy dog, he nevertheless turned toward Eleanor, sporting a cheery smile. "Such a charming little rascal, Miss Snyder! And of what breed is she, may I ask?"

Eleanor released the water glass from her satiated lips and lowered it to her dampened lap. "Well, sir..." she began, recalling how Jimmy Ray tried to coax her into finding the rightful owner, saying that a dog pure bred like this one was bound to belong to somebody. "I'm not sure. She just come to the fillin' station one day and ain't left my side ever since."

Slightly bending toward the pup which was ravenously mauling her lunch, Samuel became unusually pensive, wondering why he had not noticed what should have previously been apparent. "If I am not mistaken, Miss Snyder, I believe your Makara may be a *Rottweiler*," he stated, having become particularly aware of that breed of dog shortly after his harrowing encounter over a decade ago with the German pilot and his two-seated Junker bi-plane bearing the very name of that breed. Taking a closer look at the compact black body and distinctive rust markings, he was certain of his diagnosis, realizing that the Indian name given to the dog by his simple-minded guest was most unsuitable. "I have never seen one, however, with a full tail, being that the owners of such a splendid breed traditionally clip them shortly after birth." Samuel shrugged his shoulders, understanding the historical value of the fully bred Rottweiler, having protected legions of Roman cattle herders from robbers and wild animals as they trudged their way through the German district of Wurttemberg and into the market town of Rottweil. "You were quite correct, then, my dear, to assume that she may be a good watch-dog. But I, personally, would still be wary about placing my confidence in any pup not yet fully grown. Nonetheless," he continued, reseating himself at the table while gesturing toward the pup which was still devouring the ham like it was a last meal, "will you be in a position to afford her upkeep once she reaches maturity?"

As the present conversation delivered her mind from the impending operation, Eleanor's stomach resumed its grumbling while Samuel forked over a thick piece of ham from the serving platter and placed it on his dish. At least the doctor wasn't trying to talk her into taking the stray pup to the police station like Jimmy Ray had tried to get her to do...especially since she just *knew* it didn't belong to anyone else anyway. And, like Doctor Governey said, if someone *had* owned her, she'd probably have her tail clipped, though she couldn't imagine why anyone would ever do such a thing in the first place. She frowned, knowing it was going to be hard to convince the doctor that she *will* be able to take care of Makara, even if the pup lived to be a hundred. "Um...yes, sir...I think I'll be able ta take care of her," she firmly stated as Samuel began slicing the piece of ham for himself. "By the time she's fully growed, I should be makin' enough money ta support us both."

Samuel rested the dinner knife against his plate while dangling the ham-laden fork. "Miss Snyder...please excuse me, but...would you mind *tremendously* if I addressed you as *Eleanor*, or any other name for that matter? *Miss Snyder* seems to be a title *much* too formal for someone to whom I have grown so quickly accustomed. And, if you so wish, you shall address me by my own Christian name, *Samuel*...or simply *Sam*, if it so pleases you."

Eleanor offered the doctor a hesitant smile. Although she was glad he wasn't questioning her again about being able to provide for Makara and was pleased that he wouldn't be addressing her as *Miss Snyder* anymore, she still felt uncomfortable about calling him anything but *Doctor Governey*, being that he was a grown up. It just didn't seem right calling him anything else, knowin' how Daddy always taught her to respect her elders. "Well...sir...I mean...well," she timidly began, placing her depleted water glass back on the table, "I wouldn't mind *at all* if you didn't call me *Miss Snyder* no more. *Eleanor* would be fine, I suppose...though just about everyone, includin' my mama, calls me *Ellie* and my daddy used ta even call me *Ellie Ann*, bein' that *Ann* is my middle name, 'specially when..." Eleanor caught herself before revealing fond memories of her daddy tucking her into bed at night, lest the doctor think that she was still a child. "Anyway," she quickly restated, "I don't mind a bit that you be callin' me by any name ya' like!"

Encouraged at being yet another step closer to his final goal, however nominal, Samuel finished his second piece of ham and chased it down with another sip of water, wishing all the while that his trusted servant, Zachary, had been available to steep for him an invigorating cup of Keemun tea. "Well, then..." he affirmed with a sweep of his empty fork, "*Ellie Ann* it is...or *Ellie*...whichever suits the occasion!" Satisfied that this necessary triviality had been so expeditiously cemented, he then leaned slightly forward, addressing his compliant guest in a more serious tone. "Now, *Ellie*, my dear...I hope you will find it in your heart to forgive me for doubting that an *intelligent* lady such as yourself would be unable to provide the necessary nourishment for her cherished pet, but you must bear in mind that even many of our most *capable* citizens are struggling to keep bread on their tables during these trying times. So please...," he asked in the manner of a little boy eager to find out the contents of a birthday gift, "share with me, if you will, my *dear* Ellie Ann, this special plan which will allow you to overcome such otherwise unavoidable adversities. I won't tell a soul. *I promise,*" he whispered, tracing a cross upon his chest. "It will be our little secret!"

Eleanor remained vigilant. Up until now, she hadn't told anyone where she was heading and wanted to keep it that way so there'd be no chance that Jimmy Ray would be able to hunt her down. But telling Doctor Governey might not be so bad, she reasoned, warily following his every move as he refilled her water glass. After all, he *did* cross his heart and was being friendlier than any doctor she'd ever known...even friendlier than Dr. Gillis or Dr. Blake. And she liked the way he was calling her *Ellie Ann*. It sure sounded better than *Miss Snyder* and, somehow, even reminded her of the way her daddy used to say it. "Well...um...I'm plannin' on heading out west, sir. I'm hopin' ta meet up with a talent agent who'll get me into the talkin' pictures. I know lots of *other* girls are thinkin' the same thing," she quickly added before the doctor could object. "But I'm a really *good* actress." Smiling wistfully, she thought of the late afternoons in Ohio right before supper chores when, alone in the barn, she'd pretend to be Lillian Gish or Clara Bow, throwing both hands up in the air and swooning at the sight of Hattie, the cow, whom she'd designated as the evil villain. When Daddy once caught her, she got embarrassed, but ended up feeling mighty proud when he just stood there with hands on hips and chest all puffed out like a proud peacock, declaring that Mary Pickford may as well give back her Academy Award. "I even brought along a magazine that has some names of directors and the studios they work out of and took my best Sunday frock with me to wear during one of them screen tests they give. But...just in case I don't get discovered *right away*," she clarified before the doctor was able to put in his two cents, "I could still take on another kind of job ta earn my keep." Entwining busy fingers, she raised her ladylike chin. "There's all kind of things I could do for hire. Like...if no hospital could use me ta work in their operatin' room, I could look in the papers ta see if they'd be needin' someone ta do their bookkeepin.' I always did good in 'rithmetic and once when the Wilmington county hospital had their used book sale, I come across some bookkeepin' lessons for 25 cents. It was from the Sears-Roebuck catalog 'cause it still had the wrappings on it, so it never *did* get used. It was even marked five dollars and 75 cents, so I know I got it at a good price. Anyway, I studied it real hard. It took me six whole months ta get through it, but I passed the test at the end. They say if you took one of them classes in college, it would cost a good 50 dollars at least, so I saved lots of money besides." Eleanor defiantly braced herself against the back of the cherrywood chair. "But that'd be *only* 'til I get into the talkin' pictures. After that, it won't matter none if I didn't know nothin' about balancin' any ledger."

Fully aware that it was *he* who may be getting the better of the bargain, Samuel weighed his next few words, forever mindful that the satiated Rottweiler may soon need to go outside and take care of her own personal business. "That is quite an *impressive* plan, Ellie Ann," he began, oscillating his empty fork in mid air while stalking the rambling pup with vigilant eyes, "and an achievable one too, I might add, taking into consideration your talent and beauty. But, my dear...are you prepared to leave Makara behind in a separate baggage car for several days, all cramped up in a wooden crate with only a minimal portion of food as you, yourself, travel in comfort across our expansive country?"

Eleanor's lips bunched together like a discarded candy wrapper as Makara meandered her way toward the bright red tablecloth strewn upon the floor. Of course she wanted to carry the pup with her even if it meant sneaking her inside the burlap sack again, but she knew it would be impossible during such a long journey. And as much as she dreaded the fact that the Rottweiler would be all alone and caged up for a few days, she knew, as special as Makara was, that she'd end up surviving the whole unpleasant ordeal. Besides, she considered before speaking out in her defense, she never did hear of any pets dying of ill-use or starvation while being hauled across country in a railway car. "I...I don't think I have any other choice, Doctor Governey...Sam...Sir," she awkwardly replied as she watched him spear another piece of his noonday meal. "But I know that it'll all be worth it once we reach California." Her strained countenance suddenly softened. "Even my daddy used to say that some things just ain't worth gettin' unless the devil throws his pitchfork in."

Samuel dangled the piece of ham a mere few inches from his lips. "And what about your monetary means, my dear Ellie? A train ticket all the way to California can be quite costly aside from any room and boarding fees you will be compelled to render once you arrive there. Will you have enough money to support such an undertaking after the abortion is paid in full?"

No longer mindful of Makara who was settling within the silky folds of the embroidered tablecloth, Ellie envisioned the tan trench coat still hanging over the chair in Doctor Governey's office. She was glad the coat had deep pockets to safely store the wad of dollar bills she had stolen from Jimmy Ray as well as the golden locket she managed to snatch from Mama's dresser before darting past her drunken, sprawled-out body. She hadn't the chance yet to count all the money, but knew there'd be more than enough for the abortion, bein' that Jimmy Ray didn't trust the banks no more since the stock market up't and crashed. And then, there was always the locket she could hock if need be. Jimmy Ray claimed it was real gold when he gave it to Mama even though he could've been lying just so she'd shack up with him. "I...why, yes, sir...Sam, sir...I mean...Sam," she quickly corrected, aspiring to remain on the friendliest terms with the one person who could help deliver her from a burdened existence. "I had lots of money saved in my piggy bank that I took out before I left this morning."

Quite certain that he was about to trap the unsuspecting little sparrow, Samuel lifted the paper napkin from his lap and patted it across his mouth before speaking again. "So, yes, my dear Ellie Ann...Then I see you have thought this matter through," he asserted, aligning the refolded napkin alongside his Lenox plate. "But, my dear...are you well aware that due to the intricacy involved in such an operation, that it will be quite an expensive procedure?"

"Well...ahhh..." Eleanor hesitated, wishing the doctor would, once and for all, quit addressing her as "my dear," although she *did* understand what he was asking, regardless of such big words. "I know it costs 60 dollars, 'cause that's what my mama'd tell me time and time again. Ever since she found out about me bein' pregnant, she puts it right in my face whenever she'd be cross with me...like it was all *my* fault her boyfriend raped me. That's why I took the money from my piggy bank before leavin' home," she stated with a convincing nod, wishing all the while that she *had* been allowed to store away a few pennies of her own. "And you don't have ta worry about me not havin' enough for my trip neither, she explained with a worrisome look while twitching her foot. "I know I got plenty 'cause I been workin' at hospitals for at least two years now." Ellie dug clenched fists into the folds of her skirt, determined to reassure her gracious host. "So you see...Sam...sir...even though Mama took a good heap of it...of the money, that is, I still saved a few dollars here and there...which all adds up 'fore ya know it!"

Samuel smiled at his determined patient with a tight upper lip. Although he had planned to offer his guest a modest housekeeping position in payment for the abortion, thus delaying her journey, it was obvious at this point in time—whether this elusive ingénue was telling the truth or not—that he would be forced to initiate an alternative tactic or two while continuing to remain in her good graces. "My! How very enterprising of you, Ellie Ann. I am certain that your daddy...God rest his soul...and perhaps your own mother...would be proud of your ability to plan ahead and thus provide for yourself. But tell me, my sweet," he insisted, resolutely moving aside his unfinished lunch, "won't your mother be terribly worried about you, not having the slightest idea of your whereabouts? Perhaps she will notify the police." He glanced at the reposing pup and then back at Eleanor. "They have bloodhounds...their sense of smell much more acute than Makara's that could track your every move all the way to Michigan Central!" Quite pleased that he had ignited fear in the eyes of his prospective bride, he cupped his hand over Eleanor's clenched fists. "But I would never allow such a thing to happen to you," he nearly whispered. "If you agree to stay here for a while, I would fend off any police officers who would happen to stop by, insisting that they were surely mistaken...or," he offered, recalling his unexpected visit from Officer McCallister, "I could maintain that you had come here seeking a housekeeping position, but were well on your way by now. Whichever story you may so choose!"

Eleanor remained unusually quiet for a lingering moment. It felt kind of awkward the way the doctor was pinning her hands to her lap, but still, she secretly hoped he wouldn't let go anytime soon because, in a way, it felt comforting too. Why, if she closed her eyes, she could get herself to believe that Daddy was right there with her again...except, she realized, wrinkling her nose...he wouldn't be smelling like some stinky weed killer or, for that matter, be wearing such a fine gold ring with a sparkly blue stone set in. Immediately returning to her senses, Eleanor considered the doctor's proposition. If it was true that the police were after her, it wouldn't be 'cause Mama was worried, but because she stole all that money from Jimmy Ray. Maybe staying there for a few days, then, *would* be best, she considered, biting into her lower lip. Yet she still wasn't sure if the doctor was telling the truth about the bloodhounds or if he *would* end up lying to the police once they came looking for her. Maybe Doctor Governey thought she shouldn't be running away from home at all and was planning to tell her mama the first chance he got. Or, if she did agree to stay, maybe Mama would end up telephoning the mansion asking if she was there and talk him into telling, bein' that Mama had a way of pullin' the heart from a man the way a bobcat rips the guts out of a fallen deer. "Uh...well...," she began, realizing that if she *was* to catch the evening train, she'd better hurry along. "I really have my heart set on gettin' out ta California soon as I can. So please...*Sam*...I'd be so beholdin' to you if we could hurry along with the abortion. And *really*...cross my heart and hope to die!" she shouted, ready to express her words with the appropriate gesture if only the doctor would uncouple her hands. "You just *have* ta believe me that you really shouldn't worry about my mama cryin' over me none. I just *know* she won't be missin' me and is more'n likely glad that I ain't around ta gettin' in the way of her and Jimmy Ray!"

Offering a sympathetic smile, Samuel tenderly patted Eleanor's restrained hands. "Now, now...I would not be so hasty to arrive at such a harsh conclusion, Ellie Ann. After all, she *is* your mother and no matter what you may think, I would not doubt for a minute that she would be *extremely* distressed over your sudden disappearance." But before he could threaten her further with a probable visit from the police brigade, Eleanor forcefully yanked her hands away.

"My mama never did care a tiddly wink about me!" she blurted, her complexion suddenly changing to a fiery shade of red. "If...if she did...I...I...wouldn't even *be* here!" She used her finger to wipe away a menacing tear. "The only one who *ever* cared about me was my daddy...*he's* the one who would be missin' me. But..." she reached out to accept the paper napkin the doctor was offering. "If my daddy *was* alive, we'd still be livin' in Ohio and Jimmy Ray'd never be allowed ta come within a *mile* of me!" She paused to blow her nose. "Mama didn't care two cents about my daddy, neither; was carrying on with Jimmy Ray any chance she'd get. Would sneak out o' the house leavin' me all alone when Daddy wasn't there or be makin' up stories about havin' ta go into town ta see some doctor 'bout her female troubles." Crushing the dampened napkin between the flattened palms of her hands, she hesitated before speaking. "It was even on account o' her that my daddy died...killed him on purpose too just so she'd get him out of her way! The last time she come sick...*menstrated*...right before Daddy come down with the fever...I seen her washin' her bloody rags in the same tub as Daddy's under-clothes instead o' separate like she ought. Did it on purpose too. I just *know* she did just ta get rid of him!"

Realizing the futility of attempting to convince his superstitious guest that such primitive beliefs were indeed absurd, Samuel waited for Eleanor to erase the last few tears from her eyes before proceeding on to his next plan, noticing all the while that Makara, who had stolen a short nap upon the discarded tablecloth, was presently sniffing a trail toward her distraught mistress. "Perhaps...perhaps, then, I can help calm you with some warm ginger ale before we proceed to the operating room. Would that be to your liking, then, Ellie Ann?"

"Ya know, Doctor Governey," she responded, stormy eyes focused upon the displaced vase of calla lilies, "I can't even visit my daddy, bein' that he's been buried at the church cemetery back in Ohio. Sometimes when I'm feelin' 'specially sad or when his birthday comes around or durin' special holidays and such, I just want ta kneel by his grave so I could talk to him." Inattentive to the whining Rottweiler pawing at her skirt, she prated on. "I heard that some folks get their bodies burned inta ashes after they die and put inta urns. I wish we woulda' done that with my daddy," she woefully stated, returning pining eyes toward Samuel. "That way, I would carry him around wherever I went and talk to him whenever I like." She hesitated before taking a cleansing breath, much too self-absorbed to realize Samuel's concern about the possibility of Makara relieving herself all over his immaculate kitchen floor. "My sixth grade teacher, Mrs. Brodeur, even told us once about some tribe that instead of buryin' or burnin' their kinfolk, they do somethin' to them so they stay lookin' like they did when they were alive. This way they could keep 'em around for good. When I first heard it, I felt kinda' spooked. But now...now sometimes I think that ain't such a bad idea."

"That is all very well and quite possibly true, Ellie Ann," Samuel affirmed, somewhat surprised, yet rather impressed with the young girl's interest in human taxidermy. "However, I think it be best, at this moment in time, that we allow Makara to answer the call of nature. Perhaps," he further offered, alluding to her replenished glass, "you might appreciate a visit to the ladies' room yourself. Come...we will let Makara browse around the garden while I escort you through the hallway."

After opening the beveled door to let Makara out, Samuel promptly assisted Eleanor into the hallway, directing her to the nearest powder room. Then, quickly making his way back into the kitchen, he headed toward the breakfast nook and bolted down the basement stairs, pulling his set of keys from the pocket of his satin robe. With only a dim light at the bottom of the stairs to guide his hurried footsteps, he covered the next few yards with ease, following a path with which he was all too familiar. He stopped for a brief moment to unlock a heavy oak door, reached toward the inside wall and activated a switch, instantly flooding the room with a torrent of fluorescent lighting. Wasting not a second of time, he rushed into the operating room, thrusting the keys back inside his pocket. Upon arriving at the head of the primed operating table, which, under present circumstances, he hadn't the slightest intention of utilizing, he reached into an elevated cabinet, withdrawing a marked apothecary bottle. Then, promptly tucking it inside his other pocket, he immediately left the room and, not even bothering to relock the door, retraced his steps, dashing up the stairs.

Saddled with perspiration and quite out of breath, Samuel entered the kitchen only to find Eleanor already reseated at the table with the Rottweiler's paws propped upon her lap as the pup enthusiastically attempted to lick her face.

"I brung Makara back in before she had the chance to start messin' up your hibiscus again," she explained, noticing the defeated look on the doctor's face. "I knew that was what you'd want me to do."

Feeling like a retiring jockey who just lost his final race to a favored novice, Samuel greeted Eleanor's concern with a fatherly smile as he rambled toward the kitchen cupboards. "How perceptive you are, my dear Ellie Ann! For that is exactly what I had in mind. And I cannot apologize enough for being so *unreceptive* toward her earlier on," he explained while removing a clean glass from the lined shelf, "For it is surely a blessing that since I have made her most cordial acquaintance, she has truly captured my heart!" He placed the etched crystal glass on the counter and started toward the Frigidaire. "If you would like, Ellie Ann, I think I could even arrange for Makara to be at your side during the operation. This way you needn't feel so all alone." Satisfied by the brightened look on her face, he opened the refrigerator and removed a shapely bottle of Vernor's ginger ale, all the while tolerating his patient's outspoken response. Taking the bottle firmly in hand, he walked over to the empty glass, removed a bottle opener from the kitchen drawer and, with his back toward Eleanor, grasped its metal handle and pried open the crowned cap. "Now, Ellie Ann," he tenderly informed the 14-year-old lass while pouring a small amount of the oak-aged brew into the glass, "I haven't any fresh milk to add to the Vernor's, so you must drink it slowly," he warned, reaching into his pocket for the powder-filled receptacle. "Otherwise the bubbles might make you sneeze." As Samuel opened the bottle of chloral hydrate and sprinkled a discernable amount of its contents into the ginger ale, a sudden rush of August wind filtered through the screened window, once again arousing the tainted melody of the gruesome wind chimes.

Without uttering a word, Eleanor gently pushed her beloved pup away from her lap before timidly accepting the drink which was offered. Then, gripping the glass with both hands, hesitated for an extended moment before tilting it onto trusting lips.

chapter 74

In the Bedroom

Eleanor Ann Snyder was ten years old and the cushioned chair at the brand new Ohio Theatre in Columbus felt like a big orange water raft. It was her birthday and she was pretty, all dressed up in ruffles and blue lace with matching ribbons tumbling down wavy, dark brown locks. She was a little princess after all. The little princess Daddy often said she was. And Daddy was there too, floating right beside her, seated next to Mama. It was one of Mama's "good stretches" when she'd been laying off the liquor, so she looked even prettier than Maureen O'Sullivan. There was a big stage in front of them full of musicians playing spellbinding music and a mighty pipe organ rising up to greet them. Then a chorus of ladies with feathery fans danced all the way across the stage until they floated away. But the man playing the organ just stayed in his seat and played on and on, knowing just the right keys to press. The swaying screen that covered the whole back wall of the stage was showing moving pictures of silent film stars like Greta Garbo, Charlie Chaplain and Rudolph Valentino flashing on and off to the happy tune of the organ. A chandelier with flying horses circled overhead like a giant merry-go-round and there was light pouring out of the stars in the ceiling. And the ceiling itself was all red and golden, much prettier than a sunset. Then the stars turned into snowflakes and the flying horses came down and swooped her far away, nearly 60 miles back to the farm in Wilmington. There was snow all around and she felt cold. But it didn't matter 'cause it was Christmas time—her favorite time of year. And instead of wearing the party dress, she was covered from head to toe in boots and a heavy overcoat to block the cutting chill of the deep woods where Daddy and her just come back from chopping down the grandest tree ever. She'd made sure its branches were full and spread apart just right so the ornaments would hang proper-like. Her legs felt heavy as she dragged the Douglas fir along the planked floor of the farmhouse, filling the whole room with the smell of pine. Mama was right there, too, standing by the kitchen table next to the pot belly stove, reaching out with a steaming cup of hot chocolate. Daddy had closed the door behind them, but the wind was still coming through; an *annoying* wind that kept blowing at her face. Ellie turned her head and felt a softness against her cheeks. Something tangible. But the wind was still ruffling her hair. She looked toward the door and noticed it was open—wide open—letting in the cold, drifting snow. She extended her hand to close it, but it wouldn't budge. The softness against her cheeks distracted her. She opened her eyes and looked about. She opened them again. Slowly. The breeze wasn't coming from an open door. It was from the corner of the room. *Another* room. A *strange* room. From a small electric fan strategically positioned behind a deep metal tray accommodating a melting block of ice. And the softness against her face was from the satin casing of a large pillow—the pillow upon which she had been dreaming.

Somewhat stupefied, Eleanor pressed her elbows into the cushiony mattress and struggled to sit upright as she began to realize that Doctor Governey must have slipped some kind of sedative inside the ginger ale, all the while wondering, amid the room's warm comforting light, how long she had been sleeping. Fragments of the reminiscent dream—especially the strong, pungent smell of the Christmas tree—still lingered in her memory as she continued her journey back to consciousness. Lethargically sweeping a strand of disheveled hair from her cheek, she perceived something strange; it was not the scent of pine which had been lingering about, but the unmistakable, unpleasant weed-killing odor belonging to the doctor. And now it was clinging to her clothes. It must have rubbed off as Doctor Governey carried her into the bedroom. *But...maybe?...* Instinctively, her hand reached toward her abdomen. Did the odor rub off his hands and into the pores of her skin as he was giving her the abortion? A disquieting feeling washed over her like a deep, dark wave as she envisioned a sudden emptiness in her womb, but the hasty perception was immediately tempered by a peculiar inkling of relief. Something didn't seem quite right, she quickly realized, clumsily pushing away a satin sheet. She still felt a bit nauseous as she had intermittently during the pregnancy. *And*...gradually gaining control of her faculties, she gathered her skirt up to her thighs and groped the bottom of her undergarments, confused by the absence of a surgical pad to absorb any post-operative bleeding. She was dry. If the doctor *had* given her the abortion, shouldn't there be some bleeding? There always *was* after a woman had a baby. But maybe an abortion this early was different. Perhaps Doctor Governey was able to clean all the blood out of her right away. *Or*...suddenly abandoning the fixation on her lower body, Eleanor cupped both hands to her clothed bosom, realizing that the tenderness she'd been experiencing the last couple of weeks had not subsided. Her sedated eyes, adjusting their way further into reality, refocused upon her abdomen as an apparent feeling of solace began to cleanse her mind. *Yes!*...she was sure of it now, she sighed, attempting to grasp the significance of it all. Her body hadn't changed one bit, so it just *had* to be true...Doctor Governey never *did* give her the abortion. As that final realization began sinking in, a growing angst gnawed at the pit of her stomach. What was she to do now? Was it too late to catch the train to Chicago? *Should* she still try and catch the train to Chicago? And how would she manage to arrange for another abortion once she got to California?

Feeling as if the mattress was wavering beneath her legs, Ellie raised her head, straining to focus beyond the confines of the massive four poster bed. Her stomach growled; the last meal she'd eaten was the week-old stew she had heated up for supper the night before. Cautiously, she scooted her way toward the right side of the bed, all the while seeming as if she were slipping into another dream. The room was so big—it even looked bigger than Robert Bolder and Gloria Swanson's bedroom suite in *Beyond the Rocks!* And it had just as much beautiful furniture in it too!

Feeling like a beggar mistakenly forgotten within a king's chambers, Eleanor squinted as she continued to digest the surrounding ambience softly illuminated by the dwindling rays of a late afternoon sun escaping past drawn velvet curtains. Could it be that this was the master bedroom? It just *had* to be, she concluded while scanning an expansive mirror belonging to a mahogany wardrobe at the opposite end of the room. There couldn't possibly be any bedrooms bigger than this one—not even in a castle! But why would Doctor Governey allow her to sleep in *his* room? Wouldn't a mansion like this have rooms for *servants* that she could have used? And *why* hadn't he given her the abortion? Was it because it was much too early and he feared for her well being? Momentarily regretting that she may have doubled her bad luck by yawning without covering her mouth and then getting out of the wrong side of bed that awful June morning when Jimmy Ray raped her, Ellie clamped her lips while, this time, she slid off the right side of the downy mattress, her stocking feet finally reaching the carpeted floor.

Within a few feet sat a tufted armchair, its slim, graceful back partially covered by the cotton twill raincoat; upon its rose colored seat rested her sunhat atop the neatly folded burlap sack, and stashed underneath the chair was her traveling bag. Her shoes, unnoticeably polished amidst the absence of bright light, rested between the spooled stretchers of an adjacent mahogany table. Trusting that Makara was still in the kitchen where Doctor Governey could keep an eye on her, Eleanor hastened with an unsteady gait toward the walnut wing armchair. Was the wad of dollar bills and the gold necklace still inside her coat pocket? Or had the doctor discovered and removed them? Inadvertently reaching into the wrong pocket, she felt the oily napkin which encased the crumbled remains of the cornbread she had snatched from Mama's kitchen breadbox early that morning. Paying no attention as her stomach cried on cue, she tossed the sunhat on the floor, rested one knee upon the burlap sack and pulled the other pocket toward her, breathing a sigh of relief upon discovering that both the gold locket *and* the wad of dollar bills was still intact. Repositioning herself upon the burlap sack to gain better access of the room's soft light, she removed the cheap tin money clip and proceeded to count the dollar bills. Not that she suspected the doctor had stolen any...she could tell by its bulk that it was all there...but ever since she'd snatched the money from Jimmy Ray's trousers, she hadn't the chance to count it, being it was way too dark while hiding in the shed that morning as well as when she'd set out to catch the first bus leaving from Dearborn. And then, after sunrise, she'd been too afraid that somebody might notice her with it all and either try to rob her or, worse yet, become suspicious and get hold of the police.

Unaware that her weakened legs were regaining their steadiness by the second, Eleanor continued to count the thick pack of money, her heart growing lighter as every few bills or so increased in their denomination. "Yes!" she blurted aloud, smiling ear to ear. She had known there'd be enough for the abortion and at *least* a one-way ticket to Chicago, but never really suspected there'd be a whole $342! Why...by the time she paid the cross country train fare to California and found another doctor to give her the abortion, there should be enough left over for her to live on 'til she got an acting job. And she wouldn't even have to hock Mama's gold locket after all! Eleanor pushed the money clip over the dollar bills, the corners of her mouth beginning to droop. If she *was* able to catch a train tonight and eventually get all the way to California, how would she know where to find a doctor who would give her a real abortion? Maybe Doctor Governey would know of someone in Hollywood who'd be able to do it. *But then*, she questioned, jutting pouted lips, maybe he'd give her a hard time again about leaving this late and try to talk her into staying. Maybe it'd be better if she didn't ask any questions and just left without his knowing and worried about the matter after settling in a place of her own. But first, she'd have to get Makara, she decided, quickly swooping her shoes from the carpet. Hopefully the pup was sleeping in the kitchen while the doctor was in another room. Then, she could sneak in there and quietly leave out the back door. It was a trifle unlikely, she thought, fumbling with the laces of her shoes. But it was sure worth a try.

Feeling more in control of her senses as she tightened a lopsided shoe-string, Eleanor plopped the hat on top her head, stuffed the burlap sack within the arm of the trench coat and flung the oversized garment across her forearm. Picking up the traveling bag, she cautiously crept toward the entrance of the bedroom, her eyes full of wonder as a broadening light revealed intricate craftsmanship and rich interior design. Spontaneously moving in step to the rhythmic hum of the electric fan fading from behind, she tiptoed her way past a mahogany chifforobe, curiously eyeing a bright-ened arched alcove several feet ahead. But her determined pace soon slowed to a halt upon reaching the doorless entryway which she immediately peered through...the warm revealing light of a boudoir lamp inviting her to step inside.

It wasn't the generous dimensions of the fully-furnished dressing room or the lace-ribboned packages placed upon the embossed dressing table which first caught her attention...or even the sweet smell of assorted fruits inside a bowl of sterling silver. It was the gown. A beautiful shiny satin gown like "the blonde bombshell," Jean Harlow would wear. And it was red too. Deep red. Like a long sweeping rose gracing a golden trellis. Eleanor dropped the traveling bag and coat upon the polished hardwood floor and reverently stepped toward the brocade chaise lounge, unconcerned that the bottom of her traveling shoes might soil the circular ivory carpet. The low-cut gown which lay across the lounging chair looked just her size. And the fabric seemed even finer close up than when she had stood at the doorway. Holding her breath, she reached toward the gown, no longer feeling the weight of her own hand as she glided her fingers along its skirt, her strong nails leaving blunt trails which disappeared as quickly as they had surfaced. She was glad it wasn't wintertime after all, she thought, fondling the silky fabric between her thumb and forefinger. Otherwise her skin would be too rough and she'd spoil the dress for sure...like shortly after Saint Valentine's day when she tried on the real silk stockings Jimmy Ray gave Mama, she recollected with a shiver, and her weather-beaten hands put terrible snags all over them. She'd snuck them over to the hospital and got rid of them in the incinerator before Mama realized they were missing, but ended up getting a good ass-whooping for it just the same.

Like a stubborn icicle clinging to its source, Eleanor's fingers suddenly froze to the gown's fabric. What if Doctor Governey had molested her like Jimmy Ray had done, except this time she wouldn't have known it because she was unconscious from the medicine? And how long had she been asleep anyway? Four...five hours? Eleanor released the gown as quickly as she had bonded to it, crossing both arms to her chest, digging lackluster nails into the tendons of her upper arms. Her fearful eyes focused on the lace-ribboned packages while shaking her head. No...it just couldn't be true, she rationalized, her mind slipping back to the horrendous night when Jimmy Ray brutally had his way with her...his forceful, calloused hands pinning her down...smothering both breasts as she wrenched her neck to avoid his whiskey-stinking kisses and smoke-stained teeth...those coarse, stubby fingers squeezing the life from her tender nipples as if tightening a pair of bolts on a set of used tire rims...the horrible, ripping pain as he finally broke into her, pushing and pounding with a sickening, ongoing pleasure until every naked inch of her body had been brutally robbed of its short-lived innocence. Eleanor briskly rubbed her hands along her upper arms, focusing upon the wrapped packages as if her life depended on them. God-darn it, that Jimmy Ray for getting her all worked up again! And having her believe for even one moment that a real gentleman like Doctor Governey would even *think* of doing such a thing, let alone while she'd been asleep! She grimaced, vehemently regretting that she had given Jimmy Ray the sadistic satisfaction of watching her struggle...envisioning the stinging gleam of desire in his maniacal eyes as she remained completely powerless to block from her acute sense of hearing his sickening groans and vulgar screams of pleasure. But she had not cried. She *would* not cry. No matter how much he had hurt her, it was the one thing he *wasn't* able to take from her that night. *Besides*...she resolved, defiantly correcting slumped shoulders while taking a long, deep breath...after Jimmy Ray had gotten his way with her, she was feeling sore for days and *now* she wasn't aching one single bit. And there wasn't a trace of blood on her undergarments or running down the inside of her legs either, like there was right after. And to think that she believed for even one single moment that a respectable man like Doctor Governey would be capable of such an ugly thing!

It was ridiculous, she pouted, relaxing numbed arms and shrugging eased shoulders while feeling guilty for ever entertaining such thoughts. And what about the wrapped gifts on the dressing table? Certainly, they were meant for her as surely as the red evening gown. But why? she wondered, remembering that the only present she ever got from Jimmy Ray was an opened box of caramel truffles that Mama never finished for fear of spoiling her figure...aside from a book of paper cut-out dolls he'd won at the Ohio State Fair for shooting down a row of ducks. He even left her favorite two-wheel bicycle behind in Wilmington, claiming there was no more room on the truck. *No*...she decided with a sheepish smile. Doctor Governey was nothing near like Jimmy Ray. He was just trying his best to make her feel better about not getting the abortion—a generous man taking pleasure in sharing his wealth with a poor young farm girl like her. And hadn't Dr. Blake spoken kindly of him, too, declaring he was the best physician around and would treat her like his own daughter? A kind and thoughtful gentleman like her daddy...that's what Doctor Governey was...only a heap richer.

Feeling like an apprehensive child whose questionable virtue had been validated by the abundance of gifts awarded by a jolly Kriss Kringle, Eleanor abandoned the exquisite evening gown and eagerly began stepping toward the ribboned packages when a sudden, overwhelming dizziness compelled her to peel off the stifling sunhat and plop her famished body straight down upon the floor. Immediately lowering her head between the knees, she lingered for a sobering moment before recollecting the tray of fruit and other nourishment purposely set upon a butler tray which she had, up until now, foolishly ignored. Still feeling slightly dizzy, she slowly lifted her head and pushed the loose, dark strands of hair from her face, focusing on the velvet cushioned side chair standing alongside the butler tray. Then, after taking a long, deep breath, she forced herself from the floor and cautiously balanced her way toward it.

Bracing her weakened spine against the chair's scrolled back, Eleanor wetted dry lips while focusing upon the inviting feast which lay before her...a silver bowl laden with fruit...a painted tray brimming with cheeses and crackers...some miniature cakes set upon a doily-lined dish...a lidded bucket with shapely handles *and*...alongside all that...a set of the doctor's kitchen dishes and a glass, all sparkling clean aside a real linen napkin neatly folded underneath a silver knife and fork. Eleanor leaned over and removed the lid from the bucket, exposing an unopened bottle of Vernor's ginger ale and a smaller bottle of milk resting atop a thick layer of chipped ice. She should have known, she thought, managing to break a feeble smile. Since she only swallowed a small amount before the supposed operation, Doctor Governey was making amends by offering a full bottle now. And he'd even been thoughtful enough to include some fresh milk to tame down the bubbles. A trace of concern crossed Ellie's pallid face when she eyed a key-shaped bottle opener. As much as she craved the gingery drink, she just felt too weak to unlatch its sturdy cap. The cherries looked handy enough, though. Perhaps if she started with some of those, she'd soon feel strong enough to open the Vernor's after all.

Anticipating the thought of indulging in her favorite soda, Eleanor reached toward the silver bowl and began fumbling through several plump cherries, each smooth, rounded surface recalling fond memories of those carefree days on the farm when she went with Daddy to old man Colgan's orchard just a quarter mile down the road. Since Colgan was a childless widower, keeping up the orchard had been his hobby and he gladly welcomed the company of friendly neighbors. There were all kinds of fruit trees to be had, but her favorite was the cherry tree which grew right smack in the middle of them all. It was the tallest tree too and the most fun to climb...especially in her bare feet. Eleanor lingered for a moment, picturing Daddy in his Levi overalls holding a large pail to collect all the pickings. Daddy had been afraid at first to let her climb the tree and had hesitated to boost her up so she could reach its thick, leafy branches. But it wasn't long before he got used to the idea and even swore she must have taken lessons from a monkey before him and Mama plucked her straight out of the jungle. And she even believed him for a while until she'd been told by that know-it-all Ricky Watson where babies really *did* come from. "Your Mama and Daddy both get naked and rub up 'gainst each other," he declared in his haughty eight-year-old voice. "...just like the animals do durin' matin' season. That's how you was born," he pronounced all high and mighty-like. "You growed inside your mama and then come out just like a calf newly borned." She didn't believe him at first and even told him so. But then when she asked Daddy about the birthing part and he said not to worry her pretty little head about such *a*-dult things, she suspected it might be true...especially since he never mentioned them jungle monkeys no more.

As Eleanor scooped up a handful of the stemmed cherries, her wistful smile changed to a frown. The very last time she climbed that tree, she caught Mama and Jimmy Ray matin' just like Ricky Watson said. It was the beginning of spring and school was let out early that afternoon because the schoolmarm suddenly took sick. So, instead of going straight home like the teacher said, she headed on down to old man Colgan's orchard to avoid any extra farm chores Mama was bound to give. But she'd barely finished climbing to the sturdiest top branch of the cherry tree before hearing some grown folks laughing. Being careful not to rustle any leaves for fear of being discovered, she was surprised to see Mama and a man she first thought was Daddy...until he turned around...and that was the very first time she ever saw the likes of Jimmy Ray. Eleanor winced, squeezing the cherries within the palm of her hand as much as her weakened grasp could endure. Before she could erase them from her mind, repulsive images of that afternoon blustered through her like a cold March wind...Jimmy Ray running after Mama, playfully pushing her down on the grass, unbuttoning the front of her polka-dotted housecoat until her brassiere burst through like a bulging sanitary bandage...Mama teasin' and leadin' him on as she squirmed like a nightcrawler freshly caught, all the while allowin' Jimmy Ray to kiss her, his slobbering lips smearin' Mama's red lipstick 'til she looked like some sort o' circus clown...Jimmy Ray's groping hands yanking the brassiere from Mama's bosom and kneading her breasts as if they were two giant dough balls ready to be rolled...Mama's polished fingernails clawing at Jimmy Ray's zippered trousers, all the while allowin' him to push up her skirt and yank off her panties, both of them breathin' so heavy you'd swear they was being chased by a grizzly bear. And the long, drawn-out cries, like pleasure and pain all struggling at once to escape from a slippery pit, seemed almost inhuman. Or much *too* human. *Either* way, Ellie winced, it all seemed *so* unreal...Mama like a wildcat in heat and Jimmy Ray...Jimmy Ray like the devil himself hootin' and howlin' as if he'd just gathered up a stockpile of lost souls.

Eleanor continued staring at the handful of squeezed cherries as if gazing into a crystal ball. Although it had been the very first time she'd witnessed such behavior and found it, for the *most* part disgusting, she still couldn't will herself to look away, being it was all so fascinating at the same time. *Sure*, she was used to the animals at the farm mountin' each other every now and then and would hear Daddy groan sometimes after everyone was supposed to be fast asleep, but she still somehow believed that matin' was a thing only *animals* did and Daddy...well, she figured that Daddy was just suffering from some grownup pain that felt much better by the time morning came. All of a sudden feeling a pressure on her lower spine, Eleanor shuddered while straightening her back, making a conscious effort to once again brace herself against the walnut chair. How Mama could ever let that bastard Jimmy Ray even *touch* her, let alone cheapen her with kisses and then be screamin' with pleasure as he kept shovin' that 'snake of a thing' inside her was something she would never be able to understand, even if she lived to be as old as the Ohio River. And the animal-like groans that be comin' out of Jimmy Ray's own trashy-talkin' mouth...like a sickenin', drawn-out rumble of thunder that finally throwed up. She'd *always* recognize them filthy, sickening groans, along with that raspy, caterwauling voice of his—even if she'd be hearin' it miles away. Eleanor's frail body spontaneously shivered, cautioning her to redirect her musings elsewhere. It was a miracle that Mama didn't get herself knocked up with *triplets* after all of that, she contemplated, even though she knew by now that babies didn't get made *every* time.

Intentionally recalling the decorated packages she had yet to open, Eleanor slumped forward and let go of the smashed cherries, allowing the sweet black orbs to fall back into the silver bowl. Then, after closing her eyes for nearly a minute and whispering to ten in order to wipe away any more disturbing thoughts, she slackened her fingers and reached toward the plate of cheese and crackers Doctor Governey had provided, all the while anticipating a soothing glass of ginger ale to help wash everything down.

chapter *75*

Indulgence

Whisking away the last trace of crumbs from the lap of her wrinkled cotton skirt, Eleanor eyed a plump red peach in the silver bowl of uneaten fruit, wondering if there was any more room in her stomach to accommodate it. She had already eaten a few pieces of cheese and probably a half dozen crackers, as well as several servings of the miniature frosted cakes...and that wasn't even counting the tall glass of Vernor's which seemed to be bloating her stomach even more. But the peach looked so *good*. And she'd caught its juicy smell ever since walking into the dressing room. Besides...Doctor Governey had gone through the trouble of arranging all that fruit and she hadn't yet returned the courtesy by eating even so much as the smallest grape.

Eleanor extended her arm and grasped the ripened piece of fruit, barely gripping it within the palm of her hand. Using the fingers of her other hand to support it, she bit into its soft fuzzy flesh, all the while inhaling its irresistible sweetness as it pushed against the narrow bridge of her nose. Detecting a sudden trickle of juice running down her chin, she hesitated to grab the unused, crisp linen napkin. Up until now, she felt it a shame to dirty anything so pretty, but there was really no other choice. Quickly placing the moist peach upon a china plate, she yanked the napkin from beneath the glistening silverware, causing the knife and fork to spill upon the hard surface of the butler's table, the cacophonous clatter simultaneously merging with a high-pitched sound emanating from the corridor. Eleanor listened in wonder at the more distant sound as she wiped the linen napkin along the graceful curve of her neck. The noise resembled the chimes of a clock, similar to the chimes of the grandfather clock in Doctor Governey's entrance hall. Pressing the napkin to her mouth, she listened intently as its melody rang out, signaling the prelude to ushering in the new hour, then causing her to feel more and more apprehensive with each successive, solitary ring. *One...two...three...four...five...*followed only by the echo of silence. Having already felt the fine hairs on her forearms begin to bristle at the stroke of four, Eleanor shot up from her chair and flung the crinkled napkin onto the table. "Damn!"...here she was...whittling away her own sweet time, chompin' like some prize heifer grazing in a pasture and now she might be missin' the last train to Chicago! Jerking her head to the left, she noticed her traveling bag and coat still on the floor near the entrance of the room, exactly where she had left them. With a bit of panic, she plucked her discarded straw hat from the floor and began to move toward the arched entrance, suddenly stopping midway. *Oh, my gosh...the gifts!* She never took the time to open those beautiful packages! Her confused mind reeling like a cinematic projector, Eleanor considered the possibility of stuffing the three colorfully wrapped presents into the beaten leather bag before sensing that not even one would fit along with the things she already packed for her upcoming journey. Still detecting a faint, monotone echo in the hallway, she regretfully abandoned the alluring packages, quickly swooping up the raincoat and traveling bag as she proceeded on, her distracted eyes barely able to keep up with her quickened pace.

chapter 76

Eavesdropping

Feeling somewhat like a cat burglar on a precarious prowl, Eleanor tiptoed through the long, oak-scented corridor, unconsciously
scrunching the sunhat with her right hand while carrying the coat-
draped traveling bag with the other, her narrow vision gradually adjusting to
the surrounding lack of light. At least the floorboards weren't creaking, she
panted, continuing to navigate her way across the planked, polished wood.
Otherwise, she might give herself away. And it was bad enough that, by now,
the police might be tracking her down with them bloodhounds Doctor
Governey was talking about. Her ears practically smarting from a million and
one heartbeats which muffled the ticking of the corridor mantel clock,
Eleanor tried to focus upon the increasing light at the far end of the hall that
timidly illuminated a wide open platform and the beginnings of what looked
like a carpeted staircase. If the master bedroom was set in front of the mansion, she reasoned, and that's where she was coming from, then the kitchen
should be near the bottom of the approaching stairway where, hopefully, she
could steal Makara away and get them both the heck out of there! But her
unflagging determination soon turned to confusion as she stepped onto the
wide open landing, her puzzled gaze spiraling across the full length of a long,
winding staircase which led to no other than the mansion's grand foyer.
Eleanor began to quiver, anxiously considering her options. She could fum-
ble her way back through the darkened hallway, which would probably be the
safest route, or she could take her chances and descend the front stairway,

knowing for certain just where the kitchen would be. But before she could make up her mind, the sound of elegant chimes accompanied by a loud knock alerted her to the fact that someone had come calling at the front door.

Detecting the sound of footsteps quickly pacing toward the foyer, Ellie crouched against a far wall, out of sight, yet still able to view through thick oak rails the full expanse of the entranceway. Pushing clammy palms together and crossing her fingers while wishing with every thumping beat of her heart that her labored breathing wouldn't give her away, she became further mesmerized as Samuel, dressed in a white starched shirt, sleek suspendered trousers and polished wing-tip shoes, promptly answered the door, beckoning the visiting police officer to step inside.

"And a very good evening to you, my dear Sergeant McCallister," she heard Samuel respond as he closed the door, realizing, as the doctor pulled a bulky envelope from his trouser pocket, that the officer was none other than the good friend who had paid him a backyard visit earlier that morning.

"Top of the evening to ya, Sam," McCallister buoyantly replied, stuffing the envelope inside his jacket pocket, yet awkwardly stalling with cap still in hand. "But before I be on my way...there's somethin' I'm beholdin' ta ask of ya." Apprehensively responding to Samuel's questioning eyes, he continued. "We just received a call from the Dearborn sheriff's office," he finally blurted, rubbing both thumbs upon the rim of the cap. "Seems there's a lass gone missin' from that side o' town. Word's got it she's nabbed a good three-and-a-half hundred smackers from her ma's ol' man an' a genuine gold necklace. As a matter o' fact," he cautiously went on, "her description fits that o' the young lass that be visitin' ya this very mornin'. And I'll be a monkey's uncle if I be mistakin,' but...they say the lass be carryin' a black pup along...a lot like the one that was disturbin' the flowers in yer garden. Except...." McCallister quickly clarified, "they say she'd most likely be wearin' the old man's raincoat and a large straw sunhat her ma had suddenly been missin.' Not that I'm implyin' ya know anything about this lass skippin' town, now, but I was hopin' ya might be able ta tell me in what direction yer young visitor may be headed, bein' that she seems ta be fittin' the description."

Eleanor recoiled further against the wall, wondering if it was possible to retreat, sight unseen, back through the hallway and down the stairs which should lead into the kitchen before Doctor Governey and the officer went looking for her. But before she could even comprehend the difficulty of dragging her belongings while being compelled to crawl unnoticed toward the hallway entrance, she immediately reconsidered.

"Of *course*, my dear Sergeant McCallister," Samuel's assured voice echoed as it spiraled up the carpeted staircase, "I can very well understand your concern, being that the young lady in question certainly fits the description you so accurately depicted. However, I am sorry to report that I promptly dismissed the young lass soon after your departure and haven't the slightest notion *where* she might be headed. I suppose...," he bluffed, lifting an elbow to glance at his jeweled Bulova wristwatch, "she may very well have reached Kentucky by now if heading down South, or perhaps...perhaps she had taken up the notion of traveling westward to seek either fame, fortune or folly. Nonetheless," he shrugged before relaxing his arms along the flared lines of his impeccably tailored trousers, "I can't imagine why she would have initially sought a housekeeping position *here*. But that is neither fish nor fowl. The fact of the matter is that the young lass has most likely slipped through our fingers and, at this point, it would probably require a trailer full of *bloodhounds* to track her down."

As the grandfather clock struck the quarter hour, Eleanor kneaded the straw hat with both hands, all the while keeping a close watch on Samuel as he bid the sergeant goodbye and eventually departed the quieted foyer. So it was *true* then, she thought, gently biting into her lower lip. Doctor Governey *was* telling the truth when he promised not to tell on her—even when finding out that she stole all of Jimmy Ray's money and Mama's locket. But...even so...where did that leave her now? If the coppers *were* out looking for her, did she still have the chance to get away? *Should* she still try and run away? And what about Makara? Where was her missing pup? Was she still in the kitchen? And if she was, why didn't she come running when the officer came to the door? Was it because she was still sound asleep? Or maybe the kitchen doors were closed so she couldn't hear anything. But then again, Eleanor continued to guess, wiping beads of perspiration from her slender brow...maybe she wasn't in the kitchen after all...maybe Doctor Governey had her with him in his study. Whatever the reason, she sighed, slumping back against the wall while dropping the straw hat into her lap, she was certain that Makara was being well taken care of...just like Doctor Governey had been looking after *her*. Eleanor glanced upward with a surrendering frown, noticing that the stained glass windows hovering high above the entranceway were beginning to lose their brilliance. Even if she did happen to get away without bein' caught, chances were she'd have to wait at the station until morning to catch the next train. Perhaps it would be best, then, if she spent the night after all. Or at least for a couple of days until the search for her let off a bit...that *is*, if Doctor Governey was willing to let her stay on. And *besides*, she gathered, welcoming the tingle which suddenly overtook the numbness in her legs, inasmuch as she was itchin' to start making a name in Hollywood, it really *would* be a shame to never know what was in all them presents that Doctor Governey went through the trouble of buying for her. As if nonchalantly excusing herself from Sunday supper, Eleanor hoisted herself forward, looking down into the unoccupied foyer. Then, certain of being undetected, tucked the straw hat beneath her wet underarm, plopped the coat over the traveling bag and grabbed the worn handle before standing upright, all the more grateful of her decision as she finally began making her way down the hallway, bearing in mind the bedroom's adjoining bathroom where she could conveniently empty her strained bladder.

chapter 77

Ruminations

Balancing barefoot upon bright patterned tiles with a thick white towel securely wrapped around a freshly washed head of raven hair, Eleanor slipped off the last of her undergarments and tossed it atop the pile of dirty clothes alongside the porcelain bathtub. She practically giggled. It was such a good thing that she entered the bathroom to answer the call of nature, she thought, peeking inside the tub to see how far the bubbly water was rising. Otherwise, she wouldn't have noticed the fluffy pink bathrobe and slippers that Doctor Governey had laid out for her, along with the bath crystals, Breck shampoo and Ivory soap she'd always wanted to try. And if that were not enough, now that she was about to bathe herself, she'd be able to try on that red evening gown without getting it all soiled! Impatiently waiting for the tub to fill so that she could finally immerse herself in a sea of frothy, lilac-scented clouds, she scanned the pretty blue and yellow Pewabic tiles gracefully ornamenting the domed ceiling and arched windows, eventually catching a glimpse of herself in the sparkling clear glass of the beveled shower door. Her light olive tone seemed to melt into the glass, further accentuating dark pubic hair and rosy brown nipples. Looking down at her abdomen, she released a silent gasp. Was her belly really starting to swell or was it just her imagination? Instinctively cradling both hands over her stomach, a wondrous feeling swept over her, reminiscent of visits with her daddy to Wilmington's Church of Christ on occasional Sunday mornings. Except this time, instead of Mama not being with them, something else seemed to be missing. *It's the baby*, she realized, sensing goose bumps running up and down her forearms. *After the abortion, the baby will be gone forever.* Eleanor curled her fingers, tenderly digging into the firm flesh of her belly. Why did it have to be Jimmy Ray's? And why did the pregnancy have to happen now? She *did* want a baby of her own someday, but only after she got married. And not just only one. Her babies were gonna have brothers and sisters to play with...unlike when *she* was growing up. Just 'cause her mama never had more babies—always complaining about how much pain she went through during childbirth—didn't mean a doggone thing. There were lots of other mamas, some having upwards of a dozen kids, and they seemed to be doing just fine. And her babies wouldn't have to grow up being poor, neither. After she became a famous film star, her husband and kids could live in a mansion like this someday, each having their own bedroom with attached bathroom too. But before Eleanor could continue on with her reflections, a glance in the direction of the bathtub caused her to rush forward to turn off its gilded faucet, arresting undulating mounds of glistening white bubbles.

Feeling like a scoop of vanilla ice cream melting inside a large, frothy soda, Eleanor delayed her bathing ritual as she closed weary eyes and leaned a towel-wrapped head against the moistened tiled wall for one long, luxurious moment, reveling in the soothing coolness of the tepid water. Although she wasn't due for her weekly bath yet, being it was only Monday, it was just as well to be taking one now, she tenderly smiled. Not only had she gotten all sweaty and smelly from wearing Jimmy Ray's coat and carrying Makara while walking to the mansion, but she was anxious to get rid of the weed-killing smell that rubbed off Doctor Governey when he carried her upstairs to the bedroom...nothing that a good bottle of shampoo and a bar of soap wouldn't get rid of, she determined, still thoroughly enjoying the pure clean smell of the Breck shampoo she had used just a few minutes ago.

Purposely stalling for a while before washing herself, Eleanor could feel the bubbles popping along the pores of her skin as she slowly stirred her arms and legs, allowing the water to gently caress her body. As each soothing wave rolled across her stomach, once more she began to ponder about the new life forming inside her, submerged in its own tranquil water, her mind drifting back to the day she had waited out a thunderstorm in the Wilmington hospital library after her nursing shift was over. A certain book with the word *gestation* on its spine had caught her eye because, at first glance, it looked like *gas station* and at the time, Mama was planning on moving them to Michigan so Jimmy Ray could buy his own. Still wondering what the word *gestation* was, she had removed the book from the shelf and began leafing through its illustrated pages, captivated by pictures of tiny babies all curled up in the womb, some no older than three or four weeks of age. She was surprised to learn how early each tiny heart would start to beat and how easy it was to tell where the eyes and ears were starting to form, wondering all the while if these little ones were able to detect the dimmest light or hear the slightest sound.

Eleanor opened her eyes and reached for the unwrapped bar of Ivory soap at the edge of the tub. It felt unusually light and airy, she noticed before lurching forward as it slipped through her fingers. Attempting to retrieve the bar of soap before it had the chance to sink its way into oblivion, an air of relief along with profound fascination swept over her as it spontaneously began to float, seeming to take on a vibrant life of its own. As if mesmerized by a gypsy's spell, she watched while it bobbed through dwindling bubbles, reminding her all the more of the evolving life within her. Might the baby be floating around like that inside her womb? Would it weigh anything at all if she held it in the palm of her hand? And what about the feeling of relief she had just experienced as the soap began to float, somewhat like that of her initial reaction upon discovering that the abortion *hadn't* taken place after all? Did all this mean she really *didn't* want to have the abortion? With outstretched arms, she leaned forward and reeled in the bar of soap, recalling the radio advertisements she had heard from time to time about the "soap that floats" being ninety-nine and 44/100 percent pure, wondering at the same time what the other 56/100 percent could be made of. Gliding the lathering bar up and down her arm, she questioned the purity of the cheap, antiseptic soap that Mama had her bathe with. Not like the pretty rose-scented soaps that Mama herself used, she frowned—always making sure she kept the best things for herself. Of course, should she expect any different from a mother who was still carrying on with the man who had raped and knocked-up her own daughter? *Blamin' me for it instead...sayin' I was askin' for it all along. Like I'd want anything to do with that two-faced grease monkey!* Impetuously switching the Ivory soap to the other hand, Eleanor began to lather her right arm, vigorously working up the shoulder while easing the pressure over her chest, mindful of the tenderness she was experiencing lately. *Probably getting ready for suckling*, she pondered, eyeing darkened nipples, though not yet noticing any difference in the size of either breast. For one brief instant a memory flashed before her—she remembered many years back when Daddy held her up against the barnyard fence, pointing out a flock of newborn lambs suckling the teats of a mother ewe. Gently massaging her bosom with the soap, she wondered how it would feel to nurse her own baby, its tiny mouth alternately tugging at each abundant, life-sustaining nipple.

With soap still in hand, Eleanor crossed both arms to her chest as she entertained another recollection...one that had entered her mind occasionally but up until now was conveniently disregarded. She couldn't exactly remember when and under what circumstances she received the information, but it definitely came from the lips of her best friend, Phyllis Becker. But whether or not she had heard of the shameful situation as they sat upon the Becker's front porch swing or during their usual two-mile walk from school, it really didn't matter. She remembered it just the same. *Sally Hastings* was her name. Sally Hastings...the girlfriend of Phyllis' older sister; the one who didn't finish out the ninth grade on account of getting knocked up by her boyfriend—-the girl who ended up spending all summer with her aunt and uncle in Utah and finally giving the baby up for adoption. As if suddenly arrested by the startling sound of an outdoor dinner bell, Eleanor let the soap splash back into the water while dropping both hands to her stomach. Could she do the same? *Should* she do the same? Maybe there was some nice young couple in California like Mr. and Mrs. Lindeman from the soda shop who couldn't have any babies—people who'd raise her infant child and love it like their own. Raise it right and proper so that even if it *should* be a boy, he wouldn't end up behavin' like Jimmy Ray. And what about that crowded "orphan train" from New York Mama always threatened to put her on when she'd be naughty? Up until a few years back, it kept delivering children all over the Midwest who were hoping to be adopted...children who'd lost their parents after coming in from overseas on them cold, dirty ocean liners. Lots of them ended up being taken in by good folks living around *here,* so there was bound to be lots of *Californians* achin' for a new son or daughter too. Of course, Ellie frowned, if she did go through with the pregnancy, she'd be forced to put off her acting for another eight months or so. But, then again, she was still young. By the time the baby came, she'd be barely 15, being that it was due to be born around the time of her own birthday. And *really,* some of the most famous stars didn't even get into their first picture shows until they were a lot older. Like Joan Crawford who was practically 21 before getting a part as an extra in *Pretty Ladies.* And Marlene Dietrich was all of 28 before her first screen test that got her the part as a cabaret singer in *The Blue*

Angel. Besides, if she decided to have the baby, there'd be no worrying about finding another doctor in California to give her the abortion. She could go to one of the churches over there instead and talk to a minister or maybe even one of them missionary sisters who was always willin' to help people in need.

Eleanor shivered, suddenly realizing that in her initial haste to cool down, she hadn't let enough hot water flow into the tub. Leaning forward to reach the left faucet handle, she paused. The water was pretty deep already. Maybe she'd best let some out first. But the very thought of groping for the stopper chain and then having to replug the drain brought her to her senses; it was probably nearing six o'clock and she had dawdled long enough. *After all,* she reflected, her eyes sparkling with anticipation like a pair of evening lamplights, *there's still that pretty red gown to try on and all those fancy presents to unwrap.* And mustn't Doctor Governey be wondering what was taking her so long? Encouraged by such thoughts, she retrieved the slippery bar of soap and quickly began running it up and down her unwashed arm, eager to scour away every last trace of crusted dirt and chemical fumes.

chapter 78

Gifts

Freshly scrubbed and bundled inside the fluffy pink bathrobe, terrycloth turban and cotton-lined slippers, Eleanor Ann Snyder felt like a brand new package herself while seated at the mirrored dressing table, impatiently pulling a piece of lace ribbon from a soft, securely wrapped parcel. Having been one of three packages set atop the other two, she had decided to open it first. It felt light overall, she noticed, with a trace of heaviness at its center. Avoiding careless tearing of the printed paper, she suddenly flinched, impulsively catching the weightier object with one hand before it fell onto the floor. Ellie suddenly beamed with excitement, simultaneously tickled about the contents of the unwrapped package still resting upon her lap. It was a silver dollar! An honest-to-goodness silver dollar purposely placed upon a red satin girdle and matching pair of bloomers. Not only did Doctor Governey expect her to try on the gown by giving her some real grownup under things to wear along with it, but was wishing her well too since, when giving a garment as a gift, it was always good luck to include a coin. Especially a silver dollar. "And a brand new one at that!" she exclaimed, rubbing the shiny surface that was displaying the year "1932" beneath the graceful figure of lady liberty.

Reverently laying the silver dollar upon the dressing table, Eleanor returned her attention to the intimate apparel and began caressing the satiny fabric of the girdle, realizing she'd never seen a girdle before in such a pretty red color, being that Mama's were always a basic white. And although it seemed strange to be receiving such a gift from a practically complete stranger...and an older man at that...it wasn't bothering her in the least, being that any upstanding gentleman worth his salt would know that a real lady couldn't be wearing a fancy gown without the proper undergarments. Allowing her fingers to glide along the garter's silver clasps and tiny pearl buttons, Eleanor anticipated the contents of the flatter rectangular-shaped package still waiting to be opened. *It must be the silk stockings*, she reasoned. *Real* silk stockings with a *real* seam alongside the back. Her expectations rising, she shredded open the package, thinking of how her mama would sometimes pencil a pretend seam on the back of her bare legs to avoid extra wear on her one and only pair.

Ellie paused briefly before opening the box, bubbling with excitement while noting the insignia on the bottom right hand corner. It was from the "Hudson's" department store in downtown Detroit...one of the largest department stores in all of the United States! Ever since moving to Michigan, she'd always wanted to go shopping there, but was never allowed...although Mama made it a point to go there *herself* every so often, saying she didn't need no little girl to be draggin' at her heels. And though Jimmy Ray weren't always happy about all the money she'd be spendin' on herself, he didn't have much of a say, being that Mama still owned most of what they had. As Eleanor fumbled with the narrow lid of the hosiery box, she wondered how fast Doctor Governey had traveled in his bright red Duesenberg to make it all the way downtown and back in time, then pictured Mama returning home from her own shopping day, carrying so many packages you'd think she had grown a couple more arms to hold them all. As soon as Mama placed all those specially wrapped boxes on the kitchen table, she would hope there was something in them for her. And every single time she was disappointed. She heard there was a special department at Hudson's filled with all kinds of toys...shiny trucks and cars for boys and the newest, prettiest dolls for girls all dressed up in frilly dresses and hair ribbons. Ellie frowned, remembering the expensive china doll that Daddy had bought for her one Christmas. It was the prettiest doll she'd ever seen with curly black hair, real leather shoes and eyes that shut when she lay down. Daddy said it reminded him of her. But Mama wasn't so happy, saying he'd spent too much on it when they were still saving up for a new gas stove. She had named the doll "Mary" because she had a sweet face like the silent film star, Mary Brian. But that mean old Jimmy Ray made her leave the doll behind, along with some other favorite things when they moved from Ohio, sayin' that the Ford truck they come in could only hold so much and she was gettin' too old to be playin' with dolls anyway. And though she'd left Mary in the care of her best friend, Phyllis, she still regretted leaving her behind and missed her terribly. Detecting moistened tear ducts, Eleanor let go of the hosiery box and swept the back of her hand along each eye, then inwardly scolded herself. She was too old for dolls...*much* too old. Why...here she was...all ready to be dressed up like a real Hollywood star and she's gettin' all teary-eyed over a *child's* toy.

Adamantly reclaiming the hosiery box, Eleanor wedged her fingernails underneath the lid, finally prying it open. In an instant, she broke the monogrammed seal upon the protective tissue and uncovered the silk stockings, transforming her downcast disposition into a wide open grin. Not only had she guessed right about the box's contents, but instead of only one pair of silk stockings, there were three! Slipping reverent fingers beneath the bottom pair, she ran her thumb along the length of the black seam, cheerfully noting that the stocking remained flawless regardless of her touch. Chances were, she'd only be using one pair for now and could take the other two with her to California!

Impatiently replacing the green rectangular lid in anticipation of opening the final present, Eleanor quickly gathered the girdle and bloomers and stacked them atop the hosiery box, being careful not to disturb an elegant vanity set while sliding the treasured bundle upon the dresser. By its looks, it was a shoebox. She was sure of it, she anticipated while reaching for the larger wrapped gift, knowing that no outfit, be it for school, play or dress-up, was ever complete without the proper pair of shoes. And she was right! The paper wrapping partially torn away, the words *B Siegel...Elegant Footwear* were exposed. *Another* exclusive downtown store, she smiled, speculating that the red evening gown and underthings must also have been purchased from downtown Detroit. And she'd bet they'd be high heels too! But her jubilant mood soon turned into a puzzled pout as she pulled the rest of the wrapping paper from the box, exposing something written in bold ink along its side lip. *"Size 7"* it said. But she could only fit into a size 5 shoe. However beautiful they may be, she'd never be able to wear them and she certainly didn't bring a pair with her that would even complement a cocktail dress, let alone an elegant evening gown. Contemplating the possibility of stuffing the inside toes with some of the discarded paper, she removed the box's lid. But her hopes were soon dashed upon discovering that, although they were a perfect match for the red evening gown, these particular shoes were fashioned with an *open* toe. There was no way in high heaven, she grimaced, that the pair could be made to fit by any means. *However...*instinctively, she lifted one shoe from the box and held it in the palm of her hand, unable to detect that "new shoe smell" which always accompanied a new pair that Mama hadn't yet worn. It certainly didn't *look* too big, though. In fact, if she weren't mistaken, they'd be just the right size after all! Examining the inside of the shoe for any indication of its size, she noticed some scribbling as if in a foreign language. "Well, don't that take the cake," she softly whispered, unaware that an American store for women would be selling imported shoes. Why...she never noticed any of Mama's shoes havin' such scribblin' when she'd sneak in her closet to try 'em on. In fact, it seemed mighty strange that this brand new pair of shoes didn't come all freshly wrapped in paper. But...that didn't matter, she shrugged, admiring the satiny finish, cut-out design and fluted heel. They were still mighty beautiful just the same. And as far as Mama never buyin' overseas shoes, maybe it was 'cause they were just *too* expensive. Eleanor leaned over, cast a fluffy pink slipper from her right foot and stepped inside the shoe, not even bothering to unstrap its buckle. "Yes!" she exclaimed out loud, feeling like the Cinderella princess from the fairy tale book that Daddy used to read to her. Once her silk stockings were on and the straps of the shoes secured properly, they'd fit like they was special made just for her! Without another moment to spare, she flicked the shoe from her foot and began unfastening her robe, eager to finally try on all the wonderful gifts that Doctor Governey had purchased for her.

chapter 79

Dressing Up

Comfortably seated upon the needlepoint bench with her back to the mirror of the dressing table, Eleanor remained stark naked except for the red satin girdle hugging her already slender figure. Prudently gathering one of the silk stockings between her fingers, she leaned over, spread the bunched silk across the width of her toes and up past the arch of her foot, then stretched it along her well-defined calf and further up a proportionately long, shapely leg. She was glad she'd convinced Mama to finally let her shave them, as well as under her arms, she smiled, telling her that she couldn't be workin' in no hospital lookin' like she was plucked straight out of a jungle. And it was lucky for her that she'd shaved just yesterday mornin' too, even though a slight stubble was already starting to grow. But that was alright, she supposed, giving the stocking an extra pull at the top of her thigh. It was hardly apparent beneath the silk and once she put the long gown on, nobody would even know the difference. Pausing for a moment to secure her elastic hair band to avoid being blinded by thick, stray locks, Eleanor then held onto the border of the stocking and slowly stood up, attempting to attach the garter the way Mama always did on those rare occasions when she'd get all dressed up.

As the soft light of the boudoir lamp frolicked up and down the contours of her legs, Eleanor, having finally managed to attach the last clasp to the second silk stocking, stepped away from the table, turning toward a full length mirror situated near the gown-graced lounging chair. *Yes!* she beamed, gazing at the long, dark seams at the back of her legs. Her first pair of real silk stockings! And to think that she'd even *considered* spending the night at the railroad station or in some crummy hotel room. Why, she never would have known what she was missing! Anxious to see how the high heeled shoes would look with the stockings, she quickly unbuckled them, delighted to discover how comfortably snug they were—the silk stockings having worked better than any shoe horn. Once again assessing the full length of her legs while trying to keep her balance, she revealed a satisfying grin. They might not be Marlene Dietrich's *gams,* but they were still pretty enough. And it was just a shame, she noted, still pivoting about, being careful not to trip over the robe and slippers she had flung upon the floor, that they would eventually be hidden under the long skirt of the evening gown. But Eleanor was hardly given the chance to comprehend such a trivial disappointment before the corridor clock chimed in the half-hour, nearly causing her to stumble. Was it six-thirty already? In that case, she'd better stop dilly-dallying if she wished to enjoy all her grownup clothes before it be way past bedtime!

Like a budding artist eager to place the finishing touches on a commissioned portrait, Eleanor glided the lace-trimmed bloomers along strong, youthful thighs and rounded buttocks which, although bridled by the red satin girdle, held the promise of an accomplished woman eager to satisfy the sensual desires of her passionate lover. The bloomers felt like a fluffy cloud floating across the silk stockings, she noticed, sparing her the worry about the fabric leaving any snags. And they were so snug around the waist that she didn't have to worry about fitting them with a safety pin! Teetering briskly but carefully forward to face the scroll-framed mirror, she admired the way the bloomers complemented the developing curve of her hips. Instinctively, her sparkling eyes traveled upwards, befuddled. Her bosom was still bare and she had nothing to cover herself with before putting on the gown. Apparently, she'd been so excited about receiving the *other* articles of clothing, that it hadn't occurred to her, until now, that she'd overlooked such a thing. Could it be that Doctor Governey had *also* forgotten, or had she missed another gift somewhere? Eleanor glanced about the dressing room, then leaned over the evening gown that was still sprawled across the lounging chair. Perhaps it had been placed underneath, she guessed, scouring the gown's plunging neckline, discovering only its intricately sewn lining. Nearly giving up, she wandered past the arched doorway and into the main bedroom hallway, her puzzled gaze traversing the unmade bed and ever-functioning fan at the far end of the room. Even though the draperies were still drawn closed, their loosened crevices letting in only a small portion of the early evening light, it was obvious that nothing had been left behind. She *did* have her good Sunday slip packed in the traveling bag, but the cotton eyelet trim was sure to show underneath the low cut of the gown.

Realizing that she would just have to do without the undergarment, Eleanor stepped back into the dressing room, catching another view of herself in the standing mirror. It really wasn't as if she actually *needed* a brassiere or corset for support, being that her breasts weren't even fully developed yet. After all, she'd just started having her periods in February. Maybe her cup size was just too *small*. She grimaced, bringing to mind the size of her mama's bosom which required a size C cup. It really didn't matter if her own breasts growed *that* big, but she wouldn't mind if they'd at least growed to a size *B*. Intrigued by that thought, Eleanor began scrutinizing each delicate puff and a pair of nipples shaped like red clay anthills. They looked like *Marguerites*, she finally decided, remembering how Daddy would sometimes take her along with him to downtown Wilmington after a good selling season so he could upgrade some of the farm equipment. There was a French pastry shop at the edge of town right across from the tanner's...Josef's bakery...and Daddy would let her pick out anything she wanted to bring back home. He'd get Napoleons for Mama and chocolate éclairs for himself, but she liked the Marguerites the best...those vanilla cakes laced with coconut and a spiral of candy jelly on top. Of course, the éclairs were real good too, except eating chocolate would give her the biggest goddarn headache. Eleanor spontaneously inhaled, recalling how wonderful the pastry shop smelled even before they would step inside. "Fiddlesticks," she uttered, shaking her dampened head. "I just ate the best snack ever and here I am gettin' hungry again!" But that's the way it's been for the last few weeks, she inwardly chided, brushing glistening locks from her forehead...gettin' all sick in the morning and then wantin' to eat like a bear the rest of the day.

Wondering what Doctor Governey had planned for supper, Eleanor reached for the evening gown. Would he be cooking a meal himself now that his servant was gone? Perhaps he was fixin' to finish the rest of that ham that was left over. Or, the way she was dressing up, maybe he was planning on going to one of them fancy downtown restaurants. Ellie frowned, realizing that her keen sense of smell was not picking up so much as a boiled potato. If Doctor Governey *was* planning on taking her out, she worried while inspecting the rouge-colored gown to see which way she should slip it on, then maybe the police would still be looking for her and she'd get caught after all. But then again, she realized, noticing that the gown was void of any laces, hooks or buttons, it was likely to be dark outside by then, making it harder for her to be recognized. Unsuccessfully attempting to stretch the gown at its waistline, Eleanor finally decided that placing it over her head would be the only practical solution. *Of course*, she thought, making certain that the exquisite fabric had the least possible contact with her towel-dried hair as she guided the gown along the length of her body, maybe after she was all dolled up, she wouldn't be recognized even if it be smack in the middle of a sunlit afternoon! But during the next moment or two as Eleanor once again turned toward the inclined mirror, she suddenly forgot all about the police. Or a trip downtown. Or the leftover ham. Instead, she marveled at the stunning figure staring back at her. And a gown so perfectly fit that it accentuated every alluring curve and subtle movement of her body…especially the glimmering fabric of the flared skirt that clung to her and then dropped like a cascading waterfall every time she swayed ever so slightly. And the bodice with its plunging back and low cut bosom. Now, she understood why Doctor Governey had omitted a brassiere, being that wearing one would surely have disfigured the gown's flawlessly smooth fabric. And how wise he must be to have picked out a gown that was just her size! *Heck!* If it weren't for her small figure and dark hair, folks might *really* think she was Jean Harlow! Imagining herself to be the buxom bombshell in her latest movie, *Platinum Blonde*, Eleanor moved closer to the mirror, pretending to reel in Spencer Tracy while holding onto his patterned necktie. But as the clock in the corridor chimed the third quarter of the hour, she suddenly lost her balance, grabbing onto the mirror's mahogany frame for dear life, nearly tipping it over. Now wouldn't *that* be a stroke of bad luck, she thought, breathing a sigh of relief upon realizing that the teetering mirror remained intact. *Breakin' a lookin' glass before headin' out to California.* Determined not to get herself into any more mischief, Eleanor straightened her heels and hobbled toward the dressing table. If she wanted to appear like a proper lady, she'd best do something with that piled-up head of hair.

Lifting both hands toward the crown of her head, Eleanor let out an appreciative sigh as she removed the elastic hair band, allowing moist black tresses to tumble down the middle of her exposed back. The breeze from the window felt like a breath from heaven on her bare skin, being that the coolness of the bath had eventually worn off. It was a good thing she finally was able to pry the stubborn window open, she thought, thanks to pushing wheelbarrows and pitching hay all those years on the farm, not to mention moving around all them heavy patients in their hospital beds. Focusing upon the vanity mirror, she was pleased to notice that the deep red color of the gown emphasized the rosy flush upon her cheeks. And her eyes seemed even darker than ever, with a sparkle so bright they could cut right into the reflective glass. As the swells and curves of the ornately framed mirror mimicked her own tousled head of hair, she crinkled her baby doll nose. Why hadn't she gone ahead and gotten her hair bobbed? Then she'd *really* be puttin' on the Ritz! Of course, having to pay a whole two dollars and fifty cents for a professional cut would have been out of the question, but she could've at least had Mike's barber shop do it for less than a quarter of the price. And he probably would've done a darn good job of it!

Immediately deciding that her hair was too unruly to befit the exquisite gown, Ellie lifted a gold-handled comb from the mirrored tray and began working it through her tangled hair, all the while wondering why there'd been a woman's vanity set placed upon the dressing table. Even if this *wasn't* the master bedroom after all, she figured, detecting a stray blonde hair on the gilded brush, why would a woman's vanity set be in a mansion only occupied by an unwed doctor and his male servant? She could understand if the set was brand new like the rest of the things he had gotten for her, but, by the looks of it, they'd been here all along. And she was positive that Doctor Governey wasn't married, on account of there being no ring on his left hand finger, so the vanity set surely didn't belong to any wife of his. Maybe he was once married and his wife died of a contagious disease like diphtheria or smallpox, she guessed, smoothing out a tangled end. Or maybe he just ended up getting a divorce like some of the rich city folk were accustomed to doing. But then again, Ellie thought, coaxing the last few snarls from her wavy locks, why would such a nice gentleman like Doctor Governey get a divorce? Or why would a lady lucky enough to be his wife and bound to inherit all these costly things agree to it? *No*, she decided, carefully replacing the comb on the mirrored tray. He was either a widower or...or *most likely* his generous hospitality was often extended to other guests, male *and* female alike.

Casually separating the center portion of her hair into three select strands, Eleanor began fashioning them into a traveling braid, nimbly interlocking additional tresses as she went along. It was amazing that a doctor who only gave abortions would make enough money to afford living in a mansion like this, she thought. Even though she didn't *personally* know many doctors, she *was* working for Dr. Blake. *Worked* for Dr. Blake, she corrected herself, feeling somewhat guilty for abandoning the trustful old surgeon. As much as she was impressed by his house after being invited over last December for a Christmas party, it wasn't near as grand as this one. And there weren't any mansions like this in Wilmington, so she knew her first employer, Dr. Gillis, wasn't livin' in one neither. *Of course,* Ellie determined, twisting a strand of hair at the nape of her graceful neck, abortionists *definitely* made more money for their operations, bein' that it would've cost a whole $60 if Doctor Governey had gone through with hers. But, even so...even if Doctor Governey did an abortion every single day, that would have come to...to..."300 days x $60 equals $18,000, **plus** $60 x 60 days is $3,600, plus $60 x 5 days would be $300. All that would come to...to...$21,900 a year! Ellie curled her lips while pinching the end of the braid. *Well then, there's no doubt that Doctor Governey **can** make enough money from just givin' out abortions after all!*

Having gathered the end of the braid with the elastic hair band, Eleanor released the rope-like strand, allowing it to fall between pointed shoulder blades, concealing several distinct beauty marks. Gazing into the spotlessly clean mirror one final time to observe her handiwork, a serious look crossed the features of her translucent face. With taut tracks of hair pulled tightly back and neatly rowed along visible lines of scalp, her ears seemed a bit too prominent to suit her more feminine features. And her face appeared much rounder now. She shrugged. At least she'd been blessed with a good set of cheekbones, giving her a more mature look than the average girl of 14. Somewhat consoled, she leaned much closer to the mirror and pressed her bell shaped lips together, as if the natural color of her cheeks would somehow seep into them. If only she had grabbed a tube of Mama's lipstick upon leaving home, she frowned, then she'd *really* look grown up. Deciding she could do nothing more at the moment to improve her facial features, her eyes shifted downward along her sweeping collarbone and onto her developing bosom. She'd never worn a dress or even a summer blouse that set so low. Granted, she had hardly anything to conceal at present, but there *still* seemed to be something amiss. It looked too *bare.* Perhaps if Doctor Governey had included some kind of necklace or chain with a pendant, the plunging neckline wouldn't be so obvious. But then, again, he'd done so much for her already, she thought, glancing at the empty packages still set upon the edge of the dressing table. She *could* put on Mama's gold locket, but it probably *wouldn't* be a good idea to wear something that she just stole. Besides, that heart-shaped locket is too puny to make a difference anyway. And *really*, it wasn't all *that* improper, showing so much skin, bein' that the most famous movie stars were wearing plunging necklines. Even Jean Harlow's cleavage was so deep you could hide a pack of Luckies inside. *So*, she finally decided, standing at full height from the dressing table bench. The only thing left to do, after all, was spray herself with perfume from the atomizer on the vanity tray.

As the sweet, musky fragrance of "Tabu" embellished the youthful evening air, Eleanor took a deep breath and started walking toward the hallway door in anticipation of rejoining Doctor Governey until a steady hum reminded her that she had forgotten something. The fan was still running! As if Daddy was at her side proclaiming the virtue of sparing another outrageous electric bill, she eased her way toward the opposite end of the room with hardly a totter, located the operating switch and flicked it off. Instinctively glancing into the ice tray, she noticed that it had all melted...the last rays of daylight poking through the curtains unearthing a reflective puddle, recasting her bright, lively colors into a drab, morbid blotch. Immediately experiencing an uncontrollable shiver, Ellie sprinted toward the large rectangular bedroom window, deciding that the room was in dire need of natural light. Opening the velvet drapes and fastening each side upon their corresponding hooks, she then parted the sheer curtains, paying no attention to the imposition of dwindling daylight seeping into the brocade wallpaper and coffered ceiling. Gazing beyond the window, her attention was drawn to something foreign. It was an automobile. Not the candy apple red Duesenberg which had so impressed her that very morning, but another type of motor car. A Packard. And not just *any* Packard, but a brand new Packard *Phaeton!* She could tell 'cause it was a lot like the one Mr. Richards was bringing in for a fill-up at the station every Sunday morning before being forced to sell it when the depression hit. Except Doctor Governey's was a different color. *Imagine that*, she marveled, ogling the emerald green convertible. Not only was Doctor Governey rich enough to afford this mansion, but *two* flashy automobiles besides. As if she were back in history class about to spit out an incorrect answer, she slapped the tips of her fingers to her lips. *Could it be?* she gasped, scanning the expanse of the two-story structure at the end of the driveway. That building over there was *way* larger and far more prettier than any barn she'd ever seen. Could it be that Doctor Governey owned so many automobiles, he needed such a building to hold them all? Hardly able to fathom how one single man could be so wealthy, Ellie entwined one hand with the other, her curious eyes scrutinizing a more familiar scene.

Earlier that morning, she'd been so fearful of Doctor Governey's wrath after Makara started digging up his hibiscus, she failed to notice how breathtaking the back garden actually was. Or was it that one really couldn't perceive the beauty of the garden until viewed from a higher position? Feeling as if she were witnessing some faraway enchanted land beneath an unfolding page of mottled blue, Ellie scanned within the framework of towering trees and flowering bushes, magnificent possessions worthy of a king—a miniature stage with decorated columns descending from its crown, an arch full of honeysuckle stretching across a lily pond with a real waterfall—even the swing that was hanging from the giant elm was much more inviting than the old one back at the farm. *But...*as if she had tainted such splendid ambience by the mere thought of that old, dilapidated swing, Eleanor squinted her eyes, concentrating upon another object nearer to the rear of the mansion which should more likely belong in a junkyard. It looked like a bunch of knives and some other sharp objects attached to a large plate, all hanging from a pole. And *probably* the reason she'd been hearing all them scraping sounds while in the kitchen and library earlier on, was that when the wind blew, they'd all be clanging into each other. Eleanor winced. But *why?* Why would there be such an ugly thing at the foot of Doctor Governey's beautiful garden? Was he using such a contraption to scare away the crows, but placed it toward the back of the mansion because it was too hideous to be in the garden's center? And why would he need something to scare away the crows anyhow? It wasn't like there was any fruit or vegetables for them to be picking at. *Maybe...*she sighed, cracking her knuckles. Maybe it was something to scare away the evil spirits...although Doctor Governey didn't seem like the kind of person who believed in those type of things. *But then, again,* she thought, bearing down upon another finger, he *did* include that silver dollar with her satin girdle and bloomers. Eleanor paused as if in a daze, regretting that she hadn't a purse in which to carry the lucky coin...or the turtle bones she had brought along in her traveling bag. But that was alright, she consoled herself, looking away from the wind chimes and placing full attention upon the chameleon sky. Amid an array of sweeping clouds, a pale yellow sun wearing a distinctive halo was now near eye level, providing the perfect backdrop for a wide arrowhead of low-flying sparrows. Gazing further out into the filtered light, she noticed a bevy of blackbirds gathering upon a telephone wire. *There's gonna be a storm tonight sure as the grass is green,* she quivered. Maybe instead of wishing for an evening bag, she should be hoping for a large, sturdy umbrella.

chapter 80

Preparations

Standing at the brink of the stairway landing, Eleanor took a deep breath before revealing her adorned presence. It hadn't been difficult, once she entered the darkened hallway, to decide in which direction to proceed. It was the music! Sounding as if it were straight from heaven. Something like church music, but without any organ. And it was traveling up the *front* stairway, intertwining the clean fruity smell of polished oak with the fragrant aroma of cigar tobacco. As the sad, haunting melody of violins, an undercurrent of brooding cellos and the sweetness of French horns arrested the wide open foyer, Eleanor stepped forward and timidly peeked over the banister. Although her range of vision was still restrained, she could tell that the music was definitely coming from the room off the foyer to her right. Especially conscious of her high heeled shoes, she started down the carpeted stairway, the augmenting music encouraging each carefully paced step. Then...there he was. Surrounded by immense walls papered in crimson, Doctor Governey was seated upon an upholstered armchair reading a newspaper with the aid of a magnifying glass. Although his face wasn't in full view, thick amber hair and a wide forehead held the promise of genuinely handsome features. And an impressive stature adorned in a dark blue suit, complementary necktie and gleaming wing tip shoes left no doubt in one's mind of his physical well being. Enraptured by his appearance, Eleanor lingered on the stairs, trying to decide who he reminded her of. *Howard*...that was it. *Leslie Howard*...that famous actor from England she had been reading about in Mama's *Photoplay* magazines. It definitely seemed like him with the exception that Doctor Governey was probably taller. Gripping the banister just tightly enough to accommodate her descent, Eleanor discreetly tackled one more step, wondering when the doctor would notice her. But, as though he had the uncanny ability to read her mind, he placed the magnifying glass upon a side table, firmly folded the newspaper, reached for his smoking cigar, then promptly extinguished it.

"My dear, *dear*, Ellie Ann," he gasped, gallantly rising from his seat. "Why...my good lord! Don't you look absolutely ravishing! Please...don't be shy, my dear Ellie...step into my drawing room so that I may absorb the full vision of your loveliness!"

Feeling light on her feet, Eleanor moved with a swifter gait toward her benefactor, extending her hand in response to his offer of assistance. As if it were a tiny sparrow amidst a threatening storm, Samuel accepted the delicate hand in his own and sheltered it with his lips. Despite a sudden blush overpowering her rosy cheeks, she nevertheless sensed the coolness in his fingertips. Though a few open windows now favored the mansion with a pleasant nautical breeze, remnants of a hot summer day stubbornly persisted. Somewhat bewildered by a curious attraction to a man old enough to be her father, yet consoled by the notion that the slight chill of his hand was indicative of a warm heart, she allowed herself to relax as pent up words began sliding loosely from her tongue. "I heard the music coming all the way up the stairs...it sounded just like heaven." Releasing her hand from the doctor's gentle grasp, she scanned several exquisite objects before identifying the source of the hypnotic sound—an ornate walnut cabinet upstaging the sleek grand piano near its side.

"Yes...it is quite lovely, is it not, my dear?" Samuel agreed, nodding toward the Victrola which continued to spill forth Mozart's monumental requiem, one of the few melancholic masterpieces used for his funeral services. "I am quite partial to classical music; music from heaven for an angel from heaven." Surrounded by the familiar, overpowering scent of "Tabu", he assessed the petite figure before him. His judgment had been unerringly correct, he concluded, particularly pleased that the nipples of her developing breasts prodded the satin fabric ever so gently. That spitfire, Rosalie, at Madame Charlotte's bordello was just her size and the gown a perfect fit. As for the shoes, he had been prudent enough to bring along the farm girl's scuffed up pair so that the ladies for hire could determine which would be the closest fit.

Eleanor smiled. Daddy would sometimes call her an angel...his "little cherub" to be exact. But being called an angel was just the same. "Thank you for the pretty gown. I never had anything like it before." She almost mentioned the undergarments, but caught herself before blurting out, realizing by the sudden feverishness upon her face why they were sometimes called *unmentionables*. It didn't even seem proper to bring up the silver dollar he placed on top of them. "I...thank you, too, for the shoes, Doctor Gov...*Sam*...*Sir*...," she stammered. "They fit me even better than I ever...."

Eleanor's ramblings fell on deaf ears as Samuel stared at her, secretly recalling the liberty he had taken merely a few hours ago in the upstairs guestroom which, until now, had been solely occupied by Dr. Carvelle during his rare, extensive visits. If he hadn't been so impatient! He *should* have allowed more time for the chloral hydrate to take full effect. But he had been too excited and too much in a hurry, anticipating the many tasks which lay ahead. Then...while hurriedly carrying the limp girl up the stairs, he realized that he may have underestimated her weight and should have given her a pinch more of the potent powder, perhaps even fortifying it with a nominal amount of liquor. Having ample time to reminisce as his chatty guest continued to express an overwhelming gratitude for the multitude of treats discovered after waking from her sleep, Samuel's reflections returned once more to the guest bedroom—how he had carefully laid her upon the bed and hastily turned down the covers...how he had nearly ripped the buttons from her tattered cotton blouse while unfastening it. How *she* had unexpectedly stirred beneath him as he climbed upon the bed and began caressing the most impeccable set of female breasts he had ever laid hands upon...compelling him to retreat for the time being. *But that could be easily remedied,* he surmised, his resolve further strengthened by Eleanor's interminable gift for gab. After their visit to the club tonight, he would invite the unsuspecting child back into the drawing room, engage in a bit of conversation and top off the evening with a soothing cup of impregnated tea.

Believing to have captured her host's attention while rendering a lengthy account of shopping at second-hand stores, a crashing crescendo swiftly engulfed the room, causing Eleanor to harness her lips and gaze wide-eyed at the Victrola. "How did it *do* that?"

"The Victrola, my dear Ellie-Ann, has an automatic record changer," Samuel couldn't help but boast about the modern musical marvel which had carried a price tag similar to that of his 1930 Auburn Cabriolet. "A lift ring picks up and slides the discarded record into a felt lined drawer while attaching itself onto the next record to be played...which it then lowers onto the turntable. And *this* particular model," he couldn't help but add, hoping to profoundly impress his fascinated guest, "even encompasses a splendid RCA radio!"

Ellie stood mute for almost a full quarter of a minute as the rich tone of robust music accompanied her thoughts. Ever since arriving at Doctor Governey's doorstep this morning, it had been one big surprise after the other...his fancy motor cars...the beautiful gifts...and now a record player that was changing records all by itself. Why...it didn't even need a horn on it like Mama's old phonograph, and it sounded like the musicians were playing right there in the room; not like the cheap tinny sound she was used to hearing. And just to be inside this fantastic mansion! She had never imagined that such a house existed—not even in Hollywood! Of course, she'd seen mansions in certain movies and even pictures of them in magazines, but nothing ever prepared her for this! Eleanor quickly scanned the drawing room, imprinting upon her mind a collection of elegant furnishings as well as several tables adorned with painted figurines and fringed lamps laden with crystal. Even the fireplace mantle was so fraught with candlesticks and such, that Doctor Governey could hold a tag sale with just those very things. And the walls. They were red. Dark red. In fact, if she stood flush up against one of them, she'd blend right in. But they weren't entirely plain like the walls she'd always been used to seeing. There was a patterned border near the floor and an even more elaborate one closer to the ceiling. And the spacious ceiling itself with its enormous brass chandelier! She was sure the music from the Victrola had burst right through it! "Wha...what kind of music did you say this was?" she finally spoke up, still wondrously eying the cathedral ceiling.

"Classical," Samuel answered, bearing in mind the need to enroll the uncultured lass in a qualified school of etiquette after the wedding. "This particular opera piece was created by the renowned German composer, Richard Wagner...*The Ride of the Valkyries,*" he further explained before prompting Eleanor to be seated upon an oversized tufted divan.

As every crashing cymbal and each whirlwind melody engulfed the cavernous drawing room, Eleanor obediently slid her warm body against the cresting rail of the immense divan, feeling that at any given moment, she would discover herself being driven on a warrior boat through turbulent waters. But as she continued to absorb every striking chord, attempting to forever imprint the sonorous sounds on her mind, a gallant, familiar voice asking a simple question suddenly reassured her that she was still safe within the confines of a millionaire's drawing room. "Oh, no...*Never*," she answered to Samuel's inquiry about her experience with opera. "I always wondered what goin' to one would be like. But the closest I'd ever been to an opera was when my mama and daddy took me to the Ohio Theatre when I turned ten years old...."

Quite grateful that Wagner's forceful music was buffering yet another redundant account of Eleanor's childhood affairs, Samuel took the liberty of seating himself an arm's length beside her, tugging slightly at the bottom of his vested jacket to prevent it from puckering. "Perhaps, then," he finally interjected, detecting a slight pause in her voice, "I may one day have the pleasure of accompanying you to the opera...*if* you should ever happen to return from California, of course."

In one split second, Eleanor felt as if she had been pulled right out of her seat. During the last several minutes, she had forgotten all about California. *And* the pregnancy, she realized, her sensitive nose detecting the lingering odor of formaldehyde which had been considerably subdued by an invigorating shower and a few generous splashes of after shave. And *Makara*, she suddenly remembered, looking out toward the foyer. *Where is she?*

"Makara is fine," Samuel remarked, sensing the child's concern. "After giving her a refreshing bath, I allowed her into the back garden for a bit of a romp. She just had another helping of ham about a half hour ago." Samuel could tell by the smile on Eleanor's face that she had believed his words. *Excellent*, he thought, the truth of the matter being that earlier in the day he had filled a bucket with automobile detergent and scrubbed the filthy mutt with a tire brush before hosing it down. Then, attaching a rope to the dog's crude collar and securing her to a cast iron chair on the veranda, he indulged in his own refreshing shower before gathering Eleanor's evening wardrobe at Madame Charlotte's bordello, after which he visited his funeral parlor and a local pet shop. Upon returning home, he unleashed the pup and fed her a few scraps of meat that some of the Madame's girls were about to throw into the garbage. Finally, before Sergeant McCallister could have had the chance to suspect anything unusual in the course of collecting his weekly payoff at the five o'clock hour, he had muzzled and roped the relieved pup to the cast iron chair again. "She is now safely in the kitchen fast asleep," Samuel assured Eleanor, his strong voice rising above Wagner's crashing cymbals as he envisioned the subdued Rottweiler pawing at her new doggie bed instead of scratching his buffed veranda tiles.

Having been comforted by the thought that Makara was well taken care of, Eleanor's eyebrows suddenly drooped as she practically whispered. "You never *did* give me that abortion, did you?"

Although her question had been muted by the thunderous music, Samuel could decipher the query by the casting of his patient's eyes toward the abdomen. With a look of solemnity, he rose from the upholstered divan and strode toward the Victrola. When he opened the cabinet and lifted the needled arm from the grooved, shellac disc, the silence of the room matched his own. With an aura of fatherly concern, he somberly strolled toward a mahogany server and poured his guest a tall glass of iced water, carefully positioning a lemon wedge upon its rim. Then, gently placing a linen napkin upon Eleanor's lap so as not to soil her crimson gown, he offered her the water and reseated himself. "Please understand, Ellie Ann, there was good reason to delay the operation," he began, secretly wondering whether the child he planned to eventually adopt and claim as his own flesh and blood would be born male or female. He then leaned closer, firmly planting his palm upon Eleanor's tiny hand which was braced against her thigh. "You see, my dear, I originally had every intention to respect your wishes. However...*fortunately*...upon further examination, I discovered that the pregnancy was in a much earlier stage than I had previously anticipated...no more than four or five weeks along. *Much* too early to insure that the operation be performed in the safest possible manner, *particularly* if you desire to have more children in the future. So you see, my dear Ellie Ann, in my most humble opinion, I think it would be in your best interest to wait another week or two." Keeping his right hand staunchly positioned, he gestured with the other. "In the meantime, you are certainly welcome to be my house guest for as long as you wish. As you can very well see, I will make certain that your every desire be fulfilled!"

Looking into her generous host's apprehensive eyes, Eleanor scrunched her lips together like the gathering of fabric atop a pouch purse; she wished the doctor would remove his hand so that she could better hold onto the glass of iced water which felt so nice and cold. And he didn't seem to be very good at arithmetic either, since Jimmy Ray had raped her smack in the middle of June which would make her at least *six* weeks along. But that didn't matter, 'cause her mind was made up to giving the baby away for adoption anyway. *Heck*, she thought, taking another sip of water before sharing her decision. Doctor Governey didn't even know how to make a fitting glass of lemonade! "That's very kind of you sir, but...well...I think I'm gonna go ahead and have the baby after all." Immediately noticing the change of demeanor upon Samuel's countenance, she took a shallow breath. "It's just that...well...I just didn't feel right about havin' the abortion anymore and then remembered about how my best girlfriend, Phyllis, had an older sister who was tellin' her about a girlfriend of hers that got in the family way, so her mama and daddy sent her to Utah to live with her auntie and uncle, so's she could have the baby and give it up for adoption." Detecting a glimmer of understanding in Samuel's eyes, she immediately continued without interruption. "So I hope you understand, Doctor Governey, being that you planned on givin' me an abortion and all. I mean...you been so kind to me and everything...lettin' me wear this pretty dress and shoes and...and...puttin' out all them good things for me to eat upstairs." She suddenly thought of the bed she had left all rumpled up and cast her eyes downward, focusing now on Samuel's pair of freshly polished Oxfords. "If you'd like me to, I'll go back upstairs and change into my own clothes and then put everything back the way it was. Then I could be on my way again," she frowned, hoping that the police were no longer searching for her.

"Nonsense!" Samuel blurted, swiftly releasing Eleanor's hand and clapping his palms together. "I have a splendid evening planned for the both of us, by Jove, and it does not disappoint me in the least that you have had a change of heart concerning the abortion. *However*," he cautiously worded, taking care not to persuade her otherwise, "I think it may be prudent to think your decision over. You are certainly welcome to stay for another week or two. After all, once you are on your way, it will be difficult to find another doctor who is willing to perform the operation, should you change your mind. And *furthermore*," he quickly interjected before Eleanor had the chance to decline his kind offer, "after spending a considerable amount of time here with me, you shall surely experience a leisurely trip to California without the distressing awareness that you are being pursued by every police officer in the county."

Vaguely conscious that the linen napkin was shielding her red satin gown from any water stains, Eleanor clenched the ice cold glass with both hands, focusing upon the slippery beads of condensation. As much as she wanted to be on her way to Hollywood, her biggest fear right now was that she'd be caught. And it'd be bad enough if they put her in jail for stealing, but she'd be damned if they made her go live back home with Jimmy Ray and Mama. "So, then..., she hesitated, looking at Samuel for some sign of guidance, "will I...are we...well then...are we going to stay *here* tonight?"

"Why, heavens no, my dear!" Samuel quickly answered, rising from the divan and retrieving Eleanor's glass of water and linen napkin, secure in the knowledge that his professional assistant, Mr. Atkinson, along with the help of a young apprentice, was proceeding to receive bereaved guests at the funeral home. "As I have promised myself, we shall spend a delightful evening together...but not here, of course." Strutting toward a Jacobean hardwood sideboard after safely replacing the glass upon the mahogany server, he continued to explain. "I shall, instead, be taking you to the *swankiest* night club this side of town. But first and *foremost*," he clarified, pulling open the middle drawer of the sideboard, "we must be certain that you will not be recognized under any circumstance whatsoever!"

Eleanor's heart began to flutter as Samuel lifted a worn black metal box from the opened drawer. She'd only been to one restaurant in her whole life the time Mama and Daddy took her to the Ohio Theatre, but *never* to a night club, let alone a real *swanky* one like Doctor Governey was telling her about! She wondered if there'd be girls passing out cigarettes like she'd seen on bus posters. And dancing, too, like the picture of a flapper and her beau on the cover of an old *Life* magazine. But before she could decide whether or not it would be mannerly to ask about such things, her reflections were arrested by Samuel's invitation to sit upon one of two tapestry chairs positioned at a Baroque rosewood parlor table.

"Now, Ellie Ann," Samuel began while setting the box upon the table next to a sterling silver vanity set, "you shall see in just a short while that you have nothing to fear, for after I complete the application of these cosmetics, your own *mother* would fail to recognize you, not to mention any police officers who may happen to visit the club. And as far as those tenacious bloodhounds are concerned, I want you to understand that I would not, under any circumstances, allow such animals to soil, let alone visit, my exclusive, personal establishment. So you see, my dear," he avowed with the help of a 50-dollar smile, "there is no need to be concerned about your identity being discovered!"

Eleanor gazed in wonder as Samuel unhinged the box's rusted, scratched fastener. She had no idea, whatsoever, that Doctor Governey actually *owned* the night club! Maybe *that* was how he was making so much money! And to think that she was gonna be his special guest of honor! Feeling as if a hundred-and-one caterpillars were crawling up and down her arms, she could sense the corners of her lips spontaneously turning upwards as the doctor finally lifted the top of the metal box. The only other place she'd seen such a variety of makeup was at the five and dime store, she thought, ogling over the opened case of brushes, tubes and tin containers. But she supposed, too, that it might not be polite to ask how he had acquired such a treasure.

"Now...Ellie Ann...." Samuel instructed while seating himself to the side of his living, breathing specimen, "I am going to ask you to close your eyes and remain perfectly still while I apply some liner. This won't take long," he explained, carefully guiding a dark brown pencil along one lid, realizing, while keeping a slight distance, that obtaining a pair of spectacles in the near future was, after all, inevitable. "Your eyes are naturally stunning...but we do want to enhance them in the best possible way."

Obediently following Doctor Governey's bidding as the grandfather clock in the foyer announced the seventh hour, Eleanor remained both silent and amazed, being careful not to move one inch while he masterfully stroked and shadowed each eyelid with an ease that even her mama had never attained. Following Samuel's request, she then opened her eyes and looked upwards as he faintly lined her lower lids, again gazing straight ahead to facilitate the subtle pruning and penciling of the brows. Being extra careful not to blink as he finally tickled her long lashes with mascara, she listened keenly as he spoke up again.

"I suppose you may be wondering how it ever came to be that a doctor such as myself possesses the skill of cosmetic application," he stated with a slight quiver in his voice, momentarily overcome by the sultry innocence buried deep within the child's accentuated eyes. With little effort, he repositioned the mascara and brush within the mortician's case, then pulled from it a scuffed tube of lipstick. "It was because of my dear mother," he began in a most convincing tone, lifting Eleanor's chin with the instruction to part her lips ever so slightly. "She was a vaudeville entertainer...and, an extremely talented one at that. I would occasionally assist in applying her makeup and styling her hair before stage appearances...*particularly* when she lacked a steady hand at the gradual cessation of her career." Holding onto the uncapped tube of lipstick, he drew back slightly to observe an inviting pair of crimson lips. Quite satisfied with his work, he reached for some rose colored blush. "As a matter of fact...yes, as a matter of fact...come to think of it, you and my mother share quite a few similarities, bless her dear soul." Promptly realizing that Eleanor's vibrant cheeks needed no assistance, he grabbed a case of translucent powder instead. "Would you believe, my dear Ellie Ann, she, too, ran away from home at a young age. But not because she was with child," he explained, opening the case and gently shaking the excess powder from a large puff. "She fell in love at the very tender age of 15...with a much older man...my *father*. He discovered my mother during one of her theatre performances and, being the very beautiful woman that she was, he fell instantly in love with her." Pleased to notice the look of intrigue on his subject's face, he lovingly began to powder her nose. "But her own mother and father...my maternal grandparents, I am ashamed to admit...did not approve. It became necessary for my father to offer them both a substantial sum of money before they would give their consent so that my parents could marry legally. My mother never heard from either of them after that. But it turned out very well since they had always treated her with the minimum of kindness, the unpleasant details of which I shall spare you at the moment."

Lacking the opportunity to question the compassionate doctor before she was instructed to blot her lips on a thin piece of parchment, Eleanor quickly released her grip on the smudged paper, hardly giving Samuel the chance to withdraw it from her mouth before she spoke. "What kind of acts did she do? Did she get to dance on a big stage or play one of them Wurlitzer organs?"

"As a matter of fact, she certainly did!" Samuel declared, replacing the puff in the powder case and closing the lid. "Dancing on a big stage, that is. She was also a wonderful vocalist and many people thought her voice considerably similar to that of renowned American opera singer, Lillian Russell. And quite proficient at the keyboard as well, but, to my knowledge never utilized that particular skill on stage," he commented, responding to Eleanor's sudden change of focus toward the grand piano. "I rather like to think she reserved that special talent for my father and me. But...my dear, dear child...how I do miss hearing her play the pianoforte! Please, Ellie Ann...If you shall be so kind." He extended his hand toward the ebony concert grand Steinway. "Will you do me the honor of bringing a dear memory to life?"

Feeling suddenly stupid, Eleanor darted her eyes back toward Samuel. She didn't even know how to play a simple harmonica, let alone a piano...and such a grand one at that! "I...I'd really love to, sir...*Sam...Sir*...but I...I never really learned how to play the piano. I always *wanted* to. I mean...I always thought it would be fun to play a Wurlitzer like I'd seen at the Ohio Theatre, but we never could've afforded one. My daddy once brought a used piano home with a couple of keys missin' on it, sayin' maybe I could take some lessons, but Mama complained that the piano took up too much room and the lessons would cost a lot of money." Pouting scarlet lips, she looked downward, fixing her gaze on an unpolished pair of twittering thumbs. "I just think she was bein' selfish, though, wantin' to spend any extra money only on herself. Anyhow...," she apologized, staring back at Samuel, "Daddy ended up gettin' rid of the piano and I never did learn how to play. So I'm really *sorry*, Doctor Governey...that I won't be able to play for you."

"Why, Ellie Ann," Samuel tenderly smiled, closing up the makeup case, not at all surprised that the simple farm girl didn't know Middle C from a stake in the ground. "There is no need to apologize. I am certainly no virtuoso myself. However, it does seem a shame that a bright young lady such as you had never been granted the opportunity. Why...if you had been my daughter, not only would I have allowed you to master the piano, but would have *insisted* upon it! Furthermore, if it be the mighty Wurlitzer you desired, well..." he demonstrated, spreading his arms like a peacock in full plume, "as you can obviously see, there is plenty of room for one here! However," Samuel continued with hardly a breath in between, eager to once again steer the conversation in the direction of his fictitious mother, "you are quite correct about the queen of the windpipe instruments being featured in many a vaudeville show...particularly those which are located in larger cities worldwide like we have at the Palace Theatre in New York." He lifted the cosmetic case from the parlor table, allowing his guest not one fleeting moment to slip a word in edgewise. "My mother, however, was content to perform within some of the smaller towns in England nearer to where we resided. Especially...especially after an unfortunate incident which occurred in Paris...but one which, as I've long suspected, may have had a serendipitous outcome."

Eleanor's eyes remained glued to Samuel as he positioned the makeup box within the Jacobean sideboard and closed the drawer. She didn't know what serendipitous meant, but could tell it might mean that something bad turned out to be something good. And what could have possibly happened to his mother in Paris? As Samuel meandered back toward the parlor table, she began wiggling in her seat, finally realizing that if she didn't speak up now, she might never hear the end of the story. "Was it really bad? I mean...what happened to your mother?"

Samuel reached for the sterling silver hand mirror and held it near his heart. "As I have already revealed, Ellie Ann, it seems as if you and my mother have several things in common. You see...during her seventh year of marriage, after another brilliant stage performance, she was given the opportunity to work one summer with a traveling vaudeville company renowned for offering the finest entertainment throughout Europe. Initially, my mother was disinclined to be parted from my father for such a stretch of time, but after some discussion, they agreed to it, making future arrangements for my father to visit her during accessible weekends. And since, to their dismay, they had not been able to experience the blessings of parenthood, she was certainly free to travel without the worry of caring for any children. But that was soon to change," he sternly stated, maneuvering the sterling mirror like a principal's paddle. "She was assaulted in an alley by a drunken patron while on her way to the milliner's...and in broad daylight mind you...badly beaten and nearly left for dead! Fortunately, the horrendous incident did not leave any physical scarring, so she was able to resume her passion for theatre inside the small vaudeville house nearer to our home shortly after my birth." He lent a theatrical pause while lifting his chin. "Since I, thus, remained an only child and never bore the remotest resemblance to my father, I strongly suspect to be the product of that horrific assault, Ellie Ann...as your pregnancy is likewise the result of similar odious circumstances. However," he went on, cradling the mirror within the palm of his hand, "up until the time of their death, I never sensed that my parents loved me any less than if I were my father's very own flesh and blood. Moreover, I never thought of the man who raised and nurtured me as anything other than my very own dear father. And, needless to say, I am forever grateful for the life which I have been afforded. So you see, Ellie Ann, the manner in which a child is conceived is, in my good opinion, consequentially irrelevant, so long as there are two dedicated adults quite competent of superintending the child's anthropological...so long as there are two loving adults who will make sure that the child is kept safe and well cared for."

Several developing questions began crossing Eleanor's mind as Samuel gave his cosmetic artistry one final inspection. Would it really be possible to love her baby if she were married and decided to keep it, even though it came from that bastard, Jimmy Ray? Why was Doctor Governey giving abortions if he was happy that his mother birthed him? And what about the man who raped his mother? "Did they ever catch him?" she finally verbalized. "The man who...who beat up your mother?"

"No, Ellie," Samuel answered, sporting a discouraging frown. "By the time my poor mother was discovered, the brute had plenty of time to escape without a trace. Perhaps he is still prowling about or...worse yet...successfully manipulated an anonymous passage into this country. Of course," he declared, flicking the beveled mirror upwards, "chances are, he probably has perished from old age by now. But there are plenty more of his kind wreaking havoc on innocent young women, I can assure you of that—particularly in popular cities where they can hide themselves like snakes in the ground among the bustling crowds!" Pausing for a brief moment to lock eyes with his wincing guest, Samuel pointed the hand mirror toward Eleanor as if it were an automatic pistol. "However, Ellie Ann, my father was an extremely influential businessman who was well respected by his many colleagues, so I am *certain*, had he known of the bloody bastard's whereabouts, the contemptible coward would have been flogged and then castrated right in the center of town before being damned to an eternal grave! But enough of such doom and gloom, my dear," he declared, resolutely laying the mirror face down on the parlor table. There is nothing one can do to change the past and a beautiful evening still awaits us. Furthermore," he pointed out, thinking Eleanor's ears a bit disproportionate for her delicate features, "this hairstyle is not becoming of you and besides, a strand of hair has managed to work away from the nape of your neck."

Before having the opportunity to reach toward the traveling braid, Eleanor realized that the doctor had already stepped behind her and removed the twisted band which held it together. His hands seemed warmer now, she noticed, so why was she suddenly shivering? The heightening breeze flowing through the sheer curtained windows hadn't cooled down much, so it wasn't because of that. *Although*...Eleanor remained motionless, listening to what seemed to be the sound of...of *knives*...or something sharp scraping together...like she had heard earlier while in Doctor Governey's kitchen. A sound that would cause *anyone* to shiver. Only this time it wasn't as loud because...because...it was coming from that ugly thing she saw from the rear bedroom window...that tall pole with shiny sharp objects and pieces of glass hanging from it. Attempting to compose herself as Samuel continued to unravel the braid, Ellie suddenly realized that the grandfather clock had just finished ringing in the quarter hour, its somber echo still resounding through the vast expanse of the entranceway foyer. So *that* was it, she halfheartedly concluded, still tugging at her fingers. She really hadn't heard the sound of that ugly thing in the backyard after all, but only imagined it. All that talk about rape, murder and such had gotten her so spooked that *any* sound would have set her nerves to shattering. But now she had to do something...*anything*...ask Doctor Governey some kind of question that would free her mind from those horrible images of murder and rape as well as those never-ending thoughts of Jimmy Ray. "Have you been here long?" she swallowed. "In America? All the way from England?"

"Much too long, Ellie Ann," Samuel softly answered, welcoming the occasion to enhance his newly concocted legend. "Particularly since leaving my dear mother behind. But she is gone now...perished in a house fire while I was enjoying all that America has to offer. I was devastated, of course, and promptly traveled back to Britain as soon as the telegram arrived." He discontinued fluffing Eleanor's hair for a moment to lend credence to his contrived anguish. "Mother...nothing was spared except for the cherished cosmetic case and a few priceless pieces of jewelry which she had kept in a bank deposit box. I don't even have so much as a photograph of her," he declared, feigning a crack in his solemn voice. "To this day I regret that I had neglected to tuck one away in my traveling trunk. But being so eager to voyage overseas and certain that my mother would eventually agree to join me, it did not seem critical at the time. *However*," he stressed, once again using spindly fingers to comb through Eleanor's locks, taking care not to alter her natural wave, "the wonderful memories which are indelibly sealed within my mind can never be destroyed and for that I am forever grateful. *Now!*" Samuel finalized, reaching for the hand mirror, satisfied that he had, once and for all, successfully covered his fictional tracks, "What do you think, my dear? Have I not learned a thing or two from attending to my dear mother?"

Glancing into the mirror, Eleanor immediately forgot the pity she was feeling toward the orphaned doctor. She looked older now. Much older...maybe 18 or 19 years of age. And very beautiful too. Perhaps even more beautiful than Lillian Gish. But not as innocent looking, she noticed, detecting the seductive slant of her brows. Maybe it had to do with the way each wavy lock slinked about her face, erasing its roundness. Or the fact that her ears were now discreetly hidden. Of course, her lips never looked so inviting, she decided with a pucker. And her eyes, darker than ever; they seemed almost evil. But it was a bewitching kind of look she could certainly get used to. "I think you learned just fine," she answered, suddenly wondering if she might have preferred a bob cut after all.

"Is something troubling you, Ellie Ann?" Samuel asked, scrutinizing his handiwork, sensing, aside from the fact that it had been impractical to apply a coat or two of dark red nail polish, that something else was amiss. "Have I forgotten anything?"

"Oh no!" she quickly retorted, slapping the mirror onto her lap. "It's not that at all, sir... Sam...it's just that...well...I mean...I never expected I could look so...so.... You done a fine job, better'n *anyone* could've. It's just that I was wonderin' how...just wonderin' if maybe one of them new bobbed cuts would do me proud."

Samuel immediately converted a spontaneous wince into a patronizing smile; aside from the fact that it was unbecoming for a lady to shear her crowning glory, the bob cut had been notorious for encouraging young women to engage in unscrupulous behavior such as wearing short skirts and rolling up stockings, not to mention gyrating their wanton bodies like felines in heat while participating in the latest dance crazes—particularly that abominable 'Lindy Hop' disgracefully named after one of our most esteemed aviator pilots. "Ellie Ann," he proposed, retrieving the mirror from her lap lest it wrinkle the delicate silk fabric, "you've such a beautiful face that I am certain a blunt cut would...do you proud," he managed to articulate. "However," he continued, replacing the mirror face down upon the parlor table, "it is my very humble opinion that taking the scissors to such an attractive head of hair would be a grave mistake. Why, many a lady would sacrifice their left ring finger to possess your lovely black locks. *Of course...*" he hastily added, noticing the look of disappointment on Eleanor's face, albeit forever resolving to keep a short leash on her during their marriage as well as personally executing after the birth of her child a foolproof, irreconcilable clitoridectomy. "If you really have your heart set upon it, I can arrange an appointment first thing tomorrow morning at Virginia's Beauty Salon on Kercheval Avenue; I will even request Virginia herself, if you would like."

"Oh no, sir!" Ellie blurted, overwhelmed by the doctor's offer to have her hair bobbed by a lady beautician at a real beauty salon. "I mean..." she reconsidered, realizing that if she *did* get her hair bobbed, she could leave for California within a couple of days without being recognized; also, the timing was good for a cut, considering the moon was in its waxing phase. "...you been so kind to me already...I could never pay you back for all you done!"

Samuel smiled, contemplating that, in due time, his meager investment was bound to reap a substantial treasure. "Nonsense, Ellie Ann. Why, it is *yourself* who has been inconvenienced, having traveled many miles to obtain a service which I ultimately, by the grace of God, was unable to render. The least I can do at present, then, is to provide for your happiness in any which way I am able, be it within my power. Besides, the spiritual enjoyment I receive from assisting a patient in need is inexpressible. After all, I *am* a doctor of medicine and serving my fellow man is my *primary* aspiration."

"Well then...thank you, sir. With all the things you been givin' me so far, though, I don't *suppose* I'll need anything else before settin' out for California," Ellie responded with a touch of regret in her voice. "Except ...except maybe for some meals to hold me and my dog over while we're still here."

Although his unsuspecting guest had just indicated her willingness to stay on past the present evening, Samuel was suddenly unable to fully appreciate such a convenient situation; nervously fidgeting before her, he now realized what had been missing on her person all along. Determined to conquer his ever-increasing trepidation, he finally spoke up. "Most assuredly, it is not true, Ellie Ann...that you will require nothing else. For I have already determined that there is another matter which must be taken care of." Excusing himself, he warily walked toward the opposite end of the room in the direction of a brass embossed armoire which towered against the corner wall. Upon reaching it, he stretched upward, toward the bureau's winged crest, retrieving a small brass key which he used to unlock, before spreading open, the sturdy set of ornately carved doors. Solemnly pulling forward an inside drawer, he took out a dark green velvet case, being certain to relock the armoire and replace its key before reseating himself and offering the hand-sized box to Eleanor. "This belonged to my dear mother," he nearly choked. "I think it best that you borrow it for the evening."

Although initially concerned as to why the doctor's hands had been trembling, Eleanor accepted the rather weighty, elongated box with anticipation upon learning that it once belonged to his mother, guessing that it was probably a valuable piece of jewelry. Fumbling with the velvet edges, she finally pried the lid open, unearthing the most magnificent necklace she had ever seen. Like a winding rapids preceding a breathtaking waterfall, a strand of exquisite pearls flowed into a sparkling ruby pendant which was surrounded by a crown of diamonds. "It's beautiful!" she gasped, rubbing her thumb along the string of pearls, failing to notice the paleness of Samuel's complexion. Reverently turning the pendant over, she began reading aloud, "*Louisa & Randolph, Christmas, 1889.*"

"My father presented it to my mother the very first Christmas of their marriage," Samuel practically whispered, wondering, in response to his unyielding anxiety, if he might have, indeed, been mistaken in retrieving the pendant.

Eleanor remained entranced as she continued to examine the necklace. Aside from trying to imagine its worth, it suddenly dawned on her that if Doctor Governey was conceived seven years after his parent's marriage, then he must be...either...either 36 or 37 years old—just about the same age as her daddy when he died. Except Doctor Governey didn't have any grey hairs yet. "Is this a *real* ruby?" she finally managed to ask.

"Why...yes...it is," Samuel feebly responded. But his mind was not presently concerned with the authenticity of the necklace, or its net worth, or how it would complete the attire of his captivated guest. Instead, he was being transported into another realm...another time...another room; a room dimly lit, steeped in cigarette smoke and the odor of gin. On a cluttered nightstand stood a nearly exhausted vial of opium. He was a little boy again, instructed to sit upon a chair close to his ailing mother's bedside and read to her from the pages of *Woman's Home Companion*, deliberately retarding the pace of his narrative in dreadful anticipation of what was yet to come. "*Samuel, my darling boy,*" the ailing countess would whimper, once again rehashing a detailed account of her presence at the Devonshire Ball where she insisted that she danced with the Prince of Wales while bedecked in a flamboyant Betsy Ross costume of red white and blue. "*Paint my lips for me, dear one.*" Spindly fingers would grapple with a string of asparagus left upon her untouched dinner tray before handing the steamed, limp vegetable to her compliant little boy. "*There, there,* she'd purr as Samuel pretended the cooked vegetable to be a cosmetic brush, making sure to 'paint' puckered lips reeking of tonic and cigarettes. "*We must be presentable for the Duke and Duchess. That's a good boy. Now...brush my hair, little one,*" she'd decree as Samuel cowered toward a sterling silver brush. "*Make it nice and shiny for mother. Firm, even strokes, my darling,*" she emphasized, maneuvering his stiffened wrist along lackluster locks which barely sheathed an obscenely generous bosom, areola shielded only by a light cotton nightdress. "*Oh...yes!..such a good boy!*" As his mother would draw him closer toward her darkening, swollen nipples, Samuel's eyes remained riveted upon the ruby pendant suspended from her neck, as if it had the power to shelter him from the reality of the moment. But no matter how intense his concentration...how determined to split his mind in two...there was no escaping the swooning awareness of his mother's intentions; no extraordinary power allowing him to elude tenacious fingers roving through a pair of crisp linen knickers...feeling him...squeezing him...twisting him. Her famished lips striving to kiss his mouth as he struggled to wrench away his neck. "*Grow for me, Samuel darling. You do love your mother, do you not? Then show me how much!*" But Samuel would not...*could* not cross such a forbidden, unforgivable line. She was his *mother*, for God's sake! His sickly, demented mother! And he was barely 11 years old. Then...as if being reprimanded for refusing to perform, she would yank his hand...forcing it beneath the sheets onto her thighs, until he no longer sensed the fabric of her gown, his little hand engulfed within the sinewy hallow of sodden flesh...his scrawny wrists being kneaded against slippery, supple folds...his sensitive ears stinging from frenzied moans of pleasure.

Afterwards as his mother lay convulsing upon the bed while reaching for her opium drops, Samuel would run downstairs to the laundry room, vomit into the washtub and grab a bar of Fels-Naptha, feverishly soaping his lips and then scrubbing his neck and hands until they were practically raw. But no matter how thoroughly he had cleansed himself...how meticulous he had been at removing every trace of the repulsive grume, outrageous images of his mother still persisted into the night...as if she were being resurrected from a demonic grave...even haunting him in his sleep; a bony forefinger beckoning him to come hither; bleeding lips commanding him to groom colorless, thinning hair; sagging breasts reviving to atrocious proportions with every firm stroke of the brush. Then, suddenly, as only dreams prompted by the desires of pubescent boys have the power to invoke...the hideous figure of his decrepit mother would magically transform into a beautiful young maiden...dull, sunken eyes becoming radiant like coals in a fire; parched, ashen lips revived to a healthy red; sallow skin set aglow as if kissed by the sun. And her hair...what had formerly resembled a discarded heap of burnt straw, now lavishly long and lustrously black. But it was the maiden's breasts which would fascinate him more than any other attribute. No longer resembling an oversized pair of rumpled bed pillows, they were, instead, dainty and pert like the most delicate of flowers, their irresistible fragrance compelling him to come closer and sample the sweetened ambrosia within. Almost instantaneously, Samuel would awaken upon sticky, saturated sheets, his disoriented mind reeling from the novel sensations still carousing throughout his groin. But although these spontaneous wet dreams had ceased soon after Samuel discovered the more practical method of self-gratification, the same disturbing, yet sensual dream had continued well into adulthood—even to the present day.

"If it makes you too sad, I don't *have* to wear your mother's necklace," Eleanor spoke up, crossing her fingers in the hope that her grieving host wouldn't take her suggestion too seriously. "Maybe *you'd* best have a drink of lemonade *yourself*," she offered, noticing beads of perspiration upon the doctor's eyebrows and trickling down the bridge of his nose.

Abruptly startled for a moment, sensing that his young guest had somehow been reading his innermost private thoughts, Samuel directly straightened his back against the chair, realizing that she was instead referring to the fictitious mother who allegedly perished in a house fire. "Why...of course not, my dear...dear Ellie Ann. Rather...as I mean to say...I am quite fine." He removed a handkerchief from his suit jacket pocket, completely unfolded it, and blotted his face. "Furthermore," he continued speaking while eyeing the ruby pendant as if it were the challenger in a jousting match, "as far as the necklace is concerned, you *shall* wear it and...and 'do it proud'! It would be a tribute to my dear mother's memory!" He then leaned forward and, slipping the pendant away from Eleanor's fingers, grasped the small diamond clasp and unhooked it.

Initially reluctant to let go of the pendant, Eleanor lifted the hair away from her neck upon feeling its weight against the hollow of her breasts, allowing Samuel to secure the antique heirloom. Straining her eyes to keep the precious gemstone in view, she supposed that if sold to a jeweler, it would not only buy a first-class passage to California, but a trip around the world and back if she wanted—in a giant ocean liner too—or even one of them fancy new passenger airplanes Jimmy Ray had been talking about.

"Would you care to see how nicely it complements you?" Samuel finally managed to suggest with the utmost control in his voice while fastidiously realigning a skewed pearl.

"Uh...yes!" Ellie blundered, immediately tearing her eyes away from the pendant, grateful that Doctor Governey couldn't know she'd been thinking about selling something so precious to his heart. But her green-eyed musings, as well as the crick in her neck, no longer mattered after gazing at her reflection in the hand mirror. As she had formerly suspected while getting all dressed up, the coolish pendant, all the more dazzling upon a background of light olive skin, was just the thing her satin gown had been lacking...its natural brilliance enriching the fabric's deep scarlet color. And her hair! What had seemed a mere minute ago to be average at best, was now more resplendent than a black marble fireplace all aglow.

"There are earrings to match," Samuel blithely proclaimed, remembering that his mother had worn the set mostly around the Christmas holidays and a few other formal occasions when she was still of sound mind. But I am afraid you will not be able to wear them since they were intended for ears which are pierced. Perhaps, if you would like, I am quite capable of piercing your own. Or," he quickly jumped in, noticing the look of apprehension on Eleanor's face, "I can arrange to have the earrings redesigned...that is, if you *do* happen to reside with me for a certain amount of time. Nevertheless," he nonchalantly shrugged, "if you *should* happen to decide to have your ears pierced or wait for the earrings to be redesigned, you would certainly wear them most splendidly, taking into consideration the contrasting color of your hair...particularly...*particularly* after your scheduled appointment with Virginia tomorrow morning for that stylish blunt cut!"

For a moment or so, Eleanor wondered how long it would really take to get the earrings fixed and was even about to ask Doctor Governey, but then realized it didn't matter. If she *did* stay longer, it would only be for another day, so it wouldn't be worth it for any jeweler to go through the trouble. *Of course*, it really *was* a shame to wear such a beautiful dress and necklace only one time, but...but.... "No, thank you, sss...*Sam...*," she answered, hesitantly handing back the mirror. "I mean...I *really* appreciate you offerin' to get my hair bobbed and...if it wouldn't be puttin' you out too much, I'd be most obliged to take you up on *that*, but I *really* would like to leave no later than mid-noon tomorrow, so I could catch the train ta California before the day's too old. So you see...you don't have to worry about the earrings after all."

"Wonderful!" Samuel exclaimed, slapping his hands together. "As you wish, my dear! I believe the shop opens promptly at nine. I will telephone then and arrange the earliest appointment, or whatever time will be most convenient for you."

"Well..." Ellie hesitated, suddenly wondering if she really *was* ready to part with her long, flowing locks, "I...I'm usually up at the crack of dawn, so whatever appointment you could get, I'd...I'd be ready for it!"

"Then that *certainly* settles the matter for tomorrow morning," Samuel declared, stepping sideways toward Eleanor's chair as the grandfather clock commenced chiming on the three-quarter hour. "But as for this evening, my dear, as soon as I warm up the Packard, we shall be on our way to the club. So, then...if you will do me the honor!"

Eleanor began reaching for Samuel's hand, but had barely touched his fingertips before turning her head toward the entrance hallway which lead to the kitchen. "But...Makara!" she protested, sitting on the edge of her seat while shifting her gaze toward the front drawing room window. "That storm we talked about is bound to come while we're gone. You know...I never left her in a strange place before and she's *awfully* afraid of lightning and thunder. Really, Doctor...*Sam*...I just don't want to leave her all alone. Can we take her with us...*please?*"

Not at all surprised with his guest's unsavory plea, Samuel offered an accommodating smile. He had predicted earlier that she would be reluctant to leave the four-legged bitch behind and consequently prepared for such a request by securing layers of old cotton toweling upon the Packard's back seat. Furthermore, he had ordered a special surprise for the mutt that he planned to gather on the way to the club, which would surely make him more endearing in the eyes of his future bride. "Of *course*, Ellie Ann. Why, I wouldn't *dream* of leaving Makara behind. In fact, I have already prepared for the occasion." Bowing slightly before his mollified guest, he clenched together both fists. "She will be in good hands...I *promise*. I have already contacted one of my most reliable attendants at the club with the instruction to keep her under careful watch at all times. And, I believe there will be a few choice morsels for her to chomp on, lest she is hungry. So...what do you say, Ellie Ann? Shall we be on our way, then? Perhaps you should care to visit the powder room while I wake Makara from her restful nap and situate her inside the Packard."

"But...aren't you gonna close those windows before we leave?" she asked as she rose from her seat. "Otherwise, the storm that's comin' through is bound to give everything a good soakin'!"

Bearing in mind that according to the newspapers, the skies had been clear over Lake St. Clair for the past few days, Samuel contained his patience.

Being that the Grosse Pointe community was well known for its virtual crimelessness, and keeping the windows open would significantly cool the mansion's overheated chambers, his initial instinct was to reject Eleanor's incessant prediction. But, upon further thought, he decided against it; the little sorceress was convinced that a storm was brewing and there was nothing he could say that would change her mind. "Of course, my dear. Why...thank you for reminding me. We certainly would not want everything to become wet!" As he began walking over to one of the leaded glass windows, he stopped in his tracks as Eleanor again spoke up.

"While you're closin' them windows, I'll just go to the bathroom, bein' that I know where it is. Then you won't have to wait for me after you're done."

Samuel stalled and turned toward Eleanor, hardly giving her a chance to start toward the drawing room's entrance. He'd have one hell of a time explaining should she wander about and discover her cherished Rottweiler muzzled and leashed to the cast iron chair. "Would you very much mind helping me close the windows *first*, Ellie Ann? I think the humidity has been making them stick and I had a devil of a time getting them open in the first place!"

"Well sure!" she answered, proudly recalling how she had, with a minimum amount of effort, been able to open and shut the small window in the upstairs dressing room.

Disregarding Eleanor's near presence for the moment, Samuel pushed aside the sheer curtain and glanced up toward an almost cloudless sky, deciding once and for all to leave down the convertible top on his brand new Packard Deluxe. Then, while bearing down upon the window's lower pane, he released an audible grunt, giving the impression of a genuine struggle. As Eleanor eagerly pushed alongside him, Samuel could sense her natural sweet scent intermingling with the dissipating Tabu cologne. Detecting an unexpected tickle alongside the bridge of his hand, he realized that her long, wavy tresses were brushing against his fingers and it suddenly crossed his mind that, had he been the average, young red-blooded American male, he would not, for one minute, have hesitated to take her in his arms and steal a kiss. *Certainly*, he pondered, finally allowing the window to slowly give way, he would be the envy of the evening with Eleanor upon his arm—as long as the unsophisticated wench managed to keep her mouth shut. But, hopefully, he shouldn't have much trouble arranging that, he concluded, while, at last, thanking her for a job well done. He would introduce her to a few of his colleagues, if necessary, and immediately proceed to his private, sequestered table where they would enjoy a wonderful seven-course meal.

As Eleanor followed him toward the other open window, Samuel discreetly tolerated her verbal conviction of possessing physical strength. *By any means*, he thought, it was *imperative* that a certain somebody—namely, that gold digging flapper Maggie 'skinny shins' O'Dougherty, former girlfriend of that gunned-down Purple Gangster, show up and honor their prearranged bargain. And a pretty penny he had promised her, too, he contemplated, inhaling the rejuvenating smell of Lake St. Clair. But...all in all...such a generous amount of money was chicken feed should it happen to purchase a one-way ticket on the lucrative train to Mayorsville. Refocusing his eyes to the petite figure on his left, he couldn't help but think that should the aspiring actress, by some stroke of luck, make it to Hollywood after all, she would, indeed, be a breath of fresh air on the silver screen. Unable to disengage that intimidating thought, Samuel gave a final, forceful push upon the beveled window, causing it to shut with a loud, dull thud. Then, reassuring himself that he was bound to be victorious in his conquest, he squeezed the palms of his hands together to relieve a sudden, arthritic pain...an unpleasant sensation he usually experienced before the onset of a drenching rain. Perhaps, then, the little wench was correct, he grumbled under his breath, cordially returning Eleanor's million dollar smile. Although the possibility of threatening weather shouldn't arrive any time soon, he would nevertheless see to it that the Packard was safely secured for the trip back home, instructing the garage attendants to promptly take care of the matter upon arrival at the most celebrated speakeasy ever situated on the banks of Michigan's wondrous Great Lakes—the brazenly notorious 'Club Dalla Giungla.'

chapter 81

Second Chance

Eleanor was grateful that the setting sun still provided ample illumination as she carefully lifted the skirt of her gown and stepped onto the Packard's chrome plated running board; otherwise she wouldn't be able to clearly see all the special features the emerald green convertible had to offer. Firmly grasping Samuel's hand and reassured that her panting, freshly bathed pup was safe and secure in the wide back seat smothered in toweling, she balanced her way past the spare wire wheel and entered the immaculate automobile, promptly seating herself on the chocolate brown upholstery as if upon a regal throne. As Samuel gripped the laced leather steering wheel and backed the automobile down the brick paved driveway, abandoning it for several minutes in order to reclose the heavy iron gates, Eleanor continued to inspect every delectable inch of the Phaeton's lavish interior. It was real furniture leather she was sitting on, not the cheaper fabric in the standard motor cars she'd been accustomed to. She was *sure* of it, she contemplated, breathing in its natural, clean smell. And she'd never seen a dashboard like the one before her—-not even in Mr. Richards' Packard. Why, aside from all the gauges and other instruments it contained, the whole darn panel was made of real furniture leather too! Even the flooring hadn't been neglected, she marveled, scooting forward and stroking a high heeled shoe over rich, mink-colored carpeting...the sort that would surely be ruined should it happen to get caught in a rainstorm. "I think it be best that you put the top up when we get to the club," she asserted as Samuel proceeded westward up Pennington Avenue. "It'd be a real shame if she got soakin' wet while sittin' outside."

Shifting the Packard into second gear, Samuel turned left onto Kercheval Avenue. "It certainly would be a shame, Ellie Ann," he acknowledged, immediately switching back to third while practically ignoring the lush green country club grounds to his right. "But there is no need to worry. Not only will the Packard be safe and sound inside our private garage, but my personal attendant, Lorenzo, will replace the top for our ride back home."

About to sink both front teeth into her lower lip, Eleanor suddenly eased her bite to avoid smearing her lipstick. The only garage she'd ever been to was the one at Jimmy Ray's station and it was only for *fixin'* cars, not parking them. And it sounded like there were other people who owned the night club too—which made a lot more sense since a doctor that gave abortions probably couldn't afford to buy *both* a fancy mansion *and* a night club all by himself. "Is Lorenzo gonna be the same man watchin' Makara while we're inside?"

Reaching upwards to adjust his Fedora hat, Samuel discreetly glanced toward the back seat. Damn! Though he had tied the tattered leash to the back window handle, the toweling was coming loose and the nasty bitch was shedding her flea-spawning fur all over the previously untouched upholstery. "Yes, my dear," he managed to mumble. Nearing Kerby Avenue, he gazed westward, realizing that by making an immediate right turn, he would forthwith arrive at Vito's Automobile Laundry on Mack Avenue. "Lorenzo, as well as several other of the attendants, will certainly take care of Makara," he tolerantly explained, resolving to drive the Packard to the newly established laundry first thing the following morning.

"Is the night club in downtown Detroit?" Ellie asked, the warm evening breeze nuzzling her face as they passed by another residential street along the quiet, southbound road.

"Actually..." Samuel began, realizing that Eleanor was familiar with the prevailing path leading to the Cottage Hospital, "Club Dalla Giungla is located neither in Detroit *nor* in Grosse Pointe. It is actually in the county of Macomb, but, at present, we are headed in a different direction just because there is something very important I must attend to before we arrive at the club."

Eleanor sulked back against her seat with pouted lips, disappointed that they weren't going downtown after all, being that some of the fanciest night clubs were bound to be there. Even Jimmy Ray said as much when telling the other day that one of them got raided, complaining how folks were making the owners richer than dirt when bums were being forced to beg on the streets. But then maybe *that* was why Doctor Governey's night club wasn't downtown, she guessed, admiring how fitting her fine feathered escort appeared behind the wheel of the brand new motor car. Maybe all the places downtown were selling illegal spirits and Doctor Governey didn't want to do that 'cause he might get raided too. Maybe the Club 'Dolla Joongalla'...or whatever it was called...was just a place where folks could eat a decent meal and drink sodas without worrying about cops with machine guns busting in all of a sudden. And even if it didn't happen to be as fancy as she first imagined, maybe there'd be music and *dancin'* too...something she always wanted to do if given the chance.

Feeling as if the effort to console herself still dangled like a pair of Hooverflags on the trousers of a homesick hobo, Eleanor began wondering why a night club that the doctor part-owned had such a strange name. It sounded like another language. It certainly wasn't English. It could be French...or maybe Spanish...though French would probably be better since she always heard how good their food was. Of course, she did enjoy the spaghetti and meatballs she once had at the Church of Christ's potluck picnic. Maybe 'Joongalla' is *Italian*, she finally supposed, wondering if the doctor would think her stupid if she just went ahead and asked him about it. But before the slightest sound could escape from her painted lips, Eleanor sensed the Packard rolling to a stop, realizing that it had already passed the Cottage Hospital and was now parked along a dirt patch in front of a pet shop that the Jefferson Beach bus would quickly pass by while delivering her to the newly constructed hospital. Two spotted puppies, clearly visible through the picture window of the illuminated clapboard building, were frolicking on a carpet of hay, presently disregarding the food and water dishes that were further restricting their already cramped quarters. Suddenly wondering how long the pups had been for sale and where they originally came from, Ellie impulsively glanced toward Makara, hoping that the pups would eventually find themselves in a loving home, even though they were just a pair of *ordinary* dogs. Her musings, however, were tossed by the wayside upon realizing that the doctor had purposely stopped by this particular shop to purchase something for Makara, specifically requesting her to remain inside the Packard while removing the key from the ignition and burying it within his suit jacket pocket.

As an increasing symphony of katydids blared across a peaceful universe of dwindling farmland and virtually vacant roads scantily bordered with unlit buildings, Eleanor gazed about the enveloping darkness while waiting for her escort to return, comprehending for the first time her surroundings from a different perspective. It all seemed so strange now, she observed, even though she'd driven this road on the Jefferson Beach bus numerous times before. And it wasn't just because it was getting dark either. Aside from the fact that waiting in the Packard convertible was a much more pleasant experience than sitting on a bumpy, crowded bus reeking of body odor and diesel fuel, she now had the chance to leisurely explore her surroundings. Casually resting the back of her head against the Packard's supple leather seat as Makara's soft snores cushioned the humid August air, Eleanor beheld the changes which had taken place since she first started working at the Cottage Hospital a little over a year ago. Although a far cry from the paved, bustling streets and mammoth department stores of downtown Detroit she'd see featured every so often in the newspapers, the small, simple village *was* beginning to take on a flavor all its own. An accommodating florist and friendly druggist had already staked claims amid a scattering of farmhouses to accommodate the needs of the hospital's patients and their visitors. However, she had also witnessed a fair number of the clapboard homes either being converted into specialty shops selling everything from cigars to sodas or going down like fallen soldiers in order to make room for more sizable retail buildings, a couple of which remained uncompleted due to the ongoing economic depression.

Determined to keep her mind focused on more pleasant thoughts, Eleanor looked a little further down the road where Grosse Pointe's finest cinema, the 'Punch and Judy Theatre' was situated. Except for a half-dozen or so automobiles and a carhop smoking his cigarette while pacing the generous parking lot, the Georgian style movie house seemed void of any other occupants. *Everybody must still be in there watchin' the near end of the picture,* she thought, aware that it was already half past eight with another showing of *White Zombie* at nine. Crossing both arms over her chest and letting out a sigh, she now wished she was going to the theatre instead of the 'Club dolla Joongalla,' though she'd much rather see the matinee showing of *Tom Sawyer* which was now playing every day at two-thirty in the afternoon. Besides, she pouted, the main feature might just be too scary and aside from Bela Lugosi, there really wasn't any actors in it that she knew much about. At least *Tom Sawyer* had Mitzi Green in it—the girl who played Zinnie Wheater in *The Marriage Playground*. Focusing upon a navy blue Auburn slowly entering the parking lot, Ellie reflected upon the time she and her girlfriend, Phyllis, snuck into the local theatre in Wilmington to see the amusing drama. It was always between showings when the last of the patrons were leaving that they were able to slip into the back entrance hall and plant themselves against the wall until the ushers were finished cleaning up. Then, they'd scurry to the rear of the cinema and hide between the seats until the picture was well under way. They must have seen at least six dozen picture shows without once getting caught. And at the price of a nickel a show, it was well worth it! But it had been quite a while since she'd been to a movie theatre after being kicked out of the Grosse Pointe Park Theatre on Charlevoix Avenue where she'd sometimes stop on a detour route coming home from Cottage Hospital. It was only by pleading with the manager that she was let go without further punishment.

Well aware that several other motor cars were beginning to pull into the lot for the nine o'clock showing, Eleanor strained to catch sight of the two whimsical marionettes atop the rounded 'Punch and Judy' sign which hovered over the theatre's portico entrance. The reddish brick building with multiple chimneys and white-shuttered windows was sure a lot fancier than the movie house in Wilmington, or even the Grosse Pointe Park Theatre, for that matter. It probably cost at *least* a dime to get in, or maybe even more. And she once saw in the *Detroit Free Press* that it cost a whole dollar just for a balcony seat! Of course, she concluded, watching the doorman assist a fashionable lady and her dapper escort into the lighted building, she wouldn't care where she was seated as long as she was able to sit back for an hour or two while enjoying another fabulous feature on that big, wide, magical screen.

As a small crowd of movie patrons began filing out of the theatre's side entrance, Eleanor's heart began to flutter. Maybe those same people will be coming to see *her* someday on the big screen. But first she had to get to Hollywood, she reasoned, while two more carhops, appearing out of nowhere, promptly began to retrieve each vehicle. Feeling instantly restless, she once again focused her attention on the pet store, realizing that Doctor Governey was bound to be coming out any minute. *Special gift or not*, she fretted, glancing back at her sleeping pup, maybe she shouldn't have agreed to stay another day after all. Maybe she shouldn't even have opened any of those presents or wasted all that time feasting on fruit and cakes. Then she might *already* be on her way to California.

Realizing that it was becoming quite dark, she squeezed together her hands and looked toward the sky. A milky ray of white was vanishing into a shade of starless indigo while a cryptic moon, shrouded in translucent clouds, secreted an anemic halo. Despite the warm, smothering air, she shivered. Now that she decided to have the baby, the $342 she stole from Jimmy Ray along with the money she'd get from selling Mama's locket probably *would-n't* be enough to sustain her for nine months before gettin' hired by a movie director—even if the necklace *was* real gold like Officer McCallister was telling Doctor Governey. Now she'd *really* have to find another hospital job or maybe do some bookkeeping work. But what if... Eleanor's throat remained dry as she tried to lubricate it with a quick swallow. What if nobody wanted to hire her? Then what would she do? Or what if she *does* find work and after all that trouble, doesn't even *get* an acting job? *After all,* even 12-year-old Mitzi Green played in her family's vaudeville act since the age of three and *she*...just plain ol' ordinary Ellie Anne Snyder...didn't have any acting experience whatsoever! Even Doctor Governey's *mother* would of had a lot better chance at breakin' in the motion pictures with her vaudeville know-how, she sighed, instinctively glancing down at the ruby pendant noticing that, in the absence of sunlight, the radiant gemstone had turned a deep purple. *Of course, if this necklace belonged to me, I wouldn't have to worry one stitch about havin' enough money.* She didn't know much about the worth of such high class jewels, but did remember Jimmy Ray telling Mama that the ruby ring Greta Garbo was wearing in the picture *Grand Hotel* was like-ly worth half a million dollars. And it probably wasn't even *half* this size, not to mention all the pearls and diamonds on the necklace too! *Why*...Ellie gasped, fondling the pendant with quivering fingers...if I could hock this here necklace, not only would I never have to worry about money again but could buy myself my *own* motion picture studio!

Eleanor gazed toward the lighted pet shop, noticing that its front door still was securely shut. If she grabbed Makara now, she could run down the back fields and hide somewhere until morning before catching the bus to the train station. *No...That* wouldn't work. First, she had no bus fare bein' that all her money was left behind at the mansion inside her trench coat pocket since Doctor Governey didn't give her no purse to put it in. And she'd never

get away with asking strangers for it like some down-and-out beggar, bein'
dressed up like she was. Unless...she could run about a half-mile down where
there were more shops and then find a way to break into that small dry goods
store...take one of the dresses along with a good pair of walkin' shoes and
leave the satin gown and heels behind in exchange so she really wouldn't be
stealing. And while she was at it, she thought, envisioning the extra vial of
ether left behind in her traveling bag, she'd grab some kind of skirt or something to wrap around Makara and hope to God she keeps quiet. And she'd
check the cash register too where there was bound to be some money she
could borrow. Or maybe if she couldn't get enough money, she could *hitch*
some rides out West. Maybe even be lucky enough to find someone who was
heading for Route 66 right off. *Of course*, taking the ruby necklace would be
a much worser crime than stealing some ordinary dry goods and a drawer of
starter cash. Them small town outlaws, Bonnie and Clyde would look like a
couple o' Robin Hood's merry men once the law was onto *her*. But she
wouldn't really be *stealin'* the necklace. She'd pay Doctor Governey back.
Even *double* the cash when she got rich and famous!

As a ream of possibilities kept flashing through her mind like the forthcoming thunderstorm, Eleanor waited for a rumbling Mercedes to pass by.
Then, clenching the Packard's inside door handle, she looked around before
catching a glimpse of Virginia's Beauty Salon directly across the street. Was
she *crazy*? How could she even *think* of getting away with such a thing when
Jimmy Ray and a whole slew of police officers were still bound to be looking
for her—with bloodhounds to track her down too! Even a whole sack full of
turtle bones probably wouldn't be enough to ward them off. And what she'd
get for stealing Jimmy Ray's money and Mama's locket would likely be a slap
on the hand compared to the punishment she'd reap for robbing the doctor
out of his own dead mama's million dollar necklace! Of course, even if she
was put inta jail for life, it'd still be better than havin' to go back living with
Jimmy Ray and Mama. A cold, sinking feeling plunged through Eleanor's
chest as images of Jimmy Ray materialized, mauling her like a salivating
ogre...plump, grainy lips reeking of liquor, scorching her with that indelible
raspy, monotone voice...stony, putrid hands barricading each muffled scream
for help. *No!* she whimpered, startling a long-tailed cat which had paused to
wash itself in the middle of the street, then scurried along the dark, threatening avenue. She wasn't *ever* goin' back to live with Mama and Jimmy Ray, she
resolved, tugging cracked knuckles until her fingers felt sore. She'd rot in a

jailhouse before lettin' that happen! But...but that'd *still* be no kinda life and her dream of becoming a movie star would *never* come true.

Making a conscious effort to breathe naturally while reclining against the supple leather of the Packard's passenger seat, Eleanor could feel every nerve in her body struggling to knit itself back together again. *If* she decided to *borrow* a thing or two from Doctor Governey, it would not be tonight. After all, didn't the doctor say that his mother had other pieces of jewelry stored away too? And hadn't she noticed several more boxes inside the tall wooden chest when he had opened it to fetch the necklace in the first place...one of which was sure to contain the matching ruby earrings he had mentioned? *Heck*, she thought, tracing calmer fingers alongside the pendant's diamond border, wondering what other treasures were hidden inside those boxes. It'd even be better to sell some smaller pieces anyway since a hock shop or even a good jeweler wouldn't likely have a million dollars on them all at once. Then, maybe if *that* money was enough to get by on, there'd be no need to sell the ruby pendant being that Doctor Governey was *especially* attached to it. And if she was *real* careful to leave the boxes in their place, he might not notice that the jewels were missing until she was a famous actress. She just needed enough time to win his trust by staying for a few days like he asked her to. Afterwards, just when he didn't happen to be around, she'd sneak into the drawing room, take off her shoes and clamber along the tall, grooved chest like she used to do when climbing the cherry tree in old man Colgan's orchard. Then, with key in hand, she'd open the chest and take the jewels out of their boxes before bringing them upstairs and hiding them in the traveling bag.

As a 1930 Cadillac Cabriolet approached the corner of Fisher Road, Eleanor once again glanced toward the darkened beauty salon. In the morning she was going to get her hair bobbed. Then, in a few more days after sneaking out the mansion with the hidden jewels, not only would the search for her have worn down, but the police would be less likely to recognize her. Her stomach growled as she let out a soothing sigh. Amused by a few latecomers scurrying under a lamplight to catch the nine o'clock showing of *White Zombie*, she wished that Doctor Governey would hurry before it began to rain. But soon after the carhop had taken possession of a Buick coupe, the door to the pet shop finally opened, the generous doctor appearing like some long-awaited prince, his Fedora hat in one hand and a brown paper bag in the other.

chapter 82

Lakeside Chase

As the Packard Deluxe continued on its way, leaving the pet shop behind, Eleanor pressed the paper bag closely to her lap, bearing in mind Doctor Governey's firm instructions to "keep it under wraps" until their arrival at the Club Dalla Giungla. She guessed it might be a new collar for Makara, but didn't want him to notice the crinkling of the bag while trying to feel for it. And she couldn't even sneak a peek inside, being that the top edge was securely shut by an uneven row of staples.

"Have you noticed our beautiful new motion picture theatre, Ellie Ann?" Samuel gestured toward the 'Punch and Judy Theatre,' practically bringing the Packard to a stop before slowly turning left on Fisher Road. "Coincidentally, it too, is equipped with a mighty Wurlitzer, though I've only had the privilege of hearing its overwhelming music from my private seat in the theatre box on opening night. But, of course, I am a personal acquaintance of the proprietor," he winked while passing the Grosse Pointe public high school, "and I am certain, that, should I happen to make the request, the organist would be more than eager to perform for us exclusively."

"That sure would be awful nice," Eleanor wistfully smiled back. "But, you know...I most likely won't be stayin' for more than a few days now. Unless...unless we could maybe do it before I'm about ready to leave."

Delighted that his oblivious bride-to-be was considering a lengthier stay than she had previously declared, Samuel bore down on the clutch and shifted the Packard into third gear, ensuring a smooth drive along the remainder of Fisher Road. "Well, then, Ellie Ann, I shall see what I can arrange. Although...I am not quite sure that Mr. Kavanach will be able to accommodate us on such short notice. Nevertheless...," he confidently stated, driving away from the high school's impressive clock tower, "I will contact him immediately and try my best to persuade him otherwise. Of course, Ellie Ann, the offer to stay with me for as long as you wish still stands. And, if that be the case, we shall be able to accomplish much more than just a demonstration or two upon a Wurlitzer organ. Why," Samuel continued, delighted that he had grabbed the child's full attention, "I would be most honored to have you as my guest for an evening or two in the theatre's private loge." He paused for a moment, neglecting to admit that being permitted to smoke his cigar in that particular section of seats made the whole motion picture experience well worth his while. "Quite a few new films are scheduled to be released within the next several weeks, you know, some of which will be featuring famous stars such as Marlene Dietrich, Gable and Harlow. It would be such a shame for you to miss the opportunity of viewing such films in one of the most acoustically perfect theatres in all of America."

Eleanor needlessly braced herself as Samuel made a smooth left turn onto Jefferson Avenue, vaguely aware of the approaching Italian Renaissance style mansion on their right. She didn't know what "acoostickly" meant or even what a loge was, but she *did* know about the picture shows Doctor Governey was mentioning. The first one, *Blonde Venus* with Marlene Dietrich and Cary Grant wasn't due to come out until the middle of September and the other with Clark Gable and Jean Harlow, *Red Dust*, she was pretty sure would be showing sometime well into the month of October. And, as inviting as watching them "acoostickly" sounded, there was just no way she'd want to wait that long before headin' out to California. "I'm sorry, sir...*Sam*...but I'm afraid that a week's time is prob'ly the most I'll be stayin'. It does sound awfully nice though, seein' one of them talkin' pictures in such a fine theatre."

Samuel kept his foot braced against the accelerator as Jefferson Avenue's expanded dirt road merged along Lake St. Clair's walled shoreline. At least she had just extended her visit by a couple of days, he appreciatively contemplated, but he'd still have to convince her to stay a bit longer if he wished to eventually make her his bride. "Are you aware, Ellie Ann..." He focused upon a lighted steamer close to the Canadian shore, realizing that in a few hours time, many more boats would be sharing the compliant waterway in order to smuggle in lucrative cases of bootleg liquor which would ultimately be delivered into the hands of racketeers already perched upon accommodating docks. "Many people would consider themselves most fortunate to be living in our beautiful state of Michigan. Did you know that our Great Lakes and their connecting channels contain the largest resource of fresh water on earth? It holds one-fifth of the world's supply and nine-tenths of our country's as well." Noticing the detached look upon his student's innocent face, he immediately changed the subject. "Why...I would bet my bottom dollar that given a few years' time, Michigan will rival Hollywood itself with its miles of scenic shoreline and an endless supply of picturesque land. Furthermore, well-renowned director, Edmund Goulding, along with his enthusiastic producers, has already discovered our upper peninsula's Mackinac Island with the filming of *Grand Hotel.* Certainly!" Samuel affirmed, reflexively bearing down upon the accelerator, "It will only be a matter of time before the magnates of the motion picture industry rush into this state like a swarm of locusts, scouting out pretty, talented young actresses such as yourself. As a matter of fact," he added, pointing across the road toward a partially lighted Palladian mansion, its balustrade terrace and rolling lawn shrouded in darkness, "there is word going around that a theatrical company is unfolding in one of these lovely Grosse Pointe homes in anticipation of that very event!"

Refocusing her gaze upon Lake St. Clair, Eleanor shrunk further into her seat as the vast sheet of tarnished silver, animated only by a scant scattering of lights and a warm, accelerating breeze, seemed to engulf the moving vehicle. It *did* make sense, she reflected, that on account of the Great Lakes, the state of Michigan was like no other. Why...just about the only thing that would lift her gloomy spirits when first moving here from Ohio was when Jimmy Ray would take her and Mama out for rides along Lake St. Clair. It was the perfect remedy glancing back and forth between the blue sparkling water and beautiful mansions, thinking that maybe someday she'd be rich enough to be out in one of them sailboats or even live in a mansion of her own. And maybe she *shouldn't* be headin' out for California right away. Maybe she should find out more about that Grosse Pointe theatre group and whether or not they think it would be worth her while to stay in Michigan for a spell. *But then, again,* it'd only be a matter of time that Jimmy Ray and Mama'd be catchin' up with her.

Ellie clutched the paper bag closer to her waist, unable to rid herself of a melancholy that even the approaching landmark tower of the Grosse Pointe Yacht Association could not subdue. Scared as she really was about running away to California on her own, it *still* was the best possible plan, she pondered, as the miniature lights on the glassy lake gleamed like dozens of shifty eyes seized from the starless sky. Instinctively, she glanced back at her sleeping pup. She'd been so sure up until now that Makara, having such an exceptional soul, would be all she needed for protection. So why was she feeling especially threatened? She couldn't quite put a finger on the reason, but it was as if something deep inside was trying to signal a warning; almost as when farmers ring their dinner gongs to tell others of an approaching tornado. But, almost instantaneously, she noticed a flashing red light approaching from behind as if her worries had conjured up genuine alarm—the very moment the Packard began slowing down, finally surrendering to the persistent command of a black Ford V-8 patrol car.

chapter 83

Close Call

More perturbed about the unnecessary delay than the possibility of being fined for traveling 35 miles per hour in a 15 mile per hour zone, Samuel kept a steady eye on his side view mirror, discerning from the officer's familiar rhythmic limp and squatty build that the character in question was no other than Don Barrett, a United States Army private who had earned a Silver Citation Star for outstanding service to his country during the Great War. Immediately comprehending the futility of reaching inside the glove box for his Michigan issued driver's license, he instead unassumingly addressed the patrolman, receiving in return an overly apologetic smile accompanied by a tip of the hat.

"Goo...good evening Sam! Sorry, but...I didn't recognize you. Say...," he continued, flashing his most becoming smile upon noticing Eleanor, "when did you happen to acquire *this* beauty? The *Packard Deluxe*, I mean," he clarified, winking a military green eye. "Never seen you driving *her* up until now!" Aided by the rather weak headlights of the Ford patrol car, Barrett began inspecting the magnificent white wall tires and mounting curved fenders of the emerald green Packard as Samuel explained that the automobile, his most recent pride and joy, barely had been broken in. But the police officer's newly found fascination with the impeccable sedan was soon interrupted by a low growl from the back seat preceding an incessant series of feverish, high-pitched barks. Glancing quickly toward the direction of the pup, then back at Samuel before further scrutinizing the obviously horrified Eleanor, officer Barrett's lighthearted demeanor suddenly changed into that of a somber minister. "I don't know if you heard, Samuel," he cautiously started, his softened voice growing deeper with every word. "There's been a report down at the office of a young runaway missing." He paused long enough to silently assess the validity of his suspicions. "Supposedly, she ran away with her dog...although...although...as I remember it, I believe the lady in question is somewhere around the age of 14...yes!...14-years-old," he assuredly nodded, realizing that lurking underneath all that makeup could very well be the face of an innocent child.

"Yes...you are quite right," Samuel affirmed, suppressing the urge to reach toward the back seat and strangle the yelping Rottweiler. "Your buddy, Sergeant McCallister, was by my home this very afternoon describing the same unfortunate situation. He was returning the motor car I had lent him over the weekend...the red Duesenberg I purchased before acquiring *this* tempting beauty," he roguishly winked. "Yes, my dear Officer Barrett, one of the greatest pleasures in life is sharing one's good fortune with one's most favored comrades." Satisfied that he had rendered the officer speechless, Samuel discreetly leaned forward. "I was also told that the particular runaway in question had been abused repeatedly by her mother's resident boyfriend...in ways that would make Jack the Ripper appear a genuine gentleman." Curling his bottom lip in disgust, he continued. "I suppose...I suppose it would be more humane to commission such an unfortunate child through enemy trenches in the midst of lethal gases and hostile machine-gun nests than reveal her whereabouts to such despicable guardians. Don't you agree, officer?"

Private Barrett shuddered, recalling his own brush with death as he crawled on blood-drenched elbows through thick fog and fire before gunning down two German artillerymen and capturing another seven. Though Samuel Governey's analogy was a bit of a stretch, he reasoned while managing to impart an assenting smile, it had, nevertheless, demonstrated the gravity of the situation. "Why...yes...yes!...by all means, Sam!" he practically shouted, temporarily silencing the stunned Rottweiler. "Why...I couldn't agree with you more. I'm sorry to have inconvenienced you. Ma'am," he stated, nodding toward Eleanor, noticing whitened knuckles loosening their grip upon the paper bag. "I suppose you'd better be on your way before it starts to storm now...best to keep the inside of your Packard clean for the next person you happen to lend it to!" Without another word, Officer Barrett limped back toward the squad car, his broad bottom settled into the tattered driver's seat before witnessing the Packard suddenly lurching forward, eventually disappearing into the night as it headed north along Lake St. Clair.

chapter 84

Club Dalla Giungla

Eleanor Ann Snyder soon forgot about the encounter with the police officer as well as the contents of the paper bag while Samuel suavely directed the convertible onto a sweeping thoroughfare lined with torches illuminating an immense plot of simulated Uganda grass. She practically gasped while viewing dozens of lush green topiaries vividly shaped into various forms of life-size African wildlife, suddenly realizing that this was the brand new spectacular 'jungle speakeasy' on the shore of Lake St. Clair that Jimmy Ray and Mama had, at one time or another, mentioned. Colossal elephants, lofty giraffes and pompous tigers escorted several other enthusiastic patrons as well, all the while beckoning everyone toward the Club Dalla Giungla's Mediterranean Style entrance with its wide stone steps and a netted canopy. But even the triple-tiered, balconied speakeasy soon dissipated into a fleeting memory as Samuel passed it without a pause and veered around to the rear entrance, allowing him privileged access to the club's private garage.

Given hardly a chance to fully appreciate the expansive tiled flooring, cast iron radiators and a variety of spit and polished motor cars apparently well-fueled by a towering Mobil Oil gas pump, Eleanor, undisturbed by Makara's restless barking, remained faithfully seated alongside Samuel as he signaled the garage attendant, Lorenzo, to hold off a bit before taking possession of the Packard, allowing his beautiful guest a little time to finally open the stapled package. Further prompted by the enticing sound of orchestra music accompanying the sweet, spicy aroma of cooked meat, Eleanor ripped open the top of the bag. To her delight, she pulled out the white looped leash that had lingered in her imagination during the past 20 minutes or so...only what she had envisioned wasn't nearly as pretty. She beamed with genuine gratitude, her unadorned fingers tracing their way across the supple leather and onto the ornately decorated collar. "Are these *real* diamonds?" she asked, examining the row of alluring stones which sparkled underneath the artificial lights.

Both amused and annoyed by the child's naiveté, Samuel displayed a tight-lipped smile. "My dear...I most sincerely wish I could claim that they *were* genuine," he finally explained, raising his voice above the interminable barking. "But I am afraid it is impossible to find a dog collar with genuine diamonds in an ordinary pet store. Of course, if Makara were my own dear pet," he nodded toward the Rottweiler, wishing he could slap another muzzle on her long, black snout, "I would commission a jeweler to design one fit for a queen. Then she would be the most exquisitely adorned canine in all of Grosse Pointe!"

With waning fascination toward the imitation diamonds, Eleanor focused her attention upon the attached identification tag, exposing the engraved wording as she tilted it upward toward the light. ***Makara, 16 Pennington Ave., Grosse Pte., Michigan***.

Before she could utter a single word to accompany the puzzled look upon her face, Samuel quickly interjected. "My original intention simply was to have Makara's *name* engraved upon the piece. But the proprietor wouldn't hear of it, suggesting that a dog as cherished as Makara should be provided a place of safe return in the event of wandering away from home and becoming quite lost. When I explained to the proprietor that Makara did not yet have a known address, he insisted that I use my own, reasoning that, in case such an event occur, Makara would be returned to me, whereas I could promptly contact *you. Of course,*" he quickly emphasized, "my personal address is only *temporary.* Once you have settled down in the beautiful 'Golden State' of California, it can be easily rubbed out and replaced with your own. Although it might be a minor inconvenience, surely you will agree that it is a wise measure, indeed. Here now," he declared, taking possession of the leashed rhinestone collar. "Shall we try it on for size?" He then allowed Lorenzo to escort Eleanor from the Packard as he stepped out himself and proceeded to open the rear door in an attempt to collar the barking pup.

However, despite several attempts to appease the excited Rottweiler, Samuel eventually realized that his own perseverance and dogged determination were no match for the spirited canine.

"Here...let *me* try," volunteered Eleanor from behind, grabbing hold of the leash and collar as Samuel stepped behind her to allow ample room. "Now, now, Makara," she purred, effortlessly unhooking the dog's crude, dirty collar, "hold still...that's a girl! Uncle Sam got you a brand *new* collar so you'll look real pretty for our night out on the town! There now!" she declared, snapping it into place as the hushed Rottweiler began licking her hand. She then slowly withdrew herself from the pup while holding onto the leash, finally turning toward Samuel. "I think she'll be alright inside the club if we just give her a bone or something to chew on. Then she won't be barkin' so much!"

Feeling somewhat like a naughty schoolboy shunned by his classmates for pulling on their ribboned pigtails, Samuel nevertheless composed himself as Eleanor coaxed Makara to jump onto the immaculate mosaic floor. Although he originally hoped that the stubborn girl would agree to have the dog remain with an attendant while they both dined inside, he now realized that this was not even a remote possibility. *However,* he conceded with a resigned shrug, if his patrons could be entertained by the caged chimpanzee inside the club's 'Congo Room' rumored to be the actual Cheetah from Metro-Goldwyn-Mayer's *Tarzan the Ape Man,* then they certainly shouldn't object to the mere presence of a harmless Rottweiler pup.

Promptly removing the Fedora from his head and placing it upon the passenger seat, Samuel directed Eleanor toward an arched door held open by Lorenzo. They were going into the kitchen, she gathered before stepping inside. She could tell by the clamor of cookware and the aromas that made her mouth water. Even Makara could barely contain herself as she excitedly frisked about, determined to smell every clapboard and corner of the massive utilitarian kitchen. Eleanor's eyes became wide as shot glasses while looking about, her enraptured mind taking in all the commotion. A chef in full white uniform and tall matching hat was throwing orders around like boomerangs, over-spilled sauces hissed from copper pots and countless dishes filled to order were being flung upon marble counters. If it weren't for the seductive jazz music luring her toward the other side of the room, she thought, as Samuel stopped to ask an assistant chef to spare him a soup bone, she would have been content to remain behind and continue watching the show! But the popular Louie Armstrong song, "All of Me" soon fell on deaf ears as Eleanor entered the club's main dining room, the boisterous laughter and loud murmurs drowning out her spontaneous, open-mouthed gasp. If not for all the tables, chairs and curved booths scattered about the multi-leveled floor and so many folks dressed to the nines, it would feel like she was right in the middle of an African jungle! It kind of reminded her of Doctor Governey's library, but not so spooky, she noted, gazing past a lifelike elephant water fountain and eying primitive masks and headdresses nailed to timbered walls. And trees that looked so real with colorful birds perched throughout their branches. It was almost like something that would be part of a Hollywood set. She almost expected Johnny Weissmuller to appear any moment swinging from the rafters!

It seemed as if a thousand questions were swirling inside Ellie's mind by the time Samuel reached the front end of the dining room, inviting her to be seated at the premier elevated corner booth adorned with a leather skin cloth and two place settings of colorful bone china. Did he help with all the decorating? How many other people owned the restaurant besides him? How much did it cost to build such a place? How could all these people afford eating here when so many others were destitute and left wanting on the streets? How much money was the club taking in anyway? *And the bar,* she pondered, looking over her shoulder toward the far end of the room, vaguely aware that Samuel was securing Makara to the sturdy leg of his zebra-wood chair. If those men are selling *real* liquor, aren't they doing something illegal? Aren't they afraid of getting caught? What would happen to them if they did? But, as if to ease Eleanor's worries, a waiter in safari gear appeared at the table welcoming her and Samuel to the club, rattling off the evening's dinner specials while handing over a telephone which Samuel promptly plugged into the wall.

Requesting that the waiter leave a menu for Eleanor, Samuel graciously expressed his thanks and dismissed him for the time being, but not before discreetly peeking through the sheer-curtained window, lest he detect any trouble brewing from cutthroat prohibition agents who, like Eliot Ness and his tenacious "Untouchables," were determined to hook a few more big fish before the repeal of the Volstead Act depleted every superabundant stream. "Go ahead, my dear. Order anything you wish," he offered, removing an embroidered handkerchief from his jacket pocket to rid his right hand of the excess moisture which had seeped through the napkin of the wrapped soup bone. It was perturbing enough to be spoiling a perfectly clean handkerchief, he inwardly fumed, let alone having that worthless dog slobbering all over his beautiful planked mahogany floor.

Experiencing a break from the warm humid air which, she assumed, was being generated by one of those incredible air cooling machines now used in the finest of movie houses, Eleanor opened the menu and glanced at the bill of fare, making neither head nor tail of the tedious list of fine French and Italian cuisine. "Can I just have some *ham*?" she timidly asked.

"I think we can arrange to have some brought out as an appetizer," Samuel replied, bearing in mind the antipasto plate laden with Italian cheeses, black caviar, deviled eggs, assorted olives, jumbo shrimp, and the finest imported salami and prosciutto ham. "Or, if you would prefer, I shall order the glazed ham with a side of sweet potatoes for you. However my dear...if I may be so inclined to suggest...the specialty of the house tonight is a superb Chateaubriand served with a side order of sautéed julienned vegetables and parsley potatoes." He paused for a moment to touch her fingertips. "I sincerely believe you will find it to your liking, but if not, I promptly shall have your portion returned and order the glazed ham after all!"

Eleanor suspiciously closed the menu as a *sommelier* dressed in elegant African ceremonial garb presented a bottle of wine, accompanied by a scantily clad bus boy in native attire who placed a wicker basket filled with plump, white bread on the table. Ever since getting a whiff of the forbidden ham in Doctor Governey's kitchen early that afternoon, she was having a craving for some. But, being it seemed he was counting on her to try that 'shatoobrand' dish...whatever *that* was...she should probably go ahead and do so. Then, maybe tomorrow if she still had a craving for that ham, Doctor Governey might let her have some for lunch. "Alright," she said, wondering why the waiter had poured the red wine into only one of two stemmed glasses until the doctor began swirling it, thinking maybe he was making sure that no pieces of cork had fallen in. "Whatever you wanna order will be fine with me."

Placing the cork upon a napkin, Samuel lifted the Chateau Lafite Rothschild closer to his nose as the 12-piece band from the adjoining ballroom accompanied a Negro vocalist belting out "I Found a Million Dollar Baby." He then inhaled its spicy bouquet and savored its rich, fruity flavor before directing the wine steward to fill both glasses. "The lady and I shall have the Chateaubriand tonight, Pietro," he then told his favorite waiter who had reappeared as if out of nowhere. "But first we shall enjoy the assorted antipasto." After waiting for the bottle of wine to be placed inside a crystal ice bucket, Samuel offered Eleanor some bread and butter, then scanned the expanse of the room. He hadn't spotted Maggie O'Dougherty yet, although she wasn't scheduled to appear until after they had eaten their dinner, he reflected, noticing that Officers Bullo and Dennison had just arrived at the bar for their first round of beers. And although he hadn't yet sighted his partner in crime, Tony Terillo, he knew that 'The Tank' was present on the premises since his prized Cord had been parked in the private garage upon their arrival. Most likely, he was up on the third floor playing billiards or in the 'Rwanda Room' shooting craps. He smiled, pretending to give Eleanor his undivided attention as she unceasingly commented about every single aspect of the place while improperly buttering her bread with a dinner knife. He was in no hurry to introduce this unsophisticated tidbit to the least of his colleagues. That is, not as of yet.

Samuel glanced toward the colossal elephant statue centered inside the fountain as a few well-heeled patrons with cocktail glasses were catching the desired amount of gin for their dry martinis from its flowing trunk. "Do you like merry-go-rounds, Ellie Ann?" he asked, hoping to put a small dent in the one-sided conversation. "There is one on the second floor which the ladies seem to revel in, as well as an assortment of carnival games," he pointed upward, referring to a custom-sized carousel equipped with hand-carved jungle animals pouncing to a variety of calliope tunes. "And *Cheetah,* the mischievous chimpanzee from the recent Tarzan film, is in our Congo Room along with a few other specimens of African wildlife. So...after we have completed our dinner, I shall show you around. But *first,*" he emphasized, gently grasping the stem of his wine glass, "I should like to propose a toast." He then lifted the glass and, with a gesture, encouraged Eleanor to do the same. "To a most beautiful and lasting friendship with an exquisite, incomparable lady."

Following the cue of her mannerly host, Eleanor deposited the uneaten buttered bread back inside the basket, unaware that a vacant plate had been included at her setting for that very purpose. She wasn't sure what 'incomparable' meant, but could tell it was something good by the tone of Doctor Governey's voice, she assumed while squeezing the stem of the glass. And though she felt excited about going to see all those fun things after supper, she *was* content to stay put and share some time with him for a *little* while longer. And his *eyes*, she thought, listening to the lingering ring of their glasses; maybe it had to do with the club being so magical and all, but she hadn't noticed how blue they were up until now. Just like freshly sprouted morning glories, though the wrinkles around them seemed to deepen when he smiled. And his nose. Any other person with a nose as long as that might seem unattractive, but it kind of gave him a movie star look. Like with Clark Gable's ears or Edward G's square jaw. *Of course*, she contemplated, crinkling her own sensitive nose while Samuel seemed to encounter a divine revelation upon swallowing the fine Bordeaux. He really *ought* to start using a weed killer that wasn't so hard to wash off.

"Go ahead, my dear," interrupted Samuel. "It's quite alright. Why don't you join me in sampling a taste of heaven from one of the finest vineyards in all of France?"

Having momentarily forgotten about her glass of wine, Eleanor stared at it before taking a sip, wondering what it would taste like. The color was such a deep red, it was as though the ruby on her necklace had melted right into the glass. And it smelled strong but somewhat sweet at the same time, she couldn't help noticing while bringing it closer to her face. Not at all like the terrible whiskey she once snuck a taste of when Jimmy Ray and Mama were drop-dead drunk. Holding her breath, she tilted the glass, being careful not to drink too much all at once. With puckered lips she swallowed, all the while thinking, as the bittersweet claret inflamed her throat, that it seemed more like a drink from *hell* rather than from heaven and wishing she could just have a good wholesome glass of grape soda.

"An appreciation for an exceptional wine such as this sometimes takes years to acquire, Ellie Ann," Samuel boasted of the 1898 vintage Bordeaux. "So take your time and sip it slowly. There is no reason to hurry. The evening is still young and perhaps after we have had our fill of it, you will have grown somewhat accustomed to the distinct full-bodied flavor after all."

Terribly relieved that Doctor Governey hadn't expected her to finish the wine all at once, Eleanor carefully placed the glass back upon the table, noticing that she had left a petite lipstick mark upon the rim. It was a shame that her beautiful red lip color had started to rub off, she frowned, especially since she didn't have another tube to touch it up with...all the more reason to avoid the wine altogether. Of course, she'd still run into the same problem while eating, but at least her lipstick would be fading over something that was tasting good. In any case, she resolved, as a photographer in colorful native garb approached the table, she'd be extra careful not to let the food rub against her lips too much.

"Good evening, Sam...*miss*," greeted the *faux* 'Negro,' his white painted lips spreading from one black cheek to the other. "Would ya like yer picture taken? I can have it ready in another hour or two," he winked. "Terrific, mates! I mean...folks!" he exclaimed upon noticing Eleanor's unreserved enthusiasm. Without waiting for Samuel's approval, the photographer spread the long, skinny legs of his tripod, being careful to avoid getting them caught within the thick, stiff blades of his grass skirt. Trying not to disturb the preoccupied pup still chomping away at her soup bone, he made sure that the tripod was firmly planted to the floor before mounting his camera on top and mixing the proper amount of chemicals upon a metal tray attached to a flashgun. With a look of apprehension in the whites of his eyes, he bid the couple to sport a dashing smile, immediately opening the camera's shutter and igniting the flash, sending an abrupt sheet of white flame rocketing upwards. "Alright then, Doctor Governey!" he panted, streaking black paint above his brow while wiping off beads of perspiration, "Thank ya much! Give me 'bout an hour or two and I'll have her developed for ya by the time yer ready ta leave the club, then. *Ma'am*," he nodded with a smile. Without further delay, the photographer gathered his equipment and departed the table, anxious to court a number of other potential customers.

"Would you mind very much if I keep the photograph for myself, Doctor Governey?" Eleanor asked, eagerly leaning forward, anticipating that it might come in handy should a Hollywood director or producer request one from her, especially since she was all dolled up now. "The only other picture I have was with my daddy, and I was only ten years old then," she explained, referring to a photograph tucked away in her traveling bag which had been taken at the Ohio Theatre, the image of her mama intentionally clipped away. "I'd be sure ta pay you for it...that is, if *you* don't want it instead."

Feeling somewhat encouraged that his impressionable guest was enjoying herself enough to desire a memento of the occasion, Samuel shrugged his shoulders in total concurrence. "Why, of course, my dear Ellie Ann! You may have as many photographs as you wish. It shall be no problem for Nyle to reproduce a few duplicates. And do not even *consider* reimbursement, my dear. Your presence with me tonight is worth more than all the photographs that might fill a thousand-and-one picture books!"

Eleanor remained speechless as a warm sensation suddenly washed over her. The possibility that it could be a delayed reaction from the wine crossed her mind for a split second, but she immediately dismissed the idea, associating it more with the feeling she experienced when the doctor complimented her in his kitchen that afternoon. Except now, she didn't mind being called "dear" any more. As a matter of fact, it was growing on her as sure as the baby inside her belly. "Oh! Well...thank you, sir!" she finally blurted, happy that she wouldn't have to give up one red cent of the stolen money left back at the mansion. "I mean...but *one* picture is all I need, I think. Or...or...maybe a *couple* or so will do after all."

Samuel clenched his jaw in order to conceal a disapproving frown. He didn't think the little camera kisser would actually accept his extemporaneous offer. It was already more than inconvenient that he be required to wait for *one* photograph, as he was hoping to depart the club shortly after Maggie O'Dougherty lived up to her share of the bargain. "Very well, my dear. I shall be happy to inform Nyle of the matter. But...I think it may be wise to see the original before ordering additional prints. If it is to your liking, then, I shall have Nyle deliver some copies in the morning...granted he provides one for me, of course!"

Before Eleanor could respond to the doctor's kind offer, Pietro returned with a tray of antipasto and two tall glasses of iced water complete with lemon wedges. Makara was fast asleep by now, her moderate snoring more apparent since the jazz band was on temporary break. But Ellie hardly took notice, eyeing instead the savory assortment, interrupted only for a moment when Pietro swiftly flicked open her napkin and astutely positioned it upon her lap.

"Go ahead, my dear," Samuel coaxed, adjusting his own linen napkin as Pietro departed. "The prosciutto is divine! Or perhaps you may wish to sample some of the shrimp...or a deviled egg. If you hand me your plate," he offered, pointing to her empty hors d'oeuvre dish, "I shall fill it for you."

Promptly following the doctor's instructions, Eleanor eagerly watched her host fill the orange-colored plate with a sampling of each delicacy. The ham looked almost paper thin, she thought as her mouth began to salivate, but she still couldn't wait to taste it. And the shrimp was so big, she'd have to cut it with a knife to fit it inside her mouth...*especially* since she didn't want to mess up her lipstick. The eggs looked good too, with the yolks all fluffy and overflowin' like that. Except she wasn't too sure about eating something that had the devil's name on it. Of course, maybe she should go ahead and have one anyway. Maybe if the chicken laid the egg on a Friday, she wouldn't have the baby sickness in the morning. But Eleanor's hesitation lasted only until she started nibbling a portion of the halved boiled egg, its creamy, rich yolk suggesting that not only was it laid on a Friday, but very well could have been garnered by a Minister of God! Even the ham, as transparent as it was, must surely have come from a pig slaughtered under a rising *full* moon, she concluded while awkwardly gobbling it from her hors d'oeuvre fork. And it wouldn't have surprised her at all to discover that the moon had been a blue one too!

Sampling each hors d'oeuvre one by one, Eleanor continued making assumptions as to why everything tasted so good, sharing even the most absurd superstitions with her skeptical companion. But when Samuel matter-of-factly pointed out that the shimmering beluga caviar were actually fish eggs, she refused to bite into the embellished cracker until being reassured they didn't come out of a *cat*fish. However, before he was given the chance to explain that the tiny salted eggs were, indeed, harvested from the roe of the hardy sturgeon, a strong, bellowing voice cleaved their conversation.

"Ah, my *cumpaaare,* Doctor Sam!" the finely tailored Sicilian shouted, prompting Samuel to immediately stand up and be subject to the customary shoulder-hugging and subsequent wet kiss on both cheeks. "So herea you are! I uppa the stairs alla the time tinking whena you gonna come uppa to see me and you ara down here alla the time! Anda now I know why!" he gesticulated, opening both arms toward Eleanor. "*Che bedda signurina! Che bedda!*"

Unable to intercept his gregarious colleague before Eleanor's rosy cheeks were assaulted by a firm, drawn out pinch, Samuel immediately spoke up so as not to allow his "beautiful lady" to verbally open up an unpalatable can of worms. "Yes...yes, *Tony,* my good man. I must agree...she is, *indeed,* exquisite," he began, gesturing toward his stunned dinner guest, realizing that he would eventually be compelled to meet the challenge of integrating her into high society as well as whitewashing her age for the marriage license after receiving Lucinda's Snyder's permission to marry off her one-and-only daughter. *However,* he ruminated as Tony Terillo continued to shower Eleanor with compliments, given that even the most challenging circumstances can be remedied with the proper amount of cash, such practical matters should be no more difficult than unraveling the loosened knot from a brand new pair of unworn shoes. "Tony, please allow me to introduce Miss

Eleanor Snyder. And, *Eleanor*, this is my very good friend and business part-ner, Mr. Antonio Terillo."

Feeling somewhat like a sitting duck as Tony reached for her hand and asked if she was enjoying the evening, Eleanor couldn't help but think she already had become acquainted with Mr. Terillo, having seen the gangster film, *Little Caesar* early last winter, even though the mobsters in that film had a *Chicago* accent. And they were making lots of money from *bootlegging*, she suddenly realized, feeling an exhilarating chill running up her spine as the barrel-chested, thick-lipped Sicilian continued to squeeze her hand. *So*, she further surmised, keeping the glamorized gangster film in mind, if Doctor Governey *is* Mr. Terillo's business partner, then that might explain a lot about how he was makin' so much money. But *that's* alright, she rationalized, relieved that the tank-like Terillo had finally let go of her hand. Doctor Governey wasn't the type to go around killin' people with machine guns. "Yes, I *am* havin' a good time, Mr. Terillo," she answered. "I ain't *never* been to a place like this before! I heard 'em talked about a lot, but I never been to one...even when I was livin' in Ohio and...."

"And... *Tony*...how are Giuseppe and Angelo getting along?" Samuel curt-ly interrupted. "I must say, I was expecting to see one or the other here at the club tonight, but noticed that *neither* automobile was in the garage upon my arrival. Surely, they are alright?" he asked, placing the palm of his hand upon Terillo's padded shoulder. "This disappointing absence is not due to their encountering any unfortunate circumstances, I hope?"

Suddenly disregarding the silenced "*bedda signurina*," Tony sidestepped his way around the sleeping pup, making certain that he and Samuel were at a prudent distance before spewing out a guttural, garlic-packed sigh. "Nowa Sam...I don'ta tink there isa notting to worry about tonight, but we get a tip froma one 'o the cops today abouta maybe the Feds coulda causa some trou-ble in the nexta couple-a weeks. So I senda my boys, Gieuseppe and Angelo, to the clubs downa town. And *cugino* Stefano is atta the 'Hop,'" he explained, referring to their quaintest establishment. "Butta like I say," he emphasized, raising thick, graying brows and flashing his bullet-sized diamond ring, "I really don't think thatta notting will happen tonight." He glanced over at Eleanor who was indulging in another hors d'oeuvre, satisfied that the pre-occupied lady could not hear a word of their conversation. "And iffa they *do* bust in, asa you know, we gotta *everyting* covered. *Besides*," he added, patting the eight-millimeter ultrachrome pistol concealed within the inner pocket of his double-breasted suit, "I gotta Sonny and Luigi onna the lookout here. That'sa why I don'ta tella you before. There isa notting to worry about. Ofa *course*," Tony added matter-of-factly, reaching upward to grasp Samuel's arm with his hairy hand, "iffa the Feds *shoulda* bust in, I wanta you to getta the *fucka* outta here and drive rightta home, just inna case. Iffa one of the boys shoulda happen to get hurt, thisa way, you coulda help." He glanced at the telephone sitting on the far end of the table, then back at Samuel. "Iffa we can, we will letta you know soon as Sonny and Luigi see some trouble. Thenna you take your lady anda run for the garage and let Lorenzo helpa you outta here. But...like I tella you," he emphasized, stepping back to a more comfortable distance as Pietro approached with the Chateaubriand, "there's no gonna be any trouble tonight. So you enjoya your lady anda your meal and don'ta you worry. Maybe we coulda have some wine later on uppa the stairs, eh? *Buon appetit!*" Bringing his thumb and forefinger to his lips, he sent a swift kiss, then quickly turned and strutted his way across the dining room floor.

chapter 85

A New Acquaintance

Feeling as if she were nine months pregnant instead of only a few weeks, Eleanor leaned back into her chair, the patter of rain upon the windowsill dancing to the tune of "Puttin' on the Ritz" as the last of the bone china was cleared from the table. It was a wonder her stomach had been able to accommodate so much food, she thought, as Samuel began smoking a Cuban cigar which was offered him by a scantily dressed cigarette girl as they were finishing their 'Tropical Ice Cream Delight,' appropriately served inside a couple of halved coconut shells. The meal had been so delicious, she'd even eaten all of her vegetables. And that *shatoobrand!* To think she had almost refused to eat it, being it was all red and bloody. But then, when Doctor Governey insisted she give it a try...well...after the first taste, she just couldn't imagine leaving behind even the smallest morsel!

Suddenly realizing that she should pay a visit to the ladies room, Eleanor was about to ask for Samuel's guidance, but hesitated upon noticing that he seemed to be preoccupied about something while peering beyond the dining room table. She hoped he wasn't thinking about asking her to dance, she frowned. At first, she had been excited about visiting a night club where she could dance to a *real* orchestra with a *real* partner instead of all by herself to the scratchy tunes that played out of Mama's old Edison phonograph. But now she wasn't so sure, being that she'd never taken any formal dancing lessons. Of course, she could probably get away with some of the newer, fun dances like the 'Rag' and the 'Charleston,' but somehow she couldn't picture

Doctor Governey swinging his legs and kicking his feet. Either way, she would *definitely* have to take off her high heel shoes. Glancing downward towards the table, her eyes became fixed upon a colorful cigar band the doctor let her keep as a souvenir. The beautiful old-fashioned lady featured in the center of the embossed wrapper wouldn't have known anything about moving her dainty feet to a 'Rumba' or 'Foxtrot' either, she supposed, but she probably would *still* know how to dance any type of *'Waltz.'* Upon hearing the orchestra ending its snappy tune and easing its way into a passionate Argentine Tango, Ellie's heart suddenly jumped as she noticed that Samuel was in the process of rising from his seat. But before she was even given the opportunity to divulge her ignorance regarding the basics of ballroom dance, she was relieved to see that he was turning away from her and focusing his attention on a tall, fiery-haired lady striding toward him, the fringed hem of her purple sequin dress swaying like a fancy lampshade set atop two barren beanpoles.

"Sam! Fancy meetin' you he-a!" the nasally-voiced coquette jested with half a wink. "And ya brung ya lady too! Nice ta meet ya, doll!" Without hesitation, the newcomer leaned over the table and extended a gangly hand garnished with red painted fingernails and an impressive diamond, the low-cut bodice of her dress barely containing two loaf-shaped breasts. "Name's Maggie...Maggie O'Dougherty," she proudly announced, her pea-colored eyes practically glued to Eleanor's ruby and pearl necklace. "Not the sharpest set o' scissors in the shop, but I know my way 'round," she confidently broadcasted, abandoning Eleanor's hand the minute she accepted it to immediately fluff the bobbed edge of her frizzy auburn hair. "And my, *my*, Sam, don't *you* look mighty spiffy, *as always*. I'm surprised some gal hasn't gotten her mitts inta you yet...or *has* she?" Accentuating the flirtatious question with a quick poke to Samuel's diamond tie-tack, she immediately returned her attention to Eleanor. "I'm sorry doll, but I didn't get the name. *Your* name," she specified in reply to Ellie's quizzical look, her dark orange lipstick turning a rusty shade whenever she accentuated a word or two. "Ya know, hon, that name they gave ya at the baby fac'try after they yanked ya out and slapped ya sweet little tush."

"The lady's name is *Eleanor*. Miss Eleanor Snyder," Samuel gallantly interjected, somewhat perturbed at being deprived the opportunity of *properly* introducing the lowborn ladies to each other. "Miss Snyder is a very dear friend of mine, *Miss O'Dougherty*," he went on to explain before the ostentatious moll had a dog's chance of spoiling his preplanned scheme. "She is a guest at my residence for the time being due to a set of most unfortunate circumstances. You see," he continued, with a patronizing nod toward Eleanor, "I recently acquired the habit of frequenting a particular diner on my former servant's weekly day off, whereupon Miss Snyder would not only graciously serve my breakfast, but offer her sincerest condolences after Zachary's untimely departure. Naturally, then, since I had grown quite fond of this special lady, I was *considerably* distressed to learn that she had been evicted from her humble flat with hardly a skillet of her own to fry with." Samuel could almost sense the illusory teardrops in his ocean blue eyes as a sudden gust of rain smeared the translucent, curtained windows. "*However*, despite several pleas on my part to extend her stay at least for the remainder of the summer, Miss Snyder insists that she must move on and, of course, I shall miss her terribly." Having successfully executed the fabricated monologue, Samuel winked at his grateful house guest, then tactfully changed the subject as he directed a cautionary stare toward his co-conspirator. "So, my dear Miss O'Dougherty, would you be gracious enough to keep my sweet house guest company while I visit the gentlemen's room before showing her around the remainder of the establishment? Perhaps you could pay a visit to the ladies' lounge and engage in a bit of 'girl talk.' Furthermore," he added, while extinguishing his cigar, "if such a notion should be to your liking, I shall be most obliged to escort you."

chapter 86

Ladies' Room

A violent peal of thunder permeated the white marble walls and lace-embossed floor tiles of Club Dalla Giungla's ladies' room, causing glossy white shutters to vibrate and eliminating whatever consonance remained of the ballroom orchestra's high-stepping "Ain't We Got Fun." Amidst several outcries of amused horror among some of the other ladies who were utilizing the luxurious facility, Eleanor reached for the crystal knob of a gold plated faucet, puzzled by the absence of a simple bar of soap. Perhaps the washroom attendant would provide her with one, she guessed, discreetly eyeing a Negro woman appropriately dressed in a dark black frock and starched white pinafore handing a towel to a rouged-kneed flapper. But Eleanor suddenly felt self-conscious noticing a small basket next to the attendant laden with a few crinkled dollar bills and several silver coins. She certainly didn't want to feel embarrassed like the time she was at the Ohio Theatre and the washroom attendant gave Mama a dirty glare for giving a penny tip, not to mention being further ashamed when Mama says right out loud how lucky that nigger was for making even *that* much by just standing there and doing hardly nothing. And although she, herself, would never actually say such a rude thing, the fact of the matter was that she didn't have so much as that measly Lincoln penny to put into the Negro lady's basket, bein' that all her money was left back at the mansion...not that she would ever part with the shiny silver dollar that the doctor included with her underthings, but she would've been more than happy to contribute one of the dollars bills she'd swiped from that cheap son-of-a-bitch, Jimmy Ray. But upon finally deciding she'd be best off just running some water over her hands and then shaking them dry, a newly familiar voice pounced from behind, the rhythmic tap of high heel shoes replacing the abrupt, resonant echo of a flushing toilet.

"I sweaar!" the free-spirited floozy complained, positioning the strap of her beaded purse upon her lanky forearm as she stepped alongside Eleanor and finally engaged the neglected faucet. "Why does a gal's time o' month always decide ta pay a visit at the most inconvenient times! Of course..." Miss O'Dougherty went on, placing one wet hand beneath a basin-mounted soap dispenser and vigorously pumping with the other, "I suppose when ya think about it, there's not a *good* time for bein' on the rag. But...I sweaar! It's times like these that make me wish I was already at the change o' life...which ain't bound ta happen soon enough, bein' I'm only 38. And I ain't ashamed of it, neither...admittin' that I'm already 38 years of age," she explained, shaking the excess water from her hands into the basin as Eleanor, at last, began following the lead of her newest hygienic mentor. "I mean...!" Miss O'Dougherty shrieked as she walked toward the Negro attendant to retrieve a fresh linen towel, "some women wouldn't let go o' their age if a Fordson tractor was pullin' on it. But not me...I don't mind tellin' one bit. I mean...who do these old skirts think they're kiddin' anyway?"

As a flash of lightning illuminated a curling strand of rose-scented soap accumulating upon her moistened palm, Ellie could practically feel her unborn baby fluttering within her womb, tickling her tummy with an excitement that equaled her own. Never before had she been in such a beautiful, spacious washroom with such modern facilities...not even at the Ohio Theatre. Even the toilets were all sleek and shiny in the same pink color as each one of the seashell-shaped water basins, she marveled, vigorously rubbing soaped hands together as Maggie had done. And so many toilets too! Eleanor noticed at the corner of her eye that Miss O'Dougherty, already having given her linen towel back to the attendant, was presently massaging her hands with one of several complimentary beauty creams set atop an accommodating marble counter. There were eight of them! she quickly concluded as a few more ladies meandered in and out of the washroom stalls, an anticipated rumble of thunder attempting to disguise the indiscreet howl of flushing water. And each stall having a full-sized door of real polished wood and gold handles! Capturing another glimpse of Maggie who was now dousing herself with French perfume conveniently contained within a *Limoges* porcelain atomizer, Ellie turned the crystal knob of the faucet and began rinsing her hands, keeping in mind the need to shake them dry since she had no money to place inside the Negro woman's basket. Of course, she would have to be extra careful not to sprinkle her elegant gown and run the risk of leaving water marks like this afternoon when that overflowed glass of water stained Doctor Governey's red silk tablecloth, she noted, cautiously shutting off the faucet. Bringing to mind how she had promptly gathered the wet silk cloth after Samuel moved the water glasses and heavy vase of calla lilies to the kitchen counter, Ellie remained standing by the shell-shaped sink with dripping hands, a perplexed expression on her face as Maggie dropped a quarter into the intimidating basket. Then, as the charitable flapper glanced her way, Eleanor watched as she once again fished inside her beaded bag and pulled out another silver coin, appropriately depositing it within the wicker basket and plucking another sterile towel from the marble counter top before promptly promenading back to Eleanor.

"Here ya are," she flippantly said, flinging the embroidered edge of the towel into Eleanor's hands along with the flowery scent of Chanel No. 5. "It's one thing not bein' used ta givin' out tips in joints like this, but great gobs o' gumballs, gal! How'n the world ya gonna touch up ya kisser with no purse ta carry ya makeup in?" Without pause, she unlatched the gold clasp of the sparkly bag and pulled out a silver fluted tube. "Here ya go, baby...the pleasure's all mine."

A bit indecisive as to whether her hands were sufficiently dried, Eleanor let go of the damp linen towel and let it drop into the pedestal basin before hesitantly accepting the tube of lipstick which was practically shoved against her unpowdered nose. Then, immediately glancing into the gilded mirror, she realized why Maggie had made such a meddlesome suggestion. As careful as she had been while eating her supper, her ruby red lipstick had nevertheless smeared into an unbecoming pink hue. Vaguely aware that Maggie was presently occupied with assessing her own lavishly painted face, she uncapped the tube of lipstick and cautiously stroked it along her lips, ultimately disappointed that the dark orange color didn't agree with her skin tone nearly as much as the original shade that Doctor Governey had applied. And it didn't seem to complement the color of the gown she was wearing either. Of course, if someone as snazzy as Miss O'Dougherty had instructed her to apply it, she reasoned, disrupting her concentration for a split second

to slip a quick glance toward her temporary beauty advisor, then she supposed it would be suitable enough. But before she could fully convince
herself that the dark orange color of her lips was alluring, let alone acceptable, a shrill reprimand penetrated another crackle of thunder, abruptly
shattering all of her confidence.

"Sweet *Jesus!* Would ya look at that? Why...who on this weatha-worn,
humpty-dumpty planet is deservin' of anything so monstrously *hideous*...I
just can't believe it!...anotha godfasaken, stuck-in-ya-face, son-of-a-bitch
wrinkle!" Her face practically glued to the washroom mirror, Maggie was
pulling at the corner of her eye with a long-nailed index finger. "I tell ya, I'd
betta get hitched real soon or I'm gonna end up bein' a spinsta' for sure!
Woulda' *been* married too, except my beau went and got himself bumped off
by one o' them Third Avenue dopes. Yeaa," she dreamily sighed, her fingers
roaming the ruddy surface of her lackluster face, a three-carat diamond leading the pack, "my Joey wasn't what some gals woulda' thought of as bein' the
cat's pajamas, but aside from that skimpy-lookin' physique and bulldog mug
o' his, he coulda' put the *swellest* sheiks ta shame in the 'makin' whoopee'
depa'tment!" Maggie pulled her face away from the mirror, still gazing
straight into the center of the looking glass. "Maybe I should see one o' them
face-fixin' doctors...*you know,*" she emphasized, suddenly turning toward
Eleanor, "the kind o' docta all o' them *Hollywood* gals are goin' to nowadays."
Receiving no response from her potential cash box, other than a tightened
pair of dark orange lips, she plucked the recapped tube of lipstick from
Eleanor's fingers and flippantly dropped it inside her sequined purse.
"Enough 'bout me, though...seems all I've been doin' is runnin' off my big
fat yap. C'mon," she gestured with a flick of the head toward the ladies'
lounging area. "It's 'bout time I start bein' more polite and begin listenin' to
you for a change!"

chapter 87

"Girl Talk"

"So...*Eleanor,* you sweet little thing you," Maggie began, crossing gangly legs while seated on the edge of a pink and white uphol-stered divan, effortlessly dislodging a cigarette from a complimentary pack of Chesterfields and scooping up a box of matches from a mermaid-designed coffee table, keeping in mind the explicit instructions given to her by the rich "Doc" Governey. "What're yer plans, exactly? I mean...once ya leave here...where ya plannin' on goin,' hon?"

Eleanor wriggled in her seat, guardedly watching Miss O'Dougherty instantaneously striking the head of a match against the side of the tiny box embossed with the Club's logotype and lighting up. It was bad enough she'd been obliged to tell Doctor Governey her secret, she thought, as a peal of thunder, though subdued by the absence of windows and absorbed by plush Mediterranean blue carpeting, allowed the deferral of an immediate answer. But exposing her intentions to somebody she hardly knew was definitely out of the question! Allowing a more moderate, yet endless roll of thunder to take its course, she looked upward, wondering if the massive chandelier with sweeping crystals stretching all the way across the ceiling from its center globe, like tentacles of a giant octopus, could suddenly come crashing down. Intimidated by the notion, she pressed her back against the soft cushion of the patterned divan, choosing instead to focus her attention on the breath-taking, beautifully framed photographs adorning the walls of the lounge. They looked like they could've come right out of the pages of the *National*

Geographics from Mrs. Brodeur's class, she marveled, as her mind began soaking up images of majestic mountains, plush green landscape and tranquil rivers. But, as if the mere acknowledgment of each peaceful photograph had caused the very heavens to subside, her preoccupation was abruptly cut short by an audacious voice which rang loud and clear.

"So Ellie, ya gonna an-sa the question or not? Of course..." Maggie nonchalantly squeaked, "it don't matta ta me none if ya don't wanna tell, seein' it ain't my business anyway. I mean...if ya happen ta ask my opinion, a gal has every right ta keep certain mattas to herself."

Eleanor focused curiously upon the orange ring of lipstick discoloring the pure white paper of Maggie's Chesterfield as the seasoned smoker released the cigarette from her roller coaster lips. Even though Miss O'Dougherty had said it was perfectly alright not to tell anyone where she was planning on going, she pondered amid discomfiting silence, it still seemed impolite to say nothing at all. "I...well...I thought maybe...maybe it'd be a good idea ta take a train all the way to *Chicago*...I mean...considerin' there's supposed ta be a heap of good payin' work over there!"

Recalling Sam Governey's explicit request to say or do anything necessary to keep the little fibber from running off to *Hollywood*, Maggie took another puff of the cigarette and nonchalantly exhaled. "Chicago, *huh*?", a filmy cloud of smoke encircling her cynical face. "Well, *that's* pretty darn smart of ya! At least ya ain't stupid enough like them other 'Dumb Doras' who're all hopin' ta make a quick buck in the movie biz by skippin' off ta Hollywood! I tell ya, those gals are a dime a dozen and it's the lucky ones that get the Bum's Rush once they get there. And the *unlucky* ones...*well!*" Maggie accentuated with an overt roll of the eyes. "I could tell ya some stories that'll make yer nipples curl! Them Hollywood producers don't just hand out them *copacetic* roles to *any* gal who suits their fancy without expectin' somethin' else in return—talent or *no* talent! I should know!" Without hesitation, the unabashed socialite lifted the skirt of her dress just below the garter straps, exposing through silk stockings a lumpy, reddened scar that was acquired in a boating accident. "See this? A high and mighty directa' beat me to a pulp 'cause I refused to take part in some shameful behavia' even a *dog* would raise his nose at! And I *still* consida myself lucky, bein' that I'm still alive," she alleged, finally releasing the sequined fabric. "Not like plenty of *other* pushovers who took a beatin' lyin' flat on their backs and neva got up again ta see the light o' day!"

Eleanor remained silently still as Maggie savored another drag from the Chesterfield, hoping that the prevailing crackle of thunder might linger on enough to delay, if only for a moment, a more detailed account of what she was dreading to hear. She was starting to feel frightened again like earlier in the evening when Doctor Governey was telling her about the terrible things that happened to his mother, she realized, warily following a stream of smoke as it drifted into the green gills of the coffee table, slinked along its glass center and ultimately encircled the mermaid's swan-like neck. Only this time, it was even worse because the awful things that *Maggie* was telling her about were things that could happen to *herself* when she finally got to California. Of course, she forcefully swallowed, famous stars like Jeanette MacDonald and Irene Dunn looked so happy and wholesome on the big screen, she couldn't imagine them *ever* bein' abused...unless their singing had something to do with how good they were treated and *she* couldn't sing on tune to save her soul. And as for other actresses who *didn't* dance or sing.... Eleanor flinched as a medley of blonde bombshells and raven-haired beauties pranced through her mind. Could it really be true? Would they be putting up with being abused just to be big time motion picture stars? Would she do the same? Of *course* not, she instantly reprimanded. Hadn't she already taken enough from that wicked, wild-eyed son-of-a-snake, Jimmy Ray? But surely, not *all* directors were bound to be cruel like that, she reasoned, noticing that, aside from the thrashing sound of rain, Maggie was presently preoccupied by something which had apparently caught her attention in the seemingly vacant washroom. Maybe Miss O'Dougherty was beaten up by the director on account of a stroke of bad luck. Maybe she made the mistake of cutting her fingernails on a Friday or a Sunday. Or picked up a coin that was sitting on the ground with its tail up. Even worse yet, maybe somebody who *did* get the *Bum's Rush* got jealous and gave Maggie the evil eye.

Eleanor reflected for a moment, wondering if perhaps she *should* let Doctor Governey pierce her ears, being that wearing rings through the lobes would protect her from the evil eye. And she would *still* have them pierced to this very day if Daddy hadn't objected to Mama puncturing her tiny lobes with a sewing needle soon after she was born, insisting that Mama allow her ears to "heal" and ultimately close up. Instinctively, she lifted both hands past her neck and began fondling her earlobes, contemplating that under thorough inspection, she sometimes still could detect the scarred indentations. Daddy never *did* believe in witchcraft and fortune telling, she pouted, even once threatening to burn Mama's big black book of magic spells, and Mama screamin' and yellin' that she had a mind to leave him and then both of them getting in the biggest squabble 'til Daddy finally left slamming the kitchen door only to come back hours later meekly carrying a handful of wildflowers. But no matter how sensible Daddy was overall, he was dead wrong about such incantations and things being foolish cause she'd seen for herself, first hand, how much they really worked. Like the time she recited a certain rhyme from Mama's black book while putting *anise* seed and lavender inside her pillowcase to stop her from having so many nightmares. And how about that day when she accidentally dropped the broom while sweeping out the front of the barn and, lo and behold, just like that book says about unexpected visitors, out of the blue comes the cutler in his pickup truck askin' if Mama needs any knives or scissors sharpened. Only sometimes the spells didn't work cause Mama, bein' a lot more powerful than her, would put a hex on some of the things she'd wish for...otherwise Daddy would still be alive and Jimmy Ray...well, Jimmy Ray'd be rotting in his grave or, better yet, his picked-over bones left hanging on a tree like a forgotten piece of tattered laundry.

Eleanor suddenly froze in her seat upon hearing a sound more terrifying than the piercing of thunder, both arms going limp as they dropped to her thighs. Was...was her imagination playing tricks on her or...or...were there really masculine grunts and groans coming from somewhere inside the washroom? Was it? Could it be?...it was! She could tell by the coarse voice...the piggish, raspy panting that belonged to no other than Jimmy Ray! And the sound of someone's body banging against a door, like he'd be in one of the washroom stalls shoving his...his *thing* inside...inside...was he raping somebody else now? In a flash, Eleanor turned her attention toward Maggie. Why was she just sitting there looking all amused? Why wasn't she doing anything to help the mistreated girl? And the Negro woman...was she still inside the washroom? Did *she* care at all? Was *anyone* there to help? Why isn't someone *doing* anything? *Somebody...God...somebody help her!* Maybe if...maybe if she, *herself*, ran into the dining room and got the attention of the two police officers that were sitting at the bar....

In spite of feeling as if the room was spinning in a lopsided circle, Eleanor braced the base of her palms against the piped edge of the divan but stopped just as she managed to scoot forward. Except for the persistent downpour of rain, it was now eerily silent. Her heart rushed into her ears as she strained to hear a female voice...a whimper...a cry...*anything!* She felt paralyzed. Was someone *really* in trouble after all? And if she went into the washroom to find out, would Jimmy Ray recognize her if they ran into each other? And...and...what was *that?* Eleanor remained speechless, her eyes still glued to the open entrance of the washroom. It sounded like a woman's voice...not a shamed, horrified voice, but a cheerful *laugh.* Could it be, then? Did the person in question actually *want* Jimmy Ray to have his way with her? Had she *really* 'asked for it,' like Mama would constantly accuse *her* of doing? Maybe...maybe.... She cautiously scooted backwards, hoping that by leaning into the edge of the divan, no one from the washroom could notice her. Is it?...could it be...was it? *Mama?* But what would *Mama* be doing here at this time? For that matter, what was *Jimmy Ray* doing here? But before she could fit one more frightening thought into her already terrified mind, Maggie's voice cut through the air-conditioned lounge like a blue-white diamond on molten glass.

"Hey! This ain't a whore house, so take your business elsewhea, why don't ya!"

In an instant, Eleanor noticed a strange man with his arms around a woman's shoulders, both pausing, startled upon realizing the presence of Maggie and her, then quickly opening and scooting out the door, unable to avoid colliding with a couple of startled patrons in the process.

"Would ya get a load o' that, won't ya?...some sugha daddy and his hot-trottin' floozie usin' the Doc's washroom ta snatch a bit o' nookie!" Turning toward Eleanor to observe her reaction, Maggie's deriding demeanor immediately changed into genuine concern. "Hey...Ellie gal? You alright? Looks like ya seen a ghost or somethin'!" Receiving no response but a blank stare and a pair of unmanicured hands pressed upon a scarlet-clothed lap, she extinguished her cigarette in a starfish ashtray, promptly rose from the cushioned divan and pranced toward a hand-painted serving cart. Heea ya go...," she tenderly declared while proceeding to pour a glass of water from a sterling silver pitcher. "They don't stock up on these hea Alka Seltzers for nothin.' I tell ya...these hea things can work a hunk o' miracles...especially when ya got a sour stomach from eatin' too much, which ain't hard ta do in *this* place! I don't know how we survived a year or two ago without 'em!"

Eleanor's stomach already began to settle as Maggie dropped the large white tablet into the glass of water. Remaining silent, she warily watched the self-appointed Florence Nightingale strut toward the sofa, coaxing her to drink the bubbly fizz. Staring at the crystal drinking glass which was practically forced into her hands, she remembered the ginger ale she was given earlier that morning in Doctor Governey's kitchen before he was supposed to give her the abortion. Before now, she hadn't considered whether or not the sedative he had placed in the Vernor's could be harmful to the baby, being that she had been so preoccupied with the magnificent mansion and all those generous gifts. *Of course*, she rationalized as the new miracle drug continued to effervesce, he didn't seem at all concerned about any consequences when she told him that she'd decided to keep the baby after all. But, just to be sure, she'd go ahead and ask him about it later anyway. Maybe on the way back from the club or when they would be inside the mansion again. *Even so*, Eleanor decided, it'd probably be best that she didn't drink the water with the Alka-Seltzer in it, lest her baby be born with a fretful case of the colic or even something worse. "I...it's alright...I mean...thank you so much, Miss *O'Darty*, but it's not on account of me eatin' too much...it's just that...that..."

"Ahhh!" Maggie's eyes suddenly sparkled like the twin headlights of an Aston Martin. "I get it now! All this time with Sam treatin' you like you were the Queen of England or somethin'! I shoulda' known!" she haughtily declared, plopping down on the sofa beside Eleanor, almost causing the baffled guest to spill some of the settled potion upon her satin gown. "It shoulda' been as plain as the nose on my face that someone workin' as a waitress in some lousy restaurant can't afford ta buy an *Adrian* gown, let alone that *incredible* necklace that must've cost a wad o' dough. Not ta mention that I'd been comin' to this gin mill for I don't know *how* many years and haven't once known Sam ta be bringin' his own lady along. Not that there hasn't been any *Shebas* wantin' to get their claws inta him," she explained, fluffing her auburn hair with the palms of her hands. "And it's no wonder you got a bad case of the heebie-jeebies, then! Why, I suppose *any* self-respectin' virgin would be spooked with folks like that makin' whoopie right under her very nose!"

Eleanor squirmed in her seat. She wasn't sure whether to laugh or cry. The notion that Maggie believed her to be virginal was comical at best, but it had made the truth seem all the more unbearable. Much too unbearable to reveal...especially by confiding in a loud-mouthed busybody like Miss O'Dougherty. And besides, if Maggie leaned any closer, the sequined purse which lay between them was bound to dig into her thigh even more and maybe mar the satin fabric of her dress. "Well," she responded, placing the crystal glass upon the mermaid coffee table and standing up to imply the need to stretch, "I *really* don't think somethin' like that...like bein' a...a *virgin* really matters ta someone like Doctor Governey. I mean..." she explained with downcast eyes, keeping in mind the story Samuel had given in the main dining room to spare her any embarrassment, "...we'd just become good friends and he feels sorry for me, that's all."

Maggie immediately raised both eyebrows, focusing her attention upon the ruby and pearl necklace. "Feels *sorry* for you, huh? Just let me tell ya, gal, that feeling sorry for someone don't usually end up with that person getting to wear all the fancy things you have on now. Maybe some second-hand clothes at best...or a soup bone to throw at a starvin' dog...but a custom gown and satin shoes, not to mention that *gorgeous* necklace that must be worth at least half a million smackers!" Extremely pleased that she had gotten Eleanor's undivided attention, Maggie continued to thicken the sauce. "And you just wait, sista...if ya think that necklace is worth a pretty penny, I'd bet dollas to dumplings that he gives you a hell of a diamond when he asks for ya hand in holy matrimony...that is, if you're willin' to play yer cards right! I'm tellin' ya honey...Sam hasn't been holdin' out for nothin' and you got the goods he wants. If I were you, sweetcakes, I'd forget about goin' to Chicago and play him like a cue ball on a billiad' table!"

Acutely aware of the new life that was forming within her womb, Eleanor remained standing, wanting more than ever to part Maggie's company, painfully realizing that the worldly flapper was correct. Certain men favored women who saved their virginity for marriage and Doctor Governey would be no exception. Not that she cared about *Doctor Governey's* opinion when it came to such matters. In spite of what Maggie had said, he was much too old for her anyway. Old enough to be her father. But Miss O'Dougherty had spoken the truth sure as she had heard it implied from the gossipy mouths of upper class schoolgirls during recess. Debbie Holka was one and so was Valerie Bellard. Forever labeled as "sluts," they were no better than damaged goods for going all the way with one guy or another. Whether they had suspected it or not, no self-respecting man would want them for a wife. And she, Eleanor Anne Snyder, would fare no different. "I...I don't know what you're talkin' about, but I think we'd best be leavin' here before Doctor Governey wonders what's come of us!"

Impatiently waiting for Maggie to finally rise from the couch and scoop up the sequined evening bag, Eleanor breathed a sigh of relief as they, at last, headed toward the washroom door, hoping that the laughter and gaiety inside the dining area would help her forget all the dismal accounts which Maggie had foretold and which pierced her mind like the abrupt peal of thunder that rolled right through the soles of her high heel shoes.

chapter 88

Raid

I t didn't take long for Eleanor to start winning back her cheery disposition at the sight of Samuel bearing a single red rose which was certainly meant for her and obviously acquired from one of the lady peddlers dressed up like Jane Parker in the movie *Tarzan the Ape Man*. It was as if the song the orchestra was playing "California Here I Come," was meant just for her too. And how gallant Doctor Governey was looking as he turned toward her, a welcome smile upon his face while offering the sweet-smelling bloom! But in one instant, one single instant, it seemed...whether she first noticed the disconcerted look on the doctor's face or the abrupt suspension of the orchestra...whether it was a firing gun she was hearing or another piercing crash of thunder, or both, Eleanor realized that something was frightfully wrong. Before she knew it, sharp thorns were digging into her wrist as Samuel began pulling her by the arm. And people were screaming and scrambling in all different directions. As Samuel began running toward the entrance of the garage, she noticed that the Elephant fountain had gone all dry and every bottle of liquor that was behind the bar where the police officers had been sitting just disappeared! And it wasn't only the bottles that were gone, but the shelves too! Probably the source of the loud crash she had heard just seconds ago. Then, at the corner of her eye she spotted a Federal Agent with a Tommy gun at the far end of the room trying to get past the crowd. But not before another officer stepped in, forcefully ordering both her and Doctor Governey to rush in the other direction. As they were being hustled past abandoned tables and a floor littered with strewn cocktail glasses, she noticed that Doctor Governey didn't seem to be resisting arrest at all. In fact, by the look on his face, it was as if he welcomed the officer's commands to head toward the men's washroom.

Upon arrival in the men's room, in what seemed to be a mere split second, there was no time to marvel over the artificial waterfalls above each urinal or the mammoth aquarium decked with a breathtaking seascape and stocked with all kinds of colorful fish. Instead, everything seemed like one big blur as she was practically pushed toward an open window, tripping over her own two feet, sharp thorns tearing the fabric of her gown and piercing her shin. Before she knew what was happening, she was hoisted up in the air and face to face with a second police officer, finally realizing that both men were the same two cops who had been seated at the bar while she and Doctor Governey were having their supper. With outstretched arms, the officer pulled her outside the building, followed by Doctor Governey. Then, in a flash, the officers escorted them into the hooded Packard which had been purposely driven from the garage and around the back entrance, making certain it would not be intercepted as Samuel, at last, took command of the wheel and promptly shifted the Phaeton in first gear, peeling away on all four whitewalls toward the tranquil arms of Lake Shore Avenue.

chapter *89*

Aftermath

With the ruby necklace still intact and a starched white sheet wrapped around her dampened body, Eleanor rested upon the warm kitchen chair as Doctor Governey opened a bottle of peroxide, all the while being reassured that the medicine wouldn't sting her smarting wound. Although she felt fortunate to have an experienced doctor taking care of her, she nevertheless winced; the beautiful gown she had worn elegantly during the evening was now ruined...a wide strip recently ripped apart to stop the bleeding...and strewn upon the floor alongside her girdle, shoes and nylon stockings. And it was bad enough that the gown was spoiled, let alone her getting sopping wet from the rain coming down in buckets when they arrived at the mansion. At least Doctor Governey was able to keep dry on account of being covered by his hat and jacket, she reflected, as he saturated a piece of cotton cloth with the peroxide. But having not so much as a shawl to shelter her from the downpour as they ran from the driveway and through the nearest door, there was nothing for her to do but strip off every piece of wet clothing and cover herself instead with the scratchy sheet the doctor had retrieved from the basement. Ellie shivered as bits of rain trickled from long black tresses and seeped through the thin white cotton. At least he was polite enough to leave the room as she undressed. It had given her the willies, though. For some reason, while stripping off her clothes, she just couldn't stop thinking about how many times Jimmy Ray must have been peeking through the crack of her bedroom door before finally deciding to rape her.

But Doctor Governey wasn't at all like that, she determined as he bent forward to cleanse the wound. He was the perfect gentleman and a good doctor who would take care of her no matter what!

Eleanor took a deep breath as Samuel tenderly stroked her shin with the saturated gauze. She wondered again how Makara was doing. Aside from following Doctor Governey's instructions while driving toward the mansion to roll up her dress and press it against her wound, Makara was the first thought that had crossed her mind. And Doctor Governey had done just what he said he'd do, she thought as he reached toward the table for a piece of fresh gauze. Although she was sopping wet and dripping rainwater all over the kitchen floor, he had placed a telephone call at her insistence, only to discover that the pup had slept through the whole ordeal and would soon be safe and sound at the home of one of his business partners because, for one reason or another, it wouldn't be safe to deliver the dog to the mansion just yet. This had prompted a whole other set of questions, the first one being, was Doctor Governey in any type of big trouble? And *particularly* how did all those bottles of hooch, along with the shelving disappear so fast from behind the bar? But Doctor Governey just gave her one of those fatherly smiles, telling her not to worry her pretty little head about such things and wanting, instead, to know how her visit with Maggie O'Dougherty went. Of course, she didn't tell him about Miss O'Dougherty's awful experience in Hollywood or especially about Maggie being convinced that "Sam" had his mind set on a virgin wife. She did, however, elaborate on how beautifully the woman's washroom was decorated and complimented him once again on the overall look of the club.

"There now, my dear," Samuel proclaimed as he secured the piece of gauze with a strip of surgical tape. "You are quite a lucky lady surviving such an evening with no more than a puncture from a rose's thorn. The cut is not too deep and it should heal well."

Another clap of thunder mingled with the torrent of rain, reverberating above the kitchen's cathedral ceiling as Samuel gently released Eleanor's shin. In spite of what Maggie O'Dougherty had told her, she wondered for a moment if the doctor ever *would* consider taking her on as his wife. Or if the slightest thought of such a foolish notion would quickly be dismissed because of her lost virginity. Anyhow, she thought, feeling an uneasy emptiness as Samuel gathered the remnants of her minor surgery, it really didn't matter. Regardless of the privileged status that being *Mrs. Samuel Governey* would bring to any woman, the currently unfilled position was not for her. And besides, even more importantly, she had her own career in Hollywood to pursue. Regardless, though, she did enjoy the nice doctor's company this evening; it was a shame it couldn't go on for just a little while more. "Thank you so much, S...*Sam* for taking care of the cut on my leg. You did a real good job." Pursing her lips, she raised her eyebrows. "Do you suppose we could stay up just a little longer, though, bein'...bein' that our time out on the town got cut so short?"

Nearly letting out a chuckle upon realizing that his unsuspecting guest needed no persuasion whatsoever to join him in his previously planned cup of impregnated tea, Samuel immediately rid his mind of the vexing notion that his spanking new Packard Deluxe had barely escaped being sullied by the blood of his common guest. "Why of course, my dear Ellie Ann!" he exclaimed, immediately abandoning the first aid supplies. "The evening is still young and I cannot *imagine* spending the remainder of its better hours in the absence of your company!" He then started toward the porcelain stove, nearly brushing his shirt sleeve against one of the iron burners as he reached out to retrieve a brass tea kettle. "I think perhaps we should both engage in a cup of tea after this evening's turmoil. It is likely to sooth our nerves and will help provide the perfect ambiance for a bit of engaging conversation. So what do you say, Ellie Ann? How about returning upstairs and changing into something more appropriate while I brew the tea? Then, after you are dressed and I myself slip on a fresh, dry jacket, you may go directly to the drawing room and wait there. I shan't be very long!"

Not particularly fond of tea, Eleanor hesitated for a moment, thinking that it's only redeeming value was being able to tell a person's fortune from the arrangement of leaves at the bottom of the cup. She never did learn how to do it herself, but remembered what a treat it was on the rare occasions that Mama would read her fortune when Daddy wasn't around. No matter, though, the tea was bound to taste better than the wine she had at the club, especially if it was berry or mint flavored. "Yes, sir, that'll be fine," she answered, holding the wrapped sheet to her bosom as she scooted off the cherrywood chair. She then heeded Samuel's instruction to leave any salvageable garments behind for the time being, including the precious ruby and pearl necklace which he carefully unclasped from the nape of her neck. Finally, as Eleanor walked past the pile of wet clothing and toward the hallway entrance, she anticipated changing into her best Sunday suit which was neatly packed in the traveling bag, originally intended for one of her screen tests...the perfect thing to wear over a cup of tea in the company of a gentleman who was kind enough to share his magnificent home and kind hospitality.

chapter 90

Tea Time

Except for an occasional brush of thunder and the heavy patter of rain, the drawing room of Doctor Samuel Governey's mansion seemed strangely quiet as Eleanor once again sat upon the oversized tufted divan, sensing the fragrance of freshly brewed tea emanating from the kitchen. Although properly dressed in a three-piece jersey and dry as a wind-blown stocking, she felt more uncomfortable than ever in the stifling room void of fresh air for lack of an open window. And the room was so much darker, she eerily shivered. Being unable to locate the light switch for the brass chandelier and unsure of how to operate the Tiffany parlor lamp near to where she sat, she had, in the meantime, settled for the light emanating from the front foyer. But, in the absence of direct lighting, the vast oxblood walls of the drawing room seemed almost black. Even the many trinkets decorating each fancy table looked like menacing shadows ready to pounce on her at any given moment. She began cracking her knuckles, wishing Doctor Governey would hurry with the tea. Of course, she rationalized, perhaps it would be just as well leaving the drawing room dimly lit, being that the wrinkles in her dress wouldn't show so much. But what was taking him so long? Was he still using the telephone? She had heard it ring when she approached the upstairs hallway almost a half-hour ago. Hopefully everything was alright. Though the doctor had assured her it would be, maybe something still had gone wrong. She thought of Makara and started to worry. Perhaps something had happened to her. Suddenly, the piercing chimes from the grand foyer clock rang in the eleventh hour, causing her to nearly jump from her seat.

"I hope I have not kept you waiting very long," Samuel announced as he appeared on the threshold of the drawing room carrying a silver serving tray laden with all the things necessary for a light evening tea.

Eleanor straightened her back while attempting to smooth the wrinkles from the front of her open jacket. "No sir...not very long. I've only been wait-in' here a short time."

"Excuse me, then, for leaving you in the dark, my dear." He glanced up at the multi-tiered chandelier. "But, perhaps it is just as well, being that the muted lights will be better suited for our evening tea." Then, placing the sterling silver tray upon the same rosewood parlor table at which he had applied her makeup, he walked over to the Tiffany lamp and activated the switch.

Eleanor had barely a moment to appreciate the soft glow of the leaded lamp with its red and gold dragonfly border when a sudden flash of lightning bolted across the front windows, illuminating Samuel's white shirt and distorting the rest of his appearance. Nearly jumping from fright at the ensuing thunder and letting out an unheard shriek, she nevertheless gradually calmed down at the sound of her host's soothing voice.

"I must say again, Ellie Ann, that you were certainly correct about your prediction of an upcoming thunderstorm this evening," he stated, repositioning the Wedgewood teapot among matching cups and saucers, all the while keeping in mind which cup contained the potent dose of the chloral hydrate. "At any rate, it doesn't seem as if your storm will be letting up anytime soon. All the more reason to be in the cradle of each other's company! Come," he directed, gesturing toward the corresponding tapestry chair. "Since you are most appropriately dressed for the occasion, let us sit down and relax over our pot of tea and a bit of conversation, now shall we?" He contemplated his very young guest for a moment, thinking that her attire might not be all so bad if not for the ghastly shade of orange lipstick. *"And,* may I add, you *do* look absolutely *lovely* in your Sunday suit!" Another flash of lightning gnawed at Samuel's smile, with an almost immediate requiem of thunder crashing overhead, completely muting, for a stupefying moment, the never-ending cadence of heavy winds and thrashing rain. Without so much as a shiver, he lifted the embossed teapot and proceeded to pour the tea into Eleanor's cup, certain that in just a little while, he would be able to secretly savor every delectable attribute his comatose guest had to offer.

"Is everything alright?" Ellie blurted, noticing the preoccupied look on Samuel's face. "About the breakin' in at the club, I mean? Is...are you sure Makara's o.k. too? "

Samuel cordially smiled while handing Eleanor her tea, along with a small plate of miniature cakes, keeping in mind his recent telephone conversation with Tony Terillo. Although everything had gone as well as could be expected under the circumstances, including the disposal of liquor by means of the collapsible shelving, alcohol was nevertheless found upon the premises and the club would be fined one grand. Chicken feed. The place could be ready to go in a day or two and most of the losses recouped within the next week. At least he was quick enough to scram before the press showed up. Otherwise, he could have kissed his mayoral campaign goodbye. And as far as that nuisance of a mutt was concerned, if it weren't for trying to capture its master's little heart, he couldn't have cared less if the Feds had filled its ass with lead and used it as a paperweight for all their bloody documents. But, as it presently stood, the cops had failed to show any concern for the sleeping pup, which was now at the home of Lorenzo, the garage attendant, ready to be returned at Samuel's command. "Quite alright, I assure you, my dear," he finally answered, placing the rest of the tray's contents, save the half-filled teapot, upon the rosewood parlor table. "As I stated earlier, there is absolutely nothing to worry about. Makara is in the best of hands and we shall be able to retrieve her at any time. Perhaps Lorenzo can deliver her soon after we arrive home from your appointment at Virginia's," he calmly stated as he walked over to the Jacobean sideboard, realizing that, by such an arrangement, his trip to Vito's Automobile Laundry would not have been in vain. He then placed the silver tray upon the hardwood sideboard and promptly returned to Eleanor. "Come now...drink your tea," he coaxed while seating himself beside her, making certain to arrange two crocheted doilies beneath each cup. "I have added a bit of sugar to sweeten its taste. It will help calm you after such an eventful day."

Upon noticing Doctor Governey grasping the stem of his teacup, Eleanor practically leaped from her seat. "Wait...please wait...don't drink just yet! I mean..." she went on to explain, ready to grab the cup from her gracious host if need be. "It's just that...well...we got to exchange cups first!"

"Why...for God's sake...what in the world?"

"We got to exchange cups! Don't you know? When drinkin' tea or coffee with a new friend, you're supposed to exchange cups." She lifted her own and offered it to Samuel. "Here. You drink from mine and I'll drink from yours." Receiving no immediate response, she quickly added, "It'd bring bad luck if we don't!"

"Of course...of course, my dear," Samuel patronized, gripping the gilded handle of his teacup even tighter. "But, my dear...this presents a bit of a problem, you see. I am afraid my cup will be just a bit tart for you since I am accustomed to drinking my tea with a bit of brandy."

"That's alright. I won't mind...really!" Eleanor answered, thinking it would have been wiser for her host to have poured the brandy *after* presenting the tray.

Samuel gritted his teeth beneath a condescending smile, nevertheless appearing to remain calm. "Which means...which, of course, means that I will be compelled to drink *your* tea in a way to which I am not accustomed, being that it is sweetened."

"Well...maybe you'll like it," Ellie answered with pleading brown eyes. "'Like my daddy always said, it don't hurt to give things a try. One time I didn't want to eat some tapioca, but then when I tried it, I really liked it!'"

"My dear Ellie Ann," Samuel decreed, adjusting his posture. "I do value our friendship and believe that whether we exchange cups or not, it will continue to flourish." Noticing the unrelenting look upon Eleanor's face, he added, "I'll tell you what...why don't we just take a sip from each other's cup after which we'll finish our own. I think that would be a splendid idea and certain to bring the best of luck to any tea party!"

As Samuel reached for her cup, Eleanor started to panic. Who knows what would happen if she followed his suggestion? Maybe the terrible things that Maggie told her about Hollywood would come true. Maybe she wouldn't even make it to Hollywood. Or even worse, maybe Jimmy Ray would find her before she had the chance to leave. "I...I don't think so!" she practically shouted. "I mean...I mean, you have to really exchange cups and drink the whole thing...otherwise maybe somethin' real bad might happen to me...to us! I know! I could just feel it! After...after all, I...I was right about the storm comin,' wasn't I?"

Still reaching across the table, Samuel tapped his index finger on the side of Eleanor's cup. Perhaps he had no alternative but to humor his obstinate guest after all. For a man of his weight, the dosage was minimal. At best, he'd doze off and be spared of her annoying companionship. At worst, the sedative would hardly take effect, leaving him to tolerate her inevitable prattling until the storm was long past. Nevertheless, if he be deprived of having the pleasure of *truly* enjoying her company this evening, he may as well, in the least, treat himself to one of his choice Havanas. "Very well, then, my dear Ellie Ann" he coolly responded. "But before we propose a toast, I hope you don't mind my having a cigar. I do occasionally crave one over tea." He rose and started toward a mahogany pedestal desk, never waiting for an affirmation from his guest before retrieving the Havana and lighting up amid another rumble of thunder, after which he promptly returned to his seat with cigar and ashtray in hand. "So, my dear, shall we then exchange our cups?" Following Eleanor's cue, he once again reached for the handle of her teacup. "I propose that our friendship shall be a long and lasting one." Noticing a trace of confusion in Eleanor's eyes, he then quickly added, "of *correspondence*, of course. Why...you *will* write once you are off to Hollywood, will you not?"

"Oh, yes! Of course I will! I won't even have to bother about rememberin' your address either, since it's already on the collar that you got Makara. And I probably will leave it on there 'til I get settled in a place of my own, bein' that in case she gets lost, the person who finds her can let you know about it. This way, too, I'll always let you know just where you can find *me*." Focusing on the faraway look in Samuel's eyes as he took a sip of her tea, Eleanor felt compelled to explain the pup's situation after all, thinking it was the least she could do for someone who had been treating her like his own daughter. A bit hesitant, she decided to indulge in her own first sip before 'letting the cat out of the bag,' but after her initial taste, realized that Doctor Governey had been right after all. His tea was terribly bitter with the strong alcohol in it, unlike the fruitier taste of wine she had at the club. She'd have to finish it, though, preferably before the day was out, which would give her only about 40 minutes, being that the chimes of the grandfather clock just rang in the quarter hour a few minutes ago. "I...like I said before, Doctor...*Sam*...I'm so...so grateful about how you've been takin' to be so kind to me and Makara. And I been holdin' out on tellin' you something about her that I think you should know, bein' that you been so good to me and all." Certain that she had the doctor's full attention, she continued. "You see, *Sam*...Makara...Makara isn't *really* a puppy." She paused, waiting for a response. Receiving only a skeptical stare behind a stream of cigar smoke, she continued. "I mean...she is, but...but...she's *really* my friend."

Samuel replaced his cup on the saucer after taking a modest sip. "Of course she is your friend, my dear. It has been a well-known fact since the beginning of time that a dog is man's best friend. There have even been documented cases..."

"No...I mean she's *not* a dog. She is *now*, but hasn't *always* been. She's my friend, Makara...a lady I knew at the hospital." Encouraged by Samuel's aroused curiosity, Eleanor persevered, realizing, to her delight, that the smoke from his cigar didn't seem to nauseate her at the moment. "She was my best friend, *ever*, not countin' Phyllis. I took care of her when she was sick at the Wilmington County Hospital. I first got to knowin' Makara when she caught me cryin' one day when I went in to change her bedpan on account of Daddy was gonna sell Hattie, our cow, for slaughter. Makara said she knew a friend who might like to buy a milkin' cow and she was right! It was pretty sad to see Hattie go, but at least I was glad she wasn't slaughtered." Ellie wet her lips and relaxed her stance upon the tapestry chair. "Makara would even give me some hospital meals to take home. She didn't eat meat at all, and sometimes one of the orderlies would make a mistake by givin' some to her, so she'd give it to me which tasted much better than the slop Mama'd make for me and Daddy at home. Of course, I never did let Mama or Daddy know about it, but would sneak into the barn and hide it 'til it was safe to go back and eat it."

Samuel exhaled an intestine-like stream of smoke, placed his cigar on the ashtray and reached for the handle of his teacup. "That is an interesting story, my dear Ellie Ann, but I fail to see the connection between what you have just related and your belief that your dear friend is now a *dog*."

"Well...yes, sir...sorry I hadn't gotten to that just yet, but you see...when I'd take care of Makara, she'd tell me stories about her life. Like why she came to America and all about her bein' Hindu."

"So I suppose your friend, Makara, is...*was*...from India?

"Yes, sir," she answered replacing her cup upon the saucer. "She told me things I ain't never learned before. Like how she believed that when someone dies, they don't go to heaven like my daddy always said, but come back to live another time. I forget what she called it."

"*Reincarnation*," Samuel clarified before planting the cigar between his lips.

"Yes! That's it." Accompanied by another flash of lightning and low rumble of thunder, Eleanor excitedly twitched in her seat. "You know what I'm talkin' about then. Well," she explained, clasping her hands together, "I'd tell her about what I was plannin' on doin' too...about goin' to Hollywood some day. But I didn't see her no more once we left Ohio. I kept writin' her, though. Then I didn't hear from her no more, so I wrote the hospital and they told me she'd taken a turn for the worse." Eleanor's softened voice eased to a slower pace, practically drowned out by the heavy patter of rain. "Then Dr. Gillis sent word a couple o' months ago that she went ahead and died. But," she perked up, "two weeks later, Makara showed up at the fillin' station. I knew she was really my friend right away by the gentle, but sad look in her eyes. And I know she'd have kept Jimmy Ray from me if Mama'd let me keep her in my room instead of chained up at night in the alley. But I don't have to worry 'bout that no more. Now that I'm on my own, I can let her sleep with me from now on." Ellie paused with a hopeful look on her face. "If I stay here for another few nights or so, would it be alright if Makara slept with me in my room?"

Upon taking note that his teacup was now only half full, Samuel began to feel a bit drowsy. Perhaps he should open one of the windows to let in some fresh air. "That would be just fine," he nearly choked, rising from his seat and walking toward the window, thinking it would be in his best interest that the pup be given a thorough examination by a certified veterinarian. "It is my understanding, however, that according to Hindu doctrine, the purpose of rebirth was to *elevate* one's life as opposed to degrading it. If that is true, your friend would not have returned as an animal, let alone a mere *dog*, but rather someone higher in the caste system. Did your friend mention that to you?"

Upon realizing that Samuel was about to open the window, Eleanor began sliding off her chair to help, but suddenly stopped as he lifted the pane with ease, allowing the tinny sound of easing raindrops upon the metal window frame to penetrate the mansion's interior. "You mean..." she asked, surprised that he was able to open the window with hardly an effort, "you mean that when a Hindu dies, she'll come back a person again?"

"*Precisely*, my dear Ellie Ann," Samuel clarified as he walked back toward the parlor table to retrieve his cigar and ashtray. "Having traveled extensively through various regions of India myself, I am most familiar with the people's beliefs and customs." Carrying both the Havana and ashtray, he then walked over to the tufted divan and settled himself upon it, balancing the ashtray upon his knee. "I hope you don't mind my sitting apart from you while you finish your tea," he declared, pitching his voice across the room, "but I feel a bit drowsy and am afraid I may doze off and fall from my chair if I remain seated next to you. Of course, you are welcome to join me and may even bring your tea over here if you wish. In any case, if your friend, Makara, had been reincarnated as she believed, her position in life would have been that of a *higher* class citizen than previously held, not that of a mere animal."

A flash of lightning illuminated the wide half-moons underneath Eleanor's raised eyebrows. "You mean you *been* to India?"

"Why yes, my dear. I certainly have," Samuel teased with a boyish smile.

Despite an intruding crash of thunder, Eleanor savored the cooling breeze coming in through the open window. "I noticed some of the nice things you have here like that painted screen over there, but wasn't sure if you'd really been there. I've been wantin' to go to India ever since Makara told me all about it. I even looked up some pictures at the Wilmington library. Do you know they got palaces made from real jewels?"

"Actually, that silk screen over there is from China. But you are quite correct. The Taj Mahal in New Delhi is one such architectural masterpiece inlaid with semiprecious stones," Samuel remarked, recalling the majestic domed marble tomb. "I have traveled there, too. Nevertheless," he added with a fervent yawn, "it is a shame you will be staying here for only a few days. Otherwise, I would be more than happy to have you accompany me on my upcoming visit to Calcutta and Bombay. However," he explained, lethargically waving his Havana in mid-air, "I do understand that you have your own travels to contend with. It will be my loss, I am sure of it, my dear." Noticing the look of regret on Eleanor's face, he added, "So you see, Ellie Ann, I am afraid that your pet dog is precisely that. Nothing more than a dog, loyal as she may be. And *definitely* not the reincarnation of your dear friend from India."

Glancing toward the frosted *petits fours* and her cup of tea, Eleanor considered whether or not to join Doctor Governey on the sofa, ultimately deciding to remain where she was for the moment so that she could eat one or two of the miniature cakes and drink her tea without worrying about how to balance everything. "No, but it's not true," she finally spoke up. "I mean, I know all about what you're talkin' of. Makara told me all about it and there's a reason why she's come back a dog. It's the same reason she was livin' here and not in India anymore." Pouting orange-colored lips, she continued to explain. "She was *jinxed.* She wasn't supposed to go near a little beggar boy, but she did anyway and his shadow touched her. She came here 'cause her family didn't want her no more. But her husband came with her and took care of her 'til he got very sick and died. Even though *he* wouldn't even touch her from then on either."

With drooping eyelids getting heavier by the minute, Samuel rested his cigar upon the ashtray. Perhaps it was just as well the stupid lass believe what she chose, he yawned. The evening was certainly wearing on him and he had more important things to take care of than arguing about a common stray mutt. The tale she told, however, did make sense, though. Her Indian friend most likely resided in the South Indian state of Travancore, since the Brahmanic Orthodoxy in that region was extreme in banishing 'untouchables.' He grunted to himself, recalling filthy bodies strewn along sun-baked streets. It was just as well with him if they all were banished and disappeared from the face of this bloody earth! "I must admit, my dear, Ellie Ann, you do present a convincing case. Provided, however, that reincarnation does exist, which I, myself, personally doubt. But..." he slurred, "everyone has the right to believe what they will." Aware that the chloral hydrate was beginning to take full effect, Samuel sluggishly supported his stiffened back against the firm padding of the tufted divan while contemplating the allure of actually having the power to manipulate his affairs beyond the grave.

"Well..." Eleanor mumbled, swallowing another bite of the tea cake, "I do believe it. And I know Makara's come back to protect me. Makara really liked me. I know. She didn't want no one else to help her neither. Said I was the best orderly around. Probably 'cause I listened to her stories so much. Do you know that in India a long time ago when a man would die, they'd make his wife burn to death? It was 'cause the wife could be in the same place and keep takin' care of him. Makara said her mama told her 'bout the time her grandmamma was dragged by her own boys into the fire, kickin' and screamin' all the way. I'm glad they don't do that no more, 'cause Makara's husband died before her and...." Ellie stopped talking, her full attention now focused on the somnolent figure across the room. Like a spotlight on a darkened stage, a bolt of lightning suddenly revealed that the doctor had not heard one single word she had said, but Eleanor had hardly the chance to absorb the situation before another clap of thunder arose, immediately mimicked by the doctor's deep, sudden snore.

chapter 91

Break-in

Eleanor scanned the immense drawing room and started cracking her knuckles. Earlier that evening before heading out to the club and even up to just a minute ago as the doctor had kept her in good company, the room appeared more than hospitable. But now, despite its previous warmth and richness, it seemed to threaten her amid another tormenting patter of rain and howling wind. Even the grand piano which she had admired so dearly seemed as if it might begin badgering her with demonic sounds. And the brass chandelier with its long curving arms looked like it could plummet down and swoop her up at any given time. Maybe it was because she had never been all alone before in a mansion like this during a raging thunderstorm. She may as well be alone, she shuddered, focusing upon Samuel's slumbering body which was now slumped sideways, the ashtray with cigar still balanced upon his knee. With the back of his neck pressed against the divan's mahogany rail, his head was turned away from the distant light of the parlor lamp, obstructing her view of even the slightest expression on his lifeless face. He didn't look as if he would wake up any time soon either. Surely, her story about Makara hadn't bored him. Or had it? He probably was just tired from the long day, she guessed, intertwining the fingers of both hands while gliding a perspiring thumb across the other's freshly cracked knuckle. Older people tended to tire out more quickly. And, unlike herself, he probably hadn't taken a good nap that afternoon. Still, she wished Doctor Governey hadn't fallen asleep on her like that. Especially with the storm going strong again.

Ellie looked toward the open window, wondering when the storm would finally end. The leaded panes seemed taller than ever now, their long, drawn curtains resembling shadowed ghosts. Perhaps she should get up and close the window, she decided, welcoming the idea to keep herself busy if only for a short while. Although the rain had let up earlier, it now continued frantically. Thinking it much like a child holding onto a tantrum, she rose from her seat and walked toward the front of the room, discovering, that for some odd reason, the window wasn't sticking at all and she was able to close it almost as easily as the doctor had slid it open. Instinctively, amid the subdued sound of rain, she began to glance toward Samuel, but the sight of something else distracted her. It was the armoire. The same piece of furniture that he kept the ruby necklace in. And the matching earrings, along with some other pieces of jewelry, were probably in there too.

As if in a trance, Eleanor continued to stare at the heavy oak armoire majestically tucked against the corner wall. Feeling as if the ornamental brass which decorated the front of it was instead situated inside the soles of her shoes, she nevertheless persuaded her stagnant feet to move while cautiously creeping across the Persian rug and onto the parquet flooring. Forcing her eyes upward, she gradually discerned its outline more clearly, intentionally taking note of the decorative flute about a foot and a half above its base. If she was especially quiet, it would be possible to hoist herself up on the cabinet and grab the key without Doctor Governey hearing her, just like she thought about earlier while waiting for him to come out of the pet shop. Of course, she hadn't realized that such an opportunity would come this soon. But, how could she be sure that the doctor wouldn't wake up in the meantime and catch her? Maybe she should softly call his name to see if he responds.

Softly tiptoeing over to the divan, Eleanor waited for another roll of thunder to take its course as it sluggishly penetrated the mansion's thick walls. Disregarding prolonged snores accompanying the distinct odor of 'weed killer,' she leaned ever so close to Samuel's ear, being careful not to startle him as she whispered once, then a bit louder, and louder again for a third time without his awakening. Certain that he was fast asleep, she took a step backwards, this time noticing the cigar-laden ashtray still on his knee. No doubt, it was bound to fall off and soil the carpet, she sighed. Perhaps she should place it on one of the round tables next to the divan. This way, too, if he didn't wake up while she moved it, she'd *really* know he was fast asleep.

Feeling as if she were playing a game of pick-up sticks, Ellie leaned over and lifted the ashtray ever so gently, finally relieved that this particular maneuver also had left the doctor undisturbed.

Eleanor waited a moment or two in order to catch her breath, then stooped down to unstrap her second-hand Sunday shoes, realizing that if the storm blew over while the doctor was still asleep, she'd be able to leave that very night with the borrowed jewels. Of course, she'd have to sleep at one of those uncomfortable dirty bus stops, but that didn't matter except...except... As if a detour sign flashed inside her mind, she suddenly thought of Makara. Leaving tonight would be out of the question, she pouted, yanking off her second ankle sock. But maybe it was just as well. Being wrapped up in the excitement of snatching the jewels and all, she had forgotten about the bloodhounds that might still be after her. And it really would be best that she got her hair bobbed before heading out, lest she be easily recognized. With shoes and socks forgotten and thrown about, Eleanor started toward the armoire with a racing heart, her bare feet silently treading across the soft Persian rug with every forward step.

Taking another deep breath as she stood in front of the tall oak armoire, Ellie carefully assessed her strategy one final time before grasping a hinge with her left hand and a brass handle with the other. Then, placing a bare foot upon the narrow fluting, she hoisted herself up. Still holding onto the brass handle for support, she stretched her left arm toward the top of the armoire's frieze, her wandering fingers probing for the key as the hard wood of the tall chest pressed against her slender torso. Sensing nothing but a smooth surface for a mere second or two, she slid her hand further forward, finally feeling the weight of the metal key move at the nudging of her finger-tips. Immediately capturing the elusive key, she took another deep breath while balancing the weighted piece of metal in one hand and the rest of her body with the other. But, before she could finish plotting her leap back onto the floor, she was suddenly overcome with a gripping fear as her foot imme-diately gave way, slipping off the narrow fluting as hands and arms frantically attempted to grasp empty space, her stiffened body tumbling helplessly towards the ground.

Struggling to recover from her fall, Eleanor became horrified. In spite of the everlasting thunderstorm, she had surely made enough noise to wake up a pack of grizzly bears. *Why,* she managed to assess while still lying dazed and confused, she was certain that if Doctor Governey had even a whisper of wakefulness in his body, it would have been triggered right that very instant! Grinding her teeth, she crossed the fingers of both hands, sluggishly rose to her feet and peeked over her shoulder. He still *looked* like he was sleeping, she thought, discerning from a darkened distance the outline of his body. She couldn't see his eyes, though. Were they still closed? What if he was secretly watching her? Pretending to be asleep, but really having caught her in the act? She spontaneously shivered while blinking her own eyes in a desperate attempt to fend off her worst fear. Still failing to make out the doctor's facial features, she was eventually aided by another flash of lightning. Along with what appeared to be the sagging mouth of an old man, his eyes were firmly shut. So Doctor Governey hadn't been spying on her after all, she sighed, catching her breath. And the lightning...it was eerie enough to make even the most dashing of men look a hundred years old!

Feeling both relieved and apprehensive while a succeeding clamor of thunder shook the metal frames of the drawing room windows, Eleanor suddenly thought of the key. Where was that darn thing? It was in her hand just minutes ago. She brushed the matted hair away from her perspiring forehead and dropped to her knees as desperate eyes rapidly scanned the dark floor, nervous fingers pawing at the parquet wood. Frantically crawling back onto the plush carpeting, her palm accidentally pressed against the clawed foot of a chaise lounge. Something was moving but hidden in the shadows. The clawed foot of the chaise lounge was coming apart. No...It was the key! It had fallen against the piece of furniture. Grabbing it with her right hand, she steadied herself with the other and slowly rose from the floor, turning in the direction of the oversized divan. Her hip was sore. Rubbing away the smarting pain, she once again gazed upon Samuel. *Good,* she sighed eyeing his lifeless silhouette. He hadn't budged one bit. She suddenly thought of the baby. A fall like that could cause an abortion after all! Pressing the palm of her free hand along her abdomen and feeling nothing out of the ordinary, she breathed a sigh of relief, then brushed back together the pleats of her skirt.

Ever so grateful that she had survived the horrifying ordeal, Ellie bit her bottom lip while standing full-faced before the towering oak armoire, her intense stare, like an arrow aimed toward its target, fixed upon the enticing keyhole. With an outstretched arm she guided the key toward the hole and slipped its long, metal finger into place. With one turn of her hand, the lock chattered, then clicked. Accompanied by a prolonged flash of lightning, she pulled open the heavy oak doors, the subsequent thunder announcing the fleeting image of velvet boxes lined upon multiple shelves with the promise of the ruby necklace sequestered inside a long horizontal drawer.

chapter 92

Revelations

Clutching a small velvet box with trembling hands, Eleanor remained practically glued in front of the open armoire, bearing in mind the dozen or so other boxes which were sparingly distributed upon its darkened shelves. At once, she opened the lid of the velvet case, able to feel with her fingertips that, despite insufficient lighting, it was for certain another piece of expensive jewelry. Accompanied by the whistling of the wind and another subsequent roll of thunder, she began stepping toward the artificial light of the Tiffany lamp at the opposite end of the room. Again, as if to remind her to check whether the doctor was still sleeping, a secondary flicker of lightning cut through the drawing room, barely assisting her to discern that the contents of the box contained an array of diamonds. Instinctively, she turned toward the tufted divan, encouraged that the doctor was, indeed, sleeping. Then, tilting the open box toward the welcoming light beneath the multi-colored lamp shade, she gasped amidst a drum roll of thunder. It was a golden broach with diamonds and...and...*emeralds* probably. How much was it worth? Probably twice as much as she could get at the pawn shop, but even so, there was bound to be enough to pay for the train fare to California. There'd probably be plenty enough for room and board, too, until she found an acting job. Of course, just in case, it'd be best she took a few more pieces that she could hock *after* she got to California. But before she could comprehend one more possibility, she let out another gasp, dropping the velvet case and broach onto the carpet. Doctor Governey! He was moving! And staring at her! Her breathing stopped. Had he been pretending all this time? Following her all along? Watching her every step? Her flesh started crawling like a melting pillar of wax, adhering her feet to the surface of the floor. Completely terrified, she watched the shadowed figure rise from the divan. Frantically thinking of an excuse brought tears to her eyes. Should she tell him that she just wanted to see the necklace again but grabbed the wrong box? She was curious about the earrings? Would he believe her? Or would he see right through her? Would he be angry? Call the police? Her mind continued to race as she stared at the disquieting figure standing in front of the divan. Why wasn't he moving anymore? Why didn't he say something? Was he doing it on purpose? Making her pay for her sins? Whatever the case, he was making her squirm...exactly like Jimmy Ray would do time and time again just by staring at her! *Say something,* she almost screamed. *For heaven's sake, talk to me!*

After waiting for what seemed an eternity, Eleanor tried to speak, but nothing came out. Her face felt numb as she squinted through emerging tears. Noticing something peculiar about the threatening figure in the distance, however, she eventually felt her insides starting to revive. She squinted again. Doctor Governey wasn't so threatening after all. Instead of moving toward her, he slowly lifted his arms, turning back toward the sofa, as if he were in a trance. What was going on? It was like Doctor Governey was dreaming or something. That was it! He was dreaming. Sleepwalking, they called it. Doctor Governey was sleepwalking! She had sometimes heard of people who sleepwalked, but never knew of anyone who actually did it until now. And this whole time, he hadn't been watching her after all, she breathed, clutching her chest. He never even knew she took the diamond broach.

Mesmerized, Ellie ignored the dropped broach and its velvet case while breathing more steadily. Doctor Governey was reaching upwards and tracing something horizontally in mid air. As if he were going through some kind of ritual. Almost like an artist painting a portrait, but the strokes were smaller. Too small for a large canvas. She pushed a stray lock away from her flushed cheek. Maybe she should put the broach back and replace the key on top of the cabinet before he snapped out of it. She'd wait for the next roll of thunder, though, before actually locking the armoire. The cabinet *did* make a loud echo and in spite of the heavy rain, could startle the doctor. Besides, waking a man who was sleepwalking might just kill him. Her eyes suddenly drifted into oblivion as she contemplated the golden opportunity she would have if the doctor *did* happen to die suddenly. She wondered how much jewelry her traveling bag would hold.

Inwardly scolding herself, and aside from the possibility of never getting Makara back if she ran away first thing in the morning, how could she ever entertain such a notion, being that Doctor Governey had been so kind to her and all? Besides, there was no telling if the whole plan might just go ahead and backfire if she *did* happen to go through with it. Disregarding the entire idea altogether as bloodhounds and police cars rambled through her mind, Eleanor turned her attention once again toward the tall armoire filled with its treasures. It probably *was* best that she didn't try and take any of the jewels just yet. At least the key was still in its place so she wouldn't have to grope around for it again, she sighed while stooping down to recover the broach, all the time keeping an ever watchful eye on the somnambulistic doctor who had just reseated himself upon the oversized divan.

Having silently crept toward the armoire, Eleanor reluctantly replaced the boxed broach upon the cabinet shelf, wondering what kind of jewelry the rest of the cases contained. And what about all the other valuables that were scattered about the mansion, she wondered while shutting the heavy doors, suddenly remembering Maggie O'Dougherty's convincing declaration. *"...I'd been comin' to this gin mill for I don't know how many years and haven't once known Sam ta be bringin' his own lady along. Not that there hasn't been any Shebas wantin' to get their claws inta him..."* Was it true then? Would a girl like her really be better off marrying a man like Doctor Governey rather than running off to Hollywood? She'd certainly have the right to wear all his jewels then. And there'd be no reason to worry about stealin' them anymore. *Or* be afraid of getting caught, either by the police *or* that stinking bastard, Jimmy Ray. And how about that Grosse Pointe theatre group that was starting up that Doctor Governey was speaking of? Was it really possible that more directors would be coming to Michigan to shoot their motion pictures? And how about all the other things she'd get to do...like learn to play the Wurlitzer organ and...and...even traveling to India!

Eleanor turned the key to lock the cabinet as the next rumble of thunder was fading. She pouted while removing the key from the keyhole. Didn't Miss O'Dougherty also say that Doctor Governey would only want to marry a virgin? Maybe under different circumstances she could have tricked him into believing she was pure as an Easter lily, but he sure knew better by now.

And anyhow, *just what am I thinking?* she wondered, quickly hoisting herself upon the armoire just enough to chuck the key back onto its crest. It was ridiculous wondering about marrying a man who was old enough to be her daddy, she thought, cautiously stepping down.

Instinctively, she turned around, intrigued more than ever by Samuel's peculiar ritual. Instead of just sitting upright, he was stretching his arms up too. Up and down. Up and down. Like he was stroking something. Stroking along the length of something. But just what was he doing? It was like...like...he was brushing a head of hair. That was it! He was brushing some woman's hair. His mother's! Yes...that was exactly it. He was dreaming about helping his mother get ready for one of her vaudeville shows...especially when she was getting on in years and couldn't take care of herself so well. *Poor Doctor Governey.* He must miss her very much. She shivered, concluding that no matter what the reason for the doctor's sleepwalking, it was still pretty creepy and she'd best not pay any more attention to it. So what was there for her to do now? She certainly didn't want to go upstairs all alone. Not with the storm still going. She'd forgotten about it the last couple of minutes, but now it was frightening her again. In all her life, she'd never known a storm to last so long. Sure, she'd predicted a fierce one earlier in the day, but even then had no idea it would be like this. It was bound to end soon, though, she hoped, crossing her fingers. Maybe she could start cleaning up the tea things in the meantime. Maybe *that* would take her mind off all the creepy things that were going on around here. The kitchen light was brighter, too, and it was bound to feel more comfortable in there. Besides, she considered, plopping down upon the Persian carpet to put her shoes and ankle stockings back on, Doctor Governey was sure to be pleased that she had cleared away all the tea things. Maybe he'd even be inclined to reward her with a special trinket or bring her to another fancy night club tomorrow night. But for now, she resolved, finally sneaking toward the hardwood sideboard to retrieve the sterling silver tray and half-filled teapot, all she'd have to worry about was where Doctor Governey kept the dishwashing things.

Cautiously lifting the serving tray, Eleanor walked over to the parlor table, her improved demeanor slackening as she eyed the two teacups which were momentarily revived by a strong flicker of lightning. They were still mostly full...not drunk all the way like they ought to have been. Could this be a sign of some bad luck to come? Would something awful happen to her in Hollywood like Maggie was predicting at the club? A shiver ran down her spine as she tried to console herself amid more howling wind and another disturbing roll of thunder. Maybe she'd never make it to California after all on account of being found out by the cops who'd send her right back to Mama and Jimmy Ray. Maybe Jimmy Ray would end up raping her again. Maybe the baby would end up being a cripple or a retard and nobody would want it and she'd be stuck taking care of it the rest of her life. Maybe she and her child would end up being street urchins without so much as a penny to their names, forced to sleep on doorsteps and scrounge through garbage in the alleys....

Practically on the verge of tears, Eleanor began placing the teacups upon the silver tray. It was nonsense carrying on like this. Sheer *nonsense*, she scolded, clearing the dish of leftover cakes. The recent toast of tea was declared over *friendship*, the friendship between her and Doctor Governey. If anything, her acquaintance with the kind doctor would soon be over and forgotten. And why shouldn't it be, with her going off to California real soon? So that's all, she shrugged, picking up the crowded tray and starting toward the kitchen. The half-filled teacups were just a sign that, as much as she enjoyed the good doctor's company, it was only a temporary situation after all.

chapter 93

Spooked

As Eleanor stepped into the brightly lit kitchen, her spirits began to lift. It had done her good to leave the dreariness of the drawing room. Placing the full tray of Wedgewood china upon the counter, she gazed past the rain-spattered cathedral windows, straining her eyes through drenching blackness to discern the outline of several branches swaying to and fro, their long, spindly fingers demanding shelter from the wailing wind. Ellie let out a sigh of relief as the muscles of her shoulders began to relax. Although the storm had still refused to let up, witnessing it from the kitchen didn't seem nearly as threatening as when she was in the drawing room. She wondered if Doctor Governey was still sleepwalking and let out an involuntary shiver, immediately slipping off her shoes to feel the cool limestone tile. Maybe wearing no shoes again would help her to relax more. Mama always said that when her feet hurt, the rest of her body did too. And her Sunday shoes *were* very uncomfortable. Perhaps she'd start talking out loud, too. Then she wouldn't feel so all alone.

"Now where would he keep the soap flakes?" she questioned, her eyes scanning mahogany cupboards which overlooked wide marble counters accommodating every conceivable electrical appliance from the tall coffee-grinding machine to the flat waffle iron. The closet door in the adjoining breakfast room finally jolted her memory. "That's where Doctor Governey keeps it!" Eagerly walking into the breakfast room, she swung open the closet door, utterly amazed at the size of the storage area. Although it was too dark to recognize many of the objects inside, she suspected that the closet could easily fit not only the old cot she was accustomed to sleeping on, but two large chifforobes besides. Stepping into the oversized room, she looked upward for a hanging cord attached to a light. Noticing none, she groped around in the dark until touching a light switch on the inside wall. "Well, I'll be," she exclaimed while flicking it on. "Even my own bedroom don't have a...." Feeling the skin upon her forearms crawl to a foreboding roll of thunder, Eleanor caught her breath as she noticed a set of steps leading to the basement. That was where Doctor Governey's medical office was, she speculated. Where he had gotten the supplies for the cut on her shin and the sheet to cover her with after she had stripped off her rain-soaked clothes. Probably where he did the abortions too, she guessed, realizing that her scarlet gown and underthings had been cleared from the kitchen floor. Quickly eyeing the janitorial supplies neatly placed upon the spotless parquet and hung along the paneled wall, Ellie resumed talking to herself while scanning the cleaning products lined upon the papered shelving. There it was. The box of Ivory Soap Flakes Doctor Governey had used that afternoon, set between the Bon Ami cleanser and the Johnson's liquid wax.

With box of soap flakes in hand, Eleanor headed toward the kitchen sink again, when something distracted her. Something that took her mind off the uncleaned china. And the basement. And the large closet. Something annoying to her ears. Not only to her ears, but her insides as well. It was that peculiar, eerie sound she had heard in Doctor Governey's office that afternoon...probably coming from that awful looking contraption she had spotted outside the bedroom window after she had gotten all dressed up for the evening. Instinctively, she placed the palms of her hands over her ears, but to no avail; she could still hear its irritating screech. Like scraping a sharp set of fingernails across a chalkboard. Screech...scratch...scrape. Why in the world had Doctor Governey owned such a thing? she wondered, envisioning the tall pole laden with sharp blades and broken glass. Determined once and for all to forget about such disturbing things and assisted by a milder roll of thunder, she uncovered her ears and scurried toward the porcelain sink, cracking her knuckles and crossing her fingers, hoping that by the time she started washing the dishes, the unrelenting wind would finally have started to give way.

Eleanor removed her jacket, rolled up the sleeves of her blouse and filled the basin with sudsy water. Perhaps she should make more of an effort to think pleasant thoughts, she concluded while carefully emptying each piece of tea service and placing them, one by one, into the hot suds. Like tomorrow. After all, she was going to get her hair bobbed. And maybe get her ears pierced if Doctor Governey was still willing to do them. Maybe he would buy her another gown and take her out to eat again. Maybe they would even go see a movie at that Punch and Judy Theatre on Kercheval Avenue. She thought of the fleet of automobiles that was bound to be inside the doctor's carriage house. What kind of motor car would he drive her in this time? Maybe one of them high-class Rolls-Royce's or a spiffy Aston Martin, or...CRASH! Eleanor impulsively latched onto the teapot she had been washing to keep it from slipping through her fingers. Something had broken, but the sound hadn't come from inside the house. It was from outside the breakfast area. At the back of the house—in the backyard. She suddenly felt queasy. It was that awful contraption. It probably had fallen over from the heavy winds. But why was it making her so nervous? Warily, she placed the Wedgewood teapot upon the towel-lined marble counter, then started to walk toward the veranda window, cracking each knuckle along the way.

Eleanor trembled, altering her course to avoid bumping into the obtrusive butcher block while the sound of rain thrashed against the metal-framed window. Her nose practically against the pane, she strained her eyes to see beyond the sheeted glass...beyond the tiled veranda. She squinted. Everything was still pitch black. She had forgotten how dark it could become on a moonless night. At least there was always a street light shining above the billboard at the side of the filling station. But now...now she could hardly see a thing. It was as if the giant scorpion her mama would point out on clear autumn nights had eaten the moon and stars right out of the sky. Ellie squeezed her arms across her chest and wondered when the storm would end. If it continued much more, there could be flooding. Maybe it had already started. Maybe any minute she'd feel the water creeping under her stocking feet. If only she could see the rain pouring down. She gasped. A dazzling flash of light suddenly answered her questions. She could still see the grass, so at least there was no flooding. But something else the lightning revealed was troubling her. Something a short distance beyond the terrace. Even though the darkness had returned, she could still see it in her mind. That long contraption, all twisted and broken, strewn across the lawn. Pieces of broken glass and blades...or sharp knives of some sort, cutting into the grass. What in the world had it been used for, then? Surely, it was too ugly to be a decoration of some sort. Would Doctor Governey be upset that it had been ruined by the storm, then? Whatever it was, he possibly couldn't, she reasoned, practically oblivious to the resonant rattle of thunder. Maybe someone had given it to him and he was just too nice to throw it away. He'll probably be glad to be rid of it No matter the reason, though, it still gave her the willies. It was the storm, she decided as a sharp gust of wind vibrated the window. This never-ending storm was making her imagination play tricks on her. "Stop spooking yourself like that," she chided, quickly shuffling her way back into the main kitchen area. "Just get back to your work and mind your own business." Suddenly realizing the need to use the powder room, she decided that afterwards, she'd finally finish cleaning up and stop thinking about such frightful things. She crossed her fingers. With a bit of luck, the storm would be ended by then. She was getting awfully weary and a good night's sleep would do her good.

chapter 94

After the Storm

Her shattered nerves slowly melting away with the passing storm, Eleanor tiptoed in her stocking feet down the hall toward the drawing room with pair of Sunday shoes in hand. The softly falling rain and faint thunder allowed the resonant tick of the grandfather clock to prevail once more. Feeling refreshed from her trip to the powder room and satisfied that she had finished the kitchen chores, she yawned, wondering once again what the doctor was up to. Hopefully, he was through with his sleepwalking. The storm surely had a strange effect on both of them. Was he back on the sofa asleep? Certainly, he hadn't awakened or he'd have come into the kitchen and discovered her there. She wistfully smiled while sweeping her hair from under the wrinkled collar of her jacket. Would Doctor Governey be pleased with her? Perhaps he would reward her with a new dress or a different pair of shoes. Anything more comfortable than these Sunday shoes she took off her aching feet a half hour ago. Maybe he'd even be so impressed, that he'd give her some of his mother's jewelry. Then she might not have to sneak into the tall cabinet again to steal a piece or two.

Slowing her pace as she approached the drawing room, Eleanor peeked inside before entering, breathing a sigh of relief upon noticing that the doctor was sprawled upon the oversized divan fast asleep. The room was still dimly lit, but his immobile body and deep, slow breathing gave him away. Her eyes felt suddenly heavy. Now that the storm was over, she could sleep too. But shouldn't she wake Doctor Governey, as well, before going upstairs?

Although the amply cushioned piece of furniture was large enough to support him, a bed would certainly be more comfortable, she decided, noticing his arm dangling upon the carpet.

Being careful not to startle him, Ellie was about to lean over and tap his shoulder when something stopped her. The ashtray. She had forgotten about cleaning Doctor Governey's ashtray which was still left upon the round mahogany table. The long, fat Cuban cigar, having almost been completely smoked, had left behind a pile of ashes. She frowned. The very thought of walking all the way back to the kitchen exhausted her. Maybe she would just leave it after all. Wasn't it enough that everything else had been cleaned up? She could empty it in the morning—that is, if he didn't beat her to it. She sighed, still eyeing the ashtray and placed a hand in front of her face to catch another yawn. She was too tired to think about the matter any longer. That was it, then. She'd go to bed and clean it in the morning. Since she never slept past the crack of dawn, Doctor Governey would probably wake up later than her anyway...even if he *should* continue sleeping on the divan, which did look comfortable enough after all. The ashes could wait. The ashes...ashes.... The word taunted her. There was something about ashes. Some kind of rhyme. She used to say it as a little girl. A chant of some kind. What was it? Something about an old man. Yes. It was in Mama's big black book of magic spells and incantations. She remembered now. There was a picture on the opposite page of the chant too. A picture of fat naked ladies dancing 'round a fire under a moon as full as a sow's belly. How did it go? She closed her eyes and clenched her fists. *Ashes from a wealthy squire. Sprinkle...no. Scatter...scatter on your heart's desire.* Her face brightening, she opened her eyes, focusing intently on the slumbering figure. *If the wealthy man be old, riches return double-fold.* That was it! And Doctor Governey was old. Not real old, she concluded as her eyes adjusted to the dimness, but lots older than her. All she had to do now was spread the ashes over her heart's desire and according to the incantation, it'd be hers.

Eleanor glanced toward the tall oak cabinet. Should she spread the ashes over that? Then maybe all the jewels could be hers. Reaching for the ashtray, she suddenly grimaced. There were certainly other expensive things around the mansion. It'd be foolish to throw all the ashes on the cabinet, she decided while pulling her hand away from the ashtray. Especially already knowing how to get inside the cabinet without the help of any spell. She raised her eyebrows. Maybe the spell would work on the whole house. But where should the ashes be scattered then? Maybe over the rug. The rug was part of the house. She frowned again. The ashes would have to be scattered through the whole mansion then and that would take forever. Besides, there wasn't enough ashes to go around. Maybe she should sprinkle them around Doctor Governey. He *owned* the house. But, would it work? she wondered, forever eyeing the small crystal tray. Even if it didn't, it was worth a try. What was there to lose? She'd be careful to scatter the ashes sparingly, though, so they wouldn't be too noticeable upon the light-colored carpet.

Determining that the spell would have to be chanted softly so as not to wake Doctor Governey, Ellie reached for the ashtray, suddenly pausing as the sleeve of her jacket brushed against the table. Should she undress? The ladies in the book didn't have any clothes on. She firmly bit the inside of her lip while picking up the tray. It'd probably make the spell work better. She blushed. It would be one thing if she were being examined by a doctor, but to purposely undress and prance around the room in front of one was another. Even if he *was* sleeping. In any case, she'd best pull the curtains shut should anyone happen to pass by and look in. Of course, it'd be best that she only draw the *sheer* curtains so that any light from an emerging moon could still shine through, although the moon in the book was a full one and any present moon would be a waxing one at best. Being ever so careful not to wake the doctor, Eleanor placed the ashtray back upon the mahogany table and crept toward the window. She frowned while searching the hazy sky until, like a curtain opening on stage, a large cloud unveiled the object of her desire. It definitely was not a full moon, but it was still bright and certainly better than no moon at all, she reasoned.

As Eleanor sneaked back toward the mahogany table to retrieve the ashes, another matter began troubling her. There was a fire in the book's picture. Was a fire needed to make the spell work? She hesitated, each wrinkle in her forehead deepening as the impossibility became more apparent. *No…*she'd have to do without and hope for the best. There was no way she'd be able to set a fire in here. But…she immediately focused her full attention upon the cigar. It had burned out, but there was still some of it left. She could light it again. A lighter. She'd need a lighter. Doctor Governey had a Ronson lighter in his jacket pocket, but…Did she dare? Cautiously, she inched her way toward the end of the sofa where Samuel lay his head. His breathing seemed louder now. Although he lay flat on his back, his head was turned sideways, exposing a full head of hair which appeared darker under the dim light. Ellie's hand trembled as she leaned over to reach for Samuel's inner pocket. Holding her breath, she reached her way into the smooth silk fabric of his jacket. She felt something cool and solid. There it was, she breathed while latching onto it. He wasn't moving either. That was good. *Now, get it out. There.* But she suddenly jumped, almost dropping the lighter on his chest. Doctor Governey was waking up! *Quick. Put the lighter back in his pocket before he thinks you were stealing it!*

As if her hand had been paralyzed, though, it wasn't following her orders. It was telling her something. Telling her to wait. Telling her to calm down. What had seemed like several minutes was only a matter of seconds before she could see that the doctor wasn't waking after all. He had just grunted and changed position. Upon realizing she had finally been given the green light, Eleanor still felt as if her heart were going to burst right through her bosom. *That was close,* she swallowed, attempting to suppress her breathing while backing away from the sofa.

Having purposely stalled another minute or two to regain her composure and fine-tune her plan, Eleanor pushed aside the excess ashes with the butt of the cigar, ignited the lighter and held it against the Havana's tip. The flame burned brightly upon the sweet tobacco, but the tip of the Havana ceased to burn as soon as she withdrew the fire. *Darn!* She was going to have to puff on it to get it going. Lifting its blunt head toward her mouth, she hesitated. She had never smoked a *cigarette* before, let alone a cigar. What if she started to cough? Doctor Governey might suddenly be startled and wake up. She paused for a moment and took a deep breath. She'd just have to be extra careful, that's all. Holding the flame of the lighter to the cigar butt, Ellie brought the Havana toward puckering lips and puffed on its damp head, gradually increasing the force of her breath. To her surprise, the cigar began to smoke. And she didn't have the urge to cough either. Not only that, she realized while continuing to puff, in spite of the cigar's strong smell, it didn't taste all that bad. *There,* she concluded, gently placing it back upon the ashtray. *Everything is all set. The fire, the ashes, the moon, the....* She was still dressed. There was only one more thing to take care of then.

Having already removed her skirt and jacket, Eleanor wasted no time while unbuttoning the pleated crepe blouse, her inflamed eyes all the while remaining fixed upon Doctor Governey. She had to hurry and work the spell before he happened to wake up, she thought while guiding her arm through one of the sleeves. A teasing chill encompassed her delicate shoulders while her full white slip, accentuated by a cascade of raven hair, glowed amid a myriad of lifeless objects. Eleanor shivered slightly while placing the blouse upon her suit which was draped over the wide back of a winged chair. Still staring intently at Samuel, she paused before lowering the lace strap of her slip. The doctor was still sleeping, alright. It should be safe enough.

A welcoming coolness spread over Eleanor's bosom as the white silky fabric fell to the floor revealing a pair of pert breasts which more than sufficed the absence of a full moon. The cotton panties followed, divulging a slight bulge of the tummy which seemed to keep guard over a heart-shaped pubis modestly sheathed by a sparse coverlet of soft brunette hair. Eleanor let out an involuntary shiver as a cool draft traveled around her taut waist and over firm buttocks, finally releasing its quickening grasp between warm, susceptible thighs. With not a second to spare, she stooped down to remove her thin cotton stockings, finally baring petite, sturdy ankles and slender, agile toes. Finding it necessary to gather the remaining items of clothing, her eyes briefly abandoned the sleeping doctor as she stooped over to pick them up, her long black tresses tumbling forward. Before resuming her former posture, however, Eleanor suddenly froze while staring straight ahead. Someone was watching her! In the window...through the sheer curtains! She gasped as her whitened hands clutched the underthings against her naked body. Those beady eyes. She'd recognize them anywhere. It was Jimmy Ray! And he was staring right at her!

Paralyzed with fear, Eleanor remained in a stooped position. Like a butterfly caught in a spider's web, she helplessly waited for his next move. But he wasn't moving. He just kept staring. Eleanor shut her eyes and held her breath. She could hear her heart pounding inside her head. *Please, please go away,* she begged while memories of slobbering, putrid lips and a deep thrusting pain within her abdomen compelled her to open her eyes once more. The figure was still there. But it hadn't moved. It was still. Too still. There was something strange about it, too. Favorably strange. Eleanor could feel the life blood begin to flow throughout her body. Breathing more calmly now, she blinked several times. The image was no longer threatening. An object on a stand by the window put a whole new perspective on the face in the glass. It wasn't Jimmy Ray after all. Only a reflection from a large globe, its protruding surface projecting patterns upon the smooth, dark pane.

That does it, Eleanor quickly resolved while throwing her slip back on and stepping into her panties. She wasn't going to prance around the room naked after all. Doing the spell in her underthings should be good enough. Just because there was a picture in Mama's book didn't necessarily mean everything had to be done in exactly the same way. Besides, how in the world would she have explained herself to Doctor Governey if he happened to wake up? At least with her slip on, she could tell him she was cleaning up and didn't want to get her Sunday suit all dirty. Eleanor then hastened toward the window and closed the velvet curtains. After a short hesitation, she pushed the panels of the drapes slightly apart. The moon would still shine through the crack, she reasoned. At any rate, enough time had been wasted. She glanced at the grandfather clock in the foyer, but couldn't discern its face from the position. It must be nearly one in the morning, she finally decided, which meant she'd only get about four hours sleep altogether. That is, if she hurried up.

Eleanor let out a deep sigh while eyeing the cigar on the ashtray. The fire had gone out again. Fortunately, though, the lighter was still there. Placing the Havana to her mouth again, she relit it. It seemed to have a soothing quality, she realized, while placing it back down on the tray. The room seemed strangely quiet as she reconsidered her strategy. It would probably be best to pour the ashes into her slip before sprinkling them around to avoid burning her fingers on the cigar. Raising the bottom of her slip with one hand to form a pocket, she lifted the tray with the other while holding the head of the cigar in place with her thumb. *There,* she thought while prodding the ashes onto the white fabric, being careful not to extinguish the flame. It surely wasn't a whole lot, but there was still plenty enough to make a spell.

Holding the skirt of her slip with both hands now, Eleanor glanced at Samuel one more time before starting her chant. He had changed positions again and was on his back snoring lightly. She would quietly recite the chant as many times as possible while scattering the ashes and circling sunwise around the sofa. Eager to proceed, she released her right hand and scooped a few ashes between her fingers. Beginning her dance around the divan, her heart seemed to leap with each swaying step, her prancing toes making transient impressions upon the plush carpet as erotic hips moved to and fro to each tantalizing syllable. **"Ashes from a wealthy squire, scatter on your heart's desire. If the wealthy man be old, riches return double-fold. Ashes From A Wealthy Squire, Scatter On Your Heart's Desire. If The Wealthy Man Be Old, Riches Return Double Fold. ASHES FROM A WEALTHY SQUIRE, SCATTER ON YOUR HEART'S DESIRE. IF THE**

WEALTHY MAN BE OLD...” Upon completing the circle, Eleanor, suddenly realizing she had gotten carried away, lowered her voice and spilled the last of the ashes upon the carpet in front of her sleeping host. **“Riches return double-fold!”**

Feeling like she just finished feeding a gaggle of unruly geese, Eleanor let out a sigh of relief and dusted the remaining ashes from her slip. Would the spell really work? she thought while stepping toward the winged chair to gather her Sunday suit. If so, what would that mean? Would she really end up owning the house? How? Maybe when Doctor Governey died, he would leave it to her in his Will. But that wasn’t likely to happen for a while, she pouted while buttoning her blouse. Probably at least for another ten years or so. Maybe...maybe she wouldn’t get the *whole* house, but Doctor Governey would be so taken with her, that he’d give her lots of nice things, including some jewelry and maybe even the ruby necklace too. Then she wouldn’t even have to steal anything. Maybe...Eleanor paused. Staring at her bare ring finger while pulling up her skirt, she remembered the words spoken by Maggie in the ladies room of Doctor Governey’s club. *“...you just wait, sister if ya think that necklace is worth a pretty penny, I’d bet dollas to dumplings he gives you a hell of a diamond when he asks for ya hand in holy matrimony...”* Ellie’s eyes widened to almost double their size. Was it true then? Would she end up marrying Doctor Governey after all? Her mouth dropped. It all started to make sense now. There’d been signs coming at her all day. Signs she hadn’t paid much attention to up until now. Like the loose strand Doctor Governey found in her hair while he was unbraiding it. Or the good soaking she got from the pouring rain. And how about the cat that was washing itself in the middle of the street while she waited for the doctor to come out of the pet shop? Didn’t it look directly at her before running away?

Eleanor slipped her jacket from the winged chair and stepped toward Samuel. Was it true then? But how about her dream of going to Hollywood and becoming a movie star? She’d have to give that up. Unless...unless.... It was all making sense now about those producers coming over to Michigan. Then she really *wouldn’t* have to give up her big dream after all, she determined with a racing heart. But...did she really have a chance? Would Doctor Governey really be willing to marry her even if she *wasn’t* a virgin? And what about the pregnancy? Would he allow her to have the baby so she could give it up for adoption? Or would he talk her into having the abortion after all? Either way, she shrugged, finding peace in the serenity of his deep, calm breathing, she was certain that a man as smart and powerful as Doctor Governey would make the proper decision. But she really didn't want to think of such serious matters now. Not when there were so many exciting things to think about. Like expensive jewelry and glamorous clothes and fancy motor cars. And the places she and the doctor could travel to! Maybe even go on one of them giant ocean liners! Eleanor gazed intently at Samuel who, except for his even breathing, was as still as the air over Lake St. Clair. She did have some fond feelings for the doctor after all, didn't she? And she supposed she could learn to love him in time, even if he *was* considerably older than her. She crossed her fingers and leaned toward him. He looked so peaceful lying there. It would be rude to wake him after all. Being careful, then, to leave him sleeping, she gingerly placed the lighter back inside his jacket pocket and spread her own jacket over his shirted chest. There was no need to extinguish the cigar; the flame had already died. A feeling of relief washed over her as she stooped down to recover her Sunday shoes. Quietly approaching the long, winding stairway off the foyer with shoes in one hand, she crossed her fingers with the other while defiantly eyeing the colorful globe which, just minutes ago, had ominously imposed itself upon the window pane and caused her to panic. Being that Doctor Governey was such an important man who knew so many police officers, perhaps she might not worry anymore about Jimmy Ray.

THE END